## BOOKS BY LAWRENCE M. NYSSCHENS:

Once-Other
A Candle's Worth of Life

Once-Other heads directly towards
A New Political Civilization
here on Earth and likely for
the first time within the confines of
This Universe.

Build it together.
Travel it forever.
Keep alive a keen mind.

Anything less…
…and tomorrow belongs to the enemy.

# ONCE-OTHER

A NOVEL

BY

LAWRENCE M. NYSSCHENS

Cover artwork by Robyn Leigh Nysschens
Cover artwork Copyright © 2013, 2014 by Lawrence Martin Nysschens
Copyright © 2014, 2015, 2016 Lawrence Martin Nysschens
Paperback ISBN: 978-0-9909886-1-8

# Table of Contents

# ACKNOWLEDGEMENTS

Thank you to those good individuals who read my manuscript and provided me with their invaluable feedback. I am grateful for the time you gave and the views you expressed.

I still smile as I recall almost all of us had a similar conversation:

Reader: "Do you make good on what's in Chapter One?"

Me: "That's for you to decide."

Reader: "But is the *new stuff* promised...in your book?"

Me: "Yes!"

That this book exists I am indebted to George Erskine of Fife, Scotland. Across these many years, his words of encouragement kept me going.

While working on Once-Other, I used *The People's Guide to the United States Constitution, Revised Edition* by Dave Kluge as a reference book.

In it, Dave provides the meanings of those words that make our US Constitution what it is. This allows *anyone* to understand our Founding Documents or gain a deeper knowledge of it. His book guided me down the road upon which I have dared to venture. A path that includes further Rights and Freedom and these safeguarded.

I recommend one read it, whether a US Citizen or not.

You will be amazed and educated no matter where you may live.

As I have often heard said. "How can one grasp what one doesn't have or come to realize one has lost something—if you didn't understand it in the first place?"

Thank you all.

Lawrence Martin Nysschens.
January 2015

For the many who have asked...Nysschens...is pronounced *Nations*.

# CHAPTER 1

## OF HUMAN RIGHTS

**24**[th] **July 4008 EB**★

We the People of Here-Born, adopt the full and *original* Constitution and Bill of Rights of those United States of America, a Republic. We thank them for the document they left behind—we consider it a treasure.

With the benefit of history, other technology, and our own requirements, we have added new ideas and clarified all we can as best we can. This we have done in defense against those amongst Mankind who insist upon enslaving their fellows.

We the People of Here-Born condemn all forms of slavery whether physical, mental, financial or spiritual. We hope all of Mankind understands these are inalienable Rights, are God-given and may only be removed by God—and by God alone.

Live by Neatness alone fellow citizens.

★*See Glossary*

# CHAPTER 2

## OF THE PLANET HERE-BORN

She was once a mistress of the Sun, the beauty of a galaxy. A lady whom with each day's awakening, would wink at Brother Sun but his countenance never altered. Nevertheless, she held her smile day long as the delicate mists of her lakes, oceans and seas surrendered to him.

When day too faded, she exhaled and her breath whispered along grassy plains over mountains and through forests. Wild-life bleated their pleasure while feasting upon its scent of bush-figs and honey.

Year round rainbows of flowers circled her north to south and east to west. Their radiance shone warmer than sunlight, their beauty surpassed by her perfume alone.

The Sun named her his Great Desire.

But his passion was never matched leaving his desire unquenched. And the Sun being a wanton one, became demanding, overbearing...threatening. Nevertheless, she held her ground.

But daily, as she slipped from his grasp his anger rose. Enraged and driven by frustration he roused the molten rock from deep within her and thrust it out across her delicate landscape.

Time stood watch as the lava solidified.

Later, tiny winged pods escaped through cracks and floated upwards to darken the sky. Rain soon came and heavy with water they burst. Their seed scattered far and wide to settle on shores, mountains and seas, and there they multiplied.

But the Sun never content became dissatisfied even with the seed he had given her and set to pondering on it.

And so, after time played another hand new seed arrived—seed from beyond the Sun. They too fell like rain but rain like no other. Leaping hills of orange and red and black erupted and her oceans and lakes vanished leaving bitter salt in their wake.

She fought the violence with sighs and clouds of perfume.

But the attack multiplied ripping her open as unto death.

In desperation, she gathered her flowers, trees and all living things and buried them deep within her. There she solidified her outer beauty fearing Brother Sun's anger would rain down far crueler.

Those parts of her unable to solidify turned into a black and sticky liquid that gave forth an odor with no ties to her delicate perfume.

And she was all but done.

In a final act, she inhaled the clouds that surrounded her, those mists that once were her lakes, seas, and oceans. With this done so too was her beauty for not a whisper of it remained.

Across her now stark face, dark brown scars hardened rendering homage to a Sun's wantonness.

And new winds blew.

Winds carrying sand, the thick smell of dust, burning radiation and deadly carbon dioxide destined to choke all future life.

The Sun smug in the heavens claimed this act as his own vengeance. With his glare now firm upon her, he set to burning and baking her until she could no longer support life.

Soon all who knew her pronounced her dead. Thus, she remained barren, burnt and lifeless. After eons had passed, strangers came to her. Strangers seeking freedom and bringing hope. Some say she sighed as their first boot set imprint upon sand.

It was in the year of 3776 EB.

# CHAPTER 3

## OF ONCE-OTHER BY ONCE-OTHER

**3rd October 4296 EB**

**288 years have passed since 4008 EB when our First War of Independence was won.**

My name is Once-Other. Before though, I had *an other* name which I now keep secret. I changed from the original one when I replaced my arms and head with pre-owned body parts.

Now, my reason for swapping out body parts was to ensure no one could identify me as a Here-Born Campaigner, by appearance alone. We Campaigners operate on the frontlines of this our war of self-defense that EB has yet to declare. It follows we are vulnerable and open to capture or assassination.

We refer to this as our Second War of Independence.

It flared alive when Earth-Born recently invaded Here-Born a second time, but in a covert and underhanded fashion.

We've offered Earth-Born several warnings and appeals to end both their invasion and continued attrition upon our Rights.

In response they began to hunt down Here-Born Campaigners for no reason other than our extermination. They ought to pay attention to the last of our warnings for we have been kind enough to provide them with many such.

Now, the subject of pre-owned body parts has forever been trying upon the logic of EB tourists. Most are deeply offended at the sight of pre-owneds on display and for sale. But for us switching out arms or other appendages has become an everyday occurrence.

Despite EB's having trouble with this segment of our lives; pre-owneds were originally created by their own EB scientists. This occurred way back when our ancestors first emigrated from Earth-Born to Here-Born.

On board ship during the trip to Here-Born, EB engineers secretly conducted experiments in the regrowth of human limbs. Unfortunately, upon arrival every ship crashed. Chemical concoctions still brewing leaked into the atmosphere and from there into sand and finally from sand into other sand.

Our ancestors dearly wished to hang the EB scientists and genetic engineers on discovery of the tests and their nefarious purpose—to make all people *more* equal. Then again and at that time, our Founders did not realize that said concoctions would wrought a physical change upon us as none before in all of human history.

Instead, it was the experiments on the regrowth of human limbs the crashes revealed that our ancestors so despised, one-two-three and altogether. Furthermore, there were no handy trees about, and those ancestors soon discovered nothing much grew on Here-Born, whatsoever.

After the crash landings and with footprints barely impressed upon sand, a child was born. With the child comforted in her mother's arms, our Founders gazed about this barren world and named it Here-Born in honor of the newborn. We have since come to refer to Earth and its population as Earth-Born or EB for short.

Now. If ever you accuse us of being Earth-Born, it is a low down insult! This is due to Neatness—a code of conduct important to us. So! Beware if you tend to verbally abuse others for the Here-Born group called Desert Drivers will become a trifle physical when so insulted. Please keep this advice in mind when traveling here from abroad.

As for Once-Other here and alive this very morning; I stare into the mirror as I do every day and examine my clothes.

I am a flashy dresser with a taste for single colors from head to toe. In being as well somewhat otherwise in mind and humor, I do mix-n-match on occasion just to watch faces twitch in surprise and the surprised express disbelief.

Such like quirky humor has caused people I know to insist I'm descended of the ancient Vikings. I instead, reckon they speak to the dark red of my new hair, the width of my new chest and the Nordic cut of my new cheekbones. My lack of height they wave aside as reward enough for generations of cross-cultural matrimony.

Now these same friends are quite confident my soft voice matured as wine long encased in a barrel of soured marriage. I figure they take advantage of unfortunate circumstances altogether—and enough said of that.

At this time, as our Second War of Independence takes shape, danger dogs me every hour of each day due, as mentioned, to my being a Here-Born Campaigner. The threat of imminent arrest and imprisonment by EB's authorities hangs continuously over me causing me to do something new.

That Authorities from Earth-Born now search for us Here-Born campaigners, I am recording all the events of my part in this our Campaign, starting today. Events I hope I will live through.

This morning, duty again calls me to rejoin the search for a missing campaigner. But first, I stare out at the desertscape and consider Here-Born.

Her face is scarred by one-third a sea of rock and awash in two-thirds an ocean of sand—and nothing else. Despite these traits, our ancestors chose Here-Born for themselves and all future generations.

In their final analysis, it came down to her apparent lack of commercial value, distance from Earth-Born and so terrible a climate only fools and those seeking refuge from oppression would live with her.

These we are—and are said to be.

To our ancestor's surprise, they discovered gold and oil in large quantities though some decades later. The engineers present mused on how often it transpires that he, who flees something, often becomes the inevitable recipient of what he fears.

I hear no one laughed.

With gold and oil, we are cautious and this despite the haste demanded by those trendy business dynamos of Earth-Born. And so we have waited until recent times to export and mine. However, in our opening of oil and gold to commerce, we have invited an EB sponsored tragedy to undertake another junket amongst us.

We fight again as we did back in 4008 when we first won independence from EB. Nevertheless, this our Second War of Independence unfolds like none before and with good cause as well.

You see, Here-Born Government, technology, as well as religious and personal Rights, has evolved out here thereby creating a new and legal self-defense. We have given them fair warning as mentioned, but they persist in violating our Rights and ignore all warnings.

I am, as well, sad to say that illegal arrests by EB authorities continue. However, we of Here-Born being expectant of justice and honor in Man have gathered news of each wrongful arrest and records of the perpetrators are encrypted and stored.

They should pay attention to those warnings for on Here-Born following illegal orders or illegal laws or illegal regulations cannot be defended *except* under one circumstance—you were threatened with *immediate* death should you disobey.

All others are prosecuted and, in particular, those writing, contributing to, proposing, lobbying for or voting for illegal laws or regulations and those giving illegal orders.

So I say to them, "Beware!"

And so too must we beware.

I personally suspect something heads our way, something worse. But I know not what. Into this uncertainty, I march another day, another week, another year, and longer if needed.

We of Here-Born will not suffer a surrender nor compromise until Freedom lives again.

For us, there is no life without Freedom.

For us, it is impossible to hold onto Freedom without continued vigilance to the coming forth of a new Slave Master— one often surrounded by the obvious minions and cowering curs. Be wary of them for they crawl into view slow enough to go unnoticed...at first.

For myself, I am not sure I will survive.

I can but hope.

Nevertheless, at present all is quiet on all fronts.

# CHAPTER 4

## OF THE FIRST CASUALTY OF WAR

I crouch low atop a high dune scanning westwards across a wild and desolate desertscape. A momentary hush as the wind drops. I shift sideways, wriggle deeper into sand and inspect distant dunes as deep concerns gnaw at me.

I search for a Here-Born campaigner, Jiplee Williams, who has gone missing these last several days. We have combed the desert to no avail. For me, it is too trying this, looking for a friend while expecting the worst. Sand whispers as it slithers once again. I glance up and about then focus hard.

But no matter how much I concentrate, there is nothing to see other than naked desert. There is nothing. No one. No signs of life. Naught but sun and heat and sand.

Overhead the sky is harshly blue. In the distance, dust-devils tap-dance along the edge of a dune. Beneath their dancing feet, sand breaks free and cascades downwards, a beached wave slipping back to sea.

Gusts of wind blow sand in my face, into my eyes. Sand forever moves, tumbling and dancing to the tune of Mother Wind and her children as daily they flit and dance across sand.

From out a clear blue sky, our Sun's glare lessens not at all. A sun who is both merciless and unforgiving, and who smiles without care at Man's attempts to survive. And assuming one wishes to remain alive beneath Brother Sun courage and endurance, swiftness of mind and reactions superior to any of Earth-Born, are essential requirements.

The moan of wind picks up then subsides and behind me hot metal ticks in evidence of a cooling engine.

I briefly inspect my screaming red SandRider named Hellbent; a breakdown being Death's kissing cousin. She is almost as tall as a monster truck but built more like an ATV—an All-Terrain Vehicle. Its motorcycle styled saddle lies level at my shoulder. A fairing keeps sand and headwinds at bay, mostly.

I run a finger along the red paint and streaks of pin striping so dark-blue as to appear black. A quick check of her waist high tires—and all are good. A push on the handlebars without power-assistance assures me there is no play in the steering-head.

I kneel and glance about her V4 engine snuggled beneath the seat. This one is designed more for torque than horse-power—no oil leaks are evident. I grin my confidence in her, pat a wheel, shade eyes aflame from lack of sleep and wind-borne dust and once again search the desert. There is nothing but emptiness as far into the distance as I can see.

I check one final time and jolt physically at a sudden flash of color. I close my eyes and mumble a prayer for I had almost missed spotting Jiplee but for a bright red scarf tied around her neck. She lies high upon an opposing dune, frail, unmoving, half buried.

Perhaps I will not be too late.

I leap to Hellbent's saddle, start her, blip the throttle and she roars in defiance of sand and sun. I drop the clutch and charge down leeward. She slips-n-slides, convulses into a tank-slapper and almost tips. I catch her and angle down the steep face fighting the handlebars.

After a quick charge across the slack, we race up the opposing incline and crest the edge with all four wheels flying. They hit, bounce twice and we slide to a halt. My eyes remain glued to where Jiplee lies despite spewing sand seeking ingress beneath my helmet. Desert silence is intruded upon as my boots pound across sand.

I stop up, bend to a knee, take a moment to calm and check. Sadly, she has no pulse. I drop her hand flinching at her skin so dead upon mine. Regretful, I pick it up, dust it off, place it down with care and check for the cause of death but find none.

I sit silent, breathing fast.

A faint trace of flowers-n-honey mingled with the thick odor of sand surrounds her. I lean closer, but no signs of violence are evident. Perhaps a little hope. But no, the breath of life is gone. I lean back and examine her further.

She is dressed in khaki fatigues and brown boots. Her delicate blouse is of all colors, pink. Blonde bangs peak from beneath a pastel green cap. Typically Jiplee.

Her eyes are closed as though asleep but upon her lips lingers the strangest of smiles. I turn from it but on considering Neatness, I wipe the desert from her face and sit looking at, but not actually seeing her. Several moments on her lips once again hail my attention—they seem alive.

I reach out and a fragment of lingering memory leaps into my hand and divulges she had not anticipated the violent attack she had suffered.

Her life and her memories are gone to me now.

I sigh and gentle her hair, her cap falls free. And with my hand upon her forehead her life essence detaches and bids her human shell farewell. I sense her rise, a silver-n-gold shadow across the corner of an eye. She drifts higher seeking clouds; a forlorn endeavor for there are none and never will be.

She had often dreamed of them, though.

She and her family were and still are of a different religion to mine. Therefore, I understand she's headed for life anew and will once again live amongst us, as is believed by members of her religion—the Church of the First Faith. But harsh duty calls and despite having no wish to, I yet examine what remains of her.

In tilting her chin, the better to see her face, I discover bruises beneath her red scarf, black and terribly cruel they are. Images of powerful hands choking her return with an insatiable urge for death and reach for me.

I shrink back. My throat constricts and tightens as her final struggle strikes chords better never heard. When they fade, I bow my head and close my eyes in respect of her life, her sacrifice.

I do not know how long I sat in silence thinking about how to find the owner of those virtual hands. With no answer to be found, I glance upwards as the sun touches its zenith, the Half-Day-Moon rises and midday is upon us.

Something still nags at me, though. Something is wrong or out of place upon which I cannot place a finger. Eyes closed I send perception tendrils into the past looking, searching.

I discover dunes spread off into an endless distance. Many tower one-hundred-n-forty or more floors high. I examine them in passing. Their ever-changing tops sculpted by Mother Wind present my senses with tabletops, ribbed-tops, hump-tops, spinal-twist-tops, shark-fin tops and even octopus-topped dunes.

I accelerate *their time* backward then forwards and locked together they shift from one place to another, higher today, lower tomorrow. They remain bare sand and devoid of human interaction. Suddenly something touches my shoulder.

I return, and with eyes opened examine it. Sister Storms had awakened and now lifts delicate sand grains leaving small depressions in her wake. I brush her touch from my shoulder as she subsides. Mourner's Wind whispers an invitation to Sister Storms and they meld, becoming one.

A cold shiver zigzags down my spine. I check for danger and find but a single dust-devil dancing in the wind. Having found no solution to current circumstances, I place the call over my Nomadi, push Jiplee's bangs aside and ask of her one final question.

"Why no call for help, Jiplee?"

Here where she lies at the edge of a tabletop dune any-n-all direct mind-to-mind communications would hit home at several command posts. Still, with not a whisper had she reached out, neither had she called on her Nomadi. I can but wait and muse on how she had fallen to the enemy, but instead, my mind runs wild.

How can this be? It is not possible that she lies here as she does. Yet she does. If she was killed without evidence of how and without a single call for help...then so can I. Moreover, so can any of Here-Born.

Had Jiplee somehow lost all her skills?

Has our evolution been all for naught?

Has the enemy gained technological advantages that obliterate our evolution from speech to mind-to-mind communication during which we maintained the skills of speaking aloud as a useful tool?

No! That is impossible!

Yet I sit next to evidence of such.

And yes! Those born of EB consider speech and hearing vital, but we hold access to minds a fundamental necessity. We understand those of EB have not evolved to such. But out here and upon this barren sand-n-rock covered planet mind-to-mind communication has become a natural part of life. And although this skill developed over generations of desert life, its history still boils with confusion.

Southerners insist all is due to religion giving us spiritual skills earlier assigned to the mind. Easterners have determined that windblown sand getting into our mouths awoke evolution. Western and Northerners have no opinion either way yet will argue endless hours on the subject.

Along with it, mind-to-mind brought to life a second skill.

Why had Jiplee not used it?

Alternatively, had she lost it? If not lost, then what had defeated it with such apparent ease? And to so final a result? It is an active defense, an incredible advantage. Why had she not obtained or read, as some say, the killer's thoughts and been prepared?

I reach out to her lifeless form but with her essence departed there come no answers. I take her hand and search all my education that we of Here-Born have named one's Foundation. I seek in vain for I find no answers there either.

Head bowed I whisper, "I don't know anymore. Do you Jiplee?" Forlorn, I squeeze her hand harder hoping she will respond. She does not. I cover her and sit gazing out across the desert.

The wind drops and quiet ensues giving birth to greater concern. This campaign of ours has today become a full-blown war, and upon this high tabletop dune we have surrendered first blood. How terrible that a self-defense as non-violent as ours has invited death to savage amongst us.

And worse! She had long been a friend.

I sigh, glance at her but am unable to restrain the memories that rush at me. Nor less the duty I must undertake. To those her child and husband, I must carry the news of her death. I smile sadly as their images spring forth.

She had given to our world a boy and a girl. Both are as blonde as she is but tall and lean like Reggie, their father. It pains me that their names escape recall at a time such as this. Her son, ever quiet and shy, owns a personality the opposite of his younger sister, Little Miss Boisterous.

The first time I visited at their farm her daughter walked up to where I sat in the shade of an awning took my hand and said, "Walk with me...I like you."

I smiled, entranced a child so young had asked and with such confidence. I can still feel her hand in mine and hear the joy in her voice telling of something she has never seen, butterflies. But today I'm torn that I must bring them sad news yet relieved they receive it from a friend. I only wish....

The roar of several SandRiders shatters the silence. I have been lost in thought of times long gone and danger is about.

I lie flat breathing hard. Dust rises to tickle the inside of my nose. I wipe at it thankful there is no trace of $CO_2$. I keep absolutely still as a posse of SandRiders dance closer through the heat-haze. They storm down a distant dune dragging a sand-cloud behind. They vanish from view leaving puffs of dust to drift aimlessly and upon the wind, the snarl of engines lingers.

This could be rescue in response to my call.

This could be death. I wait, barely breathing, my hand itching for the handgun I had left at home.

Like a stampeding herd of Roanark Braer, they leap the edge of the dune I wait upon. I squint through the dust and heat-haze as various colored SandRiders fight for my attention. As times dictate, desert camouflage dominates. Up close, all are strangers except for one—Madsen Somalo, my campaign senior. This then is rescue.

I stand up and wave, my eyes lingering on Madsen.

He's seated straight-backed in the saddle of a matte-black SandRider. Despite that, his height towers obvious and so too the magnificent roundness of his belly. Sand swirls as they pull up. Set in a chubby but hard face his cold black eyes check me over as he strides across.

His large boots crunch in sand. He halts as a soldier casually coming to attention, inspects Jiplee turns to me and says, "You round-n-about sure?"

I fight a drugged-like helplessness at this unexpected accusation of incompetence. Why he suddenly thinks I am unable to tell the difference between the presence and absence of life, I cannot fathom. My internal voice whispers something a long time coming—telling of his adeptness at disguising insults as questions and thus filling them with hidden intent.

"What exactly do you really mean?" I ask him. He jolts involuntarily, remains silent, glares hard. Ignoring his glare, I look him over with a critical eye.

Sweat drips down cheeks that appear impervious to the sun. His sand-colored overalls though are no different from what I wear. He shuffles in sand and faces me square on but his eyes dart, never meeting mine.

His voice both cold and burning he says, "Have you lost sight of your last three tourists? Not exactly what we're round-n-about looking for. The jury is out on you Once-Other. I think you ain't making it. As a campaigner, my seniors have nothing but questions about you. We've a new EB tourist assigned to you. Failure ain't an option. Get it right an' all! An' you be careful of what you do or...."

I turn my back on him and gaze off into the desert. Hot air circles seeking every drop of moisture a body dare expose. The few beads of sweat lingering on my forehead—surrender up.

I wipe my brow as streams of memories rush at me. All are of Madsen's words backhand included. "What changed?" I ask and his mind snaps closed killing his retort. So he has to hide the answer. Hmm.

I glance at his rescue team who all seem suddenly and unduly interested in a distant horizon. He grabs my arm. "Nothing! It's round-n-about you! You gone an' betrayed us an' all?" he barks.

"Seems a question born of fear," I say. "I'm ignoring the insult."

"Be that heavy on your shoulders," he says.

"And yours on yours," I snap back at him.

He shrugs, glances around and commands, "You-n-all take her home."

He looks about and turns back to me. "Last time I was at Sand Lake Flats museum I paid Maggie in cash for a soda. She carefully checked my payment...as though I had shortchanged her! Glad you're not that way inclined. There's something wrong with people like that."

And he walks off.

And that is not the Maggie of my acquaintance. Stranger.

Four of the rescuers lift Jiplee's stretcher, their boots crunch-n-shuffle in sand. Canvas squeaks on the painted steel framework of a SandRider as they lock the stretcher in place. Some cough, others pant and complain. A final check and they all mount and nod to me. I nod in return. Starter motors whine and V8's and V4's snarl alive. They pop wheelies, save for the one with Jiplee on board, and speed off as engines roar and wheels spray sand.

Silence returns. The wind picks up moaning a dirge.

I wet a finger and hold it up for upon these sands wind is a predator. So know well that Mother Wind has many children each of which rises daily from its own cradle. We shall meet them all.

My finger instantly dried, and the wind whispering at my left ear, I wait until the stretcher-carrier with Jiplee on board drops from view over the edge of the dune. Taking a deep breath, I set off home to much-needed rest and replenishment.

However, I am heavy with dread.

There has always been a warmth aglow deep within me. But when I'd first touched Jiplee's lifeless body, it dimmed. And so faded my future, our campaign and my hopes of victory. But that I instantly realize, is in part surrender. And any bit of such I cannot, will not embrace.

A deep breath in, a virtual hand fans the flame of purpose and my warm light glows once again. I glance about the tabletop on which I stand. It is now a part of me. Part sorrow at the loss of a friend, part understanding of Madsen's hidden intentions.

"Who am I?" I whisper but find no answer.

I know where I'm headed as a Here-Born campaigner with certainty. But what of myself? Am I lost? What am I to become? What purpose drives me? What is my goal beyond a commitment to this our Campaign?

Perhaps this war itself will see me clear to understanding.

Three days on, I attend Jiplee's funeral under gentle lights within the adobe structure of the First Faith Church.

Inside cooler air brings relief from the baking sand outside. Floors and pews are of faux wood, which appear all too real. Overhead large fans stir air confined by walls almost free of windows. Only two stain-glass windows high up on each of the steepled front and rear walls allow sunlight in. Their stained-glass filtered light mixes rainbows which shine across the exposed rafters creating a melting pot of color.

On a table in front of the dais stands a blue urn half covered by a simple black cloth. A Priest, dressed in a long flowing red frock, waits with arms crossed and face pointed to the sky as though seeking divine inspiration.

Madsen shuffles in next to me grunting-n-wheezing as per usual. I ask him if he found what had led to her death.

"She was foolish, ill-prepared, unaware an' made a mistake an' all," he says in a hushed, breathless voice.

"No, Madsen!" I whisper upon recovery. "We must be honorable one to another. Is this Neatness?"

"You tease my patience, Once-Other. Ask no more of her incompetence! Attend to duty if you are able."

I stare at the floor my teeth grinding and glancing across note his indifference to my shattered demeanor. I'm quite confident all those present can hear my teeth grind together as I hold anger at bay. I remain staring unfocused a long time thinking on Madsen and his ongoing insults and barbs.

About to send a hard-worded query, I instead remain silent as the Priest concludes. The church doors swing wide flooding the walls and pews with sunlight. They come alive and glow as though washed and cleansed by a new measure of life.

I step outside in the wake of Jiplee's family. Her husband places the urn atop a Farewell Stone. Her children move to either side of him. We gather in a farewell circle around them.

Their memories unfurl and flow over us revealing Jiplee alive, vibrant, intelligent and attractive though more handsome and motherly than stunning. Reggie's shoulders straighten, their memories retract and he communicates.

"Understand these ideas my family, my friends, my enemy.

"We seek no revenge against those who attacked us yet failed to declare war on us. Nor do we seek conquest. We seek but a fair measure of freedom and our full measure of Rights. We desire to live in peace as do most fair people.

"Now please! Let there be no heavy-handed intrusion from our own government let alone from a foreign Earth-Born one."

"Is this too much to ask?" we mourners chorus.

And Reggie says, "Today you've taken from me something that can never be replaced. You've stolen a mother's life from her children and theirs from her.

"But even now Jiplee harbors no hatred for you despite that I do!

"We believe she lives, but we know not where. To my hate, she will lend a loving hand. Which hand will ease my pain and eventually replace it with that which we seek—our Freedom! Our Rights!"

"Amen," we mourners conclude.

The Priest hands him a Fragger.

He fires at the urn. It bubbles, becomes vapor and ten finger wide sheets of rainbows fire in all directions. A flash of bright white light and contents and urn vanish.

Reggie drops the Fragger from lifeless fingers, nods, takes his daughter and son's hands, bows to us and turning, sets off into the desert to say a final and private farewell.

But he pauses, looks back to us and says, "I thank you Once-Other. We three appreciate the time you took. The children could not have received such news from someone better qualified. Thank you."

I nod in return, sadly pleased

Madsen strides to his SandRider, mounts and heads off. I wave, but he holds his attention dead ahead. Can I trust him?

No. He is a friend who appears long-gone with no cause other than to become my senior and who lost himself in the process.

Do those higher up trust me?

Wait and see I advise self.

And it suddenly strikes me...from the instant Madsen insulted Jiplee to the conclusion of the farewell sermon I'd not received a single word spoken by the Priest.

I shade my eyes and glare at Madsen's dust-trail.

Damn!

Just then, the Priest's closing words return as though he were once again communicating them. "Our religion, the Church of the First Faith, honors all religions everywhere. For quite naturally, all those who have a religion...for each theirs is the first religion, the first faith.

"Amen."

And I sigh a measure of peace and so does Mother Wind.

# CHAPTER 5

## OF DIFFERENCES

Waves lap upon a virgin EB beach. Sand slithers backward, dark eels embroiled in thick sea foam. The ocean retreats and sand settles as it has always done.

Sentinels guard the beach standing tall and strong. Their endurance as great an affront to Mother Time as sand is. At night, they cast a dark patchwork against a star filled sky. By day, their many arms sway in the wind and their leaves dance, waving at the sun.

A carpet of decaying leaves several inches thick lives at their feet. From it, life seeps into the fertile soil, up roots, to trunks, to branches, to living leaves, and shares its wealth, its treasures, each time it rains.

The Sentinels stood tall and unyielding for eons assuming they were bound for eternity but were unprepared for a changing future. Strangers arrived, carrying cutting stones and fire. And later, came fine steel to replace sharpened stone.

The Sentinels fell to their cries of, "Timber!"

Each toppled in a slow arc shaking the land and parting the sea with thunderous crashes. And there to lie, their towering demeanor forever humbled. They huddled together stripped of branches and leaves, naked to the sun and tropical rain.

From this their Caribbean home, they traveled to distant lands to become planks, furniture, and homes. In these times, they have set sail for galaxies too far to imagine.

***

I raise an elbow staring at real wood.

The bar's counter and back cabinet are the only actual wood artifacts on all of Here-Born. Some look with envy at what they fancy is carved mahogany. Most others wave such wistfulness aside claiming it is no more than the stain of varnish upon a lesser wood.

The shelves are stocked with bottled invitations in strengths ranging from pink to green up to the various shades of golden brown. They grow darker stopping up at the darkest brown of all—Ferryman's Blast. Rumor says a single shot of which will plunge one into blissful unconsciousness...well more-or-less.

Fancy crystal stands proud amongst these invitations. A leaping dolphin with tail well clear of the water intrigues me most. Are the oceans they travel as vast as pictured?

I am alone at the bar of the Drinks-n-all sipping beer, minding my own inner store, and counting glasses with frothy residue versus those with hard liquor. Spotted like circular holes in a mirror, empty seats and tables speak of the late hour and of my internal struggle.

I'm afraid of shadows these days and wound up even tighter with the balancing act I'm performing. I have to maintain a normal appearance as a one-on-one tourist guide and pre-owned vendor, alongside my campaign duties.

My freedom and life depend on it.

The only way of doing this is to make daily life appear as normal as possible. But I struggle terribly with subterfuge. Then as well, I can feel her, touch her—Jiplee, as though we have melded. Her death now stalks me as if my own.

I've since questioned my own religion, which makes no mention of the spirit alive beyond physical death. At the same time, it refuses any official denial thereof. We of Here-Born are evenly split on whether this is fact or fiction.

Despite such competing philosophies, we do agree our Constitution embraces the idea that life follows death into an infinity of tomorrows. Therefore, it stretches all Rights into the individual's future beyond physical death and so too includes pre-birth.

In words colder than a true Artic many believers point ahead and backward saying, "Make repugnant laws, rules or regulations today and live under them tomorrow as a helpless child lacking any memory of a past. Yes, the jokes on you law-makers!"

Now if life and death were that way—but with memory intact? Would those grim and overbearing control addicts pass the laws they did back on Earth-Born—if there is no escaping their own creations?

I sigh and Jiplee's haunting words whisper from out our youth. "Having no recollection of life before birth sure don't prove you didn't live before birth. Can you recall what you did when three years old? No. But you were alive before then."

I shake her image off and run an eye over the semi-dark interior.

Synthetic tables and chairs cast as wood surround the dance floor. Wall panels are of the same. Floors are concrete covered with vinyl disguised as wood—not high class but blessed with endurance. There is a deep yearning on Here-Born for things natural.

Another security twinge but a scan of all patrons reveals no apparent threats. Dancers on the dance floor pound their heels as though digging for gold. Some wave to me. I nod but remain alert. Couples dotted by singles soloing prance-n-jig beneath the moist-n-cool breeze blowing off the cooling system.

Wild strobe lights make aliens of locals and locals of aliens. Bright colored eveningwear smiles in cheerful contrast to the brooding sand beyond these confines. I examine the dancers for danger once again and grin. Most patrons breathe air straight while all dance on two legs waving two arms. Nevertheless, three have on masks with converters changing air into the poison they breathe. The masks remind me of Jiplee and Halloweens long gone.

A shudder cascades through me just as the music ends. EB voices hit hard and loud and I regret coming here even more. I sip at my beer.

Why I drink, I'm not sure for headaches always follow. Perfume drifts by carrying a sweetness too thick for my liking. Louder music starts and more couples move onto an already densely populated floor. Elbowroom shrinks to almost zero and the sea of dancers move as one.

I think to leave and so end the pretense of normalcy for another day. I desperately need to set distance between self, drink and thought. I also have no wish to bury myself in fear nor grief nor bottle. It is time to leave.

I set off but unfortunately at the same time an EB tourist sidles on over. In his haste, he slops his beer. I would retreat but alas, he waves and so Neatness demands a minimum degree of manners.

Up close he and I are quite similar—neither too tall nor too short. He is not as broad in chest as I but sports a thick black mustache of horizontal hair begging a trim. A pale blue full-body fan-n-fit, air-conditioned suit clings to his compact frame.

Fan-n-fits provide cooling for any not born to desert temperatures. They range from casual to formal, cheap to expensive, and are worn by tourists alone. The picture of a virgin beach is printed across this one's upper body. A forest tops the beach while the beach edge cuts along a blue ocean that is wrapped around his waist.

Its beauty contradicts the scowling face he offers me in greeting. "Evening," he shouts over the deafening music. "Smooth music. Could be louder, eh? What's up?"

"I'm admiring the paneling and all," I reply.

"Cheap junk. But I get it. You're too boring to talk to. I don't care. Tell me. You know?"

"Our Ultimate Weapon of Mass Destruction?" I ask.

"Yeah. Right! Explain."

"Really?" I say and access his mind. What returns is muddled, incomprehensible, virtual beer fumes.

"Ah-ha, really-really," he says, leans closer, peers at the scars around my neck and grunts. "Seen them on others. Never mind. What's this so-called UWMD?"

He throws more beer down his throat, burps and I figure him for a drunk.

I stare at the ceiling as though thinking on his question. Ever since our politicians betrayed us, campaigners fear any mind barred to them. I personally gnaw at each one afraid they harbor secrets, hidden agendas or even actual betrayals.

Jiplee's death has compounded our anxieties and further darkened our world with grim suspicion.

He leans closer and his alcohol stained breath—is breathtaking. He examines me and raises a disapproving eyebrow at my green outfit boots-n-all. He's about to say more, but I cut him short.

"Well, okay then. You see, our Ultimate Weapon of Mass Destruction has never been used, so most of us don't know much at all. And you guys? You figure it's nothing more than rumor."

He nods as does a drunken sage upon hearing stale metaphors, and says, "Yeah. Right. Heard that one before. Rumor says it all pal."

"Thank you," I say coldly.

"What's your problem?" he demands.

"Your underhandedness, your Earth-Born politics, your oppressive taxes, your laws, and your damn ignorant educational system," I snap back at him.

He staggers backward in pretended horror. Sways for an instant, holds steady, pinches his nose closed and bursts out laughing.

I raise an eyebrow.

He sobers, waves and calls out, "Hey 'tender—same again," and points to the two of us as though he's Chief of the Generosity Clan. "Tell me more pal and watch what you're saying. Y'all got the Right to Happiness as we do, but talking that way could get you arrested."

"You're too drunk for this," I say and wave the subject aside.

"Naught. No. Stone cold sober. Come on. Go!"

I lean closer and peer into his eyes proper. They are clear and focused. Strange for someone who sways drunk as can be? Warning bells alarm but ignoring them I charge onwards a little too eager to spread the word of Here-Born Rights despite my contrary attitude.

"Well then, to begin with. You forced EB's laws on us in an underhanded and devious—"

"Hey, pal. Get a grip—it was in your face."

"Before that you left us alone. Beware! Our UWMD exists."

"Sure it does," he says.

I nod saying, "I know. You won't hear let alone listen until it's too damn late."

I throw the last of my beer back, hand him a printed copy of our final Warning Notice and head for the exit. He slams his empty mug down and reaches for me. I evade his groping fingers and merge into the crowd.

"I'm Gordon Odentien," he calls out. "Look me up sometime if you're interested. Hey! I didn't get your name."

"That's right!" I call back. "You didn't and I'm not."

He waves and starts reading the notice aloud.

"Dear Citizens of Earth-Born,

"It's Earth! Anyway....

"As in 4008, you've once again attacked our Freedom, our Declaration of Independence, our Constitution and our Bill of Rights, both covertly and overtly.

"This you've done by corrupting our politicians and enticing them to commit Treason.

"We the People of Here-Born have since voted for and initiated self-defense.

"The weapon we choose is our Campaign, our Hope. Ideas alone are its ammunition.

"Please understand an Ultimate Weapon of Mass Destruction waits in the wings.

"We will never surrender.

"We will never go quietly.

"The Committee for Freedom and Personal Rights, Here-Born."

He searches for me, waves frantically and shouts, "I've read this before, it's hogwash!"

And I cut out all sound and the club is quiet save for the *noise* of flashing lights.

Doors swing closed and from overhead, the night sky welcomes my presence upon Here-Born's moonlit sand.

# CHAPTER 6

## OF A PRIOR ARREST AND CONVICTION

Upturned eyes examine our night skies in the hope of finding distant planets upon which most Here-Borns will never tread. Closer above the desertscape circle the Half-Day-Moon, the sun, and the Star-of-Hope.

Together they imbue vast lakes and oceans of quicksand with low and high tides.

Over the heights of the far north mountains, sand-falls thunder where once waterfalls sprayed mist and cooled the air. Rivers of sand more turbulent and treacherous than water driven rapids snake into lakes, seas, and oceans...of sand.

Day burns faces and hands often beyond repair. Night threatens more so eyes and bones, the ravages of cold being harsher than that of heat. Daytime seems endless but nights measure longer lying awake listening for the hunters—it is too easy to become prey. A rapid heartbeat, a stagger to one's stride, a failure to perceive what is or a step into quicksand or blinded by driven sand are all preludes to a sudden death.

But neither days nor nights are as long as they could be.

This planet Here-Born upon its creation was rendered three times larger than Earth-Born but rotates about her axis many times faster. With her speed, she clocks sunrise-to-sunrise, a mere four hours longer than EB's twenty-four and so makes her gravity violent by comparison.

Newly arrived EB tourists stare at our night skies coddled in hotel rooms with air-cooled and carpets plush to cushion footfalls. Relaxed, comfortable, they will practice walking as toddlers do the first time out. Much as with jet lag most take a day or two or several to acclimatize.

Outside and on their own feet those endowed with courage greater than the norm whisper of how different our world looks and feels compared to theirs. More entertaining some will sometimes hint.

"How different the colors of the sand are," they will muse. "The sand is different at sunset to sunrise," and so on and often more so than a local can easily tolerate.

We, the natural born of Here-Born, are comfortable with both heat and cold. Nights belong to us, as does the heat of day. Cloaked in darkness, we race SandRiders across sand braving dangers and even death—should one's chariot fail.

The bolder ride until day erases night and fuel tanks run dry. Mind-to-mind has its advantages if one does not stray too far and holds course to within hailing distance, for aid is a simple *hello* away.

\*\*\*

The Drinks-n-All behind me I wind my way through a silent downtown. Traffic lights turn on and off as I pass by. Here and there street cleaners with Fraggers in hand vanish the city garbage as they do each night. The occasional SandRider passes me by, our sand-clouds mingle, a brief wave shared.

I glance over my shoulder as the lights of Sand Lake Flats fade from the rear-view mirror, open the throttle wide and Hellbent's exhaust note challenges the cold silence.

Hunched over and charging along the slack between dunes night cloaks all black as the Gates of Hell, wind knifes to the bone. I angle to the top of a long narrow dune, hunch down lower beneath the fairing, crank the throttle open wider and speed onwards.

It is not often I spend time riding the night cold these days. Campaigning has restricted my movements about darkened sand but has increased my searching for signs of danger. Nothing stirs out there upon blackened sand tonight.

No Poip—Police over internet protocol that is—reflect silver in the moonlight.

I shiver and tonight's biting cold reminds me of the morning all of Here-Born's teachers were arrested and imprisoned, self-included. Our arrest happened immediately after EB forced a new curriculum upon us.

Never before had any of us imagined how dangerous a weapon against young minds an education system could become. Instead, we at first viewed the new curriculum as a stupidity so thick one could roll it down a dune.

Our Here-Born schooling system, based on competence, vanished the moment verbatim learning replaced conceptual understanding. As a greater crime, EB's system demands unquestioning acceptance of theories and adds penalties for those who chose not to do so.

Now still, those penalties commence with unspoken condemnation of any who dare to investigate for themselves and peaks in the refusal of further education—something never openly stated.

Their system also denies students the right to complete daily schoolwork by breaking the day into periods so short nothing can be finished. Bells or sirens announce the beginning and end of the day and the end of every class.

Students are forced to quit doing what they are doing when the bell or alarm sounds despite the work being incomplete. They then study something else—imagine running a business that way!

This study regimen instills compliance as an involuntary response to command stimuli (the bell ringing) and so unquestioning obedience to those in charge.

This study regimen of breaking the day arbitrarily into sections is based upon tests and experiments done on dogs. Food was placed out and simultaneously a bell was rung. Next, only the bell was rung but there was no food. And the dogs salivated each time the bell rang expecting food.

But these tests results were inconsistent, and those conducting them appear to have overlooked the fact that We the People are not dogs, let alone rats.

We Here-Born teachers drew the line at school uniforms devised as they are to make us equal by being dressed the same—the death knell of individuality via enforced conformity.

Last though not least, all students had to and still must, regurgitate exactly what they had memorized onto examination answer screens. Responses, when provided as demanded by their system, bring reward—a diploma—but one not backed by competence nor by any skills of application out in life.

Worse, the economic value of each student remains based upon the *grandness* of the Institute issuing their certificate. All Certificates are earned by memorizing what one has studied and then giving the *correct answers*.

And damned be it to a student's actual competence, ability, or quick mind for the Certificate is the all of their Educational system and thus a person's economic value.

We teachers were not fooled and continued to teach our own system which is crafted to lead students to what's called a Moment in Time. A Moment in Time is the instance in which our education comes together as all the pieces fall into place conceptually. My son will shortly undergo his. I look forward to doing my first with a child.

Upon our refusal to kowtow to EB's curriculum and illegal demands, we teachers attained instant infamy all the way to the sacred halls of the House and Senatorial Hub of the United Countries of Earth-Born. There they decided what to do with us teachers over coffee and cookies, or so I heard.

"Once-Other!" snarled my then wife, Deidre. "How can you expect to earn a living breaking the law? You've been let go, laid off, outlawed. What's going to get it through to you? Teachers are history. It's illegal to teach. You might as well be a crucified doctor, flaunting the law."

"Deidre dear," I replied. "I am a teacher so I teach. They will have to arrest and imprison me to stop me."

"And you think they won't!" she spat.

Two weeks later our doorbell rang at 3:00 a.m. on a cold Sunday morning.

Despite their humanoid shape, their cheerfully bright silver bodies and their soft desert-camouflage military coveralls, Poip dragged me roughly out my warm and comfortable bed. A real-time demonstration of their complete lack of emotion or any other human trait, whatsoever!

This despite promises they were *human-friendly*.

"I knew nothing good would come of you," Deidre snarled as my feet hit the cold floor.

So did our marital relationship finally wreck upon the rocks of mutual bitterness. Thankfully, I'd taken precautions and asked my good friend, Bordt Nettler, to care for Deidre and Karrell our son.

Poip kicked the front door open and pushed me out.

My beloved lanky blonde headed boy with big blue-eyed watched from his window as they dragged me away. Wounded by the fear and grief landscaping his young face, I bade him understand.

"They haven't taken note of why we fought them to win our freedom, Karrell. They should venture over to the monument in Capital Square, Washington, Here-Born. It stands in honor of our heroes, our patriots.

"There they will discover that half our original population gave their lives in the war for our freedom—our independence. Never forget Karrell—no offer of wealth should be considered worthy of surrendering up one's Rights, one's Freedom, one's Honor, one's Neatness."

He smiled and dropped the curtain.

Trial and conviction were packaged, preordained and rapidly executed. Sentencing was the same all round—three years in prison.

We were marched off to prisons unlike any on Earth-Born.

# CHAPTER 7

## OF JAIL TIME, ECONOMIC VALUE AND A NEW TAXATION SYSTEM

"Being in chains is more trying than dying," a plump-n-short teacher declared as hundreds of us dressed in bright green prison garb shivered in the cold morning light waiting to enter our new *home*.

The first set of brown steel gates swung wide as the sun touched the horizon. We shuffled forward in groups of a hundred, were processed one at a time, and led to holding pens until all were done. Some of us covered our ears in protest of harsh Poip voices bellowing orders from all directions.

"I shall see this day paid for," Madsen whispered staring down at sand.

With the sun climbing quickly, a second set of gates rolled open screeching their thirst for but a sliver of grease. Stoic prison Poip dressed in khaki fatigues herded us inside. Single story adobe dormitories with dark brown bars welded to door and window frames bordered the main thoroughfare.

A row of palm trees ran the length of the sidewalk their feet hugged by green fern and rose bushes. Palm branches swayed in the wind as though pointing the way.

"Welcome!" said a prison Poip. "You will be conducted to quarters. There you will remain until called. Make no noise, keep smoking to a minimum and enjoy the free time."

As one, we glanced fearfully around and then set off.

Ahead, the prison property stretched a mile wide in both directions and forty long. I took a deep breath and smelt the good side of cows, pigs and wheat on the breeze and more pungently—the bad side.

I glanced left and smiled knowingly at the two-story schools, workshops, and apprentice halls. Inside these inmates in pursuit of a better life beyond the restraining gates learn and practice economic techniques of their own choosing.

Silver lights flashed across window panes as Poip waved us on in their standard jerk-n-go fashion while nodding as though they understood what had brought us into their care.

We marched one mile and two-hundred some sand-paces to our dorms our feet shuffling a rhythm in sand. A few teachers hummed a worker's dirge around the shuffle. Several pairs of calculating eyes assessed us from darkened windows as though we were ambulatory food.

Under harsh Poip glares, our dorms admitted us to gray walls, concrete floors, low ceilings, no fans and bed-bunks that we promptly discovered were registered as patented torture devices.

"I suppose as teaching goes, hands on has its value," I quipped on entering. No teacher laughed though plenty glared fierce enough to knock a head off.

On the following day, Madsen and I twinned up to neither of our satisfaction. "I've spent more time with Once-Other than I care for," he declared.

Poip nodded and twinned us anyway.

We began work at the lowest rung performing primitive manual labor, which old timers referred to as Dung Duty. On a strict schedule, we awoke at five and started our day milking unruly cows. On that first day, I was barely able to avoid having my head staved in by kicking hooves and my buttocks perforated by horns far sharper than seemed natural.

Done, we were on our hands-n-knees cleaning pigsties very hands on accompanied by olfactory overload. Next, we collected cow dung even more hands on. Pushing squeaking wheelbarrows, we carted vast quantities to the wheat fields where we dumped portions onto a dung pile spreading the remainder ever more hands on and fly swamped.

"Not pleasant," Madsen said as we held raw dung dripping in our bare hands.

"I don't know," I replied. "At least the fresh stuff's warm. May be kinda good on freezing mornings. For a while anyways." He was not a happy camper.

Six weeks of Dung Duty concluded along with the enforced use of a mess hall reserved solely for *dung dealers*—temporary and permanent assignees.

"How better the food tastes," said Madsen a week free of Dung Duty.

"Smells like food," I added, agreeing with him for the first time in decades. I then grinned wider. "Prison may be bad but not as awful as on EB. Cheer up Madsen. You know how it works."

He grunted mid-chew, remaining silent thereafter.

Now!

Punishment for punishment's sake is not welcome on Here-Born, let alone for revenge. Instead of incarceration we remove those found guilty of crimes from society. This is more to protect others than to punish an offender.

Once in prison, they will find two roads available to them.

Only one of these leads back into society.

Rehabilitation Road is available on self-determined request alone. This because no individual improves unless each personally desires it. With that in place education and internships are available while incarcerated.

I've checked and no prisoner to date has survived a program by faking a desire to better him or herself. It's too much hard work and intense application.

But! Inmates preferring to hew a criminal's tack never get the chance to practice their skills on others again. Oh, they get better quarters after their sentence ends but they will continue working the basic trade they have.

In this way prisoners who have no wish to get straight and honest and become economically valuable and viable never leave prison. However, at any time if one decides to shed the criminal's ways—he is welcome to travel Rehabilitation Road.

On the other hand, by working a fruitful job while imprisoned prisoners become skilled in their chosen career paths and earn income from beyond the confining walls and fences. This income is used to pay staff salaries and all the expenses of their own incarceration for the duration they stay or until death takes them.

There are no taxation dollars for prisons in our system. Their inmates alone finance them. Although! A portion of Here-Born taxes does end up as bonuses paid to individual prisons. It is in payment for the number of prisoners released who stay to their chosen occupations and commit no crimes, from then on out.

But should too many go back to a life of crime upon release—the Courts simply stop sending the guilty to that prison and out of business they'll go. In this way, prison staff must not only rehabilitate inmates but also create economically valuable and honorable individuals.

"What?" EB tourists scream. "That's cruel and unusual."

My rebuttal is always, "Who sends criminals back into society knowing they intend to continue a life of crime?"

EB's tend to stare in silence some with jaws dropped open like flytraps.

"Only those who are uncaring or who profit by it or both," I add.

"Why?" they ask again and frown in confusion.

So be it.

I was fortunate in my career allocation once Dung Duty ended.

When a young man I had undertaken an apprenticeship at the SandMaster factory. These are massive eight-wheel-drive armored vehicles with front-n-rear steering and twin engines. Due to Deidre, I never graduated—about which I do not think let alone speak.

With that background, I took up work at the local Hunduranda SandMaster dealership. I enjoyed the work and seldom ran across Madsen and his darkening moods. He quickly noticed and sneaked about trying to surprise me. I avoided him all the more. And so we played prison tag for some while.

After many months, a prisoner approached me in the yard one still and hot morning. I recognized him as one of those who had viewed we teachers as ambulatory food. He was tall, lean, almost hairless, cold-eyed and nasty. I had earlier noted him hovering about my periphery. Others had warned me that he brooked no backchat.

Without an introduction, he said, "Got'ah me no economic value Once-Other."

"You'll spend a damn long time doing manual labor," I said forcing a steady voice, stomach quaking.

His eyes said he understood.

"You want personal economic value?" I asked and licked at chapped lips.

"What'ah I do?" he asked.

"You sincere?" I queried and without waiting for a response added, "You know...this comes as self-determined only?"

"Like'ah my life way it is. Kind'ah works for me."

The criminal peeked out at me.

"You know where that leads?" I managed to say and sound calm.

He nodded yes.

"You cause damage? Any harm?"

He confirmed without looking at me.

"No matter how long your sentence you must make up for what you did. The victims or their family must agree."

"I hear you-n-all. But'ah why? Got'ah me six years only. I'm counting seven here."

"Who sets a criminal free to do what he does?" I asked.

He shrugged a no comment.

"Tell me. Have you at least worked out compensation for the damage?"

"Got'ah me nothing to offer."

"Listen."

I took his elbow.

His skin cringed from my touch and he glared down at me. I waited, heart racing, my stare fixed out across sand to where wheat swayed in a gentle breeze. Something about his demeanor changed, his skin smoothed over, he moved off and we headed towards a distant wheat field.

I let go his arm, saying, "I've heard of a prisoner who, on release, spent the rest of his days working a hard job and caring for the lady he had injured. This he did through to her old age and dying day. In the end they say, he cried during her funeral."

"Ye-ah?" he barked.

"No dung. Look." I pointed at a wheat field. "No telling where real benefit will come from. Would you have guessed people living in deserts on Earth-Born? And now—wheat fields in a desert."

"Damn'ah," he mused, pulled out a knife and opened it, his eyes on my face. I figured he was contemplating how different he could make it look.

I swallowed noisily and said, "Be very careful with this. If you pretend to want a new and productive life only to get out of prison...it will not work out. Also, if once out you commit crimes again, you will end up back here. But...you will never be offered Rehabilitation Road again."

We stood in silence for endless minutes, me sweating as he cut at the thick calluses manual labor had rewarded him with. A few moments on, he snapped the blade closed, squared his shoulders and walked off without a word.

He thanked me upon his release—and there you have it. Just attain economic value while incarcerated on Here-Born and upon release one already has employment.

Upon my release, I gained full-time employment with the Hunduranda SandMaster dealership at a qualified, professional salary. Deductions from my first paycheck alerted me to a new and illegal EB tax.

Can anyone believe that over on EB you pay higher taxes the more productive you are? That is how they reward success—by penalizing it?

Now Here-Born's lawful taxes are...well!

On Here-Born, 10% is the highest percentage anyone will pay in taxes and that is anyone or anything. From there it drops in 2.5% increments. Therefore, it goes 10%, 7.5%, 5.0% and the lowest taxes anyone or entity pays is 2.5%.

Deductions are those items we spend money on which can be subtracted from our income before we are taxed. These include all the essentials of living life. Such as rent, the upkeep of one's home, transport and gasoline, expenditures for doing business, food, water, maintenance and whatever else living life and working costs.

Further deductions include all items on which government may spend our taxes. All of which we have listed in our Constitution. Then we deduct all insurance, any Healthcare, and all education.

We get to deduct these all figuring no government would want to tax the mere act of living, which is what all those expenses represent.

Now, all of these you can deduct for yourself personally if single or for all your family members if married and living in the same household. Many extended families live together in extended homes. Often these are connected via enclosed paths. Each distant enough to ensure privacy yet close enough to form a tightly knit household. The advantage gained is the collective family income total is used instead of per individual.

With deductions subtracted from overall income, we have found out how much of our yearly income is taxable. In other words, what your profit is.

So, those of us who show a profit of up to fifty thousand dollars per year over and above the deductions pay 10% in taxes—the highest percentage that we have. Those who show profits higher than fifty thousand pay lower percentages in taxes. This means that here on Here-Born taxation rates work in reverse to Earth-Born.

Therefore, those who show a profit greater than fifty thousand dollars will pay a lower tax percentage...and so on down to 2.5% being the lowest.

Unbelievable! Is the kindest EB attitude on hearing this.

But. The high percent is an incentive used to *drive self* to earn more. Here success may only be rewarded and never penalized—by law.

Some EB's find it interesting what happens with a lower tax rate—the more you earn.

First off, you will pay a *greater amount* of *dollars* in taxes to Government due to the higher income and second you get to keep a *higher percentage* of your own hard-earned income. I believe other times referred to this as *win-win*. But what of cheaters?

For us, cheating on one's taxes is almost unheard of.

And why?

Well! If you fake it by showing larger deductions, you end up showing less profit for the year. This can put you into a higher tax percentage bracket. On the other hand, if you make your deductions less than they should be you will show a profit greater than it is, and that is fraud.

What happens to you when you commit that fraud is not a happy thing.

A public list of names of all the persons and businesses who refuse to pay taxes at all or who cheat hoping to pay less at a lower percentage bracket is available to all individuals, all businesses. Soon as ones' name appears, many will no longer employ you or do business with you—but deciding so is at their personal choice alone. There are no regulations that demand anyone do this.

That is a stiff price to pay for a few dollars more or less.

But! How does our legal side of life feel about someone doing either of these two?

Well! Go ahead and thank you for the extra dollars—is one way. And losing your entire income due to unemployment or the refusal by others to do business with you is a harsh penalty that many never recover from. And if you want to come back to full financial prosperity it's a long road.

You first sign a commitment to pay what you owe from the past and what's due in the future. If not. There are few ways of getting income once on that list. Most are menial jobs located out in the open desert. All of which are run by individuals who prefer to profit from another's misfortune or misdeeds.

Few survive long out there.

So take your pick.

And! Beware anyone adding a name to the list that should not be on it. You will be liable for loss of income and criminal charges are levied against you as well.

Yes. Here-Born's taxes are not merely fair but it's criminal to attempt changing or adding to them...let alone actually changing them.

Looking up from the past, I find myself naked in front of my bedroom mirror. I pull pajamas on, pause and examine the moonlit sky as I do each night.

I was once a teacher but am now a vendor of pre-owned body parts. Pre-owned parts are as difficult for tourists from Earth-Born to understand as our tax system is.

"That's so revolting," is how most tourists react to human parts on display and for sale.

To which I am inclined to say, "Despite rumors to the contrary we are not robots nor zombies. We can and do die."

If anyone still appears confused, I'll add, "The fleet which brought our forefathers here, crashed. They had miscalculated gravity—badly. Experiments on the regrowth of human parts were underway onboard. During and after the crash-landing chemical compounds escaped into the atmosphere.

"These evolved to become *preservatives,* which we now use to treat injuries. In this fashion, pre-owned parts came to thrive as a business." Few do much more than gag despite so eloquent an explanation.

I got divorced soon after my release from prison. My now ex-friend Bordt Nettler and ex-wife Deidre then got married.

I later become a campaigner. Conducting a campaign as a pre-owned parts dealer made more sense as contact with tourists is a natural part of a pre-owned vendor and a one-on-one tourist guide's daily life.

Therefore, for the second time my career with SandMasters ended but this time at the Hunduranda dealership. The first termination happened with the factory itself. Something I do not care to discuss, as I've mentioned.

With teeth brushed and in bed I bid the day farewell amidst thoughts of Peter Wernt, my new EB tourist and campaign target.

In what condition will I find his Foundation?

Which is what we call his education.

Which is the target of my campaign.

And the target of our Hope.

# CHAPTER 8

## OF POIP, PRE-OWNEDS GALORE AND A STRANGE EB TOURIST

**Sand Lake Flats Review—Morning Edition**

Those of Earth-Born fearing a disruption of society position themselves upon EB's Foundation.

We know Society's foundation is, after all, its education system.

However, on Earth-Born education remains the domain of Government alone.

Their students monitored via testing will find their brightest identified and offered education at its *best*.

These students cannot help but accept and by doing so become molded into conformity by a Foundation tunnel-visioned in design, in result.

Thus is attained a conformity of viewpoint to the satisfaction of an old, old need.

The *need* of the fearful to be relieved of fear.

In addition, the afraid celebrate each graduate with their own victory cry.

*This bright one will not upset the applecart!*

Sadly, the brightest of their young believe they remain alert to when brainwashing may begin.

And in that *alertness* they discuss issues in words that are an exact copy of what they'd heard on the *News* the day before.

None realize this.

Yet all declare said words are their own heartfelt opinions.

Tragic?

Tull-Tor Hawkur—commentator.

\*\*\*

The morning sun slips stealthily onto sand. Temperatures soar despite the shards of morning-pink lingering in the sky.

A hangover manifests a faint throbbing at my temples. Pleased at its mildness, I hunch down over the handlebars and tickle the throttle open. Hellbent responds and we accelerate across sand headed for my shop Pre-owneds Galore of SLF.

Dust swirls seeking entry to my eyes, nose, and mouth.

I snort and chuckle but keep a keen eye on the way ahead.

Minutes on, my path across sand weaves back-n-forth some. I bend my arms at the elbows to lessen the degree of body motion feeding back into the steering and our tracks straighten. I run an eye over sand to find a treacherous surface awaits this morning's unwary commuter—this courtesy of last night's Antarctic blowing out the southeast.

Mother Wind creates our roads as flat stretches of sand—many being old riverbeds now eons dry. Each day and every night she leaves freeways and highways in her wake but never in the same location. But always headed in the same two directions. Out here, tar turns soft and mushy by day, hardens at night and often cracks beyond repair making it worthless.

Those of her children who awaken during daylight hours are contradictory of nature. From the north comes Sister Storms, from the southeast whispers Mourner's Wind, from the north-east wafts Arzern's Delight and from the southwest gusts Chef's Call-out. Only two rush about at night, the Antarctic and the Arctic.

I cut the long way around what looks suspiciously like quicksand. The relentless dust swirls up and about me. I chew at the taste of it flat and gritty in my mouth. Mid-chew Peter Wernt leaps to mind and so too the dangers of bracing up to a new EB mind. Every EB tourist encountered is a new universe of thought, a new challenge, making entry to each Foundation unique.

However, with entry gained, I plant our ideas of Freedom and Rights within and perhaps they will spread these on returning home—this is our Hope. But not as easy a task as it sounds.

Of late, I have struggled more than before while getting little in the way of results. Each my recent tourists were full-blown failures, not one having expressed enthusiasm for our Here-Born Rights. I groan as Madsen's face springs to view carved hard as Rocklands rock and as disagreeable.

As a senior, he does not camp happily when failure is involved. But his recent threat spat at me out upon sand was too vague for my liking. Campaigners are all volunteers. Why then does he impart useless threats? Especially when they say naught of any ill that may befall me. His words cling to me now, bloodthirsty worms wriggling about in search of edible thoughts.

During bouts of deep introspection, I imagine he has revealed my real name to Poip and visions of Jiplee's fate besiege me. Any-n-all reasoning stumbles and falters and I dangle betwixt flight and obligation. I cannot help myself. He is too grim. I fear he will betray me, as did our elected officials sell out our entire nation.

Therefore, I now hide certain thoughts from him. Yes. I've not been forthright of late. In self-defense, I've decided to keep secrets and to hold back certain bits of information. On the flipside, I have many unanswered questions. Who murdered Jiplee? Is this EB's response to our campaign once we announced it—it is no secret? How did the killer identify her? Was her last tourist involved? But Madsen worries me most of all.

Only of late have I realized that if he is saying things to me that are critical of mutual friends...then he is saying the same to them about me. Witness his comment about Maggie counting pennies.

There are many that do such rumor mongering...while pretending to be a friend to one-n-all. Such persons insist they merely *share worthwhile information about others for one's own benefit.*

I shudder at the effort of laying to sleep worrisome images and ideas. It's a struggle, but I generate extra energy for self and accelerate down the last dune towards town. Looking out ahead my heart flutters with sudden trepidation. Barriers block access into town this morning. A double line of Poip does duty behind several rows of orange colored drums.

Ahead of these a Poip pair, the A-one and B-one models of a two-part system, do duty. B-one stands off a short distance as A-one interviews each commuter. I join the waiting line of SandRiders but keep a watchful eye busy.

Some of us twitch involuntarily, the tension of pretended ease being more than they can handle. Poip busily move with their perpetual stutter motion. The wind sighs around our silent protests. Exhausts burble at idle, tires scrunch on sand, heat offers no mercy. Poip voices almost hurt.

I stare at my fuel tank and run a fingertip along a pinstripe, my eyes busy elsewhere. Nervous tension drifts on the wind. Commuters scratch at armpits and scalps. Engines idle while others tick once shut down.

Dressed in military fatigues, the silver-bodied Poip move briskly, methodically, questioning commuters one at a time— their uniforms snap-n-crackle in starched stiffness. Robotic Poip voices grow sharper and cut the wind more than usual.

Once assessed most commuters head for town. Others find themselves shoved into Poip-wagons. With each wagon full, they head off into the desert, the snarl of exhausts resounding a victory call.

I reach the front breathing too fast, knees weak and grateful I'm seated. Sweat drips down my back. I manage a smile.

"You Once-Other?" the A-one asks as it looks up from the data displayed on its Nomadi screen.

"I am," I reply.

"What's your real name?" A-one demands.

"That information is not available," I reply and raise an eyebrow in query.

"In the interest of happiness I advise you to disclose," A-one says.

"Whose happiness?" I ask it.

A-one steps backward throws its arms wide and says, "Once-Other, please take a timeout and attend to a bulletin directly from the Director of the Department for the Assurance of Happiness, Earth." It pauses and points to its twin. "A moment as my friend downloads."

Its *friend* buzzes and whines, a coffee grinder about to let go of life, and falls silent.

A-one says, "The Bulletin has been downloaded. May I have your attention, please?" And grasps its handgun.

I swallow at a suddenly dry throat despite having been briefed that this action on the part of Poip is a test. A test to discover we campaigners—none of us has figured out how precisely such a test is supposed to work. I hold to a relaxed outward attitude and even manage a smile.

A-one lets go of its weapon and once again throwing its arms wide, says, "Welcome to Earth's delivery of law and order and the assurance of happiness for one-n-all.

"The people of Here-Born can now demand happiness as an entitlement. It is well worth your while to understand that the sole task of Poip is to ensure the happiness of all citizens.

"Please visit our website where you'll discover happiness is by law an entitlement. We hope happiness participants will tell others how much life has changed for the better with happiness now guaranteed.

"Attention! One and all!

"No one may violate your right to happiness.

"Now! Moving on!

"We do understand the need to withhold real personal names on Here-Born despite how unhappy that makes others. Under current law, we have embraced the idea.

"Have a nice day fellow citizen. Your friendly Director of the Department for the Assurance of Happiness, Mister Warrent McPeters."

I ride across old sand-snail burrows unaware of the handlebars moving from side-to-side and the crunch of tire upon sand. All I can sense is Poip-scan boring into the back of my head. I rub the nape pretending I am unconcerned and glance into a rear-view mirror. As a group all Poip turn from scrutinizing my retreat and focus on the next in line.

I sigh but cannot smooth away all anxiety.

They'll arrest me someday—once they know my real name.

On that day, I will vanish.

I nibble at my lower lip.

We are in a real war and up against an endless parade of laws and regulations eroding our freedoms and rights. At times, all seems hopeless. Still, in the strangest manner a ray of hope peeks out from between the clouds of doom-n-gloom— it comes by way of results, campaign results.

By all accounts, our ideas of freedom and rights have driven certain EB tourists quite mad, screwball-snorting as one report claims. These campaigners warn that affected persons tend to wander off into the desert and are never seen again.

Strange hope this is indeed.

Nevertheless, despite the deaths EB tourists keep coming— that gives us hope.

But our struggle isn't lightened in any way. Recently, a lady tourist handed me her business card assuming I'd broken an EB law or two. And by way of an invitation to hire her she said, "I'm a Criminal Attorney, Once-Other."

"That's very honest of you," I replied changing one of her nouns into an adjective. She was not amused.

I turn my attention outwards as the city of Sand Lake Flats embraces me.

Out upon open sand scanning is easy. Sand hides none; sand hides all...yes...a quandary. At the entrance to any city, scanning changes from relaxed to tense. I check down alleys, behind store windows looking for foreigners and locals alike.

I examine each for signs of danger but find none or perhaps fail to see where there is. I relax a little and allow the city's welcome to touch me with its own peculiar tradition. Yes, there is an animal readiness about SLF.

The city sprawls upon a valley floor some insist was once the bed of a lake or frying pan of the gods. It is prey to sandstorms violent of velocity and pernicious of disposition. Emergency Fraggers stationed throughout the city provide recovery from such sandstorms.

I note that on the sidewalk, a man stands with an ear bent to Nomadi, back to me, yet his eyes follow my progress reflected in a shop window. I reach for his thoughts but find them in do-not-disturb mode. A cold hand clasps at my throat.

Why would he block me? He glances at his Nomadi screen, holds it up and searches for bandwidth. I look up at the towering profile of SLF and realize he was merely concerned my presence came between him and a tenuous connection.

I peer overhead where perhaps a sniper waits. All I find are hundreds of tall communication towers boosting Nomadi signal for residents and businesses alike notwithstanding the odd dead spot. From overhead, the city's combination of tents and single story buildings entwined by a daisy chain of high-rises forms an organized pattern...if you squint.

Attention back on what's nearby, I veer left skirting the city's edges headed for the purple-n-gold striped circus tent and fairgrounds located south of the Mall's east parking lot.

SLF Mall stands two floors tall, is oval in design and shimmers green in the sunlight. Ocean green I believe.

I zero in on my store scrutinizing it for anything out of place. To my relief, tie-downs are taut with knotted loops still hanging as they were last night. It is a large rectangular tent with its main entrance facing west.

Its roof is finished in reflective silver in homage to our sun and doubles as solar panels. Walls are pastel green broken by vertical white stripes. One can see through the tent walls when the sun hangs eastwards and at the right angle.

Nothing appears out of the ordinary and my heartbeat eases. If sudden death awaits one, it's normally carefully hidden in full view amongst all that is familiar.

Which is likely what Jiplee discovered but far too late.

Inside, I roll up sections of the north, east and south sides allowing passersby and the breeze to enter. I pause, step outside and scan my surroundings a habit of those who live upon sand and know its dangers. Yes, scanning the horizon for signs of sandstorms comes as natural as does breathing.

A few dust-devils dance along the edge of a distant dune. None are dangerous though few *not* of Here-Born understand the suddenness with which they can grow into monsters.

Across sand, all is clear this morning.

I check closer to *home.*

To the south lies the circus tent, the fairgrounds, and a carousel mostly occupied by tourists and performers. Westwards one has a clear view of the Mall, its east parking lot and entrance. To the north and east, open desert flows to the horizon and onwards to the barren northern mountain ranges and the Rocklands proper.

I head back inside and check the anti-fly system located between displays of fresh pre-owned parts. Today its pump dutifully thump-thumps. A good sign for they are finicky appliances for which the flies are assuredly thankful.

I remove older pre-owneds from coolers located beneath the counter and lay them out neatly along the special-deals counter. I check all hanging legs and arms for Neatness, ensure they are properly aligned and in formation, most are. Only the fingers refuse to hold still—there is just no Neatness with fingers.

Despite this, my pre-owned business thrives as does sales from items on shelves and hanging racks. These are mostly paintings, potted cacti, stuffed wild animals and used pots, pans, secondhand Nomadi, desert clothes and SandRider parts. My slowest selling items are all but useless EB clothing.

A quick glance to the rear confirms gray-blue Arzerns, stuffed birds of prey that is, are where they should be. Their counterparts, stuffed beige-n-brown sand bound Water Criers, cluster together in a corner under a tattered tarp. Around the walls and along walkways cacti stand to attention in tall flowerpots.

Near the entrance, a faux blackwood table waits bolted to the floor and untouched since yesterday. I lay a single fingerprint in the thin film of sand before wiping it down. This I'd learned in prison—good luck for a day. With morning preparations complete, I relax at the table sipping ice-cold water.

Across the parking lot, a Poip pair exits the Mall. They halt upon seeing me and lean close to one another in imitation of whispering. Unease swamps me.

Has Madsen betrayed me? Why did he ignore my farewell wave at Jiplee's funeral? Has he already committed a dastardly deed? Have I been compromised?

I watch and even at a hundred sand-paces their incessant buzzing irritates. After several minutes, they head off. I sigh in relief. One of them glances back and my heart races. I bite my lip and gaze upwards. In the sky, the last traces of pink, turn blue. Unlike sunset, the pink of dawn often lingers until noon.

Abruptly the environment tunes up brighter, sounds hit louder. SandRiders drone by at low rpm. Distant cries of laughter and fear waft across from the carousel. Tourist's voices, sharp and edged, cut in from the parking lot. The red Mall doors slide open hissing protestations at the inbound rush of throat burning air. The waiting crowd surges forward, jostling and pushing to be first in, first out of the heat.

I check the Mall parking lot and note a tall, slim built EB tourist headed my way. I examine him in detail as this is likely Peter Wernt, my new tourist. I also ponder whether he is more than a tourist for he could be an undercover agent of EB's Poip.

Wait and see, I advise self.

His top-of-the-line, silver-gray fan-n-fit suit and a snug full-face helmet speak of a moneyed life. Its face-shield, closed against the heat, hides his eyes. His boots imprint loudly upon sand, his breath snorts through the helmet vents like a bull, head down pawing at sand eyes focused upon a bloodied matador.

I swallow the last of the water and stand as he strides in. His boots pounding on the floorboards reflect a hint of military life. I smile as we shake hands and note this Peter Wernt is more confident than most.

He slides his face-shield up, reveals an unsmiling face, glances around and wrinkles his long narrow nose as though a foul odor had drifted by. Now most all tourists shudder in disgust on seeing pre-owned parts for the first time. Some even present one with an impromptu display of recent meals—others simply faint away.

Not this Peter Wernt though.

His eyes flash like Poip lights as ideas skitter across his face.

I reach for them but they vanish.

Keeping a firm grip on my hand, he checks over my all white outfit—boots-n-all.

"You Once-Other?" he asks in a manner indicative of another bad odor wafting his way.

And I'm thrown back to brown bars on doors and windows and wherein wheat fields at high noon hard faces drip with sweat toiling beneath a blazing sun. Backs bend tilling a desert sand earlier prepped for planting with a mixture of rich EB soil.

A short distance away, empty drums of rich-n-moist earth stand in silent witness of hard labor. Digging tools thud, men curse the heat, empty barrels echo as they bounce tossed carelessly aside. I question how Peter's innocent greeting managed to send me so far back in time, back to prison.

Nothing comes to mind.

Dismissing the unanswerable, I address his question.

"I am, and you are Peter Wernt, right?" I reply.

He takes a half step backward. "Ah? Well...oh? Yeah. I am." He glances at the fairground, the Mall, the horizon. "Yeah! I understand why no pictures—only chat."

I brace up ready to defend self from this verbal stain when Franciscoa, an elderly and rugged Here-Born gentleman and my campaign slash shop-assistant, walks in.

Peter raises an eyebrow at the sight of Franciscoa's light olive coveralls, red cap, red shoes and strange face. He wouldn't know why Franciscoa's skin is stretched tightly across high cheekbones nor why the whites of his eyes are permanently yellowed. All in evidence of the damage wrought by excessive Crier poison upon his body when we were all very young.

He had almost died out upon the desert on one damn hot day. At full howl, Franciscoa's engine gave up the ghost and shredded itself when a connecting rod snapped at the small end, spun around like a helicopter blade and made minced-metal of the internals.

In the next instant, the wheels locked up, launching him over the handlebars into a Crier warren. Six of them attacked him with their sting-claws emptying their poison sacks into him. Franciscoa survived because friends were there and someone had anti-venom, though not enough.

He spent six weeks in hospital. Even now he still suffers. Yet as always he is aglow with life and perpetual cheer despite the continued presence of poison-induced pain coursing through his body most days and every night.

I grin fondly as he adjusts his cap revealing a barren scalp shaved clean by the same poison. He rushes over, grabs my hand in a bony grip his eyes fixed on Peter.

His face splits into a wide smile. "Now Mister Tourist—would you agree your education is your Foundation?"

Wernt speaks rapidly but utters no sound.

"Wow! This one pure swallowed his tongue," Franciscoa says directly to me, chuckles, pumps my hand again and heads deeper into the tent. There he selects a canister of preservatives, holds it to his ear, shakes it, smiles as the contents slosh and goes to work.

I turn to Peter hopeful of a something I have long sought. A missing something within every EB tourist I have met. Moreover, I again hope that maybe, just maybe this one will have it.

Will he comprehend what their Department for the Assurance of Happiness is doing? My countenance hardens at the real meaning of their motto: *Our monitoring ensures your Happiness*. Wait and see I advise self.

"Walk with me," I say and his mouth snaps closed.

Taking his arm, I head deeper in amongst my goods until miscellaneous wares surround us. I hold up, glance about and find current conditions sound. I turn and check Peter's reaction when he is this close to my pre-owneds.

At first, his face holds smooth and calm. However, within seconds a slow tick starts up around his eyes. It crosses to his mouth, leaps to his nose in a strange jerky fashion and for no reason I can fathom keeps on ticking.

I wait for its demise.

And wait some more.

It ticks on.

Perhaps he is a little low on calcium, or magnesium, or even vitamin C, or potassium, or perhaps all. I hide a smile from my lips, let go his arm and intent on accessing his mind walk deeper into my store.

He reluctantly follows, examining my stock of pre-owned parts as his face smooths over. I stop-up, he steps in and stands close. I sense there is something further different with this one. To begin with, and it's a first altogether, he's relatively calm in the face of pre-owneds despite that manifest tick.

We examine various pre-owned in silence for several moments. He touches the toes of one, snaps his hand away and grimaces. I reach over and check for his thoughts and find them blocked. Okay. Not a problem. Access to EB minds can at times take longer.

I move on. "Most of my pre-owned stock is under this counter inside a cooling locker. Would you like to examine some of those, Peter?"

He shakes his head and leans on the counter, chin cupped in his palm.

"No. Well. Okay. Now—a couple of essential items. Tours are one-on-one. Okay? Also, I, ah, well...you are a magnificent tourist and we customarily give a reduced price too—"

He stands tall and says, "Spare me the false compliments."

"One of those eh?" Franciscoa says the naughty twinkle of an old man in his young eyes. He stoops over and sprays a set of pre-owned feet with preservative.

"Looks that way," I reply and say to Peter, "I understand but I know you are. No! Please don't deny it. Okay. Good. Hold it. Now. You'd like to know about this all and my pre-owned business as well I figure. Right?"

I tune to his mind and nothing.

"Weird Once-Other," Franciscoa says. "Real dangerous."

"I'll solve it, Franci."

"Make it fast," he says and over sprays an arm.

"Preservatives are expensive...ease up will you," I say.

"Money. Money. Money. Were you EB born Once-Other?" And he chuckles to smooth over the insult.

I turn to Peter, who takes a half step closer and gazes down his nose at me. We lock fully head-on for the first time—and another difference is apparent.

His eyes are as cold as last night's Antarctic blower. Behind their frozen wastes resides a something I recognize but cannot place. It's something—something I've seen before, but where? And the ice barrier shatters. In prison in the eyes of hardened criminals. My heart stutters like a SandRider running out of gas.

I make a note to be more than careful with this one and to have Madsen check on whom this Peter is—in depth. "You want to know about our customs...my business?" I ask him my voice a little shaky.

He rubs his chin, gives my stock the once-over and says, "Preservatives as well," and waves at the sky and sand as he who knows of what he indicates—but actually does not.

I begin my campaign.

"Okay then...and briefly at this point. Preservatives make for pre-owned sales and the swapping out of body parts in general. But we'll come to the details later—much later in fact. Now stay with me and pay attention, altogether.

"There's much you need to learn when it comes to surviving upon these heated sands—keep in mind that death stalks Here-Born incessantly. It can strike when you least expect it and it's final. Which I'm sure you know—it being death and all. So, beware of Here-Born she's a cruel and unforgiving mistress."

He pops a finger into his mouth, wets it, wipes his eyebrows down. "Yeah well, let's find out who you are. So yeah. Cutting to the chase here. What's the bottom line? We never did finalize." He crosses his arms and waits tapping his foot.

I examine him in silence.

His eyes are still deader than any I have seen outside of prison and about as cold as the black slots Poip pass off as eyes. Caution bows in. I open the door to it, take a mental step backward, measure Peter's hidden thoughts, consider his foul distemper...demeanor and make my calculations.

In conclusion, I modify my price upward by several measures. With a flourish, I show him five fingers at one thousand per finger and cross them with three to multiply by. "The price of a one-on-one tour, Peter."

His chin drops like a rock down a mineshaft, his eyes sharpen cutting into me. But upon my face shines a confidence born of years of successful sales.

I assuage his dagger eyes with a smile and certainty.

Peter's mouth works in silence and stops open. He closes it and says, "Fifteen thousand? Yeah. Ha! That include everything? We've chatted, but I am looking you in the eye. Some jump, eh?"

My hard face confirms pricing.

"Wow. Isn't that like...high?" Franciscoa says.

"Stay out of this Franciscoa," I order.

"Does Madsen approve?" he asks.

I chop downwards with a virtual hand and say, "Do your chores. Price has nothing to do with him. This is my business."

"Still! You know Madsen."

"What's with you today?" I demand looking in his direction

"Oh? You noticed! Had a realization...last night—it consumes me. Tell you later Once-Other—maybe at the Drinks-n-All."

"I hear...you...," I say and glance to where Franciscoa is staring, his mouth suddenly hung open.

A demon is stabbing at Peter's cheeks from inside his mouth, a steel punch desperate to escape. They grow larger as tiny volcanoes of skin thrust up, flatten and pop up again. All the while, his cold blue eyes never waver from mine and then the impossible happens.

A cobra's head appears in each of his eyes.

They hiss...long and low.

# CHAPTER 9

## OF POSSIBLE ILLNESS, A NEW ECONOMIC SYSTEM, HIDDEN THOUGHTS

I wait for them to vanish. They instead extend fangs dripping poison. I blink. They are still present. But?! Are they imagination? Real? What to do?

To gather some semblance of reality, I glance at Franciscoa busy spraying hanging Pre-owneds with preservatives. He slips in and out of focus. I shake my head in hopes of clearing it, but instead a cacophony erupts—bells, whistles, engines, screams, thundering sandstorms.

Then silence followed by more painful noise.

Bells toll as loud as a mile-long lane of cathedrals calling their congregations to Mass. My head threatens to split in half. Not feel good in any way, altogether. Whatever is going on with this tourist Peter Wernt is unique. The noise ends. I blink once again and this time the snakes and fangs do vanish.

I should bail out and take my chances with Madsen's foul disposition. Wait! I glance around. All seems normal. My heart beats steadily. The wind blows. The sky is blue. My tent has white stripes. But what to do?

At best, I should end this tour. Yes. End it now.

In an incomprehensible contradiction I instead say, "Yes Peter! Everything, and in all possible ways is non-negotiable at fifteen thousand and you pay immediately. Yes, you do!" Adjusting mind and thought I add, "We've got no credit system out here but if you like, please feel free to refuse and leave."

I step back with arms crossed and copy him by tapping my foot while presenting a stern countenance from behind which I inspect possible futures, a single question in mind.

What is going on inside this tourist, Peter Wernt? No answer returns—indicating another failure to envision a future. Until I get his thoughts as I should, answers will be few and far between. This is more dangerous than any previous campaign—I am *deaf*. Caution in all I do is a must.

Is there an alternative?

Yes. I should send him off without hesitation. But who knows how important he may be. Especially if he has personal contact with hundreds, thousands or perhaps even millions back home on EB. That we need!

Also, Madsen will soon update me on this Peter Wernt. If it turns out, he has vast contacts—that is hope. Hook into many from EB with the details of our Rights.

Peter rubs his cheeks as though they hurt, grunts, smiles and says, "Direct eh. Uh? Oh yeah. Right. Okay. No credit system at all. Difficult to believe."

He hunts through his fan-n-fit.

I take the opportunity to introduce him to something no EB understands. "On Here-Born we operate with a balanced economy, Peter. No inflation, no deflation. Balanced. So no credit."

"Impossible," he says as they all do.

I blip a mental throttle and change down into high rpm campaign mode. "Well. The quandary of credit and inflation is similar to the riddle of the chicken and the egg. Which do you think came first? Allow me to answer. Neither. They are created as one and at the same time."

"Yeah! You lost me Once-Other."

"No chickens without eggs, no eggs without chickens as far as the creation of chickens goes—all chickens. So. No inflation needed without credit. Both of which are created as the chicken and the egg. One has no role to play without the other."

He makes to speak, but I wave him silent. His eyes reveal he is not pleased.

"Under *your* inflation prices rise faster than savings, Peter. So. You cannot run an economy using inflation without also having a credit system. You will not find much use for credit within a balanced economy because prices do not rise and rise.

"And! Inflation is a manufactured condition—not a natural one. Your Foundation lies to you about the what, the wherefore and the why of inflation. Of course...there is the financing of massive projects by corporations. Investment returns solve that."

"I don't believe—," he says.

A loud thud as Franciscoa stumbles drops a canister and kicks it. It rolls and bangs into a flowerpot.

"What's going on?" I ask him.

"I'm a little edgy. Don't worry."

"Keep the noise down, Franci. You're interrupting my work."

I turn back to Peter, he to me and I say out aloud, "I know our economic system is hard to understand but the details are written in our Constitution. I'll let you have a copy before you leave."

"Waste of time Once-Other. I would never read it."

"If you—" and my mouth locks up in shock at what I just sensed.

Did Peter get Franciscoa's and my mind-to-mind communication? He had glanced at Franciscoa and I'd gotten the distinct impression he knew what I'd said mind-to-mind. This includes the follow-up response from Franciscoa but that is impossible. EB's cannot, do not communicate mind-to-mind.

Now if *this one* can...he must have electronic equipment hidden about his person.

A quick inspection reveals nothing visible.

Franciscoa says, "We're kinda low on preservatives. I'll get more. How much?"

"Five gallons will do," I say hoping he gets my need to concentrate on Peter.

"No kidding—big spender."

"Franciscoa!"

He grunts waves to Peter, nods to me and heads off.

Peter's cold eyes follow him far longer than curiosity would. I concentrate entirely on Peter. He senses my scrutiny and turns to me. A thought shadows across his eyes and gone.

He looks to the floor, meanders his attention to the rear of the shop as though deeply interested in my store. I wait him out. Our eyes meet and hold, but he remains silent. I crook a finger to indicate if he is staying—payment is due.

He nods and pays.

As he does, I reach out to his mind in new ways. A beep from my Nomadi announces his payment arrived but what he's thinking does not. And from out last night's adventures at the Drinks-n-All, recall strikes me.

Odious Odentien's mind also seemed closed to me. But that was due to excessive alcohol. Or so I had thought. What if it's not drinking hiding their thoughts? Could this be something new? Something I've not been briefed on? Are EB's intoxicated all the time? Could that be the cause of my difficulty with Peter and Odentien? Without EB minds available to us our Campaign is doomed to failure.

I shudder at visions of how Madsen will be camping if I fail once again. I swallow at a dry mouth and say, "Thank you, Peter. Now, and before moving on, allow me to configure proof of payment so that Toip can verify taxes as paid."

From out of nowhere, not even from out of the oppressive heat and without warning an involuntary flutter of nerves assaults me. My mouth locks closed and my heart beats unevenly. My fingers feel detached. I flex them, but they remain numb. My left arm aches and my legs turn into soggy paper. I struggle just staying upright.

I manage to hold still for an instant and once sure of maintaining dignity say, "Where shall I begin your tour?"

"You okay?" he asks.

"I'm good," I lie. "Where would you like to start?"

"What's ah? Toip? What's this Toip thing?"

Where does such a nonsensical question come from? Toip *is* from EB! Peter Wernt *is* from EB. Can he be that ignorant? No! Impossible. Bells alarm again yet provide no hint of why he pretends to such vast ignorance. Dare I question it? Would he be offended? No! Don't do it born of curiosity alone for it's not critical…at this stage.

I swallow hard. He watches me a fixed grin in place. This may be a hopeless campaign. What to do? End off? Keep going? Well. We have made our choice of weapon. Something will come up. I must be careful with this one, though, and very alert.

I take several deep breaths and resolve to discover what this Peter hides up his skin-tight sleeve. With luck good or bad, all this weirdness and sneering may simply be whom Peter Wernt is. And so I continue.

"Toip means *taxation over internet protocol.* You must be familiar with the Toip and the Poip, Peter?"

He shakes his head no.

It's a little early to straight out call a new tourist a liar, so instead I say, "No? How astonishing. Hmm? Well. We'll cover those later as they crop up. We'll also meet a Poip pair." And I hope pretended ignorance and lack of awareness will open him up.

"You're not very good at this, are you Once-Other? What's Poip?"

This time, I am prepared. "Poip means *police over internet protocol.* I'm real shocked you apparently don't know that yet you're from EB, but let's move on with your one-on-one."

"You telling me I'm stupid?" he asks. "A liar?"

Brakes screech and rubber burns upon an imaginary tarred road. I have one response to severe insults and I'm about to actually bow out when Madsen's words of old wander on back, as they were intended to when he drummed them in during my training.

"No matter what an' all. No matter who an' all. He or she may be all of a high value. So round-n-about never allow personal feelings, likes or dislikes to get in the way of your campaign an' all. You open every Foundation, ain't nothing more to the task ahead. Plant the seeds of Freedom an' Rights an' grow they will."

Peter lifts his face shield higher, points to his forehead and indicates questions.

I calm irresolute Once-Other and Madsen fades from mind as I answer. "Yes, you can use your recently purchased third-eye camera. My? It's perfectly embedded in your forehead. It's damn close to invisible with that imitation skin lens cover. Damn fine work it is."

With his elbow up I note a small bulge near his armpit.

These at least I know of, but each differs in purpose.

Beyond the common though, devices exist which keep minds hidden. Scramblers or nullifiers we call them. He will have declared it on arrival so Madsen can find out for me. But for now I'll assume Peter to be more than an everyday tourist.

But at this time, I don't know what the *more* is.

"Costs extra I imagine," he says.

I smile inside. If nothing else, I can make this endeavor profitable or end it right now. "The same again Peter," I reply in a cold, flat voice.

He glares at me for a long time, then pulls out his Nomadi and pays. And you could have knocked me out Rocklands hard with a single grain of sand—not a protest, a counter offer.

Nothing?! Unheard of! Scary!

Nevertheless, I quickly accept and configure Toip fumbling in my haste with mind run amok. Who would pay almost four times the price of a tour? And why when he could leave and join another pre-owned vendor's tour? I must get at his innermost self. Must use all questions correctly, effectively.

As do any-n-all of Here-Born's Free Marketers, I stream questions that are the starting point for estimating a future. We also extend perception forward and back in time when assessing the current, past and future timelines for answers.

So the life of the Free Marketer is filled with questions— many are never answered. The others do provide answers and thus open doors within our minds. Those doors offer a view of the future and enable us to predict and to estimate.

This is our skill. A skill bare and devoid of all but facts.

Yet, buried deep within me the poet of my youth yet lives.

And so I have a threesome: My recording cold and true, my view of the facts themselves, and the poet now long dead which yet arises to lend a hand to life and livingness.

Peter lets loose a cough.

"Ah yes! Where shall I begin? Where in all my pre-owneds shall I start? Ah! You know? Pre-owned fingers bother me the most." He about faces and films the hanging arms his head swaying in concert as the arms swing in the breeze.

I note the whisper of wind, the shouts, and laughter drifting in from the carousel. From behind me comes the hiss and gasp of the Mall doors opening and closing. The rumble-n-burble of SandRiders parking seems normal and reassuring.

Nodding to myself, I cut them all out and concentrate on Peter. "That's right. Point down this way and then along those fingers. You've got it."

"I don't need a Director," he snaps and continues recording but in a fashion unlike any other tourist.

He zooms in on the unruly fingers, drops to a knee and shoots low along a row of arms. Goes prone and records torsos displayed near the tent wall. Stands and examines the stuffed Arzerns suspended overhead as though in full flight.

He grimaces, shakes his head at something he finds distasteful, goes quickly to his knees and walks forward on them towards a pair of male legs for sale and pauses.

I redirect his attention. "See that Arzern over in the far corner. Left a little. Good. You're looking at the largest one ever captured—lived to a ripe old age that one did. Wingspan is a good five sand-paces. As you can tell, that is around twenty-five of your feet. Most are only about three some sand-paces."

"Yeah. Killer information Once-Other. Remind me to let you have a bonus."

I send his acid remark to where water on a duck flows and say, "That big! They can take a man. Pay attention, please. Who knows when you'll encounter one?"

"Yeah," he grunts, stands and moves closer to the pre-owneds, pulls out his Nomadi and works the keypad looking for all like an accountant. He stares a long time at the results. Smiles with grim satisfaction, pockets it, moves closer to the pre-owneds and zooms in for close-ups.

With sudden insight, it dawns on me.

He is estimating the value of items—heads and torsos in particular. Could a sale be imminent? Is that what he is hiding? Or maybe he suffers from an incurable disease—one invisible to the eye. Who knows how many pre-owned parts he may need? Well now!

I select an arm from under the counter; hold it at arm's length, point at it and say, "Shoot this one and you'll understand?"

He moves in close, shoots and shakes his head in reply.

I point and say, "Okay Peter. There. No, over there. How restless are those fingers? Nothing less than molecules of cheese trying desperately to escape being digested. Damn fine trouble fingers are. Neatness having gone missing altogether."

Questions chase each other across his face. I await their utterance. But he asks none. Instead, he bites his lip and stares at the floor. I clear my throat. He looks up and in his eyes the snakes writhe.

I swallow an urge to comment on them fearing they are imagination alone and say, "Keep watching and note fingers don't lie still. Shoot them. Okay. Good capture. You see what I mean. No? Okay. Let us ask a question. How does a vendor such as myself present Neatness if fingers move and point all over, all the time?"

I raise an eyebrow, he shrugs.

"Be assured...it's never!" I answer on his behalf.

He brushes sand off his legs but freezes at the burble of a SandRider driving close by. I listen as well, but the exhaust note is different from Madsen's. I sigh in relief glance over to ensure the flies are being kept at bay and again Peter coughs.

"This whole Neatness thing...an idiot's delight—right?" he asks.

I bite my tongue. "Important to us Peter."

"Whoopee!" he whispers.

One deep breath later I place the pre-owned arm back beneath the counter, ensure all of it is in the shade and tuck the fingers away. All done, I ready myself for this verbal combat Peter has packed along with his emotional baggage.

He stares off across the desert and whispers "Can't imagine living here. Sand and sun, sand—and so quiet! So few voices."

We stand close, listening. I play my attention over and around him. Still nothing. I keep trying and glance about as I do. Poip questioning someone is louder than usual. SandRider engines seem muted, windblown sand scratches at tent walls.

Peter becomes aware of my probing.

He turns and looks me in the eye. Hard-boiled hatred stabs at me for an instant and then vanishes. Now this I must understand, and soon. And the fastest way there? Give no hint of the importance access to a mind is.

Many tourists have come and gone since last I was forced to batter my way into a Foundation in this fashion. I've not often failed. This because my method is direct and simple, but not easy.

When forestalled I use my campaign like a blunt instrument. A battering ram so to say. No mental wall has held up; all castles have succumbed. As each one shatters torrents of hatred spew forth as he or she attempts to regain equilibrium.

That is when I move in and get the thoughts of those who work at keeping me out. And so I begin a more dangerous strategy with this Peter.

First comes the gentle probing with a virtual crowbar as the lever. Then the battering ram should that fail. In that he appears tougher than others screwball snorting as reported earlier by other Campaigners along with death out in the desert, should not be an issue.

I gather resolution to myself, nod pleasantly and say, "You're right. This desert is enormous, planet-wide in fact. It's damn dry and damn dusty all of everywhere. There's nothing but sand-n-rock across our world and silent save for the wind.

"Now up north towers Iron Ridge Mountain from which Iron Rock Falls feeds to the Lowlands. But! What is not sand is rock so hot you cannot walk on it as it right off cooks your feet if you do. Well now!

"We've named all flat rock the Rocklands and yes...after itself though spoken of as a scar. And! We'll come to all those later."

The light of interest in his eyes turns hard then dims as he looks inwards. Light returns to them and he reaches over to shake hands. Surprised, I hold back. He keeps his hand out. I clasp it, shake, make to release but he holds on...and his thinking self, engulfs me.

I stagger mentally at the impact of vivid images of snow and desert and summer mingled with winter and night with day. My pre-owned parts blur, the tent walls vanish. Not a sound whispers save for the tread of boots crunching in sand spread across the faux floorboards by our winds.

Who has entered my store? Wait and see I advise self.

As though from out a vast distance Peter says, "Do you take medication, Once-Other?"

Struggling to break free of the surreal creature that holds me immobile, I squeeze Peter's hand real hard. The images vanish and Peter's face appears before me. I stare in awe as his eyes grow brighter, his mouth twitches like a possessed rock-n-roller and his eyebrows slam together.

Then all freeze in place as though time stands still.

One by one they unravel. He grins like nothing happened, releases my hand and wipes sand off his glossy silver-gray sleeve. He checks the contents level of the Quaaseon gas flask hanging at his hip and is satisfied. He adjusts cooling to warmer and waits, a child at a bus stop and the bus is late.

First, I search for the owner of the footsteps to find only Peter present. Who walked across my floor? I glance at Peter.

He smiles of secrets.

This has become weird—too weird in fact. Not the battering ram nor crowbar I envisioned. Yet there's a message in those images. A hidden one I can but sense.

To buy time in which to examine them further, I pretend to inspect Peter's suit in detail and to my utter speechlessness, he turns as though on a fashion ramp. At a loss for words, I mutter, "Excellent...er...silky fan-n-fit...um...quality Peter."

"You better believe it," he says holding his arms wide, wrists locked. Suddenly a buzzing alarms from within his suit. He pulls out his Nomadi steps outside and walks off a distance.

From inside my store, with my back to Peter I work on getting his conversation. Sweat drips down my brow as I all but strain at it. Those perception tendrils I so prize seem suddenly disabled, hidden from me as though they are no longer mine.

I keep pushing outwards though, but they refuse to materialize. I try reaching him without them. After several minutes and receiving nothing, I glance over my shoulder.

His feet splayed upon the hot desert, Peter pumps his Nomadi in the air and slips it into a pocket. He walks back inside, stands close and says, "Okay. You look hot. Yeah. What's this idiot's notion *Neatness* all about?"

Mind numbed, I yet nod sagely at this my latest campaign and personal failure. Now, irrespective of what I tried, I failed to receive a single scrap of his conversation. But! No EB tech blocks at so consistent a level. How then can this be?

Also, what has happened to my perception? This is the second time now. Out upon sand seated alongside Jiplee I had found nothing when I sent tendrils across sand. At least that time I perceived the obvious—sand.

Am I seriously ill? Is sickness the cause of my shrinking skills? I must have a check-up. And damn! Perhaps I should have listened to Peter's conversation instead.

And damn again.

However, I brace up, swallow my frustration and set resolve to undefeated. Taking his elbow, I walk him towards my hanging pre-owneds, stuffed animals, stuffed birds and thriving cacti.

A quick check of our surroundings confirms we are alone—regular clients receive notification well ahead of time when a new campaign begins—with no such reason given.

I check once again. Is someone hiding behind those barrels over in the southwest corner? No. Well. At least scanning is still operational.

I clear a throat and mind dried by pitiless winds. And once again driven by the urge for a free tomorrow for Karrell and all our children, I proceed.

"See these arms over here. Note how they keep to a neat row, altogether. They will at times twitch a little. But if you speak in a kind, cajoling, but firm like voice they'll behave themselves."

He rubs his eyes as though they hurt beyond repair. "Did you not understand?" he says. "Your stock doesn't disgust me—comes close, though. Only on this sanity forsaken planet can horror shows be treated as normal."

Ignoring that, I plow onwards. "Doesn't support Neatness. Understand? Ah. Look over...little right. Focus. Fingers! Oh, how they wiggling around and get out of line. You get that?"

"Aargh! What?"

"No Neatness Peter."

"You a control freak or just plain stupid?" he growls.

My smile ticks, a stuck clock determined to make time. I ease my mind into neutral and edge him closer to my stock.

He attempts to step around me.

I block his escape and say, "On Here-Born Neatness earns extra points. Reputation points that is. Oh! Wait. Are you familiar with our motto? No? Ah! Explains all...that does. Pay attention now it's—*never let there be many when Neatness makes one.*"

# CHAPTER 10

## OF NEATNESS, FINGERS AND CACTI

"Awfully comprehensible Once-Other. Awfully so."

"Peter. Neatness is partly tidiness but more so *wholeness*. Pride from honor and...."

"Who cares?" he snarls yanks his arm free and covers his eyes with both hands as though fending off reality. After a slow heartbeat, his hands swing open like shutters do.

Flames leap out them, turn into glowing pincers, slam into me and lock on. I try to wrestle free but am unable to move. I focus my awareness inwards and scan for their point of contact, the point of paralysis.

All clear inside my head and within my upper torso. But there in the pit of my stomach attached left and right of center, the virtual pincers. I grab them with my inner-self and pull. An explosion erupts.

I stagger backward as the pincers rush about, jackhammers racing along nerve ends. I scream. They mount upon and ride my scream but in the instant sound exits my mouth they vanish and so too sound.

I glance around...still just the two of us here.

I focus on the refrigerator and head for it, legs leaden. Hands shaking, I pour water, add ice and glance over my shoulder. Peter had not followed. Instead, he stands with his back to me, hands on hips looking across at the Mall.

I fear this EB may be dangerous.

No! Wait.

Are there any Desert Drivers close? They have the skills to do this. If it is one or more waging a mind-to-mind war against me I must find out who and why. A quick scan of the crowd and beyond comes up empty.

I examine Peter once again—still nothing.

After brief though careful consideration, it comes to me that this Peter Wernt seems much like certain students from my earlier life. Slow to start but likely quick to the finish. Unlike them, he possesses a strange and mesmerizing power. On the other hand, if he does not—is there truly something wrong with me?

Only time will tell.

I head over, hand him some water and speak as does a teacher of young children. "Some details for you. Due to fingers not lining up there's no inherent Neatness. None! Out here, we pay extra for Neatness. Human beings, those ingrained with sloth, find it all too easy to be sloppy. *Sloppy is many. Neatness is one.*" I spread my arms appealing for understanding.

He snorts. "I am not a child Once-Other. Don't speak to me that way."

And he sulks like one.

Switching to a brisk tone, I point from legs to heads, to torsos, to a row of arms suspended high overhead. "Focus on those arms. Alright. Now. In general, arms are always straight except for—hey? Are you there *arm*...trying to ruin my reputation?"

It snaps back into line obedient-n-all.

I glance at Peter and wait but get no response.

"Now moving on, Peter? I told that arm to get back in line and bang-zip—in line, neat-n-all. Damn fine altogether. But Ohh! Please don't ask how it heard me. We've tried to find out but failed."

"The story of Here-Born, Once-Other. The full, complete, unabridged version."

I turn away and walk off talking fast in a low voice—he follows leaning forward, ears cocked to my every word.

"Fingers! They point everywhere and wiggle-wiggle they'll go. Wiggle, wiggle, wiggle! No Neatness with those damn fingers. How big a bad we talking here? Sure tarnishes a vendor's name, one-two-three and altogether. I had a sound name before, but now...well," and I nod at the parts surrounding us.

"I kinda like how they wiggle," he says.

I shrug his words off and hurry him across the floor until arms, legs, torsos and heads surround us. Let's see how he deals with this. Well damn! He remains cold of disposition, close to frigid.

I pull him clear of the pre-owned. He shakes my hand off and walks away. Bumps into an arm and lurches, bangs his head against a foot and totters there. Perhaps a crack in the armor?

I grab his sleeve and steady him.

In his eyes, thanks blink for but an instant.

I scoot in between the tent wall and a row of hanging arms. Hurry to the opposite end, exit and turn to Peter, who had followed. Keeping him trapped between stock and wall I say, "Note the arms hanging nice clean and neat right above my head...wha-what did you say?"

He pushes his way out waving his arms as though dispersing flies, stops mid-wave with his arms held up, looks me in the eye, drops his arms and says, "The décor."

A cold hand crushes my reasoning.

Is this one privy to the notion that all this talk of pre-owned parts and our Rights is merely a crowbar applied to open a resistive mind? This will be challenging if he's actually caught on this quickly.

And worse! I have no choice but to continue my search for his thoughts. Without them, I've no way of measuring the impact of my campaign.

I swallow a sand roughened fear and continue. "Oh...the décor," I say taking an additional physical and mental step backward at the abrupt change of focus. Then with self-control in hand, I turn and head off for the opposite end of my store.

He paces me. "Yeah. Who contrived this? Not sure that's the right word."

"I did," I reply feeling accused of something. "You like what I've done?"

"Not even faintly. Yetch."

"I do," and pointing add, "Note those magnificent blue-gray Arzerns looking down hungry like at my Criers."

"What's with you guys and the gore and the predators?" he asks.

"Well...look at those cacti plants," I say stopping up.

He looks shrugs indifference and turns away.

"No-no, Peter. Pay attention here—look again. Cacti grow straight up like tree trunks. Now. You'd best be careful of the blade arms growing out of them. Oh, how innocent they appear. But if you get too close they'll lop your members off...and there you go, instantly dismembered."

"They move by themselves?" he gasps. "Like they're alive?"

"Damn right you are. Alive, hard as steel...sharper than a razor blade."

Outside a wind gusts and sand drifts by. I remind self to have Franciscoa clean up after I've gone to the Mall with Peter.

Peter straightens his shoulders, stands taller and says, "Do you own everything here Once-Other?"

"Wha...ah?" I gasp then collect self. "Has nothing to do with anything. Let's stay with the tour, far more relevant. Oh? You don't think so. Well! Get this good...survival out here on Here-Born requires knowledge and competency. Knowledge and competency! Damn large amounts of competence in particular. On the other hand—who owns what is private info and second only to never revealing our real names."

He leans forward. "I hear you don't tell...why?"

"This is not part of a tour," I reply stiffly. "Now. Moving on...."

But my train of thought abruptly vanishes down a dark tunnel. I chase after it. Stop up and look around—darkness surrounds into which my thoughts have gone AWOL. I rub my eyes and search the dark. A distant white spot. I lean closer. Clouds of light appear. I make to turn but am unable to move.

Another motion attracts my attention and I glance there.

It is Peter.

In a slow, graceful fashion, he reaches out and pulls at a pre-owned finger as though flushing, grins and says, "Do we

84

need to do this? Do you have to hide your name and ownership details? Come on. Do you own everything?"

My mouth and vocal chords attempt an involuntary response then freeze upon my Foundation's command. I collect self, placate a quivering jaw wishing to stutter purposefully, and examine Peter.

He scrutinizes me in return. After a comprehensive mutual inspection during which nothing untoward leaped to view, I list what I've learned of him thus far without mind-to-mind.

He suffers weird rages, his thoughts are wholly blocked, his interests stretch beyond the norm and for an unknown reason he paid four times the costs of a tour.

Was that just to be with me? A chill suddenly shudders through me. I swallow it and consider Peter further.

Now. He possesses a commanding power...no wait...maybe there's something wrong with me. Perhaps I have a condition which now begs attention. I've enough poison residue within me that reactivates at irregular intervals. I also tend to brush aside signs of illness.

I end my searching for reasons, pause and collect self. Calm returns and I decide to address possible health issues but later.

"The ownership is?" Peter says.

"Not part of a tour," I reply. "So moving on and please listen up—this is important. Alright then. You've been told the Rocklands is damn hot enough to melt the soles of your boots. Wait! Listen! Cactus-blades dismember in the blink of an eye. Cacti themselves grow out of holes or gaps in the Rocklands and appear to be innocent to the uninformed."

"Yeah. Whatever."

I nod grimly. "No *whatever* here. Pay attention, please. Okay! You're on the Rocklands, the soles of your boots are melting, smoking, bursting into flames even. Bang—your attention is captured by all that unwanted activity around your feet. People walk on them you know. Kind of important they should be in good shape and not half cooked-n-all!"

"You exaggerate. How come the rocks are that hot—if that's true?"

I smile, surprised he's listening. "Excellent question. Even though the visible rock lies low and mostly flat, beneath the surface much of it descends to the molten core."

He nods and says, "Okay. Makes sense. What about daily customers? How are they handled when you're on a tour? Does Franciscoa cover for you?"

My jaw drops figuratively in invitation to any virtual flies chancing on by. "You know his name?" I ask hard pressed to sound calm.

But reason prevails. "Ah well...ignore that...he meets a lot of tourists. Now I understand...you're interested in more than a one-on-one tour." I check him over once more still worried about what is really going on.

Now Peter seems at moments able to control circumstances as well as what I do or say. If he is doing so, so much personal power is stunning to behold. On the other hand, if I'm suffering from something—it and old poison still present could be causing my loss of control. This can happen when lack of sleep and continued stress takes hold of one who has residual Crier poison within.

I take a deep breath, calm my heart, brace up my Foundation, my techniques and inspect his fan-n-fit again but other than the bulge under his armpit, all is good.

Good—all but for his thoughts!

Once again I reach out to access his mind but find it still dark, still impenetrable. I'm shut out as we of Here-Born can do. I try circumventing any drug present, but the same thing blocks me once again.

I attempt alternative protocols to the same worthless result. I sigh, withdraw, zero in on some cacti and head towards them. "Please, just for now listen up. With one's attention stuck on his feet it's all too easy to miscalculate the distance to a cactus let alone the length of its blade-arms."

His face assumes a thick coating of *whatever*.

"And one-two-three you're semi-dismembered. Careful there!" I pull him back just as a blade arm swings at him.

He gulps and turns his cooling down. "Okay. Yeah. Heh-heh. That was close! Damn fine important as you'd say. Is everything in here yours? Are you the sole owner?"

I ignore his ill-mannered and persistent question. "So! You've now learned a little something about desert survival." I turn away and walk off.

At my table, I pour two glasses of cold water. A glance over my shoulder finds him staring out the entrance again, his mouth a thin hard line.

I lean over and check outside.

No one is about.

I sip water.

He continues his watch upon the desert.

Is he searching for something, someone? I wave him over.

He ignores me.

I point at my stock. "I've got one or two undamaged heads you could choose from and use if the fancy tickles you."

He takes a backward step, holds a hand up as a stop signal, covers his mouth and takes another step back his face ashen.

I head over. "Drink well," I say as I hand him a glass. "You should buy a head and take it back to your hotel. No? Oh.

Think it through. You can replace your current one...after lopping it off...with help of course." He staggers as from a blow.

I press onwards crowbar inserted, hoping to break in. "Peter. Peter. Think, please! The family back home will be damn surprised. Look. I'll make a good price for you, you know, seeing as you don't need one right now."

"No!" he snarls.

"Oh? Okay. But go ahead think it over."

"Just the tour Once-Other."

If not a sale—then what?

Peter shakes his hands as though they are wet and then caresses that bulge.

"You alright?" I ask.

"Stupid questions irritate me," he says.

"What's the bulge?" I ask.

"Bulge?" he says pretending innocence.

"Under your arm."

"Nothing. Why you asking?"

"Curious," I reply.

What an interesting no answer.

But. Why does he need to hide what it is?

Is it dangerous or just a typical power pack for his fan-n-fit?

On the other hand, does it house the electronics that block access to his mind?

Nothing comes to my mind and damn!

He turns away his eyelids ticking faster than before.

Wait, I advise myself for once I do get at his mind all will be clear as our sky.

Now if Peter were of Here-Born, I would tackle him down to the floor and investigate that bulge.

I should not and would not do that with an EB—their Happiness entitlements forbid such direct physical inquiries. Poip mostly react to such actions as a violation of EB's Right to Happiness.

Suddenly, a jarring scream rends the hot desert air and Peter jerks as though shot.

I chuckle but in mind alone.

He frowns a question at me.

I continue to chuckle behind a straight face.

His frown tightens as he raises both eyebrows.

# CHAPTER 11

## OF SYMPTOMS, HAPPINESS ENTITLEMENTS, POIP AND TOIP

Resisting the temptation to point with a pre-owned arm and its wiggling fingers, I instead gaze off toward the carousel from where the scream had come. Peter shades his eyes as they follow mine. I glance at his underarm. Hmm? Perhaps...I worry too much.

He cocks an eyebrow in question.

I tend to it. "Pay those screams no mind. There. Over there. No, there! On the carousel. Folks in fun mode and terrorized altogether. Now should someone lose, or damage a limb...good chance they'll shop here. Yes. Competition is intense. But. This is an excellent position. I sure get lots of turnaround business. Heh-heh. Little joke you know. Turnaround?"

He snorts in disgust and examines the showground.

Beyond the carousel, the large purple-n-gold striped circus tent waits poised in silence for patrons and artists alike. To its left a lone hand clad in a dust covered cowboy outfit cleans a corral with a Fragger keeping a keen eye on some semi-broke horses huddled nervously in a corner.

Further back eight SandRider acrobats practice jumping acts like horse riding performers do.

My curiosity finds Maureen, a tall black-haired fortune teller dressed in shocking pink, as she walks by the locked stalls her hands held high, palms open. Even at this distance I enjoy her perfume, a mixture of honey-lemon and scent of flowers.

She stops, turns on the spot, focuses on us, jerks as though struck, drops her hands and says, "Be careful Once-Other."

"Get on with it!" Peter snarls his face almost touching mine.

I prattle out, "When you observe no Neatness you will know you are dealing with a particular type...a real bad person."

"I don't get you. Figure I've paid an amateur or a con artist. You do refunds Once-Other?"

"Okay...no. So now. Moving on...what the?" Somehow, a mighty hand flipped a switch and turned the sun off. Vision gone I listen instead.

Windborne sand brushes against the store sides. There are no voices; no engines revving nothing save for the smell of dry desert upon my senses. I shake my head but darkness clings like a virus bonded to its victim. I fumble about, a child lost in a dark tunnel.

From out the surrounding blackness and speaking as though across a vast and black space Peter says, "Tell me Once-Other. Who were you before?"

My mouth snaps open in instant response but once again, techniques from our Moment in Time kick alive, and I remain silent and immediately virtual clamps lock painfully onto my arms, legs and jaws. I send perception probes down into my body in search of their purpose. This time, they come alive and red patches of energy leap to view.

I inspect them, but they reveal no data other than that they are located behind my eyes. A pulse turns on. Its beat quickens and sheets of energy wash over me like an ocean battering headlong against a dangerously steep beach.

Red switches to gray, to green and back again.

A pause as the colors gather into a ball suspended in the center of my head. The ball glows brighter and explodes throwing me sideways, but I manage to maintain my balance. I probe beyond the red to where clouds of white foam drift.

I reach for them, but they dissolve and vanish.

Warmth touches my eyelids. I blink, sunlight appears and Peter stands before me silently staring off northwards tapping a foot in that way of his.

My eyes ache as though dipped in acid. I rub them and they burn with greater pain. I close them to little relief. A hand appears inside my head and circles. Sharp fingernails dig at my inner skull tearing like a dog searching for buried bones. I hold back the urge to scream.

My arms snap in close, pinned at my sides.

I struggle but am unable to move.

Fear's devilish voice whispers, "Others have mentioned similar daytime nightmares, Once-Other. Real horrors they are."

I know such nightmares invade seconds before the closing moments of life out here upon sand. There are deaths from heart attacks, strokes or a painless cancer with its peculiar sudden death syndrome. There are no symptoms, no warnings either and so a life vanishes without giving notice.

I need help.

I blink and light returns.

Peter still stands in front of me shading his eyes from our angry sun his gaze fixed northwards across the barren northern desert.

A sound from below. I glance down. He is still tapping his foot, an impatient parent awaiting a reticent child's response.

I decide to visit a doctor as soon as possible. But for now I need to eat and ease my physical self and so, taking him by the elbow I set out across sand not realizing views north and south had switched without my turning around...or so it seems.

Tongue still sluggish I yet manage to say, "Come on. Let me show you the Mall and if there's time we'll go down the goldmine museum around which this Mall is built. It is a real shaft, a played out mine."

He resists bringing us to a halt. "Only on Here-Born," he mutters. "A Mall and goldmine all in one. Oh...how I sigh."

I drag him along gnawing at my tongue until pain supplants anger. "Some info for you. The main shaft plunges two-thousand sand-paces to the first Level or Drift."

He makes to speak. I wave him silent. "Underground, where a shaft ends is called the inset, plat or shaft station."

He sneers. "Two thousand sand-paces deep eh? Yeah! How truly *uninteresting*. Please, *do* keep going."

"Well...a second shaft descends another fifteen-hundred sand-paces. Oh? You got one sand-pace measures about five feet long?"

He glares at me.

"So you did. Okay. You'll find out more once we've toured the Mall."

"If I must," he says.

Here now and for the first time I have cut short a campaign step and this for two reasons. One, I may suffer a serious health problem. Two, I am in a dogfight—a mental and spiritual one.

Which fights can often escalate into violence. Similar dangers plague all campaigners. At this point though without Peter's mind available I cannot judge one way or the other what exactly I'm grappling with. I need his thoughts—and fast.

Hopefully, inside his mind reside the explanations I thirst for. May all the gods we believe in help me if this behavior is simply his primary personality.

On the other hand, I do suspect a hidden agenda although it may also turn out to be a pathetic bargaining style on his part. Or, perhaps he likes to intimidate others and for no real reason at that—there are enough of such individuals to go round.

However, I am lost without access to a mind and so too is this one-on-one campaign. How foolish we of Here-Born to have relied upon a single skill—our ability to access another's mind. How dangerous when it fails. I calm self, sigh and decide, though more like hope, that Peter is nothing more than an abrasive character and who is grossly rough around the edges-n-more.

We trudge across sand our footsteps louder than normal.

But the voices and engines close by are muted as though afraid.

In the parking lot, several riders search for an open bay. The Mall doors hiss as they open and close. Shoppers walk by, many chatting mind-to-mind. A few greet me, glance at Peter and nod a silent one to him.

"So eerie...this silence," Peter says.

I'm about to respond when a Poip pair exit the Mall, check us over and abruptly march towards us, their odd and exaggerated stride on full display. The A-one hand-signals for us to stop.

I take a deep breath, exhale slowly and say, "My goodness damn gracious. Didn't I mention meeting Poip later? And here's a pair right before your very eyes."

"I should care?" he says.

In contrast, he examines them in detail.

"Ah, Peter. Note how EB technology still has a damn long road to travel. You know what I mean?"

"No. What?"

"Look there! Poip sink up to their ankles in sand. See? They cannot walk well and definitely do not dare run unless urgent. And if they do...real slow they go. Need to lighten them up for walking on sand. You should test on EB's beaches and deserts to see how that works."

"What's your gripe?" he says.

I ignore his question. "I never liked the empty black slots which are supposed to be their eyes. In the first place, they have no eyes. Now. The one with A-one indented in its forehead is...okay you figured that one. The B-one retrieves data and downloads to the A-one."

"I see," he says rubbing his chin with a satisfaction I don't quite understand.

"They are a violation and represent all your attacks on our Rights," I say.

He jolts as though directly responsible. Gives me a searching look, seems satisfied, smiles and says, "Lost me Once-Other. Appears they want to speak with you."

The A-one points at me. "Once-Other, citizen of Here-Born, recipient of income this morning. Please present your Nomadi for examination and validation of Toip."

I take Once-Other the campaigner by the scruff, shake him free and campaign onwards. "EB Toip-n-Poip are not legal here," I reply.

A-one shakes its head in disagreement, exactly as programmed.

"Yes, they are!" I growl.

"Hey?" Peter says. "Easy. A-one's just asking a simple question. What's with the biting attitude?"

I glare at him and he backs off flapping his hands in faked angst.

A-one says, "Here-Born's Constitution was modified under the Earth slash Here-Born Trade Accord. From Section 1112, Page 7856...allow me to quote."

"Sure," I say and note Peter grinning as though he had won something.

The A-one hums lost in a binary trance. It awakens and says, "For the protection, development and distribution of Here-Born's gold and oil resources across State and other borders or any boundaries, real or otherwise, Earth guarantees the following entitlements: Happiness, Security, Protection, Education and Monetary Equivalence."

"You'd best comprehend those simplicities, Once-Other?" Peter whispers. "Clear and sound when understood...keeps you within legal boundaries."

I glare at him. He waves his hands again and backs away.

A-one says, "In exchange Toip as supervised and controlled by us Poip was adopted under a Here-Born Yes-vote thereby enabling both Toip and we Poip and the Assurance of your Happiness."

"I know!" I spit in return. "But Toip violates our Here-Born tax laws. And worst of all your Representative, Jimmy Cromwell, lied to us about the Bill we voted on. The copy given us had most of the Regulations damn well missing. We voters didn't understand that—another violation in and of itself. And so too is *regulations to follow.*"

Peter throws his arms wide. "Come on. You can't change anything. We're talking Poip for crying out loud."

Though I won't be silenced, I do take note of the sudden familiarity Peter has with Poip. "Cromwell bought off many Here-Born politicians. With this devious act completed, all the votes of Here-Born citizens on Earth-Born were included in the vote."

A-one tries to interrupt, but I wave it silent. "Which appeared honest, but wasn't. Cromwell and our own no good damned criminal politicians cheated by issuing *all* of Earth-Born's citizens with Here-Born citizenship. Damn illegal immigration and naturalization *and* without ever arriving. Plus! Damn Voter fraud to boot."

"Our Monitoring Ensures your Happiness," A-one declares coldly.

"I am happy!" I snarl.

"Once-Other provide your Nomadi for examination. I've noted an Argumentative Attitude Specific Simplex Syndrome..."

"I'm more than familiar with what AASSS is," I interject.

"...which violates Mister Peter Wernt's Constitutional Right to Assured Happiness. He does not appear happy at this moment. While you were speaking and with what you said his Happiness index has decreased. A final request is being made of you! Present your Nomadi for examination forthwith or suffer the consequences." They brace themselves and edge closer.

"I have the right to protest, to express my views," I declare.

"You should be more courteous," Wernt whispers.

Oddly, A-one pleadingly waves us silent and says, "Once-Other—my dear fellow citizen. Please. A timeout requested by Happiness HQ. Please allow us to present two bulletins from the desk of Mister Warrent McPeters, Director of the Department for the Assurance of Happiness, Earth. A moment as my partner and valued friend downloads for us."

They slip into silent mode.

"You should be more respectful," Wernt insists and adjusts his fan-n-fit just as Chef's Call-out blows. His stomach growls in protest of its emptiness, and I smile.

"We can have breakfast when these two are done with us. Keep in mind days on Here-Born are twenty-eight hours long."

He rubs his stomach and sniffs at the wind. "Where do those appetizing aromas come from?"

"Out the southwest, but only when Chef's Call-out gusts," I reply. "Outdoor chefs set up and operate open flame broilers across there."

A-one awakes. "Bulletins are downloaded and have been transferred. Would you like a video playback of Mister Warrent McPeters in all his magnificent presence or audio alone?"

"Audio only!" Peter barks in a harsh, strained voice.

"Thank you for waiting," A-one says. "I require your full attention in this matter." They wait as twins do for our response.

We nod yes.

"Citizen Once-Other! The Department for the Assurance of Happiness wishes you a good day. Here for you is the information. Please maintain a sufficiently attentive mode."

It pauses, draws a heart shape in air and smiles. "Bulletin One outlines how exactly Happiness was legislated as a Right and an entitlement. No one may violate these Rights. Criminal charges are laid against those who do. Arrest and imprisonment will result...for as we all know...our monitoring ensures your happiness."

I nod.

"Bulletin Two states...protests, undue concern with other Rights, expressed dissatisfaction, continuously harping against established Rules, Regulations, Laws or Trade agreements leads to making oneself very, very unhappy."

A-one pauses and looks at me with its head cocked to one side much like a mother gazes with fondness upon a somewhat rebellious son.

"Once-Other. You are hereby being informed that new legislation prohibits you from making *yourself* unhappy...which conduct violates your own Right to Happiness. Arrest of self for violating the Rights of Self to the Assurance of Happiness is probable.

"Thank you for your attention. Mister Warrent McPeters, Director of Department for the Assurance of Happiness, Earth and at this time, Here-Born. Have a nice day."

They nod to each other and A-one says, "Please present your Nomadi Once-Other."

I hand it over as always hoping Peter notes that Poip act here as they do back on EB. Nothing works as well as a real-time demonstration of Poip in action. Furthermore, foreigners will often realize something new inside of the familiar even though they had never thought to consider such when home.

A-one plugs my Nomadi into a hip socket, scans it, nods as though happy and hands it back. "Once-Other, you have configured taxes due to Earth in the manner required. Thank you for your loyalty, your contributions to the joys of Assured Happiness, to the wonders of the Earth slash Here-Born Trade Accord and for exercising your Right to Obey the Law."

Peter whispers, "So simple."

The A-one examines and computes him.

Peter thrusts a hand into his pocket and leaves it there.

I assume he's reaching for his Nomadi.

A-one says, "You are Peter Wernt ah..."

A burst of static noise cuts across the heated air and dies as suddenly. I am unable to spot the source of it.

"...you are actually...welcome. On Here-born, we Poip monitor and ensure the Happiness of all persons of whatever race, color or creed. Enjoy your time here and have a nice day."

They salute, about-turn and head towards the carousel marching in step and ankle deep.

"And now?" Peter asks.

But I'm not ready for questions.

I'm considering what just happened.

That is the first time a new version Poip hiccupped in any fashion. And the burst of noise was possibly electronics kicking alive and controlling that Poip. Lost deep in thought I am jolted awake as Peter strides off headed for the Mall his boots crunching on sand.

I look him over...am I going under...can this be happening? No! Impossible! What a wild idea—Peter able to control Poip?

I quickly follow him, catch up, grasp his upper arm and pull him down to one knee. His suit clings silky-smooth to my palm. I shudder and release his arm.

The corner of his left eye ticks. He rubs it. "Once-Other?" he asks in a shaky voice.

"Look out across the surface. Tell me what you notice."

He licks his lips, looks at the endless expanse of sand, frowns and says, "Sand?"

"That's one damn fine important observation on your part."

I walk off leaving him kneeling, frowning.

Moments later, he follows kicking at sand.

But I am worried. It's just a sense of something odd. Something out of place upon which I cannot place a finger, perceptive tendrils nor any other awareness.

And questions rouse themselves.

Why had Peter been so eager for audio only?

I think it over but nothing makes sense other than his self-centeredness and his urge to change what others like or suggest...and probably just for the hell of it. On the other hand, am I missing something, something important?

No answers present themselves.

How strange such emptiness where before answers flowed.

Wait and see I advise self.

# CHAPTER 12

## OF SAND, COLORED GLASS, WATER CRIERS AND SAND-SNAILS

Black cargo containers hitched to sand colored SandMasters hurtle across the endless desert, a rumbling dust cloud headed for a setting sun. Cargo holds choked full of natural quartz sand, tax suspensions to the maximum. Tire footprints cut trails across sand deeper than any other Here-Born vehicle. Taking Here-Born into account, sand seems a worthless cargo.

Yet, there's a purpose to these cargoes destined to undergo a metamorphosis. They thunder onwards crossing basins, up and over dunes, barreling along old riverbeds for days while others travel for weeks.

Their cargoes originate from five distinct areas each providing unique impurities which impurities dictate individual color and qualities.

There is lead oxide to bring out the clear sparkle of crystal.

Iron oxides shade green.

However, no sulfur was present on *the* day—no amber nor hues of brown that is.

In the requirements for the Mall of Sand Lake Flats designs demanded green and green alone. The architects insisted amber and brown be noticeable by their absence alone.

After unloading and climbing mechanical hills, the loads fuse with fire. Liquefied quartz runs the finishing slope to float as sheets upon liquid tin. Passing through kilns each cools, is measured and cut into sheets of float-glass.

*** 

I throw my arms wide embracing the Mall.

"Some highlights Peter. Obviously, it's an oval design with outer walls and the domed roof made of transparent green glass. Does the exterior shimmer as an ocean does? All the green tint, right? Hmm? Okay. Maybe not. A tourist once mentioned that those white columns along the walkway are replicas from a Greek temple or something?"

He does not look nor reply.

I point to the roof. "When you're far back enough the steel headframe of the goldmine is visible."

He backs up but we are too close and he appears disappointed.

We step inside to a cool moist climate, quiet and refreshing. Several toddlers play on swings in a kid's playground. One sits with arms crossed bawling and kicking her heels. Nothing feels quite as strange as hearing a child cry mind-to-mind.

I glance about for any danger but find none.

Peter flips his face shield fully open.

The conditioned breeze is sweet with the spices of India and Earl Grey out of England. Here and there aroma streams of pizza, hotdogs, peppers and BBQ waft by.

From another direction, the occasional smell of chlorine from a swimming pool catches at my throat. In it, several teenagers splash and laugh as they shoot water at one another.

Further EB voices cut the air jarring loud and hard.

I point upwards. "Peter...the ceiling allows sunlight in but reflects heat—ninety-eight percent. The stores are all on the perimeter leaving the center open for aesthetic fountains, refreshment islands and kid's playgrounds.

"Note how the floor tiles start out black, shade dark brown, to brown, to beige across to brown and dark brown and return to black again. Granite tiles they are, rough to the touch—don't slip here. They are born of Here-Born many ages ago. You have anything like this back home?"

He laughs but not because he is impressed.

I stroke my chin as though thoughtful. "Note the shoppers admiring kitchenware and those bent over peering at protective clothing. Get it? No. Okay. No one wears a dress or kilt out here. You would not want to be caught by wind let alone a sandstorm wearing one. Also. There's the escalator for those who prefer their stair climbing be performed for them."

He sighs and taps his foot.

"Up on the top floor...the finest Nomadi dealer in all the universe. You care to upgrade yours?"

He taps his foot louder.

I turn my back on him and that foot and head for the Top of the Mine restaurant. About to follow he pauses at a store window and examines some wildlife paintings. "What's this?" he asks.

I return and say, "A sand-snail...a delicacy for us...ah Crier food. They live out in the wild desert though some species still live close to town."

He moves over to a painting of a Crier. "Yeah. These are so weird. Beige, black, white. Crazy skin folds around its neck, thick hind legs, large back with that long hair covering it and hanging down its sides, sort of a wolf's face and human-like eyes. I glimpsed them beneath the tarp in your shop. Is this what Water Criers really look like?"

I nod and he raises an eyebrow.

"Right. But beware of their teeth and their sting! The sting is under that fold of skin on its rump. Just here. When one of them has a hold of you your only defense is to find their stun point—if you are unarmed. It's located behind the head at the top of its neck amongst all the folded skin and fur...over there. Doesn't help much unless you know what you're doing. When pinched they go under—so to say, okay?"

He nods thoughtfully—a calculating look in his eyes.

Those his thoughts are the ones I need.

"Also. You'll find the stuffed ones in my store under a tarp are low priced compared to others. Hmm?"

He waves my sales pitch aside. I step closer and touch his elbow. The elbow pad is rough, sand scratches my palm. He goes rigid, struggles with something, relaxes and says, "This have something to do with why you had me inspect your desert?"

"Yes...well done putting those together. Tomorrow we'll head into the wild desert and I'll teach you how to find water."

"Tell me now and don't think I appreciated your childish compliment," he says.

I bite my tongue. "I'd rather show you...better than telling you."

"I prefer to be informed well ahead of time."

"No doubt you do." And I walk away.

He follows slapping the soles of his boots loudly on the tiled floor. Shoppers glance his way and shrug...*it's an EB.*

Inside the Top of the Mine restaurant, old mining lamps serve as overhead light fittings. Antique Laser-gas drillers and early Fraggers line the sidewalls in silent testimony of an evolving technology.

Wax figures of miners from years long gone, dressed in dirt-splattered coveralls with helmet lanterns ablaze, lean over tables illuminating meals. Behind the counter, a small converted heat-treatment furnace serves as a pizza oven.

I take a deep breath in, which rewards me with the enticing aroma of coffee, sausages, bacon, pancakes, and eggs. We take seats with a view out the front window facing down concourse towards the main entrance.

Wernt checks the restaurant over, sits back and scrutinizes photos of mining activities adorning the walls. He zeroes in on pictures of Fragger units, some blasting while others have miners draped across them. He smiles as though he understands something. Inside I smile too. If he thinks Fraggers are our UWMD he follows in the steps of most every EB tourist.

Audrey, a waiter with long auburn hair and dressed like a Mongolian maiden hands us menus. "How are you doing with this one compared to your last?" she asks mind-to-mind.

"I'm having trouble getting his thoughts," I reply.

Taken aback she studies him a moment. "Best solve that one," and out aloud says, "Where have you been? I've missed the sight of all that new red hair you have these days," and she chuckles.

"Ah Audrey. Volcanic activity closed LAX-EB for six weeks. No one was able to obtain passage to Here-Born. But how is your husband? I hear his SandRider broke down quite far north."

"Yes, it did. Luckily he had the new FindMe app running. So we found him."

"Good to hear that."

She nods and points to the menus. We order and she leaves. Peter stares off into the Mall. I do too.

After a few minutes, he stretches and groans in pleasure. Mid-stretch he leaps to his feet and unhooks the Quaaseon flask at his hip. Gas hisses as he does a recharge using a small metallic backup canister. Done, he tucks the empty into a pocket.

My interest is piqued. "Peter. Quaaseon flasks cool a fan-n-fit suit around four to five days per charge. Right?" He nods confirmation.

What was he doing? Most tourist will not roam on their own. Then again, it is none of my business. I'm about to query again but I stay my questions as Audrey arrives with food and drinks.

She hands Peter his coffee but deliberately shakes her hand causing the teaspoon to slip off the saucer. I place my fork down, catch the teaspoon mid-flight and return it to the saucer with a clink of stainless steel on ceramic.

Peter barely blinks.

"As slow as all the others," Audrey says.

"Too true," I reply as Peter glances back and forth between us.

"Doesn't he look like he got our mind-to-mind?" Audrey asks.

I nod.

"Thankfully they can't," she concludes and heads off.

However, if he can and has been then I must urgently get with Madsen about that bulge at Peter's armpit. As Madsen has often enough said, "Failure with this tourist ain't an option."

Such reminders bring a sour flavor to my mouth.
I sip some coffee.
Ah! Much better.

# CHAPTER 13

## OF THE POWER OF WALLETS AND GOVERNMENT ASSISTANCE

I turn to Peter as Audrey enters the kitchen. "When we're done eating, we'll go underground. Okay?"

"It's an idiot's world out here Once-Other. I should never have come. An agent could better do what's needed."

"Oh? What needs doing?" He ignores my question and starts eating.

I'm about to follow suit when a commotion outside the Mall entrance attracts our attention. Poip had stopped an elderly Here-Born lady and demanded her Nomadi.

She searches her purse, looks up and takes an uncertain step backward. Poip take a determined one forward. She stares long and fearfully at them then hands over her Nomadi.

A-one plugs it in and checks. A moment later, it wiggles as though ecstatic and without further ado—they arrest her.

"Looks like she screwed up," Peter says.

"Yes...sure does. So sad it is."

He laughs, wipes his nose and says, "You people...so much to learn."

I wait for more but nothing. "Well...*gifts* bestowed upon us by your Rulers. *Elected* officials so to say?"

He grins and says, "You don't approve of me. Do you?"

An icy wind slithers across my shoulders. Not because of what he said—but at not knowing if he *is* getting my thoughts. Are the tables turned? Alternatively, am I a neurotic loon newly converted to that madness?

Without being obvious, I scrutinize him but find no visible technology—just that bulge under his arm. I calm my heart and sample the future—tidbits of info snuggle in.

It'll be best to keep this Wernt tourist off balance as much as possible. To do so without qualms I assure self that he seems tougher, hardier and more resistant than other EB's. It is common knowledge that certain EB Foundations do not crumble easily.

This we discovered is due to their education. It's deeply embedded—almost as though implanted into their minds with tremendous force or threat. And this Peter is definitely unpleasant—to say the least. He will survive a ruined Foundation without mishap...or so I assume.

I do know of one such tourist who survived—a truly hardy and robust character I'm told. And so it is unlikely Peter will go screwball snorting and vanish as others have. And this despite his strange behavior.

I lick my lips at having forded a river of personal doubt. A climb up the opposite bank finds clearer purpose and intent awaiting me. It is time to move on. "Not you personally. Those Earth-Born laws and taxes you forced upon us. Allow me to outline how our tax system works." And I dive right in without waiting for his okay.

When I'm done explaining he doubles over laughing. Tears stream down his cheeks and gasping for breath he says, "No Government will hold off at fixed percentages like those. I figure they will need more and invent ways of getting what they want. Right?"

"Too true," I reply.

"There you go! Yeah. Wasting my tour time with your idiotic tax system. How dumb are those percentages? Just how stupid an idea is that? Yeah. Wish I'd missed that experience. Come on—wakey-wakey. Yeah! Who believes the *more* you earn the *lower* a rate you will pay. Get real."

And he pours himself a cup of coffee.

Around us the hum of conversation, clink of crockery, and breakfast aromas swirl and float as though alive and seeking recognition. I sigh, breathe them in and say, "Well. Our Bill of Rights outlines a single method by which Government can increase taxation revenues...."

"There you go—wasting my time again." He throws his arms wide appealing to one-n-all. "Anyway," he says, "our laws rule. Yeah. Wait. Er? Well...what if someone refuses to pay *your* so called taxes."

"A fate I consider worse than prison."

"What's that mean?" he asks.

"Refuse to live by our system, rules, laws...here!"

I pull out my Nomadi, browse to a website and show him the screen. "See that list of names? Okay. Those people have refused to pay taxes or cheated. Make this list and most no one will hire you, mostly no one will accept your money and absolutely no one will do business with you.

"You either sign on to make up what you owe and begin paying or you end up a hermit eking out an existence in the wild desert."

"That's an idiotic, moronic law!" he growls.

"It's not a law nor a regulation, Peter. We do that as a personal decision. No one forces us. So. If you wish to take their money or hire such a person, go ahead. But keep in mind that many will not do business with you once you do. There you go! Oh. I know our taxes are...were different. I'll explain further."

"This is not what I paid for Once-Other. Don't waste my money."

He blows to cool his coffee and slurps at it.

"Peter. You wanted to...."

He pulls back from slurping, spills coffee, his mouth snaps open in protest but I cut him off. "No! You wait! You listen!" His eyes widen but I rush on. "You asked me to outline our customs and business practices. Right?" And I hold my breath.

He pats his cheek eying me and says, "Er? Yeah. Right?"

"All I'm doing."

His eyes dart from Fraggers to waiters to lighting and hold steady. A cunning comes to them. "Okay oh wise one. Educate away. But don't think I'm persuaded. And I've noticed you're selling your Constitution and Bill of Rights. Warning alert—"

"You see," I cut in, "our Government stands ever dedicated to working with us via our Treasury."

He laughs. "And they soon come visiting. Right?"

"Damn right you are. Three government contractors visit you—say what?"

"Far worse than on Earth," he repeats.

"Well, worse or better than EB I don't know."

"What kind of tour guide says *I don't know*?" he sneers.

I gulp and say, "Our Treasury, using Treasury Contractors, works endlessly to take in more-n-more tax dollars."

"No!" he blurts, stands, throws his arms wide, waves to one-n-all and sits down. "And so it unravels. Feel free, go on, keep going. How small and amusing. Ha! Ha!"

He sips coffee glances at a gray haired lady applying makeup and winks at her. She smiles at him dabs at her lipstick and directly communicates that she feels my pain.

I grin. "Okay. Now. All Treasury Contractors must first and foremost be experts in communication. Not some communication system. Communications directly person to person for the purpose of gaining understand.

"That's the fundamental requirement just to qualify for this work. They will also need to be expert in one or more technologies. Such as business administration, production, management, marketing, human resources including staff assessment, training. All these in any one of the fields of commerce and industry.

"These contractors send out teams to private enterprises regularly. They investigate how you or a company is operating and how well financially you are doing. Typically three different teams arrive at the same time."

His mouth snaps open but I wave him silent. "Each presents a proposal to improve your productivity and so increase your income and profits. They charge for their service. It's the only way they are paid but the inspection is a no charge item."

He waves an invitation for me to wake up. "Never bite the hand that rubs the back that feeds the pack."

"Ah? Okay. That made no sense...now ah. Okay. Their program guarantees higher income for you or your business."

"Yeah sure," he says.

I swallow. "Well they...they estimate as a percentage range how much your income will increase once a program is fully and correctly completed—you pick which one to go with."

"Any dimwit can spit out a number," he says, pulls out the empty Quaaseon canister and taps his chin with it.

I wave that aside. "Now when they're wrong. And or when increased revenues or profits are far less than estimated, they have to come back at no cost to you. And! Fix what needs doing to get that promised increase."

I sit back and fold my arms.

"What?" he says waving his arms like a windmill beset by bedeviling crosswinds.

The empty canister slips from his grasp, floats and lands on the floor bouncing towards the aisle. He drops to his hands and knees and shuffles after it managing to grasp hold of it just as it rolls under the elderly lady's table.

"Been a long time since a man got to his knees for me," she says and we smile.

Peter sits down again and I drop a ticking time bomb into his Foundation. "If they don't or can't increase their customers' income they will go bankrupt."

"Whoa. Lost me right there. What are you talking about?" And he leans forward.

I lean in as well. "Here's what I mean. The *only* way our Treasury can earn more annual revenues is by raising productivity on Here-Born. You get that?"

He nods, I rush on. "Okay. Good. Urgh! Maybe not! Look. These contractors guaranty one greater income and live or die by their own word. Fail to do this often enough and you'll soon be bankrupt."

His face goes blank as most tourist's faces do.

I drive in harder. "Yes. To those from EB, the thought of a Government assisting citizens and companies to earn more and be more successful comes across as foreign as wingless stones flying into the sun to nest and raise their young."

He blinks and snarls, "BS!"

"Wha...no Peter."

He grins as one does after hearing something incredibly stupid. After biting my tongue, I pause for a moment as the pain subsides. He waves me on his full blown sneer masquerading as a smile.

"Our Government *must* increase the income of all working individuals, all corporations and any business," I add and wait but he waves me on again.

"That's the only way they can get more tax dollars into the Treasury on Schedule 1-4...which is the only obligatory tax on Here-Born. It's all in our Constitution. You really should read it but read it all before screaming in vain or should that be in pain."

And I smile but to no effect.

He waves all of everything aside. "Whatever the 1-4...will not work. We've analyzed it, dissected your system—this way and that way—up and down. Never going to pan out. Period."

I note how he claims to have *not* read something he then claims to have analyzed. Tucking that info away as contradictory, I continue.

"Hear me out here. Our Government assists us to produce more and in doing so they contribute to the success of all. Please comprehend...you're hearing something new, understanding it may take a while."

He yet again waves all I've said aside. "Has never happened and never will. No. *You* get a grip. Ongoing real-time legislating with detailed regulations to follow is the ideal. Wake up. You live by our Law now."

I bat those words aside. "Works here. Yes...wasn't achieved in all of human history until Here-Born. Your barrier to understanding is never having read our Constitution. Read what is written there and you will understand.

"Now, maybe you've gotten a glimpse of why passing new Laws isn't the primary activity of elected officials on Here-Born. To the contrary—that's the last action from politicians we desire let alone encourage."

"So they do this increasing production tap dance?" he asks.

"What else would a government do other than that and running...?"

But he bats my words into no-where-sand as too painful to consider.

I push on. "Get this. Those Government contractors provide the service I mentioned and one can hire them at any time—so help is waiting a Nomadi call away."

His head shakes saying both no and I don't believe this.

"Oh it works and Treasury certifies all contractors."

His mouth cycles four or five times before any sound exits. "That...that...that goes against the grain and the natural order of things—of the universe. There are standardized methodologies, Once-Other. A three-week visit to Earth will see you clear to understanding some very simple basics. Just as I have...." His mouth snaps closed and he glances furtively around.

If I could just access his thoughts, I would know what he didn't say. That was likely an important thought I'd missed.

Nevertheless, I provide him with the last piece and say, "If a contractor continuously fails bad-on-bad happens to them."

"What?" he asks more interested than he lets on.

"They are investigated and so too the Government officials who selected them."

He grunts. "Why not removed? That's the logical sequence in your illogical world."

I sigh at all that is EB and say, "Out here criminal laws are used against criminals *alone*. Which means they only kick in *after* you are found guilty of a crime—never *before*. Near the end of your tour, I'll give you excerpts from our Constitution and Bill of Rights to take home with you."

"Dream on if you wish," he says and pours himself another cup of coffee and sips with the air of a superior.

Time to back off. I wave Audrey over, plug my Nomadi into her cash register, pay and add a tip for her.

"Why don't you use wireless when paying?" he asks.

"Close to impossible to piggyback a direct connect."

He smiles as does the thief. "Ah. Yeah. Just steal the handheld." I nod, grin, and we head out the restaurant.

He glances around the open expanse. "What's The Missing Twelve?" he says pointing at a poster.

I'm saddened and walk in silence for several seconds. "One unfortunate and tragic event. We remind ourselves with posters like these across our world and... well...long ago twelve infants went missing."

Something strange flashes in his eyes. I'm about to ask what's happening when my mind goes blank and my legs turn to water. I stagger and almost fall but just as quickly strength returns. Perhaps the stress of campaigning has gotten to me.

In silence, I set off for the gold mine museum entrance.

He follows neither eager nor dragging his feet.

# CHAPTER 14

## OF BOYCOTTS AND HERE-BORN'S VANISHED BEAUTY

Headed down the escalator, Peter notes an empty store with a *Closed Down* sign posted. "Yeah! Someone went out of business—on Here-Born? Oh, wow! Your Department for ensuring increased production sure as hell works. Right Once-Other?"

"Some history with those stores."

"You don't say. Go on, justify why all this increasing productivity, improving employees' skills isn't just pure one-hundred percent proof BS."

"They provided what appeared to be one damn fine product," I reply.

"Yeah?" he asks.

"Terrible side effects came later," I say.

"That all?" he says.

"Well...they mostly sold a skin cream...did an incredible job of keeping one's skin smooth, soft, crack-free and glowing under this sun of ours but..."

"Sounds like a good product."

"...red blemishes appeared some while after having applied it—and they stayed."

"So what?" he says.

"Not pleasant," I say and roll up a sleeve.

He peers across and examines my arm.

"They still itch," I say.

"Yeah. Why would they close down? Your Government fixes everything. Right? Spare me the lies here."

I release my tongue from the grip of teeth. "Nothing to do with improved sales or increasing revenues or profits. A quality issue for us buyers. A something we deal with harshly."

He sneers.

"Peter! We can make a withdrawal from our wallets and surrender up cash for goods—or not. That places quality control in our hands, the buyers—one-hundred percent. On Here-Born We the People are the economy despite what those from EB may think and are educated in."

"True everywhere. Buyers are—"

I cut him off. "Maybe so. Maybe not. Hear me out...news travels something rapid here. We wanted their cream...it was fantastic...my skin was so moist. But! For whatever reason, they were not able to fix the issue or would not. The decision to stop buying we make as an individual buyer personally. Took a while to happen but in the end no one was buying."

"A long winded way of saying you boycotted them—something illegal on Earth. We hate boycotts...outright coercion—brutal force. That's blackmailing others to do what you want or else!"

I smile my driest of dry smiles, anger flickers inside his eyes. I say, "Calm down now. Okay. Alright. Now listen up. You've just revealed the horrific liability of your education or

Foundation as we've named it. So much of what EB tourists say is perverted and twisted to mean something else. You....'

"How dare you?" he demands.

I slap his protest aside with a sharp gesture. "I'm not talking nor even thinking boycott. A boycott most often comes about due to opposing groups forcing their views on others. In doing so they attempt to destroy a business for personal reasons...only!

"So boycotting is a form of punishment for failing to comply with a political agenda. Not done on Here-Born! People's rights include the right to buy or not to buy. We are willing to try something new and equally capable of judging a product. That doesn't mean we've called for a boycott."

His mouth snaps open, his opposition so powerful I can almost see words dangling on the edge of his tongue. I ensure they dangle there a moment longer.

"No Peter! Listen to me! Others will still be buying. We do not demand they stop. EB's Foundation is so drilled into you all you hear is *boycott*. How stupid is that?"

"Boycott!" he says, folds his arms and glares.

I sigh and say, "Not a boycott. It means that when I buy something for the first time...I am investing money and assessing a product. As does any investor with research well in hand."

"Boycott!" he snarls.

I crease my brow. "About them...even after they opened a handful of additional stores hoping to clear their inventory not a single sale transpired. We'd closed our wallets from north to south and east to west. The only option was to cut their losses and head back to Rio-Tero."

His eyes brighten as a child's upon finding a longed for Christmas gift then he scowls. "An awful planet," he says and glances about guiltily. "Tero II is more like Earth but better. I don't understand why they choose to live in a desert on Tero as you do here." He looks around once again. "Not that I've ever been there—so bang they go under!"

I note his attempt to downplay his knowledge and interest in Tero and Tero II. Why would he need to hide being interested in them? No answers come to the fore. Damn! Too many questions…unanswered.

Is this how Jiplee lost her skills?

And another unanswered question! Damn!

I continue. "They were paid not a single penny more. On Here-Born, We the People are the economy as I've said. Most governments of this Inter-Constellation Arena Thirty don't know how economies work or worse…lie about it."

He raises an eyebrow.

I sigh and stop for it is time to call his hand. A tick turns on at his temple. True, many EB's are sensitive to changes in others or if someone fixes attention on them. Most are not.

And I test him. "Tell me Peter what's going on here? What are you after? Me? Something else?"

The tick accelerates and he presses a finger to it. His sneer makes a dramatic appearance mid mouth; his eyes tighten focus. "You paranoid Once-Other?"

I spin away and head for a display window next to the Museum entrance which shows a dissected view of Here-Born's geology.

A triumphant smile beaming, he follows strolling casually. At the window he gasps, goes to one knee and stares his fingers snaking across the glass front. "This is different," he whispers.

"Let's move on," I say.

He waves me back. "No. No. Wait. A solid inner core surrounded by an enormous molten outer one but the rest of Here-Born is...different."

"You're right. Come, let's go. You're not the first tourist to figure on how much gold and oil is in all that rock."

He waves me back from the few paces I had moved off.

I return—interested in his interest.

"Take a moment would you," he says. "Look! That solid inner core...huge! Surrounding your molten outer core here...a solid rock formation...it's a massive interior mountain almost the size of this planet and...over here...a towering mountain ridge rising above the surface...the sand."

"Iron Ridge Mountains," I explain.

"Look here," he says, pointing to one of many large sections of blue, "there are oceans of water buried inside this underground mountain...and these water-veins? See how they spider-web up through the rock but never quite reach the surface except as geysers—and twenty active volcanoes?"

"The black cavities are oil. Let's move on...."

"One moment Once-Other! This encased water is close to your outer core. I can imagine it's boiling and being pushed up these veins."

"Especially across the Rocklands," I add. "You got it. Come on."

"Would you wait? Here where the narrowest water veins reach upwards they appear to end between say...fifty to two-hundred feet down and this *chocolate* covering...all Rocklands?"

"Right you are. Well okay. An oil surrounds all under-sand water. Let's go inside."

"No-no. Tell me more."

"Peter...ah...we're not talking oil like what we drill to export. Heated this oil solidifies into a waxy wall or cover."

"What kind of oil—never mind. Nothing like this on Earth. Quite unique—some planet."

Surprise! Campaign Step One done and early at that.

Yes. On Here-born things are different.

I march my campaign onwards pleased at the unexpected result. "So. Near the outer core the water is naturally heated. It rises up the fissures into sand and the waxy-oil forms a pipe up which the water moves. Wax pods dome at the top when pressure no longer exerts from below and holds the water in place under steady pressure."

"Unbelievable...incredible," he whispers.

"Yes...," I catch a glimpse of someone from the corner of my eye.

Madsen comes hurrying out the Museum wiping at chocolate cookie crumbs on his loose fitting Hawaiian shirt. I glance at his baggy white pants flapping as he walks and meeting his eyes note how the worry reflected there hardens.

"Once-Other!" he barks at me. "We can round-n-about find no records of a Peter Wernt. He ain't existing *except* in the Departure Records at LAX-EB, Arrivals at Port-SLF an' in the Here-Born Residentia's register. Damn unusual an' damn worrying."

"Thanks Madsen but I'm good with him—just had a breakthrough. Probably a computer glitch."

He glowers. "Perhaps. Stay alert an' all. You round-n-about get me?"

I ignore his last, take Peter by the arm and head through the Museum's main entrance. Madsen strides rapidly off soles squeaking across the floor tiles. He jolts to a sudden halt.

"You been eating cookies-n-all?" His wife Victoria snaps as she marches into the foyer.

"Now Vicki dear," Madsen says. "Nothing really. Just a tiny one. Very."

"I'm supposed to believe this?" Victoria growls.

He opens his arms and walks towards her.

She waits for him with hands on hips, feet spread apart and a thick scowl pasted across her face. Her black shirt and red pants hang loose about her and black boots crease more than her brow as she rocks back-n-forth.

Madsen reaches for her hand but she snaps it from out his grasp and says, "You been seeing yourself in the mirror come mornings or you close your eyes an' all?" And she turns and walks off. He trails along wiping his brow, head bowed.

I grin, take Peter's elbow and we enter the museum where he notes a sign and says, "Let's do a self-guided tour Once-Other."

I nod agreement and we stride off towards the cage but he stops, points and says, "A large diameter pipe next to the cage? Shouldn't we see one or two skips?"

I'm enthused by his knowledge and I now understand his disappointment at not seeing the mineshaft rigging above the Mall roof.

With pride evident in my voice I reply, "Well Peter, we're looking at a collect-n-grind mechanism which avoids hauling ore from below sand in skips. Inside the pipe crusher screws grind and haul ore to the surface in one action."

"Hmmm. Interesting. But pointless—unnecessary."

I hold stillborn a nasty response as the Museum Curator stops next to us. And as always, I'm saddened by tragic history.

We've crossed sand trails many times over the years spanning childhood to adults and married-n-all. He's always been polite and very scholarly.

Once when he was shopping on a day off he had his wife with him. She reminded me of others I had worked with back when I was a teacher. By appearance, she suited him well. Yet despite our frequent hellos, our relationship never progressed beyond cordial.

Some while ago his wife went missing out in the wild desert. We tracked the homing device only to find her SandRider lay beneath three-hundred sand-paces of quicksand.

It was never recovered nor were her remains.

He appeared a broken man for many years barely greeting others let alone making conversation. He has never truly come out of it and I fear he is now married to the museum.

He stands silent a moment, pats the sleeve of his light brown suit which is a shade darker than his hair and says, "Good morning Once-Other. On a solo tour? Not joining a Group?" He stretches to his full height and towers as tall as Wernt but twice as broad in shoulder, more-or-less.

"I prefer personal service," Peter says.

"Right you are Sir. And—oh? Once-Other is one of the few not on staff who can do the complete tour. Enjoy. Hope you like being underground."

# CHAPTER 15

## OF FRAGGERS AND REFLEXES

The focused industry and capabilities of Man penetrated her defenses. Steel drills, bit ends armed with cutting diamonds bored inwards exposing her treasures to plunder.

She sighed, as pieces of her old outer beauty were taken captive. Yet she had an urge to service those scurrying about sand and rock where once her perfume ruled. Her urge awakened by old memories of a sun grown merciless.

Though saddened by the plundering, she still on occasion smiled her old smile, for once again upon the wind sailed the scent of growing plants and other living things.

How much she had missed them.

***

Every time the Walmer siren announces our downward progress, Peter touches the bulge under his arm. At the third Walmer alert, I decide his armpit hides a good luck charm or a memento and dismiss it.

Five and a half minutes later, we arrive.

"Welcome to Station One, Level One," I announce.

Without warning cage-fear grips him with fangs real as Crier's teeth. He presses himself against the cage wall his glazed eyes darting in search of danger. I watch him carefully expecting an attack. He backs into a corner.

I point to the doors as they hiss releasing the locks.

He remains rigid, unmoving.

The doors slide open to reveal pitch black save for the rectangle of light cast out the cage. The thick smell of wet rock tumbles in and washes over us. The silence is eerie filled only with the creak and groan of stressed support beams.

Peter stares at the dark hole awaiting us. I wave him on, he shrinks further back and cowers, a terrified gazelle unable to spot the predator but fully cognizant of a threatening presence.

"Peter?" I ask, coming up onto the balls of my feet ready to move suddenly and quickly.

After three shuddering breaths, he calms a little, spots the collect-n-grind intake and takes a deep breath. He shuffles closer to the doors and inspects what is visible of the crusher-screws. Instead of being more afraid as most are, he relaxes and Peter the Confident reasserts.

"Hmm, yeah, impressive," he says and leans outwards.

I let out a breath, reach around the door, grasp the rough steel lever and throw the power switch. The main lights flicker. A loud electrical thud and they turn on hard to light up the Level walls.

At first glance it appears one is viewing the sides of a building. Arched balconies stacked five floors high recede into the distance, alien condominiums on a moonlit boulevard.

Sparing me a glare to which I remain stoic, Peter slow walks scanning the walls and ceiling as he goes. After a half dozen paces he halts and gasps at the sight of a day-glow yellow six-wheeled carriage supporting a mounted Fragger Unit.

We head over, my hand at his elbow steadying him. He stops abruptly and stares wide-eyed at the high-frequency guns protruding from the center of a three sand-paces diameter dish.

I let go of his arm and wait. He moves closer to the unit.

"Looks like an old Gatling but massively so," he mutters as he examines the low-frequency guns that surround the high-frequency ones. He glances my way.

I remain stoic, move across and stand close to him.

He turns away and runs his hand along the smooth four finger caliber barrels. He takes a deep breath reaches over and scratches at the matte black finish, the painful screech of fingernail on metal. He inspects his fingers tips squinting in the low light and looking up says, "Photos did not do this justice."

He steps closer, shudders and strokes the edge of a low-frequency unit a little too fondly for comfort. He glances at me, giggles and caresses the high-frequency unit with yet more passion. "This a weapon?" he asks in a husky voice.

To his surprise, I face him head-on and lock eyes.

With Here-born speed, I step to his side. He remains focused on the point I just vacated. I tap his spine with a knuckle and zip back in front of him. Only now does his focus switch to where I touched him.

Step two, confirmation test done.

I have the edge in reaction speed should he go screwball snorting. Furthermore, he has no idea of how to survive alone in the desert. To get water requires stealing it from a Water Crier. Without superb reactions, survival is unlikely so I would need to be there for him.

I drive my campaign onwards. "It's time to drop a small, though retrievable deposit back there in the cage."

His eyes roll over white. His mouth pops open and his nose twitches...well more-or-less. Whatever he suffers from is getting worse.

"Calm yourself," I implore as the whites recede.

"You are violating my Rights, Once-Other."

"Oh? No. We have some damn odd traditions out here Peter but not that strange. Now. Moving on. After negotiations to export gold concluded everything happened fast."

He brightens and waves their flag in my face.

"Yeah. Processed. Shipped. Sold. Yay. Earth."

"Too right and very EB. There's more to this...we've been aware of gold for as long as oil."

"Yeah?" he says incredulous disbelief sliding across his face.

"We had no technology to mine with—that was acceptable to us. Your Nice Blast & Munitions Company of Denver-EB wanted us to use their product for blasting and negotiated with us every day once we discovered gold."

"Don't exaggerate," he growls.

"More-or-less. Possibly not on weekends. All came to naught because we were and are still not willing to go around setting off explosions designed to rip holes in our planet in a random and senseless manner."

"Yeah. You used whatever and never announced *whatever*."

"You're about to find out."

"I should care?" he says.

"Just a tour. A one-on-one tour and well paid for."

"Okay. What's with the retrievable deposit thing?"

I indicate *not yet* and say, "Took centuries to create this." I pat the Fragger carriage. "Keep in mind these are destructive and that the central issue was ensuring no one could turn a tool into a weapon—no matter what. Industry and commerce had to wait until we resolved that. Which is why it took so extended a time. The mining side was devised some centuries ago."

"You people take the cake. How long has your economy been nickel and dime? How long has poverty been rampant, Once-Other?"

"I don't know about the widespread poverty, the nickels nor the dimes, but Freedom and Rights have been rampant ever since our independence from Earth-Born. As you obviously have down cold, Peter."

"Whatever. So you got this weapon. How's this work?"

"It's not a..."

"Yeah. Sure. How?"

"First the deposit," I demand.

"Wha...come on explain."

"I want to outline a damn important concept. Afterward, we blast."

"Explain!" he says.

"No. Let's take a few basics of your EB education and drop them into the cage."

"Like what? Why?"

"To assist in understanding. You can collect them on the way up again. Okay?"

"Once-Other!"

"Now-now Peter. Take everything you understand of atoms, protons, electrons and neutrons and place them in yonder cage as though making a credit deposit to a Nomadi."

He turns to the cage and all I perceive is a thought-motion crossing his face.

"Thank you," I acknowledge and parry the questions sprouting like tufts of rare desert grass. "Now. We of Here-Born consider matter, anything physical, was a wavelength fixed between two tiny particles—both of which were points to begin with. Each one smaller than an atom. But other forms of matter exist and these are simply solid...no particles involved.

Rock groans in anguish. We both glance across. Peter holds his breath.

I add. "So in one form solids came from tiny particles when they pulled closer together reducing the wavelength and distance close to zero—and they stuck together—like the opposite poles of magnets do.

"Now. Our Fragger converts solids formed from particles back into wavelengths and the original distance reassert itself. Others refer to this last as an explosion. But with pure solids, those not formed by particles joining, we get an implosion leaving just the original space there. Did I say that so you got it?"

"I kinda get...kinda not. Have you seen those wavelengths your theory assumes?"

"No, but we can measure them."

"Then your theory is as much a theory as you claim ours is," he says.

"Well yes, Peter."

He grins without warmth, steps in front of the Fragger and examines the complete unit. After a few moments he glances over his shoulder at the wall of rock. "Looks like a huge spoon was used to scoop the rock out leaving those arches in place as natural support. There are no signs of drilling to bed explosives. How's this work?"

"On Earth-Born you play with atoms and can now blow up the whole planet. Right?"

I wait and he nods yes.

"What took so long were our endeavors in self-defense—we never release anything as a weapon or could be changed into one until we've developed an active defense."

"Good idea," he says. "But why?"

"Every weapon ever created ends up being used against its creator. How stupid do you have to be not to figure that's coming?"

He glares coldly at me.

"So Peter, our laws prohibit the making of anything that can be turned into a weapon without first designing and manufacturing a defense against it. This is in our Constitution and Bill of Rights."

I fold my arms and grin.

"You sure sneaked that one in," he says.

"I sure did. You see, the Here-Born Constitution and Bill of Rights have value."

"You're pushing it. How's this work?"

"We shoot energy into an object as reversing waves or…as a negative-solid of an existing solid," I reply.

"As what?" he asks.

"With particles, matter becomes liquid. Liquid turns gaseous. Gas becomes light waves an explosion results during which the original wavelengths once again manifest…to give you the short explanation. Negative solid vanishes solid."

"This *is* a weapon," he says.

"This one only works when mining for gold."

Peter smiles but not because he believes me.

I open a metal cabinet mounted on the side of the carriage, remove ear protection headphones and hand a set to Peter without a word, climb on board and he follows.

I power-up the Fragger.

"What's this?" he asks holding up the headphones. "To protect our ears?"

I nod yes.

"This *can* be used as a weapon," he says.

"You can cause ear damage down here. Out in the open? No."

"Yeah. But Fraggers will destroy buildings. Same as rocks Once-Other."

"Yes. This kind of rock for this Fragger—none other. No gold and it won't work."

"Okay. Got that. Not a weapon. How do you get the ice-cream scoop effect?"

I glance his way and note he does not expect me to believe he thinks it is not a weapon. "Vectors that curve the blasting paths," I reply.

"Your Ultimate Weapon of Mass Destruction!" he insists.

Which brings Step Three into play. By denial, we get tourists to believe Fraggers are our Ultimate Weapon of Mass Destruction. And it's time to *prove* it.

"Well, Peter. Time to demonstrate."

"Aren't we a little close here?" he says glancing back-n-forth between Level wall and Fragger unit.

I ignore his question and point over my shoulder. "These two electronic storage units are critical. You understand?" He shakes his head.

"Okay. They provide power in exact quantities and qualities."

"Sounds over complicated," he says, glancing back-n-forth from our position to the cage, apparently estimating distance.

"Too little or too much power and nothing happens."

He grins coldly. "Ultimate Weapon of Mass Destruction. Right here. Right?"

With yet another tourist I ask, "What makes this a weapon? Power high?"

He shudders with excitement and hollers, "Excessive, vast quantities of. Ya-ha!"

I point. "Okay. Up here and we have Full Power."

I hold my fist above the fire button. He dives out his seat, lands on the carriage deck and rolls off the edge. Hits the Level floor hard, curls into a protective ball and our eyes meet just as I slam my fist down.

The barky-bark of a miniature dog alights upon our eardrums.

Moving with the abrupt, jerky motions of the truly angered he uncurls, stands up, brushes his suit off, adjusts cooling lower, clambers back up, sits down and folds his arms.

"Now. Any damage? A single pebble lying on the floor?"

"I'm not amused by your antics Once-Other. In fact, you *are* violating my Right to Happiness. I'll be reporting your unnecessary and cruel behavior."

He deliberately looks away from me, pulls a facial tissue from a pocket and blows his nose as loudly as a sandstorm alarm at full howl. Coming from out the dark the sound of tiny feet running across rock informs us all rodents within several miles are frantically scurrying for safety.

I tap his shoulder; he turns eyes hard as Rocklands blackrock to me.

"Well Peter! Report me for having a poor sense of humor if you must. Perhaps you can get me arrested for violating your Right to Happiness with humor. Maybe not."

Daggers fire out his eyes. "Let's do this," he growls.

I adjust the settings slide over and indicate for him to assume the Operator's seat. He moves over, makes a fist and slams it down hard and fast.

# CHAPTER 16

## OF A COLLECT-N-GRIND'S DANGERS

The Fragger winds up filling the Level with the bone shaking beat of a massive bass drum. Violins screech in agonized protest as the electronic storage units let loose a groan as though outraged at being wakened.

Streaks of energy fire out the Fragger's guns and strike the Level wall. Rock bubbles, liquefies, hisses and white clouds billow. Flat ten finger wide sheets of rainbows fire in all directions. A searing flash blinds and a rock-shaking thunderclap almost deafens. An instant of silence and rock fragments clatter to the Level floor forming a half circle around the explosion point.

Dust chokes and we both cough.

I recover first. "There you go, as easy as falling down after drinking too much."

"Okay. That was impressive. Now what?"

"First off...a Fragger's power can be set anywhere from so gentle matter dissolves like sugar stirred into coffee or all the way up to ripping solid rock to shreds. Now we examine what we have."

He twists his lower lip, shakes his head no but says, "Okay."

We cross to the other side.

He kneels, touches a pebble and snatches his finger away. "Yeow! That's hot."

"Well...you know...an explosion...heat."

Muttering unpleasantly under his breath, he removes a Nomadi extension aerial from a hip pouch, extends it, flips some fragments over and gasps. He leans forward and reaches further into the half circle, turns another over...and I sense his puzzlement. He does one more then moves around the debris to the rock wall where the explosion occurred.

He turns several over, pauses deep in thought and says, "The rocks over on the outer edge show a high quantity of gold. Closer to the blast point here less color is visible. Do the fragments here at the point of the explosion have color deeper inside?"

"No. Not at all." I pause and after a brief silence he reluctantly waves for me to continue. "We tune our damn fine Fragger to gold-bearing rock not merely plain old rock. The more gold in it the greater the reversal, the larger an explosion, the further pieces fly."

He nods in an absent-minded fashion, taps the small ice-cream scoop shaped balcony our Fragger blast made and says, "Your Here-Born theory at play?"

"Yes."

"Hmmm!" he says and slaps his leg with the aerial.

He glances down the Level, walks to the outer edge of fragments, turns to me and says, "You said this mine is played out...look at the outer pieces here. Real rich! On Earth this is almost virgin."

"Not by our standards of gold per cubic sand-pace."

Judging by his expression, I had removed or shifted a stone within his Foundation. But he hardens his demeanor and says, "Yeah. Now?"

"Now we collect-n-grind," and I head towards the cage.

He takes a step backward as the crusher screws kick alive with a metallic snarl. I motion for him to move further back. He does so keeping a careful eye on the gaping mouth.

I steer towards the rubble.

He skips around in front and walks backward watching the screws whirl, eyes wide, a wild excitement rushing about his face.

Horrified, I halt the collect-n-grind. "That's damn awful dangerous. One slip and you will be drawn in...to become very second hand indeed. Please step aside. I'm not mincing words here."

"Not funny," he says and though not wanting to, does so.

I wait to ensure he remains clear and set off again. He steps further away as the mouth ingests fragments with loud bites followed by a rumbling thunder as crushing and grinding kicks alive.

I shout over the cacophony, "Okay. I'm about to do something damn dangerous. Keep back, don't approach. No matter what happens—stay clear."

"Why?" he asks.

"No one making a mistake doing this lived to share the error of their ways."

He backs up further and waves me on.

I lean in mere fingers distant from the intake screws searching for the catch-lip indicator. A faint green light confirms sensors are on and the gap from rim to floor reads correctly.

I check on Peter; he watches me intently. "Any issue with the clearance and the lip will snag and dig in. The mouth then lurches up and swings about, a hungry monster looking for a quick meal."

"Got it," he replies and backs away tapping his chin with the empty Quaaseon canister.

I turn back to the crusher screws and in that instant Peter slips and stumbles. The metallic ring of his empty Quaaseon canister bouncing along rock penetrates the deep rumble of the collect-n-grind. I step clear of the mouth and glance over my shoulder. The canister bounces towards my feet.

Peter lands in a pile of legs and arms. He leaps up, and I note he is more agile than I'd thought. Uncertain, confused, he shuffles his feet back-n-forth. He decides, spins on his heel and sprints for the sole safe place...the waiting cage.

My boot arcs downwards until mere fractions of a finger above the bouncing canister, and contact. My leg shoots out from under me and my foot heads for the intake screws.

Peter glances over his shoulder and accelerates harder.

His raspy breathing loud in the confines.

I glance down and then back at Peter.

He's already in the cage pressing the button, his face drawn tight across his cheekbones, his eyes lit by an unholy glow.

I fall down—my head-n-torso shake-n-jerk something awful. My screams fill the Level to echo against uncaring face-rock.

# CHAPTER 17

## OF SPEED AND CONSEQUENCES

Our eyes hold as Peter tosses the headphones to the Level floor, the cage door hisses, slides closed and it's adieu to Peter the Tourist. I get up, dust myself off, sigh, walk a circle and smile.

Now! How do I happen to be standing upright and unconcerned when but moments ago my leg was being devoured by the collect-n-grind?

Well! A part of me likes to show off.

First off, I deliberately stepped towards the metallic canister. At the faintest hint of contact, I lay myself down upon the Level floor in a rapid fashion. I flapped my arms as though my leg was being devoured with mechanical dedication—my leg hidden from Peter's view by the collect-n-grind.

I yelled and screamed like my favorite rock star Malstrado the Rat. All the while, I admired Wernt's dynamic running style and the resonance of his howling. It appears he was athletic during his more youthful days and perhaps has a trophy or two.

I quickly checked the distance from my foot to the intake screws.

Peter continued accelerating with short, powerful strides. After an additional six, he glanced over his shoulder and on his face shone a desperation strange to behold. It spoke to me in terms of painful fear and triumphant glee.

His attention back ahead and still accelerating he broke into a medium stride and moments later into a full-length one.

I screamed louder as though my leg was in its final throes, courtesy of the collect-n-grind's voracious appetite. Peter leaped into the cage and slammed his palm against the Sand-Level button. Our eyes met as the doors hissed closed.

In his was a strange and ugly satisfaction.

The cage door fully closed, Once-Other chuckled, stood up and brushed rock fragments off and questions roused themselves from a light slumber.

Did Peter actually slip, stumble and fall? Was dropping the canister an accident? Alas, no thoughts, no answers. Where-oh-where are his? Does he have an agenda? Yes. But what? Why did he run away? Fear? Guilt?

Or...are one-n-all modern day EB's hopelessly lost and utterly detached from responsibility they'll flee all mistakes...the inevitable pointing-finger, pointing?

Do they have any clue of how personal strength grows when one stands true and announces one did it him or herself...especially when failure is distinct yet one is willing to have learned a lesson? And perhaps had to face ridicule.

Sadly, it appears Peter is done with this tour and I'll never discover what his presence on Here-Born was about, nor get my questions answered. I'll soon have to face Madsen and explain why and how I'd lost yet another tourist. He's of no tender a disposition when failure's involved.

With myself, though, I am angry. I'd pushed Peter hard mistaking his unpleasantness for strength of will and mind.

How wrong I was. I should have known better.

But it's time to clean up and so regrets are laid aside.

I complete the crushing action, reverse the collect-n-grind, ensure it docks cleanly, shut it down and silence returns. I remove the headphones and hang them on a hook.

The hiss of sand slithering through cracks and falling to the Level floor echoes softly around me. Moments later, the hum of the cage descending rattles alive. After endless minutes, the doors slide open to reveal the Curator and fifteen tourists. His face painted with concern relaxes when he notes I am okay.

"Your tourist Once-Other. Wow. He arrived above sand all alive with fear and mental storms in abundance. He sprinted across the foyer and vanished one-two-three altogether. He has a strange almost professional running style. You okay?"

I thank him, impart assurances and wait as the noisy tourists disembark. He thanks me for the lights being on as some of his group are quite quaking with fear.

"Is Madsen above?" I ask.

"He's gone," he says and chuckles his understanding.

The tourist's thoughts crowd in on me. A young Asian lady dressed in white silk slacks and shirt and hiking boots appears to possess a certain degree of self-control.

I smile and nod to her.

Her lips return my smile reflecting another one in her eyes.

The man walking behind her, dressed in a red-n-black checkered fan-n-fit suit, seems like in mind to her. But his thoughts reveal a desire to conquer her and include plans to do so later. He glances my way and assumes I'm competition.

I nod to him. He glares in return and I name him Mister Conqueror but consider her a Lady.

Several children rush to the collect-n-grind and examine the intake screws.

"What's this for?" a young boy asks.

"I'll show you later," the Curator says and heads down the Level.

"Tell me now," one of them whines.

"Showing has more value than telling," the Curator replies.

"Ah gee!" they groan and follow.

The solitude of the cage settles my turmoil and ruffled campaigner's feathers. The cold metal container cools my mind and thoughts. Our rattling progress upwards serves as an invitation to Here-Born's heated sand to request my presence upon itself.

I close my eyes, listen to the cage rattling and search sand both now and of the past for answers.

What had caused my failed endeavor and adventure with this Peter Wernt? No matter the angle I look at it from nothing makes sense.

Nothing other than Peter is weird, altogether.

How else can one explain the facial twitches, the almost rabid hatred of all things Here-Born and his unwavering dedication to the glories of EB?

# CHAPTER 18

## OF A SOUTHERN LADY

I'm lost in thought when the halfway Walmer sounds. And what just happened minutes earlier reverberates anew within me. I'd gotten the thoughts of the Earth-Born tourists who now wander below sand touring a dark goldmine—two of them clearer than the others.

Why not Peter's then?

Can't be me and not all of them either. Peter only?

No, from my night's drinking there is odious Odentien as well. The cage slows as further questions arise. Could Wernt the Madman be lurking intent on doing me harm?

What if he's an accessory in Jiplee's murder?

Heart thudding hard I brace up as the doors slide open.

I peer about the foyer but there is no sign of Peter.

I shrug and head for the refreshments stand moving briskly. A glance ahead and my face relaxes and my smile broadens at the sight of Maggie Schwartzlauda, an intriguing wisp of a brunette with deep green eyes.

She waves to me from behind the counter and a smile twinkles in her eyes as she mouths a hello. I wave in return and admire her while pretending I am not.

We've been close since childhood. She had moved here from down south with her parents. Back in school, we once shared a brief kiss in the class tent when we were alone. Strangely, that was all that happened. That in part thanks to me and in part because of Deidre's attitudes.

Enough said.

Maggie was a good athlete and competed in marathons, beating all other girls and at times the boys too.

Today, she is dressed in a tight fitting orange and white striped uniform and is busily making fresh popcorn. I consider her the guardian of all things popcorn, corn dog, soda, chocolate, candy, male egos and roasted sand-snails. The first and last of those being my favorites.

I lean on the counter.

She leans on the counter.

"That Peter Wernt sure can run something way fine," she says.

I grin despite sensing something is amiss. But I dismiss such thoughts as she places her hand over mine, digs her fingernails in and says, "How's our single man these bright an' sunny days?"

A tingle rushes through me and to cover it I ask, "Where's he now?"

"Wernt you mean?"

"Yes," I reply.

"Gone I figure. Madsen ain't gonna be happy."

Her words turn my blood into ice. I wait until all has warmed and say, "You notice any change come over Madsen these last years...months?"

"No way can I say I do. But I don't see him often as you do. What happened with you an' this Wernt?"

I get the distinct impression she is holding back and watching her carefully say, "Damn Maggie. I got nowhere with him. Something was going on, with him I mean. He even asked if I am the sole owner of my pre-owned parts store. Where did that come from?"

"You're right," she agrees, "where under the stars an' moon an' sun did it come from? He's maybe been reading Here-Born fiction an' is now mighty confused?"

Still pondering over Madsen, I say, "Madsen's southern accent comes across stronger than yours. But he's been here longer than you—how's that?"

"Different regions, says the wise answer. Ya did naurt know thaaaat?"

"Now you're thickening it like in the books. I've known him since we were ten. How does he keep an accent that long?"

In almost perfect northern English Maggie says, "That he has, dear Once-Other." She laughs, sobers and continues, "Where he comes from, the far south, I don't know any 'as lost their accent even when leaving around ten years old an' never returning. They kinda keep it forever an' on. Or so my mother informs me while looking down her nose at his accent. Anyway. What can I do for you in this cool an' peaceful Mall?"

With reluctance, I gently remove her hand from mine and point to an extra-large sized transparent container its sides decorated with popcorn falling like rain.

Her eyes and face light up and in a husky voice she says, "To eat now? You just had breakfast an' all."

"How do you know?" I demand.

An enticing burble mixes with the huskiness in her voice as she says, "Where handsome goes, news round we ladies who are not all too concerned with riches an' possessions, travels way faster."

"Later please," is all I can muster blushing some at her sideways reference to Deidre.

She takes a container from the shelf as though midst the act of undressing, trickles corn through her fingers while watching my reaction in the wall mirror. She smiles secret thoughts, and with her eyes on me attaches the container to the popper and turns it on with a seductive stroke of her delicate hand.

The corn slowly expands until a little of the fluffy white becomes visible. She suspends popping, seals the container, brushes her fingers down the back of my hand, and in a tight, urgent voice she says, "Press right here...an' the popping completes."

"Thank you," I reply barely able to whisper.

"Remember," she says stroking the container, "be sure an' pop inside of ten hours."

She leans back showing off her beauty and laughs something damn naughty, altogether.

With tremendous reluctance, I take my popcorn now no longer merely semi-popped corn and head off with a last lingering glance back.

Her face set and contemplative, she waves as I exit the Museum door.

# CHAPTER 19

## OF TRADITIONS, CO2 CAPTURES, THE INFLATION FALSEHOOD

Back at Pre-owneds Galore, and with desire's urges somewhat under control, I fasten a loose tent flap, take a minute to clean sand out of the nooks-n-crannies sand likes to collect in, and damn!

I've wasted precious campaign time and expended energy to no effect with Peter. No worthwhile product gained. Nothing. Damn again!

Worst of all...there is the specter of meeting Madsen.

If any chance of success existed, I would hunt Wernt down. Unfortunately, by now he'll be in a state of high escape ready to board an Inter-Constellation flight back to LAX-EB that inevitable finger pointing in my direction.

EB tourists never hang about once they make a break for home. A sudden sense of danger—someone is behind me. This someone has stood there for some minutes. Long slow minutes ticked by during which I had been too internal.

Lack of awareness invites failure. Failure to perceive danger is often the final error made upon sand.

At the scuffing of boot upon sand, I turn slow and easy—and sigh in relief. Jenk Nordt waits ten paces from the entrance.

He is a direct descendant of the original Northern Settlers most of whom stand about one-n-a-bit sand-paces high and four wide, more-or-less. The exact silhouette of an armored tank endowed with thick black hair hung to its hips. Jenk walks wherever he travels—they all do.

Not that modern transport isn't used as required.

I suffer a moment of heat suffocation at the sight of him in full leather and a black, white and beige ankle-length fur coat over the leather. His feet are large and wrapped inside fur-lined boots. Fur-lined gloves cling snug to his hands and are strapped tight at his wrists.

Yet, not a single drop of sweat blisters his brow.

There are none hardier, bolder nor possessed of a stamina compared to Northerners. In the north temperatures are a good fifteen to twenty-five degrees higher than down here. When traveling in the south they dress up against the *cold*.

I'd met Jenk soon after I became a pre-owned vendor. It was partially by accident.

Early one long ago Sunday morning I was out test-driving Hellbent having taken possession of her the previous afternoon. I was miles-n-miles from anywhere with half a tank of gas already burned.

Hunched low behind the windshield I at first figured I was looking at a dead fly that had splattered itself on it. But it began to grow larger. Soon it was evident that out ahead someone was walking across sand.

I pulled up throwing a larger than normal sand-cloud. When the dust settled, I almost choked at the sight of Jenk dressed in fur and leather striding swiftly across sand.

He halted and examined me and Hellbent. "A cheery good day to you fellow traveler," he said.

Mind locked by shock, I merely waved.

"I am bound for Sand Lake Flats and there to meet with a Once-Other. I am party to pre-owneds and tend to gather those of a higher quality. It would be of great service if you would describe him to me and perhaps impart a whisker of knowledge of the kind of man I am to meet. How do you feel about that? I see your vehicle is out of the same city."

"My name is Once-Other," I replied and Jenk slapped a knee or two and burst out laughing.

"How coincident. How welcome." And he offered me his hand. We have been firm friends ever since.

I check him over in detail.

His outfit, cut from the skin of a Roanark Braer, speaks volumes of his hunting prowess. Braers are beige-n-black deer like animal with a donkey face and Kudu like horns. They roam the Highlands and bray like donkeys at the faintest hint of danger.

I believe they eat cactus and being shy beasts possessing their skins requires hunting skills *par excellence*.

With an eye I measure Jenk's height and width and smile.

There is a history behind the Northerners' physical attributes and skills. After our ancestors had arrived, they figured out how to take advantage of the changes wrought by preservatives. Using the knowledge gained, they have developed their physique to what one sees today—short and stocky crosses sand easier than tall and gangly.

Negotiations are imminent though. I prevent myself from looking directly at why so. But under his arm, Jenk carries a bundle wrapped in a Braer's hide.

With Northerners being socially formal, I wait as Jenk removes his gloves and arranges his fur cuffs and collar into a more orderly affair. He then pulls his coat open, left and right, revealing he has come unarmed.

"A good and cheery day to you Once-Other," he communicates and enters my store. His feet glide across the floorboards without a whisper. Where he stepped, no imprint of a foot is evident in the perpetual film of sand.

"Welcome Jenk, honest collector of pre-owneds," I reply.

"Allow me a moment to impart an observation," he says.

I nod and wave him on.

"This dear world of ours, Here-Born, despite the centuries passed is still famously a frontier world. Or infamously. As you know, strangers from all around this Inter-Constellation Arena Thirty come here. Many of them are dangerous and adding Jiplee's death to that mix, danger multiplies."

"I know," I grumble and concede.

He bows extends his bundle towards me and says, "So please remain alert. But for now. I've been down and away for some months and on this my return, I've come directly to Pre-owneds Galore. With grace, I request the right to present this my latest collection. I do confess though, not all are worthy of your store."

"I appreciate your directness—it's refreshing how down-to-sand you are, Jenk. Welcome. Come! Let's drink some damn cold water."

"I am honored," he replies.

I turn, he follows and my step feels clumsy by comparison.

Seated, I dispense water for us.

We hold the glasses high and take an instant to examine the honor in the other. Jenk nods. We clink glasses and drink the water in one breath, drop the glasses, stand and switch places. Each stamps on the glass the other had used. We shake hands again and sit down where the other had sat.

In the bundle are three arms and two legs.

I examine the first arm in detail, place it to one side and check the remaining items. These four appear in excellent condition. I flex the fingers, check the elbows bend smoothly, toggle the toes back-n-forth, rotate the ankles-n-knees and all work well.

"Well now Jenk. These are excellent but this other one doesn't work for me."

"That I predicted Once-Other and I'll gladly accept twenty-five-hundred for all four."

"No doubt you would Jenk. No doubt you would."

I present him two fingers bent at the knuckles, sit back and await his response to my bid of one thousand. After a few seconds, he holds out two fingers extended requesting two thousand. I counter with three fingers bent at the knuckles for fifteen-hundred. He agrees to that and we shake hands.

"Let me verify all's well with these, Jenk."

Using a tiny spot of blood from each, I check if any are Criminal Pre-Owned Parts, C-POP that is, but none are. Verification and clearance certificates download.

I print two copies per stock item and give Jenk his ones.

"Well, Jenk. Damn fine parts indeed."

"To echo an honored friend and business acquaintance— *damn fine* as you've often said Once-Other."

We chuckle as I transfer payment and eCopies of the certificates to his Nomadi. He wraps the remaining arm with the

Braer's hide, ties it and his attitude abruptly sours. "Maggie informs you've lost your tourist...oh dear. What's happening honored friend?"

I bite my already mangled tongue. "Nothing altogether. Something was wrong with this one."

"I was informed and as southerners say...*Once-Other blew it*. How many times is that now? This my dear friend affects all of us dependent on campaigners...that's no tourist going home spreading our ideas of freedom...of rights. Has something come over you? Have you lost your will to continue? Or maybe you've changed sides...as Madsen hints upon."

My temper explodes. "Damn him! You notice anything about Madsen...never mind! Jenk! I did everything I possibly could. This tourist was weirder than any before. Enough! Let's drop it—got Madsen to deal with altogether."

"*That includes* every Here-Born Citizen Once-Other. We are all affected! Correct?"

"Talk about something else or damn leave."

I cross my arms and stare off into the northern desert.

After a thoughtful silence during which he tapped his cheek, he says, "Okay, old fiend. I leave matters in your hands."

"Did you say *fiend*?" I ask.

"Yes...*friend* Once-Other."

And we laugh.

He falls silent staring out at the desert. I sense him longing to be walking across sand but he turns to me and asks, "Tell me Once-Other...what will you do now your tourist has left?"

"Well...there's Madsen to see even just to request the next one. Perhaps I'll take a little time off, visit Reggie and see how they are all doing. You know...with Jiplee not long...."

He nods thoughtfully and says, "Tragic what happened. It will be good finding out who did this. It makes a man edgy. Dear me and blast all ancestors."

We sit in silence listening to the wind when suddenly he jerks as in a sudden realization.

"You know Once-Other, and I'm changing the subject on us, I'm pleased we voted Meredith Nother into the Federal Senate for the Upper Highlands. Jolly excellent."

Relieved, and withholding my failure to get Wernt's thoughts, I dive in saying, "Oh damn. You are? I myself could not believe it. Her program read as wishy-washy to me. All filled with holes—so to say."

"Well. Okay. But no."

"You're happy with her in Office?" I ask unable to keep the dismay out of my voice.

"My friend. More to her than meets the eye. Not that what meets the eye isn't outright, and in all possible ways attractive." He blushes, wipes his mouth and says, "Okay. Well. Look. On this trip I found a few CO2 captures had overflowed some fifty to one-hundred sand-paces."

"Dangerous," I offer.

"Yes. Now listen to me. Up around Tower Dune City work has already started on deepening, enclosing and widening them just as she promised...if elected. What a shame! Something tragic...."

I allow him a minute.

"Yes?" I ask.

"Blast all sandstorms, Once-Other! Bloody horrid mishaps! One of the workers had faulty equipment...which failed. He succumbed in a standing position. No one noticed until the Walmer declared lunchtime had begun. By then it was too late."

"Damn shame. But tell me now Jenk...are they losing it?"

"Okay! Okay! I get it good friend. So to conclude. They made a detailed check of equipment after that."

"Bit late...better than never. Hmm? Breathing pure $CO_2$ is a quick way to go. Oh, wait!" I glance at the parts I had just purchased.

"No-no my dear friend."

"No?" I say.

"Yes, no. These are not his. $CO_2$ makes for useless parts—like poison does."

Assured, I take some damn fine EB cigars from out their cool-n-moisturizing container. Offer him one, he accepts, we light up and watch as the smoke rises in wisps above us, catches the breeze and sails off towards the exit and parking lot beyond.

Eying his cigar, he says, "Oh yes! Oh dear! EB this very day doubled prices for trees and all things flora."

My mouth drops open. "What? No. What happened? How do you know this?"

"Again...up around Tower Dune City. The Senate Committee delved into it...those of us present paid attention and then some. Just another below the belt blow from EB's economic practice of inflation come to stab us dead-eye in the buttocks—rumor says the cost of EB soil will be next."

I suppress an urge to add more damn criticism. Instead, I grasp the opportunity to express some of my own difficulties. "Changing gears Jenk—that's what I'm having trouble with. Damned inflation! To date not one EB tourist has understood our economy. Not one! They go brain dead and I cannot get them beyond inflation and the belief that deflation is a greater evil. Now this is a good time to check something with you. You mind?"

He waves me on.

"Can you guess if EB tourists know inflation without credit is impossible?"

"What my dear friend are you going on about?" he cries in horror. "That's your outline? You have lost your marbles?"

"It was just a ques...never mind. Look...okay...try this on. When prices go up very fast, most people cannot save enough to buy something expensive before the price goes up again.

"So the only way to sell a big ticket item is to provide credit. You must have credit available when you run on inflation or no one or very few can buy your products."

"Not particularly good but I suppose it'll squeak by."

"Wait will you! Those two are created, inflation and credit, as the chicken and the egg, both at the same time as neither can exist without the other. What you think?"

"True. True. Still not absorbing. I'm falling asleep here. In fact, I'm both sleep sitting and sleep talking. Who on all of Here-Born, native or visitor would want to listen to you?"

"You did."

"Ah! But I'm not paying. Why are you leaving out so much?"

"Damn Jenk. Okay. With inflation raiding your wallet you will soon need a higher salary just to purchase the same amount of goods you did on your former salary. But as soon as your earnings increase you end up in a higher tax bracket over on EB."

"Awful shame that is," he says.

"Right. Now Government gets in on the act with licenses, parking fees on *public roads*, permits, sales taxes, property taxes, value added taxes, citations and more. Damn. EB tourists don't even realize all those damn fees-n-citations are simply extra taxes on top the other taxes. I mean...dog licenses! What?"

"Good one Once-Other I...."

But he has me going so I hush him and rush on.

"Can you believe Earth-Born's citizens are happy when they're told their taxes won't be increased right now but will be increased later? Do they assume having taxes increased later is a gift? Do any of them understand their tax rates are always lowered—temporarily? That flat rate or sales tax only systems soon see the rates rise as high as two hundred percent and higher. No. More is needed to fix it as we have done here. They are...."

"Unequivocally tragic," Jenk snorts. "But how is Karrell doing? Living with Deidre and what's his name?"

"Bordt Nettler! He's fine. Don't interrupt. Damn shameful economic politics Jenk—something all their politicians are in on. Elect someone into their current EB system? A waste of time. What they need is our UWMD." I pause for breath then rush on now that I have a captive audience.

"I sometimes wonder! Do they know that the original Declaration of Independence of the United States of America cited excessive taxation, and without representation, as some of the reasons for disconnecting from the King of England? And more so cited oppressive laws that ushered in endless regulations written by unelected officials.

"I've no doubt the merry old King of England was astounded some dared protest his taxation demands."

Jenk chuckles and waves me on.

"But look at their taxes and laws now—more regulations than anyone could ever shake a fist at. How well those who write their ongoing parade of endless laws have fooled them. No one on EB has noticed that all new laws come with a line that says...*regulations to follow!*

"And no one looks up and sees how they never get to agree with regulations but are subject to them. It's worse than when they waged their War of Independence against England. They have a crippling Foundation in action Jenk. None of them has figured that when everyone gets the same tunnel-visioned education with its fixed views and ideas and solutions then elections can't change anything..."

I struggle to breathe evenly. Jenk waves me on.

"...because all elected officials have the same education despite differing schools, colleges, and universities. It's the ideas taught that are the same across all institutes of education back there. And since everyone uses his or her Foundation in life nothing ever changes. And so Jenk...all their solutions are the same but worded differently."

Jenk rubs his eyes and says, "Lost upon the path they're educated to see. Blinded."

I jump back in.

"Their elected official's so-called solutions have the same results—and things get worse, then worse than that? And why? Their whole Foundation is based on wrong, even false information—how can they expect someone to make changes for the better when his or her Foundation is no different from the last? This comes from a curriculum designed and run by Government! God help them!"

Jenk shrugs, I keep going.

"Which means all students have learned the same things as those gone before and none have ever dared question his education let alone went out to investigate if what he's learning works or not."

"An endless merry-go-round it is...but not merry at all," Jenk quips.

"Right," I reply. "That they have many different schools and colleges means nothing. These all teach the same ideas, and if you don't write those down during the exam you fail. And so no certificate and so no or low employment. Even when graduates cannot find worthwhile work, they still do not question their education. Wow."

Exhausted physically, mentally and emotionally we sit silent for a few minutes.

The wind blows. Dust-devils dance and die.

I sigh and say, "Ha! Of course, things technical in nature, tests prove that...one way or the other. You hold a rock up, let go, it falls. But it's not like that with life in general...and less so with politics, economics and finance. A lot wrong there, there is. Few of them even know the difference between a free market economy and capitalism! Those two are not the same!"

"Tunnel-vision Education at its worst to say the least," Jenk concurs. "And you've something of passion I see."

"Damn right you are! And worse! They don't understand our economy. You should be here sometime. It's amazing. That our Government keeps the amount of money circulating balanced against the value of services and products available is rocket science to them."

Jenk rubs his chin and says, "Most unfortunate. Not too bad on your part Once-Other. Pretty good. I'd advise you tell them what you've just said—quite enlightening it was."

He stands up, slaps my shoulder and heads off into the desert leaving me with much unsaid. He waves and calls out, "Dearest Maggie said for you to be sure you pop your *corncob* within ten hours."

"*Popcorn*," I shout back.

"Words Once-Other. Jolly old words!"

I smile at that and at the small dust-devils that dance into my store once again seeking out comfortable nooks-n-crannies in which to lie down and slumber.

They do and I glance around.

In the Fairground, Maureen the fortuneteller welcomes a client and lets me know she is pleased I had taken good care of myself earlier. She adds a wink, pushes her dark hair aside, and with a seductive swagger leads a mesmerized EB male into her store.

The roar of a SandMaster shatters the silence and my relative calm. I check northward sand, heart pounding as it emerges from its own sandstorm and stops atop a tall dune. The engines groan and fall silent and sand settles like mist in a downdraft.

For several slow breaths nothing stirs. Midst taking a deep one, a cold shiver runs down my back. Cold enough to elicit goose bumps. I hold my gaze northwards, unblinking.

Two men exit the SandMaster and lean close as though plotting a conspiracy. The one in black leather would be a Desert Driver and the owner. The other is tall and thin, which reminds me of Peter Wernt but this one is dressed in a white Nomad's thobe and a pale blue ghutra. They point around as though marking territory, shake hands and board.

A roar blasts out the exhausts of its twin engines revealing it had been fitted with a Dual SandMaster Free Flow system. The tailpipes have a distinctive whistling sound as it accelerates revealing there is a bend, hole or bump in one or both exhaust pipes through which air leaks.

With a long and tired sigh, I get down to admin and tax duties.

Engrossed, I'm taken by surprise when the light turns orange heralding sunset.

I rush to my closet, grab a full-length fur coat and pull it on just as all becomes dark. I lower the side sections, lock the faux wood doors and board Hellbent with thoughts of a quiet evening ahead.

I pull my bandana over nose and mouth, fasten my helmet and set off. Overhead, the stars cluster around the brightest one, our Star-of-Hope. I smile as her light caresses my face.

# CHAPTER 20

## OF MAGGIE, THE LADY AND MISTER CONQUEROR

Trundling Hellbent along the fence dividing my property from the Mall parking lot a familiar figure detaches from the home-going crowd and heads towards me.

I smile at Maggie's silhouette. "Goin' home 'lone Once-Other?" She calls out, broadcasting her question so broadly as to alert all within range.

Several glance our way and smile. Yes. That is Maggie being Maggie.

I smile inside my helmet and stop up. She flips the cut-off switch places her hand over mine and asks, "Have you an' all popped your popcorn?" And she chuckles as naughty as all can be.

"No...," and that single word catches in my throat.

"Don't you leave it too long," she says, gives me a penetrating look and steps onto the rear footpeg. She pauses, smiles, swings her leg over settles in and says, "Tonight's a night for One Grain o' Sand."

The rough noose of fear named after Jiplee encircles my heart. My imagination pounds with Maggie's screams as those hands, which took Jiplee's life now take Maggie's. I push neurotic images aside, calm self as best I can and hoping to bow out without being fried alive by a woman scorned, I pause and look for her eyes proper.

Our eyes hold each other much like when we were children and in love. "Oh my. Now wait Maggie. Listen to me please...you know my involvement, attitudes such as Wernt's that of others and what happened to Jiplee...I...you know...it would...you know? Dangerous." Not fluid by any stretch of the imagination but at least spoken.

Her thoughts flick into private-mode, she nods yes, wraps her arms around me and whispers, "Friends an' all Once-Other no matter the future." But a sadness lingers upon her words.

Nevertheless, I'm relieved and I fire Hellbent up and we race off into the night.

Arriving at the One Grain o' Sand, I check the time and note we have an hour left before EB and other tourists enter bringing with them their need for speaker driven music. Until then, music plays over special equipment for those using mind-to-mind alone.

We hasten up the stairs, pay the entrance fee, the double doors open and we are inside a nightclub as silent as an empty church according to those who require sound. Only the ring of cutlery and crockery meeting, the gurgle of poured drinks and the odd cough breaks the silence. We both sigh in relief at the respite from the pounding of tourist voices.

Overhead, neon waterfalls tumble downwards spraying mists of blue light which then surge back up. As the mood and tempo of the music changes so do their colors. Above them, neon planets dip and swoop like swallows orbiting a pulsing sun. We dance with abandon.

After six or seven fast numbers, Maggie heads for the DJ.

She returns, smiles mischievously, takes my hand and places her other on my shoulder as a true classic, *Surrender* by Elvis Presley moves us. We're close. She snuggles closer. Her eyes twinkle in an enticing fashion.

"Only friends Maggie," I whisper around an aching heart.

"Only friends an' all Once-Other," she whispers back with a chuckle that says she means otherwise. And she presses yet closer. Right then *Surrender* ends much to my relief but to Maggie's disappointment.

I step away, let out a longing sigh and check for an empty table. We seat ourselves and order drinks. The DJ switches to music in live audio mode and tourists enter shattering the relative silence.

The EB Lady from the goldmine arrives with Mister Conqueror and they take a table close by. She spots me, smiles and waves. I wave back. Mister Conqueror smiles as well but not because he is happy to see me.

"Dear-dear me—careful now an' all you hear Once-Other," Maggie confides and leans closer as though whispering in my ear, "EB women *don't* use that ol' hell hath no fury like a woman scorned an' all."

"What?" I blurt. "They do too."

"Ah yes," she confirms. "But these days when she shows a man she's interested an' he don't up his interest. Oh-oh. Or worse, he don't become way interested an' real fast an' all...hell hath no fury is but a tiny storm in a coffee cup compared to what an' all hits some unsuspecting male."

She laughs and slips her hand over mine. "Trust me—I know," she whispers.

"Now you're starting a war," I groan.

"Hope not with Mister Conqueror as you call him," she says a little devil dancing in her eyes.

At the other table Mister Conqueror deliberately reaches out, takes the Lady's hand in his and smiles coldly at me. The Lady glares at him and attempts to pull her hand away but he holds on tight.

"Oh. You think of her as the Lady—capped an' all."

"Well. I think she's a Lady, Maggie."

"Just pullin' your leg. Lighten up some."

I communicate to a waiter, he arrives and we both order chicken peri-peri. While waiting for our food, Maggie stares at me oddly then asks, "Did you go an' do something...made Peter Wernt run for home?"

"You're asking me this? What's it got to do with you?" And instantly I regret my harsh tone.

"Don't," she says. "Please don't. I'm curious. An' that's all."

"It's a sore point with me. Okay? He was the most irritating person I've ever met. Here." I show her my tooth-battered-tongue. "Every one of them self-inflicted in defense against my taking his head off and refusing him a new one."

"Okay. I got it. A challenging tourist an' all."

"He was up to something," I muse.

"Oh?" she gasps.

"I'm not sure what," I quickly add hoping to avoid further questions.

"What his thoughts tell you an' all?" she asks.

"Well, I...let's get off the subject and enjoy our-selves...okay?"

Maggie is about to demand an answer when our food arrives allowing me to wave the subject aside and dig in after waving a fork to stifle her questioning.

We eat ravenously. Sweat breaks out on our brows. Maggie wipes mine then hers with the same napkin folds it and pockets it.

"Maggie," I groan.

"Once-Other?" and she pretends not to know what is what but frowns when my attention switches to a new arrival.

# CHAPTER 21

## OF THIRD-EYE CAMERAS AND A POPPED SHOULDER JOINT

With music pounding my senses, I watch an EB tourist wearing the same style third-eye camera as Peter walk towards us. He is shorter than Peter but has thicker arms and legs and a large barrel-shaped head from which golden brown hair falls to his shoulders. His fan-n-fit is similar to Wernt's but a deeper gray.

Maggie frowns when she notes my interest and asks, "What you checking on?"

In answer, I reach out and touch his arm. He stops. I withdraw my hand in that physical contact aids getting thoughts and say, "One damn fine third-eye camera you've got there, Mister."

"Thank you very much," he says and his thoughts reveal that I should keep my hands to myself.

So. A third-eye camera does not automatically block their minds from us. Maggie frowns further questions, which I ignore for nature calls upon me.

Washing my hands Mister Conqueror enters, steps to the center and waits, hands on hips, glaring at me. Unlike in the goldmine, I find no thoughts available or perhaps he has none.

"Good evening," I say aloud.

He makes a fist and grinds it in his palm. "You Here-Born folk composed of miscellaneous used parts—"

"That's pre-owned Mister," I cut in.

"Whatever the hell! We are talking used parts and like any other *piece of property* needs to listen up, wake up and get real. I'm gonna teach you a lesson...stay away from our women and keep your used parts to yourself."

He snaps his fist backward.

I sigh at such slow reactions, step around him and note his focus remains where I no longer stand.

His arm hits maximum rearward motion.

I take a step towards the exit.

His arm pauses ready to punch.

I take another step towards the door.

He throws a punch.

I take another step.

His shoulder does a crunch-n-snap under the full fury of it. I take another step towards the door and push it open. His agonized scream hits as the restroom door swings closed behind me.

Maggie looks up and says, "...an' their men have grown way more jealous an' all."

She pats my arm and communicates she understands my decision to head on home. I'm about to ask but she assures me she'll get a ride back to her SandRider and hands me my popcorn.

"Now you know tomorrow will be way too late an' all for popping." She giggles like a naughty little girl and hooking her arm through mine walks me to the exit. There she pats my arm, gives me a quick kiss, and eyes searching mine says, "I still remember our childhood kiss Once-Other. Something a woman never forgets." She tweaks my nose and heads back inside.

The doors swing closed. The night is cold as always. The moon is high. Sand drifts as crosswinds fight for possession of each grain.

Hellbent's four wheels leave sand as I crest the last dune and accelerate down windward. Looking ahead I note something odd and troubling. Usually well lit, tonight home is a dark patch upon a pale, moonlit desert.

Where are the nightlights?

Did they all die at the same time?

Heart pounding, I pull up the driveway and let her idle with the headlights on taking a few moments to admire the house despite the tight fist in my stomach urging me to investigate immediately.

# CHAPTER 22

## OF HOME AND DEIDRE'S WEAPONS

Home is similar in design to the Mall but her roof curls low down the outside walls. Chutes in its overhang allow hot air and wind driven sand to escape upwards. Fraggers installed in the roof remove piles of sand at the press of Nomadi button.

Forcing myself to ignore the nightlights, I conduct a standard inspection of the exterior and find sand piled up against the eastern wall in particular—it was a southeasterly blower.

I clear most away with a hand-held domestic Fragger. While sweeping up the remains with an ancient straw broom I chuckle at the diverse technologies of a handheld Fragger and a handheld broom. At the last window, I freeze as though bereft of life. On a glass pane, are two oily palm prints with a smudge between them?

Images of Jiplee, lifeless in the desert flash alive. I glance about, nothing moves and no sounds caress my hearing. I check but find no vehicle tracks nor footprints thanks to the wind.

A somewhat frantic search at the front door yields an empty mailbox and parcel receptacle. The door mounted communications recorder is blank. I pause, take several deep breaths and now it's time to inspect the nightlights...I can wait no longer.

Removing a flashlight from Hellbent's toolbox I shine it along the eaves and my heart stops—every light bulb has been smashed. This has never happened before. Did someone do this deliberately? I stroke arm hairs stiffened by a now racing heart—they calm, lie down and settle as does my heart.

I park in the garage, check her over and nod satisfied at duty done but still shake inwardly at what I'd seen outside.

Inside, the door lock clicks closed behind me and Once-Other the worrier comes fully alive.

Maggie was the one who delayed my departure. Did she do it intentionally? Was it planned? Worse. Has she been compromised as many of our politicians have been? I struggle but manage to contact a more logical self...and it's no. I have known her too long. She obviously more than likes me.

"This is so Once-Other," she had said on her first visit here. Still she...no. I control a rampant heart-n-mind and glance about.

Modest furniture leans towards useful rather than decorative. Walls glow a pastel blue, overhead pale-white ceilings smile at one. The kitchen stands alone dominated by a chromed antique coffee maker—my pride and joy. In the lounge, lighting focuses on my favorite chair, Della Comfort.

Tonight the green indicator light on the comm-link flashes. I'm drawn to it like a moth to candlelight. But the level meter demands attention first, it's glowing red.

After a quick inspection, I discover that my house has tilted three degrees off kilter, which may keep me awake all night being that I am sensitive to tilt.

Eager to get back to my messages, I rush into the Configuration Room and open the control cabinet doors. The screen displays a narrow keel descending two-hundred and a few more sand-paces beneath the ten sand-paces deep foundation.

Two horizontal wing stabilizers mounted midway down help keep home true in the strongest of sandstorms. They are twice as long as the house is wide.

On Here-Born digging into sand is no way to attempt laying down a foundation upon which to erect a building. Sand runs back as water does. Instead, Fraggers are used. Placed at strategic points they fire into sand creating the trenches into which are lowered foundation keels and all other required parts.

These are special Fraggers similar to the ones provided on vehicles of all types. When fired they vanish sand and harden the new surfaces. What is then lowered into such or driven out of such must do so fast and accurately. Melted-n-then-solidified sand does not wait for the tardy before breaking up once again.

I correct the settings and enable manual mode. The house rocks-n-shakes as the level indicator drifts back-n-forth. Once centered, I set it back to auto-mode, which has limitations and head for the lounge pondering on what caused it to tilt.

The wind of my journey had not seemed significant enough. Had a ball rock shifted below sand? Did a new water vein pushing upwards cause an upheaval? A sudden hard gust perhaps? I shrug concerns aside as Karrell's recorded message fills my mind with cheer.

"Hi, Dad. Miss you a whole bunch. Now don't you worry about me. I'm okay out here with Mom and—she says *hi* by-the-by."

He sounds cheerful enough but an undertone lurks. I make myself comfortable on Della Comfort, complete popping the popcorn, close my eyes and allow his voice to engulf me.

"So Dad. I am after all earlier protests a child of habit. This I know for sure. Every night I take a walk before sunset as we three used to. I can't help myself...it's not the same without you, though." His mother says something in the background but without connecting it to the comm-link.

"Okay, Mom—hangdog-garb. You know what Dad? She never said anything about why she left with Bordt Nettler...your friend. I figure that it's ex-friend now. Mom? I got that." Her stringent tone provides no words nor concepts, but her attitude and aggravating disposition hit loud and clear.

"I won't tell him, Mom. Okay?"

Silence for a minute.

Then speaking faster, he says, "As I was saying...the other day Mom had a visit from some EB guy and a couple of Poip...I couldn't pick up any details. When she spoke to me later she said *damn you even more*. Also that I'll soon find out what it means to be the son of someone like you and mumbled how it should have been a life sentence."

Her snarl cuts in again without concepts reaching the system.

"Oh?" Karrell says. "You meant don't tell Dad that. Oh? Oops."

She connects and says, "I'm not a fool Karrell. You did that deliberately!"

"Can I do this call now?" Karrell snaps back at her making me proud of him.

"This isn't the end of this," she says and silence.

I sigh as the decayed flotsam-n-jetsam of a wrecked marriage surfaces. Each piece composed of unspoken threats declaring that none dared do or say anything to upset her as consequences would be far too dire. So awful in fact, no one could actually imagine the horror and emotional pain about to descend upon one.

My heart races driven by times best left to cool a while longer. Karrell's voice returns.

"I'm fine Dad, don't worry." And there's an adult chuckle mingled in his words.

I pause playback.

What would an EB and Poip want with Deidre?

No cause comes to mind.

I hit play.

"So hey Dad. Doing pretty good at school these days. Been burning the eLibrary late at night." Deidre's voice cuts in with no words nor concepts once again.

I wait.

Dejected Karrell says, "Well, Mom just said calls cost money and money doesn't grow on a Crier's back. Goodnight. Hope to communicate direct next time. Bye."

Home grows silent and cold as the lights start their shutdown. I curl up on Della Comfort yearning for Karrell's love and happy countenance.

How I miss him.

# CHAPTER 23

## OF DANGER AND CONFESSION

Mother wind, the designer, the road builder, the manipulator, brings death second only to Brother Sun. She'll often flit across sand brushing lips along her baby while whispering a mother's secret love. A playful twinkle in her eyes she scoops sand into pockets of her own design.

If temperatures change and she's rendered uncertain of direction, she pauses and thus sheds her collection gently.

But when she drives with a raging heart and stops suddenly she'll fling back to this erg, this dune-sea named Here-Born, every grain with a violence no mere human can survive.

Mountainous dunes rise upon sand and beneath each lie the bones of many an unwary traveler.

***

Although the wind sleeps late this morning the sun awakened on time.

A glance out the window reveals a desert quiet and tranquil with not a dust devil in sight. Perhaps I imagine it but if not, the real crunch of sand permeates my toothpaste. I gag a bit, spit out before a proper brushing, rinse and call oral hygiene done.

My next morning action? To brew a perfect cup of coffee.

I fill the paper filter to the top with four heaped spoons of freshly ground bean—the darker the bean the better. One mug of water goes in and she is set to brew.

I wait next to her until every last drop snakes through the grounds. Add a measure of fresh cream—the final touch of excellence—no sugar or other flavors mar my coffee. Once ready, I carry the mug everywhere I go as tasks unfold and it empties.

We of Here-Born use the time between six and ten in the morning as personal hours. In this fashion, we change our twenty-eight-hour day into twenty-four for the benefit of Earth-Born tourists and businessmen alike. We agreed to this for economic reasons not to bow to a politically correct demand.

Due to clocks ticking on two worlds far apart, our calendar dates were once different but we have since synchronized. We were ten years ahead of Earth-Born at that time. No one recalls why or how this happened.

Both worlds accepted the later dated year—ours.

The correction took place at Midnight on New Year's Day back in 3584. For us the year was 3584, for Earth-Born it was 3574. The agreement states days, weeks and years are the same for EB and us. This is possible because Here-Born has no seasons other than damn hot and damned hotter. Our one concession was this *wasting* of personal hours each morning.

In the garage, I pull a tarp off an old four cylinder, air cooled motorcycle and gaze upon reliable and classic EB technology at its finest. They had been *extinct* over on EB until we of Here-Born resurrected them in pure desperation for a form of personal transport.

Sipping coffee, I admire her lines for a few minutes and smile at the history of my work. Back when I began restoring and modifying this classic Bordt Nettler asked, and now that I think of it with a sneer Wernt would envy, "Why bother?"

"Well, Bordt, damn fine and impressive altogether," I replied. He sneered more-n-more and I never bothered explaining.

That Deidre's sneer harmonized with his should have come across as something of a clue. A clue to what was happening between them. But I wasn't home often enough to expose it and was then gone to prison for three years and compounding all I'd asked Bordt to take care of Deidre and Karrell while I was imprisoned. Appears he did a sterling job, as Jenk would say.

I wash and polish her frame, side covers, wheel rims and fuel tank. Done, I stand back, admire some more, salute her with the empty mug and with the four hours gone, obligations beckon.

I lock the front door, glance up at the eaves and frown still confused over what caused all of the light bulbs to break. But I'm jolted fully alert by the roar of a SandMaster at full throttle. The same bent or holed tailpipe from yesterday whistles across sand. I push up against the front door and scan the horizon.

Desert Drivers this close when I'm alone?

Cold shivers cascade through me.

I wait. Finally, the roar fades.

I calm self and heart and curious to know more about last night's visitor I set off to inspect the nose and hand prints. Turning the corner, I'm again brought up short. A fresh set of footprints leads to the same window and back into the desert.

I kneel and examine them.

They are of an ordinary boot worn by most, tourists included. My heartbeat uneven, I track their return over a small dune from where they head off into the distance and disappear. I wait listening but hear nothing further. Do they belong to the Desert Driver? No answer.

Several minutes on, I walk back with one or two nervous glances over my shoulder. About to re-enter home I pause and ponder if I will need a handgun today.

Like most Here-Born citizens I attend biannual training for we are all soldiers. So, I own a variety of weapons as do all citizens. Here no application nor a permit is required to purchase, to own, to carry—open or concealed. Our Founders were determined honest folk would never be legislated into being victims. I think the circumstances over.

Though the footprints are strange and disturbing, there are no signs of ill intent other than the smashed light bulbs. Of those I have recently met, Wernt has been critical of me but he's EB bound while Mister Conqueror has no way of finding me.

I decide I do not need one, mount Hellbent, check her over and accelerate away.

Hunched down behind her fairing I snick up each gear, snap her into fifth and then top. Racing along a flat-topped dune my speed sneaks up towards ninety-five mph. I hold the pace as we cut through the warm morning air spotted here and there by pockets of hotter air. I smile as the engine hums and purrs and allow thinking to wander over to Wernt and Karrell.

About Wernt I worry—troubled by an inexplicably blocked mind. I'd tried accessing him in multiple ways with different styles and alternate protocols and failed. If all EB's learn to do that, our campaign will falter and fail in the face of hidden thoughts—and goodbye Freedom.

At least I've no need to get with Madsen about that bulge under Peter's arm anymore. And Karrell? How is he doing? He sounded so unhappy despite the forced cheer in his voice. I can't figure why his mother said he would regret being my son. What tragedy would bring about such a decision on his part?

I am answerless.

Also! Why did an EB tourist and Poip visit her?

I've too many questions and too few answers.

I'm awakened with a vengeance as the left front wheel slams into an empty Crier burrow. We lurch left. Arzern feathers fly as the handlebars twist in my grip and smack against the steering stops. Battling a tank-slapper I drop down two gears and accelerate.

The rear wheels bite deep and the front-end lifts.

I hit another burrow, launch into the air again and fly over the edge of the dune. Midflight I kick down a gear and as the tires touch sand I drop the clutch and bang the throttle full open. Hard acceleration smooths out the tank-slapper.

I hold my attention a few feet ahead watching for soft sand or rock. I drive her harder in preparation for a race across the slack and the climb up the opposing slope.

Wait! This dune is extremely steep. Why?

I glance up.

To my horror it's not a dune but a capture-ditch I'm racing down. One quarter filled with $CO_2$. To my right $CO_2$ intake tunnels roar inducting the $CO_2$—inviting it to become reformed. Is this to be my final error?

The suction from the intake fans drag at me. I hunch down lower, steer left and open the throttle wider. The handlebars shudder as I fight the suction. Even my hardened palms cringe at the abuse.

Hellbent's wheels whine and swish across sand. I glance down. At current speeds and angle, I've no way of turning without tumbling head over wheels down the slope. I can but accelerate and hope to make it across the slack with a dead engine. Once engulfed by $CO_2$ the engine will die—starved of oxygen.

I drop a gear, twist the throttle fully open and hunch down out of the wind. The exhausts thrill to their task roaring a high RPM medley, the tires bite deeper.

I steer further left away from the $CO_2$ intake. Seconds later the scream of tortured metal shredding shatters Hellbent's singing voice. I pull the clutch in to prevent the wheels from locking and freewheel ever faster-n-faster as the capture-ditch drops down steeper-n-steeper. At near vertical I take a deep breath in preparation for $CO_2$'s insidious embrace.

The thick yellow cloud leaps forward and wraps its deadly wisps around me stinging and bringing tears to my eyes. The bandana around my mouth and nose barely protects me from the $CO_2$ that swirls about seeking to suffocate.

With a thud, the suspension bottoms on sand. We bounce high and flip sideways. I leap clear, land feet first, tumble several times, come to my feet and sprint for the opposing slope bearing left to stay clear of the intakes.

Hellbent tumbles by missing me by mere fingers.

From the corner of an eye I watch her break apart as pieces fly in all directions like scattering flies.

I reach the slope and charge upwards, boots slipping.

My chest heaves begging for air.

I pinch my nose closed.

My heart beats thunder louder, threatening to burst through my chest.

I trip on a tiny outcrop of rock and drop to all fours but keep climbing. Both lungs scream in agony. I glance to the crest—it is too far.

Sand splashes my face and my legs turn to lead. Every cell screams for oxygen. Blood runs down my chin. I bite down harder but cannot hold back any longer. Still, I do for several seconds more and my mouth snaps open of its own accord. I breathe in and though foul it is mostly air.

I sprawl flat on my face nose buried in sand, gasping and slide downwards. I dig hands and boots in, hold still and rest. Limb by limb my strength returns, my breathing settles and my heart calms.

I crawl to and across the crest, drop flat and remain prone.

In the distance terraced desert unfolds to a far Sand Lake Flats. The goldmine's headframe is clearly visible towering above the Mall and silhouetted against a bright blue sky.

Though I'm not close I am not too far. I have a long, tough walk to the freeway. I'll get there but not with the ease of Jenk Nordt.

I stand up, ensure I'm on firm sand, dust shirt and pants off, check my survival kit and Crier fan are good—they are. I take a deep breath, remove my bandana and shake sand out of it, and glance down to where Hellbent lies twisted and broken on her handlebars and saddle.

A rear wheel turns idly. Gasoline trickles out the fuel tank. One long sigh says loss is more than expected. As I brace up for the long walk into town the roar of an engine rips the silence apart. I drop to sand, hold still and follow the distant dust cloud's approach.

A dark blue fairing with white lightning slashes becomes visible. No one I know owns such a SandRider. It slides to a halt, sand-dust settles.

A large and dangerous looking rider wearing a black full-face helmet, dressed in camo-jeans and a knee-length khaki tent-top dismounts and pauses almost invisible against the desertscape. He draws a handgun and turns a circle scanning it along his line of sight.

I squeeze down lower and watch as he holsters the weapon and steps to the edge of the capture-ditch. He stares down at my broken SandRider, glances around, shrugs and with his back to me starts taking his helmet off.

He suddenly freezes, spins on his heel his attention directed at me. "Once-Other! Once-Other—you okay an' all?"

"Ah Madsen," I reply. "Wearing so baggy a shirt hides a rotund outline...fooled me. Nevertheless, a complimentary silhouette it undoubtedly provides."

His immediate response I did not record.

On one hand, I am relieved but at the same time I'm hoping to avoid the subject of Peter Wernt...for now at least. I stand up and walk towards him clapping my hands to distract him. "You are a welcome sight at such a trying time. How did you manage to find me so quickly?"

He ignores me looking down at Hellbent and his face shades a little pale. "What happened round-n-about?" he asks.

"You have a new SandRider?" I counter.

"New paint job an' all. Speak up. What?"

"An oddity here there is, Madsen."

"Would you explain," he growls and rubs his ample stomach, which responds with a grumbling request for an immediate refill.

I examine the events from last night and this morning. Add together what fits and enlighten him about the palm and nose prints, the footprints and the broken lights but hide my failure to get Wernt's thoughts.

He pats both his chins as he listens and they bobble as he mutters in a garbled whisper. Done, I wait as I've always done from the earliest days of our youth.

He sighs and says, "Who an' all could this be? You lost Peter Wernt so it ain't retaliation for whatever happened between you two. We'll get to all an' more later. I'm round-n-about unhappy over losing him so early in a tour. What's with you?"

I shrug hoping he will move on.

He glares at me and waits.

I consider matters again. "Does not appear to be anything strange or odd except for that SandMaster I keep seeing and hearing."

"SandMaster?" Madsen gasps glancing to the horizon.

"Yes," I confirm, speaking as calmly as I can.

"I think Once-Other better tell me about what an' all is inside this Peter Wernt."

After a few seconds of desperate effort to settle an unruly stomach I give up, lick my parched lips and say, "I couldn't get his thoughts...at all." He double takes his eyes bulging. "I...I tried every protocol I could think...nothing but fragments, meaningless."

And as happens when he's mad and upset he comes close to incomprehensible. "We *will* talk...you-n-all hiding...round-n-about. You're facing a Court Martial for negligence, Failure to Report, withholding vital information an' anything I can think on."

"I was going to report as soon as we met today...anyway," I counter.

He examines me as though seeking honesty from an irretrievably corrupted good-for-nothing, turns away and ideas cascade through his mind.

What would a Desert Driver an' all be doing down here? Who would be hiring one? Who can pay that much an' all? Did a tourist hire one? How would a tourist know about Desert Drivers an' round-n-about where to hire one? How can an EB tourist keep his thoughts an' all from us? Is Once-Other...?

On the last, he blocks me...nevertheless, I know.

He's thinking of me and treason co-joined in unholy matrimony. And all for the imagined love of personal wealth—EB dollars in payment for betrayal.

# CHAPTER 24

## OF VEHICLE MAINTENANCE, REGULATIONS AND HAPPINESS

I unhook the tow-cable from Madsen's SandRider. He hands me his emergency oxygen system, lets it go too soon forcing me to catch before it hits sand. I hold to silence and peace—for now.

The walk down the steep side of the capture-ditch does not reflect Karrell's evening strolls. My breathing resonates loud inside the helmet, driven by intake fans the oxygen tank slaps against my back and the tow-cable drags along sand.

The rear wheel no longer turns. Gasoline no longer leaks.

I hook up and step away. A groan of broken metal, a whip-snap of steel rope and she's back on her wheels but will never be the same again. I pat her a fond and sad farewell.

"Would you an' all switch that cable Once-Other," Madsen shouts. I bite my tongue.

Back at his SandRider, I stow the emergency oxygen equipment and unhook the cable. He winches it in and says, "Better your SandRider than you an' all."

"Yes," I reply. "Let's get her hooked up and head on into town." Instead of moving, he stands silent staring at my SandRider his thoughts hidden. I move to hook her up. He grabs my arms and says, "Not round-n-about auspicious timing Once-Other."

"I didn't plan it, Madsen. Something's wrong here...."

"Yes. Something's wrong an' it's you—far as I see. How can you be so negligent? Don't you know breaking down can be fatal? I just happen to be out-n-about this way."

"So...you're saying it's happenstance...you being round-n-about here...are you?" I snap at him.

"You have a troubling mind," he snarls.

Hackles at full stretch I yet hold back about my suspected heart problems. Half an hour later I am still biting my tongue as we merge with the work-bound traffic on the Eastern Freeway.

This morning the Freeway lies hundreds of sand-paces further west than last night, thanks to the wind and shifting sand. Around us, riders swarm down the dunes, ramp onto the freeway, accelerate hard and race for downtown.

Many take to sharing their observations and opinions.

"Wow! Once-Other wiped out."

"Mister Ever-so-careful had an engine break on him. Oh dear, oh dear."

"For sale. Slightly used SandRider. Get a free arm as a bonus."

"Were you guys romancing or something—at high speed?"

"You miss a turn?"

"You swerved for a Crier?"

"You mistake a capture-ditch for an off-ramp?"

To escape Madsen and I switch into *do not disturb* mode. The traffic thins and suddenly a SandRider cuts in too damn close for comfort. The fairing brushes by my left knee, clips our front wheel, lurches and keeps going. We reach out to the other rider and Maggie's chirpy laugh responds.

"Are you still doing your makeup in traffic?" I ask her.

She laughs harder and kicks down a gear. With front wheels pawing the sky she vanishes inside a dust cloud.

"That Maggie is little too wild an' all," Madsen complains.

I chuckle as that too is what makes Maggie, Maggie.

"Where we taking her...your SandRider?" Madsen asks.

"It's worth less than sand now but I'm curious. Soonsaan's?"

"Okay. He's not round-n-about too far."

As Sand Lake Flats comes into view a Poip pair step out from hiding behind a small dune. Their *eyes* flash blue Poip lights as they wave us off the road. These two are earlier models to yesterday's ones and are programmed oddly compared to the newer versions.

They ignore us and head for my SandRider chatting to each other in electronic language. The A-one kneels and inspects the engine then *sniffs* at the fuel tank, the chassis and wheels.

Suddenly the saddle I'm sitting on feels hotter and roughened by sand. I wiggle some, which elicits a scowl from Madsen. I shrug it off and we step down.

The Poip consult, their voices buzzing loudly, almost frenzied. Done, they turn to us. "You have suffered an accident of what nature, Once-Other?" A-one asks a trace of human warmth spread like butter across its voice.

"There's some dust on your arm," I reply and we watch.

The B-one extracts a brush from a slot in its midriff and dusts A-one off.

"Round-n-about same-old-same-old program," Madsen chortles.

"Yes. Good thing verbal communication is required with them." We smile at each other—a rare occurrence these days.

"What is the nature of the mishap?" A-one asks me.

"You assume the worst an' all...because?" Madsen shoots back at them.

The A-one wrings its hands and says, "Current status of fuel tank, evidence of a piston top driven through the engine casing. There's bent handlebars and steering column, sand particles in various and unusual locations and traces of $CO_2$ and methane on everything. Please answer the question."

"Not accidental," I say.

"Accidents endanger happiness. Happiness is assured. You must provide correct information. Fines and possible prison time are given those providing false data."

They shuffle closer to one another as though seeking mutual comfort. Madsen and I ponder how anyone on EB had envisioned programming Poip with childish human traits would make them more acceptable to us.

Madsen steps forward indicates the horizon and says, "In an' round-n-about all these vast reaches of desert...happiness is evident." He steps back.

Electronic language whips back-n-forth and the A-one says, "We are not able to conceptualize those words."

"I'm saying happiness ain't worth much without willingness an' all," Madsen clarifies.

A longer silence ensues. "Are you pleased your SandRider crashed?" A-one eventually asks me.

"Crashing willingly can be a happy thing," I reply.

Lights turn on in the black slots supposed to be their eyes. A-one steps closer hands clasped. "We thank you Once-Other for your dedicated, honest and continued testing of vehicles at your own expense per *our* Vehicle Maintenance and Safety Codes. We appreciate dedication and in particular compliance with all the new Standards and Requirements."

Madsen glances at me, we do a mental shrug. They jiggle ecstatically. A-one takes another step forward swings both arms to fully embrace Here-Born and bellows, "Behold!"

We do. Alas. All of everything remains desert, sky and a blazing sun.

A-one gazes at us with its head tilted sideways; abruptly rights it and says, "A commendation has been entered into your record with the Department for the Assurance of Happiness. This serves against future misdemeanors, gross errors, crimes but not high crimes. Have a lovely day, Citizens."

Their attention back on the traffic, Madsen and I share a smile and are about to mount and continue into town when they spin around and square off on us.

"One moment," A-one says and not a single note of warmth tickles our ears.

"Fresh as morning baked bread from the ovens of Here-Born. Yes! A message direct from the desk of our exalted Director, Mister Warrent McPeters."

A flutter of ghostly hands flits through me. I tighten my gut trapping them. Yet they flutter on.

A-one continues in a warm voice. "In the interest of harmony, happiness and the joys of the Earth slash Here-Born Accord we invite you to take but a tiny measure of your time and listen to our esteemed Director's new and enlightening speech. And while listening please dwell upon its subject matter with riveted attention.

"Once comprehended and for the benefit of the All, you may deem to provide vital information in return and bring forth happiness for one-n-all."

Being cautious we agree to a measure of enlightenment.

"Thank you for your kind attention," A-one says. "May your days and nights from this time on reign both glorious and fruitful. A moment as my valued friend downloads the bulletins. As you are well aware our version provides only audio." A-one lowers its head in recognition of its awful shortcomings.

We nod sympathetic understanding.

"We are regretful of this fellow citizens. It is widely known that the visual impact of our Grand Director, Mister Warrent McPeters, has attained a cult status never before realize in all the eons of Man's life...

"...both on Earth and amongst the stars!

"Today, images of Him are cherished by many in actual wood frames as well as in pure hearts. Lifelike pictures are available from Megatrone Images of Nova Vista, California, Earth. Purchase three or more and get a discount."

A-one points heavenwards, holds still then carves an arc from the horizon up into the sky and to the opposite horizon. "But for now...enjoy the sunshine and early morning air as the bulletin downloads."

# CHAPTER 25

## OF REAL-TIME LEGISLATION

"Check time, select morning, afternoon or evening and continue. Check time, select morning, afternoon or evening and continue. Check time, select morning, afternoon or evening and...."

Obviously, A-one is having a bad day. B-one presses a reset button on the back of A-one's head. A-one powers down and boots back up.

I grimace. Why is it that Earth-Born's finest technology resulted in Poip and Toip? Government dreams beating out personal ones I suppose. How do they manage over on EB?

I cringe as A-one, now operational, squeals in its purely electronic voice, "Good morning damn fine citizens of Here-Born. Thank you for your time and all of Earth wishes for you both to have a nice day and not just round-n-about but altogether."

We sigh at colloquialism at its worst screeched by an electronic soprano. Gradually electronic language buzzes louder and the warm voice returns.

"Madsen Somalo, Once-Other. On Here-Born many things are true while many are not. Alas. A quandary my friends. What then...is or isn't true?" Recorded applause plays and fades.

"To the point citizens. We've received news, disturbing news altogether. What could the subject matter be? Damn fine question citizens Once-Other and Madsen Somalo."

A-one waves at the desert, nods and says, "Allow us to provide the details for your enlightenment and edification." It pauses, wrings its hands in angst and continues.

"Growing from seed in our garden of compassion is a bush of grave concern. Yes, Citizens! We are concerned about your current happiness and your continuing happiness."

They stare down at sand. Glance up as one and A-one points to its companion, they nod agreeably to one another, bow low, indicate desert, sun, sky and end with their arms held wide in invitation. "Due to our deep, deep concern we are reaching out to you citizens."

Trumpets blare. Both drop to a knee, cup a hand behind an *ear* and clasp the others free hand. Faces turn to the sky as though God is about to speak. Instead, they bellow in unison and two-part harmony, "And now! For your enlightenment! Mister Warrent McPeters!"

Trumpets blare louder and end abruptly mid note.

McPeters' voice is dry and electronic. "My dedicated citizens, Beloved brethren, fellow travelers along life's trail now coordinated by the Earth slash Here-Born Accord. This is Warrent McPeters appealing to you in full sincerity. For we who live by the rule of Earth law and who love all moments of pleasure brought our way by exercising our inalienable Right to Obey the Law—hear me now!"

A-one and B-one drop to their knees and gaze into the sky as if God had actually appeared.

"Brothers!" McPeters cries. "We've received news of the nature your campaign. How kind of you to clarify it for us. But! What is this stain that has birthed so foully? Too painful is the pain of seeing happiness squandered in so callous a manner. "Oh Brothers! How can this be? How sad. How tragic!"

Both Poip nod sagely.

"But wait!" McPeters bellows. "What is it in reality? Well. Nothing significant. You see fellow citizens we know this is merely a homegrown, garden-variety, everyday GMT. That is Grassroots Terrorist Movement brothers. Moreover, and topping all...one bent upon ruining your present and future Right to Happiness. Pathetic? You bet."

A-one and B-one shake their heads as though the worst catastrophe of all time had occurred.

"But wait!" McPeters cries in anguish. "We suspect—this is not grassroots but instead just another convenient ATM. Yes! AstroTurf Movement brothers. One without any life of its own and no matter how much one feeds or waters AstroTurf—it will not grow. Dear Citizens! It won't grow! Now...to the motto of the day. *You need our help. We hope for yours.*"

A-one and B-one stand up and take a step towards us with arms held wide like mothers do as a child rushes in.

Madsen and I fight an urge to burst out laughing for though we laugh mind-to-mind the physical side remains evident. We manage to nod and appear solemn.

McPeters continues his offer.

"You will, in return, be rewarded as follows.

"Any Here-Born citizen who provides information about the campaign will receive ten thousand dollars in credit, tax-free, paid directly into his or her account. You could also be exempt from Earth taxation for three years at our own financial requirements discretion.

"You'll receive as well, ten two-way, Inter-Constellation Lines First Class tickets with no expiration dates to destinations of your choice. Please help us, help you help your fellows."

We are aghast. Madsen struggles like a worm wiggling free of sinking sand. He takes a deep breath and turns hard eyes briefly in my direction. "Heard talk of the where-about an' all of this campaign an' all," he says to A-one.

I'm about to reach out and implore him but A-one speaks.

"Well done Madsen Somalo. Enlighten us one-two-three, altogether."

Madsen nods momentarily contemplative. "Round-n-about an' all—it ain't located where an' ever you'd expect!" he says and once again sends me a threatening glare.

"Mostly it's up around Iron Rock Falls...a campaign of something bad. It's been going on for more years than I can recall. A secret born of years-n-years of dedicated silence. I do not know how long an' all but...been up and running longer than I care for. Straight up criminal. In need of correction for some time...spreading like a cancer to all sectors of Here-Born."

Both models edge forward bobbing their heads eagerly.

I'm terrified. Is Madsen a traitor?

"Continue," the warm voice urges.

Madsen takes a deep breath. "The campaign is vigorously indulged in by those who wish to be the first to free climb Iron Rock Falls. Like I said, been growing secretly for a long-long time an' all. Too many lives have been lost. Endless hours of production...lost an' all? Loved ones never again seen. Needs be stopped for its own damn good. I hope this helps me, help you more than round-n-about."

I am as aghast as are the Poip.

A-one jiggles its head and turns off.

B-one hums with activity and shuts down as well.

B-one comes up.

A-one awakes and says, "A moment as my trusted companion downloads the latest Legislation for the Assurance of Happiness."

B-one hums again—falls silent.

In a cold and official voice, A-one says, "Information downloaded and transferred."

Madsen glances at me.

Without warmth A-one says, "Citing the new Earth Combined Houses Bill 227-437 titled: Happiness, Rights to, Addition 440-601.

"And Referencing Sub-Section 299-45 of the Vehicle Maintenance Code. With added References to Sub-Sub Section 889-7 Part 114-56, Number 1002-34, Titled: Providing Information and attempts to sabotage Happiness through Vehicular Maintenance Negligence and Suspect Verbal Engagement under the Traffic Violation Sections."

A-one pauses as though taking a deep breath and says, "This new Legislation is dated today and passed into Law via the Happiness Monitoring Act. Which Law in part states: Consistent and topical Conversation is a legal requirement as, while and when answering questions and or providing information in reference to vehicle maintenance under the Misuse of Mechanical Devices Section.

"Rights exist purely for the Assurance of Happiness as required under the Modifiable Constitution of Earth.

"Thusly, referencing amendments numbered 1785 through 2026 which in part states: Laws are required to ensure Happiness for the general, amalgamated, ethnic, non-ethnic, collective, dispersed, and any other specific or nonspecific public or individuals or groups.

"It is herein decreed that violations of these Laws may require immediate attention or not, due consideration or not, even exact formulation or not, some with or without formal form, some congruent or otherwise. Valid for all current or imagined positions, situations and possibilities.

"Thus by these legal truths we do here solemnly on this day, at this time, declare and enable the People's Rights to Living Law."

"What's this?" I ask Madsen.

He shrugs.

"Under Section 911 Sub-Section 104-764 Page 288-934 it is hereby declared that Living Law provides instant Legislative Processing. This guards our Rights to Happiness in the face of any and all violations, potential violations both deliberate and otherwise.

"Whereas real time violations are committed in real time it follows that all moments of dissent are violations of one's own Right to Assured Happiness and of the Rights of Others to have Rights."

They bow to us and A-one continues.

"Disclaimer for ADD-Dees and others; Legal assistance will be provided to any who suffer from one or all genetic diseases. This includes such as the epidemic Dissenter's Mental Lapsus and Thought Paralysis Diseased Disorder comprising Types 1 through 70889 whether the primary ADD-D infection is present and dominates all other diseases or not.

"Furthermore, assistance will be provided to all current, past and future active or passively infected subjects as well as all other citizens in respect of the contagion that such contagious diseases perpetuate."

Madsen and I figuratively scratch our heads.

"This law subjects as well, all personal contacts, family members, friends and/or other persons, known or unknown at the time of violation, whether they are influenced by similar or dissimilar locations, or during occupancy or non-attendance in said locations. Includes all present or future dates and times. This embraces as well persons other than those described both known and unknown.

"Treatment, citations, fines, and fees may be levied upon those who have been close to or within the contagion arena at the time a crime has been committed. And includes prior to the time and post the time of any and all crimes or potential crimes.

"Distances from contagion points are calculated at all possible mileage, possible travel distances to any and all possible and probable locations be they inhabited or not.

"Time required writing this new Legislation, 27.06 seconds.

"Time required voting legislation into Law, 12.53 seconds.

"Costs of the new law are $ 2091.01 per violation.

"The amount and effect of this law is extended and compounded by the process of the ad infinitum laws of natural extension and normalization as and when required.

"Designed, written, approved, costing done and voted into Law by Mister Warrent McPeters. This done as authorized and on behalf of absent members of the House of Representations and the Senatorial Hub of the Federal Government of the United Countries of Earth.

"Percentage of House and Hub Members absent during voting, 100%. Default Voter Who Votes for Absentees, Mister Warrent McPeters.

"Yea Votes 100%. Nay Votes 0%.

"Thus passed into law this day. Today. Date. This date. Time. This time.

"This law embraces Situation Z which states that under questioning by any and all Authorized Government entities or persons at any time, in any place, on any subject a Respondent's Rights are hereby clarified:

"A Respondent's Answers are necessary and must be correct per Government stipulations.

"Any claims made and all data provided by Government Representatives are always correct and always accurate and always true.

"Failure to provide the expected correct answers violates one's and all others Right to Happiness.

"Fines imposed for this violation are calculated in real time and are paid in real time."

Our mouths hang open in horror; our minds as blank as the first page of an unwritten book.

"Once-Other and Madsen Somalo the sum of $ 2091.01 plus a further $ 500.00 for Administration Fees, another $ 850.54 for Voting Fees and possible paperwork has been deducted from each of your accounts.

"Once-Other. An additional $ 1730.99 has been deducted from your account under citation number 763-908, Poor or substandard Vehicular Maintenance per the Assurance of Happiness Commingled Legislative Act. Written, enacted and legally binding on today's Date, at this Time and in this Place.

"Furthermore, a $ 500.00 Administration Fee and another $ 850.54 Voting Fee and possible paperwork have also been deducted for this second violation.

"We, of the Department for the Assurance of Happiness wish you well, a safe journey, thank you for your contributions to maintaining Law and Order as well as the Assurance of Happiness.

"With sincere thanks from me the esteemed Director, Mister Warrent McPeters.

"This includes an appreciation for your selfless exercising of your Constitutional Rights to Contribute to and Obey the Law. We bid peace and sanity to you and all those you may encounter today, tomorrow and for all your life at work or at play.

"Have a nice day citizens."

Several minutes tick by before we are able to think, let alone clearly.

"Anyone writing laws worded like that on Here-Born would be charged with treason Madsen!" I whisper.

"I know an' all! Bad-on-bad Once-Other and not round-n-about at all."

"May not be as bad as we think," I reply ever hopeful.

He glares at me.

I shrug his glare aside.

We turn toward Salt Lake Flats suddenly a strange and altered destination.

# CHAPTER 26

## OF HIDDEN ENEMIES

Unaltered though, is Soonsaan's SandRider Sales, Repairs and Maintenance. It prospers beneath a circular red tent nestled in the city center of Sand Lake Flats. Is located at the tip of Two Mile Square Mall and faces west to the setting sun. Its rear door opens onto Circle Road where the coffee shops are rumored the finest on all of Here-Born.

Soonsaan's high peaked roof flies a beige flag depicting a red SandRider cresting a dune. Sections of the tent's walls are transparent allowing one to see into the showroom where the latest models gleam in lighting designed to enhance one's desire to own. Parked outside and roasting in the sun are several pre-owned SandRiders bearing *For Sale* signs.

It has always puzzled me that Soonsaan and Maggie had not gotten married to one another. Something is odd there. As teenagers, they were inseparable. Briefly, I'd been jealous but that faded after Deidre scowled at me.

We made a foursome tearing across sand on hand-me-down SandRiders, lying on our backs staring up at the night sky. Days now long gone. Circumstances now long changed.

We pull up in the Service and Repairs bay just as Soonsaan exits and his smiling face smiles broader at the sight of us. I grin at his spotless red overall, which belies the mechanical nature of his work.

He's short like Jenk but leaner. Broad hands dangle from long sleeves. He spreads his arms wide in welcome, shakes his head and ample black hair flares a dark fire about his face.

He holds still allowing us three an instant in which to examine one another. Unable to keep his enthusiasm at bay he rushes forward.

"Once-Other! Uh, Madsen. It's wonderful you're both...at the same time."

We hug long and hard.

"Oh? What? Hmm?" He drops to his haunches and examines Hellbent. "Well?"

"Forgive me Soonsaan. I was deep in thought when it happened."

"Tell me," he demands.

"Strange sounds were coming from the engine but I failed to hear them clearly," I reply.

"Hmm. What kind we talking about?" he says.

"Well...hard to say...something like ga-eer...ga-eer...softly or perhaps my thinking muted them."

He runs a finger along his upper lip and says, "Ga-eer eh? We have a clue on our hands."

"I ain't getting other than most of nothing," Madsen complains. We ignore him.

Soonsaan inspects the hoses, sniffs at the oil reservoir tank, fiddles with the hose connections and tugs at each.

"What you reckonin' Soonsaan?" Madsen asks.

"I'm thinking Madsen."

"Yes—round-n-about?" Madsen prompts.

Soonsaan waves him silent and checks under the oil pan.

Madsen's face drops at being ordered about.

Soonsaan mumbles, "Ga-eer? Hmm? Metal filings? Hmm? Main bearings? Hmm? Maybe the small ends too. Hmm? Here—I'll be right back. Hmm?"

He rushes inside and emerges moments later with a spanner and a catch-can. "Once-Other—hold this under the feed pipe...to oil cooler...hmm?" he says handing me the can. I do and Soonsaan works the connector and the O-ring free and oil gushes into the catch can. "Let's take a look-see...hmm?" he says.

In his Analysis Lab, which is filled with high-tech equipment for the taking of all possible measurements and their persuasions, he pours some of the oil into a small pan. Pops it into the analyzer and watches keenly as the display evolves. "Interesting," he mutters and adjusts the settings and the spectrum changes. "Hmm? Uh-hmm."

We wait expectantly.

He grunts, nods, rubs an elbow, whistles through his teeth, steps back and examines me in an odd fashion. "Hmm? Hmm? You got enemies Once-Other?" he asks.

I stagger backward as though all of my fingers had found their way into a hot power outlet and stammer, "No. Well. I can't think of any. Can you?"

"Seems you do," he says.

"Why you say so an' all?" Madsen asks as puzzled as I am stunned.

"See this here," Soonsaan says. "The red with a bluish tinge tells tales...hmm...it's the remains of an EB lubricant. Hmm? One not in use on Here-Born. Can't even get any here. Hmm?"

"But why an enemy Soonsaan?" I ask.

"Hmm? Well. Has value on EB—as a general lubricant. Temperature ceiling is too low for Here-Born use, overheats easily, molecular structure alters. Hmm? Can't be used here."

"Ah...yes?" I say.

He stares at me long and hard, sighs and says, "Hmm? At too high a temperature doesn't just thin and break down as oil tends to do. Instead, its molecules fuse into a solid lump."

He taps the display thoughtfully, dips a finger into the oil and rubs it between his finger and thumb. "Do that," he says.

Madsen and I can feel the rough particles crunch together.

"That's bad," Madsen says.

"Hmm. Right. Hmm? Now. Even our early morning temperatures are higher than the hottest EB desert at high noon in high summer. We engineer our oil here for our conditions. You can feel the difference between solidified oil and metal particles from the motor itself. Hmm?"

Madsen and I do another dip, rub the oil between thumb and forefinger and nod as one. Soonsaan traces a line around the red tinged with blue.

"What's that?" I ask.

"Hmm? Cool blue and red hot," he says. "We're looking at partially seized molecules. It's worse when added to other oil. Hmm? The darker blue...pieces of metal."

For a minute we all think our own thoughts.

"Someone added this to your oil reservoir," Soonsaan says. And I say, "Hmm?"

"Someone who brought it here intending to cause damage," Soonsaan adds.

I nod in cold understanding.

"Hmm? So the question about enemies."

"I can't think of any," I say.

I search deep for enemies—known and unknown.

None comes to mind.

Soonsaan adds to my woes.

"How do you figure it got into your SandRider?" he asks.

Keeping those footprints in sand a secret, I shrug and he pivots and heads down a dark alley. "This is footprints in sand, Once-Other," he says. "Someone is coming at you. You must find out who the hunter is."

I nod, thoughtful, heart beat uneven.

Soonsaan says, "Now Once-Other. Yours is a dead engine. The chassis and suspension may still work. But if I spend time and money testing...cost more than I can get. The best option? Recycle."

"Oh no," I mumble.

"We'll do so free of charge of course...if you are okay with...," he concludes.

I nod yes and note his constant *hmm's* have gone missing.

He points.

I turn with a sense of loss in the direction of Hellbent but with sudden insight to his sales techniques, I ask, "What? No trade-in value?"

"I've plenty work to do an' all," Madsen says, pats his belly in revelation of the actual truth and leaves. I watch him head off feeling a little guilty at my sense of relief.

Soonsaan smiles and says, "I understand."

"Been some years now," I add.

We both glance at Madsen checking his SandRider over.

Soonsaan whispers as he says, "Tragic slide downwards he's had. Inexplicable too. Hope all turns out the best for you.

Don't see much hope for change in him. Best you rise above it…above him."

"Been thinking along those lines, Soonsaan. We've been friends so…."

"Do along them Once-Other."

I nod yes though lost as to how.

In a whisper laced with a strange power he says, "But for now…come with me!" Moving off involuntarily, I still manage to take a deep breath, break free of his grasp and stop up.

"Come Once-Other," Soonsaan says a smile of innocence twinkling in his eyes.

"Do we need to do this now?" I ask and make to head for the rear exit.

He takes me by the arm and says, "Hmm? Allow me to show off our new models. Nothing more. Hmm?" I again lose my own will and follow as though a natural extension of him.

# CHAPTER 27

## OF BUYING AND SELLING

His showroom is spotless with that strange lighting hanging like ethereal mist. The smell of new metal, rubber, polish and fresh oil tickles my nose. Waves of contrasting colors assault me as Soonsaan gives my funny bone a gentle squeeze and marches me forward. At our entry two salesmen in beige pants and red shirts look up, note it is Soonsaan and get back to making calls.

The SandRider that catches my eye sits high upon a pedestal in the center of the showroom. Its six wheels stand proud, hunched and ready for action. She has two up front and four in the rear. Across its fairing, a wild graphic advertises her engine as a V8.

Being familiar with Soonsaan's skills, I focus on a smaller model parked on the floor in a far corner. I saunter on by and examine her up on the pedestal without appearing to do so.

Her six tires seem designed for high speed and properly grooved for soft sand conditions. Their profiles and treads suggest undefeatable traction. And for all future passengers, her rear seat is blessed with a backrest. And both seats are longer, wider and better padded than Hellbent's. Deep green metallic paint glows under the subdued lighting and seems alive with the anticipation of adventure. Stretched along her fairing, orange teardrops fly away into a fantasy of speed.

I struggle to control desire, a racing heart and glance at the sticker on the windshield by only moving my eyes.

A First Aid Kit along with a Navigation System that includes Remote Locate for when you are separated and not sure where to find her reassures one of a better survival potential. Then there's a tow-bar. Winch. Nomadi connector. Satellite Access Module. Music System, with and without noise making speakers. Emergency Oxygen System and topping all, an auto-deploying tent.

Goosebumps attack my legs and arms. I refrain from rubbing them aware of Soonsaan's attention playing over every square-finger of me like radar.

"Who wants to pollute with a V8?" I ask.

He claps and glances at me. "Technology. Hmm. Carbon monoxide gets burned before hitting the atmosphere. Hmm. Now it is carbon dioxide. That ends up in capture ditches populated with conversion units. With carbon removed, O2 releases into the environment—like trees on EB do. We've no rain, so no acid rain. Nitrogen stays nitrogen."

"We don't need more CO2," I say.

"Polluting? No. You know this already. Hmm Once-Other?"

"Ah yes," I say. "A pocket of air saved me this morning."

He nods in understanding, pats my arm and points.

"The tent system is a real pleasure," he says.

I nod disinterestedly.

"Hmm. Pitches at the touch of a button. Fulfills all needs from moments of personal solitude to interludes of romance, to emergency housing, to breakdown, to coming home and finding your house tilted or maybe buried. Hmm?"

He pats a front wheel.

I head towards the lesser model as he adds, "We've already installed the five-hundred horsepower kit."

"That's not high on my priorities list," I lie.

"Of course not," he assures. "Just making idle though informative chat. Hmm?" We both know no such thing exists in his showroom.

"The required stress tests on h...it?" I ask and chastise self for almost saying *her*.

"Five-hundred trouble free miles of the High Desert...certified. But oh. With six-wheel drive, she hugs sand like nothing before. No chain drive. Shafts. Bullet proof. Almost no chance of a drivetrain failure. Central Transfer case with eight ratios. Ten gear transmission. Hmm?"

I mentally reconfigure her drive train, note the asking price and keep going towards the smaller one in the far corner, which has but four wheels.

With enthusiasm, I examine what is visible of its V4 engine. Sit astride the saddle, grip the handlebars and hunch down below the windshield as though there is wind blowing through my hair.

Soonsaan observes with a knowing eye, rubs his elbow, squeezes his nose and glances back-n-forth between the six-wheeled beauty upon the pedestal and back to where I sit enraptured and enthralled.

"I like this one," I enthusiastically remark and glance down at the gear lever.

"A magnificent machine, Once-Other. It's been honed to a new perfection of speed, agility, reliability, and endurance."

He crosses his arms as I check the smaller one over.

I work the clutch lever and ask, "How quickly does it find neutral when hot or cold."

He drums his fingers on the saddle in that nervous way of his, locks them together as though about to pray, stretches his arms out forwards with palms outwards and cracks his finger joints. As always, I shudder.

"She's well worth every penny if you're being chased by either too satisfied or very dissatisfied ladies. Hmm?"

He's about to continue when Francisco, face landscaped with joy, rushes up but on seeing me it changes to concern. "Once-Other," he communicates, "I thought you were in the store...few minutes ago."

"Why?" I ask.

"Well. The front door was open and there was an outline of someone inside."

"Someone has entered my store without permission?" I ask of no one but self.

# CHAPTER 28

## OF UNEXPECTED AND LAME EXCUSES

Head tucked behind the fairing, knees tight to the saddle, elbows bent and hands gentle on the handlebars I storm through downtown, weaving around SandRiders and avoiding pedestrians.

Turning tight around a corner I just manage to miss the tent pegs of a traveling carpet vendor. He leaps backward, expresses his displeasure in crude, though precise sign language, kicks at sand and heads into his tent.

The street is relatively quiet but pedestrians tend to cross without looking left-n-right-n-left-again. Behind me a sand-cloud billows larger than those made by the four wheels of my old SandRider. Ahead, a mother and her child retreat in horror at the sight of me bearing down on them. Both shake their heads in chastisement.

I open the throttle a little more, hunch down further out of the wind, glance at the high-rises to my left and make a hard right winding the throttle open to the stops.

More-n-more fists are shaken as I speed onwards. In self-defense, I broadcast my predicament to one-n-all present. Various acknowledgments return. Some arrive colored with encouragement while others are shaded with caution advised. Most though complain about the sandstorm billowing off my six new wheels.

Breaking free of downtown, I zero in on Pre-owneds Galore. Despite my haste, I note that even this early hundreds of tourists are lined up at the carousel. We're looking at one damn fine tourist season this year.

With the sun shining from the east and still at the correct angle I too discern a silhouette inside my store. I slide to a stop, hit sand running, charge inside and slam to a halt as a massive mental short erupts rendering me virtually dead on arrival.

Seated at my table is Peter Wernt.

He is dressed in the same silver-gray colored fan-n-fit. His Nomadi, alive and active, lies next to a glass of my water. He has my ID Check connection drawn close and his brow wrinkles and furrows as he strives to gain access.

Something is indeed wrong with this man—this EB.

What it is I have failed to discern. I must tread here with care. I cannot afford a bout of screwball snorting. Also, I've trouble enough with Madsen as well as that nagging fear in my gut which has now become a natural part of my life within this campaign of ours.

Nevertheless, I'm aware of EB's who have no respect for the property of others and who will tamper as they please and without permission. Perhaps that is Peter, a man without consideration of others.

Wait and see I advise myself.

I rock on my heels listening to sand scrunch beneath my boots. The seconds tick by and he slowly becomes aware of my presence. He turns, stares a moment as though seeing a ghost, and says, "Well damn Once-Other. Good morning to you, one-two-three."

I wait, silent.

A trace of doubt slithers across his face.

I tap my foot. His eyes linger on my shoes.

His brow creases with questions. "Yeah. Ah? Once-Other? Yes. After what happened I thought...no longer...good you're alright and damn fine indeed."

He slow-grins as though we are friends enough to share this parody of our speech mannerisms and waves at the table. "Yeah—please excuse the natural curiosity," he says as a cold calculation flashes in his eyes.

I unclench my fists and waggle my fingers. They relax as anger eases. I present him a stiff smile that nevertheless hides my snarl.

He stands and extracts a pack of cigarettes from a hip pocket. Flips it from hand to hand, shows it is unopened and says, "I picked up a faint whiff of tobacco around so I brought this brand with me today. I hear they're sought after out here."

He offers me the pack.

"Did you not consider me dead?" I ask ignoring his offering.

He glances to the entrance, back at me. "Yeah. Right. Oh. Okay. Kinda yes—kinda no." He drops the pack onto the table as though it's worthless and sips more water.

I wait, silent.

His eyes narrow, a new light turns on deep within them and he says, "You told me to keep a distance...no matter what." And he peers over the glass brim at me.

"This is true," I concede.

The lights in his eyes switch to a triumphant glow. "Yeah. I panicked...left you down there—can't deny that. Journey alone in the cage did something...don't understand what. Scrambled my mind, emotions...."

"Well, okay Peter," I say hoping to stem his blatant lies.

Now without a doubt something is very wrong or dangerous or both but about which I have no clue. Further questions plague me. Danger *for* whom? Myself alone? Our campaign? Is he merely weird?

Unfortunately, the road to any answers requires spending time with him. I gulp and accept my own challenge. And with my goals redefined, I resume my campaign but add this new path of discovery and set course towards finding out whom Peter Wernt is and why he is here and all else worth knowing.

I inexplicably break out sweating. Peter notices but says nothing. My temperature drops as suddenly. I walk over and inspect the ID Check connect. It's powered on but without my Nomadi, he cannot log into remote databases.

"Do you verify against violent criminal parts?" he asks.

I note he made an effort to sound conversational.

Again, doubt rages. I should send him on his way. Something is more than bad here—rotten. It in fact smells to high heaven yet remains hidden.

I consider his questions, him, my predicament and Madsen's face if I bow out on this one now. I decide once again, right or wrong, to continue my campaign with this EB while hoping for answers to unanswered questions.

Where had Peter been when his Quaaseon flask depleted?

Is there a connection to Jiplee?

I embrace Once-Other's Foundation, purpose and skills for perhaps winning with this Peter Wernt may still be possible. And so the battle resumes. This one to be fought in the fields, mountains and valleys of two minds—each with mutually foreign and unknown landscapes and conflicting purposes.

My goal I understand. But what is Peter's?

With this unspoken declaration of war, I answer his question. "Well Peter, like all pre-owned vendors I'm connected to Local, State and Federal databases with a certified ID Check connection. The one before your eyes with which you fiddle...without my permission."

He deliberately touches it and asks, "Do you really?"

"Let me show you. Here I place a spot of its blood." I pull the receptacle open, he looks in and I slam it closed. "Then I add a drop of Bondo-stick-on which...."

"Bondo-stick-on?"

"We'll come to that in due course."

"Yeah. The later *whatever* thing."

"As I was saying...Bondo-stick-on extracts the DNA code and embeds it into the sensor plate of a translation chip."

I point to the chip's location and say, "DNA is streamed to all databases. An ID Check certificate as an eCopy downloads. I'm sent a clear record or a violent criminal one. I provide every purchaser with two copies."

He grins as I do when recognizing lies and says, "You sure? Never mixed up two or more...forgotten to check?"

"No mix-ups, no forgetting. We use ID Check to register all new stock and each sale. Unless an impossible to hack database is hacked—no errors possible. So! No C-POP."

"You've never sold Criminal Pre-Owned Parts?"

"Damn accurately stated, Peter."

"Hard to believe Once-Other."

"Why do you ask?" I say.

"Ah? Well...you know...the attitude on Earth."

"We are not all criminals nor zombies."

He stares off into the distance as though alone.

"This your first trip here?" I ask.

"You've already checked my background," he replies coldly. "You're right."

Does he know his background is muddy, though more so empty? If yes, then he is incredibly calm at sudden probing questions. The less I tell him of what I know the better. And so I withhold that we cannot find any historical records about him. Does he even come from EB? Is Peter Wernt his real name? We change ours why not them.

The sound of a particular SandRider alerts me to Madsen's presence. "Updates to participants gone out Once-Other. Oh. Wernt's back. Damn fine but peculiar. I'll reassign the new tourist. This time...don't blow it an' all."

I bite my tongue.

Madsen adds, "Who is he? Why's he here? Was he involved with Jiplee? I want everything. He's an EB. Whatever is shutting you out—find it. Look for hardware on his person—there's nothing he can use from a distance. Givin' an order here an' all. Failure's no option."

"Just about had your attitude...." But I abruptly drop the connection with Madsen for someone is attempting to break into it.

We switch to safe mode.

# CHAPTER 29

## OF SANDMASTERS AND ONE-TWO-THREE

"Yes!" Madsen says. "All's good for the party this weekend. I can't wait to celebrate one damn fine new SandRider, one-two-three an' all."

I search for the intruder amongst a group of shoppers weighed down with bright green plastic bags. None registers as intrusive. We configure a deeper communications pipe. Madsen sends me a stream of urgent information and a terrible sadness descends upon me.

"No questioning this Once-Other," he says.

I swallow a hard, dry lump.

"Franciscoa decided this? I ask.

"Yes...his alone an' all."

"Right," I whisper laboring under the weight of what we dare not communicate.

"Comes to many an' all Once-Other," Madsen says.

"Yes...still...," I reply barely able to muster any words.

"Live by Neatness alone," he says and the old comradeship from our youth flickers alive for but a moment. He drops the connection, winds the throttle open and races away.

Once again, danger has increased but this time my old friend and companion Franciscoa has willingly stepped directly into enemy fire. I look up from the sudden sadness and my eyes find Madsen retreating toward the horizon. Hope wishes that Franciscoa comes through his chosen path alive.

Through all my troubled youth, prison time, loss of my parents he was always there despite the poison that makes his life a Hell that I have but the faintest symptoms of by comparison. "Come back alive dear friend," I broadcast wide and far but receive no acknowledgement from him.

With a tired sigh, I once again embrace my campaign duties and examine circumstances for clarity and possible clues to Peter.

It's clear to me that this skirmish with Peter is unlike any previous one-on-one tour. Still, I'm reluctant to admit it may be more than a tour with a strange and peculiar EB. Keeping a hold of that allows for my deepest wish live on. I want Peter interested in our Rights and Constitution no matter how dim a hope that may be.

Perhaps, when all is said-n-done I worry needlessly. Maybe he's a thoroughly unpleasant personality and nothing more. He could also be medically drugged and thereby close to mindless—but what switches his wild manifestations on and off I have no clue.

I jolt at his touch.

"You alright?" he asks his elbow nudging me.

There had been no sound nor hint of his approach. Had I been that introspective? From out the northern desert and sudden as a thundering duststorm, sounds that same SandMaster driving hard. I search sand but it is beyond the dunes and out of sight. I hold to full alert as a chill runs down my spine.

"What on Earth...Here-Born?" Peter says.

"A SandMaster," I reply, voice shaky.

"Come on Once-Other," he growls.

I take several deep breaths.

"Well...one damn fine eight-wheeled vehicle it is...used by Desert Drivers. Fitted with one engine up front and one in the rear—they're seventeen-cylinder radial engines, air and liquid cooled, from way back on EB but updated here."

His mouth hardens at such useless information yet he says, "Radial engine? What's that?"

"Okay. Imagine a wagon wheel. Now imagine the spokes have cooling-fins around them. Next, envision that inside the spokes are pistons sliding up and down.

"Now see the pistons connected in the center to the wheel-hub and spinning it round-n-round very fast. Now fasten a propeller to the hub and imagine an airplane with this radial engine mounted in the front. There you go—radial engines."

"I'm not really interested but at least get done with this," he says and looks to the sky as though seeking divine patience.

"Now! Radial engines came to us by way of EB—as I've mentioned. Back then, they were built for light tanks and the airplanes of World War I and II, some earlier, and others later. Many saw service in other ways. Production ended around the 1980's. You understand the change of dates we're talking 1970's in EB reality?"

He glares.

"So you do," I confirm. "Okay. We found them as museum displays and junkyard relics. Over time, we redesigned and manufactured them ourselves—modernized them as well. Same way we did with all our internal combustion engines."

He laughs without mirth and says, "Hell no! Here is what happened—Here-Born stole some engines and reverse engineered them—straight up theft. Period! And from us no less. Who are Desert Drivers anyway?"

"Oh. You know about these engines. Well, you're wrong!" He makes to protest; I wave him silent. "Desert Drivers are descendants of Here-Born's original soldiers. Back then, they had no duties other than those of a soldier.

"They, with the general public as recruits and volunteers, won for us our Independence from Earth-Born. Today their offspring live as Desert Drivers with minimal to no contact with others."

"Interesting. More."

"Their interaction with the Nomads is greater than with us the Free Marketeers. Population breakdown for you Peter. One Desert Drives, two Nomads, three Free Marketeers."

"Tell me about the others?" he says.

Inwardly I smile at his interest. "Some of us believe that back in those early times, Desert Drivers split off from the Nomads. Before then there were supposedly us, Nomads and Northerners but there's no proof of this."

He sighs in exasperation and says, "Do you or don't you know?"

I wait long enough to watch his simmering demeanor head towards boiling point. Just before he boils over I say, "Northerners and Desert Drivers are now one group. Desert Drivers own and run the electrical power grid with many power stations located around Here-Born. They also run all things mechanical in design."

"Where are the large bodies of water, fast-flowing rivers? No one's mentioned nuclear power."

My virtual antenna hums and sparks, he has just confirmed he is getting information from other sources. Why would he? Well. Why not?

"Damn right you are. We lower thermocouples deep into the boiling water below sand. You remember the rendition yesterday."

He jolts physically. "That's where? That's how you make electricity?"

I nod and smile. "Sure. Out on the Rocklands steam geysers exist. That's where thermocouples are driven into the depths of Here-Born. It is mostly solid rock all the way down—where they blow a path already exists. Oh? Thermocouples are two different compounds reacting to heat and creating an electrical current—we use unique materials, make gigantic ones and so generate usable electricity."

"Seen no grid," he says.

"They are either on the desert surface or buried below sand depending on what happens with the wind."

"Yeah sure."

"Peter. I'm talking about flexible pipelines...conduits that is. Big ones. Designed to withstand high winds and driven sand. They whip around like sidewinders during sandstorms. Most of the time though, they'll rest quietly beneath sand...who knows where they are?"

"That's all?" he asks.

"No further information is available. They own it and run it and maintain it."

"I see," he whispers.

"On the other hand Nomads own and run electronic systems. Not electrical. Electronic. You understand? Inter-planet connections, boosters and all other communication systems.

Oh! You need to understand Fragger technology to understand boosters."

"I see," he whispers.

"Our commercial basics for you. We are business orientated—Free Marketeers. Nomads run communications. Desert Drivers command power supply and mechanical systems."

"That fair, Once-Other?"

"Whatever fair is...it's the way we evolved."

"I see," he says.

"Oh. Many believe Nomads became cannibals but no evidence is available or was eaten."

"How about a couple of straight answers here," he growls.

"Ease up and listen, Peter. We figure Desert Drivers and Nomads are in continuous conflict over sand, territory. Nomads I believe live a simple but exact and honorable life. Desert Drivers are more aggressive and unpredictable—some insist violent."

"Yeah. One hell of a lot of words to say nothing."

"Try this on. Possibly Desert Drivers and Nomads do have our economy in their hands. But. All three groups work together forming one economy. None can continue as economically viable without the other two. All three play economics together. And there you have it."

"Have what?" he growls.

"Why we say one-two-three so often."

He licks his lips with the satisfaction of the underdog having conquered the alpha male and says, "Sounds like they're tied into your UWMD Once-Other."

"Sure, rumors galore...no one knows for sure. They don't advertise let alone—"

"As you would say...damn informative indeed," he whispers and rubs an earlobe as though it itches more than usual.

We step outside and I point with pride. "This is brand new and you are to be its first passenger."

"Where's the name like on the other one?" he asks.

"Purchased it this morning. I think I'll paint her name right here—midway between the four rear wheels and the front ones." I run my hand along the lower fairing beneath the speeding orange teardrops. "Hellbent II. What you think?"

"Looks kinda dangerous—orange teardrops and all."

"Not really Peter. Just don't jump or fall off at speeds well over a hundred miles an hour."

"What the hell?" he asks.

"Peter? The higher the speed the more bones you break— the greater the pain."

Needless, to say...he is not amused.

# CHAPTER 30

## OF PETER'S MANIFESTATIONS AND ONCE-OTHER'S CONDITION

Peter shifts his weight in the saddle as I navigate around an old warren. I smile at having recently come a cropper due to one and turn my attention southeast to where Mourner's Wind originates. This morning she slumbers leaving the air thick with heat.

Upon the vast desert, nothing stirs other than Hellbent II and its dust plume. We climb up the face of North Guard dune. At its peak, a tabletop unfolds to the horizon. I smiled contentedly at how Hellbent II navigates sand on six wheels with ease.

Ahead of us lie many hours of droning across sand headed north. Invitations to nod off will be constant.

Later we charge down old riverbeds, eons dry.

Our companions are consistent, heat, sand and salt. The latter preferring a diet of eyes, lips and lungs. But licking one's lips leads to bleeding. Then pressing them together, without any preservatives present, glues them closed.

Nevertheless, when salts attacks one often longs for wind despite knowing it will compound one's misery. I wipe mine carefully and glance at the sky. It's clear as always.

Again I check the southeast, still nothing visible there.

That we are headed dead North requires I remain fully alert to any storms headed our way. But to stay awake during the long drive I set about feeding Peter's Foundation a diet of new ideas mixed with Here-Born descriptions. All the while, I am hoping they will serve as an antidote to his rigid attitude.

Fragile hope indeed.

After an hour of racing through heat, sand, and more heat, I get the distinct impression he's not listening. He remains silent and disinterested. I cover the many wonders of Here-Born anyway. Four more hours out and with not a single comment from him, I lock wheels and slide to a halt saying, "So Criers are dangerous, ordinary and outright frightening. Right?"

"Whatever," he snaps back.

"We've no *whatever* out here. Be careful Peter."

"Yeah! Whatever."

He dismounts stiff in leg-n-back, brushes his suit off, checks our location over and glances to the horizon. Desertscape unfolds in all directions. Maybe he notes sand out here is a little orange in color—perhaps not. He looks a question at me.

I ponder his hidden mind once again but find no resolutions nor solutions. I attempt accessing it and still nothing. I sigh in exasperation, squat down, scan the desert and find what I'm looking for. "Now. Something like we did outside the Mall."

"Not that BS again," he says.

"A little different this time."

He jerks back-n-forth as though attacking and fleeing in the same instant. An animal rage flashes across his face. He licks at a fleck of foam on his lip and crouches like EB apes do—arms hung loose, head swaying.

I back away and turn sideways to what appears to be an attacking stance. "Peter?"

"Once-Other?" he says.

"You alright?" I ask.

He shudders and shakes violently enough to rattle his teeth together. His eyes roll up white and back to normal. He drops to his knees and grunts. I take a cautious step forward but he waves me away.

"Give me a moment Once-Other."

"Do you suffer something?"

"It'll pass. Wait."

He wraps his arms around his chest and squeezes. Within a minute the shaking subsides. He takes a few deep breaths, gazes around as though seeing where he is for the first time, notices me and says in his usual voice, "Thank you Once-Other. It's done. Okay. Let's do this."

He stands up and steadies himself.

"You sure?" I ask.

"I'm good. Don't worry."

"Sure?"

"Yeah! Tell me what to do."

"Okay then. There is something out here. But if you search as though you already know all there is to see...you won't see anything new. With me?"

"Yeah. Kinda."

"Look at sand like a child in a playground does for the first time."

He looks-n-looks. After some minutes his face changes and a smile evolves. "There's...patches."

"Yes. Describe them."

"They're about two and a half feet wide and four to six long, faintly sunken. Above each...a whisper of vapor. I'd never have...something to thank you for...I guess."

He reaches over, we shake hands, and a blade stabs at the inside of my skull. I drop to my knees, struggle back up and manage to remain upright. But at the same time I cannot tell if it is actually happening or not.

Similar to Franciscoa, though less so, I've been poisoned by Criers and slashed and cut more often than I care to recall. I've also broken bones hitting Crier burrows while riding a SandRider.

Other scars tell their own tales. In addition, I replaced both arms when I became a campaigner. My head I changed out as well but with help of course. Therefore, what rules me rules Franciscoa: Crier poison.

Once inside...always inside.

In a voice hoarse with heat and dust, I whisper encouragement to self, swallow and take several deep breaths to no relief. I wait, after several seconds my vision clears and a little strength returns.

Is a heart condition worsening?

Perhaps.

Even so, damn poison is the real culprit—now as in the past.

# CHAPTER 31

## OF WATER CRIERS, WHAT IS AND WHAT IS NOT DANGEROUS

I shake my head and Peter withdraws from reaching to steady me.

"You okay?" he asks.

I nod yes and motion for him to follow. "Stay on mine," I say, pointing at my footprints. "I don't want you stepping on a Crier burrow and getting bitten or worse...stung."

I gentle down prone and leopard crawl towards a cluster of Crier burrows. I pause, come carefully to my hands and knees, lean forward and hold still a few feet short of a burrow.

The Crier stirs awake and lifts its pouch a little. I hold my breath waiting for it to relax again. The Crier vibrates its pouch-cover cooling itself. After a few moments it stops and snuggles down.

Old pain revisits and an ancient meat grinder assaults my head. I take several slow breaths and pain slips back into yesterday. I nod for Peter to follow. He goes to his hands-n-knees and crawls closer.

The Crier senses Peter's movements, stirs uneasily and starts standing up. I wave frantically. Peter halts. We hold still for several minutes.

Eventually, the Crier relaxes, wriggles lower and sand pours onto its back hiding it completely. The sting-claw cover peeks out momentarily then disappears beneath the covering of sand.

Heart beat faster, I edge forward one hand and knee at a time. Behind me, Peter steps into the hand and knee indents I had made. Sweat drips down his face. He wipes some away and turns his cooling lower.

"Hot out here," he whispers.

I nod at the obvious.

He raises an eyebrow in query.

I nod towards the burrow and in a low whisper say, "Note Peter. No, there—the faint hump right at the tail end."

"Oh? Yeah. Explain."

"In a minute. The hump lines up towards the center."

"Yeah. Okay. Get on with this so-called tour."

"Follow an imaginary line down the center of the back to the folds of skin just visible. Right there is where the stun-point is. Only practice in finding it helps if attacked. We have real live ones to learn on. And they're not tame in any way."

"Yeah. Yeah."

"But! The sting itself is not particularly dangerous." And I smile within.

"What? After all you've told...how enough of their poison can get you dead. You're trying my patience, Once-Other!"

I'm pleased some data I'd passed on found a home. "Well no. You see—a sting-claw is a sting-claw and nothing more. Now back of it is a poison sack, which in itself is not dangerous either. Wait-wait. In the sack is a potent poison which as you probably guessed isn't dangerous either."

"What is?" he asks in a cold, hard whisper.

"Excessive amounts of poison inside your body doing damage...though...being stung is itself damn painful altogether."

His eyes of woe-n-stop reject my humor. "I'll definitely be reporting you for endangering happiness with cruel intent...a violation of assured Happiness."

"If you must report—you must report. Now—pay attention if you don't want to get stung. We're about to do the difficult part. As I mentioned earlier—Criers stand around four of your feet high just under a sand pace. Top of its head down to sand."

"Yeah, I got that. All-damn-together!"

"Okay."

He calms some. I smile at him. He glares at me. I nod ahead. We crawl a little closer, stop-up and examine the patch.

"To repeat. Folds of skin and fur protect its neck. The sting-claw is on the tip of the pouch-cover covered by a fold of skin...here. We say pouch-cover...but it's more a trunk lid decorated with long dark hair and hinged behind the neck. Opens like an auto's trunk."

"How come this one is not coming at us?" Peter asks.

"Nothing much hunts them...they fear no enemies except Arzerns. They'll retreat from built-up areas solely to escape the noise. Interesting item about Criers and Arzerns—communication is by a form of mind-to-mind."

"Yeah. Tiny mind to tiny mind," he says.

"We can hear them snarl and Arzerns scream but we can't pick up when they communicate an attack or a strategy amongst themselves."

"Genetics Once-Other. Eons of programmed behavior."

"Not from our view," I say.

"The blind leading fools to imaginary points-of-view," he says sneeringly.

I wave it aside and say, "Look here!"

He pushes closer inspects what I'm pointing at, backs away and says, "Yeah. What?"

"Crier fur is a combination of regular hair and feather-like hair—very slippery. But now! There's no other way to do this, Peter. So watch carefully, stay alert and last but not least the only way to get Crier water is the right way."

"Where do they get water? I've seen no surface water nor did I see some in the museum rendition either."

"In a moment. Pay attention please...this may save your life. Here's what. Crier jaws are like that of wolves, fangs-n-all. Teeth for biting, holding, chewing."

He hisses saying, "Altogether! Cut out the BS and answer my question."

"Not yet. Genetically speaking, Criers were large dogs or wolves who somehow survived the disaster when Here-Born turned to desert. We have not been able to establish how they escaped the catastrophe or if they were introduced after it by settlers or perhaps by God. Nor how they evolved those pouches."

"Still no answer! What here is fiction, speculation or science, Once-Other?"

"A little of all I suppose," I reply.

He nods and smirks.

"Now! Moving on. Their long black back hair grows on their pouch-cover. The cover connects just behind the neck about there. Beneath the cover is a pouch. Inside it right behind the neck, are two teats. One for water. One for milk. Wait. Wait.

Their young live in the pouch until they're old enough to venture out on their own."

He stares at the sketch I'd made in sand exhibiting an odd rapture of interest and frustration. He cocks an eyebrow but I'm not ready to answer.

I partly unfurl my Crier fan.

"What's the large eye on it for?" he asks, pointing.

"It's like a Crier's eye. We use it to hold their attention while getting water."

He grabs the fan and opens it fully.

"How's this work?" he asks.

"You hold the fan close to its eye, very close...rocking it back-n-forth like this." I rock his hand back-n-forth, and he nods. "They slip into a trance. Don't go for water until then. Once they're in a trance, reach over, hook a finger under the sting-claw and gently lift it to expose the teats. As I said one for milk one for water. We drink water from the teat to *their left.*"

"Sounds awful. Disgusting."

"Not when you are dying of thirst Peter."

"I guess not. Whatever."

"No whatever...if there's a young one in the pouch we try another."

"Why?"

"They bite and sting as well."

He swats at flies and says, "Oh yeah. Why not drink their milk? Nutrition...right?"

"First let me say that you should have purchased anti-fly from me. I have a spray can in my SandRider. Care to buy it?"

"Just answer the question," he growls.

"Well okay. You can drink the milk but...that's how I got stung when doing my final survival test."

He leans close. "You got stung? Tell me how oh wise one."

I grin at which he snarls silently. "I'd been told not to drink the milk but we were desperate for food, for nutrition, so I drank some."

"Yeah?"

"And got stung."

"Would you tell me!"

Thoughts and emotions streak across his face and into his eyes. I reach out for them but he waves a hand by his eyes and they disappear. Did what's under his armpit erase them? If yes, can it be disabled? Thus far no luck in doing so and not that I haven't secretly tried over-n-over.

Will I lose here with a tourist once again? "Keep going, Once-Other," I say mind-to-mind and to myself. Sitting back, I stare across sand taking time to remind self of all I'm doing.

This defense of ours at times seems tougher on Here-Born soldiers and campaigners than violent conflict. Hope is all we have. Hope that we can bring into being within enough Earth-Born citizens a realization of our Here-Born Rights, our Constitution and our way of life.

And not just an ordinary Life.

But a Life free of government interference.

In addition, a political structure in which We the People hold *all* the power and are the true guardians of Freedom. Yet, a society filled with conflicting cultures and customs...living side by side without racial hate yet with adventure for all.

We of Here-Born refer to our system as a New Political Civilization. And proudly so.

I sigh.

Peter glares some, frowns, glances at the patch and waves me on again.

# CHAPTER 32

## OF DRINKING WATER AND STING-CLAWS

I acknowledge his wave with a grin. "Okay. Now! Criers do for survival alone and nothing else. You will never find one sleeping or resting in direct sunlight. Well now...okay, an answer.

"I discovered Crier milk is worse than I'd been warned. Damn awful altogether. But I was starved. I puked and lost my grip on the sting-claw. More important than being stung, their poison has a cumulative effect.

"After the first time stung, be shy. The next will be twice as deadly at half the quantity. No matter how long between episodes."

"Interesting," he mutters.

"Now. I'll open the pouch but you drink the water. Okay?"

"I don't think so. Doesn't work for me."

"Just once and you'll know how. You should go a few times. Definitely help if you get stranded."

"The hell with you Once-Other."

"I can't force you, Peter, but—"

"No!" he snarls.

He stares at the Crier burrow and rubs his ear. Glances my way and seems to find something about my face of which I am unaware. "Come on Once-Other, don't take me so...ah jeez...okay...meeting halfway. When the pouch is open maybe I'll drink—and the taste is?"

"Damn fine Peter."

"Yeah. Everything's damn fine! You still haven't told me where they find water."

"Here's how," and I pause for I am no fool.

That he found signs of dejection on my face is pure conjecture on his part. Which once again begs a question. Is Peter steering me towards something? Alas, I have no idea. Damn! Without his thoughts I'm *blinded*.

Yet ever hopeful I say, "Well now...Criers roam the night appearing to *cry* at the moon while circling in a decreasing radius. They use a form of sonar as echolocation to detect water. They'll circle until zeroed in. We could experience that live tonight."

"I'll pass," he snaps back.

"Well okay. They do so only when digging a new burrow. Now. Once water is located they head out and collect Arzern feathers along with any bone-strewn about.

"Back at the chosen location it digs into sand. And here's something strange. Its companion burrow dwellers all help with the digging. Each Crier has a gland located at the end of the sting-claw cover from which they can excrete a wax-like substance. Using it they *cement* feathers together to create a nest."

He makes to interrupt. I wave him silent.

"While waiting for the feather-n-wax to harden they chew the bones into gravel like pieces. Next, they bite open a hole in the center of the new nest and dig down into sand creating a pipeline. As they dig down towards the water they use their wax to seal the pipe with feathers-n-bone-gravel."

"What the hell?" he says.

"I'll back up for you. They dig downwards with their front paws and scoop sand into their pouch. Next! Each one returns with sand in its pouch and dumps it."

I draw a diagram in sand and say, "The feathers-n-bones-n-wax are used to make and seal the pipe they're digging. They shuffle these along held between forelegs and rear ones. Once it hardens the pipe is about twenty fingers in diameter, wide enough to accommodate them and it's flexible."

"Quite fascinating," he says.

"Yes. Below sand, they attach the pipe to the waxy-oil pod that seals off the water rising from below. Ah? Remember, in the museum. Pod over water? Good.

"Next. All the Criers turn face upwards. The first one down, being the last one going back up, slices the pod open with a hind-leg claw. Their feather-like hair acts as a seal to hold the rising water at bay and the Criers return to the surface.

"The last one out is of course the burrow owner."

I glance at him and he waves me on.

"The burrow owner settles in, camouflages itself by scooping sand over its back and gives the top end of the feather pipe a new wax cover with a plug in the center of it. That attaches to a mouth in its belly, through which it drinks. If danger is about they can instantly detach the plug leaving the water pipe sealed.

"And as we say, *waste not, want not*. Please note! There's a double negative there. So if you want something you must first be able to waste it!"

"Thanks for the info despite that I've no use for it," he says.

"Imagine if you will. I board my SandRider and race away never to return. So! Look around. What do you see?"

"Sand Once-Other."

"Pray tell...how are you going to survive...alone?"

He smiles like a child caught with forbidden candy. "Ah? Oh yeah...you got me there. Let's do this." He pauses and adds, "I'll definitely drink a little water."

Pleased, I reach over and fan sand off the sting-claw, expose an eye the same way and tick-tock the fan until the eye glazes over. "Move around. Come in from the opposite side facing me when I lift. Remember. The teat on its left. Don't touch the other one."

"Yeah."

He edges closer. I hook a finger under the sting-claw. The folds of skin around its neck cascade back-n-forth like ocean waves upon a beach. I wait until the Crier calms and then lift the pouch.

"This one's edgy. Be careful. Don't drink the milk."

"Yeah. I got that."

The tail end of the pouch stiffens. "Don't move!" I command in a hoarse whisper.

Peter's face turns ashen, sweat pops out on his upper lip.

"He's suspicious. Hold still. Wait for my okay."

I tick-tock the fan in a wider arc moving closer-n-back at the same time. Once it's relaxed I open the cover another fraction. I sigh on finding no young present, open it wider and nod towards the teats.

Peter edges closer, stops and asks, "Why milk, absent young?"

"They share those duties. You'll always find some."

"Ah."

"Recycled daily," I add. "Don't drink any."

I open the pouch fully. He leans in instead of working his way to the other side as I'd instructed. I grin at that. That's EB tourists for one-n-all—always forgetful. I bend my elbow so he can get under it while keeping a watchful eye on the Crier's tail and head.

Peter shuffles forward blocking my view. He leans further in and the sting-claw cover tenses and relaxes, and I sigh. Peter exhales, takes several sharp breaths, pauses and takes a long hard suck. He swallows, shudders and lurches backward slamming into my arm. My finger holding the sting-claw slips free.

Peter stumbles off and drops to sand puking Crier milk plus the remains of his breakfast. The fan shifts sideways on the Crier. It spots me and with fangs bared lunges. In the same instant, the pouch-cover opens fully and holds, poised to strike.

I snap my fan closed and thrust it into the Crier's mouth with a mere two fingers distance remaining between its fangs and my face. It bites down hard and pauses for a second then jerks backward pulling me off balance. I manage to wrap my free arm around my throat.

The Crier's pouch-cover descends over my head and tightens like shrink-wrap. The sting-claw touches down softly behind my ear and its hind-legs swing up and settle on my arms. The Crier pauses savoring its moment. The sting-claw thrusts deep and pulses, injecting venom until the sack is empty.

Pain from hell explodes in my head.

The pouch-cover tightens.

My skull creaks.

Its razor sharp claws slice at my forearm in search of a path to my throat.

Out there, Peter thrashes in stomach wrenching agony punctuated by groans of utter disgust.

Damn this feeling of hopelessness, I must fight, I must win. For if I die here, Wernt—who has not learned to survive will die as well. That would not good for Peter, not good for my campaign let alone my Neatness.

Worse! I have little time; Death already caresses me with its insatiable desire.

# CHAPTER 33

## OF CRIER MILK AND POISON OLD AND NEW

My blood runs freely and preservatives kick-alive. Earlier poison awakens and joins the new and together, drive a powerful current of red-hot needles into my brain. I hold on for dear life as the Crier pulls at the fan seeking to sink its fangs into my hand. If it does, it will instantly release my head from its pouch and take me at the throat.

Its vicious growls send shivers down my back.

Wernt groans.

The Crier pauses, listens, then rages on.

I must somehow switch hands and get my free hand onto the fan so I can reach its stun-spot with the hand desperately holding onto the fan.

The pouch-cover squeezes tighter flattening my nose and barely able to breathe I pull the fan closer to my other hand. My arms shake with effort. I kick at sand, as does a wounded animal in the throes of death.

My hands touch each other.

With a final desperate effort, I switch hands and of its own accord, my free hand searches for the base of the Crier's skull.

My other arm I surrender up to keep its claws at bay.

I reach upward, grab hold and squeeze but the Crier's attack rages on. I pinch harder. There comes no surrender, no respite. I adjust my grip and pinch as hard as I can and the Crier finally goes slack but its sting-claw keeps pumping.

Head screaming in agony, vision blurred by dripping blood and cascading pain, I ease the sting-claw free. With extreme care, I lift the pouch-cover off, roll away, stagger to my feet and sway as though beset by raging winds.

Nearly blinded, I head for my SandRider taking care not to step into a burrow. My knees suddenly give. I struggle back to my feet and keep going. I stumble by Wernt who lies prone next to a rank pool of his own design.

"I'm sorry Once-Other. Didn't mean for...." and he heaves once again.

I note there's a difference between his words and his emotion despite the lightning, bombs and needle storms assaulting me. Contrary to those words, his attitude seems almost triumphant in nature.

Nevertheless, I keep going for now is not the moment for petty foibles. Each step I take sends fists from my feet upwards to explode inside my head. Each one threatens to lay me flat upon sand and from there never to rise.

I trip over my own feet and collapse across Hellbent II's rear wheel. I drag myself up and reach for the emergency kit. Slip sideways, strike my head on the saddle, slide down it, bump the footrest with my chin and end up flat on my face, nose buried in sand.

I turn my head sideways and breathe.

Wernt's footsteps shuffle closer. He stops, braces himself, drops to his hand-n-knees and convulses. Grim, I yet smile inside. Like me, his stomach does not deal well with Crier milk.

There are those who can take it, we are not of that ilk.

I climb to feet unwilling to bear weight, cling to the saddle and rest a moment. I jolt awake swaying and almost fall. I open the emergency kit, grab a scalpel and hand mirror. I pause for breath then locate the poison blister in a rear-view mirror. Another deep breath in and I cut the two and a half finger wide poison blister open edge-to-edge.

Blood and poison pour down my neck, under my collar and drip to sand. I drop the scalpel and squeeze the blister fighting a darkness that threatens to send me crashing to sand. I keep pressing until no cream colored poison is visible. Barely able to stand I fumble about the emergency kit for a spray can of antidote, and forcing the blister open spray inside it.

Several industrial sized smelting furnaces explode spraying molten pain in all directions. Bombs of the planet busting variety erupt between each exploding furnace. I land on my hands and knees and glancing over my shoulder find Peter lying flat on his face.

Between his dry retches and my personal lesson in tactical bombing he groans pitifully. He rolls away from his latest deposit upon sand, curls up, hugs himself and rocks on his side moaning a dirge.

That dirge of all lost and demented souls.

I smile the coldest of smiles, never in the annals of this universe's history has nutrition come with such horrific, foul and vile flavoring as Crier milk. It's a worthy defense in both action and design.

I drag myself to my feet and swaying, apply an antidote pad to the wound and wrap a bandage around it. With my last strength, I reach over, press the SOS button and slip to sand.

Resting with my back against the front wheel, I watch Wernt rocking back-n-forth. Inside my head bombs, lightning and needle storms perform a symphony dedicated to a World War II bombardment. I pop an antidote pill into my mouth and chew.

Once swallowed, I shuffle away from the blood-n-poison patch leaving it to the flies. I check the bandage and it's good. I take a sip of water and about to offer Wernt some but reconsider. Yes. It's the last thing he would entertain right now. I examine my tattered and ripped arm and scoop sand over the wounds.

"What for?" Peter asks in a dry croak.

"In sand across all of Here-Born are preservatives. All released into the atmosphere and sand back when the first wave of immigrants arrived. This is why we don't need refrigeration for many weeks...with pre-owned parts."

"That makes no sense—argh!" and he pukes once again.

When he is done I add, "The crew on board those immigration space-liners carelessly miscalculated the size and therefore the gravity of Here-Born. We are far larger than Earth-Born yet our day lasts only four hours longer. Here-Born rotates far faster than Earth-Born."

"And...?"

"Your scientists were conducting experiments. They were trying to preserve and regrow human tissue. The crash landings released their newly engineered cocktail into the atmosphere."

"Whatever!"

"No, Peter, no...."

He closes his eyes and groans.

I examine our vicinity and find nothing dangerous lurking about. Therefore, other than sand, sun, heat, and night with its deep freeze, all is well. We are by SandRider, some four to six hours out of Sand Lake Flats. An Evac will take far less time to reach us but it may be dark by then.

I should prepare for night but find myself unwilling or perhaps unable to move. I pat my new favorite, Hellbent II. Its homing device and expanded emergency kit may yet save our lives. And if push comes to shove the tent will see us through the night.

I give a silent thanks to Soonsaan's sales techniques.

We are relatively safe, somewhat hydrated, have extra water and food should not be an issue. Unless it is food we are to become.

I smile as Peter heaves once again, another dry one.

My eyes close of their own accord and darkness descends without invitation.

From out my inner darkness my old school teacher's words echo, weaving and slithering around the savage pain inside my head. "Water Crier poison is hallucinogenic Once-Other. Wild visions of water have killed more tourists than the direct effects of poison. You'll find most of them end up drinking sand in the belief they're consuming water."

"Not I," I whisper and cross my fingers.

Darkness.

# CHAPTER 34

## OF NO COMFORTABLE A SEAT AND VISITORS

The sharp edge of tire tread presses hard against my spine. The muffled tread of boots crunches upon sand. A droning hum draws closer. Madsen's voice sneaks to the fore and drones on. Words mingle with the roar of exploding furnaces, the groan of a bomb-bay door opening. The screech of plummeting bombs.

The butt of a Browning five-oh thuds at my shoulder.

My eyes open and night fills my senses.

Madsen shouts from mere fingers away and vanishes.

He returns and stares in silence while his hand at my shoulder shakes me awake.

There's a dream comes in the moments before death.

Why mine is of Madsen, I cannot tell. Why is it not instead Maggie or Karrell? I accept nonetheless. What else can one do? My hand floats into view seeming to move of its own volition. It touches Madsen, Browning says farewell to my shoulder and a hand touches my cheek.

Madsen raises his nose in a questioning fashion.

"Ah yes. You're not welcomed Madsen. But it's good you're here...despite that you have become a Rocklands sized pain in the rear these last years. I must be alive—I can feel you."

I offer him a hand.

He pulls me to my feet.

At the Evac, he links his fingers into a foothold. I step up, the Medic grabs my arm, hoists me, swings me around and straps me into a seat in one fluid motion. He gives the pilot the thumbs up and with sand swirling we take off.

Through the open hatch, Madsen waves farewell midst running a check on Hellbent II. I glance across at Wernt. He's curled up in his seat, groaning in agony but okay save for the effects of Crier milk.

The Medic hovers over me clucking like a mother hen. He connects an IV-line, starts the antidote drip, checks my pulse and without warning shines a blinding light in my eyes. He holds it there, mutters his approval, undoes my bandage, checks the wound and ever-so chipper says, "This will hurt a little laddie," and he sprays antidote.

And he lied—it hurt a lot.

I glare my displeasure at him. He ignores me, slaps a new antidote pad on and using my bandage wraps it tight. He fixes an oxygen mask in place and as he turns to Wernt says ever-more chipper, "You'll probably live, laddie-me-boy."

He shakes and opens a can of Milk-n-Fix and hands it to Peter—desperation and questions quickly populate Peter's face.

"That will fix you one-two-three," I say. "But! Pinch your nose closed and drink it all in one breath. Then hold your breath as long as you can."

Hurricanes of doubt rage across his face. His eyebrows dance a jerk-n-jump in perfect time with each other. "You sure?"

"Go ahead. You'll be fixed more-or-less instantly."

"Yeah. Right. Instantly."

He pinches his nose closed, drinks and waits as his face turns red. He lets out a long breath and surprised says, "Relief already!"

I smile but he turns away, rests his head on the seat back, closes his eyes and nods off. With his eyes closed, with Crier milk still in play and hoping his defenses are down, I search for his thoughts only to find nothing but barriers.

Perhaps the battle raging in my head inhibits my own natural skills.

I desperately need to know about this EB named Wernt. And for that I require his thoughts. I must obtain them for my campaign and because I have an urge to know what and why he switches between somewhat pleasant and raging wild and back again. So right now it is time to consider this Peter Wernt in greater depth.

I do so only to chuckle at what I find after having removed emotion and upset from the equation.

Yes. He is interested in me. Yes. I do not know why. Yes. Like all tourists he is curious about our UWMD. True to form he rejects our political ideas. Yet despite these I am positive some campaign items found a home within him. What they are...I do not know. I dismiss him sit back and wriggle myself comfortable.

The beat of the Evac's blades pulses inside my head. Thinking dives for cover and I doze off. I'm awakened by a change in their tempo. Looking out the open door reveals Sand Lake Flats Toxin Center. It's a single story building built of adobe, painted medium-brown and located some ten miles southwest of the city.

The Evac lands amidst its own sandstorm.

Wernt and I smile at one another as we make our way into Emergency, each under his own steam. ER staff interview him briefly, conduct tests and affirm he can leave. On the other hand, needles as well as several probes find their way into me.

One is inserted where I least wish to be probed. I'm left to my own uncomfortable self sitting on a chair with no center cushion. A hole in place of a seat proper suffices.

Minutes later Peter is at the door.

He smiles in deference to the least favored probe I mentioned. He appears hangdog, sheepish and awaits my invitation. I wave him over. He enters and to my damn fine surprise checks over the new bandage around my head and asks in a voice thick with compassion, "You okay Once-Other?"

Chills meander up my spine threatening to freeze my brain. I halt them and consider the EB tourist before me. Now by all possible standards this Peter Wernt is damn smart. Perhaps smart enough to appear stupid, which trick—if you are very smart is not easy to pull off with any conviction.

He pats me on the shoulder and says, "Yeah. I figure we both need some time off. You more so than me I'll bet. I'm okay with getting back to our tour Monday morning. Monday work for you?" He waits, a little boy who has asked for the money to buy what he was told he cannot have.

"Fine with me," I reply.

He offers his hand and we shake.

Images flutter in. They break apart and fly around as though seeking to escape confinement. None of them makes any sense. A large wheel stuck in either white beach sand or snow. Overhead are darkened skies from which snowflakes drift. An infant wrapped in a shawl, a blazing sun over a desert. The images vanish as he releases my hand, smiles with a knowing glint in his eyes, walks to the door, waves and leaves.

Never in my entire campaigning career did I ever meet an Earth-Born as peculiar as Peter Wernt. I close my eyes hoping to doze off but a soft sound stirs me awake. The door swings open and Madsen enters—a growling irritation plastered across his brow.

"Round-n-about damn an' all Once-Other. How can you be so incompetent?"

"Much too close a call Madsen," I say ignoring the verbal barb.

"I've informed everyone including your ex—"

"Oh no. Not Deidre."

"Not wrong Once-Other. An' I know this is round-n-about the last thing you want. But. I'm told a massive a dose of poison got into you an' all. You be in a troubling physical state. Too close, real close."

He holds two fingers up pressed tightly together. "That close to wasting expensive training an' all." He taps my head. "You keep your body, mind and spirit together an' all. I'm out of here. Way late. Got a long ride ahead dropping off your San-dRider."

He exits does a double take, glances back at me, chuckles and heads off.

Maggie enters hiding her concern behind a forced smile. Seeing her still dressed in her work uniform but without a counter between us lifts a weary heart.

"You're sure a no damn good pirate sailing carelessly on this girl's emotional seas," she growls, her husky voice thick with emotion.

"Nice of you to come too, Maggie."

She sits on the edge of the bed and takes my hand. "Not good an' all! Head swollen like a Roanark Braer's...three days dead in the sun an' smelling 'bout the same."

"Yes...way close," and she smiles at my taking on her accent, "Wernt accidentally sipped milk instead of water an' all. Nothing more."

She examines me long-n-hard and asks, "You sure an' all?"

"I could smell Crier milk. He regurgitated some...and then some."

"I mean. Real accidental? We got the goldmine thing an' now this."

"Hadn't thought on it in that way," I say and consider her concerns.

A little wild I conclude. How can anyone plan to have me step on a refill canister to cause severe injury or death? And while they're falling to boot! There's few on Here-Born and none on EB. Period. Who in his right mind would drink Crier milk after a warning? None except those about to die of hunger and who would simply die of hunger while puking.

"I don't...." I say but a nurse enters and indicates it's time for me to rest and recover.

Maggie kisses my cheek, touches the bandage and then kisses my forehead.

"Take care you," she whispers and leaves with a long look back.

The nurse smiles, tucks the blanket in and pauses. I frown at the strange mix of emotion emanating from her. "What?" I gently ask.

"Franciscoa is our uncle."

"Oh. Our?"

"Maggie and I," she says.

"Oh right! Sorry I don't—didn't mean to be...."

"It's okay...he explained in detail before...."

"Oh. Yes. Madsen told me. Great benefit to us all...I hope. Let it not be in vain."

"So do we Once-Other. It is the *Time* he said...for active self-defense. You know what that means?"

"May all EB citizens be warned," I reply.

She nods grim agreement pats my shoulder and leaves.

I sit back and think over what is coming.

Yes, and true.

We the People are not happy.

We the People will not drink sand instead of water for as the idiom goes: *A smooth tongue makes not water of sand.*

Now it is time to rest and later...we shall see what we shall see.

# CHAPTER 35

## OF OUR MONITORING ENSURES YOUR HAPPINESS

The Department for the Assurance of Happiness

Los Angeles Regional District

Motto: Our Monitoring Ensures Your Happiness

Date: Confidential—as are all

Document: 798-631

Document Type: Assurance of Happiness Transcript

Requesting Authority: Mister Warrent McPeters

Issuing Authority: Mister Warrent McPeters

Subject Matter: Peter Wernt, Number Six, Number Eight

Location: Here-Born Residentia, Here-Born in general

Methodology: third-eye camera/local Poip/audio-visual monitoring.

Transcript Processor: Ms. Agnes Soulone (pronounced: Soul-one)

Technical Disclaimer: That the button provided above when pressed plays the original audio-visual version of this report on the opposite page is quite misleading.

No warranty nor guaranty ensures that audio-visual will play. That technology is no longer valid. It's been cancelled due to apparent bugs and the art of reading is substituted.

Refer all questions to the Dot Soft Corporation.

Thank you.

Transcript:

This is Agnes and please excuse my inserting how to say my last name. No one gets it right unless I do. Peccadilloes!

Here now I'll start this transcript:

At last the wind has settled, the sand lies quiet and this monitoring record opens on the green and white striped sides of Pre-owneds Galore.

Feet splayed upon the sand outside of Once-Other's store Peter Wernt takes a call on his Nomadi. He listens. His mouth twitches. His eyebrows bob. From inside Once-Other attempts to overhear the conversation but pretends he is not.

Peter Wernt, his back to Once-Other and both hands cupped around Nomadi, listens intently. Audio begins at the tail end of the call.

"...new Writ of Property is approved and confirmed with no modification to the current one, Property ID dash109."

"Yeah!" Peter says and pumps his arm as though he had just scored a championship-winning goal.

Call ends and static squiggles wash across my monitor screen. Another recording starts.

Judging by the zigzagging of his progress as seen via his third-eye camera, Mister Peter Wernt is staggering through the sparsely decorated reception of the Here-Born Residentia drunk or incapacitated in one way or another.

His head bobs so much the camera POV weaves alarmingly. Personal opinions are not part of my job description but it makes me so woozy just viewing this.

Oh dear me!

Back to work I go.

Wait!

A glance out the window and the wind blows leaves along the sidewalk. Trams hustle by their lines blurred by dust thick on the window pane.

Never hear them, what with double glazed sound proof windows. Windows designed to reflect sound and prevent visual intrusion from those curious as to what exactly we at the Department for the Assurance of Happiness, Los Angeles Bureau are getting up and down to.

Secrecy is what it most of all is. Whoops! That's a no-no.

Back to work I go!

Numbers Six and Eight are waiting in the dining room idly playing with their food. Why are they named Six and Eight? I don't know. Let me research that.

On checking no data is available. Dear me! How odd.

Oh! You will need to excuse my transcription style even further if you are new to Transcript Verifications and Corrections. For those who judge my work you will soon notice I tend to ramble on as though I am speaking to someone. But you'll get my meaning—so moving along briskly.

I must admit I like Number Six's full body suit, dark green against a white top and red pin in her black hair—most becoming. Peter joins them and takes her hand firmly in his.

Number Eight growls discontentedly his eyes glued on their hands, his unease evident by involuntary motions. The poor fellow is pulling at his sleeves, combing his bangs with his fingers and checking his appearance in a wall mirror.

He's apparently afflicted with low self-esteem despite the gaudy red and black checkered fan-n-fit. He still favors the arm injured when he tried punching Once-Other.

"You teach that Once-Other a lesson?" Peter Wernt asks him.

"I sure did," Number Eight says.

"No, you didn't," Number Six says.

"Okay. Okay. I tried. I made the right moves—wrenched my shoulder. Still hurts!"

I pause playback and smile...that Once-Other sure is fleet-of-foot. Continue.

"Anything to report?" Peter asks Number Six and holds her hand the same way he held onto Once-Other's when they first met inside Pre-owneds Galore.

"Once-Other is divorced," she says. "He's the sole owner of the store but with their business rules or the lax rules of Here-Born, I'd still get everything confirmed by him." She squeezes his hand.

"Anything else?" Peter asks a little cold for all the hand-holding.

Number Eight passes across his Nomadi and Peter downloads. "What am I downloading?" he asks.

"His inventory, domicile and possessions. He's got no debts." Number Eight strives to make the information sound far grander than warranted.

"There's no credit system here...no one has any debts," Peter snarls exasperation easily traceable in his voice and on his face. The lens loses focus as it darts left and right making me nauseous and starts a little pain in the middle of my head.

"How's that work?" Number Eight asks and crosses his legs as though his bladder is about to let loose.

Peter leans towards him and says, "You pay in full and up front for everything. What do you think?"

"That's dumb," Number Eight says and crosses his legs the other way. His foot starts twitching; he grabs it, holds on briefly then lets go.

Number Six shakes her head and rubs the bridge of her nose as though assaulted by a sudden headache.

Peter sits frozen in time eyes fixed but unfocused on a wall mirror. He wakes with a jolt and glances around as though unaware of his location. He notes Number Eight's foot is twitching again, shakes his head and looks to the ceiling.

"Yeah," he says and leans in on Number Eight, eye-to-eye. "If any of you had to suffer his endless going on we'd have left a no BS'ing a long time ago. His rants about so-called Rights and Here-Born's other alleged *treasures* infuriate me!"

"Why not finish him off?" Number Eight asks and grabs at his own tongue as though there's a hair on it and wipes his wet fingers on a sleeve.

"I'm enjoying his feeble attempts at figuring things out," Peter says then snarls, "What happened? Once-Other turns up alive and well after he *died* at the bottom of that dumb-ass Museum. No call? You don't figure on reporting in Eight?"

Number Eight's voice whines like a fly caught in a jar. "I called, but you were out of range. I put the oil in his SandRider okay. You were there. You saw me. Where were you when I couldn't contact you?"

"Out in the desert. Damn extension aerial didn't work. Go Figure." He leans across the table, grabs and pulls Number Eight nose-to-nose. "When I need you to know where I am, what I'm doing and what I think...be sure and understand...I'll brief you."

"Okay. Mister...Peter."

Peter's face twitches his nose jumping up and down.

Number Six smiles quietly to herself.

Number Eight wipes sweat off his brow.

Peter lets him go and starts eating.

Six and Eight follow suit.

I can't stop staring at them eating.

Oh dear, the food...so good.

When last did I see real orange juice?

Behind me Skellumer clears his throat.

I force myself not to glance over my shoulder. I can imagine what's on this face. Threats of being reported are what. Despite him, I'm excited by this new project my Supervisor awarded me.

Strange though, my Supe provided no info other than these Assurance of Happiness recordings themselves. Then again, he's a mere two-day old baby on his first tour of duty down here at the Department for the Assurance of Happiness.

He'll learn. Real soon.

However, there is something strange...no...something different...almost alien about him.

Hmmm? Yummy.

Oops!

I sigh and gaze across at our standard allotment of ADD-D suffers—a perfect mix of male and female. They watch TV all day because they are unable to work.

Dear me, how trying on them. Well, at least they are paid the same as we are making us all wonderfully equal. What happiness real equality ensures.

"Hallelujah!" I whisper in closing down another day here at the Department for the Assurance of Happiness.

# CHAPTER 36

## OF ONCE-OTHER'S SECOND MOMENT IN TIME AND DEIDRE'S CONCERNS

Firm hands at the helm, canvas cleaved to the wind, brave hearts challenge the Cape of Storms with rudders, keels, courage and trust in their God alone.

The Atlantic Ocean's temper, held high in all their esteem, takes no prisoners. Angered, she rises to tower overhead menacing all who dare sail upon her. For those who do climb her waves, dead ahead looms naught but a darkened sky.

These brave sailors confront mountains of water high as a Here-Born dune. After the face is conquered eyes widen as vessels plunge downwards like a SandRider charging into a capture-ditch. Those sailors who survive tell no tales—a silence in honor of souls taken by the sea and there to keep others of a like destiny company.

Later came catamarans with arms to steady them upon the ever-changing ocean and with keels so deep before entering harbors or shallow coastal waters they are raised. From the plans of catamarans were extrapolated concepts of ships upon sand.

The Here-Born desert is too an ocean having no vegetation save cacti and rare patches of desert grass to bind it. Rivers of sand flow across her like those of water. Sandfalls plunge and thunder as loud as Niagara.

Her desert currents out power the cold Benguela current which is driven to full power by the South Easterly Trade winds charting a course from Cape Point northwards along the southwestern coast of Africa.

Tents were the first structures on Here-Born and are still the most common. Fixed to a hull they sail sand well enough if a storm is gentle. However, square angled houses and buildings break upon a violent sandstorm.

Yacht and Catamaran designed homes came later. They'll ride sandstorms almost as well as yachts upon an ocean.

We build very few tent homes in these times based, as they are, on a shallow hull though hull enough to float if upright.

But whatever its design is...home is home.

*** 

Madsen races off towards the horizon. The dust plume that billows from his SandRider's wheels swells larger and thicker. Halfway to the horizon he vanishes hidden by his own sand-cloud.

I'm still aggravated by what he'd said to me in the Toxin Center last night. What does he expect—for me to be infallible? With effort I dismiss him and his attitudes and glance about.

Saturday morning shines warm and windless. Yes, I am home once again and though worse off for poison, I am alive.

I find no messages from Karrell at my front door. I check Hellbent II and all appears in good order, engine oil included.

I walk the exterior. Sand is smooth, clear of any footprints, the windows clean of smudges.

I scan the horizon but nothing strikes me as dangerous.

I enter home.

A fast inspection assures it rests level and no message waiting lights blink. Courtesy of Crier poison bombs explode, lightning crackles and needle storms needle inside my head and in concert with one another.

In self-defense I brew a cup of strong tea. Seated in Della Comfort and sipping contentedly, I stare out the window.

Sand drifts upon a distant dune following the sun. Wind gusts sand against the window pane to pitter-patter like I imagine rain does. The grains float down the panes in hypnotic patterns and puzzles.

I imagine real rain, slipping in mud, stamping snow covered boots in the entrance way, picking up mail as hail pelts me. Ideas of other places and things and none part of my life.

Suddenly new ideas find their way into my thoughts as though born upon drifting sand. I close my eyes and the ideas entwine, clasp one another and tighten into a ball. The ball evolves into a clenched fist and executes a quick ninety-degree turn. The fingers unfurl, spread wide and waggle like bait on a sand-snail's tail.

I cannot resist so obvious an invitation and plunge my perception inwards to inspect this strange apparition. It dissolves upon sensing my scrutiny. The tiny fragments I do contact smack of Crier poison. I flinch at the taste of them.

Nevertheless, I reach back in and again the hand darts off swimming now with the strokes of a jellyfish. It stops a short distance away and chuckles with evil glee, then fades into a translucent oval. A finger pops up and beckons.

I reach across and touch it and voices from my past come alive. I drift closer and individual words find me.

"Hear me. Heed me."

I nod in acceptance.

First, Peter Wernt leaps to view. His appearance as vivid and robust as though he is actually here beside me. In the same instant, something dark and snake-like slithers by and tucks itself into a corner, hidden, yet a presence felt.

Poison's bombs continue exploding, marching onwards at a staggered pace. Cymbals clash then skitter across jangled nerve ends. The tempo changes to a marching beat. The voices grow stronger and more demanding as they question me. "Can an EB calculate the arrival underfoot of an empty canister?

"If yes, such skills are stunning. On Here-born, only Nomads possess such unbreakable concentration. On the other hand, Desert Drivers can take Nomad calculations and act instantly upon the findings.

"Desert Drivers are, if nothing else, people of action.

"You, the Free Marketeers are renowned for your skills to plan into the future with the greatest of ease. You of Here-Born know full well it takes two to tango—but it takes three to create or to resolve."

I mumble to self, "Therefore, Peter dropping his empty canister must have been accidental."

But the clouds of doubt roll back in, spread outwards, and turn into thunderclouds. They form up as though a firing squad. As one they bellow, "What you, Once-Other, don't know about Peter could fill countless tomes in a size six font at that."

Personal revision...perhaps it was not an accident.

I sigh exasperated and park ponderous reasoning.

Done, I turn inwards and track down the dark something that slithered in along with thoughts of Peter. When I find and touch it, it breaks into tiny drops of gold colored water. They drift closer each one vying for my attention.

Faces appear as I caress one. Some smile, some frown, others laugh. I catch a drop and a collection of data falls into my virtual inner-palm. I caress a few more to discover that each holds bits of information.

I slide closer and they change into squares. I spot one with unique characters on it—time stamps. I check them over.

Nothing but dates and times from the past, from the present, some from out my Foundation and many places I cannot recall. Yet all are familiar as though I lived back then but cannot now remember where nor when.

They group together and fuse into a golden ball.

I grasp it and a scroll drops out and unfurls to become a yellowed newspaper dated many centuries ago. My viewpoint finds the headlines then the story below. I read quickly and analyze once done.

Using generalized statements, individual priests on EB were accused of molesting young children. With no evidence presented in support of these accusations the case moved forward.

The, so-called, guilty were condemned with ferocity not only in this article but in the general news media as well. By the end of the piece, a whole religion was destroyed based on unproven accusations against a few individuals.

"Should those reporters have generalized as much?" I ask of no one in particular.

Another newspaper begs my attention and outlines how religion was ultimately destroyed. This was done using a calculated progression of condemnation by association.

Well thought out it went: Seeing, as priests are bad, their religion must be bad. And if one religion is bad then all religion is bad and if all religion is bad so too is Religious Freedom bad.

And goodbye to Religious Freedom whether the priests were ever guilty or not! An atrocity I say. Here-Born's Constitution—the Freedom of Religion section drifts into view. I read it despite that I know it verbatim.

It reminds me why Freedom of Religion was and is so important to us. It also reveals that Religious Freedom alone ensured EB reporters and comedic commentators the right to condemn. Giving them the very Freedom of Speech they practiced in their condemnation of religion.

Without a religious background and its role in the Constitution of the United States of America—such vitriol as their condemnation of religion would not have gone unpunished. In other lands people were beheaded for far, far less.

How I wish I could be present if and when one of these so-called *comedians or reporters* came to understand *where* their Right, their Freedom of Speech that they so strongly insist upon, *truly* came from. I must get Peter Wernt to take a copy of our Constitution home with him.

Another article appears and intrigued, I make myself comfortable but the chime of the front door bell jerks me out of my thoughts. Which chime also comes without real world audio.

The front door swings open to reveal Deidre, my ex-wife, standing on the welcome mat looking as she always does. Her mouth cuts a tight thin line, the Fires of Hate burn in her blue eyes, her nostrils flare spraying Eternal Damnation three-hundred and sixty degrees and five miles deep.

Other than that, she is quite attractive.

Blonde hair flows over an elegant tight fitting blue suit. Her pale beige-pink lipstick offsets clear nail polish. Her high cheekbones are a delicate prelude to dainty hands with long thin fingers reminiscent of a piano player despite that she is essentially tone deaf.

At the sight of her my first impulse is to shoot Madsen in the foot without warning nor any explanation thereafter. Happily though, standing next to her and holding her hand is Karrell our son. But to be more accurate she has a firm grip on his hand.

"Once-Other," she says pronouncing my name as though spitting out foul syllables present in her mouth by circumstance alone. "We were concerned. Very concerned. Weren't we Karrell?"

Karrell nods yes looking as though he means no. She glares at him but says to me, "Business Once-Other? I hope you aren't suffering financial loss...in any way." And there you go—reason enough for her to be here.

I make her wait as I consider any advantages to be had. Her smile freezes in place when I make her wait some more—then to wait further.

Soon it's iced in place possible only with someone as cold as Deidre taking into account the average Here-Born temperature. Just before she explodes, I say, "I see you've brought Karrell over for his Moment in Time with me, his father."

And the ice of her smile cracks. "That wasn't...."

I cut in and say, "It's perfect timing...with business going well." Her eyes light up and the ice melts a little. "At the same time here I am, a touch injured but with the whole weekend ahead. And here you are inquiring after my personal...*health*. What could make more sense or be more perfect?"

"Well Once-Other," and she gags on my name once again, "I was only interested in...if you...would be able to have him this weekend due to your...you know?"

"Yes, I know," I say and shudder without visible evidence of one. She reminds me in certain ways of Wernt, nothing save for unpleasantness lives in the open.

She turns to Karrell and with forced cheer says, "Karrell honey, aren't you as glad as I am that Dad's well and able to have you spend the weekend?" Karrell looks at her as though she had spoken in a foreign tongue. "Karrell honey?" she insists her voice hardening.

"You said it's time to assume ownership of Dad's business," Karrell says.

"Oh Karrell, you are such a tease. Isn't he just Once-Other?"

"I don't remember anything about the weekend," Karrell insists.

"You should pay more attention sweetheart!" she says.

"We didn't bring a change of clothes," Karrell says.

"You have some. Don't you Once-Other?" she asks.

"I do," I say.

She swipes a case closed gesture and says, "There you go— kissy me bye-bye-bee Karrell baby."

He takes a step backward in self-defense. Deidre follows, grasps his hands, yanks him close and plants a kiss. "You see Once-Other. He thinks twelve is too old to be kissed by his Mommy."

She sets about tickling him as though he is a baby. Pulls at his cheeks, pinches them, leaving red spots. Abruptly she strides to her SandRider, mounts, starts up, kicks into gear and races off.

We watch her pink painted and pink-chromed SandRider throw up dust. She waves without looking back and it seems more the signature of Deidre the Attorney closing arguments than a farewell.

Karrell relaxes as Deidre slips from view over an eastern dune.

I close the front door hoping to save myself an unscheduled dusting with a Fragger.

Not likely on Here-Born.

# CHAPTER 37

## OF A MOMENT IN TIME AND PROMISES MADE

"How do we do a Moment in Time, Dad?" Karrell asks.

"Strange happenings taking place, Karrell. Minutes ago I experienced something akin to a second Moment in Time for myself. But let's get to you. We'll head into the desert and spend the night under the sky, the stars, the Half-Day Moon and of course, the Star-of-Hope."

"Tonight?" he asks.

"Yes—tonight."

"I'll get clothes and warm stuff," he says.

"I'll get everything else."

We head in different directions, moments later I hear him rummaging about in his room. I'm sure *it* misses him as much as I do. Perhaps, I should have been more attentive to Deidre.

Her face appears before me and I realize it would have made no difference; we were traveling life on disparate paths with conflicting ideas of what is important and of what a family is for.

In my opinion, she sees children as an inconvenience and at best, something owned but of no exchangeable value—then maybe my own pet peeves from times long gone are here being recorded. But! Too often to recall she expressed misgivings about having Karrell but never to his face, but assuredly to mine.

For me, children are the tomorrow of a nation. They carry forward what we teach them—the right, the wrong, the crazy, the calm and the sane. Therefore, we teach them well—I hope.

I sigh, fill and pack water bottles.

Half an hour later, outside the front door lies a far from neat men only kind of pile. Karrell glances around the desertscape and asks, "Where to Dad?"

Abruptly, I'm back at my own Moment in Time. A smile eases in on me, an old glow warms from within and my father's words return as mine. "A place peaceful and quiet. Where the night sky is black, no city lights wink, the stars and moon shine and nothing reflects upon a dark desertscape."

"Sounds good, Dad. I wish grandpa were still alive. I miss his words. They were always filled with good stuff to know and that smile which never left his face. Dad, why did he dress as though he had one set of clothes?"

"Here-Born Karrell, is tough. Lives are mostly short courtesy of sand and sun—for all of us. He was a simple man, Karrell. Lived to do for others what he was able. He lacked an urge to own. Your grandmother was often driven to distraction by that. Granddad would sometimes wander off into the desert for weeks and reappear without warning nor fanfare. She cried at night. We lived in a tent. I'd hear."

"Yes. I was born in it, remember."

"May they rest in peace," I add.

"Amen. You remind me of him, Dad."

I smile a thank-you to him and head into the garage, drive Hellbent II out and watch smiling as Karrell jumps up and down. "Wow-wow-wow. Will Bordt...and Mom be jealous? You have the latest one Dad. Oh wow wow. Hangdog-garb. Oh wow, wow, wow six-wheel drive!"

"I'll take that as approval," I say.

"Oh yes," he replies.

We laugh as one, my joy at his joy tightens my throat and regrets of a marriage long gone sour stab me once again. I sober and slap his back.

He walks around me and slaps mine. "It's the beauty of it, Dad."

"I understand Karrell," and my joy mingles with his and we hug for a long time. He pulls away and I can tell from his eyes he misses being hugged. I fight regret for several moments.

She comes alive beneath us. I slip her into gear and we race across hard-packed sand. Karrell holds on tight and looks back at the dust plume hugging our tail.

I mention what I should have long ago. "My main hope for you, Karrell, is for your heart to beat in harmony with a mind at peace."

He thinks a moment and says, "As long as you are here and I can reach you...all I need."

"If you need me I will come—no matter what," and he tightens his arms around me and lays his cheek upon my back.

"Keep in mind Karrell, a Moment in Time is illegal under EB's laws. We don't want to be caught and charged with the crime of exercising our own education."

"My thoughts are sealed, Dad. Hangdog-garb."

Miles on, I pull to a stop atop a towering dune some ninety floors high, and it'll do perfectly.

# CHAPTER 38

## OF KARRELL'S MOMENT IN TIME

My mouth hangs open in utter amazement. Karrell has eaten two hotdogs and three hamburgers faster than anyone I have ever witnessed. Ketchup and mustard dribble down his chin.

He licks at it and smiles broadly. "You've not experienced the gradual increase of my appetite," he says and chuckles. "I eat less when I'm down."

"You've grown into a sound and vital young boy, Karrell."

"Hangdog-garb," he whispers speaking across time to all our ancestors.

"Yes Karrell, as you said, *it is so, so let us begin.*"

"Okay, Dad. Let's."

I glance around at Hellbent II then eye the edge of the dune. Tiny waves of sand tumble over as Arzern's Delight casts about in hopes of joining with another wind so as to grow stronger. The heat lessens and the wind whispers quietly promising sand a restful gully in which to spend the night.

I take a deep breath and begin. "From the first moment you studied it...recollect every instant spent on the new EB curriculum and their parrot fashioned tests."

"You want what?" and he spits each word.

"Please, just follow my lead one-two-three altogether."

"Well...okay." He considers for several moments and nods yes.

"Excellent. Create a burning sun trapped inside a bucket. Toss EB's education into it."

He chuckles, bursts out laughing and says, "Wow. What a relief."

"Now! Let's address your Here-Born education. As you are aware, on Here-Born your primary education covers the basics of EB's and our history, political systems, and life and living skills. Later when you're around fifteen, you'll be getting into your career choice, the doing of it and study of it. Then comes further study but only when and as you need it and if you so choose, altogether.

"So. Till now you've done the basics of manners, our history, reading to a high level, handwriting. Now handwriting you did until fast but legible. Then there's the basics of mathematics for life and living, literature, and creative writing, listened to music, learned an instrument, and played some music.

"You will also have covered all the general forms of government and, of course, our Constitution, Bill of Rights and the Letter to all Citizens. So! I figure you're at Level *G* or *H* given you're already twelve. Right?"

"*I*," he says.

"Oh. Damn fine. Damn, damn fine altogether. Only two more Levels to go. To begin then, examine *A* from start to finish over-n-over. Until you get a conceptual understanding."

Several minutes later, he smiles as the dawn of greater insight grows within him.

"Excellent," I say. "Now. Address Level *B* through *I* one at a time, do the same."

He grins wryly and sets to his task. Two hours later he looks up at me and the smile of a Moment in Time sparkles in his eyes.

He hugs me beaming like a newborn sun. "Thanks, Dad."

"Okay. As you know Level *J and K* will slot in when you do those. So you won't need to do this again. Now. Using all concepts, *A* through *I,* create a circle in front of you."

He takes but seconds to complete.

"Loop strings from the circle's center through each of *A* through *I.*"

After a while, he nods yes.

"Next. Examine each concept *A* through *I* from the center until full conceptual understanding unfolds for your entire Here-Born education."

I wait in silence. After some time, he turns to me with light shining about his face. And I am moved to repeat the words of my father. "Good evening young Man," I say.

Karrell smiles a million or more lifetimes' worth of joy.

"Wow, Dad. And you had me wait this long. Damn."

We chuckle.

"Now Karrell. Give me two ideas from the outer circle of *A* through *I* and one or two from the inner concept. Okay?"

"Okay. At Level *G.* Perceive what *is* not what you think you should be seeing."

"Right."

"At Level *H.* First, imagine a new future. Next, use actions and data from the past and present plus new ideas and create a future."

"Right."

"An inner concept...competence in action first requires competence in understanding."

"Damn, damn, damn more than fine altogether, Karrell."

Formally, he shakes my hand and asks, "Anything more?"

"One last thing...."

"Thought so," he says.

"Well, Karrell...we're fortunate my current EB tourist is a perfect fit. His name is Peter Wernt. I'll outline everything I've experienced and what was spoken of over the last few days. Okay?"

And he nods. "Okay Dad."

"While I'm doing this assign items to your Foundation and note where each fits."

"Done deal, Dad."

"One other thing...I'm recording most everything."

"Oh?" Karrell says, frowning.

"Some things I won't record. Those hook into our primary treasure, our UWMD...I won't record them in case something happens to me and my Nomadi falls into hostile hands."

"Are you okay Dad?"

"Yes. I'm good. Times dictate this and my work demands it...you'll get why but make no mention of any details."

"Okay, Dad. You scared me there."

I shift about until more comfortable on sand and outline what transpired between Wernt and myself through to sitting here doing Karrell's Moment in Time. I watch as he arranges the information, extracts parts and assigns them to his education and discards the irrelevant.

Block upon block his Foundation grows until with a jolt he gazes up at the Star-of-Hope and says, "I've fit each item."

"Now. Get *the* one thing you know nothing about. Get that. Thread its idea through all."

"Okay."

For much longer Karrell sits deep in thought, his forehead furrowed. After some further time during which he frowned more-n-more his brow abruptly unfolds. He turns and stares with wonder upon the dark desert and says, "Oh my hangdog-garb! I know how to deploy our Ultimate Weapon of Mass Destruction."

"Damn right you are!" I declare.

He eyes dim, he frowns again, rubs his chin and falls back into deep thought. After several minutes pass by, he turns to me with a sense of loss and says, "Dad...it won't work! Something is missing. I get the potential...at the same time too much is...not...."

"Here, make yourself comfortable and I'll outline the end piece for you."

He stands, stretches, slaps sand off his pants, sits down and I begin. "Listen well, but stop me if you must because I'm going to give you details and examples—real fast."

"Hangdog-garb."

"First, in the Preamble to our Declaration of Independence our Founders mention a fundamental concept to waging and winning a war is to divide and conquer your enemy."

He nods yes.

"The best way to do this? Find your enemy's strengths, adopt them as your own, pervert them then attack and destroy your enemy from within—with these...their very own strengths.

"The United States of America was attacked in many different ways and a prime example was by perverting Freedom of Speech into the Freedom to Lie. Then was added condemnation of those who don't or won't lie and those who don't accept lies as truth or fact."

He nods yes and gazes at the hamburger patties warming at the edge of the fire but changes his mind.

"There's also the perversion of words by changing their meaning, their definitions.

"For example, conspiracy was redefined to mean something only *insane* people believe. No mention was ever made of the fact that those who wish to enslave and control others have a plan on how to go about it."

"Yes, Dad—I already know that!"

"Here's more...people, through education are taught an economy is a pie of a fixed size—pie graphs are shown as proof of this. Therefore, by using perverted logic, the richer others become the less pie there is to go around and so the rich are stealing from the poor.

"But that's false information—an economic pie expands and contracts naturally. The more individual success taking place in an economy, the bigger the pie grows. The more a Government takes out of the economy, regulates or legislates into it—the smaller the pie gets. Any questions so far?"

"No, Dad."

"Okay. Religion was destroyed by equating bad Priests or an individual church member's personal wrongful deeds with a whole religion.

"Freedom of Speech was further destroyed by condemning any who spoke out in criticism of politicians who wanted successful people to pay higher taxes, and all other reasonable criticism was attacked the same way. Those Politicians promised to distribute the extra tax money to the poor.

"Yet they kept the poor dependent on government and in poverty by giving them just enough in handouts to stay alive, and nothing more. Therefore, and thereby, the poor became slaves to government handouts.

"This was kept up until the entire Constitution, and Bill of Rights of the United States of America was destroyed. Okay?"

"Yes."

"All these actions I've mentioned fall under one title...propaganda. The Nazis, as do all socialists or slave masters, ran propaganda to demonize targeted groups of people. First, they attacked hobos and transients. Next, the physically and mentally handicapped. Then tiny minorities like the gypsies. And so they came to their actual target...the Jews...an industrious and productive culture. All these groups were condemned as useless eaters and exterminated or almost so.

"Later came Mao Zedong Communist leader of China and Joseph Stalin Communist head of the Soviet Union. But Mao inverted his targeting by starting with the wealthy and productive people then working his way down to the workers themselves. Which method was also used by the socialist active in the USA.

"Later yet, in the United States, the Governor of a State with a Jewish last name actually condemned some of his State's citizens for drinking too many sugar drinks. And even for eating too much sugar foods and for becoming overweight.

"He concluded by saying his State could no longer *afford* these obese people. Which was the same propaganda used by the Nazis...useless eaters but with a modern twist...cannot afford them...pretty much the same idea as useless eaters but more politically correct.

"Now! After our ancestors had emigrated to Here-Born, we evolved into three separate groups. Those are we the Free Marketeers, the Nomads and the Desert Drivers, yet we stand united by the concepts of Here-Born citizenship, Honor, and Neatness. Okay?"

"Okay."

"Now should anyone of us, Nomads, Desert Drivers or Free Marketeers, come under attack, each group understands they may soon be attacked as well.

"To defend ourselves and defeat any enemy and in particular an enemy from within, an Ultimate Weapon of Mass Destruction was created. Good so far?"

"Good so far."

"The UWMD was designed so one-third of deployment was a natural part of each of the three Here-Born groups. In doing this, the knowledge and capabilities required to deploy our Ultimate Weapon of Mass Destruction was divided by three.

"Now, when attacked there's no defense for any one group unless we unite and implement."

"So you're saying we need the Nomads and Desert Drivers and Northerners as much as they need us?" Karrell asks.

"Damn right we do."

"But if we split in a permanent fashion. Some argument or upset. Won't that be the end?"

"If that happens, one person, or many, from each group or even each State, must rise above any upset and lead the way to a unified defense of Freedom. This represents the depth of Faith our Founders had and laid upon future generations. States are expected to band together in self-defense. And violent conflict is the absolute last resort. More often than not, building something new alongside the old will end the old sooner or later."

"Oh." He thinks and asks, "Anything else?"

"You've learned encryption and high encryption?"

"Yes."

"Take your understanding of our UWMD...encrypt it then encrypt a second time but deeper."

"Okay."

"Place all this into a folder. Encrypt the folder."

"Okay."

"Now write upon that folder as your only response when questioned. *Well now. You see. Our UWMD has never actually been deployed. So, most of us pretty much don't know what it is. And so you guys figure it's nothing more than a rumor.* Good?"

"Okay. Done."

"Link it to your inner-mind-mechanism, Karrell. So even if you're drugged or probed in any way it's all they'll find, altogether."

Done he nods a little pale in face.

"Your Moment in Time, one-two-three and altogether. Like I experienced when I was young, and your mother as well."

"Not sure about Mom, Dad," he says.

"Why's that?" I ask a little afraid of the answer.

"Mom's mentioned her Moment in Time. She did not sound good with it. Nowhere hangdog-garb. More like nothing changed for her."

"Hmmm. May explain—altogether. Thanks, Karrell. I think I'll drink some...."

But the sky turns orange and minutes later the heat is thick.

We change into cooler clothing, pack and head on home.

# CHAPTER 39

## OF DEIDRE'S MOMENT IN TIME

Charging homewards across the desert I take a moment to address what's on my mind. "That EB tourist who came to visit your mother...was he tall and thin and wearing a plain silver-gray but expensive fan-n-fit?"

"No to both Dad. He was around your height but not as broad in the chest. Why you asking?"

"I'm curious...she said you'll regret being my son...even more."

"Well. I have no regrets. You see...if I need you I know you'll come."

"Yes, I will." I pledge.

We race over the top of the final dune.

Glancing homewards, the sight of Deidre's SandRider parked at my front door turns me cold. She turns from knocking at the sound of our approach, wipes sand from her jacket, enough lifts to mist around her.

She has apparently driven here in haste.

I dismount as, with eyes averted she strides towards her SandRider in that stiff, angry way of hers. Her three-finger high heels sink fully into sand with her every step. She mounts, tosses her hair, crosses her arms, and with eyes narrowed and mouth a thin hard line, waits in silence staring off into the distant desert.

I understand that I am not worth even seeing. I walk over as angry as she appears to be and say, "What are you—?" But she cuts me off.

"Once-Other!" she barks. "I'm sorry. Something came up. I need Karrell at home...today. Nothing I can do about it. A legal matter."

"What...ah...a legal concern and Karrell? What more-or-less?"

"Well...it involves myself and Bordt but Karrell needs to be present. Once-Other! There's no need for that."

Her lips twist into a snarl at having picked up my thoughts on the subject. Somewhat critical and unpleasant they were, and not of the kind one wishes to share with recordings.

I swallow another harsh retort threatening to erupt like a long frustrated volcano, and with nothing more to be gained say, "Karrell mentioned your Moment in Time to me, and I'm curious."

"Now you want to know!" And she points her nose to the sun and the back of her head to me. I get the impression she is hiding something with regards Karrell.

Something terrible.

"Deidre," and I choke on her name, "just tell me." And I bite back fears for Karrell.

She looks back and says, "Only if you don't make a fuss and Karrell leaves with me."

My heart races with sudden bad intent, galvanizing limbs to action as my thoughts erupt with violent desires. My nose pinches closed as I inhale and pops open as I snort out. A gleam sparks alive in her eyes.

The corner of her mouth twitches a smile. She runs a finger along her upper lip, inspects it and frowns as though puzzled. She has always had this effect on me. She has always enjoyed it to the fullest.

"Well?" she says. I swallow the bile of bitterness rising in protest and acquiesce to her blackmail with a stiff nod. "Okay then," she says. "The fast version...I was the same when I came back."

"No change?" I ask.

"Let me know if I'm wrong. That's-what-I-just-said!"

"Right. Right. Ah? Who did you go with?"

"A parent."

"Yes. Which one?"

"My father."

"Now don't take this the wrong way. I've had a successful Moment in Time and it appears Karrell has as well."

"Damn successful," Karrell says his eyes twinkling.

"Say it," Deidre barks and spares Karrell a chastising glance.

I utter my words with all the sincerity I can muster—on behalf of Karrell's future with her. "Take some time off. Go to your parents. Grab your mother. Head off into the desert. Do a Moment in Time with her."

She glowers at me but behind the flames of spite realization lights up but hard Deidre rises and quashes both. "Mount up Karrell," she barks. "Let's go."

She points her nose up again, but something grabs her attention and she freezes rigid as stone. I follow her line of sight to Hellbent II ticking as she cools behind me.

Deidre examines it and then me in detail. I sense calculations of price and cost clicking over behind her forehead. They end and her eyes widen and inform that she is not happy with either.

As I recall, she never seemed happier and more loving than during those times when I struggled. Not that she failed to point out my failures—real or imagined. Of course, unless money was rolling in the door bed was a cold and lonely place despite double-occupancy.

"Get on Karrell!" she commands.

He climbs up slowly, deathlike. His eyes plead for my intervention but I must let him go. I cannot sour this into a custody battle as much as she would want me to.

She waits expecting contention.

I take a step backward and Karrell's face drops. He stares down at sand and my heart breaks. Triumph dances across her face in partner with waves of glee. She smiles with cold deliberation but her icy glare shatters as Karrell jumps down, rushes over and hugs me long and hard.

Despite her SandRider being lost to view out ahead of its own sand-cloud...I can still feel his arms around me.

Listless, I while most of the day away curled up on Della Comfort.

Similar to what happened out on the open desert last night, Crier poison hits me all day long and about an hour apart. Each time it hits my vision blurs, my limbs grow sluggish and my heart beats faster-n-faster.

I consider taking my classic for a ride but decide Karrell should partake of that first ride. I spend the day reading, writing, eating and snoozing each time the poison claws at me.

Throughout a restless night nothing much changes.

Come morning, I find myself slightly improved but poison still announces its presence with strict regularity.

I spend my personal four hours checking Hellbent II and giving my classic motorcycle another damn fine wax and polish before cleaning up the garage and self.

Today, while dressing in front of the mirror I mix-n-match colors.

Red shoes stylishly crumple black pants into which is tucked a pure white shirt. Around my waist a two-finger broad red leather belt highlights my trim hips.

I generously apply Fat-n-Grease by Hardins, which holds my red hair stiff in even the strongest wind and provides additional responses from the surprised.

To top it all I fasten a stars-n-stripes bandana about my neck this morning.

# CHAPTER 40

## OF FRANCISCOA'S CHOICE

Far beyond several intervening dunes a flock of Arzerns circle against a bright blue sky. Beneath them, though out of view, lies a Crier warren.

With the wind in my face I catch the faint sound of wings beating the air and the gnash of beaks in anticipation of the feast. The smell of sand is thick and dry with faint traces of Crier odor musty, sweet-n-pungent.

A Great Black swoops down and drops from view behind a shark fin dune. Moments on it climbs back into the sky a Crier clasped in its talons.

Wings thumping at the air the Arzern levels off and glides, releases the Crier and plunges down in pursuit. The hissing snarl of a Crier at death's door mingles with the screech of an Arzern's delight. I jolt at the thud of Crier upon sand and the vision of an Arzern landing to feed.

I hunch down, tickle the throttle open and Hellbent II responds with a subdued snarl. Beneath me a sudden dust devil leaps to life and Hellbent II's front end drops into soft sand. Six tires fight for grip, sheets of sand spray and I pray it is not quicksand.

The tires howl protests as Hellbent II lunges forward in starts-n-stops. Dust shoots up under the edge of my helmet and beneath my bandana seeking my mouth, eyes, ears and nose. One or two grains sneak by and into my eyes. I blink them away. One refuses to leave. Tears gush fighting the grain grating as though sandpaper. I snap the face shield up and grab a handy-wipe from a pocket as Hellbent II coasts.

I clean my eyes, face and nose altogether, wipe the visor clean, pocket the handy-wipe, pull the bandana back up, kick down three gears and yank the throttle open.

Instantly, I find myself staring straight up into the sun. The front wheels suddenly drop shooting the sun upwards and out of view and the desert surface reappears. A loud thud as the wheels hit sand bounce-n-grip.

The full-blooded howl of her V8 comes on song—the flash of the rev-counter needle almost too fast to track. I hang on for dear life arms at full stretch. Snaking, I swerve down an on-ramp and accelerate onto the freeway. Once in my chosen lane I back off allowing her to amble along engine burbling easy and lumpy.

Commuters storm by. Some congratulate me, others mumble an envious, "Damn."

While headed down the last dune into Sand Lake Flats Maggie pulls up to the left and Madsen on my right. They both frown at my mix-n-match. I smile without evidence of one.

"Way all colors, Once-Other," Maggie says and glances at Madsen who looks me over shaking his head in disbelief.

"Good morning you two," I say, ease my speed and add, "Oh! Madsen? Any reports of new technology from EB?"

"Why an' all?" he asks.

"Just curious," I reply.

He stares ahead and says, "You round-n-about have a reason. You-n-who needs that info?"

"No one and nothing altogether," I reply. "I'm interested in how Wernt's thoughts are hidden."

"We need to discuss something—urgent," he snaps back.

"At my store...it's closest," I say.

"No," Maggie says. "Pull off—there at the foot of the dune—it's way closer."

"An' now!" Madsen says. "We ain't for fun."

"Okay?" I say glancing back-n-forth between them but their faces remain blank, their minds in blocked mode. We park facing each other and remove our helmets.

Three engines tick their cooling. Madsen rubs his temples. Maggie stares into the distance. Their attention circles as though choreographed until both focus on me.

They remain seated—their eyes unable to hide how grief-stricken and angry they are. Recent events circle like hungry Arzerns wings linked blocking out the sunlight.

I expect the worst from faces as solemn as these. Has my road as a campaigner ended? Madsen will know if I've been dismissed for recent failures as well as Wernt's hidden thoughts. Then add my failures to report and what more-n-all he can conjure.

He may suspect betrayals on my part with regards the reports I've not given. At best that is negligence. But, strangest of all—what's Maggie doing here? Why are these two together? I hold all questions at bay, hide what I'm thinking and wait.

Into the ticking of cooling engines Madsen says, "Awful Once-Other...Franciscoa has been taken an' all."

I'm shocked and a little ashamed to be relieved by the news.

The sudden tears in Maggie's eyes stun me though.

"He's my uncle an' teacher," she says dabbing at an eye.

I nod and assume this is why she is here.

She wipes her cheeks and says, "It was bad-on-bad when you an' all were sent to prison. Has an effect...your loving uncle suddenly a criminal? But he's a good man. Hits home way hard." And her tears roll freely.

Uncertain if it's right by her, Madsen dismounts, steps onto the foot-peg of her SandRider and wraps an arm around her shoulders.

She rests her head on it for but a moment then pushes him away, dries her eyes, smiles woefully and barks, "Don't you an' both dare mention this. Not ever you hear. Not even 'tween yourselves. I will castrate you! Both of you an' altogether."

I wave such terrible deeds aside saying, "You got it, Maggie."

"Kinda important you remember," she adds.

"We'll do so," I assure her.

Madsen now back in the saddle waits, his face blank. She glares from him to me and back a few times, appears satisfied at what she finds, folds her arms and turns to Madsen.

"Better tell him an' all," she says.

For a moment they both stare at sand.

Madsen sighs.

Maggie flaps her hands. "Get on with the telling," she commands.

"Well?" he says. "Franciscoa was round-n-about the Drinks-n-All last night. He disappeared after saying, loud an' all, that he *ain't* part of this campaign of ours—but sounding like he is. Later someone picked up a call for help. Not certain if it was Franciscoa or not. Happened after closing, most patrons had left."

I rock backward too stunned to say anything.

Maggie glares at Madsen.

"Okay, an' round-n-about Maggie," Madsen says. "Took place in a dark corner of the parking lot. No further details are available at this time. We sure ain't got who abducted him nor how. Informant suspects Franciscoa's communication was blocked an' all. There was probably no time-n-all for a Nomadi call. We've assigned several Rescue teams. They're out-n-about searching."

With tragic suddenness the meaning of our chatter about Franciscoa's retirement curves full circle—he'd put himself out as bait while understanding that this may be his final act. With his thoughts blocked and taken as he was in the dark of night rescue may be well-nigh impossible. I figure he'd grown tired of living with poison and pain though he never showed it.

Wait! Was this what happened to Jiplee? Worse! What of my illness? Are these symptoms warnings? I force those fears back into the dark hole they leapt out. But mental images of myself laid out upon the desert as Jiplee was—and as dead—assault me. Yes! It could happen.

Though struggling for calm, I yet manage to hide my internal battle from them. "Too damn fast and too damn suspicious," I manage to say. "You know what? I was there the night before Peter Wernt's tour began."

"Anything unusual?" Madsen asks examining me in detail.

Am I not trusted? No. Not by Madsen. That's clear enough.

"Not really," I reply. "I had a few drinks. Then more. Spoke to one or two acquaintances. A tourist. Nothing unusual."

Maggie folds her arms and with eyes never leaving mine says, "I'm not concerned with that an' all. Anything happen with that tourist?"

"No," I reply.

"What you two talk on an' all?" Madsen asks.

"Nothing unusual. Normal, everyday, questions."

"Like what?" Maggie growls in return.

"Didn't you get what I just said? The usual Maggie! Scars. Pre-Owned. Heat. Sand. UWMD. Nothing about our campaign. I gave him a pamphlet is all."

"Okay—hang back an' all," Madsen says waving his arms in a settle down appeal. "Wait Maggie. You calm down now Once-Other. Ain't this round-n-about why Jiplee didn't, or couldn't, call for help? An' what's happening ain't no plague of old but something new." We three shudder at tales of old. I dismount and lean against Hellbent II's front wheel.

Hundreds of years ago a plague ravaged amongst us. For endless years mind-to-mind vanished. No cure was ever found because the afflicted remained in a permanently blocked-state.

Medical specialists unable to gain access to their minds failed to discover the cause, nor did they come up with a cure. I shudder at the number of deaths recorded but am thankful it eventually ended.

Maggie clears her throat and I return from the past. "I'd best send Peter Wernt on his way and join the search," I say.

"You are ordered to continue," Madsen says. "Others will deal with this. You stay to your campaign.

I accept his order with a cold nod.

Maggie climbs down, walks over, steps on Hellbent II's foot-peg, wraps her arms around my neck and whispers, "You! You know an' all. Right? Not personal. Don't make it so—for me. Okay?"

"Alright, Maggie. I get it. Friends are at risk. So are we. But I can't put a finger on who or where the attack is coming from. And I'm not sure if what Madsen says links to it or not. Damn strange altogether."

"What more about Peter Wernt?" Madsen demands as Maggie returns to her SandRider.

For their benefit I review Peter once again and say, "Right. Okay. Yes. He's damn awsomely peculiar. Let's see uh...he's interested in our UWMD as they all are despite his pretenses not to be.

"Humph! Yesterday I found him trying to access my ID Check connect. Pretty bad manners on his part. Most of all I'm unhappy with his reason for leaving when my leg was apparently being chewed. But responsibility is so low amongst EB's any excuse will do so...."

"You all sure that's it Once-Other?" Maggie asks.

"I am. I understand this man now. Know him pretty well in fact. We've been through a lot together. He's shown no interest in our campaign, irritation at best for our political system, our Rights in particular and insists I'm wasting his time with those.

"Actually, he fights back with loud protests...and rudely so. He is not interested in our politics, our taxes, our economy— the only thing he responded well to is the rendition of our planet's structure, the inner and outer core, in particular, …oh! And the size of Here-Born's interior rock.

"Damn? How could I forget? He suffers one or more afflictions." I tap my temple to indicate their probable location.

Madsen dismounting, says, "Round-n-about an' all—that's the depth of what you know?"

"Madsen," I growl.

He turns to me brushing at sand on his sleeve. His eyebrows creep up his forehead and hook there like question marks. I bite my tongue killing a curse.

He's about to speak, but I cut in saying, "No. I was suspicious of him, but it turns out he has a weird personal interest in me. That's true more than anything else. He's asked me personal questions—only. I mean, even who I was and if I'm the sole owner of my store. But you're right. What's wrong with him I just don't...his thoughts...."

They both stare at opposite horizons as though struggling to come to terms with the obvious lies of a ten-year-old. Maggie turns to Madsen who is inspecting his engine, and waits.

"That be troubling more than enough," Madsen muses and turns our way fiddling with a shirt button.

"Right," Maggie whispers and runs her forefinger down her nose, inspects it and seems satisfied. I blink reminded of Deidre doing something similar.

Silence hangs hot, the wind murmurs questions, questions about my getting Peter's thoughts or not. If yes, then I'm lying to them. I wait. Madsen says, "If this an' all ain't him—then where they attacking from? Who is?"

I force myself to relax, flex my fingers, sigh and say, "We conduct multiple Talking Tours Madsen—not just mine. Who says we're even looking for a tourist when as many EB's are here doing business."

"You realize it's twice now, Once-Other," Maggie says wiping my words away with a swipe of her hand.

A dust devil dances in between us before I can reply and dies before our eyes.

"Twice?" I ask.

"Yes," she says. "Once in the goldmine an' once with the Crier. Twice you've been injured or come close while out an' about with this Wernt." She taps her temple her eyes hard and grim. "Dangerous? A criminal an' all?"

"I don't think so, Maggie," I reply. "He hasn't done anything I'd consider a real threat. Without his thoughts though, I've no certainty." They both glance off across sand as those who have questions they fear to ask.

In the opposite direction, a sand-snail peeks out from beneath sand. Its periscope eyes riveted on Maggie as though aware she'll roast him given the opportunity. Her eyes follow mine and so do Madsen's. The instant she spots the sand-snail its eyes retract followed by a scurrying retreat beneath sand.

We all laugh. Madsen and I glance at Maggie who appears a little embarrassed, face flushed.

She faces me and is about to press her concerns about Peter Wernt, but I cut her off. "Wait! You're on the wrong track with Wernt. I was as well, at first. Now you are. He's not dangerous. Now, and at best as I can tell without access to him, Peter is...a mild to wild epileptic. Perhaps medication is the cause of his thoughts being unavailable."

They frown their disbelief.

"Okay. Here's my full take on him. He's got to be on medication altogether. Got to be! Times he's calm and relaxed, times he's pure nuts. Excuse the coarseness of—it's all that comes to mind. I've seen what happens to him. You should be around when he has his bouts—real revelation. Never imagined something like...can happen to someone, one-two-three and altogether. Once he ah...never mind. On the other side, he appears to be interested in me personally."

They wave me on. I oblige. "He's aggravating to put it mildly. Self-centered and worse but if he's an active enemy...he has it well hidden. And of course, he loves all things EB."

Madsen lets out a long slow breath, washes his hands together as though he's done with something or someone. He glances at Maggie, the far desert and thinks for a moment after which he stands taller, turns and examines me.

His face softens and he says, "Alright, an' thank you Once-Other. Like Maggie said, nothing personal. I'll put out a High

Priority Alert to all campaign members an' Rescue Teams. We need be extra careful. I ain't looking to lose Franciscoa. Jiplee was about one too many altogether."

"Okay Madsen," Maggie says.

"Good idea," I add but remain alert; for what he says isn't always, and is often the opposite, of what he concludes.

Madsen's eyes harden. "You ain't been on form of late Once-Other. You be awful careful. Maggie an' I'll tune in with you—until he leaves. No! Not to keep track of you an' all—just backup."

I nod as he-who-is-not-fooled.

Now. Due to Madsen's ever darkening nature I keep my bouts of giddiness, disorientation and Wernt's strange images when he and I shake hands, to myself. Furthermore, news of ill health would not help any.

A SandMaster's roar cuts the silence. We freeze at this aural evidence of the hunter. Its exhaust note grows louder. We are unable to move, glued to sand. Only my eyes dance as I search the desertscape. However, I cannot find a sand-cloud nor the SandMaster itself.

Maggie swallows and steps towards her SandRider. Madsen holds the tip of his nose between forefinger and thumb.

"Same one," I say.

They both nod. We wait, hearts pounding.

The engine roars louder as the driver drops down six gears.

I listen more intently and yes it's up-dune—there's a different music when braking against engines and descending. Rapid gear changes tell he has topped the dune. Within minutes, it is quiet.

Inside my mind the roar of exhausts resounds.

How different I muse, the sound of those engines in the hands of a Desert Drive yet so sweet they sang in my own hands.

We glance at each other and shrug.

We mount and head off downtown.

The wind flutters by warm and pleasant. Hellbent II glides across the hard-packed sand of the freeway. I glance northwards to where that SandMaster is headed.

What's he doing down south? We see them on occasion but not often. Why has this one dallied so long? It's been several days that I've heard him. I take a deep breath of fresh, hot out the oven Here-Born air and smile grimly.

Yes, EB's have a terrible time with heat as did our Founding pioneers. Twenty-five percent of those original pioneers died of heat exhaustion within the first two weeks of their arrival. This despite the survival skills each possessed naturally and for which they were chosen. The three-quarters left became our three different population groups.

Tourists have it harder on Here-Born. Brother Sun has taken many of their lives when they were merely strolling around town. The inventors of fan-n-fit suits must have made a killing. They are also responsible for the tourist explosion.

So then. Thank you to all fan-n-fit inventors.

I glance to the sky. In the distance, a single Arzern heads west. I grin at Here-Born and ponder over what scorched and left her all desert-n-rock. There is proof that long ago water filled our sand oceans, lakes, and rivers.

I should take the time to get our naturalists invigorated in search of further answers.

I wave to Maggie and Madsen as we enter the outskirts of Sand Lake Flats and peel off eastwards.

Attention back on the road before me, my mind hunting ahead to Peter Wernt when out of nowhere the impossible occurs.

A frozen breath of air wraps its arms tight around me and whispers, "Is Freedom dead? Have our Rights vanished...forever?"

# CHAPTER 41

## OF A DESERT DRIVER

I ride uneasy in mind. Chef's Call-out thick with warmth and the aromas of bacon, sausages, pancakes and coffee, ambles by and smooths my mental goosebumps away. I sigh. Hellbent II burbles a V8's throaty tune.

Peter Wernt grabs my hand as though I am a long lost relative recently named the sole beneficiary of a vast family fortune—to which he feels entitled. I flinch at the blades of gray light firing off his fan-n-fit but brace up and pull my hand back.

But he holds onto it and says, "Yeah! One hell of a slipped-down-dead Friday that was but here we are. You're looking good. You okay?"

"Thank you. Kind of you to ask."

"No, no Once-Other. I'm grateful. Got to admit that...well...from your...was not a good experience."

"Very observant of you, Peter."

Stepping closer, he squeezes my hand and as unexpected as hail falling a storm of images rains down upon me. Each virtual hailstone slams into my Foundation, shatters, and turns into a picture revealing a glimpse of Peter's past.

I gaze fixated as several automobile wheels churn across desert sand, then in snow then back to desert. Suddenly tropical trees sway in the wind and endless waves of the bluest of water break upon a pristine beach.

Dripping random fragments, I emerge from the image storm to find Wernt watching me intently, a trust me smile on display. He releases my hand and says, "I've empathy for those with whom I've shared the dangers of adventuring."

I shake the remaining images off. Now more than ever I need to understand why at certain times I get Peter's thoughts both when touching and not touching him. I must solve this.

Suddenly the desert vanishes one-two-three, altogether.

Darkness surrounds me. I peer into its depth.

Vague images flash by too fast to grasp. I concentrate harder. Peter appears and disappears. A sudden sandstorm swirls and breaks burying me beneath its two thousand sand-paces height. I retreat from suffocation, climb upwards into my head and search for yesterday's words.

After an intense search, I find them. They are my father's.

He speaks of mental lapses friends of his had suffered—those who had previously been stung by Criers. I embrace his words, bow my head and paddle up through sand. My chest heaves. My head pounds and I'm about to surrender, but sunlight returns and Peter materializes standing before me.

In a thick, wooden voice I manage to say, "Okay. Interesting and thank you. Now, come inside and we can continue with your tour and well paid for it was."

"Yeah, Once-Other. You sure took me in a big way."

"I did?" I stammer.

His smirk materializes left of mouth and centers. "Yeah. I paid double. What with the tour fee price and the same again for the use of my third-eye camera. Quite the shrewd business-man you are. Been told by others what they paid. The highest is ten percent extra for a camera. Quite astute you are."

I smile for I had actually charged four times for his tour not merely double. I wait for a follow-up, a demand for a refund—but no, nothing. Yet he feels he has overpaid. That he is not demanding a refund says something. But what? Does he think I will feel obligated or somehow indebted to him?

"My prices are my prices," I remind him and self.

"Yeah. They sure are."

I update my watchful companions Maggie and Madsen and am shocked that neither was aware of the image storm I'd encountered. I hide my disorientation spells once again and make a note to self to get a checkup. "Tomorrow we'll skip a day. Got a doctor's appointment."

After a momentary hesitation and a sharp glance my way, he nods, turns and meanders down an aisle of arms. He touches one and sets it to swinging and moves on touching hands, elbows, fingers, forearms, and biceps.

"We should spend time here today and get into the finan-cial side of pre-owned parts," I say.

"You buy for less than you sell. There's more to know?"

"Should we head out to the Oil rig then Peter?"

He strolls along a row as though lost in a dream, brushes hanging arms with his fingertips and sights down a row of legs then straightens some twitching fingers. They go right back to twitching. He holds them jammed together, releases them, they twitch on.

"Yeah! Like you said. There's sure no Neatness with these fingers Once-Other. None at all. But you're damn fine recovered. Damn courageous that was?" He smiles as if he is a true comrade-in-arms and meanders over to several torsos in the rear.

I catch up with him and inspect his eyes. There's an agenda happening that much I perceive. But the details elude me. Also, he has a new sense of confidence, a certainty of future results.

"Trying to figure me out Once-Other? Am I good? Bad? Worse than bad?" He touches the bulge under his arm and peeks sly-like at me. "What's the estimated value of your stock, assets, and goodwill? You can tell me. Do you even know?"

"Damn fine nothing to do with you. Can you stop doing *the whatever* you're doing?"

He turns on me with his eyes flashing hot-n-cold, steps closer on legs stiff as tree trunks and with unexpected power says, "Who were you before, Once-Other?"

My muscles turn to water and my arms hang heavy. My neck gives and my head flops to one side. My knees and ankles threaten to give. I struggle to stay upright while tracking two ghostly snakes as they enter my chest and slither towards the one place where entry is forbidden, my UWMD folder. Still, over-n-above all else I am analyzing events.

Anything more physical and violent and I would know this is Peter's doing. With Peter electronics would be at play and the vibrations would be evident. But so high a level of control over others can only be achieved by a Here-Born and worse—by a Desert Driver. If it's the same Desert Driver, he would need to be close...real close.

I stagger sideways, hit my head on an overhead frame and pain drives the snakes away some. But poison's symphony races to duty its flame licking at my brain. Through the waves of pain, a metallic clinking resounds.

I grasp at it and focus on the timbre of each ring. Vision partially returns. I glance around, but Peter is no longer where he was. The clinking rings out once again coming from outside the tent. I step to the entrance.

Peter squats next to my SandRider tapping the wheel rim with a large screwdriver. He turns to me, smiles and says, "This doesn't even make a scratch on the wheel rim Once-Other. That's quality for you."

"Yes Peter," I say while quenching the fires within with images of waterfalls cascading through my head. As the flames die, my mind races onwards desperate for answers to Peter's strange and weird behavior. Nothing.

He toggles the screwdriver between his fingers a bemused look on his face. I glance at my toolbox and find it open. He re-enters my store and replaces the screwdriver. I close the toolbox.

"For a moment it appeared you had a heart attack," he says. "I figured I'd best get ready for an emergency as we must do back on Earth. So I went right out and checked your wheels for soundness as is required when an Emergency appears imminent—it's the Law back home. But you look okay now. You all right?"

"Yes I am," and I scrutinize him for thoughts both in his mind and on his face.

He must realize I'd never believe they have laws anywhere close to that stupid. He examines me smiling coldly. The poison retreats from its current skirmish, the snakes slip fully back into their dark den, evaporate and vanish. My strength returns, eyesight improves.

I glance around the crowd outside and some window-shoppers but cannot spot a Desert Driver. I turn to Peter to find him standing with his back to me.

He gazes across the desertscape all relaxed in his air-conditioned suit his hands at ease upon his hips. How had he turned so fast and in complete silence? Am I going senile from Crier poison? Am I missing moments in time?

In case not I scan the desert again. Nothing. No one. What if Peter is simply a relay point? If so, he would not be aware of what is going on, which would explain his innocent demeanor and perhaps his split personality.

He speaks, voice now less compelling almost comforting, "You okay Once-Other?"

I nod yes.

"Well then? *Who were you before Once-Other?*"

My mouth once again snaps open in auto-response but at the same time a scent wafts by and saves me. Like those legendary EB sharks, I'm tuned to the scent of blood upon the air. Yes, indeed. Fresh is about and close by.

"Once-Other?" Peter insists.

I shush him; sniff the air, estimate direction, and my eyes follow my nose. Wernt's eyes follow mine and we see him more-or-less, one-two-three as one. It is one bad-on-bad Desert Driver.

I control the weak knees sight of him engenders, request calm and endurance of self and change gears. "Inspect this one in detail and you'll know bad when you see bad," I whisper to Wernt. I wait—but he says nothing.

"Peter? No. Okay, I'll explain. His clothes are old and worn. No Neatness with those. Black leather jacket all torn and tatty. One sleeve empty of arm. Broken nose pointing all over and never replaced nor repaired.

"Deep blue eyes with a history of pain in them. Dark brown hair loose and flying all unruly upon the breeze. No Neatness there either. His black leather pants and boots are...well I see you get the point."

"Yeah I do," Peter says.

I point to my own dramatic self. "Note my shiny red shoes. My black pants neatly ironed with the sewn-in creases. The red two-finger broad belt, my white shirt so immaculate it deserves a Neatness Award and...which should be pending...my hair so well contained with Fat-n-Grease by Hardins one can count each strand with ease. In this way, one comprehends good but he's bad-on-bad."

Wernt ignores me and stares intently at the Desert Driver. I touch his arm, but he ignores that as well. I nod understanding and provide him further enlightenment.

"Get this. First off. He is a Desert Driver so watch yourself. Bad manners will have you dead in all-of-an-instant. More-or-less. Also! He's missing an arm and you'll note how he scowls when he peers morbid like at those pre-owned fingers you touched that are still askew.

"But! Despite that he is without an arm, please do not speak to him as you have to me. As I said, it will get you dead."

We watch the Desert Driver's approach and much of my fear vanishes. After all, he has but one arm. Is he the one who attacked me?

The virtual snakes return, entwine my lungs and I fight just to breathe. They dissolve as mysteriously as they arrived. I take a deep breath and say, "Come closer Peter. Even the bad-on-bad appreciate Neatness—you'll see."

"You don't know him? Never seen him before?"

I wave his questions aside. "This one's been on the Rock-lands and with his arm hung free a cactus-blade lopped it off sudden like—and now? Here he is. But where else would he go? My store stocks pre-owned parts that none can compete with.

Still, it's strange he made so basic an error. Well, business is business."

Wernt rubs his arm as though it hurts.

"Now. Where will a one-armed Desert Driver get a girl with all her limbs if he doesn't have them?"

Peter frowns in response.

"Nowhere is where," I say.

"Why didn't you take better care of your wife?" he whispers.

I gasp struggling to understand but as quickly dismiss it and laugh at myself for being a trifle neurotic. He had obviously muttered about his own wife. Whatever happened between them, I do not know for equally obvious reasons.

I sigh but snap back alert as in my peripheral view two bright silver apparitions reflect sunlight. I glance at them and everything changes for the worse.

# CHAPTER 42

## OF SALES TECHNIQUES AND A PRE-OWNED ARM

A Poip pair lurk amongst the tourists crowded around the carousel. They zero in on my Desert Driver prospect and stroke their chins—as programmed to do. They glance at one another their heads bobbing like jack-in-a-box twins.

Electronic language buzzes clear as sunlight.

They grip their holstered weapons and pause.

One leans across and whispers to the other—not that they can actually whisper.

The Desert Driver spots them, glances at their markings, their uniforms with guns-n-all and his countenance sets grimmer. The sales bells jangling in my head start to fade.

I lean towards Peter. "I hope to make a quick sale here. But as you can see, all comes down to timing. On the other hand, being ankle deep Poip are not fast sprinters...as you are, Peter."

He double-takes on that and snorts his displeasure.

I examine the Desert Driver in detail and figure he'll want around a five-thousand-dollar arm, mid to high range that is but not of superior quality. Now, as he has no time to bargain, he'll have to pay what I say, which will be more than that.

Much more.

He walks faster but keeps a firm hold on his stump to prevent it bumping into anyone, or anything. Though preservatives allow us to replace damaged parts they do nothing to lessen the pain.

He arrives and without a greeting, examines my stock of pre-owned. Wernt checks him over in detail. I scrutinize Wernt and notice something is not right, or out of place, but I can't place a finger on what.

The Desert Driver glances at Wernt and dismisses him out of hand. He then glares hard at me and a warm, radiating energy glides across my skin. I brush my palm down my arm and stare off into the desert as one with little or no interest in sales techniques does.

Yet I'm deeply curious that such a warmth comes from a Desert Driver. The seconds tick on by. Across sand, the Poip wait for confirmation downloads to complete. The Desert Driver's eyes dance back-n-forth from Poip to pre-owneds and back.

"Are you perhaps interested in a leg?" I finally ask of him out loud.

"Leg?" he snarls. "Are you stupid? An arm!"

Having deliberately said the wrong thing I present him with my best—*I've been corrected altogether smile* which he and all others know is faked. There're times during sales when irritating the buyer, ones who have little choice, can have a positive effect. Or so I've been told. Apparently it short-circuits straight thinking.

Glancing at his remaining one, I retrieve similar arms from beneath the counter and lay them out for him. He inspects them, selects one with enough muscle yet is youthful, but not too young. He holds his selection to where his severed one would be and checks for compatible length, hairiness, coloring, and form.

He glances at the Poip then asks, "Do you have quality preservatives?"

"I only have quality," I assure him. "Quality enough to ensure gradual growth and an eventual ninety-five percent match between a new and old."

"Okay. How much?"

I indicate to Wernt that he should take note of this sales demo. Strolling out into the sunlight I inspect the distant horizon while working my Nomadi.

"Damn all sand—I asked how much?" the Desert Driver says.

"Not much," I reply.

"What?" he growls.

Once-Other, the salesman, suddenly turns hard–n-fast, steps in face-to-face and shows him five fingers, three times and crosses them with two to multiply by.

The Desert Driver's face turns red, shades to blue then to green...more-or-less. Meanwhile, he speaks rapidly but utters no sound. Likely he's not well-practiced in the verbal arts of communicating.

I shrug, smile a sympathetic smile and my eyes glance ever so casual like at the Poip. They are now headed our way their grievous and dedicated intent apparent to one-n-all.

Next. Born of many, many years of practice, I allow one eyebrow to climb slowly but most assuredly up my forehead and my eyes to grow ever larger-n-rounder. A bead of sweat pops out on his lower lip.

He licks at it. "I'll never forget your internal face Once-Other." Nevertheless, he pays but as he does I once again feel faintly disorientated.

# CHAPTER 43

## OF PRESERVATIVES AND BONDO-STICK-ON

I check the Desert Driver over, but no attack emanates from him. So he's not my attacker. I hand him an injector bottle of Bondo-stick-on, an ID Check Certificate, the pre-owned arm in a wrap, extra preservatives and a battery pack with which to jump-start it.

He retreats in ungainly pain. As the crowd swallows him, he spares me a long hard glare. The Poip reset and follow him.

I touch Peter's arm and say, "What a perfect opportunity. Here. Take this bottle of Bondo-stick-on. It and preservatives are the secret to pre-owned parts."

He removes the cap and without asking sniffs at the contents. He immediately doubles over and gags and struggles back upright.

"Ask next time Peter. Now preservatives—you okay?"

He controls the gagging further and says, "Yeah. Get on with it!"

I wave at the general view, buildings, tents, people, desert and sky and spot something up in the blue. "Oh look...out there in the distance...an Arzern in flight. It's unusual to see one or two on their own. They are flock-orientated. This one is probably setting up to drink some Crier water. Which we'll come to later." His eyes narrow.

I smile within and say, "Okay and moving on. Preservatives are everywhere. In the air, in sand, and some believe in the light. More important than that—it gets into your body pretty damn quick no matter where you hail from."

I note his typical every-day-tourist disbelief.

He turns away and heads deeper into my store brushing his hands along a line of legs, and glances over his shoulder at me. He smiles with a high factor of minus-warmth and walks by a cactus but far too close.

I follow quickly as he says, "Yeah. Riveting stuff Once-Other. Keep up with me here."

He hurries off behind a five sand-paces high display case containing Criers wrapped in the hides of Roanark Braer.

Glances beneath a tarp briefly, gazes up at the Arzerns hanging from the tent's cross-beam, looks back at me and says, "Yeah. I figure you should keep going with all this...stuff. I get how *critical* it is. Yeah. Get with the preservative things and ah...the altogether."

I desert him, retreat to the table and pour us each a glass of cold water.

He walks back slow and easy kicking at the film of sand on the floor. His rubber soles spit-sand-n-squeal on the faux wood floorboards. He stops in front of me, waits several seconds, takes the glass and says, "Yeah?"

"Peter...all began when our ancestors first arrived...as you already know. The ships, including the one housing the central lab, crashed when landing and what they were working on fused into the atmosphere. The result being that you can now lop off a limb, even your head—with help of course, and it'd be no trouble at all because you'd just glue another one on."

"That's how this works? I never imagined...this can't be true. Glue?"

He empties his glass and holds it out for more. I oblige him.

"Still takes a day or two to grow on and another three to heal...what did you say?"

"Glue?!" he says.

"No Peter. Bondo-stick-on is a cellular converter."

"Huh?" he says and pulls out a chair, sits down, raps my ID Check with a knuckle and peers at me as though inviting a protest.

I ignore the invitation and say, "Okay. I'll slow down some. Bondo-stick-on converts pre-owned limbs or members to the same cellular and chromosome structure as your current ones. We just call it a glue as a quick time reference. You know? A kind of non-acronym-acronym."

He shakes his head as though ridding himself of something foul.

I add, "Preservatives work with Bondo-stick-on and together allow for this my business." I wave at my store and goods.

He slams the glass down on the table, stands with hands on hips and glares at me. I take his elbow and head deeper into my store. He resists. I insist.

I guide him around a cactus. "Once preservatives get inside you, your body structure changes and you can almost be without a head and not be dead. Not for too long, though. Heads need fast replacement under anesthetics during an operation. They are not like arms. Accidental decapitation equals accidentally dead. You know? No?

308

"Okay. Look. There's the whole spinal cord and those nerves to join. Strapped immobile while recovering is the worst. So heads must be changed out fast. Damned quick in fact. Heh-heh. Thereafter Bondo-stick-on works."

He stops up and says, "What? I'm not getting it. You aren't any good at this—are you?"

I withdraw teeth from tongue and get him moving again.

"Look. Experiments first conducted on board ship—were secret. They were testing natural regenerative compounds that individual creatures have. The kind able to regrow limbs or members previously dismembered. They tested with lizards-n-all? You know? Grab a lizard by the tail and it comes off. Defense mechanism. Then they grow another one. Get it?"

"Incomprehensible Once-Other," he says and glances back at the table.

I firm my grip on his elbow and continue walking. "Patience. Long after the crash landings we developed preservatives into Bondo-stick-on. Okay?"

He frowns but waves me on.

"After applying Bondo-stick-on externally the blood semi-clots. You will bleed consistently but slower. Preservatives within sand or the atmosphere will already be inside you. These prevent excessive bleeding immediately you're wounded. I'm talking slower bleeding via semi-clotting and the preservation of tissue in one action."

"You've lost me," he says.

We halt and I reply, "Okay. You apply Bondo-stick-on to the wound, press and hold the pre-owned in place. They bond together. Inject Bondo-stick-on into the blood stream. Okay? No. Ah? A little technical but...we all have a personal DNA. A blueprint in the chromosomes. Right?"

He nods yes.

"Excellent. Here's how this works. Bondo-stick-on reads your current DNA code while spreading through your body and on finding a different DNA, goes to work. Pre-owned parts, of course, have the wrong DNA. Right?"

"Yeah. Good so far."

"Quad-mitosis kicks alive in the pre-owned parts, the cells split into eight separate ones. Your actual DNA code gets embedded into the new cells as they split overwriting the old DNA. And so you get eight new cells—damn instantly.

"Ah. Yes. Regular mitosis is the action of a single cell splitting into two new cells. Where you had one, you now have two. Quad-mitosis means it happens four times. Four times two is eight new cells. Okay?"

"Yeah. Right. Thanks for the math lesson. Give me a moment here."

He turns away, fights back a bout of gagging, wipes his mouth with a facial tissue, blows his nose and asks, "How does Bondo-stick-on figure the right code?" and he gags again.

"Ah yes! One needs to be real sure and inject Bondo-stick-on into an original body part. If you do it into a new part, it will read the new DNA as your DNA and convert your entire body to the DNA of the pre-owned."

"That an issue?" he asks.

"Not unless being very dead is okay with you."

He jerks back-n-forth as though attacking and retreating at the same time. He slowly calms but continues flexing his fingers as though he is at someone's throat, which makes me shiver. I pull myself together, walk back and replenish my glass and without any for Peter, return.

"Well. Should pre-owned parts languish in stock too long, they'll age like jerky and can't or won't jump-start and, of course, don't work. Pre-owneds need be fresh with particular attention to heads being fresh."

"Okay," he says and wipes his mouth his eyes on my helping of water.

I take a sip. "Here's what's interesting. Some of us believe preservatives were at first conceived by Earth-Born politicians and manufactured in one awful and damned worthless experiment. We still figure that the experiments were an attempt to make us more equal, one to another or so they say. How stupid an idea—we are all equal?"

And he takes the bait full on.

"We are all equal," he snarls.

"Not damn in our Here-Born Constitution and Bill of Rights," I snap back at him.

His eyes roll over white and his knees give. I reach over and steady him. He straightens, pushes away and stares accusations and condemnations at me.

I sigh in deep satisfaction...here at last and across a sea of protest and sand. Foundation ahoy! It had taken a direct verbal assault upon him to shatter the emotional armor he has in place.

Now I'll target his mind and find his hidden thoughts.

I sally forth.

# CHAPTER 44

## OF EQUAL MEANS EQUAL AND DIVIDE AND RULE

"Now, Peter. On Here-Born it does say all people *are created with equal Rights* and are endowed by the Creator with certain Inalienable Rights. Among these are Life, Liberty and the Pursuit of Happiness." I pause.

He waves me on.

"This includes the Right to defend one's life or property. It also includes defense of family, friends, groups, community, possessions, neighborhood, city, village or town, County, State, Country, Planet and most valuable of all—one's Sanity and that of others.

"The Right to be armed and able to defend yourself stands paramount.

"There are more inalienable Rights, or as some say, unalienable—the same thing—can't be taken away—can't be removed nor altered."

He waves his hands in my face as to awaken the dead. "Lies. All you Here-Born citizens are equal."

"No, Peter. Not even close. Listen!

"Our Founders examined this *all people are equal* thing and had certain misgivings and many questions. Example questions for you. Did God create us equally? On the other hand, does it mean we are all created equal one to another? Which one is it? These two are not the same idea."

His face pales and he snarls, "You conceited fool. Where the hell do you get off?"

"Listen...I understand that long ago back on Earth-Born when you killed God by killing the belief in one and thereby that Rights come from God...you also killed a Constitution and Bill of Rights.

"That's when The End is.

"For by that time, the Spirit of Man was long dead."

"Moron!" he snarls.

A few seconds of silence and his face collapses in shock as I break down laughing.

"You find that funny? You think I'm so dumb this whole tour thing escapes me?"

"No. It's just that with the moron insult being so popular amongst EB's it seems you don't know idiots by definition have a lower IQ than morons. So...calling someone a moron could be a compliment." He may have been angry, but now he is apoplectic. He clenches his fists so tight both arms shake.

I drive harder at his Foundation. "People being equal one to another is impossible. Think on it. No two of anything nor anyone are exactly alike, let alone equal. Not even twins are equal. Get what I just said. One's a moron the other an idiot. Equals not equal. Some live for government handouts others strive for personal success—not equal either.

"I'm taking into account equal by definition means well...equal and nothing else. You know? No? Okay. It means one is exactly the same as another! That's what equal means—and nothing else."

He tightens his fists further and grinds his teeth his head shaking as much as his fists.

"Easy, Peter and listen up. People cannot be legislated into being equal—not matter the lies saying it can be done. Now! Should you attempt to do so, it inevitably comes to pass that someone will set about the task of making us all *equal*.

"And if not willingly then forced to be *equal*.

"Also equal was never in the Bible nor any other religion. All people are equal, is a fond belief of Communists and all other Socialists.

"Now! Once they're in power, they set about forcing others to believe it as well. But should you wish to pass on believing such...the Communists or their other names...Progressives, Liberals, Socialists will force you to believe it or kill you.

"Which if you care to note...being killed or tortured into believing or vanishing into a work camp never to be seen again...isn't exactly equal despite that it is Communists doing it to you."

"Impossible in a shared assets community," he says.

"Doesn't work, Peter. Equality is always promised as taking away from others what they worked for and giving it to those who have not worked for it. Always. Always. Always."

"You're playing with words. We are all equal Once-Other."

I wave that aside. "Giving the wealth and success of others to those who failed to earn it—terribly cruel."

"Nothing evil about sharing the wealth of the few with those less fortunate. The wealthy must just suck it up and deal with it."

"It's a terrible cruelty to those receiving not to those having theirs taken away, Peter."

His face flashes red then white then green...more-or-less. Between the varying colors he spits, "Your idiot ideas are wearisome. Time you shut up about this. I've had enough! I'm paying here!"

"May at first be difficult to understand."

"No!" he spits.

"Seems to me that you don't exactly know what a Communist Party that has gained power sets about doing. Their theory or system says that all property and wealth is owned by all the members of a *classless* society.

"So, first they confiscate all wealth in the name of the Party.

"And then the communists-slash-liberals-slash-progressives run the economy and political system of a country with absolute power. Extensive restrictions are enforced on personal liberties and freedom and individual rights are overruled by the collective *needs* of the masses.

"And! Who exactly decides on what the collective needs are? That would be the Committee, or Party or Dictator. Not exactly equal either. And! These committees most often *don't* decide what a collective group *needs*...they instead decide what they *don't need*.

"They don't need cars, personal phones or handhelds, good clothes, shoes, food, a comfortable bed, children, income, love, nor a home.

"There one-two-three is the death of any society. Any!"

He taps his foot.

I sigh and change tactic. "Do you have a child?" I ask. He staggers backward as though shot through the forehead.

I change again at his unexpected reaction and lunge for his educational jugular. "Giving people something they have not earned forces them to depend upon government for every-thing, even to eat. That's slavery. No one is more dependent on handouts than a slave."

He pinches his nostrils closed and stares down at the floor-boards. His pinky spasms. He grabs it and glances at all the restless fingers around us. I chuckle behind a straight face.

He waves me on and I ponder why he wants more—but briefly. Could it be I'm achieving the next step—the seeds of our Rights planted and ready to be nurtured?

I rush on. "An example of real help can be found in our prison system. But it only works upon and at each person's self-determined request for that help. No matter the individual, no one can be forced to improve let alone to accept real help. Except of course under threat, pain, and or drugged. With those, you never end up with an active and proud individual.

"Real help is actions such as assistance in becoming edu-cated and the learning and practicing of economically viable skills. Or there's personal help that assists one with perception and the understanding of the various parts of life itself."

"Criminals getting educated. Sure Once-Other—just as soon as Here-Born freezes the hell on over."

I apply the wave off to his words. "On the other hand. Those who champion the poor but who don't at the same time work to make them economically viable and valuable—have built for themselves a running platform upon the backs of the poor."

He goes rigid, steps closer his eyes fixed on mine. Fires flare within his. I note far more hate than I can understand. What drives him? What gave birth to so much hate? I sigh deeply, longing for but a whisper of his thoughts, for but an instant of access to his mind. I try once more and nothing.

I quietly say, "And as time rolls by he'll need more backs to stand on. This kind of champion gets trapped into needing more-n-more poor people who must also stay poor. And!

"How can anyone condemn those who are successful while the poor are improving and gaining greater success for themselves? So!

"To champion anything like the poor—poverty and neediness must be continued and or even nurtured. Here-Born logic for you."

He folds his arms, steps closer and glares from six fingers away. "Logic of an ignoramus you mean."

"If you like, Peter. But consider this—if education gets sabotaged so that the poor never get to understand their own Rights...who will they turn to, to explain those Rights? The very people who lead them...those who depend on them being and staying poor, uneducated and ignorant.

"Such *leaders* need them to remain poor and so they ensure poor folk never become properly educated and have no skills with which to make themselves economically valuable. And how would one ensure that condition for ones' followers?

"Simple! Destroy school systems by making it impossible to understand or learn anything. Encourage drug use. Make Mental Health, *recreational* and psychiatric drugs freely available to those who will take them without question.

"Force others to take them via government regulations for so-called *diseases* like your ADD-D. Encourage all forms of drug usage. Drugged becomes mindless eventually.

"And all the while the redistribution of wealth provides recipients with just enough to survive on but in continued and eternal poverty. And not a penny more.

"At higher educational levels...teach falsely. Pervert education into guilt-driven theories and propaganda of the abuse of one group by another.

"Destroy individual thought and reason by making group think all.

"Now. That by any name is slavery. Okay. Okay. Calm down."

He shudders but controls himself and says, "You really should shut-up about this Once-Other."

"I hear you. But the idea that *All people are equal* was reasoned by our Founding Fathers to be an unworkable philosophy. But it's a damn good idea if you want to replace natural birth with clones. How can one get closer to *truly equal*? With clones. They are much closer to being *equal*."

He glares at me with the moron insult in his eyes and says, "What about employers who cheat their workers? Explain that one Once-Other!"

"That falls under criminal law. Not the Bill of Rights."

"All are equal on Earth. Change the subject."

"One last item. To be anywhere close to *equal*, all people must have the same salary, the same authority, the same position, the possessions...at the very least. What position in life should we choose for all People to be so as to be equal...that of President?

"Will each have equal power to command all the other three hundred million Presidents who are equal to each other? You see? We can't have a single President because right there we would no longer be equal! How stupid do you have to be?"

"Shut-up," he hisses.

"Okay," I reply, think on it and ask, "Do you know why there's no credit system on Here-Born?"

"No. And I don't care."

He turns his back on me and stares out the entrance to the distant desert. I check as well but other than sand and sky there's nothing further to see.

Quietly I say, "If we the people have a credit system, it will come to pass that the Government will have credit as well."

"Nothing wrong with a good credit system," he counters.

I smile at the opening he presents. "Except when you can no longer pay the debt down. On EB, nations defaulted on their payments. Property, land and natural resources were awarded to foreign countries, the so-called debt holders, through International Courts."

"Right Once-Other and perfectly reasonable. If you owe, you pay. If you default, you lose. It's a matter of honor...of meeting your commitments. Of Neatness!" And he sniggers but catches it and controls himself.

"Yes. That's also known as something else. Do you know what?"

"Would you just tell me? I don't give a damn but tell me."

"The redistribution of wealth. And how can that be? Simple. Borrow madly on behalf of your country. Sell your debt to other so-called poorer countries. Default on your payment. They take action against your government to collect on the debt.

"Courts award them land, factories, buildings, property, businesses in payment of *your debt*. The foreign country now owns all that was your country...including all foreseeable taxes. And you're done...your country and your personal wealth have been redistributed...by those you voted into office!"

He turns his cooling down. "You are an idiot. Get off this stuff." I don't but do note he'd downgraded my IQ.

"If you pay a foreign country interest you're essentially paying taxes to a foreign government—one you have no representation in? And so they have power and sway over your country. Power and sway you have no vote in let alone a veto!"

His face turns bright red and purple well more-or...but his Nomadi buzzes breaking the moment. He pulls it out without taking his eyes off me, stalks out into the blazing sun and sand, answers, listens, turns and comes back with fists clenched his face a landscape of rage.

"Change the subject Once-Other!" he shouts.

"Well, okay. You now know something about Desert Drivers, Poip, preservatives, where all these pre-owned parts come from and a little about our Bill of Rights."

He walks to a row of arms and touches one. Reduces the temperature of his cooling suit a trifle and caresses its control dial. "How many political parties are there?"

And I'm taken aback at this sudden change. Is he actually interested? Doubtful. Then why stay on the subject? Does he think there is something worth knowing? Or is this interest the opening move of his hidden agenda?

I sail onwards in the hope of discovering what and why.

"Political parties are illegal here."

He jolts as though hit over the head with a rock.

"The divide and *conquer* concept is used by politicians to divide and *rule*."

"People need to be ruled...all the time," he says shaking his head.

"As you mentioned earlier, Peter, an idiot's delight and without doubt that blows away your notion of all being equal. Now! Out here it's common knowledge that people are easily controlled by two opposite ended political parties.

"Just generate enough hate between them. Follow that up with racial hatred, cultural hatred, class or income hatred by which time a country has pretty much been conquered.

"Then! All that's needed is for a leader to step up and make promises everyone wants to hear and more...wants to believe. The simple promise that all people will be made *equal*."

His face goes slack. His shoulders sag. He resists for an instant but too far off kilter he almost falls but manages to grab onto a chair and steady himself.

I drive onwards. "On Here-Born political campaigning is illegal as well. There is an Election Website and nothing more. To run for office, you upload details of the programs, laws, bills, propositions, and any regulations needed to implement them. No more than fifty pages in all. Letter size. Minimum font is ten.

"And of course, your full resume. Do we check backgrounds and achievements...or what? And the winner must attain 52% or higher. The same 52% is needed in a runoff."

With his arms waving he says, "Are you telling me Here-Born politicians must outline what they will do in office in writing ahead of being elected?"

"Yes, Peter! But there's more. When running for office on Here-Born you have to disclose all your staff and consultants' political philosophy, current endeavors and their resumes, including education. Oh! Lobbying is illegal and any failure to fully disclose is a High Crime."

"What!" he screams.

"And there's more. Federal, State, County, and City elections are held in different years. In this way, voters can concentrate on one level of government at a time. This includes any Propositions and the regulations proposed. Which we never vote on for the final time during an election.

"All final voting on Propositions and their proposed regulations, if any, happens in the years after Federal and State elections. Federal Propositions the year after Federal elections and State follows the same pattern.

"All county and city Propositions are voted on by the residents at any time as their Propositions and Proposed Legislation are local.

"So we have a six-year voting cycle...all told.

"And as you already know...at all levels and with regards all Politicians, Propositions, Laws or Legislation and any Regulations...there is an un-elect and a repeal website constantly up and running.

"Legislation, Laws, any Regulations, plus all elected officials can be removed from the books or from Office at any time by We the People. That's at and from all levels of Government—from Federal to State, to County, to city or town or village. As we say amongst ourselves...*never shall one single vote said to be...nor ever be counted as worthless.*"

"Sounds long and tedious," he murmurs.

"No, not really. So! Next! For a full month before any election and ending one week before Election Day we have a Political Convention for Federal and State Elections.

"For State elections, conventions are held in a different County each election cycle. Any County and City Conventions are always held in the County or City itself.

"Federal Conventions are held in two different States each election cycle.

"During Conventions one can meet any candidate face-to-face and even one-on-one. Here is where the media host question-n- answer shows that are broadcasted planet wide.

"No questions are forbidden...not even stupid ones.

"Something further...during the full length of any convention TV crews as well as private citizens will broadcast most every moment, every question and every answer. This makes it possible for those not in attendance to tune in or search and find what they wish to view.

"In the final week after debates, that may have been organized, are complete, each person running for office gives a half-hour speech—with no questions allowed so they must be clear and exact.

"Well, Peter. Now you've been introduced to our Bill of Rights and Our Constitution. There's more though and, of course, there's the Letter written by our Founders addressed to all Citizens back then and those of the future.

"Welcome to Here-Born, Peter."

He turns his back on me and leans forward as one does when blood has drained from the head and pooled in one's toes.

# CHAPTER 45

## OF WHAT AND WHY TREASON IS

"You alright?" I ask of Peter.

With a glance telling of his displeasure in me he staggers off to my ID Check, helps himself to water, spills some, looks at me a little guiltily and says, "That's pretty much pointless Once-Other. That website and those write-ups are worthless. Very few voters understand...."

"No," I cut in. "Not really. Not here. Here we are fully educated by the time we graduate High School in political philosophy, political power, and political economics.

"Which includes all the different kinds there are...democratic, democratic republic, fascist, communist socialism, Nazi socialism also known as National Socialism, liberalism, progressive, conservative, any and all kinds of dictatorships. Rule by kings and queens and any other ruling class people may invent such as tribal ones with their chiefs.

"And there's something else that makes a damn big difference out here as well."

I watch as interest races across his face, but I remain silent. Peter's lips quiver. His eyes bulge he swallows noisily and waves me on.

"I'll admit to repeating myself here. But it is critical! We've enacted an un-elect website which is permanently open. We can un-elect anyone at any time. As soon as un-elect votes equal seventy-five percent of all the votes cast to elect you— you're fired.

"We use Nomadi to vote so only those who voted for you can vote to un-elect you.

"The same is true for all Legislation, Laws, and Regulations. We can repeal these, in the same way we un-elect an elected official. And these Rights, as well as others, are what we've added to the Original of those United States of America which we adopted after our First War of Independence.

"Oh yes! Now our Superior Courts...are very different as well." I pour some water for myself and sip. He drinks his down and holds out the glass for more.

I refill it.

"How so?" he asks.

"Well. Every Court decision made and every law passed and every court ruling given must by law be checked against our Declaration of Independence first.

"Then against our Constitution, the Letter To All Citizens Present and Future and our Bill of Rights to ensure no ruling violates them or attempts to alter them.

"If any do commit such a violation he or she is immediately charged with Treason against We the People."

For once he is speechless. He stares without seeing. In his eyes, I perceive something go click. His sneer vanishes, his face pales, he turns cooling to a lower temperature, staggers to a straight-backed chair, sits down and hangs his head between his knees.

In the background pre-owned arms sway in a sudden gust and settle. EB voices trail in from the carousel and the sound of the circus tent slapping against faux wood support poles seems muted beneath the moan of wind.

"I didn't know," he mumbles, remains sitting for several minutes then looks up a strange glint in his eyes. "Once they upload all of what they are running on they'll campaign. Yeah?"

Barely able to catch my breath at the breadth of his change I say, "Political campaigns are illegal as well. Anyone can run for office taking into consideration that personal wealth, fundraising, and personality have been removed from play.

"That being due to the election website. And!

"Advertising in any other way to get elected is illegal. Let alone championing the poor just to get elected then abandoning them.

"We are interested in what you've done, your future vision, how you'll deliver your vision, but not in what you have to say—charming or otherwise.

"*Never* judge a person by what they say, Peter.

"Instead, one must observe their actions and the results of their actions.

"Also, always note when they fail to act and the results of doing nothing. Did less confusion arise from either doing something or doing nothing? Or more confusion even chaos result? It's chaos we don't want."

He tries interrupting me. I keep going.

"Elected officials are limited to two terms, twelve years in total and may not run for any office or be a public employee or political consultant thereafter. This is from City to County to State to Federal."

He stands up, but his legs wobble and he sits down again, wipes his hands on his suit and straining to sound relaxed says, "Too much inconvenience."

"We don't surrender our rights-n-freedoms for a more convenient life."

He thinks, his face blank and says, "What's with all the treason in your founding documents?"

"You've read them?" I demand.

He waits with a straight face.

"Let it be known, Peter...elected officials pay a high price for betrayal.

"You'll find written in our Constitution *betraying the trust of the People is Treason! And which still includes waging war against us. Any war! Be it attrition, economic, direct war or invasion, social, destruction of your Constitutional Rights, propaganda wars whether waged by word of mouth or over the media, destroying the value of our currency...all are forms of war. All!*

"Better not make promises you do not intend to keep and do not waiver from your stated path. Both are treason. This stands true for all us of Here-Born. All. So!

"True for politicians. For News media persons. For military. For Police. Everyone. On the other hand, those guilty of treason are not executed. They will spend their lives in prison working a worthwhile job—if found guilty."

He flaps his hands in anguish and says, "You mean if someone writes a law or regulation which violates your Constitution they'll be charged for merely attempting?"

"Altogether!"

He waves at the ceiling like an octopus struck by infinite confusion. "Why?"

I hold to calm hoping he's Foundation opened and he is now seeking new ideas. "Any system that has no consequences for acts against and violations of a Constitution breeds uncaring and criminal politicians.

"You should read the documents I'll provide.

"It's interesting what happens out here if legislation and regulations which violate our Constitution are passed or even proposed...you'll now understand why lobbying is illegal."

He bats my words aside as too painful for consideration and asks, "How do you rationalize the politicians you said are imprisoned for what you insinuate they did?"

"We discovered they had provided every Earth-Born citizen an illegal Here-Born citizenship. That's too large a can-of-worms to hide. It's Treason. We zeroed in and everything else followed."

"I see."

"They'll never be released. Treason stands as treason—always."

"Unless of course Earth intervenes," he mumbles.

For several moments, I am unable to speak. We had not thought of interference from EB in this matter. More than a simple something is wrong here—with this Wernt.

I send what I have heard to all citizens nearby as well as Maggie and Madsen. Not a single confirmation returns...evidence no one received my communication.

Someone is blocking my communication.

Someone I cannot identify.

Someone close but hidden.

My mind runs wild overcome by hidden dangers.

The shoppers milling about spin and dive as though walking up the side of the carousel. I close my eyes and clear my mind. Balance both physical and mental return.

I look out across sand just as Arzern's Delight picks up. Several dust-devils leap to life and rush about greeting each other.

But the wind dies and so do they.

# CHAPTER 46

## OF PETER WERNT'S HIDDEN HAND

A sudden rush of Crier poison assaults me; it is all I can do to stay on my feet. Peter's face swims before me bulging like the magnified face of a fish peering out a clear bowl. He smiles coldly, strolls out onto sand, checks around and says, "Poison still bothering you Once-Other?"

Pain greater than the Crier sinking its sting-claw into my neck strikes with a vengeance. Multitudes of marauding sting-flies attack my brain their bites hitting as one—I stagger but fight to keep a footing and just manage to regain my balance before falling.

A gentle explosion around my head. A cold light encircles me and locks on. I run as fast as I am able, desperate to escape what all is attacking me. My lungs burn with effort, my legs shake.

But I cannot move, nor turn, nor break free, a cactus planted and defenseless against the wind. Is this another man-ifestation of those snakes, their fangs, and that hand?

Are they all the same thing?

There comes no answer.

I hold still.

I listen.

I hear Peter scuffing at sand with his boot.

The terrifying presence of a predator engulfs me.

A brief silence and his boot settles on the floor, scrunching sand. And what I'd thought was a one-on-one tour with one damn odd and weird tourist comes to an abrupt end as Peter draws his sword.

From a point deep within my very self his cold voice says, "Once-Other my resilient guide, campaigner, enemy of Earth, a so-called patriot of Here-Born. Time for those revelations you've been pondering on. You figure you're so smart...but you're not."

His laughter mingles with the light, grabs hold and throws me towards the faux wood floor. As I fall and far too late I realize that I'd misread his intention from that first glare up to its revelation in this moment.

All this while Peter's thoughts had remained hidden. Tucked away so skillfully I'd failed to consider myself in danger. Oh, how wrong I was. Like none before he has conquered me better even than Deidre ever did.

I slam into the floorboards shoulder first. Pain shoots from head to toes, to arms and down to fingertips. And how Jiplee and Franciscoa were taken dawns belatedly upon me. I too have failed as a Here-Born citizen and worse, as a Campaigner.

I look up, but my eyes refuse to open. Convulsions rip at my arms and legs. The doff-doff of Peter's boot kicking at sand returns. That and his voice are all I can hear.

"Come on Once-Other," Peter hisses. "Where's your power? Where's your gumption?"

My mouth snaps open. I attempt to cry out vocally, but sand fills it. I gag and spit. Sweat runs down my neck and drips beneath my collar.

"Come on!" he shouts.

I reach out and embrace the Star-of-Hope and a little strength returns. Enough to gain control of my mouth and spit out virtual sand. "Tell me, Peter, what are you doing here?"

He burst out laughing with not a single note of mirth. "You haven't figured that *one* out?" he asks.

I ignore his question and desperate to escape what imprisons me, I switch attention inwards and examine the convulsions that rip at me.

Running inner perception tendrils amongst them, I discover they are actual energy beams. Each has a sting-claw hooked into a muscle. The beams contract and expand snapping my muscles back-n-forth in a painful fashion.

I force an eye open but maintain my inner view of the beams. A quick outward glance confirms my arms and legs twitch in tune with what's inside me. Fully back inside, I play my viewpoint along the convulsions until my inner view vibrates as fast as the energy beams.

I increase the speed of both and the beams blur, lock up and fuse together. Rays of silver light flash, dip and dive, coil around one another and tighten into a ball. The light switches off and all is dark and vibration-free. But deep inside something waits, an energy coiled and dormant.

I reach for it and it explodes violently.

Razor blades of silver energy shoot outwards from the pit of my stomach slicing through everything in their path. I retreat from them and for a beat my heart stops, stutters, then beats on.

Hot, dry air rushes through my nose and mouth as I deliberately breathe in-n-out rapidly. A sliver of inner power returns. But I need something to counter the blades of pain.

Taking bile from the pit of my stomach, I create a ball solid as Rocklands black. The silver blades attack and shatter upon it like crystal glasses carelessly tossed aside.

I open an eye. Darkness reigns but overhead a blue sky stares down at me. Wait. There is a blue sky in place of the ceiling of my tent?

Doff-Doff!

"You okay Once-Other?" Peter asks.

I gulp air, flex my arm and leg muscles, clench my jaws and wiggle my fingers. Sensation and control meander on back. I stand up and stagger blindly towards his voice. My feet stumble in sand and I land on my hands and knees.

He laughs louder, crueler.

Where are my friends? Where's Madsen? Why is no one coming to my aid? I broadcast an emergency call but it dies a mere three feet out.

Wernt grabs my shoulder yanks me to my feet and the blue sky vanishes. I blink rapidly. Shake my head to clear it and glance about to discover a horror. I'm still where I was, in my store standing on the same spot on the floor. Not a single step towards Peter had I taken. Neither had I fallen.

I examine him where he stands a few feet off and find no evidence of what gives him the power to do this. The two likely suspects are that bulge at his armpit and that Desert Driver.

He steps closer and with his face mere fingers away says, "Come now Once-Other. Yeah! Time you quit dancing in circles. Figure it out!" Try as I might I am unable to speak.

"I'll take silence as a no," he says. "Allow me to enlighten you Once-Other. This *is* personal. This *is* about your UWMD. This *is* politics. This *is* justice. This *is* vengeance as well. Yeah!"

He glances down and taps his foot. Sand scrunches gritty and uneven. He looks up at me and adds, "And! This is *not* a vacation, a one-on-one tour nor anything damned else one-two-three all-damn-together!"

I flinch for his voice hurts in both volume and force. I take several deep breaths exercise muscles and refresh my Moment in Time. Peter waits his face landscaped with contempt. I breathe harder and work my muscles faster.

"Once-Other, for the sake of pretense we will continue this tour of ours. Sublime of me?"

I try to speak but cannot.

"It will give you time to figure this out. Check over my questions...they are actually answers."

I dig deeper, gather my Here-Born Foundation together and call upon all my training but to no avail—weakness pervades.

Wernt examines me as the bully inspects the skinny guy with glasses attempting to brave danger and says, "Damn fine challenge...eh Once-Other?"

Again I call for help. Again no one responds. Jiplee's face flashes before me—I turn from it and concentrate on my predicament. For what assails me has got to be impossible—no Earth-Born can control us without sophisticated technical equipment. Could it be that both technology and Desert Drivers are at work here? Or worse!

Has Earth-Born reverse-engineered our Fraggers into a weapon that controls people? Or even worse than that, is this actually Peter only—an Earth-Born? But they don't possess such abilities and that everyone knows.

Stepping out onto sand, I stumble, regain my balance and continue towards the Mall. A faint headwind picks up making forward progress twice as difficult. At every step that whisper of a breeze blows my foot back to sand but I keep trying.

If I make any progress or not, I cannot tell.

Needle storms and sting-flies assault my mind.

Red and black pain blinds me.

I stop and feel around.

A finger touches Hellbent II.

I lean against her front wheel.

So some progress I've made...good!

A few deep breaths later and my vision clears a little.

No one is close by.

Near the Mall and about the Fair a few tourists mingle.

No one looks our way.

Hope appears.

Maureen enters her store, pauses, and waves to me but if she communicated nothing arrived. I try to wave back, but my arms will not move. I send her a message to receive none in return. Wernt's footsteps approach and stop behind me.

I turn and face him to find his eyes aglow with the flames of hell, his smile thin and tight, his fingers flexing and his eyelids twitch and a low growl emanates from his throat.

I hold myself tall and ask, "Who are you Peter Wernt?"

And the no good damn tourist shoves at my chest. I land upon sand and look up just in time to see his hand move. But all to see is a flash-n-blur. Where did such speed come from? His reactions were so sluggish.

Yet with Here-Born speed Peter's hand reaches the bulge I'd been ignoring. And my mistakes are worse than anyone could imagine. It's an underarm holster, not something that is blocking his thoughts from me.

"Why are you pointing that handgun at me?" I ask.

"Get up," he says.

I struggle up and brush sand off my clothes with leaden arms. He points to the crowd with his free hand keeping the gun hidden from view.

"What'd you mean?" I ask.

"Move," he orders and points.

"Why?"

"Move. Don't plan to be back."

"What do you damn think will happen to my pre-owneds?" I demand.

He glances at the crowd and checks the two Poip standing at the edge still searching for the Desert Driver, and it hits me.

Moments ago I had seen no crowd. Damn! I'm in greater peril than I realized. Peter, and perhaps another someone is running control on me. Shutting down my perception, turning on-n-off my senses, inputting thoughts and emotions into me...against my will.

I swallow real hard, take a deep breath, glance at Peter and ask with a tremulous voice, "What you want you damn criminal tourist? What Justice? For what revenge? Are you quite mad? Do you want my money? No! You a pervert wanting to do bad things to me? No! Okay. What do you want then?"

"We're headed for the Rocklands...Highlands. Northwards."

"The Rocklands? Why the Highlands? Why?"

"I'll provide enlightenment when I want to," he declares as though he is a god or something.

"A gun can't kill me. You know? Preservatives-n-all."

But he's not stupid. A gunshot does cause damned enormous quantities of pain and death comes as part of that equation. As if to confirm he stabs the muzzle into my kidneys and I stumble forward gasping in pain.

"Okay. Okay, I'm walking but...your money's used up. Also, I'll be charging double once again. That's for my time and those parts which will go dry—if I'm gone too long."

He caresses my kidneys with the muzzle and hisses a dry throaty chuckle at my ear. "So you charged me double. Neatness eh? Sure....now yeah. When I'm good and ready I'll explain why that won't happen and why I don't give a damn. We have a long journey ahead. Do what I say and nothing else. Yeah. So now. Move it!"

I take a deep breath and note Peter's deodorant is stronger this morning. It hails from EB...*Mild & Manly* it's called. He makes to jab his handgun into my kidneys and I move it working my way through a crowd who apparently remain unaware of our presence, and say "I charge as I like. You pay or you don't." He nods, smiles coldly.

After a few paces, Peter points straight ahead and I almost fall over backward. "What?" I gasp. "Follow him?"

"Get going," he growls.

"The Desert Driver? You're in cahoots with him?"

Wernt points and sneers.

The Desert Driver melts into the crowd.

The Poip continue searching for him.

I consider Peter as though I had gotten his thoughts and much adds up but too late. His attitude towards me was present from the moment we first met, so he had an issue with me from before our meeting each other. Damn! Why did I not realize that?

Yet we've never met. I don't recognize him nor any relative of the same name. What is his issue? He has no visible scars around his neck so that is still the original. "Why are you doing this, Peter? I am innocent of all crimes which may have been committed in an accidental fashion."

"Keep your one-on-one tour up," he growls and scans the crowd. I search it as well, but no one pays us any attention.

Shoppers mill, head for destinations both in and outdoors scuffing sand with each stride they take. I reach out to nearby ones, but no one responds.

Peter steps closer to me. "I said keep talking!" he hisses and slams the muzzle into me again.

"Argh! Damn! Okay! What? Whoa! Let me consider. Okay. During the Great Population Redistribution some three to three-hundred-n-eighty years ago when our ancestors first arrived...argh. I don't feel like talking. Okay, get it out my face."

He pulls the revolver back glances about and spots the Desert Driver. The Desert Driver points beyond the crowd and heads off keeping an eye on the Poip. But they spot him and set off in pursuit.

Curiosity, the kind that so loves to cling to one, rears its questions. "What did I do to make you so mad, Peter? Did you want a pre-owned I didn't offer? No. Okay. A male or perhaps female head so you can be a major talking point back home? No. Have we met before? No. Relative buy the wrong part? Too expensive? No."

He double-takes on something I'd said, examines me and says, "Do the tour Once-Other. Keep your actions natural, or die here now."

"How would that be possible? Remember? Preservatives."

But I'm faking it again—bullets kill. In the same instant, I realize that in continuing this Talking Tour it's harder to reach out to others mind-to-mind.

He nudges my elbow. I glance down. With a subtle fanfare, he pulls a poison-filled injector vial from a pocket and waves it under my nose. "Direct from Earth exclusively for you. A deadly one. You won't be worth a bent nickel as used parts."

"Pre-owned...and you're threatening murder."

"Yeah," he says in a long slow growl. "And I don't give a damn! You'll find out why soon enough. Now get moving! The faster we make the open desert the sooner you get answers."

"What's that mean?" I ask to cover any visible evidence of a sudden realization. He waggles the handgun as though he is a super-human, nods ahead and I set off.

But deep inside where no Here-Born has ever been, I'm thinking. That poison has particular shortcomings that few beyond our world are aware of. Knowing this gives me hope of surviving this...ah...this *whatever* Peter has in mind.

Scant hope indeed.

His handgun slams into my kidneys and knives of pain once again pirouette from kidneys to liver and back again.

"I'm walking, I'm talking," I manage to gasp.

# CHAPTER 47

## OF ONCE-OTHER'S PERSONAL BAGGAGE

Sand crunches beneath our boots as we follow the appearing and disappearing Desert Driver. Pain grips my senses inviting me to lie down and accept unconsciousness. I keep walking though, hoping there will come an opportunity by which to escape.

Each time the Desert Driver appears he glances over his shoulder then vanishes and finally does not reappear. Wernt pulls me to a halt and anxiously scrutinizes the bustling crowd.

Citizens stroll by, Shoppers-to-be hustle urgently; some greet me and nod to Wernt. There is understanding in their eyes. Crier poison can make one look like something half-chewed-n-half-dead that the cat dragged in.

Desperate to communicate circumstances I reflect predicament in my eyes and the gun muzzle rams into me. My legs give, but Peter grabs my arm and holds me up. I bite my lip and suck air as sheets of pain serve up another helping of sliced kidney. Passersby smile sympathetically again assuming Crier poison is the culprit.

The pain ebbs, dissolves and like a black storm cloud the Desert Driver appears before us. He and Wernt nod in agreement. The Desert Driver about-faces and heads back into the crowd. His new pre-owned arm still wrapped and carefully tucked under the remaining one. Wernt nudges me with his elbow and we follow.

The crowd thins. A SandRider cruises by. Wernt sneezes in the dust stirred. The driver, a stranger, ignores us. Ahead, though almost hidden behind a tent with its nose barely visible, is the Desert Driver's destination.

"Just don't ask me to get into his SandMaster," I say. "They are wild and mad trucks. Half alive and half mechanical."

Wernt's gun nozzle threatens at my kidneys. I gulp air in anticipation of greater pain, reconsider and manage to gasp, "Unless of course you need me to."

I head briskly in its direction. With his gun nibbling at me I beg of him, "Please be more respectful of my kidneys."

"Seems like you know some about SandMaster—yeah?" he says sounding amazed.

I offer no response.

"Keep talking. Tell me what you know. Now." He motions with the handgun.

"Okay. Okay! Here's what. I spent much of my career choice while in high school at the SandMaster factory, the aft section manufacturer. My father worked at the assembly plant and often took me to work with him."

The Desert Driver materializes alongside Peter—we halt— they huddle. "He's lying," the Desert Driver says.

"He is?" Wernt hisses.

The Desert Driver grins cruelly and says, "He also worked at the factory after he graduated. He lied by omission but," and he turns to me, "how many...two...three?"

"Three," I enlighten him.

"Yeah. Three years in, he errored-out...to become a teacher. Imagine that!"

"Pray tell Once-Other," Wernt says with faked politeness.

"Go on!" the Desert Driver says, a knowing light in his eyes.

And it appears he knows about that which I don't think on and don't speak of. I pass on troubling my inner self with needless questions of how he knows. But! It is still my all-consuming embarrassment from way back altogether when I first worked on SandMasters—long before prison and working for Hunduranda.

To many others, such occurrences may seem trivial and no-good a reason for a lifelong burden of emotional pain. It is that to me. I'll reveal what he knows just to keep that gun barrel at bay and those rounds within it sleeping. But I do so with great reluctance and under duress and threat of pain alone, might I add. For he is Earth-Born and they are now enemies and any information imparted is valuable information.

"Well okay Wernt," I say. "When one test drives a SandMaster exact procedures must be followed."

"Exact procedures being key all the way down," the Desert Driver adds and rewards me with a dry chuckle.

"So what happened?" Wernt asks his impatience threatening to explode upon my kidneys. They both shuffle closer creating the impression we three are huddled in conversation.

With a heavy heart and for the first time ever I outline how I'd been influenced by the need for a woman's warmth in my bed and the consequences thereof. "Consumed with emotional distress and upset with Deidre, my then future wife but now ex-wife, I blew the rear engine of a SandMaster while testing it."

"What's so bad?" Wernt asks genuinely amazed at a seeming triviality.

"No one ever did before, no one has done so since," the Desert Driver says and laughter fills his eyes with nasty. "But that's not all. Tell him the rest of it."

"Yeah," Peter says. "Go on."

I grind my teeth in protest and consider not doing so.

Wernt raises an eyebrow and waggles his handgun.

As ground kidneys do not augur well for a grand escape, I say, "With testing over and while on the way back I blew the second engine. I called for help, but no one cared to pick me up after I reported what happened.

"I arrived soaked in death-defying sweat, tongue thick with thirst, covered in sand and was errored-out so fast my mouth was still hanging open as I left—severance check in hand.

"Compounding insult upon damn insult I had to pay twenty percent of the costs to repair the engines and never completed my apprenticeship one-two-three altogether.

"Needless to damn say—said payment came out my check. Which check's value was a fraction more than the digital bits used to send it to my Nomadi." And as happened back then I once again die a little inside and fall silent lost in yesteryear and its unfortunate events.

The Desert Driver yanks me back to the here-n-now. "Tell him how come and all," he says.

I hesitate. This Desert Drivers definitely knows more than he should. How? No answers persist. Wernt waves his handgun again and shows me the vial of poison as an exclamation point.

Speaking slowly, I say, "Okay. The night before Deidre and I had argued long-n-hard. Tempers flared when she told me she was pregnant. Damn. Okay. Still rocks me sideways now as then."

I sigh and continue. "Well anyway, altogether. We were in no financial state to support a child. She screamed, cried, howled and sobbed. Desperate for sleep I agreed. She kissed my cheek rolled over and went to sleep. I lay awake most all night ruing that surrender."

"And," the Desert Driver says and laughs as though he'd just thought of the funniest of jokes.

I add what he is referring to. "The next morning she dragged me to the chaplain, and we were married. A glint in her eye she kissed me once and I went off to test a SandMaster in enough turmoil to make errors inevitable."

"And?" the Desert Driver insists.

"Some weeks later she found out she wasn't pregnant after all."

"Oh yeah?" Peter exclaims. "So you weren't and still aren't particularly bright Once-Other. I figure it's just as well we chose you?"

"What you mean Peter?" I ask my voice thick with trepidation.

"All will be revealed. At journey's end—all will be revealed...yeah ah...what you mean—you worked on the aft section?" He shudders his eyes darting to those about as though assassins surround us.

I check the crowd but find no threats present. How does he go from such virulent anger and disdain to shuddering fear in so small an instant? Where-oh-where are his thoughts hidden? How does he block his mind so effectively from me?

Obviously, I'd read Wernt wrong. He is a threat to our campaign. Why else would he be in cahoots with a Desert Driver?

I retreat from internal questions afraid they will open a path to what I am hiding—my only hope. Hope for a life continued beyond this travail despite that there's little chance of it now.

Nevertheless, I am carefully plotting an escape with success hinged upon immaculate timing. Wernt has threatened to inform me altogether—at our northern destination in the Highlands.

I must get that information from him and with as much detail as possible. As important, I must endeavor to live long enough to convey what he reveals to those tasked with monitoring aggression against us and with our defense.

I swallow hard-n-dry and even at my Foundation's protests, I know I cannot trust this Desert Driver despite telling Karrell we must. This one has chosen the path of treason. This Desert Driver's actions are treason—treason compounded by inaction.

If he's been bought it will be the end of his freedom— should I live to tell my tale. So he wants to see me dead as well!

Peter is a different but similar story.

He needs something from me and that he wants to be away from populated areas spells out clearly that I am embarked upon life's final journey. For now, all I can hope for is a moment to communicate the information Wernt will reveal.

I wait until he threatens me again.

He does and I get down to what he demanded. "Well. And ignorance is about here. Okay, Peter. Easy. Two separate vendors build our SandMasters. One for the forward and one for the aft section.

"Here's the joke. If something goes wrong with your SandMaster, you have to dismantle the chassis. It's designed to do that. Now. Once that's completed you send the malfunctioning section to the proper vendor—fore or aft."

Peter nods looking bored, which makes me glance anxiously about only to find many shoppers scurrying to enter the moist cool of the Mall.

A faint breeze stirs and Peter licks at the sweat on his upper lip. The Desert Driver kicks up sand and grins as Peter twists away and covers his nose.

I raise an eyebrow in question. Peter waves any questioning on my part aside, indicates for me to continue and crosses his arms the handgun pointed in my direction.

A thought leaps up, hits me right between the eyes and rocks my head backward.

"What?" Peter demands.

"Nothing much," I say buying time to figure an answer.

"Best come clean Once-Other," Peter says.

The Desert Driver examines us an amused grin in place.

"Just a reaction. I felt my predicament in clarity and altogether."

"Good for you," Peter says and waves me on.

So! He doesn't have total access to me. Chalk up one for Once-Other. I move off thinking hard and fast hoping this Desert Driver will not be able to access my mind.

Now Peter has been digging for information ever since he first arrived. Although most of the data was not of a confidential nature, he did delve into the workings of our society in detail. Great data as far as an invader or wanna be a slave master goes.

Does it point to Peter being a vanguard?

The prelude to an invasion?

His questions in retrospect, have been more pointed than most tourists almost as though planned. Has EB danced a double twist? Are they using our self-defense campaign to garner information with which to target each of our campaigners?

Was Jiplee found this way? Damned be Madsen for his damned evasive attitude and lack of answers. Damn. Here I am in need of everything that he knows. Damn! I must...must live long enough to find out what Wernt hides and convey that to our patriotic defenders.

The handgun nibbles at me.

And so for the Record: What I now do I do for Karrell, even Deidre and Madsen, Maggie, Franciscoa and all fellow citizens.

Goosebumps rush down my chest and back and I sense that this my calling may likely be far greater a responsibility than life itself—my life.

I sally forth my gut a tight knot. "Here's the punchline Peter. Comes a real significant financial pain if the trouble with your SandMaster happens to be amidships. Okay? No? Well. Which end do you send? Don't know? Okay. It's both and you still have to dismantle it."

I look up and the desert colored SandMaster towers over us. Wernt nudges me closer. I smile, grim at old times returned along with the smell of gasoline, grease, and baked steel.

As is true for all SandMasters, the tops of its tires come up twelve fingers above my head. It runs on four wheels each side, eight in all. Between the center two wheels, a five-rung metal ladder provides purchase when stepping up and entering.

A sand-pace full sliding door closes flush, one per side. Both have fixed-closed bulletproof windows. The rear is upright and flat. Two massive rounded air intakes stand proud mounted facing forward on the rear corners of the roof.

The sides of the driver's cab have one square window apiece and a triangular one behind it—the sharp ends pointing rearwards. All bulletproofed as well. The cab itself resembles an old airliner cockpit above a sloping nose. The nose looks sharply down cutting like the prow of a ship.

Above the cab, an enormous oval air intake for engine cooling makes one envision the open jaws of a Great White about to feed. I imagine the mechanism through which the front and rear steering works.

There's a large double steering-box controlled by a steering-wheel within a steering-wheel. Computers enable the four front wheels and four rear wheels to be steered independently or to be locked so as to work in sync.

The hiss of compressed air and the door pops outwards and slides open. "Get in," Wernt snaps and pushes me.

The Desert Driver watches, his face cold, expressionless.

Inside the temperature of a smelting furnace embraces us.

I glance around the standard cabin with two front seats and drab olive painted benches behind. The cabin comes with standard off-white paint.

Despite his fan-n-fit, Wernt gasps for breath. The Desert Driver enters and seats himself in the driver's seat glances over his shoulder at us and hits a switch.

Side ports slide open. A faint breeze stirs the heated interior. The roof sighs and raises twelve fingers above the armored sides. Desert wind rushes in-n-out mixing the choking gasoline fumes and sweltering heat.

I stare at the control panel populated with modern screens surrounded by replicas of WW II gauges. I glance around the rigid steel structure and the barely padded seating surfaces. Memories harken back to better days. I shrug them off and grin at a familiar clunk-clunk then smile broadly.

The Desert Driver is busy pumping the primer-plunger with his wrong hand because his arm on the primer-pump side is missing. He growls under his breath. Well! He should have opted for the Electronic Primer Kit upgrade. But! Having to prime the cylinders means he has been parked a long time. Just to buy an arm?

No. Once-Other's fate is part of the mix.

Wait and see I advise myself.

I glance at Wernt. He gazes unfocused across the distant desertscape. "Wernt," I whisper.

"What?" he says, grumpy at being disturbed.

"You see those toggle switches square in the middle of all the display screens?"

He leans left and right. "No. Where?"

"Directly in front of him," I reply, pointing.

Peter shuffles sideways along the seat. "Oh yeah?" he says.

"Mighty interesting they are. On the far left are the Starters—one for each engine. The four alongside the Starters—left and right Magnetos—two for each engine. The two switches *way* over on the right are Boosters—one for each engine."

"You use Magnetos?" he asks his words dripping with contempt.

"Damn fine modernized and ninety-nine dot nine-nine-nine, five nines reliable—purely electronic systems don't cut it out here. This desert has its heat and sand and other dangers—as we've covered earlier and altogether."

Wernt nods understanding, pinches his nose and says with sincere-insincerity, "I appreciate you're continuing to earn your tour payment, Once-Other. Yeah. Keep going." He wipes his sweaty palms on his suit and lowers the temperature.

"Well okay. You start a SandMaster one engine at a time. First toggle the Starter lever and hold it closed—they are spring loaded. Engage Magnetos one after the other. Then the Boosters and hold as well."

He shakes his head as to rid himself of what I had said and with a hissing snarl says, "Yeah! Real essential information. Thank you oh so much Once-Other."

I slide around his hissing voice and say, "Important for one reason and one reason only." I wait.

His nose twitches. "Okay. What?"

"Requires two hands to start a SandMaster one-two-three and altogether."

The primer plunger goes clunk-clunk, the black leather dressed Desert Driver snarls like a wild animal trapped by shadows and fearful of them. He closes the rear-engine starter-switch and holds. The starter shrieks as though suffering under the throes of roller-bearing dementia.

He closes the magneto switches—one after the other. He leans forward and holds the Booster closed with his chin. I smile at that—he will never let another touch his SandMaster's controls nor ask for help.

The exhaust coughs spewing thick white-blue smoke and bellows a hard continuous roar as all seventeen cylinders come alive. Engine bay cameras show no fires. He keeps to a medium rpm as the rear engine warms. Once idling smoothly, he starts the forward engine, warms it, syncs them and both snarl a double roar at which Wernt jerks and almost leaps out his seat.

With heart suddenly cold my attention snaps onto the sound coming from the exhausts. It is the same whistling note I had heard out in the desert, near home, and around Sand Lake Flats.

So it was Peter dressed as a Nomad doing a deal with this Desert Driver—I should never have dismissed that. But! How did he contact them? We don't have access to Desert Drivers let alone the public from EB. Mid thought, the muzzle of Peter's gun appears beside me.

"The tour," he hisses. "How many times must I tell you to keep talking?"

I continue but behind the talking I am planning with increased urgency. How am I going to inform Madsen and any others what I've figured out about this Peter Wernt? I have no answers right now, but it's time to get Peter's attention off of me as much as possible. "SandMasters have two enormous central computers—," I say.

"What for?" he snaps.

"Hundreds of sensors here Peter. All the graphic indicators around and above the start-up switches are readouts. Two entirely separate computers control everything. One for the rear, one for the front." He lowers the handgun and waves me on.

Relieved, I continue. "There are so many computations going on that at times the two computers argue over where to go."

"Who designed that idiot Here-Born piece of so-called technology?" he asks and the Desert Driver sends him an evil glare that Peter fails to notice.

"Well, I believe the manufacturers, two of them, sure did a damn fine job of disagreeing with one another. EB vendors of course."

"Ah...how expertly you slid that one in." He sniffs the air, glares at the gas tanks and says, "You know gasoline is passé on Earth? Right?"

"Okay," I reply entirely disinterested.

Sudden gunfire erupts.

Wernt hits the floor and curls up into a tight ball.

The Desert Driver and I stare blankly more startled by this than by the gunfire. Peter peeps out from behind his arms and blushes. I note that he didn't let go of his handgun, though. He stands up, brushes himself off, sits down and crosses his arms and stares dead ahead.

The Poip pair charge toward us at a rapid stumble, ankle deep, guns blazing. More shots ricochet off the armored bodywork. One screams by below the raised roof, deflects off the rear gas tank and showers sparks in all directions.

I hold my breath in fearful expectation but thankfully no explosion. Again something new and unpleasant—gunfire without warning.

Due to their weight the Poip make little and far from rapid progress. They keep coming, though, their fire pattern getting more-n-more accurate.

I glance at Wernt. He bites his lip and jerks with each shot fired. At their third shot, he accidentally fires off a round. It ricochets several times whining as though unhappy at not finding a worthwhile target, clangs against the ceiling and screams off across the desert.

The Desert Driver glares at him. I glare at him.

He stands up and waves his handgun in apology. We freeze as the muzzle passes us by. He gulps on realizing where he is aiming, seats himself and points it elsewhere.

The Desert Driver gives him another glare and honors me with one as well. Then he laughs with a peculiar off humor, draws his handgun, fires back at the Poip without any real attempt to hit them, holsters it, tightens his seat-belt and grabs the controls.

"Argh...here we go," Peter mumbles, ejects the spent round, tosses it overboard and loads a fresh one.

The door slides closed with a hiss-n-clunk and seals. The song of two powerful engines easily leap multiple decibels as their voices curve up the rev-counter. We accelerate off and I'm pressed firmly into the seat's backrest, as is Peter.

352

Gasoline splashes in the twin-gas-tanks.

"You hear that splashing?" I ask Peter.

"Yeah. I've been wondering...I mean ah...how much?"

"The sound of three thousand gallons of gasoline."

"The what of what?" he says.

"There's two engines, two gearboxes, twelve gears in each. There's shifting sand and steep dunes. But most important of all—not wanting to run out of gas in the deep desert makes three thousand gallons a minimum requirement."

"How many miles per gallon we talking here?" he asks.

"Well...on average we're talking one to three *gallons* per mile." His mouth drops open like a flytrap.

Lucky for him none are about.

We charge onwards.

Sand swirls over us then trails as speed increases.

Once out of range Poip gunfire ceases.

Within minutes, we break free of Sand Lake Flats headed northwest along the Eastern Freeway.

Now.

This is not a journey I'd planned. Not an outing either.

There is one purpose only, my impending execution.

Despite this, I must keep my mind busy elsewhere.

Tomorrow is where. For therein lies that for which I campaign—our children and theirs.

May I serve them well.

May my life bring peace to Here-Born.

Despite this, I have not surrendered nor given up.

I can but hope I will survive.

# CHAPTER 48

## OF RELATIONSHIPS, WATER CRIERS, ARZERNS AND ROANARK BRAERS

Beneath the SandMaster's wheels, the Freeway unfolds at a steady eighty-five mph. Wind howls in concert with the roar of exhausts. Behind us sand-clouds blow off our wheels blocking out the sun.

After fifty miles of this he swings right and heads up the Northern Freeway. The empty Northern Desert is no place to be—not even in a SandMaster.

There, sheer mountain faces rain rocks to pound at the only road around them—Dead Man's Alley. Getting to the Alley means navigating around rivers of sand with rapids worse than any EB river. Their turbulent flowing sands wind southwards from the mountains, but unlike rivers, one cannot swim in nor sail upon them.

More importantly, we will need to be wary of quicksand so difficult to discern stepping in and vanishing is often the sole method of discovery. Only Desert Drivers and Northerners know the safe route.

Despite the heat, cold shivers race down my spine. I take a deep breath and cast out mental images of impending death.

However, they remain. I sit back and close my eyes.

As the hours elapse my hard seat grows harder.

Next to me, Wernt drips sweat despite his fan-n-fit suit. He lowers the temperature and glances at me. His gaze lingers as that of passersby at a stranger's funeral. The Desert Driver drives onwards his teeth clenched against pain.

The Half-Day-Moon rises heralding midday. Sand beneath our eight wheels switches from soft as the pillow that welcomes one's head to slumber and semi-hardened...not ideal in support of several tons of steel thundering along at high speed.

Significant damage would occur should we hit a ridge of packed sand or worse, a Ball Rock hidden below the surface. Yet he does not slow down by a single mile per hour. Swift flying birds of steel born of shredded gearboxes and engine parts haunt my imaginings.

Despite eight-wheel-drive the SandMaster slides, lurches and once or twice almost tumbles across the rugged terrain. Each time the Desert Driver's expertise brings us back on course. By the same token, I am thrown left-n-right in my seat, not comforting in the least.

I look around the Desert Driver to the steering wheels and find he has his severed arm hooked onto the rim of the outer one and his good hand grips the inner steering wheel. Pain is present in his eyes, anger as well. Nevertheless, he will never give in to either.

His eyes remain on the way ahead. His back and arm muscles bulge as he wrests a path through sand.

Next to me, Wernt's fingers remain tight around the pistol grip. He spies me watching, lets out a long slow breath and eases his hold on the handgun. He has held on to it with white knuckles ever since first pulling it out. How deep does his fear run? So deep he can't relax?

How strong is his commitment to his purpose?

Deadly, I fear.

I shuffle in search of comfort, fail to find any. I sit still as possible and stare at the desertscape in hopes of forgetting an aching posterior. Without warning, we slam into a Crier field, bounce over burrows and in our hard seats.

The Desert Driver holds to a steady speed and steers diagonally across. The warren ends and we storm by a pile of bleached Crier bones, evidence of the pillage and plundering of Arzerns. In corroboration, scattered Arzern skeletons lie in silent witness of a counter attack. Mostly Criers flee Arzerns but when two or more are trapped together, they'll stand and fight.

"Peter," I say, "note that Arzerns have feasted on Criers here." He glances outwards, nods and raises an eyebrow in query.

"Criers and Arzerns conduct the strangest of relationships. I mentioned informing you about this. Well. You know Criers have water but how do Arzerns find water—there's none on the surface?"

"I care deeply about their predicament, Once-Other," he says.

"You wish for this tour to end now?" I ask.

"Yeah. No. Tell me. Where *do* Arzerns get water?"

"From Criers," I reply and he jerks as though struck across the face.

"What? And they eat them?"

"Yes. The old and sick are culled by Arzerns. But Criers provide the sole source of surface water for all animals. Roan-ark Braers as well. To survive Arzerns and Braers, and most all other creatures developed a *safe-call*. It calms Criers and allows the birds to land and drink their fill—they never feed at the same time—and Braers are offered an open pouch as well.

"But, how do sand-snails get water? Those tubes Criers fashion down to water leak a little. That serves sand-snails more than adequately." I smile at him.

"Interesting relationships. You okay Once-Other?"

Poison has come a-visiting. I close my eyes in hopes of less-ening the pain. The muzzle of Wernt's handgun touches my ear—not a feel good moment. I glance sideways to find his fin-ger hooked around the trigger. Each time the SandMaster lurches he involuntarily takes up the slack.

I swallow several gallons of virtual sand for through the head is dead. After several more deep and careful breaths I say, "You can put the gun away. I've nowhere to run."

He blinks and glances about as though seeing our environ-ment for the first time. "Don't lose sight of who is the in-charge here," he says and lowers the revolver.

"Thank you," I reply in honest relief and shuffle about but find no comfort.

After many more hours, Peter abruptly says, "Tell me again how you claim radial engines got here."

"I don't care to—find out for yourself." His gun settles at my temple and with a foreshadowing grin he snicks the ham-mer back.

"Extremely persuasive Peter. So okay! We discovered that a Mister Conway had a collection of radial engines and had pre-served and maintained them in a desert museum, in Arizona-EB. Our engineers quickly determined they were, and still are well suited to our conditions."

"What's this radial thing again," he says.

"Twice is once too much. Use My Answers dot Search Engine...you'll know."

He jabs me three times in the kidneys hissing, "Manners. Manners. Manners. Yeah. Continue!"

In a pain strained voice, I do. "Okay. Just a tour and well paid for—on both sides of that coin. Damn that hurt. Okay. Okay! We found the owner, James Conway the Tenth, unwilling to sell even one of his precious engines despite owning many hundreds of them. Right after he refused to sell them he suffered a sudden heart-stopping moment...and his heart never started again.

"Immediately his son, Thomas Conway the Twenty-first, expressed interest in selling what then became his radial engines. In fact, he called before the funeral and sold them more-or-less, one-two-three all gone. They are troublesome engines, though...very—,"

"Yeah interesting, but let me add a correction...as *I've* already mentioned. Per our historical records Here-Born actually stole and reverse engineered them. You are all thieves, dogs, lowly hyenas in the night."

The Desert Driver glances at Peter then at me, chuckles and says, "What little problems?" and laughs but not because anything seems amusing to him. He floors the accelerator and the SandMaster leaps forward headed ever northwards.

There's nothing I can do about Peter's plans other than to cloud all I'd earlier imparted with useless data and hopefully hide what's important from him.

"I suppose if I must, I must," I say. "He's referring to a Hydro-Static Lock brought on by incorrectly shutting the engines down which can cause oil and fuel to seep past the valves into the lower cylinder's combustion chamber. Neither liquid fuel nor oil compresses. So when starting the engines...things tend to break quite dramatically if you don't first check."

"Stealing wasn't enough," Peter says. "Now you create imaginary problems and blame us for them."

"Perhaps you should tell me what's actually going on Peter."

He ignores that.

In silence, we both stare out across the desert.

I inhale two deep breaths of the clear air and notice I'm enjoying the drive despite that it's my last. The sky seems bluer than ever and even sand glows alive like never before.

Sand grains cling to my clothes, snuggle closer and whisper how much they will miss my presence upon themselves. Off in the distance, dust-devils dance a requiem as the wind sings a dirge in anticipation of the ghost I am to become.

We charge onwards for endless hours of heat, sand, engine roars, transmission howls and seat pounding.

Without warning the Desert Driver swerves off the Freeway dives down a steep bank and heads into virgin desert taxing the suspension across the rough terrain. Wernt and I grab handholds and hang on as we bounce in our seat.

The winds gust harder, the SandMaster shudders like a loose window beset by a hurricane. Beneath our wheels is another Crier warren long since abandoned. We lurch and fantail across it. My elbows threaten to pop from holding on and bouncing about in my seat.

I bend my arms to relieve the stress. Wernt wraps his legs around the bench leg and snarls at me. The Desert Driver struggles as both steering wheels twist in his hand and the crook of arm. His good arm bulges, the injured one shakes and sweat streams down his face. His eyes remain fixed on the way ahead and on instrumentation...a loner fighting the elements and in his element.

The empty warren ends abruptly. Wernt's eyes widen as we plunge downwards into a ravine. "Yeah, how steep can we go and the wheels will still...?" he asks.

I smile and the Desert Driver smiles.

Wernt tries smiling as though we are all making idle chitchat, but it fails to mount properly. He stands up, scans ahead, overhead, backward, east and west while murmuring to himself. Can he be charting a course? Has he the faculties to do that without charts or hardware?

The Desert Driver glances briefly at me—hard, cold and indifferent. He neither sends nor offers to receive a communication. He is making an assessment—that much is clear. Wernt turns to me and the Desert Driver looks back to the control panel.

I ponder on why he checked me over but can find no answer. I take a sip of water. Wernt follows suit. "Refreshing!" he says and chuckles dryly.

The SandMaster drives up a gentle slope and exists the ravine. Ahead the way is rough and broken. The SandMaster roars and heaves across the rocky terrain once again reminding us that it is military built with a single goal in mind—traverse desert as fast and reliably as possible.

The Desert Driver engages eight-wheel-drive, steers northwest, swerves left and races up a steep incline to the top of a high dune. All eight wheels fly free as we crest the edge to land upon a tabletop bouncing like kids on a trampoline—more-or-less. He switches to four-wheel-drive bears hard right and storms onwards.

We travel north without stop. Engines, tires and gearboxes whine-n-drone in concert. A little before nightfall, he pulls to a halt. Brakes screech and sand spurts. "Time for a refill," he says and shuts down the engines by cutting off fuel until they die.

I gaze about and frown. So does Wernt.

Out there the desert is quiet, desolate.

Distant winds blow sand-clouds off the edges of towering dunes. Here-n-there dust-devils dance to the whim of Mother Wind. Simple dances, short and sweet but the music ends and the uncaring winds deny further life.

The SandMaster ticks and groans while hot engines grow warmer before cooling. The loud ticking as they cool, distinct in the silence. I glance upwards. No Arzerns hang in the sky.

Around us not a whisper of wind stirs sand.

The Half-Day-Moon watches all with a straight face.

There is no sign of life about let alone a gas station.

Nothing lives out here.

The door slides open. Air rushes in.

I turn to it with arms spread offering body moisture to gain faint relief from the stifling heat.

Wernt rubs his calves while staring northwards, eyes unfocused. In the distance soar mountains so high they vanish into the blue. Nothing else exists this close to Iron Ridge Mountains.

# CHAPTER 49

## OF GASOLINE STOPS AND ESCAPE OPTIONS

The Desert Driver indicates for us to remain seated, exits, kneels next to the SandMaster and scans the surface as I did when searching for Crier nests.

Wernt grimaces and wipes at the sweat under his collar. In deference to my aching posterior, I disobey and stand up to receive a hard glare from the Desert Drive but nothing else.

I quickly become as interested as Wernt is when the Desert Driver extends a flat sensor screen from his Nomadi on which an arrow blinks. He heads off following the pointing arrowhead. Ten paces on the pointer changes into a dot. He kneels, scoops away sand at his feet to reveal the head of a gasoline pump.

Wernt's mouth drops open, but he quickly covers it by pretending to yawn. "Long days, Once-Other," he says.

I grin inside.

The Desert Driver returns and detaches a Fragger unit from its exterior mounting on the SandMaster. Back at the gas pump, he frags sand exposing a hose coupling. He wipes it down with a super lube-n-clean cloth, connects his Nomadi and enters a code. Heads back and remounts the Fragger. He then unlocks a long, narrow storage compartment on the lower exterior of the SandMaster to expose two flexible six-finger diameter hoses.

He hooks a center coupling in one to the other forming a 'Y'. He connects the single end to the gas pump and the other two to the twin-gas-tanks. He hits the activate button and the hoses snap up to suspend like a frozen two-headed snake quivering in the sunlight.

Pumping gas at full go, it howls like a demented banshee rock star at a make or break audition. One determined to beat out all competition and so become the Head Wailer. Wernt covers his ears but watches with keen interest, taking mental notes while pretending disinterest.

Howling ends.

Minutes on, we again thunder across desert our perpetual dust cloud trailing us. Two hours later we ramp back onto the North Freeway headed northwest.

I doze. Peter dozes.

I awake. Peter awakens.

A high wind awakens and night embraces us with its regular suddenness. The Desert Driver nods towards a compartment. I open it to find several fur coats. I hand one to Peter and slip into the other.

The roof closes.

Another bout of Crier poison hits me.

I wait and after a while it passes.

Peter curls up on his seat and dozes fitfully.

I consider opening the door and jumping overboard, but chances of survival are too slim this far north. Along the same lines, traveling at over a hundred miles an hour speaks of broken bones should I try.

Instead, I curl up, close my eyes and sleep surrounded by the roar of the SandMaster's twins and the howling wind.

Day becomes night, becomes day.

Through each, engines thunder our presence to any-n-all who may be close. I suspect no one is about and any that are would not care. At daybreak on day five he hits the brakes and the SandMaster plows to a halt. I remove the fur coat, stumble out and stretch as joints pop.

The Desert Driver hits a button. A kitchenette opens presenting hot coffee and bagels.

I climb back up and we eat with vigor having not eaten since leaving Sand Lake Flats. I look the kitchenette over and despite its olive green color there's nothing quite like a touch of civility upon the hard aspects of military life.

With coffee and food settled, we set off and travel all day through the billowing sand. Fatigue assaults Wernt and unable to make himself comfortable he sleeps restlessly.

Late that night beneath the Star-of-Hope and the Half-Day-Moon we halt and both engines shut down. Hot metal ticks beneath the whispering wind.

The Desert Driver checks his new arm, nods in satisfaction, stows it, curls up on a floor mat, pulls his fur coat tight and without a word spoken falls asleep.

Peter and I follow suit.

Outside, the ominous rumblings of Thunder River alert us to its closeness and the reality that flowing sand drives its currents, flying rocks are its rapids and $CO_2$—its mists of death.

# CHAPTER 50

## OF A SEVERED ARM AND REVELATIONS

The morning sun awakens and lights up the magnificent eight-mile width of Iron Rock Falls. Over sheer cliffs Wellspring Lake's $CO_2$, sand, and rock tumble. At the foot of the Falls, they churn whirlpools and charge off headed southeast to become Thunder River.

Across the plateau north of Wellspring Lake spread the flat plains of the Highlands, which most all hardy adventurers insist is endless. Iron Ridge Mountain cradles both the Highlands and Wellspring Lake with arms and towering peaks of solid rock.

On Here-Born, we have desert and then we have *desert*.

In the center of Wellspring Lake sand-n-rocks erupt as though there is a volcano below. Rumor says the rocks and sand near Here-Born's core explode upwards like popcorn. A final thrust breaks the surface sending rock and sand into the air then on crashing back into Wellspring Lake they head for the plunge over the falls.

EB's become confused by the name *Wellspring Lake*. It makes them think of a water lake. No, it is a lake of sand and rock and $CO_2$. There is no surface water on Here-Born.

I listen carefully to the thunder of sand and rock and the cacophony seems more distant in the morning light. I glance about and off to the northwest is a vast section of Rocklands.

I shudder. The other two stand a way off looking northwards and talking softly to each other.

We breakfast on croissants and coffee courtesy of this Desert Driver and for me the last meal. Paper cups and plates incinerate without smoke using a handy Fragger.

With the usual roar of engines, we set off headed for the Rocklands. I express my concern over this despite my prior understanding of Peter's purpose. "Do we want to get this close to the Rocklands?"

He smiles a reminder to me.

I nod sage-like to hide a tightening gut and say, "Okay Peter. This is...where...." I leave the rest unsaid and stare off at the Rocklands. To date, I had not seen this great an expanse of rock. Now that I have I confess it is not the mystery I'd imagined. Nothing more than dark brown rock and cacti. I lean forward for a better look.

Above its surface heat waves dance like cobras swaying to a master's flute. Cactus plants imitate shape-shifting aliens enticing the unwary to come closer. As far as one can see dark brown rock bubbles an illusion of boiling chocolate.

We slide, do a skip-n-hop and shudder to a halt.

The Desert Driver cuts the fuel. The engines growl a while longer, cough and die. He sits thinking for a few moments. A movement to my right grabs my attention. I look there and find the muzzle of Wernt's handgun a mere finger away.

He taps my front teeth with the muzzle and smiles, a predator contemplating an opportune meal. With an effort I pull my attention off him, turn away and out across the Rocklands something grabs my attention altogether.

Close to the edge of the Rocklands at the foot of a tall cactus lies a severed arm. One which is now well beyond any value as a pre-owned. I'm unable to fathom what anyone would be doing out here in this life forsaken wilderness.

A sharp chord suddenly strums through me. Vibrations tingle erect the hair down my back and arms—I shiver and fight the urge to glance at the Desert Driver. Something wild just happened and I cannot for the life of me fathom why.

At this late hour, a communication arrived from this no-damn-good-n-treasonous Desert Driver. It impacted like a force ten wind driven straight into my face. I grapple with the fact that he has offered me access to his mind.

Fearing he will withdraw the offer I push caution aside, quickly accept and track what's available through many twists of encryption layered one over the other. Four layers in I find what's he's made available.

The first images are of him sitting around a fire with a few other Desert Drivers. They are talking, but none of the content is available. The next shows him standing near my home peering ahead as though expecting the unexpected.

I reach in deeper...and there they are...those footprints...leading to my house and back out into the desert.

Anticipation leaps ahead predicting Peter Wernt will step into view. But it's that damn odious EB tourist I'd met at the Drinks-n-All some days back, Gordon Odentien! He is still dressed in his pale blue fan-n-fit with mustache still not trimmed.

With a sickening thud, I recall Karrell's description of the EB tourist that came to visit his mother—built like me but a little stockier.

Odentien exactly!

I quiet self and continue inspecting what's offered.

And another familiar face!

Mister Conqueror waits, with something in hand, atop a small dune dressed in his red and black checkered suit. A closer examination shows he has an EB oil can in hand. So he added that oil in my SandRider.

The last image brings me close to gasping involuntarily.

It is the severed arm lying next to the cactus plant but a few sand-paces away from where we are. But it's freshly severed. I focus on the Desert Driver, but his face remains blank. I glance at Wernt; his attention is still focused on the Rocklands.

I engage the Desert Driver's offering again.

In the image, there're no signs of life—just the Rocklands and the severed arm. A blur of rewind and the arm disappears.

Rewind stops on bare rock and plays forward.

The roar of dual engines starts as a faint grumbling and grows louder. After a minute or two a SandMaster races into view and stops, rocking on a taxed suspension. Dust flies as though a sandstorm was under way. Engines die and this Desert Driver climbs out with *both* his arms intact.

He gazes across the Rocklands for a long time face chiseled by the granite hand of hard decision. He takes several deep breaths, squares his shoulders, comes to attention, marches to the Rocklands and steps onto it.

Wisps of smoke rise from the soles of his boots forming clouds like mist adrift above a waterfall. He heads for a cactus. Stops a safe distance off and pauses to look off northwards his chin held high.

He salutes with a crisp, determined motion. Pulls his arm out the leather jacket sleeve, leans over and holds it out. He steps closer and in one blinding flash the cactus slices it off as cleanly as does a butcher's knife swung with skill.

He staggers backward clutching at the stump.

His mouth open he sucks in air.

His loud gasps of pain mixed with animal snarls bark a warning to any who would dare to cross him. He turns and heads back towards the camera, growling as he stumbles his face creased with pain.

He stops and stares into the camera for a few seconds. Blood from the wound drips slower-n-slower as preservatives kick in and go to work. He pulls out a Bondo-Preserve bandage and binds the stump tight.

He takes several slow breaths his focus on sand at his feet. He looks up and stares into camera, eyes hard, face expressionless. The corners of his mouth twitch a smile that does not reflect in his eyes. He nods a confirmation of something I do not get and steps around the camera.

It swivels to follow him.

Back at his SandMaster he boards, the door hisses closed, dust flies and access ends.

And I had noted his arm was severed below the elbow. That left length enough to grasp and hold the outer steering wheel of a SandMaster. Hmm?

"My name is Mawlendor Ozerken of Plaeth City, Far North Highlands," he says.

And I'm stunned almost comatose—we never reveal an actual name!

For the life of me, I cannot fathom why he provided those thoughts let alone his name. I examine him in detail, but his face remains carved in stone. A flash of motion to my right.

Peter slams his handgun into my kidneys and pain explodes from kidneys up into my head and down to my toes.

"Have you gone deaf?" he screams. "I said get out!"

Flecks of white foam spray out his mouth onto my shoulder. I brush them off and exit doubled over.

He follows handgun at my spine.

I stop. He stops.

The hammer clicks back.

The distant horizon suddenly seems close. I sense grains of sand drifting over its edge. A little beyond it sand-snails dance their mating shuffle under the critical scrutiny of an all-female audience. Sand brushes like sandpaper beneath them. Periscope eyes sway seductively.

The wind dislodges the rim of the horizon and sand cascades covering the sand-snails. For a moment, the surface remains smooth, intact, and to all intents and purposes virgin.

Periscope eyes pop up and glance about. A distant roar approaches. I smile, my mind has come alive for my body is about to die. I ponder on what Peter thinks I am guilty of, but nothing whispers back to me. I turn to him, but that roar now rends the silence asunder.

Another SandMaster barrels in with brake-pads screaming in protest. A cloud of dust spews over us. Squeaks, roars, and groans fill my senses as the dust-cloud settles. The door opens and hope takes a fatal shot between the eyes.

Gordon Odentien and another Desert Driver step out. Odentien still wears his beach and ocean fan-n-fit while the Desert Driver is in leather much the same as Ozerken.

"You should have called me," Odentien says doing a Nomadi with thumb and finger. He snickers reaches back inside, grabs a hold of something, yanks hard and tosses what appears to be a large burlap sack to sand.

In the next instant, I am colder and more heartbroken than I have ever been. Pain beyond the wounds of war cut through my heart. Worse, a deeper sorrow punches with fists carved out of Rocklands black rock. These blows are for Maggie and my Toxin Center nurse, not for me.

Nevertheless, I am relieved neither of them is here. If Maggie were she would seek revenge and attack without consideration—and in the next instant be dead herself.

Franciscoa flies out the door and lands on sand in a limp heap his head at an impossible angle. I stare at his body and my heartache becomes anger, cold and vengeful anger.

But I paint a calm upon my face and turn to them ignoring Wernt's muttered warning and his handgun now back at my spine. Odentien and the other Desert Driver tense up, hands drift towards holsters.

The newly arrived Desert Driver steps away from Odentien his eyes glued on me. I look him over. He stands tall and thin with close-set eyes in a face as cold as Ozerken's. His nose is long and thin like Peter's.

After a brief internal struggle, I turn my back on them and stare across the desert.

The crunch of footsteps in sand moving closer to each other. I glance over my shoulder and find them at Ozerken's SandMaster deep in conversation. From out the blue, the new Desert Driver says directly to me, "I'm Pe'truss Wagenaara."

I'm speechless at another such revelation.

I inspect him again, but his face remains blank with nothing further communicated. Why do they want me to know their names? That violates a long-standing history.

We began hiding our real names when mind-to-mind communication spread throughout Here-Born. We quickly found that when one's real name became known others were able to access our thoughts and minds without permission even when we blocked them. But only if they possessed the required skills.

Nowadays, once someone knows your real name he or she can also gain access to the Here-Born citizen's database. It contains all our personal information.

In view of this and because I campaign you will not find my real name nor even that of Once-Other written nor advertised upon my store. Without an introduction, no one even knows to call me Once-Other.

And it hits me.

Ozerken had called me Once-Other when he was in my store—when he threatened that he would never forget my name. It's not advertised on my tent walls. Neither had I told him so Peter must have.

Now, these two Desert Drivers have given me their names, their real ones. This speaks of trust, giving someone a true name. I assume they trust that I will soon be very dead. Do they want me to know whom my co-executioners are? I presume future viewers and readers understand that my participation in this recording my end abruptly—so be prepared.

I look up from my thoughts as louder chatter, in which I still cannot discern any words passes between them. They fall silent and as one they nod yes, turn to look at me and their combined attention hits like a flying rock.

I placate my racing heart with false promises of a future, glance at the sad state of Franciscoa and grit my teeth.

They all remain where they are except for Peter. He marches towards me an executioner for whom grim duty calls.

My mouth locks up tight as with startling suddenness his eyes blaze and his face contorts with rage. He rushes in and hits me across the cheek with his handgun.

A bright flash of lightning, a thud and darkness swoops inwards, but I manage to remain standing. I wipe a sleeve across the blood running down my lips and attempt to find Peter from within the darkness, but too much of my attention remains fixed on the large gash in my face.

I raise a hand to it and my blood is warm upon it.

I sense that I am swaying, going down.

I fight it, more afraid of falling down than of taking another hit.

I fear as one fears the predatory beast when helpless. Pleas garner no sympathy from the hunter. Instead, it advertises here lies a meal, freshly maimed, awaiting consumption.

During a long struggle, which even I realize takes but moments, I manage to drag my attention from my face and look outwards but darkness persists.

I whisper promises of sunsets never before seen. One at a time my eyes open and I see. But my legs give and I sink to my knees and from there I ask the one and only question that comes to mind. "Why have you hit me with that gun of yours?"

Like never before his nose twitches in harmony with his mouth, his eyes, and even his ears. Several times he attempts to speak, but no words disturb the air.

What he does eventually spit-n-snarl ventures beyond insane—even for him. "You killed my son, Once-Other. For that, you will die a painful, agonizing death."

Okay and be damned one-n-all! Hell hath no fury like a lunatic consumed by indignant outrage at being wronged—no matter how delusional. What nightmarish mental acrobatics are required to invoke such a wild and unfounded accusation?

He, a complete stranger until but a few days ago has no justification for this. I gather all of Once-Other, firm up my resolve, my campaign techniques, my Foundation and express them.

"No. I tell you no. I did not kill your son. In fact, I have never killed anyone. I have never even seen your son. Has your child come to Here-Born? No! There you go. No way could I have killed him. I have never left Here-Born. Period."

"You sold C-POP, Once-Other. Oh yeah. Don't shake your head *no*. Yeah! You sold C-POP. *That's Criminal Pre-Owned Parts*! And that violent criminal pre-owned part came from a known killer. A killer sent by your sale to Earth. You are guilty and you will die."

At last an explanation of his crazed fascination with C-POP.

I make to stand, but he kicks me in the chest. Odentien, Ozerken and Pe'truss draw their weapons fan out and cover me. I settle back, stare up at Wernt and as quietly as I can inform him of the correct details.

"No one here believes pre-owned parts can be violently criminal by themselves. That's as stupid as believing a gun can kill on its own. But, you can leave one on a table for all time and it will do nothing but collect dust—if no one touches it."

He smiles but not because he is happy. "Guns are banned on Earth as it should be," he declares. "Would you be in this predicament if that were true here?"

I elect not to enlighten him of the obvious being that it is *yes*. I would still be here for he is a criminal and repressive gun laws only rob the honest of a means of self-defense while criminals do not obtain firearms legally.

"Tell me. How can one pre-owned arm with a hand attached be criminal all by itself? How in all of Here-Born's heavens, rock and sand can you expect me to believe that monkey of a lie?"

He wags a finger in my face. "Once-Other, you sold my wife the arm of a violent criminal. My wife took the worthless thing to her hotel. There she removed her damaged and useless one—with help of course. She then attached a used no yeah...a no good pre-owned arm bought from you. From you! She then came home to LA, California, Earth."

He struggles to breathe. I indicate for him to take his time, but he gets right back to it. "She awoke one morning from what she thought was a good night's sleep. Sh...she found...during the night her new arm and hand had strangled our beloved son to death."

And a crushing weight releases its hold upon me.

And I understand his reaction to my question about a son.

He forces the barrel of his handgun into my mouth.

I note how unpleasant metal tastes.

"You will die out here Once-Other."

Only an EB Foundation could be this confused and ill-informed. How do they survive over there?

Far off in the distant reaches of my mind I am puzzled over and above all the pain, the threats and my pending death. Puzzled over why I have no recorded sale to a Wernt. Either Peter continues to lie or something is further amiss.

In self-defense, I respond to his integrity mutilating accusation after extracting the barrel from my mouth and pushing it aside, much to his amusement. "What you in fact mean is that your criminal wife...okay, okay...I apologize. Still. Your wife killed him. It cannot be the arm. Your wife did. It's like you and that gun you're pointing. It cannot shoot until you aim it or make a no-good-damn-error while asleep in your head, as you've already done and pull the trigger."

"Once-Other!" he snarls.

At this late and fateful hour, Once-Other continues his campaign. "Wait. Wait. That is why on Here-Born you must train well to drive a SandMaster—with no license required. But to bear arms is a Right, training is also needed but no license nor permit required to buy, to own or to carry—open or concealed."

No response is forthcoming from Wernt the Lunatic.

He steps back and indicates for me to stand.

Being obliging I stand up, dust myself off and look at him.

What he now says is worse than all his previous accusations.

"Nice try Once-Other but no coconut.

"You see, the Peoples Court 90213 found that arm guilty of murder...not my wife. The arm is guilty of murder. And. I've been given the authority to execute you as the sales vendor and therefore, the source of the crime."

"What kind of mad criminal court can find such a stupid thing?" I ask.

One damn loud thunderclap rips apart the desert air.

Wernt's no good handgun spits fire-n-ball.

At first it appears he missed from three feet away.

Then, looking down I note my blood leaking out onto sand, not a feel good scenario. Preservatives kick alive a second time and clotting prevents further rapid bleeding.

Next, the pain finds me, joins that from my face and hurts more-n-more and all over and altogether. I manage to glare up at him. It is clear to me that he is mad inside his head and inside his heart. I cannot grasp how he can think I killed his son when even after being shot I continue shaking my head in denial.

Ozerken, holsters his handgun, climbs into his SandMaster, exits with his pre-owned arm in hand, clambers on top, sits on the raised roof and sets to attaching it.

Wernt walks a circle around me, expels the used cartridge, loads a fresh round, holsters his revolver and says, "Your moment of enlightenment Once-Other. Yeah. One-two-three. *You people* are so odd. Yeah. Quaint. You ready for this?"

"What if I prefer to pass?"

"Isn't he the wise one now? No! Not even if horses were pigs and wishes could fly." I frown at such a meaningless idiom.

He notices what Ozerken is doing, loses interest in me but points a finger saying I should remain where I am, walks over and joins them.

Gordon and Pe'truss put their weapons away, lean on Ozerken's SandMaster, light cigarettes and puff away with deep satisfaction. It strikes me just how casual Desert Drivers can be around gasoline vapor. An open flame is not recommended within fifty feet of a SandMaster. I dismiss them as pain sends me reminders of itself.

I force sand into my chest wound clenching my teeth as I do. I am hoping sand will control the bleeding further and allow me the time in which to recover. Although preservatives result in immediate clotting and slower bleeding, movement induces normal wound bleeding once again.

There's nothing I can do about the pain other than to deal with it. Obviously, I'm to die out here. But if I can get a little more campaigning done I'm good—not with death but with duty. What would Madsen say if he were here?

"That's round-n-about typical Once-Other. Trouble parades natural an' all."

Many times I've thought of why he and I are...were friends when he's so prone to criticize. Perhaps there is no answer other than friends are friends.

Atop the SandMaster Ozerken bites his lip, sprays a saline solution on his arm stump and taking a sterile cloth from his kit dabs it dry. He opens the container of Bondo-stick-on, applies some to the wound, some to his new arm and rests a few moments breathing hard through his mouth.

Wernt paces while the other two smoke. He halts and all watch as Ozerken joins the pre-owned to his stump. After holding them together for some minutes, he nods to Pe'truss who steps up and injects Bondo-stick-on into the original arm.

And quad-mitosis kicks alive.

His new arm across his knees, Ozerken gazes out across the desert and Rocklands his face expressionless, but each time quad-mitosis kicks he grimaces. I know the pain of pre-owned parts converting as well as any being somewhat composed of such myself.

And in that fashion I came to choose the name of Once-Other for I was once *an-other* person, as I've already mentioned.

And now finally, Wernt experiences how Bondo-stick-on works, how an arm changes right before one's astonishment— much like watching a child grow but in an accelerated fashion.

Five minutes later the pre-owned has attached well enough that the fingers become a trifle unruly. Ozerken holds them still and glances deadpan at me.

Wernt walks back, stops five feet away and says, "Let me repeat my question to you. Who were you before?"

I explain to him in beautifully simple words that I had bought this pre-owneds business around two years ago and that I'm primarily put together with pre-owneds.

"Once-Other!" he snarls.

"Note my joints. My arms...look...ever so different. The scar on my neck...."

"Once-Other—stop!" he says.

"Perhaps your wife bought her arm from the previous owner or a different vendor, altogether. Right?"

Another violent thunderclap, greater pain slams into me and darkness descends. Nevertheless, I hear those no good Desert Drivers laughing and Wernt's footsteps crunching in sand as he walks away.

And a dark warmth wraps its embrace around me.

Out where I can no longer see, Wernt's footsteps stop. "You've earned your pay Ozerken. Pe'truss. Let's talk bonuses."

Now taking all of everything into consideration such as that Earth-Born travesty of a curriculum that sent me to prison counts as one, that ex-wife as two and this Wernt as three.

One-two-three in a row right here, right now.

We all know that bad-on-bad always comes one-two-three in a row. Which is another reason we say it so often.

# CHAPTER 51

## OF RELIANCE ON OLD SKILLS, REALIZATIONS AND NEATNESS

When unconscious, time is hard to track as it tends to change values. In some moments, it is longer but during others shorter than sixty seconds per minute. It is similar to dreams where some are short some are forever long. Yet, both are pretty much the same length. One dream expands time, another compresses it.

After several days or seconds, or minutes pass a very unpleasant but distant noise erupts, draws closer, grows louder and forces my eyes open. And my eyes see and time resumes its regular value revealing only minutes had ticked on by.

I lie upon sand too close to the Rocklands for comfort. Ozerken and company are as they were. However, that awful sound is nearer and around its edges I can hear footsteps in sand. A shadow falls across me.

Looking up I find Wernt headed my way and what an awe-inspiring sight to behold. The Crazy Criminal Tourist has flipped over the edge—altogether.

He suddenly howls in a maniac's high-pitched wail and curses and swears most foul. Abruptly he stops up dead in his tracks, shudders, turns into a statue carved from rock and his eyes roll over white. Yellow foam froths out his mouth, perhaps it's a feeble attempt to cleanse the soul within. Doubtful.

He walks a circle shaking as a cactus beset by violent winds and malevolent earthquakes, falls to his knees and onto his side and twitches round-n-round, up-n-down and over-n-under until sand all but covers him. His fingers do a final twitch and stop. Well, too-damn-bad is about as much as I care.

Pe'truss goes over and checks his pulse, pats his cheek and walks back to the SandMaster shrugging his shoulders. I struggle to one knee and spit my contempt upon sand. All three of them laugh with wild and evil merriment.

May they all spit sand forever!

With more bravado than any ability to carry through, I declare, "You will regret the harm done to Franciscoa and to me. You two Desert Drivers, you should know better. You will find no easy return from treason. A life sentence awaits you both. And...."

Ozerken holds his finger up and I involuntarily stop speaking. "Think through our time together Once-Other—think it through," he says and raises an eyebrow, which oddly enough conveys encouragement.

Pe'truss nods yes—it appears to encourage as well.

Gordon Odentien, puzzled by all this glances back-n-forth between them. The two Desert Drivers ignore him.

More fascinated by the pre-owned arm than my predicament or these Desert Driver's odd words, Odentien loses interest in Peter and me and watches the new arm growing and healing.

Ozerken waves Pe'truss over and indicates the battery pack with a nod. Pe'truss attaches the electrodes and flips a red switch. The arm jerks and dances. He cuts the power and Ozerken waggles his new fingers. Odentien gapes in astonishment.

"Excellent product Once-Other," Ozerken says. "Top quality."

"Thank you," I reply and glare accusations.

They trumpet a short burst of hard laughter.

"Makes no damn difference," Pe'truss informs one-n-all.

A small movement captures our attention.

We look to where Wernt lies and his legs twitch once again. Next his fingers twitch, his head jiggles and the mad tourist suddenly leaps up and lands on his feet as though he'd just arrived by falling out the sky.

Wild-on-wild blaze the fires of his eyes and his words...oh how terribly he swears. But most grievously he swears as he comes at me all snarling and spitting foam with eyes that do terrifying things.

They roll this way-n-that-way, n-up-n-down. His face glows red and his tongue turns purple and his skin sprouts big black blotches and...well...more-or-less.

I struggle to my feet, stand tall but the raving mad tourist fires into my chest a third time. I land on my back. This compounds the earlier bad-on-bad with a second one-two-three but with bullets alone.

With no time to dwell on it, I look up into the blinding sun. The mad tourist looms into view and snarls, "Admit you are guilty of murder in the First Dot One."

"I'll not admit to something I don't understand and didn't do."

"Then die some more," he says. Taps my cheek with the hot gun barrel, presses the muzzle against my forehead and leans in. "You have been an interesting campaign item Once-Other. Oh yeah? Surprised? Yeah. We're running a campaign too. Duh. Didn't realize that did you?"

I pull mind and emotions together, cut past pain and all of everything else and ask, "How do you keep your thoughts from me Wernt?"

He bursts out laughing, collects himself and says, "Didn't I tell you to look at our time together. Did you? Yeah. Nooo!" He leans in closer. "Here's a little clue for you. Think of a number."

"Two, for the two of us?" I guess.

"No."

"Three or maybe four for you two and those two?"

"No. How sadly lacking you are, Once-Other. How terribly depressing an empty mind must be. Sigh." And he smiles as though touched by my shortcomings.

But I know the number!

It answers a question I've had about Peter for some time but which I had forgotten. It drifted up from hiding amongst the hazy mists of my poison-infested mind as soon as he mentioned it.

When he and I were at the Mall of Sand Lake Flats he had said something and due to all the adventures with Criers and Peter the Sprinter—it slithered into hiding. But now I've found it and I understand what, if not who, Wernt is. But worst of all...he's played me all this time. He even faked slow reactions.

The answer discloses as well how he has been able to control me and hide his thoughts. Danger from EB has once again ratcheted up several notches. Some of those on Earth-Born have developed the skills and powers we have and are using these to take control of we campaigners and politicians as well, it would seem.

That is what happened to Jiplee, to Franciscoa and to me. Who knows how many of us there are in the desert as dead as all can be. Damned be Madsen for withholding information from me.

On the other side, like most all Here-Born's, I was sure that EB's don't have and would never have anything near our mind-to-mind skills. Clearly, some of them are well ahead of us.

What Peter had said was by all accounts rational, appropriate and worst of all, the casual conversation of a typical tourist. And so I lost sight of it. My failure to assign any significance to his words kept them hidden.

How simple what he said was.

How cunning if planned.

How troubling, such cunning is.

And all he'd said was, "What are the Missing Twelve?"

How deadly a question.

Twelve. Twelve lost children...and Peter is one.

And Gordon is two.

Mister Conqueror in his red-n-black checkered suit is three.

The Lady is four.

That leaves another eight somewhere.

It's been thirty-some years since they vanished. Thirty long years during which Earth-Born's plotters raised twelve Here-Born infants and molded them into weapons against their own people.

Now I understand why I cannot get Wernt's thoughts and how he was able to dig into my mind searching for that one thing they so desperately seek—Here-Born's UWMD.

Without our Foundation, he knows nothing of our Ultimate Weapon of Mass Destruction. And that's their campaign—finding our UWMD not just we campaigners.

No one had thought to search Earth-Born for the Twelve.

Wait! Perhaps then...I had sold his wife an arm.

Why then are there no records of such a sale?

Straight from the all-encompassing beige and orange sand of our desert the answer hits me right between the eyes. I stagger backward despite being prone and it takes several moments to recover before I can speak.

"Peter Wernt? An interesting name Peter."

He smiles with joyous evil.

"Yeah?" he says.

I search his face but nothing twitches.

I say his name but emphasize the last one differently.

"It appears that Peter *Weren't* your name—Peter Wernt. No background to be found under that name."

"Ah. The campaigner, the vendor of pre-owned, once a Teacher of Children...has awoken."

"I have no record of a sale to a Mrs. Wernt either. What's your real name Peter?"

"Let's be fair here. You haven't told me yours. I won't tell you mine."

We look at each other for a long time with a repulsive mixture of comradeship and enmity while our faces remain devoid of such. I try to see into his mind, but it's still blank and at best foggy. But now those images I'd glimpsed earlier make sense.

"You were taken Peter...whatever your name. From sand, you were removed. You arrived upon Earth-Born in winter.

Snow was falling. Later you lived in a tropical paradise at or near the beach."

"Yeah?" he says.

I nod towards the SandMaster.

"That no good Odentien's air-conditioned suit was purchased in a tropical climate. Yours, being plain-n-all, in a climate with winter snow. Am I right?"

"Yeah," he whispers and pats my cheek.

"What is your name Wernt?"

"Wouldn't you love to know?" he gloats.

"I'll never forget your face Once-Other." Ozerken had said when he bought his new arm. I'd felt faint at the time and deciding the giddiness was physical promised myself I'd see a doctor, but that wasn't it. Ozerken only has my current name, no doubt told to him by Peter.

Therefore, Peter attacked me—not Ozerken.

Peter must know my real name.

He has also slowed my heart and suffocated me.

But from our side of Neatness, we of Here-Born have found doing bad has a steep price. Soon one loses his or her skills. There's many a fugitive out in the wild desert lost to us and mind-to-mind.

But not so Wernt.

I must find a way to pass this information on to others.

Damn! I've landed here through my own failure to perceive what is.

How terrible to one proud of observing what he sees and to have missed all this. Without access to his thoughts, I've made terrible mistakes. How limiting such reliance upon our single talent has been.

We cannot afford to continue like this—obviously our strength has been turned into a weakness. But what if I had met

Peter's wife? Then he would have no need of my real name just to target me as a campaigner.

Is he so powerful he can do what he has done without knowing my actual name? How terrifying a thought!

Damn! Too much doubt and uncertainty prevail.

Perhaps I did so damned excellent a job with his wife that she spoke to him of our Rights-n-all. If so, that allowed him to target me as a campaigner. And from me he hopes to get other names and target them.

Not all tour guides are campaigners so EB must find a method of sorting us. Peter is likely hunting from one to the next and our criminal politicians then look up our real names for him in the database, as they possibly did mine.

Those Database Records exist from birth on forward. They also provide the dividing line between criminal and honest citizen with the required shades of gray between. This includes any journey into and out of those classifications.

The only data not in the database are the details of our Here-Born campaigners. Keeping those records would be too risky once the devious deeds of our politicians had been unearthed.

Therefore, Peter wants into my mind and there to find both our UWMD and other campaigners. However, with me he has failed to get in that deeply. Chalk up one for Once-Other.

But I fear we have underestimated what they are doing.

How much worse than we've realized...our politician's betrayals?

# CHAPTER 52

## OF THE ASSIGNMENT OF RIGHTS AND INTERNAL CONFLICTS

My situation seems hopeless, but there is one thing that gives me hope. Though it is unlikely to change anything at this time, perhaps some good may come of it when I am gone. But with no time to gentle in as I should, I have time alone for a full-on frontal assault.

"Peter...many of our Religions believe the real self is a being, a spirit if you like and that we're not only the body we're living in. Today, most of your side of Mankind is no longer aware of such a separation. I'm not talking the kind of spirit like in stories, which goes bump in the night."

"Oh shut-up Once-Other," he groans.

Needless to say...I don't.

"With this idea in place we of Here-Born added unique concepts to our Bill of Rights. On Here-Born, all Rights are assigned to the Individual, the spiritual being within—not only to the physical being."

"I don't give a damn what you believe. Dead is dead. Spare me the BS."

"Peter. It's the first time in human history where politically, Rights are assigned in such a way."

He touches my forehead with the muzzle of his handgun. "A bullet through the head ends all Rights," he whispers.

I steel myself for one last attempt. "I understand these ideas seem insane and incomprehensible to one such as you."

He grinds the muzzle into my ear and hisses, "Your campaign's done. Your life is done. So, take what's left of it and enjoy the sun and the sand."

An idea sneaks up on me. Yes—I can still do something about this Peter Wernt. I change gears and go after what is so horrifically wrong with him. "You know what?" I say.

"No. But you're going to tell me no matter...yeah?"

"Listen carefully," I say as a teacher does to his favored and most talented student.

He leans in with exaggerated interest. "Yeah?"

"It appears to me...that you the Here-Born is in conflict with you the Earth-Born raised. So comes to be your *affliction*. All that twitching, the eye rolling, those spasms and that terrible tearing apart going on within he who isn't Peter Wernt."

"Sure going to be a pleasure executing you," he whispers voice thick with hate.

"Thank you for confirming it, Peter," I reply with grim satisfaction.

I examine him in detail and find the seed planted and there with luck, it will grow until his Here-Born side wins out. On the other hand, will the blood of his past deeds well up above his elbows and choke decency's manifestation? Only the future will tell which he chooses.

He strokes his handgun a little too fondly and says, "You Once-Other were chosen...he, Franciscoa, came to us voluntarily advertising his connections. He was tougher than he looks and, unfortunately, Gordon, in the heat of the moment, lost sight of how much power...."

He crooks his arm makes a sudden jerk-n-tighten motion and says, "Snap! And Franciscoa was no longer with us and none of us had a clue on how to fix a broken neck with a used part. Yeah. Okay. I got the BS name. He went without providing us a single lead...you following me...the names of other campaigners...I need them. Like the one we sniffed out and left in the desert. You sure found her remains faster than anticipated."

"We campaign in the hope you'll go home whatever-your-name-is," I reply and my heart thuds heavy at evidence of Jiplee's final moments.

"Oh spare me—we know better," Peter snaps back. "We chose you before any mission personnel was brought on board. You did a *damn fine* job on my wife Once-Other—dead giveaway. All her talk about this Right and that one, on and on she went. Too tiresome. So you're involved but we're careful in what we're doing. Don't want to eliminate anyone without just cause—go figure how much that would reduce the potential workforce. Get me?"

"Is that more of your insane *justice*?" I ask.

"Oh no. That arm did kill. You are subject to the Authority of a Writ of Execution. Don't misunderstand me here."

My teeth grind. "You should have figured it out for yourself. A Here-Born cannot co-exist within an Earth-Born raised *and* wage war upon us."

He waves it off. "Whatever! What about Madsen? Maggie? Of course, Franciscoa's involvement was evident. Any others you care to reveal?"

"What are you on about Peter?"

"Jenk? Deidre? *Karrell*?"

My heart stops beating for several moments as I compose my inner self and wait.

He grins. "Deidre was more than helpful. She doesn't like you very much! We had to stop her babbling on and passing us info...just to get away."

"She likes but one person," I say.

"And that is?" he asks.

"Herself," I growl.

Chuckling he nods agreement. "So Once-Other let me say this right. You've been informed justice enters in here as well as revenge for what you did to my son. Shut up! You've also been told it's your and our campaign locking horns here. Now I'll show you this."

He briefly reveals his Nomadi screen that displays, *Writ of Execution*. He leans closer and reads.

"Once-Other is found guilty of Murder in the First Dot One Degree. He is a vendor of pre-owned parts, a resident of Here-Born and his previous identity is unknown. Good so far? Yeah. Now! Get this.

"This Court proved murder in the First Dot One Degree. We define Murder in the First Dot One Degree as knowingly selling a C-POP resulting in an unnatural death. A Writ of Execution is granted *to me of course*. Legal Authority empowers *me of course* to process this Writ of Execution upon the subject: Once-Other of Here-Born.

"This Writ may not be transferred, used as a Negotiable nor sold. Let it be known that unnecessary cruelty is not recommended. The manner of, forms of, actions of, are open to the wishes of the Executor. Think of this as part of my campaign. Aren't we Earth-Born sublime?"

"Quite mad Wernt," I reply.

He sets his Nomadi to record and says, "Maybe we can come to a compromise here...if you'll just admit to selling my wife a C-POP, Criminal pre-owned part."

"Never going to happen," I say, choosing my words with care so they cannot be edited to provide the answer he is looking for.

"We'll see. We'll see."

He works the settings.

How easy it will be for them to twist the sale of a pre-owned part into the deliberate sale of criminal parts.

And then?

Turn that into a terrorist attack?

And then?

Start Earth-Born's war machine in so-called defense.

But! On a personal level, Peter is very mistaken. I will not confess to something I did not do. Not even to save my life.

If I do so I will lose all Neatness and Honor, never to be regained—not even in death. For when I am dead my loss will transfer to Karrell and saddle future generations with dishonor until a son or daughter rises to undo it.

Still, I am in two minds about dying.

First off, I'll miss friends and family very much and right now I struggle not to think of them. Second, the critical information I have learned needs be passed on. Nevertheless, death will answer one question—am I or am I not wholly a spirit glued to the body until death do us part? I hope to confirm this one way or the other despite that dying is not an ideal test bed.

Pain hits, my throat constricts and I fight for breath.

Wernt glances dead-eyed at me and continues to work his Nomadi.

Done he stretches, sighs and says, "A couple of deep breaths Once-Other. In and out and in and out. Feeling better? Yeah.

Moving on. Writ of Property is assigned to—*me of course*. I've checked and you are the sole owner of your store. Right?"

I should have figured it out. How often had Peter examined me and mine as though he was the owner, not I? It was not a pending sale as I had thought but pending theft.

"You won't be able to buy out a partner and take over. Yes, I am the sole owner." Not that it does me any good in death.

"Thank you kindly Once-Other," he says.

I glance across to the SandMasters, but none of the others pays us any mind.

Peter works his Nomadi humming to himself, spares me a glare, a cold smile and an insulting wink. His fingers blur as they dance across the keypad. Calculations end, he looks me in the eye for several moments, shows the screen to me long enough to read *Writ of Property* and the same EB Court number.

His voice a soft hiss drifting across sand, he reads, "The following Properties are awarded *to me of course*. One pre-owned parts business. All inventory and equipment. All banking accounts and deposits. All other commercial and personal assets. This includes one home located northeast of Sand Lake Flats, Newfound Sand Flats, Here-Born. All vehicles, all contents, other items, and equipment are included. All business and personal debts are dissolved upon Transfer of Ownership."

He looks up smiles and says, "Well Once-Other that's one-two-three. Right?"

"No," I reply.

"Oh?" he says, "You don't get what I've read? Okay. Here's why and for your edification. One. All your business and personal properties are mine. Two your life is mine and three...."

"And three?" I ask stunned and breathless for I have not yet heard the third one.

"Three I'll enjoy knowing for as long as I live. You will die twice out here Once-Other."

He stands, chuckles and heads to the SandMaster. They huddle whispering. Several times one or the other glances my way then dives back into the conversation. After several minutes of intense conversations their talking ends.

They all look at me and nod in group agreement.

Wernt returns carrying a rope. "We're taking you up to the Highlands as I promised, but in the morning. This is to ensure you do not make off during the night. I've offered them a bonus if you live till then. So if you have a religion now's the time to pray. Don't take this personally—I need some time...prior to the final act. It's been a little upsetting...getting to know you."

He ties my feet and hands.

"In the morning then Once-Other—dead or alive."

He heads off as happy as such can be. The bad-on-bad Desert Drivers laugh without humor as they usher their passengers onboard.

Ozerken strolls over and drops a fur coat down next to me. "Stay alive until morning. We get a bonus if you do."

The hiss of doors, the roar of four powerful engines, the whine of gears meshing, the swooshing of sixteen wheels spitting sand and the two SandMaster head off.

And the wind dies and silence reigns.

I'm alone and though prone I'm stumbling down a one-way-sand-alley along which the Minions of Death search for the spirit that is I—whispering my real name to me.

No, I will not place it on this record.

Wernt may be listening.

# CHAPTER 53

## OF A SIP OF DEATH, A TOUCH OF HOPE, A SANDSTORM

Seated upon the crest of a high dune, the sun burning fiercely and surrounded by Arzerns, I await death. Hands and feet freed, legs and arms crossed I make no attempt to escape. Death has been accepted our differences reconciled, her arrival welcomed

Around me, sand is soaked with my blood-clouded sweat.

The sun's heat reaches inwards seeking to turn blood into powder.

I scoop up sand and wash my face and hair. Another scoop is used to bathe my chest. Confronting pain, I force some into my wounds despite that it no longer matters.

Later.

Comfortable, hands resting easy upon my knees the final darkness beckons. Will I find a place of no identity? Or will I instead have a new identity and another chance to find loved ones and to be loved as many of our religions say happens and many believe?

Though some insist they know this is true.

I glance down to find damp, darkened sand.

Perhaps my sweat has done this.

The loud beat of wings intrudes.

A Great Black, giants amongst Arzerns, lands, waddles closer and stops two sand-paces off. It curves its neck and stares me in the eye from various angles. It steps backward, preens itself with one eye on itself while the other checks wet sand and me over.

Its just over two sand-paces long wing stretches out and settles over darkened sand. Tentacles covered with suction pads slither out from between wingtip feathers and dip into moist sand. Moments later with sand now dry the tentacles vanish. The Black stretches its neck until its razor sharp beak reaches three some sand-paces high and screams.

In full-blown panic, Criers lunge out their burrows and scatter.

From their hiding place beneath sand Arzerns launch screeching with delight.

An old Crier rushes by. A Black swoops down on the slow, aging one. Six finger long talons wrap around the old Crier's neck, sink in and blood spurts. The predator soars back into the sky and circles. A tentacle slithers out from beneath its tail feathers dips under the Crier's pouch-cover, attaches to a teat and sucks out the milk.

It switches teats and consumes the water.

Nothing on Here-Born goes wasted.

The Crier falls and slams into sand with a dull thud. The Great Black descends, lands, hops to the Crier, scans the surroundings for several moments, a soft diner's murmur of delight and it feeds.

I note that I am cold, bone-deep cold.

The Great Black before me bows several times its gaze fixed on something above my head. Without moving, I glance up.

A large block of ice rests on my head. With a crackle-n-crunch, the ice expands downward like an overgrowth. Cold pierces my eyes; they remain open despite the pain. The view of the Arzern distorts as the ice extends downwards, bulges around my shoulders, scurries down my torso and splays out to cover my legs.

The Black edges closer to me. It stops and glances about, then pecks at the ice. Chips spray into its face—a brief backward flight-n-hop. Wind from its flapping wings showers water off the melting ice. Wet spots dot sand. The Black watches me as though I am a museum exhibit.

"I hope we round-n-about live through this. I ain't making judgment here, but you know an' all getting stung can get us dead an' all?" said Madsen a long ago in the desert when we were young.

Now I see that since that day on which I had placed his life in danger, his attitude towards me began to change. Perhaps he lost trust in me...perhaps in himself as well. I shall miss him despite his criticisms.

Perhaps visions of one's life do play before death.

The fleeing Criers scream louder.

So does the Black in front of me.

A gaggle of Criers collide with each other in panic and rush in circles. Yet others stand back-to-back their blood stained fangs gnashing in self-defense.

To my left, a panic-stricken gaggle rushes by. Arzerns swoop in to rise with old and weak Criers held tight. Overhead their numbers darken the sky and Madsen says, "You be in a troubling mind?"

He's not here, though. Is this the all of my life? Is there nothing else? Have I no accomplishments, no moment worthy of remembrance?

The Great Black hops forward and pecks at the ice. Each blow of its beak thuds against my forehead igniting explosions and sending more dark-n-wet specks onto sand.

And Wernt says, "Wake up."

I blink and the sunlight hurts my eyes and I hear soft shuffling sounds.

Now comes the end of Once-Other of Here-Born for the Arzern is coming in for the kill. I turn my eyes up to watch my last moments reflected in the Black's eyes and so to record my last instant for those of the future.

Instead, I find Wernt tapping my forehead with the muzzle of his handgun. Beyond him, Pe'truss and Ozerken smile triumphantly. Bonuses all round kind of smiles.

Odentien stares off into the distance, expressionless.

"Good morning Once-Other," Wernt says. "Yeah. You made it. A little blue in the face but otherwise damn fine."

He hauls me to a sitting position leaving the fur coat on sand.

Ripped and shredded remnants of clothing are all that remains of Franciscoa. I parry the rage that threatens to erupt and end all possibility of escape. There's nothing I can do now but survive. Survive and bring justice to Franciscoa, to Jiplee and to all Here-Borns who have been lost in a war as yet undeclared.

My stomach flutters and acid rises to my throat. I swallow and glance about. Crier tracks everywhere. Why was only Franciscoa taken? Was I alive enough to keep them at bay?

Unlikely.

Ozerken glances at the fur coat and his eyes twinkle.

I follow his line of sight to find the tag of a repellant sachet protruding out a pocket. I note a tear with slight heat burns along the edges with the contents long since gone, leaked into the air.

Ozerken must have added a detonator and timer to the sachet and hidden them in the fur coat. The timer he would have set to activate after their departure.

Breathing deeply, I catch the faint trace of Arzern scent, which keeps Criers at bay. Mingled with it are remnants of the thick smell of $CO_2$, which kept the Arzerns at bay.

I glance about. Neither Odentien nor Wernt is suspicious for now the contents are almost odorless.

Strange Ozerken did that.

Well...bonuses were involved.

Wernt offers me water and I drink sparingly.

Ozerken retrieves his fur coat, shakes it out and tosses it into the SandMaster.

They sit me up proper.

Wernt holds me upright while Odentien cuts the ropes and feeling returns along with pins-n-needles. Pe'truss and Ozerken squat down on either side of me. Pe'truss with Bondo-Preserve bandages in hand.

Working together one applies new sand to my back while the other does the same to my chest. Pe'truss holds sand in place while Ozerken wraps the bandage and ties it tight.

"Don't die on them Once-Other," Wernt says. "More bonuses up if you make it to the Highlands."

The Desert Drivers nod and grin coldly.

I'm more than just damn puzzled by these two. Why use Bondo-Preserve bandages on me? Would they not prefer to save such expensive items for someone who will live? Even a fool knows that where they leave me I will die or already be dead.

I'm stood up by Wernt and walked to the SandMaster.

In passing, I give both Desert Drivers a sneer of disgust that each ignores.

The SandMaster charges off shuddering across a Crier warren strewn with fresh carcasses. My wounds scream in protest as I bounce in my seat.

However, there is no succor here.

We thunder onwards. The roof rises and hot desert air rushes in. As we pass by the edge of the warren, a single remaining Great Black feeds. It pauses, looks at us and nods as though it knows me and has taken a moment to bid me a final farewell.

Wernt puts his feet up and snoozes.

The pungent odor of gasoline lingers mixed with the faint traces of coffee and bagels. My stomach growls in protest. But I ignore hunger and look out upon our Here-Born sky soaking in its splendor as does one who has been condemned to die.

The sudden scream of tortured metal rips my attention off of my wounds. We lurch left and plunge downwards. Is this a dune or a capture-ditch we plunge into? In answer, $CO_2$ pours in under the raised roof. I push myself against the backrest and place a hand over my mouth and nose.

Wernt snaps his face shield down and plugs a temporary filter over the intake. His dead eyes find mine. They express as much sympathy for me as a butcher does for the meat he is carving.

Ozerken's hands flash about the control panel. He yanks the driver's windshield closed. The roof lowers and the reverse system kicks in sucking the $CO_2$ out. One damn fine but temporary fix. He reaches for the periscope-n-intake, which provides overhead views and a fresh air intake but changes his mind. At this speed, it could snap off and we have no way of repairing it out here in the far desert.

I lean back to ease my pain and Wernt's handgun touches my ear and he says, "Don't make me have to clean the floor as Ozerken threatened. Yeah? You get my meaning?"

I nod and turn my attention back to the no damn good Desert Driver.

His left foot riding the hydraulic suspension pumps he drives to the right across the forty-five-degree angle of the capture-ditch. The high-pitched whine of hydraulic pumps cuts painfully into my head.

I imagine the hydraulics raising the left-hand side of the SandMaster and keeping us horizontal as we turn. With only moments left before air reserves for both engines run out and they suck $CO_2$ and die...I cross my fingers.

Wernt holsters his weapon and I sigh.

His attention fixed on our degree-of-tilt, Ozerken reverses the lean angle and the SandMaster levels as we come around facing back up the ditch wall. Eight wheels slip-n-grip their way to the crest. We leap the edge just as the rear engine stutters on a cocktail of air and $CO_2$. We bounce several pogo-like bounds and I clutch at my wounds.

Both engines clear their throats and snarl with renewed vigor. I note that we all sigh in relief.

Eight wheels settle upon sand and I relax some. Ozerken floors the accelerator and turns full-lock left with the front wheels and full-lock right at the rear. His SandMaster snaps around facing along the length of the ditch well clear of the edge. We are back on course but not free of danger.

Beyond the northern horizon, sand-clouds rise to blacken the skies. Black-n-brown pylons of sand climb upwards to darken the sky. When fully grown, they shatter and rain sand down upon the desert floor.

"Whoa! Yeah—wow!" Peter exclaims.

Several whirlwinds of a good seven thousand sand-paces in diameter rise up from out the remains of the sand-cloud and turn day into night. They bump into each other, join at the hip and dance as one, dipping and spinning as though at a barn dance. And they all fall-down-n-down in a torrential downpour of sand.

Even Ozerken jolts involuntarily at the sight of so massive a sandstorm.

"Are we safe?" Wernt asks and we ignore him.

From out the downpour, a tornado rises so high I am unable to see the top of it. With sudden understanding, I realize what had happened.

"Peter," I say. "A tendril of the wind that's driving this sandstorm slammed into us and the SandMaster ended up in the ditch as easily as a spent match carelessly flicked aside."

"Yeah, whatever," he says.

I look ahead in too much pain to care about his foul demeanor and his *whatever's*.

At full power, the storm charges straight at us seeming furious at being thwarted.

"This is not the ideal place to be even in a SandMaster," I whisper to self.

"Hold tight," Ozerken commands.

And the storm hits a straight-arm blow to the SandMaster's chin lifting the front wheels clear of sand. The front steering goes light in Ozerken's hands. The SandMaster shudders and tosses her head, a cornered bull—exhausted and afraid yet fighting.

The front wheels drop-n-grab, engines scream and with gearboxes moaning in anguish the SandMaster counter punches.

Both Wernt and I have a firm grasp on the bench we sit upon, knuckles white with tension and faces devoid of emotion. Yet I can sense his heart beating as fast as mine is.

The wind feints a retreat but delivers another hard-n-fast uppercut and almost floors the SandMaster. Engine revs drop like a falling star.

Ozerken disengages the clutch preventing a stall. Selects a lower ratio, drops the clutch and the revs leap upwards to sniff at redline.

He powers down another two gears and briefly bounces the revs off the limiter. I cover my ears the noise of gears so high I am willing to let go of the bench.

Ozerken eases back and holds her just below redline. The engines scream in anger. My heart keeps pace as the howl of exhausts duck-n-dive around the howling wind. We crawl towards an adversary who at any instant may switch directions and flip us over with the greatest of ease.

Wernt sweats profusely behind his face shield. His eyes dart but never focus. He licks his lips and grimaces.

May he taste fear for the rest of his life, I muse.

As I look away, he says, "Shut-up!"

And mind-to-mind, mind you.

I once again cling to my seat as all eight wheels slip-n-grip.

My curiosity gets the better of me. Peering around him, I note that Ozerken's new arm struggles to hold onto the steering-wheel. I sit up straight and look over his shoulder at the driver's screens.

In that instant, a sixty sand-paces wide dust devil swerves towards us and breaks across our bow. The SandMaster shakes and shudders, a dandelion dancing to the violent will of Mother Wind.

I slump back onto the bench.

Wernt sneers, turns his cooling down and grabs a hold of the bench.

I clench my jaws at the screech of engines screaming as though afraid. A sudden gust and the rear wheels break free and we spin hard left. Ozerken steers into the slide; the wheels grab then slip and catch again as he counter-steers.

"Not a merry activity...dancing with the wind," I groan aloud.

"Come now sweetheart," Ozerken whispers.

The SandMaster takes another one on the chin lurches up and sways to the right front wheels clear of sand, its engine revs threatening destruction.

Ozerken curses beneath his breath and drops a gear on the front and two on the rear. Both rev-counter needles lunge for redline. The rear wheels bite hard, lock up and drag the front end down. He hits the same gear front and rear. Engines settle, but the wind still batters us.

"Thank you to all personnel, designers and...even testers," Ozerken says sparing me a glance.

With his SandMaster shuddering as though coming apart at the welds, we crawl forward across sand to plod onwards conquering less than one sand-mile per hour.

I check outside. The wind gusts thick with swirling sand. Visibility drops to ten sand-paces. I cross my fingers. For should sand fill the engine bays it will choke the extractors and we are all done for. Without cooling engines rip apart and scatter themselves across the landscape.

No drive power amidst a sandstorm of this magnitude would be terrifying to say the least. Unless tumbling across the desert in several tons of armored steel is to be considered fun.

Sudden silence descends as the winds die.

Overhead the massive cloud of sand mushrooms open like a curtain thrust aside by the wave of a gigantic hand. The eerie silence lingers as clear blue skies appear.

The SandMaster crawls through the eye of the sandstorm, engines screaming in defiance, gearboxes whining—like those who know what mighty a force still comes.

But with the wind gone a dread lingers within the silence.

One of us does not know this and he speaks.

"It's over?" Wernt asks.

# CHAPTER 54

## OF SAND COVERS ALL

No one answers and he gets it, slumps down in his seat, crosses his arms and stares at the floor. I gaze outwards at sand. In the distance, swirling circles of sand-clouds gather themselves ready to hurl Nature's fury at us once again.

"One damn fine storm you've brought us to," I say.

"It doesn't change anything," Wernt says.

Ozerken ignores us.

I turn away and stare unblinkingly at the drive-by-camera screens.

On the screens, the desert ahead is flat. Here and there sand-geysers spew fifteen sand-paces high leaving ghostly apparitions to hang motionless for an instant. Then they crash back to sand in imitation of a torrential tropical downpour.

Some are large enough to swallow a SandMaster or two.

I adjust the Bondo-Preserve bandages and pat them down.

Wernt eyes me and pats the grip of his revolver.

Which, with my acceptance of impending death, sets my mind towards duty and Neatness. I must somehow end his campaign but I have so far found no way of doing so. No appeal to this treasonous Desert Drive will work. Any physical attack on Wernt by myself would be too easily thwarted.

My death will only enhance his will to destroy us, to steal our wealth, to enslave us all. Helplessness engulfs me and I silently curse Wernt, Odentien and both these damn no good treasonous Desert Drivers despite how worthless such cursing is. Wait! A possible answer.

Yes. This leaves me with a single defense for now; my attempts at sowing confusion on what-n-all I've told him to date.

I silently curse them once again. Wernt looks up and chuckles and even Ozerken glances over his shoulder at me, a cold smile in place. But I am the first to notice a change and my attention leaps outwards beyond our confines, beyond any tactic.

Out there the wind blows with greater violence. Our engines scream louder in defiance. Yet I hear Wernt's heavy breathing and the Desert Driver's leathers squeak-n-groan as he leans to his task.

"Hang in there Once-Other you don't want to deny your fellow patriots their just and due bonuses," Wernt gloats and smirks. The satisfaction in his eyes strolls along my wounds and deepens with each step it takes.

I make to reply but without introduction nor any forewarning a huge sand-geyser erupts across our bow leaving a gaping hole in its wake. The SandMaster plunges in nose first. I groan in despair at the sight of a massive Ball Rock rushing upwards from below sand to greet us.

"God help us," I murmur.

Wernt spits and glares at me. Ozerken's eyes snarl at Wernt. Back to his tasks and in a blur of speed he points drive-by-cameras to under chassis view.

We slam into the Ball Rock with a dull thud-n-crunch followed by the screech of agonized metal. Peter and I fly off the bench as the left front tire jams into a crevice and we stop dead. My head slams into Ozerken's back, bounces off and I land on the floor—chin first.

Peter falls on top of me.

So concentrated on his task Ozerken barely notices.

Wernt digs his elbows into my back as he rolls off. I struggle up and onto my seat and strap in with shaking hands. My wounds express their displeasure at these antics with blades of pain and renewed bleeding.

Wernt crawls up onto his seat as well, his hands shaking.

Overhead the howling wind returns in all its fury. Ozerken kills the engines and switches the rear mounted drive-by-cameras to look ahead and licks his lips. Driven sand beats at the lenses reducing visibility to literally zero.

Steel groans in further agony as the Ball Rock settles dragging us deeper. We hang on as every square finger's worth of armored steel cries out in anguish.

Overhead raging rapids of sand pour in and quickly cover the viewports. Ozerken engages periscope-n-intake and kicks over to cell power. Outside the bullet-proof windows and windshield, a wall of sand hugs tight against the glass.

Our suddenly tiny world is beset by electronic groans as the engines shut down, and cell power comes online. Periscope-n-intake pans three-hundred and sixty degrees as it rises to reveal the desertscape above. Sand drums against the lens climbs up and buries it. It rises again.

With Here-Born suddenness the sandstorm passes. Silence, eerie as the graveyard, surrounds us as we wait in what may be our grave.

"We're done for," Wernt says.

We of Here-Born ignore him.

Sweating, I watch as Ozerken raises the periscope-n-intake until it breaks completely free of sand. A gauge indicates we are beneath ten sand-paces of it. Five-hundred some sand-paces back, Pe'truss' periscope-n-intake thrusts up above sand as well. They too had fallen foul of a sand-geyser.

Barely able to breathe evenly, I watch Ozerken working to extend all our lives beyond this moment, this grave. His hands flash about the controls. One after the other Fragger Units power up. Wernt hisses air through his teeth, adjusts the temperature of his suit downwards, half closes his eyes and I note, pays full attention to Ozerken's actions.

At each critical point, he makes mental notes.

As always, I perceive what he is doing but not the content. I curse silently to myself and Wernt sniggers. I fear him and the knowledge he's acquiring. How can these damn Desert Drivers allow this? Are they not patriots?

Ozerken taps the cell power indicator—it drops a quarter dial. He nods and motions we are to remain seated and not move. We nod in ready agreement, but he is already running Fragger programming. Done, he cuts the blowers driving hot surface air in. With his hands poised above the controls, he glances at us and says, "Eyes closed—bright lights coming," and fires the Fraggers.

A throaty electrical moan-n-thump. Its power rocks the SandMaster. On the screens, sand turns into liquid, bubbles and flat sheets of rainbows flash outwards. I quickly close my eyes and bury them in my palms. A sudden blinding flash of white light.

I glance about, but all to see are bright spots dancing before my eyes. I blink, squeeze them and focus.

Ozerken works busily at the controls.

Over his shoulder drive-by-cameras show success.

Sand above and around us is gone. The newly designed surfaces have formed into a wall of molten sand and hardened.

Ahead a ramp to the surface awaits us. The rear of the SandMaster had dropped and we now lie level. However, the surfaces created by Fraggers in sand do not last long and tend to crack at inopportune moments thus allowing sand to pour back in. Those poor souls buried are never found.

"Look where you have taken us," Wernt hisses.

No one replies. I shake my head at such wild illogic.

Ozerken opens a hatch in the roof and examines the sky, appears satisfied, indicates for us to remain seated and gets no argument. He stares long and hard at me, and I know why. He has taken a time-out to inspect me and Wernt and the interior of his SandMaster.

Wernt appears puzzled though but remains silent watching all.

Besides sand walls possibly collapsing around us, at any instant the storm could return and bury Ozerken beneath thirty feet of sand. If that happens, Wernt and I will keep him company for the next few hundred years, maybe longer altogether—unless I am able to get Wernt and myself out before all power fails.

It is a moment of courage for Ozerken. A timeout in which to say, "Adieu, break a leg."

He climbs up, closes the hatch and his boots thump along the roof.

After several seconds of silence, he appears and waves into a drive-by-camera, goes to one knee and feels around the crevice beneath the trapped wheel. He nods and pans his Nomadi across the A-frame, wheel, suspension mounts, brake caliper and disc.

The output appears on-screen superimposed over standard system diagrams. They align precisely indicating nothing has bent nor broken.

He nods pleased. I sigh more than pleased. Ozerken changes settings and scans the crevice in which the wheel is jammed. System displays the capacity and shape of the crevice.

A schematic with dimensions inserted evolves on-screen. Ozerken enters a code into his Nomadi. The schematic rotates and fills with rocks of various size, each one numbered.

Wernt takes careful notes—laboring at his task some now that stress hits.

# CHAPTER 55

## OF TIRE REPAIRS AND ARGUMENTATIVE COMPUTERS

Has Peter stretched his skills beyond their abilities? He glares at me as one genuinely insulted—perhaps not then.

I dismiss my questions as Ozerken hits the quick release on a Fragger unit, plugs his Nomadi into it and downloads the information as the Fragger powers on. He lays his Nomadi on sand, pulls on a set of gloves, aims the Fragger at bare rock and fires.

A single rock fragment flies off its shape and size conforming exactly to number one in the schematic. Juggling it hand to hand he places it into the crevice at the indicated position and fires at the rock again. Another fragment flies off. He repeats over-n-over.

After the last fragment is in place Ozerken sets the Fragger to a pencil beam. He enables auto detect and aims at the rock-edge next to the tire. With rainbows and white light firing in all directions, he cuts away the sharp edge against which the tire is jammed.

The SandMaster settles on the rock fragments he had placed into the crevice. He nods in satisfaction and oddly we three all glance to the sky at the same time. At the sight of bright blue skies, we sigh as one as well.

His movements sure and exact, Ozerken leans in around the back of the wheel and cuts off the opposing crevice edge ensuring it will not cut the tire when we drive out.

His face carved hard as Rocklands black-rock, he leans close in and inspects the tire by running his Nomadi across the surface. It beeps loudly and he lies prone, checks the inside sidewall and locates a deep gash where the tire had jammed.

Grunting his displeasure, he gets up and from a side compartment extracts a tire repair kit.

Working quickly, he attaches its connector to the rear of the Fragger, aims at the gash and fires but this time he strokes the Fragger as though painting a wall. Every couple of seconds he glances to the sky.

Each time he does, I bite my tongue wishing he would stop doing that...it is a waste of time and we need to get out of this hole.

Wernt suddenly leans forward as the rubber of the tire wall bubbles, smooths over, hardens and one-two-three the damage is repaired.

Ozerken opens the front engine bay and frags sand until it's cleared. He then removes sand from the rear engine compartment. Quickly returns the Fragger to its mount and clambers up the side to the roof. There he pauses and inspects the sky again. After a moment, he drops in through the hatch and looks us over his face flushed with pride.

Seated and business-like he lowers the periscope-n-intake, adjusts focus on the under chassis drive-by-cameras, fires up the engines, blips the throttle and the radial engines snarl eager to perform.

Screaming a high RPM protest song over having been so unceremoniously silenced, we slip and slide our way upwards as the ramp crumbles beneath us. We all hold our breath as the SandMaster abruptly shudders and then slides backward.

Images of sand pouring in from overhead swamp me. I hold my breath as the tires grip-n-hold-n-slip. With engines screaming, we roll back toward the waiting grave. Sand-clouds spew off our wheels and surround us providing yet another preview of life within the tomb.

Without apparent cause, my back comes alive burning as though sliced open by a whip applied by the hand of pure cruelty. I close my eyes and concentrate, inspect my back to find there are no wounds. But vague images of a hand swinging a whip inside a darkened tomb hover over me.

Eyes opened, I stare hard at Ozerken and the fires across my back subside.

The wheels hunt traction yet we slid backward.

Ozerken curses.

Wernt stares at the floor his face twitching. With the raging screams of spinning tire on sand, the rear end drops into a sand hollow the wheels themselves had dug. In the same instant, the computers begin to argue with each other and all the dash readings light up maximum.

The SandMaster shudders rocking back-n-forth.

Sand breaks away beneath our wheels.

"What...?" Wernt says, but I wave him silent.

His face pales.

I channel my hearing around the roar of my beating heart and evaluate the shudder. Our rear wheels have turned left; front ones steer a half-turn to the right. The engine revs high screaming a demented howl as though inviting death to the hunt.

My heart stops as Ozerken cuts power, reboots both computers and synchronizes them. We slide slowly backward into the grave. I close my eyes. Wernt mutters incoherently.

The engines roar into life, gears growl, wheels spin and we lurch sideways. The sudden thrash of engines, the howl of exhausts and the scream of tires slipping on sand. Ozerken corrects steering, reduces power at the front, sets traction control to a higher auto setting, drive to fully auto, and whips his boots off the foot brake and accelerator.

Groaning like an old man woken too early we climb slowly upwards. A shudder shakes the SandMaster as though it is a fragile skeleton fighting a windstorm. We totter on the edge of tomb and sand. Screams. Howls. Suddenly direct sunlight hits and we all smile in relief.

Twenty some sand-paces along the top of the dune Ozerken changes into high-ratio and floors it. Behind us Pe'truss' SandMaster emerges shedding sand from the roof like a Crier shaking itself after sand-bathing.

Ozerken points us northwest away from the storm's path and runs system tests as speed builds. All checks come up good.

He glances my way his countenance set like the face of a clock; expressionless save for the inevitable passage of time.

Yes. I know. I have very little of it left.

We charge along the canyon bed that runs the length of Iron Ridge Mountain. I look back but am unable to discern Iron Rock Falls far off to the east. The dry riverbed we travel is the only road that goes around, up and over the mountains to the Highlands above and beyond. It is also the most dangerous route on all of Here-Born when it becomes Dead Man's Alley.

With rugged rock walls to our left and right, we thunder onwards. The roar of exhausts bounce off the walls multiplying their cacophony. Soon I long for the rasp and grate of Poip voices directly into my ears and at close range.

At noon alarms sound. We have reached Dead Man's Alley.

Loud thundering and clangs welcome us to rocks falling upon us from the heights above. I peer outwards to where rocks thud into sand like a boxer's gloves against a soft chin. Sand splashes high when soft but where sand is hard the rocks hit and tumble along, solid tumbleweeds.

Wernt's right foot shakes as though he is attempting to flee for safety despite that there is nowhere to run. I smile. He grabs his knee, squeezes, and the shaking eases.

Ozerken, his attention fixed on the overhead view drives around a salvo of rocks. Yet he is unable to avoid them all. Loud clangs reveal how many plummeting down from the heights of Iron Ridge Mountain make contact.

Who drives this road more than once? Desert Drivers do.

I glance at his back rippling with muscle as he wrestles with the steering. We dart around three and between two. He brakes hard and swerves left, accelerates, swings right around two more. He floors it just as a four hands wide rock smashes into the windshield. A spread of dust and fragments leave a rock-spot across glass. The windshield glass remains intact.

We thunder onwards close to unscathed thanks to over-head cameras and his skill. He smiles to himself and pride creases his face once again. He turns his head a fraction left and his eyes, reflected in the control screen, find mine. I'm rendered brain-dead by this first Here-Born styled direct contact between us.

I watch with my eyes turned to him, but my face pointed outwards towards sand. He glances left, back dead ahead then straight down and back at me. I look down to find the press-stud end of the strap around the handle of his knife hanging free.

Our eyes meet once again. His are alive with dedication.

So, the Old Soldier still lives in this Desert Driver.

But why did he show me this? He has not hinted at any allegiance to me, to Franciscoa nor any call to unite. If he wanted, Wernt would lie dead in an instant and I would be free to go about my life and campaign. Yet nothing.

Pain flares alive savaging any further thought. I fight it as Crier poison assaults my mind in combination with burning from the Bondo-Preserve bandages at my chest and back. Despite the bandages, both pains multiply and suck my attention inwards—not a good thing.

I will need all my reserves, my willpower, my physical strength, my Here-Born Foundation and desert skills if I am to take advantage of any opportunity and snatch life back from my impending execution.

I stroke the goose bumps that creep up my arms. Roll my head as to relieve pain while observing Wernt from the corner of an eye. He appears exhausted as he dozes eyes closed, arms slack and feet splayed.

I consider potential advantages beckoning.

First, I must get possession of Ozerken's dagger, the fur coat, and some Bondo-Preserve bandages. I feel around my leg pockets and find my Crier fan is secure. I shift about on my seat and, as comfortable as is possible slip into a light slumber with hopes of recuperating.

I awaken on my back lying upon sand.

Wernt stands spread-eagled ten paces away.

Ozerken leans over me his foot on my chest, handgun staring at the spot between my eyes. Wernt walks closer his handgun cocked-n-ready. His boots crunch in sand each footfall clear enough to count the grains of sand rubbing against each other.

I feel alone but am not alone.

Beyond him, Pe'truss and Odentien lean against Ozerken's SandMaster puffing cigarettes, indifferent as anyone awaiting the arrival of a later than usual bus. They whisper-n-snicker like old comrades do—but opportunity knocks as Ozerken nods at Wernt and turns side on to me.

Diving forward and up I grab the knife handle and pull it free of the sheath. Wernt cocks his handgun. Ozerken spins around and his revolver finds my chest.

Wernt fires. Ozerken fires. And each fires again.

I gasp at the sudden numbness wondering why there is no pain. Then all changes. Four flesh tearing, bone splintering explosions slam home. A fist of extreme agony punches upwards into my head. It explodes, my internal light turns off and all is dark. Away in the distance loud whooshing thunderclaps followed by sand shaking thuds beat a heavy rhythm.

But it doesn't end. Over-n-over pain slams into my chest then rockets up to explode inside my head. Sand presses against my cheeks. A grain finds its way under my lashes where tears attack it. My eyelids twitch as it scratches, a moment later it floats to a corner and slips into that place such irritants go. I may be dead. How to find out?

I look out ahead but see only the red that comes from staring with my eyelids closed while facing the sun. Shadows fall across the red, my eyes open and I find myself flat on my back upon the desert sand with Wernt's boot heel pounding my chest.

"Wake up Once-Other—we're here," he says.

I leap at him but find my hands tied.

"What? You think you can just fly up at me. Get real. Yeah. Get real."

He pats my cheek with the barrel of his revolver.

I glance around to find Ozerken sitting on his SandMaster. His attention focused on what he is doing, applying Bondo-stick-on to the joint in his arm. Apparently, I was dreaming or perhaps predicting. Nevertheless, I am grateful the gunshots were born of my imagination.

Unfortunately, the pain from Wernt's heel at my chest is all too real. He steps back and kicks the sole of my boot, looks over his shoulder, notes what Ozerken is doing, glances my way and says, "Don't move!"

In that instant, the arrival and roar of Pe'truss' SandMaster distracts everyone. I grab this slim opportunity and lunging to my feet, I flee. After several paces, my poison infected vision clears and I find myself running towards Iron Rock Wellspring visible in the distance. I shudder at images of the horrible death that awaits all who dare to error and step in it.

Northerners included.

I swerve hard left, then left again and Pe'truss' SandMaster roars down on me. I crash into its sharp-edged nose of steel. My upper left arm snaps with a sharp crack. I fly over backward, land on my back winded and gasping in pain.

Wernt, Pe'truss, Ozerken and Gordon Odentien surround me, handguns pointed at my chest, eight dead, uncaring eyes aimed between my eyes.

In a dreamlike fashion, I examine their hardware.

Wernt's Buckminster .357 Mini three-shot revolver makes for easy concealment. Pe'truss and Gordon have Colseter .45 Autos while Ozerken's eight-finger barrel .50 x 35 seems tiny clasped in his hand. But it looms more menacing than the others thanks to its enormous air cooled barrel. Its muzzle appears large enough to crawl inside of and hide. Save for Wernt's, every weapon is powerful enough to bring down a Roanark Braer with the greatest of ease.

Once-Other makes for an easier kill.

Wernt shakes his head as a disillusioned father does at evidence of a son's irretrievable failure.

"Waste of time and effort," he says.

They all grunt, relax and ease back.

I turn away and gaze off towards Iron Rock Wellspring where a virtual juggler performs beneath the surface tossing rocks into the air, a touch of entertainment for the condemned campaigner.

Timing them, I discover that every ten seconds sand-geysers gush obscuring the distant sun. I watch the columns of yellow-brown $CO_2$ blast upwards like the foul and fiery breath of a giant fire-breathing monster. Even at our distance the thunderous cacophony of rocks falling back into sand is close to deafening. The sharp smell of $CO_2$ burns my nostrils and makes me lightheaded.

Odentien steps closer picks up the fur coat from where I'd dropped it and tosses it down next to me. I assume my tormenters have little intention of spending much time here though it is an excellent place to leave someone to die—should that be one's design. The excessive heat has already parched my tongue.

Looking closer, I note Wernt's face is puffed and sweaty despite his suit being turned to its lowest setting. I once again marvel that Jenk Nordt travels this sand on foot. Such toughness is undoubtedly admirable.

I cough. Wernt smiles.

They all back off a little except for Wernt. He comes closer, sits down and places his lips against my ear. His voice oddly distinct against the rolling thunder of Iron Rock Wellspring and soft and throaty like a lover, he says, "So Once-Other. Here we are. The final curtain. Yeah?"

"Get on with it Wernt," I snap in return.

"Patience," he says. "Yeah. Patience. Now listen up for once will you. You know one, you know two and now I've decided I must tell you three."

"I don't give a damn Wernt."

"You will, Once-Other! You will. Yeah."

He digs out his Nomadi, flips it from hand to hand, works the keypad, reads the results, smiles coldly and says, "Here comes three of one-two-three and death number one of two. I don't know if you realize what a pleasure—knowing you died twice."

He waves the others away and they head off towards the SandMasters parked alongside each other. Wernt makes himself comfortable in sand, crosses his legs and taps his Nomadi screen.

"Allow me to present number three, Once-Other."

# CHAPTER 56

## OF A FINAL THREE OF TOO MANY ONE-TWO-THREE, ALTOGETHER

Peter leans in close and I figure it's to further prevent others from hearing. He sniggers and says, "But first—a quick recap. Yeah. Yesterday I went over the transfer of your business and personal assets to me and that your life belongs to me. Now, this next section has a smattering of legalize. Yeah!"

He pauses, smiles and adds, "I'm sure you'll grasp meanings."

"I'll hold my breath Wernt—just for you."

He chuckles and taps the Nomadi screen.

The distant thunder of rocks crashing back to Here-Born's sand sound softer. The tang of $CO_2$ is sweeter than I recall. The murmur of voices drifts across from those grouped around the SandMasters.

Wernt shuffles until more comfortable and smiles as his hands float with a gentle motion as though upon a breeze. I am saddened that my life's road has ended. As he reads his voice lilts like a singer weaving a tapestry of notes both bitterly sad and sweet.

"Here's three Once-Other. And one two three…here goes! In keeping with the fact, all Citizens are Assured Happiness and with particular reference to Section 800-376 of the Violation of Happiness Act and its relation to the Compensations and Remunerations Act."

He looks at me. I frown in ignorance of his song.

"It'll come to you," he says.

I sneer, much as he does.

He chuckles and continues.

"With reference to the Back Pay Act Sub-Section 1134 Titled C-POP Murder in the First Dot One Degree…we quote: Compensations for all Definite Actions or Apparent Equivalent Actions are rendered as actionable."

He pauses, smiles and continues.

"In Consultation with the Happiness Assurance Enabling Back End Receipts and Payments Act, which cites pertinent procedures can and must be undertaken per the Irrespective of Location paragraphs of the aforementioned Section 800-376.

"In which paragraphs it is stipulated that certain actions are executable and what remuneration is receivable for Murder in the First Dot One Degree. Irrespective of whether such acts were committed in the past, present or any probable future as well as after, before and or during the fact of or similarity to any such previous or potential future Acts.

"Therefore! By the use of these Legal Truths the following has been promulgated and thus declared as Truth in Justice."

He shuffles his posterior in the heated sand again attempting to render his skinny frame ever more comfortable.

"Are you tracking this as well as you can with Crier poison still active?" he asks.

"Quite mad you all are Peter," I reply.

He snorts and nods as though he understands me.

"I'll continue to the benefit of your enlightenment. Yeah. Here we go.

"In consideration of the Deed committed by Once-Other, the consequent result of the Deed, the continued reminder of the Deed, which reminder is obvious by its absence. It is hereby declared and rendered lawful, truthful Justice and is congruent with Property Rights under the Expandable Constitution of Earth and the Bill of Modifiable Rights.

"So here is number three Once-Other. Listen up now!

"Hereby, Property Item D-109 is assigned with all Owner-ship and Executive Rights *to me of course.*"

He smiles at me, eyebrows raised in question

"One long-winded way of saying nothing," I answer.

"Oh yeah? How's this? Description of Property Item D-109: Karrell, the child of Once-Other and Deidre, Age 12, Gender Male, Location Here-Born. Said Property Rights and Posses-sion assigned *to me of course.*"

And I die inside.

And I think of murder most foul regards Deidre and her *a legal matter.*

Nevertheless, Wernt was right.

I will die twice today.

How did Earth-Born come to this?

What are the laws that permit this?

Who are the people enacting such heinous law?

Wernt's knee jams into my solar plexus and holds.

With a gasp of pain, my mouth snaps open.

He thrusts the poison vial in, clamps his other hand over it sealing mouth, vial and nose. He lifts his knee. I suck in as he hits the eject button. Poison squirts into my mouth. He pulls the vial out, clamps my mouth and nose closed and pumps his knee in-n-out. There was no need for the last—I swallow all without resistance for it is my one slim and almost pathetic hope.

Overdone this particular poison will at times be rejected by the stomach. It would have been wiser to inject it into my bloodstream. Not that I'm complaining.

Now. Much depends on how soon I can eject most of what is already inside. Slim hope indeed, such being dependent upon how insidious a stomach finds the action of digesting this particular poison.

Nevertheless, I count the seconds until they leave.

Peter stands up, tosses the vial aside, nods down at me with a sick satisfaction, scoops up sand and washes his hands with it. "Die once more Once-Other," he says and walks away.

But I'm thinking. I'm planning.

I'm taking what has happened over recent days and hooking the past to where I'm right now. I shuffle over and lie on the fur coat hoping to hide it, glance their way and watch as they huddle in the shade of Ozerken's SandMaster all the while hoping they leave soon.

Wernt makes payments with his Nomadi followed by handshakes all round. Odentien enters Pe'truss' SandMaster, the door hisses closed, the engines scream and they storm off to descend Iron Ridge Mountains after once again climbing its heights.

Wernt waits for relative silence, waves, blows me an insulting kiss, climbs the steel ladder, waves once again, enters the SandMaster and looks back at me from inside and laughs with evil satisfaction.

Ozerken turns to enter the SandMaster but checks himself, does a double take, walks over and yanks the fur coat free. He hangs it over his shoulder and heads back to the SandMaster his knife still hanging free. I had counted on that knife, that coat.

"Ah. Thank you very much Ozerken," Wernt calls out, turns and rummages beneath the rear bench.

At the rear of his SandMaster, Ozerken flips an exterior compartment open. He searches through the pockets of his black leather jacket. Extracts three items, tucks them into the pockets of the fur coat, tosses the coat into the compartment and slams the cover with force enough that it bounces several times before settling.

Wernt pulls something blue from beneath the seat, glances my way and waves it like a flag. It looks much like the pale blue ghutra worn earlier when a SandMaster had parked near my store. His cruel laugh confirms it.

The door hisses closed, the engines roar and they charge off just as the poison begins its symphony of death. The first attack comes at the joints starting with the fingers then the shoulders, elbows, knees and lastly...ankles.

I have but precious little time.

I am alone and I will die alone.

Rolling to my knees and keeping my broken arm tight against my hip, I insert a finger as far down my throat as I can. Poison and other unpleasant contents erupt in a fashion that declares Wernt's earlier hurling was but a sneeze by comparison.

After calming self, I thrust my finger in over-n-over until I dry hurl. For now, that is all I can do. Perhaps the overload will be rejected. I can but hope.

With a fan, I can get water, with a knife, sand-snails but none without a knife.

But thirst kills first.

Perhaps in taking water I can kill a Crier without a knife.

I spend a moment imagining what one tastes like.

Not good I decide.

However, there is something more significant and of a greater urgency needs doing. I must orientate before delusion sets in. I scan the desertscape and it already takes longer than usual.

# CHAPTER 57

## OF STRUGGLE, ORIENTATION AND INTERNAL REPAIRS

I pull out my Nomadi only to find a red cross over my Navigation services. I glare up to where the satellite would be, curse it out, check recording is working and tuck the Nomadi carefully away a little puzzled that it's still in my possession.

I cast about for direction. How close I am to the quicksand shores of the Lake itself, I cannot tell. I could be within sand-paces or a mile or more.

Behind me, southwards, Iron Rock Ridge drops some two thousand to twenty-five hundred sand-paces to the Lowlands.

I envision myself climbing down it and shudder. With one good arm alone I will not be able to descend its face honed by windblown sand to edges so keen as to rival that of Ozerken's knife.

I struggle to my feet, hold my broken arm across my chest and keeping it secure set off hoping the tracks in sand I am seeing are real and not delusion. With each step I take poison-induced paralysis creeps deeper into my mind and into my every joint and every muscle.

I look out ahead.

The distant horizon is free of storm clouds.

I march on.

A gusting wind creates and destroys tiny dust-devils much like a child makes funny faces one after another.

Later...my feet stumble.

I stare at them but can find no reason for halting.

I peer ahead to where dust-devils dance, their tops curved over like ocean waves breaking to splatter sand-drops across my face. I close my eyes, steel my inner-self and nearly blinded continue towards a destination unseen.

My boots drag in sand.

How do Northerners travel here on foot?

I could do with some down-to-sand advice from Jenk—altogether.

Time ticks on, heat thickens.

The sun seeks out every drop of moisture that exposes itself and absorbs each like a monstrous sponge possessed of an insatiable thirst. My tongue hardens. My eyeballs scratch on lids.

Hordes of insects buzz about inside my head, settle and feast upon thought until nothing other than pain makes sense.

Yet I smile for if my lifeless body is found my hair will be neat and tidy thanks to Fat-n-Grease by Hardins. Perhaps posthumously, I'll receive a Neatness award for this beautiful white shirt and superb dress etiquette.

But...wait!

There's something else here and though it's out beyond the immediate it begs my attention. What is it? No answer.

I stop.

I listen.

The distant thud of rocks dropping back into Iron Rock Wellspring sound like giant fists punching a well-tuned set of drums. I lean towards the noise to better hear for it's far too loud. And! Yes. Quicksand is close.

I must move on but in which direction?

Blinded, poisoned and with only the thudding of rocks on sand to guide me, I reach out and embrace its cacophony. Next, I separate each drumbeat into distinctive sounds and block others out thereby creating a personal selection.

From these selections I envision a musical tempo to which I march listening for the lessening of their noise.

Am I too confused to tell the difference?

I march on with hope my sole companion.

A strong gust of wind halts me. I open my eyes to find the desert gone. I rub my eyes and sand reappears and vanishes, and appears and vanishes.

I glance up.

Overhead the Half-Day-Moon rises to greet me one final time. I march on but stumble over feet grown unwilling to take another sand-resisting step.

Pain eats at my strength with a boundless greed for power. I kneel—hoping to gather what reserves I may still possess. Eyes closed I reach inwards to the broken arm bone. At first I cannot approach but I know I must for if I do not—here I shall die.

I edge my inner view closer to the broken bone and pause to build courage. With a little gathered from distant successes I sidle my internal perception nearer and reddish pain grasps at me and holds on. I retreat in a panic. The red ball of pain remains fastened to me.

I halt within. I wait within. I focus within.

Red pain pulses and changes to black, to red and back to black like an EB traffic light gone psychotic and uncertain of duty. The pulses accelerate becoming harder, realer.

Pain intensifies.

I retreat and gather resolve.

I return and assess the red separately to black and discover red draws me closer as black pushes me away. I latch onto their beat and follow them with naught but the hands and the point of view I had placed within my body. Which hands are as virtual as those that Peter Wernt used to invade my mind. Yet my internal point-of-view is as valid as seeing sand before one's eyes.

Pain flashes faster-n-faster.

I work a virtual arm around the red, another around the black and hang on. Black flames into white and vanishes but red remains red and pulses on. I match red's new pulses and in-sync add an offbeat and red's rhythm breaks apart. It shoots off across the sky, a high-speed cloud riding a wild tornado.

For a moment all is still.

I wait.

I listen.

I hear.

I see.

In the distance sand-clouds loop around the drumbeats of falling rocks—and plunge back down into Iron Rock Well-spring—and fly up again.

And pain beckons to me.

I return inwards and anchor myself.

From the center of my body I reach for and touch every beat, every pulse of pain that remains, making them my own.

They slip free and tumble down into my legs.

Muscles twitch. Yet I make them work. And I stand.

Muscles twitch.

Muscles work.

I open my eyes and embrace a vision of the blue sky.

"And he walked," I whisper.

I set off but something further is wrong.

With my legs demanding the right to collapse altogether, I stop and force them to stand still.

I listen intently intrigued at how loud rocks falling back into Iron Rock Wellspring sound.

I step forward and my foot drops down into quicksand.

I twist about in midair and throw my torso backward, land with my upper body on firm sand and my right leg buried in quicksand.

I am at the edge of Wellspring Lake draped over the border between sand and death and slipping into the grave.

Disorientated by pain and poison and led here by the will of those two villains, I have walked eastwards towards Wellspring Lake not westwards along Ozerken's tracks.

I have made a terrible life-threatening error. I must backtrack and now. I cannot afford to lose my trail. It leads back to Ozerken's. I need his as it gives direction and guidance crossing the mountains down to the Lowlands.

I push down with my left knee to find it's on compacted sand. I grip at sand with it and with my good hand working as a paddle, pull myself free as my teeth grind against pain.

I pause, look around, orientate and crawl in the right direction. At a safe distance I stand up, brush off one-handed, check for direction and with the Lake at my back I scout about.

After some minutes, some blinking, some reassuring, I set off once again. Sand puffs up at my every step. I march onwards fighting Crier poison, Wernt's poison, heat, thirst, fatigue, fear and worst of all—the urge to give up, lie down and sleep for all eternity.

Ahead my old footprints recede into the distance down a long dimly lit tunnel. I keep going. The tunnel vanishes and becomes a tiny patch of sand. I don't know whether it is real or pure delusion—but I walk. Several World Wars of pain are under way in my head and arm, chest and back.

Much later my footprints vanish.

I stagger to a halt, tunnel-vision dissolves and I glance about. To my left is an indentation in sand.

I hurry over and find dry blood. Mine I hope.

I scan the area; spot some tracks made by a SandMaster and follow them. Tunnel-vision returns with Ozerken's tracks in sharp focus. Later his tracks vanish. I halt and gaze out ahead but nothing. I take a step forward, still nothing. I turn around keeping a careful watch on direction.

Wait! Behind me—marks in sand. I scurry over. They are of a SandMaster executing a sharp left. I follow as they twist back-n-forth across sand. He must have hit semi-quick-sand and careened out of control. I kneel and test the surface but find nothing to skid upon.

What happened? Ozerken is a professional.

I examine sand while noting my broken arm no longer pains me. I hope that the swelling has locked the bones in place. I stand up. My head spins.

I hold still until all of everything comes into focus. I look outwards from his tracks and a tiny outcrop of Rocklands, a minute brown pimple pasted upon the vast desertscape grabs my attention.

I stagger across just as a gust of wind blows lifting its eastern edge and my heart races with sudden hope. I charge forward teeth clenched against the explosions in my arm and chest.

I fall onto the brown and reach out as doubt laughs contemptuously. I bite at fur, rub the coat down my chest, bury my face and drink deeply of its musky flavor.

I hold in my hands the coat Ozerken so carelessly tossed into an exterior compartment. Oh, joy! I laugh long and hard but force myself to stop at the precipice of sanity and reason.

His wild skid must have flipped open the compartment allowing the wind to blow the coat free. I struggle to my knees and fumbling, search through its pockets with memory charged desperation. What had Ozerken slipped into the pocket as he walked to his SandMaster?

Into my good hand, he deposits three vital items. No four!

I sit back, consider Ozerken anew and as a greater quandary.

By all Here-Born standards his dedication to Wernt's criminal actions bespeaks of treason. This odd and pathetic attempt to help me survive will not mitigate in his favor should his role come to light. He knows this. Why bother providing these at this stage?

But not one to stare a gift Roanark Braer in the mouth I lay them out on the fur coat—my heart beats faster as soul-crushing doubt assaults reason. Is this all my imagination? Are these three items actually here?

On the coat rests a healing preservative injector, an anti-venom injector and a roll of Bondo-Preserve bandage but not a single drop of water. No food either. As valuable as these are their benefit is compromised by the lack of water.

And four...is the coat itself. It will provide protection from driven sand. Blown sand can slice away flesh as easily as a butcher's knife.

Dry protein biscuits would have been good. How tasty they are when softened in water and eaten with the sauce of intense hunger spread over. Gingerly, I reach out and confirm they are real, as real as my poison fogged mind can estimate and just in time—my body is breaking down.

Poison is working its way ever deeper-n-deeper leaving a trail of dead tissue in its wake. Obviously, Peter Wernt intended my final dying would be painful, long and drawn out. My purging has slowed the process, but my body is now breaking down as my fingers stiffen more-n-more.

I've almost no time left.

I pull my shirt up, hold the seam clamped by teeth and twitching jaws, expose the long needle of the anti-venom injector, plunge it all the way into my stomach and depress the plunger. Not wanting to pause in case I never again awaken, I roll up my left sleeve. Shaking I rest my broken arm on my thigh and move the separated pieces until the broken bone lines up as best I can judge.

Fighting the darkness slamming into me like a sledgehammer swung in the hands of a professional, I inject the healing Preservative into the break. Wild fever rampages as I wind the Bondo-Preserve bandage around my arm making them tight enough to keep the bone in place yet blood flowing.

I push my right arm into the sleeve and curl up just as my light turns off. And I know I may never awake so what I now record is for you....

If I should fail to awaken—hopefully a new and patriotic writer will continue my work. He or she will find all my actions with thoughts included on my Nomadi. Perhaps find more than they will care to know of me. I hope he or she will continue what this Here-Born named Once-Other started and if you care to travel the road that I have, please do a good job.

Make me proud as well as any I leave behind.

Patriots are all that a nation can count on in times of distress.

True now, in the past and will always be so.

The brave and the willing are often not the obvious.

They are almost never the loud and noisy but instead, are the quiet individuals who are driven to action by an unrelenting abuse of their Rights by others. These quiet ones are hindered some by a willingness to wait for those others to cease their oppressive natures and so become worthy of representing them.

Please do not wait too long.

Also! Never surrender and never go quietly nor apathetically into slavery no matter how attractive getting free stuff looks nor how easy *not* having to work sounds.

Keep in mind that all hunters offer their prey a free meal whether it's hung from a snare or served-n-caged in a one-way entrance. Free meals are always bait! And so one should know that those offering free stuff are the Hunters and those receiving free stuff are the Prey.

And the Hunter always demeans those who speak out against their hunting of humans, whether in flesh, as souls or spirits. And so he defends his right to bait and thereby add to his collection those ensnared because they are *owed stuff*.

And so it follows that one must always defend self, family, community and your sanity as well as the sanity of others. Without the right to our own sanity, we can be deemed insane by merely being accused of demonstrating some emotion, some upset, some momentary outburst.

With such a *crime committed* one-n-all can be medicated into zombie-like deadness and soon all are walking vegetables.

All that is needed is for one to be found emotionally disturbed and therefore, dangerous to self and others—by law.

Sadness, anger, fear, happiness, too much cheerfulness, antagonism, grief, regret, apathy, frustration—any such natural feeling could be deemed insane. So too can any reaction or emotion be legislated and named a disease and thereby require drug therapy or time in a quiet and secure facility. One with locked doors and bars on the windows and there to allow others to observe you and all—*for your own well-being.*

Those *observers* will tend to earn a living *caring for sufferers just like you.* They will surely want many to care for. One could say they have a stake in finding you emotionally disturbed, unstable, in need of medication, quiet cells, and observation.

And who knows what they will make you into with drugs and their side-effects. It happened back on Earth-Born many centuries ago. So vanished Earth-Born's freedom and soon thereafter their collective sanity was buried in the cemetery of Freedoms and Rights.

But as for now...I am not sure I will survive.

If by fate, I don't awake:

Live by Neatness fellow citizens—one-n-all.

# CHAPTER 58

## OF FEVER AND VOICES

I awake shivering yet the sun shines. I blink several times and the sky changes from day to night and back again. I stare upwards, the Half-Day-Moon plummets from the sky, crashes to sand and waves of bright yellow sand tumble over the horizon.

Darkness descends.

Later.

The Star-of-Hope shines upon me—its light cold and uncaring of events.

Yes. Okay. It had to happen. I am quite mad, or quite dead, or quite both. It is both day and night at the same time. Am I alive as a spirit alone or is my body still part of life?

Did Jiplee know the difference?

I don't.

Perhaps in the end Jiplee found the answer—I hope I will.

Is that why she had a smile on her lips?

Sand laps at my cheeks followed by the soft flutter of wind through my hair. The sun bakes down. I awake hot and shivering, the sun shining from behind.

Not a whisper of a breeze stirs sand.

A sticky moisture clings to my eyes, my nose, my mouth.

I wipe at it. A thick smear of blue residue drips from my fingers. I tear a piece of Bondo-Preserve bandage off and wipe it all away. By all accounts, I am alive but wretched. How I'll escape the Highlands and reach the Lowlands I have no clue.

My skin crinkles parched as hide too long cured. The high temperature of the Highlands is without a doubt dehydrating me. Despite the heat and to keep a firm grip on the fur coat, I work my left arm into a sleeve as well and stand up.

On my feet, I head to the vertical edge of Iron Rock Ridge. I lie down, peer over and confirm what I already know. Falling away from the edge is an eighteen-hundred vertical sand-paces, perhaps more, climb or fall to the Lowlands below.

I back away, sit down cross-legged, contemplate possibilities and find two options. Well, three.

One, walk the length of Iron Ridge Mountain making my way slowly but surely up, over and along the western precipice of the Iron Ridge horseshoe to the Lowlands and die on the way.

Two, climb down Iron Rock Ridge to the Lowlands and die upon cooler sand or with bad luck fall to my death—which latter could be considered good luck.

Three, sit here idle until I pass away.

There are no warm-n-fuzzy options in any direction.

I park thinking in hopes of recovery and lying down pull the fur collar up to cover as much of my head as possible and sleep again. Some while later the deep freeze of night embraces me. Though more unconscious than asleep, I can feel my body shaking and shivering, but from fever not cold.

Later.

The wind blows, and I know Ozerken's tracks are gone.

Later.

The fever breaks and I awake as does morning.

Rising to my feet I scan sand.

Off in the distance are several Crier burrows.

A while later I reach one.

Hunger gnaws as I wave the fan with my healing arm and lift the pouch-cover by hooking a finger under the sting-claw. I drink my fill hydrating as fast as I drink. I rest and drink again, and rest and drink again.

Back at the cliff's edge I sit for hours gazing at the distant Lowlands. Nothing moves down there. I lie prone intent on thinking the situation through. But my wounds break into a medley of pain. I curl up, ensure my healing arm is comfortable and allow sleep to take me from suffering.

When I awake an inspection of my chest wounds reveals that all is not well. They are not healing and signs of gangrene are already visible. I scoop sand into the wounds, wrap them closed and hope for the best.

Much later I awake thick and groggy but this time something woke me. I listen, but all is silent. Pain takes me away.

I crawl up from darkness once again and lie still for again something stirred me awake.

The hairs on my arms stand erect. I gazed about heart racing. Is it Criers or Arzerns come to feed? Both? I listen—silence except for the wind whispering a final farewell. Suddenly a voice speaks from out the sky and I know I've gone quite mad.

"Once-Other dear friend. Once-Other. Are you with us honorable one?" Jenk Nordt's voice stirs me fully awake.

I look around and sand, wind, sun and self is all I find.

I chuckle in insanity's face and prepare for the final sleep.

"My good and honorable friend Once-Other. Are you surviving dear friend of mine?"

Is he communicating across a vast distance as impossible as that is? Surely not over Nomadi. Didn't Wernt and those no good Desert Drivers relieve me of my sole method of communication out here?

"Jenk? Where are you?" I send as far and wide as I can.

"Jolly good Once-Other. I've hailed you some two days. Where are you?"

"Ah, Jenk. I'm on the Highlands close to the edge of Iron Rock Ridge. A damn no good Desert Driver and that worthless Wernt left me here to die."

"We are appraised of conditions."

"You are? We?"

"Later honorable campaigner. But for now lend unto me thine ears." And he chuckles.

My head swims as hope-n-despair whisper their little infidelities in my ear. But I should know better for mind tricks exist at the Gates of Death. I listen intently, but all is silent. I dismiss the voice, lie down and place out the welcome mat and unopposed, let Death enter.

"Take this with grace please—no friend. No. I...we are...this is Jenk...I'm on the Lowlands but too far to reach you in time. Please. Please stay with me. I'm sending help. Are you tracking?"

I embrace the voice I hear as a simple farewell gesture. Yes! Why shouldn't my last hours be filled with pleasant, even delusional conversation? No reason at all I reason. Is madness not what takes most every EB tourist's life despite that we blame the sun and sand?

Let Once-Other then travel the same road and meet those earlier travelers. "I'm awake, Jenk. Speak to me. Let me enjoy these last hours talking to myself."

"I'm honored in receipt of your attention, Once-Other. Yet we seem set upon separate paths. How strange at this *early* hour you bid me farewell. Come friend. I am speaking to and with you. Considering circumstances, it appears you are a trifle disorientated. Is that so?"

"Damn Jenk. How real you sound."

"Once-Other! Friend! Heed these words. I am distant—yes. Yet I am connected as impossible as it appears. I am in desperate need of your indulgence. I beg you to converse right here and right now and altogether. I need this despite that you may consider all to be delusional. Can you oblige me my dear friend?"

A tiny spark of hope. "Okay. Yes. Okay. I can."

"My deepest thanks go out across distant sand to you. Pray, tell—how far are you from Iron Rock Wellspring?"

"More or less?"

"More or less."

"Far enough to catch a whiff of CO2. Near enough to hear rocks falling."

"And distance to the edge of Iron Rock Ridge?"

"About thirty some sand-paces."

"Excellent, Once-Other. Go there. Check left, check right. Tell me what you find, friend."

Quite amazed at how far I'm taking this game I drag myself over, scan east, west and down. "Rock and sand, Jenk."

"A no result on looking with any clarity worth mentioning. Out along the lip Once-Other. East and West but first...pull yourself together, invoke your full Foundation and perceive."

Fear drowns hope and I chuckle at how I've chided myself using Jenk as a source for my own voice. Yet, I take a minute and refresh my Foundation, clear my vision and to my surprise something appears.

"Out west some hundreds of sand-paces stands a squarish rock, Jenk."

"Go to it!" the voice commands.

I stand up and swoon.

The flat desert and the distant horizon come together weaving a landscape of confusion. V-shaped gullies beckon; knife-like dunes invite me to slide along their cutting edges; into such I'm loath to tread. I drop back to sand, drag myself further from the edge, stand, spread my arms wide like a tightrope walker and when my head stops reeling I head for the square rock.

"You get there yet?" Jenk asks.

"No."

"Confirm when you have."

"Where are you Jenk?" I ask.

"Not an unreasonable question Once-Other. Didn't he tell you?"

"Who? What?"

"Ozerken."

"Ozerken? That no good damn treasonous criminal."

"With my own patience in hand...I beg of you—patience. Didn't he tell you to think all of most everything through?"

"Ah? Yes, he did."

"Did you dear friend?"

"Yes. He's guilty of treason."

"Rather does require thinking through all, Once-Other."

"Through what? Come on. Tell me."

"Honorable campaigner. You know that does no good. You'll find the answer yourself but later, not now."

"Okay. Damn. Alright. I'm at the square rock. Oh? It's is not a rock."

"Excellent. Look inside."

I open a door and find a hoisting-chair attached to a pulley inside the *rock*. "Are we connected Jenk?" I ask.

"I'm here friend."

They didn't take my Nomadi! How strange! My legs collapse. I remain seated for several minutes. So he didn't take my Nomadi. Make it five items Ozerken left for me.

Now. With nothing further worth a penny inside my head, I ask what comes. "What do you know about the contest to free climb Iron Rock Ridge?" And I labor back up to my feet.

"Welcome back. Long since been conquered Once-Other. Let's concentrate on getting you off of the Highlands. Okay?"

"Okay," and I smile at this mind-to-mind of ours. "I am thankful we don't need to use verbal speech for my dry and hard as rock tongue fills my mouth. What would we do here if our technology required speaking? I would die listening to your attempts to reach me. Right?"

"Right my friend. Well now. What's your complete physical state like?"

"I'm okay. My broken arm appears to be healing but my chest wounds are not. It could be gangrene. I'm suffering more-n-more pain from the bullet wounds and my head spins when I stand. I'm not sure of how much more I can take. Drank some water but have had nothing to eat. I'm weaker than ever before. You understand Wernt poisoned me?"

"I do. Ozerken leave you Bondo-Preserve bandages?"

"Just enough for my arm," I reply.

And my thoughts run rampant and rapid.

How is it that Jenk knows Ozerken? Is Jenk part of their treasonous conspiracy? Damn! At this moment, I'm unable to see clearly let alone think properly. I'd best leave that until later. Perhaps Jenk is friend enough and is not sending me to certain death. "The ones wrapped around my chest are pretty much used up," I add.

"Dear me. Well then. Let's get down to business shall we? The faster you're off the mountain the sooner we can get someone to you. Now—the lift is mechanical so you'll need to work the handbrake, but in going down one working arm will do. You ready to do this?"

"I hope so," I reply noting the uncertainty in my response.

I pause and generate as much peace and confidence for self as I can muster given circumstances. I close the door, take hold of the handle on the top and pull. The box tilts, I step aside and it drops to sand.

On careful examination, I note that the chair though covered by a layer of sand, is itself in good order. The ropes are sound and the pulley mountings do not budge when I test them. That the chair has one leg only does not appear odd to me. In my view, a chair can be designed with as many legs or as few as its creator chooses.

"All checks out good," I mutter.

"Get into the seat and strap in," Jenk commands.

By all appearances, this chair was made for tiny people as it swings back-n-forth each time I put weight on the seat. After several attempts and failing, I sit back, think it through and am struck by a flash of inspiration.

I'll throw caution to the wind and lunge out into space, do a half turn in the air and land backward in the seat. In the instant of landing, I'll grasp hold of the pulley ropes, hang on like mad and steady myself by planting my feet on the wood ledge against which the chair rests its single leg.

In good physical condition, that's a challenge. It will be impossible with a broken arm and so I dismiss all thoughts along those lines...but wait! If this is a dream—anything should be possible. But on second thoughts, why scare Once-Other of Here-Born, even in a dream.

"Jenk?"

"Yes."

"How can we be talking? Are we not too far apart?"

"We're linked up Once-Other. Nomads configured a virtual pipe between our Nomadi. They set yours to Locked-on and invoked auto-answer. They charged your battery using Power over Wireless. I recommend you add PoW to your service in the future. Listen, I'm doing this with you, not Madsen. I'm closer to you than he is, is why. Are you in the seat?"

"No."

"Get in," he commands.

This then is not a dream so lunging out into space would not be good advice, despite being my own advice. I examine the chair in detail listing each item.

It's suspended from four ropes. Okay. Four ropes. Hmm? Ah. They join a single rope hanging from the pulley-winch system above. Um-hmm. The brake mechanism attaches to the single rope as well. I reach over and push the brake handle aside.

I try getting in. Each time I do the chair swivels, swings backward and I almost fall. I retreat and inspect it once again but in detail. A crossover harness hangs over the top of the backrest. I reach for the harness but my knee bumps the chair and it swings away.

"I can't get into the chair Jenk."

"Seems your mental capacities are down and away, Once-Other. Retrieve them and look. But look with your Foundation—not as though you know everything and have seen all before."

I look-n-look.

Some while later I am still looking.

I sense Jenk pacing back-n-forth.

I stop looking at the chair and its single leg and rest my arms on the small wood ledge against which the chair bumps. Idly I trace out with a finger a slot in the ledge that curls back on itself.

My thinking stops. My seeing stops.

All I sense is my finger sliding along the slot. It's so strange an action that ensnares so much of my attention. I will not be able to descend Iron Rock Ridge. I can't help thinking on how I may, though. I figure the trick is to enter the chair forwards, head first, crawl under the four ropes while turning to get seated.

It can't be done with only one good arm.

"Are you in?" Jenk asks.

"Yes, I'm in."

"Well! Excellent Once-Other. Now take hold of the brake."

"No point to that."

"Once-Other! Here-Born's damn fine and respected campaigner. You are ordered to pay attention. Now pay attention!"

Jenk's voice slices through my reverie. "Oh? Okay, Jenk."

"Recover yourself one-two-three. Invoke your Moment in Time. Right now! Examine the chair. Use it. Get seated."

"Okay," I reply and turning, crawl away from the edge.

Standing on unsteady legs and drunk with heat, I stagger off into the desert. A distance in I kneel, scan across sand, spot some burrows, crawl to them and drink my fill.

# CHAPTER 59

## OF A PAINFUL DESCENT

I remain seated close to the Crier burrow taking a few moments to calm and collect self.

Calmer, I invoke my Moment in Time but instead of mine Karrell's Moment in Time appears. I'm moved to smile, once you've done it right a Foundation works no matter what. And my own Foundation kicks alive sparked by his success.

Hydrated by Crier-water, back at the edge of Iron Rock Ridge, heart filled with determination, I inspect the platform and hoist-chair as though I had seen neither before. It clicks together, thanks to hydrated clarity and a Foundation absent any government control and free of regulations and vested interests.

Okay! The single leg fits into the curved slot. The one I'd run my finger along. I pull the chair closer, hook its leg in place, push and shove trying to dislodge the chair but it remains firmly locked in place.

My back to the chair I slide in while keeping a watch on the chair's leg. I reach over my shoulder, grab the harness, pull the two straps over my shoulders and slip the eye loops over hourglass fasteners. And pause as my wounds express their protests at such activity.

Recovered some, I unhook the chair, grab hold of the lever, squeeze it and drop three some sand-paces leaving my heart and stomach on the platform above. They catch up and I breathe easier.

"Once-Other?" Jenk asks.

"I'm in and already around three sand-paces down, Jenk."

"Now you're doing excellent indeed. Gently lower the chair, friend."

Going down gusting wind pushes me towards the cliff forcing me to kick off. Razor-edged rock spins by in slow-motion. Giddy, I yet make steady progress during which Jenk remains silent.

I ponder how we can be communicating as we are too far apart for mind-to-mind, even those closest must be some distance away. But had I not already asked him about that? No? Yes? I don't recall.

"All going well, Once-Other?" Jenk asks.

"Did you provide details about us talking across this distance?"

"I did," Jenk says.

"Right. Okay. Yes. I'm descending."

"You still sound a trifle confused—watch the harness they are tricky altogether."

"Okay. But tell me again?"

"If you insist. We are connected over Nomadi. Please keep yours safe."

"Oh yes. That's right. Excellent. I will. Thank you."

"How are those wounds holding up?" he asks.

I inspect my arm. Make a fist several times accidentally flex the wrong hand releasing the brake and plunge downwards.

Rock rushes by and as I drop faster-n-faster the blur of rock drowns my senses. Bile rises in my throat.

After a struggle, I swallow and look outwards.

Rock switches to desert and back to rock over-n-over.

My head spins faster.

My mind short-circuits, my vision blurs.

Yet deep inside I know there's something I can do.

But what?

I rally my will and glance to the sky where appears the instrument telling me what to do. I reach up and apply the brake. The chair stops dead bouncing at the end of the rope. A series of sharp twangs and showers of sand hit my eyes with unerring accuracy.

I wipe at them only to cause greater discomfort.

I sit still holding my breath waiting for the rope to break.

My arm shakes.

The chair swings wildly.

My foot slams into the cliff.

Razor sharp blades of rock cut into my legs shredding my pants and skin. I kick off, swoop a fast loop and hit the wall with my knee. Fiery pain leaps up-n-down my leg. I kick out and my boot slams into rock.

My ankle joint explodes and catches on fire.

I force my eyes open despite the pain.

Through tears and grating sand, I find myself swaying back-n-forth.

I glance down at my leg to find my foot disjointed, hanging loose and useless. I know that ankle cannot take another such collision with rock and neither can it be walked on.

With no protective clothing, any gust of wind strong enough to slam me into the rock-face of Iron Ridge Mountain would be more than I can recover from.

I kick off with my good foot only to spin wildly. On the next swing back in I drag my injured foot down the cliff face searching for a hold. My ankle protests with pain reminiscent of Crier poison at work.

After several tries, I get a foothold on an upturned edge and steady myself. My heart pounds in my chest, hot desert air wheezes by my teeth. I swallow hard, let go of the brake lever, flex my fingers and answer Jenk's question.

"All appears well with my arm, but my chest wounds require attention—as I've said."

"Thank you Once-Other. Perhaps you should think over and through—Ozerken."

"I'd prefer to be back on solid sand before doing that. I'm ravaged with poison despite most of it being expelled. The antivenom saved my life—that I'll admit. I give many thanks to Ozerken but no forgiveness. I need more and soon."

"I understand," he says.

I rest a moment until Jenk's voice jerks me awake.

"You still with me Once-Other?"

"Yes. I was just resting for a few minutes."

"Make that two hours Once-Other."

"Oh?"

"Let's get going shall we?"

"Okay."

Warily, I continue my descent.

After what feels like weeks the desert floor appears some ten sand-paces below.

With impatience, I release the brake a little too fast, plunge six sand-paces and jerk to a stop. The eye loops pop free, the harness snakes up my chest. I snatch at it but miss.

A sudden gust of wind thrusts me into the cliff-face. My forehead catches a sharp edge of rock. Body and mind fuse to become whirlpools of confusion and pain.

I cling to the seat; blood pours down my face.

The desert spins wildly.

Pain rakes its claws up my arm as the chair spins faster.

My boot catches on rock. My floppy ankle pops back into place amidst blinding pain, and I lose my grip on the brake lever.

Another wild swing and my other foot slams into the cliff face.

The seat tilts like a small boat upon a rough EB sea.

Helpless, I slide out the chair feet first.

I lunge upwards, grab for the overhead rope and miss.

The chair and I part company.

# CHAPTER 60

## OF PROMISES MADE

The sun switches on-n-off. The Half-Day-Moon flies away a blur too fast for the eye to follow. The Star-of-Hope zigzags across a darkened sky, a sidewinder in search of relief from burning sand.

Beyond that fragmented reality, the Carousel Galaxy explodes wrapping streams of red cotton wool around the Half-Day-Moon, a suffocating embrace of fire and smoke.

Bright light burns my eyes, tears stream down my cheeks.

I close them and find some respite.

I hold still.

I listen. There is only the whisper of wind.

I doze.

Gentle touches of wind then wind enough to stir me.

I try to awake but cannot.

Much later thunder sounds from out the far distance.

I jerk awake glancing in all directions at once. My eyes are drawn towards the horizon. An obese giant dances closer growing taller with each stride it takes. Its enormous belly splits open. The halves explode and spread upwards to hide the sun.

As this menacing monster of a sand-cloud looms closer dark ovals evolve between cloud and sand. Beneath me, sand vibrates faster hurting the arm held tightly across my chest.

I cannot reckon why sand vibrates.

I wait, insanely curious.

The shapes beneath the clouds take form.

I blink several times to find billowing linen hanging on a washing line. My eyes focus further and the forms settle and evolve into large black-n-white horses. My chest and back vibrate to the beat of their hooves. In a feeble attempt to hide I press my back against the hot face-rock of Iron Rock Ridge and pull the fur coat over my face.

My mouth grows drier and my eyes scratch on sand as they move behind closed eyelids. Sand chokes and tickles my nose. Thunder ends and an eerie silence descends. Sand drifts down to gentle upon my hands and face as mist surely does.

I peep out from within the coat.

At a safe distance stand a small herd of horses. Each watches me as though they are on a tour at the zoo. After several minutes of mutual examinations, the leader throws its head high, whinnies and looks expectantly at me. I shrug, hunching my shoulders in question.

Bemused questions scurry across their faces, dive into eyes and hold, suspended in pools of black water. As one they turn to the stallion. His attention remains fixed upon me, his eyes locked on mine.

But I have nothing to say that he'd understand.

He rises up onto his hind legs, paws at the sky, whinnies and attacks sand with his hooves. Dust billows.

My nose itches more. I scratch and sneeze.

The stallion shakes its head. His magnificent black mane fans out around his white face and reminds me of Soonsaan. He stamps sand three times with his hoof, looks at his herd then back at me.

I struggle up and lean against the cliff face. I take a step towards them, but my bad ankle gives. I fall to my knees and try as I may, am unable to regain my feet.

The stallion bobs his head saying, "Wait here," and pounds sand once again.

Once-Other, feeling a little silly, slams his good fist into sand three times and waves an acknowledgment just as sunset descends and all is dark and cold.

The horses shake their heads in unison and, in the sudden cold, blow vapor clouds out their nostrils. They turn and gallop in circles, marking the spot I assume.

They face the way they had come, glance over their shoulders, shake their heads in warning, and gallop off into the night the mist of their breath thick upon the cold air.

I wave them adieu and pull the fur coat close.

Night becomes morning, morning becomes day.

I soon lose count of the changes.

Staring open-eyed into the burning sunlight, my focus dissolves turning all into shapeless clouds of dust dancing through shimmering heat.

Suddenly the wind dies.

I sit up, remove the fur coat, lean against the furnace-hot face of Iron Rock Ridge, drape the coat over me like a tent, and find faint comfort from the beating sun. I awake lying flat on my back on top of the fur coat with arms spread wide.

My face burns, blistered by a baking sun. Some blisters have popped their serum already crystallized. My mouth sticks closed; too dry to open, my tongue is too solid to swallow.

I try standing but am unable to. My legs feel dead and even my good arm refuses to rise upon command. I remain on my back waiting for a something. I know not what and yes, I may never stir again. I can sense it...a body too far gone. One that has given up the struggle and is now ready to give up the ghost.

What's to become of Karrell...? A thought as sudden and unexpected as drenching rain would be. Something I had said to him is important. But what did I say?

I think for a long time, but all comes up blank.

He vanishes from my thoughts.

Later.

Opportunities offered and missed come knocking upon memory's door drowning out all else. Ah. Maybe Maggie was the one. We could have spent some damn fine romantic time together had I been ready.

She, her parents and mine, had long been friends. Friends at school, in church and out upon the sands of Here-Born challenging the elements on SandRiders so old I winch at our foolhardiness.

Then bow in Deidre. At first warm and loving, eyes that promised more than any man could wish for. But once I took the hook the fisher-women appeared guarding her catch from any that might approach. And so Maggie drifted away though never too far and remained a friend no matter.

Maggie's face dances before me now. Her silky hair wafts in the breeze. Her eyes smile as they always do, beckoning me come closer. Her naturally radiant lips venture closer and her last kiss lingers upon my cheek. In my mouth the flavor of popcorn resurrects.

I chuckle drily.

We are still well suited one to the other—yet nothing. I had made excuses about Deidre, on the rebound, danger and all. But to be honest, none of that was ever true. I knew it. Others knew it. We all knew it yet here I am still single.

I pull the fur coat tight around my waist and smile.

Yes, the Old Soldier lives in my heart as well.

What is real? What is delusion? Does survival depend on my separating them? And Karrell? Where is he now? I can but dread the circumstances he must now face.

What strange and contradictory characters Ozerken and Pe'truss are. First, they help get me killed. Next, they help me survive and finally...they leave me here to die.

*"No matter what, regardless of where, if you need me I will come."*

Yes. That, more-or-less, is what I'd said to Karrell. Had I said so too hastily? With too little thought? Is this the final moments of Once-Other of Here-Born?

Karrell's face floats into view. His peak achievement at his Moment in Time once again dissolves his eyes into pools of liquid diamonds. How proud that moment is for me, for him.

How grand an achievement it is for him, for me.

I lean closer the better to see his eyes and my head explodes as a tornado of pain twists within it. I stagger but manage to keep my footing and with arms held wide I stare down at sand in disbelief. After a few moments and as my boots come into focus I figure it out.

Yes. I am standing. Yes. They are right. Once-Other hates to surrender hates to give up. How did I come to stand? I have no idea and I don't give a damn. I take a step forward, pause and then another one.

I know not where I go...nor how. I grasp that direction demands marching towards Karrell no matter where he is or what he has been subjected to. Along that road travels hand-in-hand our campaign. Damn right to keep going and wrong of me to consider surrender.

I know too much. I've heard too much.

I croak my defiance in a hoarse whisper, "Death! I bid thee farewell."

And I wave adieu to Death's hopes.

But I'm not sure if it's too late.

I examine the desert in detail.

Several Crier burrows are close enough to reach.

"Forward march," I command.

I march forward...well...stagger onwards.

I drink and consider eating raw Crier, but pass.

Back at the foot of Iron Rock Ridge I sit down and examine my condition to find a fire burns in my chest and my left arm creaks when I make a fist.

I check my Nomadi to find it is cracked and broken. After a full inspection, I ascertain communications no longer work but that recording is still taking place. I nod my satisfaction and smile at those future students and others who may someday study this record. But in the minus column, there is now no way by which to find me.

I stare upwards and soon the sun turns green.

The moon fades to black.

Beige clouds surround me. Rolling thunder moves sand.

I feel it in my bones. I use its vibrations and focus.

Out upon the horizon a sandstorm once again heads my way. This one has ovals between billowing sand and flat sand as well—but these are dark brown—not black-n-white as before.

I gaze upwards and it's daytime.

Perhaps the horses have returned, and having bathed are brown.

Though they gallop, they do so with a strange loping gait. Their heads hang low, their bellies are large and swollen and their necks extended. My nightmare becomes insanity as the horses thin and distort into wispy ghosts.

An eyeglass appears before me. In it, shape-changing cacti dance in the heat-haze. They merge to become brown petals standing upright. The petals become horses, they shift-n-waver and separate into beige blotches. They regroup, outlines sharpen and shapes stabilize to become camels racing across sand.

In mere moments, they plow to a halt before me blowing hard in protest at having galloped under Here-Born's sun.

Camel toes shuffle, necks crane, eyes blink.

Voices murmur, someone coughs but silence descends by command of a powerful voice. "Hold!" a male voice declares.

The camels stare at me as I stare at them.

One ambles on over, stops when close, lays its head upon sand, stares me in the eye and laughs as though enjoying one damn fine joke.

I glare long and hard trying to rationalize what I see for camels ordinarily, do not laugh and neither do they evolve from horses.

I rub my eyes and focus. Ah!

A man is laughing.

He peers around the camel's neck and his deep black eyes are crying—he is laughing that hard.

I for one am not amused.

"Take him," he commands and hands lift me.

At first I fight them but cease as water touches my lips. I pull in a mouth full and swallow. I reach for more, but they take it away. Someone smears a fatty compound over the blisters and gashes on my face and legs. Foul smelling though soothing it is.

A wet blanket appears and wraps around me and much to my peace of mind, my temperature sets to dropping.

Darkness beckons, a bony finger crooked.

I wave it aside, reach out and embrace the gurgle of water as it splashes over the blanket. Soon I am so cold I shiver.

# CHAPTER 61

## OF ARTISTIC UNIVERSES

I awake to find the camels and their foul breath are gone, peace and quiet reigns. Without moving, I glance about and find I recline post-slumber-wise inside an expensive tent.

Wool and mohair rugs in desert shades of sand-brown, beige and black cover every square sand-pace of the floor. Some are plain in color; others have geometric designs threaded into them. Soft light radiates from lamps shaped like candles. Overhead, a spiral fan stirs the air. Scattered emerald-green lounge cushions provide seating with a view of the entire tent.

Centered in all this luxury is one damn comfortable bed upon which I lie beneath dark red covers. The comfort and opulence are not what concern me the most.

And so I recall the Nomads with a severe degree of trepidation. Rumor says they treat you with grace on first acquaintance, keep one well fed, hydrated, bring you back to health and up to weight and cook and eat you.

My heart pounds despite trying to calm internal rants.

I sit up, spot my clothes and am about to embark upon an escape when from outside comes the shuffle of shoes upon sand. I pretend to sleep.

The tent flap moves.

Eyes half-closed I watch from behind my eyelashes.

A nomad female enters and stops just beyond the entrance.

I am all of a sudden ravaged by hot-n-cold, which has nothing to do with the other fevers plaguing me. I open my eyes fully to better see her face and am struck by a greater assault of hot-n-cold. Thoughts and excuses involving Deidre and on the rebound vanish in a blinding Fragger like flash.

She is dressed in a cream, single-piece silk suit that clings as though a natural part of her. Steam rises from a golden bowl she holds in delicate hands. Draped over the edge is a white facecloth. Under her left arm, she grips a green bottle of liquid soft-soap, over her shoulder hangs a tan towel and in her eyes a smile awaits presentation.

It lights and Once-Other, the poet long buried, is reborn.

My heart skips and sings and accelerates for her smile was made in heaven with love and care. Around it her golden brown hair glows a halo of wonder and health. Never in all of time has a smile said as much with so little, to but one. Never in all my time have I wished to be smiled at over-n-over.

A breeze touches her revealing partial lines of her beauty beneath.

I gaze up in search of her eyes to find them watching me, and I understand with a profound and desperate need that I must look into their emerald beauty every day for the rest of my life. I can have no meaningful life without engaging them each morning upon waking, nor can I live without saying goodnight to them every night for the Light of Life lives in them.

Life and light dance and twinkle there so powerfully that any may behold their dance, but only a few will understand.

Here they say, we present for your consideration a free spirit. One with no wish to be owned by another and who has no desire to own another. Yet they glow with an abundance of love. Until this moment, I had not known what nor whom I had been looking for—for all my life.

I continue to stare.

She allows me the privilege and time to do so. All the while she remains poised, calm, neither challenging nor demeaning of my looking.

In return, she examines me.

Finally, our eyes meet head on and in that instant, a new universe is born. A personal one, one not of the physical universe nor any other, yet we occupy it. Beyond our presence, it's empty—but a different kind of empty. Nothing is missing for there has never been anything inside it. Instead, it's a new canvas created for a single lifelong work of art.

Together we are the artist.

The brushes and paints in a multitude of colors, textures and hues are the emotions and adventures of a life together. Colors are of courage, of love, of achievement, of goals attained, of friends and children held, loved and departed. Of quiet moments together. Of raging battles of will. Of battles of war but always...of two artists and a single painting.

She glides forward, a breeze across the landscape of cushions and carpets. She places the basin down, looks me in the eye, smiles and touches my injured arm now wrapped in clean Bondo-Preserve bandages.

I boil-over and am quite convinced steam is rising from the top of my head. Amongst all these raging emotions I realize there has been no Neatness in my conduct, to one degree or another. So far I've said nothing. No, thank you. Not where am I? Not who are you? Not how did I get here?

Most assuredly, I have stared my fill. "Thank you for this magnificent tent in which I have just awoken," I say.

"Pleased to meet you Once-Other. But please, think nothing of this. You may not know it, but you are not merely some lost soul rescued from the grip of our desert. And neither are you simply a business contact of Jenk's...but a friend of his. Jenk is part of us. Therefore, you are a part of us. Welcome."

"Thank you. I am honored."

"I'm going to wash you," she communicates in a whisper.

I'm both happy and genuinely afraid. On Here-Born we wash all food before cooking—positively washed and absolutely clean.

"You will be absolutely clean," she says, smiles mischievously, dips the cloth in the water, applies soap and looking deep into my eyes, begins.

Her cool hands mingled with the warmth of the water whisper a cleansing breeze across my skin. Goose-bumps arise to play havoc with skin and mind. I give her a smile but a short, closed mouth one for my mouth tastes like the bottom of a birdcage—not that I know what one tastes like. In return, she blushes wonderfully and peeps sideways and shy-like at me, which makes me blush as well.

She washes my chest with gentle care. "These bullet wounds are bad Once-Other. We are preparing some pre-owned parts from your own store to replace them. But not until you are a little stronger and the danger has lessened."

She touches the entry wounds, smiles and continues washing. After several minutes, she all of a sudden gives me a bold glance and leans in closer.

Her closeness is both familiar and comforting as though we have known each other with intimacy for a long time. Deep inside, hidden from all others and perhaps even self, Once-Other the survivor hopes she's not looking hungry like at him and mentally thumbing through her repertoire of recipes.

Despite this fear, I am reminded of my youth. Many times I'd stopped and stared and stared. Often, the lady stopped as well but we both moved on...something was wrong or missing.

Now I understand.

She glances hard at me, decides something and says, "Are you married Once-Other? I've heard no—but I'm curious to hear from you."

I lie in silence stunned by her question.

She waits her hand poised to continue.

"I have been single a long time," I reply.

"Ah. How long so?"

"Recently dawned upon me that when I was married...I was yet single."

"How recent did that dawn upon you?" she asks.

"Moments ago."

She nods and says, "You must engage many girlfriends amongst your own. So many as to occupy all your attention...and stamina."

"Well no," I gasp.

"Are you playing with me? Taking advantage of a simple Nomad girl?"

"No!" I cry out.

She leans in close, gazes into my eyes, down to the I within and melds with me. After a moment, she pulls back and her smile curves the first brush stroke upon our canvas.

Mine the second.

I am lost to despair when she finishes up, gathers the basin, the soap, the face cloth and towel, nods to me, heads for the exit and pauses.

"We have our customs and if you wish—I can initiate them?"

"Any trials by danger?" I ask.

"Perhaps we Nomad women are danger enough," she says and smiles.

Swirling pain engulfs me.

I force myself to find her through it and she's still standing there. I nod yes or hope I did.

"Sleep well Once-Other."

Pain assaults me and when I again focus she's gone.

I lie back to the rustle of clothes at the entrance once again. At first, I'm disappointed to find a different Nomad female standing where she had. Secondly, I whisper to myself, "Most beloved Half-Day-Moon, save me."

This one towers fearsome large, muscular all over and her face glowers like the dark side of the Half-Day-Moon. She smiles and magnificent flat-edged teeth display—teeth well suited to chewing meat—any meat.

She steps cautiously closer and checks me over. Wipes large hands on a red desert-suit as though unsure of herself, and sighs deeply. Pushing deep-red hair off her face she takes a step closer and her emerald eyes twinkle as she says, "My daughter likes you more than I can understand."

Praise be all sand, heavens, the Half-Day-Moon, the Star-of-Hope and preservatives for this frightening individual gave birth to my heavenly designed beauty to whom I'd just surrendered my heart. I try a smile but fail to mount it.

Nevertheless, her eyes brighten, she rushes over, grasps my hand in a painful manner and asks, "Do you like her?"

Once-Other can only think of her calloused hand that holds his and nod an honest yes. She gives my hand a squeeze.

Sharp nails shoot up my arm into and then out of the top of my skull. Damn! This woman does not know her own strength.

She smiles at me.

"Call me Dew," she says. "Everyone does."

She waves to someone outside and releases my hand.

"She has many sisters," she says grinning hugely, proudly.

She hurries out as they enter in a flurry of smiling faces. Their desert suits too are of silk and their eyes glow in mixtures of black and emerald.

They stand ooh-ing and ah-ing then set upon me.

Their touch is as soft and light as a delicate film of sand upon an arm. But I'm once again afraid when they poke at and measure my limbs. It strikes me they measure for the pot and with a poke here-n-there are looking for where best to dismember.

In one fluid motion, they turn me over, poke at my behind and laugh real loud when someone tickles my foot. They hold me down with much shushing-n-hushing followed by some subtle stroking.

I smile my pleasure, but the heartbeat calling for immediate escape returns when they measure me this way round as well. They roll me back-n-forth, laugh some and shush each other while continuing to measure-n-poke when, without warning, all are silent.

At the entrance stands Dew smiling from ear to ear. She glances outside, nods to someone, takes a step sideways and waits.

A magnificent tower of a Nomad man with straight black hair and deep brown eyes staring from out a handsome desert hardened face steps into the tent. They are the same eyes that had laughed when I lay at the foot of Iron Rock Ridge.

He stands alone for a moment his arms crossed, his dark brown and black desert-suit tight on his tall, lean frame. Not a single grain of sand mars his knee-high black boots.

She enters, stands next to him and when she smiles my heart skips several beats and melts. She perceives this and her face reflects her own heart's smile. She takes his arm and pushes him towards me.

He hesitates, steps closer and says, "My name's Benwarr."

He glances at her and she waves him on.

"But to the point Once-Other. Our customs typically require...." He glances at her again.

She waves fiercely.

"Well. What I'm to say would under ordinary circumstances take many months—at times years before being mentioned. Months of casual acquaintance. But...in these days, due to conflict between worlds, with lives at risk, with casualties already...we no longer wait."

He glances her way again and she waves him on once more.

"Now Once-Other. My daughter wishes to commit to you. Do you wish to commit her? No. Damn and wait. I'm not getting this right. Okay. First, and in clarity's direction, we are not talking marriage. To commit simply allows two individuals to develop a relationship—something we Nomads require under our concepts of Neatness. Well? What do you say?"

My first knee jerk reaction says this is much better than being eaten. But when I meet her eyes an emotion deep inside my heart explodes—one I know well. One that has been missing for a long, long time. She feels it as well and I nod yes.

Benwarr smiles as if I had just now saved his life instead of he'd saved mine. He waits for her approval, she smiles it to him and I dare say beams of light began to shine from her eyes.

He steps forward and shakes my hand, which lights a pain all the way to my other hand and down to my toes. He pulls me to my feet with the greatest of ease, holds me steady as I sway and gives me to her.

"And thus you are committed," he declares sounding happier than his face reveals.

So I'm committed and no one-two-three—here we go. But this is much better than being eaten if eating people, they indeed do. Now, what of Maggie?

As wonderful as she is, she and I never experienced a moment such as this. I can only hope she will understand.

Benwarr steps aside and she takes my hand and kisses me.

Well now! With my being shot several times, those two attacks of poison upon me one more recent than the other. The pain-on-pain of a broken arm, the solidifying nighttime cold and murderous daytime sun. One dislocated and again relocated ankle. Then as well there's the hunger I suffered with exceptional toughness.

All these, along with the descent down Iron Rock Ridge, hit me one-two-three and more between the eyes. And so I am robbed of the meager strength I'd recaptured during my recent sleep and I pass out standing up.

The last impression as I fall, is of them laughing and commenting on how powerful my committed one's kisses are seeing as a single one has knocked me out cold.

Even I chuckle some.

They fall silent as Benwarr recites in an official but welcoming tone, "He's a fine man as well as an excellent tourist guide and a magnificent campaigner. Rest well Once-Other. We must plan as we have much to do. For these, we need your input.

"Though you haven't been told, as of last week you've been promoted from Captain to the rank of Colonel. This we've done in honor of your conduct and dedication to duty and the damn fine execution of your functions in the Here-Born Army. And allow me to add...not a small jump and well earned...despite Madsen's contrary reports and failure to inform you."

"Which is exceptional especially for one who believes we are going to eat him," Dew muses.

They all laugh a happy, carefree laughter.

The shuffle of shoes upon carpet as they turn to leave and a thought crosses my mind right as darkness takes me utterly and one-two-three altogether.

What is my committed one's name? Why has no one told me? Is it something terrible?

As night progresses, I sense her warmth next to me and the cold air around us. Her hand takes mine and she curls up alongside me as the Healer of Wounds.

From far away come the beat of drums and the strumming of guitars along with many voices in song. Inside the lyrics, the name of Once-Other is mentioned. But when the night's deepest cold arrives, that morning hour when the old and sick die, a freeze creeps deep into my bones.

She returns and lies with me and a unique warmth flows out of her and into me. Her voice communicates she loved me the moment they found me out in the desert. That I shouldn't worry, she will give me all the life she harbors. And with that she will help bring me through this encounter with death I must now face.

Her arms are strong, her breath sweet upon my cheek. Her natural perfume tastes of what legend and bottled perfume says is the scent of roses. Her hair tickles and down near Death's door I chuckle a little.

But hammering pain returns.

And Death's door swings open.

Once-Other sways towards forever darkness.

Her hand grips mine harder and I realize how cold I am.

The warmth of her travels up my arm and into my heart and all my pre-owneds scream their pain at me right where they were joined and glued.

Which pain commands me to die.

Faster-n-faster the pain-on-pain rushes back-n-forth until her touch recedes and her hand slips from mine and I'm alone in the dark and very, very cold.

# CHAPTER 62

## OF A VISIT WITH PRE-OWNED AND DEATH

In that eerie zone between life and death, the air seems solid with cold. Distant sounds ring familiar, others thud, but I'm unable to identify what they are. A sharp flash of silver. How can it be? I see no light. The clink of metal on metal.

A scalpel appears and slices across the darkness.

In my peripheral, something edges closer.

I glance over to find a ribcage hanging in midair.

Ribs detach one at a time and fly away, spinning like boomerangs, though destined never to return. I recall my pre-owned parts business and the cruel criminal tourist calling himself Peter Wernt. I growl at Ozerken and Pe'truss, two bad-on-bad Desert Drivers with their four dead eyes.

At my ear, Wernt whispers telling me to die some more. I smile with grim humor wishing Wernt had been awarded Deidre as well—she'd make life on Earth-Born a worthy misery for him.

I drift along featureless tunnels. Beneath me, black sand slithers across black rock its dry, eerie shuffle sending shivers through me. Yet I feel no emotion. No pain. No fear. I am content, numbed by cold into indifference despite the ominous dark.

I angle left sensing a bend in the tunnel. I drift aimlessly, mind numbed yet drawn onwards by an invisible guide. I emerge upon a blackened plain. Soft lights turn on overhead and pulse.

I ride a gentle breeze upwards.

Questions embrace me.

What do I trust self with?

Is persistence a worthy trait?

Isn't it wise to know when to end all endeavors...even that of living?

A sluggish mind struggles to comprehend them.

Something distracts me.

I examine the dark beyond the pulsing light to find only emptiness.

I sense a something, though, and check once again. Nothing. I listen instead. Yes, a sound. A soft distant one. A voice.

One I've heard before.

A voice laced with concern calling across a vast distance.

I search for the source but cannot find it.

The groan of a hatch opening, a bright white light switches on with a violent electrical snarl.

I turn to find someone standing at a door alongside the edge of Death's tunnel. White light shining from behind hides the person's features. Yet I sense we are kindred. I move closer and recognize her but cannot recall a name.

In her eyes, shadows reveal an internal struggle. Quivering emotions say it is fear she fights. In her hands, she clasps a pre-owned ribcage—a strong looking and handsomely muscled one.

I reach out, but my arms won't move.

Shocked at this, she swallows hard and smiles her courage and whispers as one does when wishing another back from the grave, "My name is Roses D'elti, daughter of Benwarr and Dewana D'elti. Everyone calls her Dew."

She waves and blows a kiss.

It touches my cold lips leaving a trace of herself, a sampling of warmth.

I reach out and fumble about.

Her warm-n-soft fingers find mine.

Her warm-n-strong hand grasps mine and tugs me gently, firmly.

I slide forward as though escaping quicksand and slowly pass by Death's Door and it swings closed behind me. Death's Scream of anguish follows me, demanding I return.

I flounder, but Roses is close, warm. Her arms hold me tight but gently. Her life flows through me warming my body and spirit from the inside outwards. A peacefulness born of assurance invades my mind and I sleep.

I awake to find her breath sweet upon me, her hand wrapped around mine. I am in pain yet content. It appears that Once-Other's life goes on as goals and purposes beckon.

My eyes close and deep down at the center of sleep, I sense she's here and so I am safe and can sleep without fear.

When I again awake the world is a painful glaring light but immediately a cool-n-soft darkness gentles over my eyes.

I smile and sense her one in return for we are upon our canvas where no distance intercedes between thoughts and emotions, nor between the inner life we all cradle knowingly or unknowingly within ourselves.

Her voice tells me not to open my eyes for I've been gone far too long and the light may blind. The cool softness of the wet cloth over my eyes grows cooler and water trickles down my cheek.

I lick at it.

She whispers telling of how she'd kept me clean altogether, which includes my birdcage mouth and we chuckle over that. She further hopes I'll be happy with what she did and can't wait to find out if I approve of the pre-owneds they'd fit me with.

For an instant boomerang ribs flutter by.

She tells me further that there had been no need to change all my body parts. My head is still the same one along with my legs. What changed were my ribcage and an arm. She whispers that I must be thankful Peter Wernt didn't use hollow-point ammunition for had he done so I would not have survived.

Her sweet mouth kisses me, I groan, she laughs, sits back and touches my cheek. With her hand on my cheek and her smile upon my senses, I sleep.

Later when I awake, Roses still holds my hand and still smiles.

I communicate with intense urgency, but she shushes me and says, "We understand about Wernt and Karrell. My father has gone to check on Karrell."

A sliver of hope flickers to life.

"I hope you like the pre-owneds we fixed you with?" she says.

"I will be happy with *most* all that you are and what you do," I reply.

She kisses my cheek and pours water into the cloth and whispers, "I hope that that *most* is true. The last thing I need is endless agreement with all I say and do."

I nod agreement and she says, "Sleep now. One I love".

She lies next to me and places a comforting arm gently across my chest. I sleep in a dedicated fashion and no dreams wander upon sleep's landscape.

Later when voices awaken me, night is about.

Soft lighting shines easy upon my eyes.

Looking around I find Benwarr returned.

"Live by Neatness alone," he says.

And I smile for Neatness is One and One is All.

He rubs his eyes and says, "In this lucid moment allow me a question, Once-Other."

I agree.

"Did you manage to reach this Wernt's Foundation?"

"Yes indeed," I answer.

"There's Hope then but...we are about to harden our response. I...we need you fit and strong as the moment for defensive action—both here and on Earth-Born can wait no longer. Rest please—no further questions at this time. There will be hours enough for that later.

"The way ahead will be difficult, more dangerous. You must recover. We need you ready and able. Until then...rest well friend. Oh! You recall being told you are now a Colonel?"

I nod yes but cannot rest easy until I impart some of what I've found. "I need to debrief. I've critical information. I...."

"Rest Colonel Once-Other," Benwarr commands.

Roses pushes me back and says, "More tourists than before are coming. It's a good sign."

I'm not so sure it is. Not if they are like Peter Wernt. But I hold my peace. She looks to the entrance as a tall Nomad enters.

His face is a younger Benwarr and he carries himself with the same grace, dignity and sense of power. Roses rises, walks to him, hugs him. She steps back and checks over his dark brown and black leather suit, tugs at a sleeve, adjusts his shirt collar and checks him once again nodding her approval.

He looks at me over her shoulder. "Welcome, Colonel Once-Other. I'm Droght, Roses' brother, Dew and Benwarr's son, needless to say."

Roses steps aside.

He bows and seats himself next to Benwarr.

Next, all those beautiful sisters enter. Benwarr smiles with pride as they seat themselves.

Roses' mother coughs and says, "Those new ribs you have there Once-Other—they sure do look tasty."

And all of everyone laughs.

Roses comes over and takes my hand kisses it and in her eyes a playful pixie dances.

And the lights go out but for me alone.

# CHAPTER 63

## OF BETRAYALS AND REVELATIONS

Wind-driven sand stirs me awake. With eyes closed I listen as it drums against the tent. And as I did when a child I imagine it sounds much as rain does. The freezing temperature says night is about, rampant pain means healing is about.

Across the subdued howl of the wind, Jenk's voice wakes me fully. "My honored friends, a trying time these past weeks," he says.

I glance around the tent.

Dew and Benwarr sit facing me, their daughters huddle close by. To one side, Madsen sprawls a grim grin in place, part of a cookie in hand the balance busily chewed on. Next to him sits Jenk, who expresses his pleasure at seeing me alive with a faint nod. He then smiles in acknowledgment of what transpired out upon sand—and coming from him hits home as one damn fine compliment altogether.

To my surprise, Maggie is here as well. Her face glows with calm and love, her eyes shine brighter than ever before.

She checks the entrance then says, "Dear me Once-Other—you sure do seem fine despite...." And she checks the entrance once again.

"Hello, Maggie. Surprised to...," I reply.

She waves me silent and says, "I'm pleased you won against sand an' all," and she shares a look with Roses, a secret one. One I hope is not born of conflict. Again, her eyes find the entrance and linger a moment.

Roses opens a cooker. Ceramic clinks against metal to foreshadow the intoxicating aroma of lamb stew. My stomach comes alive and growls worse than Peter Wernt's ever did.

Everyone laughs.

A sudden silence and what my attention is stuck upon takes control of me. "What of Karrell?" I ask into the silence.

Benwarr nods, looks directly at me. "To be short and clear Once-Other. Seems a road traveling in directions we are not sure of. I'm afraid we may be navigating quicksand. I cannot confirm this with any certainty. I...we sense a danger as none before. We'll come back to Karrell later when I'm sure."

"Thank you Benwarr," is all I can find to say. I swallow the foul seeds of fear whelming up to choke me and turn to Roses.

With a spoon in hand, she frowns a question at me. I reach for the bowl, but she waves my hand aside, kisses my cheek and feeds me ensuring I do not eat too much nor too fast. She allows me small sips of water but pulls the glass away when I try for larger ones.

Maggie watches with joy, leaving me a little puzzled.

I note the absence of conversation. A glance around confirms all attention centers on me—my armpits start to itch. I wiggle my arms attempting to rub the itch away but to no effect, and tribulations come knocking.

Is something wrong? Are they withholding crucial news about Karrell? Something else? Worse! Am I still dying? Am I just delusional?

A scuff of sand at the entrance and Droght D'elti enters. A large smile breaks across his face the instant he spots Maggie. She comes to her feet and walks urgently to him. They hug long and hard. Maggie pulls back, turns to me, chuckles and says, "Friends no matter what Once-Other?"

"Friends," I respond, relieved and happy.

"They are committed," Roses says and fills my mouth with delicious food taking my attention off troubesome questions, but now all of everything makes sense.

I nod yes in response to her smile and she feeds me another spoonful of stew. I chew slowly, savoring every nuance of the not too spicy sauce, vegetables, and lamb.

When I'm done, and with my raging thirst somewhat in abeyance, I sit up higher on the cushions. Roses remains next to me, attentive though neither sympathetic nor intrusive.

Benwarr clears his throat.

"Once-Other we await—" at the sound of footsteps from outside he turns to the entrance.

The tent flap swings open.

I jerk-n-spasm and lurch upwards intent upon a violence I cannot command. Ozerken and Pe'truss step inside, stop up and assess me with their four dead eyes. They nod, in a satisfied fashion mind you, and take seats.

Roses digs her fingernails into my arm and forces me to lie back.

"Allow me a minute one-n-all," Benwarr commands and glances at each of us in turn.

With his attention back on me, he says, "I understand this is sudden Once-Other. But! Time and circumstances don't allow for gentle gradients. We here today...are all Patriots. Patriots alone. Wait. I'll explain. We are the unofficial, unelected, campaign leaders of our three Here-Born groups. Each one of us elected for him or herself a duty much as you've taken on the functions of a campaigner. Our responsibilities are different, though. What we do is monitor aggression towards us keeping our fingers on its pulse...at all times."

Everyone nods understanding. Roses as well.

Benwarr looks a question at me.

I glance at the Desert Drivers but hold to a hard face.

Madsen nods as though he understands something others don't and says, "I informed him...we've nothing other than questions and doubts about him."

And my anger explodes.

"I've about had your...."

"You gone an' betrayed us?" Madsen shoots back.

Benwarr holds up a hand and silence ensues.

Without comment nor reprimand let alone disdain, he says, "Dew and I represent the Nomads. Madsen and Maggie the Free Marketeers. Pe'truss and Ozerken the Desert Drivers and the Highlanders are represented by Jenk and his brother Hansen, who's on his way."

Stupefied by the after-burn of Madsen's attack, my mind races to integrate what Benwarr had just said, and I break out sweating. Roses wipes my brow. Her fingers brush across my forehead and stir alive my current, though meager, mental faculties.

An answer pops into view and resolves a question that has hung about the outer edges of my awareness for some time.

How did Maggie know Peter Wernt's name back in the Museum? Now I get it.

I sigh, examine Madsen, who glares in return. My concerns at the change come over him threaten to swamp me again. But this time I am able to present them a duck's back down which they slither from view. And this thanks in part to Soonsaan's words and suggestion about Madsen.

I let out a long, slow breath and wave Benwarr on.

"At this meeting," he says, "we'll need information Once-Other, for here tonight we must decide the future of our campaign—our self-defense—that one which is within our Constitution. And so! With that decision in waiting, we formally request your participation."

Overwhelmed, I mumble, "I am honored."

Roses hugs my good arm then pats it. Maggie smiles her hug to me. Droght nods approval. Madsen grins thanks looking pleased for once—or pretends to be. I notice Jenk and the two Desert Drivers seem content as well.

I'm uneasy, though, suspicious of the latter two. Do they expect me to believe their conduct out in the desert was in the interests of Here-Born when their every action placed me in greater danger?

Do these people know whom they are dealing with?

Roses touches my shoulder, nods towards Benwarr.

"Allow me to clarify further Once-Other."

My attention drifts from face to face. After assessing each, I nod for him to go ahead.

"As we've all experienced with our own Moment in Time—each of the three sections of our population owns one-third of the knowledge required to deploy our UWMD. Desert Drivers and Northerners sharing one-third. So hear me now, Once-Other. While you and Wernt were with Ozerken and Pe'truss, you'll have witnessed some of their campaign actions. Actions based on their third of our UWMD."

He pauses, scrutinizes my reaction and thoughts, eyes intense, penetrating. I nod yes. Nevertheless, my stomach churns with violent emotions.

Benwarr smiles, nods and says, "Excellent. Now Once-Other. Let us all please realize that just as they don't fully understand what you can, were and are doing, so it follows that you have not comprehended their actions."

I consider his words, but anger still clouds my reasoning.

I wave to them, requesting a few moments. They sit back and wait. I muster my Foundation and visit my Moment in Time. I take the information provided by Benwarr and assign each datum as needed, discard others, think the remainder over and my anger slowly dissolves.

"This is true," I concede but still hold to some reservations.

Their faces break out smiles, their eyes share relief and happiness.

Jenk waves a thank you. So does Madsen and they both break into chuckles on noting how something else becomes apparent to me.

I chuckle as well and their faces ask a single question of me.

"It appears," I say in answer, "you are as cunning and slippery as Wernt and Company. They know nothing of you. Wernt suspects and that is all he still has—suspicions."

Everyone chuckles and slaps a knee or two.

"Tell us what you've learned, experienced," Benwarr says and leans forward.

Perhaps due to their certainty in me—something, with a snap-n-spark, changes within me. I zero in to find it is similar to that which grew within me when my Moment in Time expanded. New ideas tumble by my perception, expanding my mind, my skills. I align them.

Clearly neither Pe'truss nor Ozerken will tell me the reasons for their actions nor their inaction. What's real is I am here, and alive. Furthermore, those actions may have left Peter Wernt with the mistaken idea that we are a divided people. That alone could be a powerful advantage. I smile as reservations dissolve, accept both of them for whom they are and dive right in.

"Peter Wernt is not Peter's name."

Everyone rocks sideways at that.

I allow them a moment to absorb that significance and add, "Worse. Peter Wernt is one of the Missing Twelve."

Gasps of horror fill the tent.

"They were kidnaped by Earth-Born agents and transported to Earth-Born. They have been trained to accomplish Earth-Born's agenda. Odentien, the Lady and Mister Conqueror are of the Twelve as well—leaving eight others."

They gasp again and lean forward.

"Peter can block our monitoring his thoughts. Which he can turn on-n-off—just as we go into a Do Not Disturb mode...but I couldn't find a break-in method.

"You must understand—there is a power to him. He immobilized me at times, caused me to imagine I'd moved, events had occurred or time had passed—when none truly occurred."

Faces pale. Roses hands me water. Sipping, I examine their faces on which ancient fears have come alive. I get to the worst of it.

"He was able to dig into my mind, search *almost* anywhere he cared and could control me physically. Yet I kept him at bay...to a significant degree. I don't know if we all can—he seeks to access our UWMD folders.

"It did come to me that he doesn't have our Foundation—so he must steal what's inside those folders from one of us. That said, I think he failed with Jiplee.

"I now realize that could be what she was telling us when in death—she smiled. And to my own anger, I was right about Peter Wernt's Quaaseon canister being almost empty when he and I had breakfast together. Damn! Also...Peter tried killing me several times. Inside the mine and with Crier poison he came close."

I look at Maggie without saying anything and tears whelm up in her eyes. "Oh no!" she sobs.

I nod slow-n-sad and say, "Peter murdered Jiplee and our friend Franciscoa. But Odentien committed the actual act against Franciscoa."

Benwarr bows his head and we hold to a respectful silence.

Droght comforts Maggie. She buries her face in his shoulder, her arms go tight around his neck and she sobs softly.

Roses places a hand on my shoulder. We stare unfocused at the tent walls. After a few minutes, Benwarr waves me on with a tired hand.

"What happened to Franciscoa and Jiplee informs all of us just how powerful Peter is. I believed he must have known Jiplee's real name to do what he did to her, but I'm not certain of that anymore. Nevertheless, that's what they are doing. Using one campaigner to find the next.

"Our politicians must have looked up our real names for them. I can't see them giving anyone from EB complete access and getting away with that. As an aside, Peter claimed that Odentien killed Franciscoa by accident—under questioning."

"Damn!" Benwarr growls and Dew places a hand over his.

I add, "That Wernt is in conflict with himself—is certain. It appears his Here-Born side fights with the Earth-Born raised side."

They all take a note of that, and I continue.

"They are running their own campaign to counter ours. Wernt revealed that they intend to release our criminal politicians."

Their faces pale.

"They're noting everything we do. How Fraggers and SandMasters work. Details and details, all under the guise of being tourists. Based on their predisposition to violent attack, I'd say Peter is searching for some horrific and brutal weapon which he reasons our UWMD must be."

"This is round-n-about worse than I imagined," Madsen whispers.

Everyone nods agreement and though unspoken, ask for more.

"From what he said it appears that Wernt's wife killed their son after she purchased a pre-owned arm from me and returned to EB. Or so Peter claims. The Earth-Born Court found me, the vendor, guilty of what they call Murder in the First Dot One Degree. Murder by Criminal pre-owneds and so C-POP was judged as having committed the crime.

"That Court awarded Wernt possession of all my assets, canceled my non-existent debts upon change of ownership and granted him Property Rights to take ownership of Karrell and license to execute me."

I crumble, as grief breaks free of its restraining chains.

I lie back, eyes closed. Roses places the cool, wet cloth over my face and takes both my hands in hers. The wind drops and a deeper silence pervades. From behind the face cloth and into a silence thick with dread, I express our one ray of hope.

"Wernt was aggravated by his wife upon her return to EB. She went on-n-on about our Rights, and still does."

"Damn fine indeed," they chorus and our spirits lift.

"Which is how he found me. He let on they intend to kill all campaigners. But they don't want to exterminate in a random fashion. They want campaigners dead and no one else. As he described it, *they do not wish to reduce the labor force more than needed.*"

Roses removes the facecloth to reveal their shocked and angry faces.

"I am sure there's more, but nothing further comes to mind. Oh, wait! I swear he was able to control Poip but have no proof of that. Something happened. Poip were about to address him, but A-one hiccupped and appeared to change direction."

Benwarr struggles with his own horrors and urges for revenge. His face calms, he inspects me and quietly says, "Thank you for the critical information, Once-Other."

A grim silence follows.

# CHAPTER 64

## OF VOTES TALLIED AND DECISIONS MADE

After several minutes Benwarr glances around and all nod confirmation. He takes several deep breaths and speaking in a strong voice says, "With what we've heard today and with what we've garnered from others, we can now decide. Let us all invoke our Foundations, our Moment in Time and when done we will vote."

Each in turn looks to me and says, "Thank you Once-Other."

Benwarr turns to Jenk and says, "Is Hansen tuned in with us and can we get his vote?"

Jenk nods. Despite being seated, each faces me and bows his or her head with the tiniest motion leaving me shocked beyond words.

Their eyes closed, Madsen, Maggie, Jenk, Pe'truss, Ozerken, Dew and Benwarr work the information through. After an hour and as each completes, they look up. Without a word, one by one, they hold out a hand.

Each one a closed fist, a Yes-vote.

Next they vote certainty of their own personal understanding and conviction. Again, every vote is a closed fist.

Benwarr confirms.

"With our Declaration of Independence, Constitution, Bill of Rights, Letter to All Citizens Present and Future and our complete political and educational systems having been invaded and perverted we have come here today and voted."

He glances at each once again.

All nod their confirmation.

"With this Yes-vote and its subsequent Confirmation vote by the People we do on this day invoke Here-Born's Right to self-defense. Self-defense as written and outlined in the Letter to All Current and Future Citizens by our Founders, which Letter is part of our Constitution and Bill of Rights.

"And...with this Call to Arms We Declare on behalf of the Citizens of Here-Born, our Ultimate Weapon of Mass Destruction that Constitutional self-defense is activated as soon as our citizens confirm our findings and our call to action."

Once more he finds verification with each one present.

"I hereby declare we do so with great regret. We wish this were not our remaining option, but our campaign has not sufficed because our Mother Earth-Born no longer feeds us but instead—she now feeds upon us."

A moment of silence. "And so it is done!" they chant as one.

Benwarr gazes upwards then marches us through the Gates of no Return.

"This decision will be set into action following the vote of and by our Citizens. As with all grim and vital decisions a sixty-nine percent Yes-vote is required in confirmation. As we all understand, this is not sixty-nine percent of the number of votes cast.

"But it is and always will be sixty-nine percent of our entire voting population—those citizens eighteen and older. Yes...several Founders wanted to make it ninety-seven percent as is required to change our Constitution. They decided not to do so for this requires war and thus immediate action.

"Now. Send word to all voters, to every Nomadi. The UWMD voting website will be live and active from sunrise tomorrow at Time Zone SLF. It will list data provided by Once-Other and all other campaigners and contributors alike. The site will be open for forty-eight hours. Let the voting begin!"

They withdraw their fists and once again with a strange intensity turn to me, and Benwarr asks, "Upon a Yes-vote, how should we proceed Colonel Once-Other?"

I am speechless, jaws locked tight in respect of ancient times when we still communicated verbally. I stare, unseeing.

They wait.

My focus shifts, shades gray, resolves, tightens and sharpens. I examine each of my soldiers-in-arms, measure them, lingering longest upon Madsen. His demeanor seems that of someone awaiting instructions—strange attitude for a senior. Where's the critical comment? The demeaning facial expression?

But even more to my amazement, upon each face is carved full trust and complete assurance in Once-Other, though less so with Madsen. I am exhilarated, honored and damn outright terrified; with every error I make people will die.

Roses takes my hand and says, "Your battle has been at the forefront of this war more than any. No one has as much hands-on with Earth-Born's ways, as you do."

She waits and with reluctance, I nod yes.

"And there's more Once-Other...but please my love, allow me to quote Tull-Tor Hawkur!"

I wait, smile oddly.

Softly she says, "In your searching, search for Those who are possessed of a sound mind...who have a straightforward view of what *is* and who favor self-defense in place of attack.

"Yet who will attack in self-defense when needed.

"For These shall be of extreme value to one-n-all.

"But, know well if such self-defense is of and for every man, women, and child of Here-Born. For then, none will be found more ardent in their love of Freedom.

"Despite contrary opinions; many such individuals exist.

"You will know them for their eyes will meet yours and the light within their eyes will not dim with hidden intentions. Nor will they glance away from eye to eye contact in fear of having their true Self discovered by another.

"Their hand shall hold yours firmly when you shake it, and their goals shall be true for all. Their deeds will reflect their word and their word clear to see in their answers and their do-ing...no matter any internal strife he or she may suffer under."

She waits silent, expectant.

I sigh and she smiles, squeezes my hand.

And I assume the proffered mantle, woven of trust.

I turn to my Foundation and the Free Marketeer's skills of projecting into the future, a future, and lay out what I behold as well as I can.

They lean closer, brows furrowed, eyes intense.

A hush descends and settles upon us and I begin.

"They will soon invade.

"Prior to the execution thereof, facts will be twisted, false ones invented, and motivations speculated on but declared as legal truths and presented to the Rio-Teroans as factual evi-dence.

"Rio-Tero will green light EB's invasion based upon these so-called facts.

"EB's facts will be of acts of terror supposedly committed by us. This will include the use of pre-owned parts in Terrorist Acts. They'll *prove* pre-owned parts are being sent to murder their children. Sadly, real deaths will be used as proof positive and altogether. As with Peter Wernt and his son's death."

I glance around the circle of attentive faces.

They all nod yes, remaining grim and alert.

I hasten on.

"I cannot say what will be the cause of those deaths. All that will be hidden. C-POP will be judged guilty as I have been. They will declare this planned terrorism on our part. With such reasoning, they may or may not declare war but they will invade."

I look them over to find no doubters.

What has become of Madsen's biting tongue?

"Now...to what we can do.

"Fragger Unit Companies under the command of Desert Drivers will deal with the invasion using the Basic Procedure of Dishonorable De-Clothing. We'll call upon all active-duty citizens to stand to arms. Desert Drivers will execute our defense once our strategic retreat lures EB's forces into errors."

Benwarr holds his hand up and looks at the two Desert Drivers.

To my complete amazement, they nod yes.

He waves me on.

"Citizens in prison, but who have the required skills should be offered a role and appropriately rewarded with amnesty upon individual success.

"It must be a self-determined decision by each to sign on.

"Select and prepare all sites for De-Clothing and lead the invaders there once they've landed. Also. Clear all citizens from the invader's path by retreating under the *just in time* methodology.

"Protect retreating citizens with platoons of *performance riders* attracting and occupying the invaders attention and efforts. Ahead of them, citizens retreat along the roads that lead to your chosen sites.

"They must be well clear at the critical moment.

"Select several sites of varying locations and distances as we don't know the hour of attack nor where. Inter-constellation ports are the obvious targets. No visible signs of preparation must be evident."

I pause to collect my thoughts and note my audience waits, barely breathing. Jenk urges me on with a nod.

"With EB's latest incursion to Here-Born, Wernt and others will suspect we are alert to their foul purpose. They will expect us to invade Earth-Born, attempt to deploy our UWMD via a standardized and violent assault. They will prepare for this invasion and so tie up resources...to no benefit."

Madsen, Maggie and Jenk grin and nod yes.

The others think my data and outline over with brows creased.

I add. "Earth-Born's Toip and Poip will monitor all Here-Born financial transactions as well as all travel to Earth-Born—these will be strictly policed. They will lease or hire, perhaps even purchase additional scanners and weapons from the Rio-Teorans. All their Sky Defenses will be active and their troops placed on standby.

"They'll watch for large numbers traveling to EB from Here-Born.

"They'll monitor for huge financial transactions—provide them these.

"They realize we possess no invasion fleet and will expect us to hijack one or more of the Rio-Teroans civilian or Space Fleet ships and invade EB."

"And hope we die in the attempt," Madsen muses to tacit agreement all round.

Roses uses the moment to hand me water. I sip and continue.

"We need to ensure they are certain an invasion of EB will happen and that our UWMD will be deployed in the manner they believe.

"Have volunteers attempt to smuggle Fragger Units or parts of one through their Customs. This action will fix their attention upon and confirm such an invasion. Also, let slip into their hands plans which almost, but don't quite confirm such an invasion. They will put the rest of it together."

I glance around and all are still attentive.

"Create several of what appears to be massive military buildups. Keep them camouflaged from off planet surveillance but ensure enough detail can be captured so that the wrong conclusions will be drawn.

"It's to be a huge subterfuge, like the fake armies set up by the British and Americans and other Allies prior to D-Day of WW II. It must hide the true nature and target of our UWMD.

"Stealth and deception are critical.

"We must never lose sight of Peter Wernt and the other eleven. He's intelligent and underhanded. I hope his tour was at least successful in convincing him that Fraggers are our UWMD."

They all nod their agreement chuckling over our deception.

"We can further blind him by taking advantage of his own lies, his intelligence, his deviousness but most of all, his expectations.

"Those expectations being...he knows what *he* would do under similar circumstances. I'm hoping he's incapable of imagining that we would be or do any different. With this, we take advantage of an EB trait long since erased from us of Here-Born—the only way to fix a problem is with force, punishment and brutality.

"This is our one gamble...and my personal one as well. I will be going to EB to find Karrell. I promised him that if he needs me, I will find him.

"There, I'll link up and provide my Free Marketeer skills and the duties of a Colonel at the same time.

"I need to drive Peter Wernt into a knee-jerk reaction and hope he leads me to Karrell—at the same time I'll integrate with this, my plan.

"So my personal success hinges on this plan and its success.

"My finding Karrell and our overall success are for me, linked. I am unable to separate them. When I try, one must surrender itself to failure so that the other might succeed. As one, they both succeed."

I pause as Madsen shakes his head no.

"We'll talk about that an' all...later," he says.

I wave it aside as irrelevant and he scowls as I continue.

"To reduce our risk we must take certain actions."

They lean forward, eyes bright with attention.

"Yes?" Benwarr urges.

"Present to EB small bodies of tourist arriving a little more frequently than before. Mix real tourists with campaign staff. Make it real. They will laugh at us, with contempt mind you, and so succumb to being over confident."

"I don't see that working...maybe with good acting," Ozerken says.

"We must engender the belief that it's a few invading simpletons," I add.

"Maybe," Madsen says.

"I'm half yes, half maybe on the last item," Jenk says.

The others remain silent.

I add the cherry on top.

"All the while our UWMD executes we must maintain a state of *Obviously Invisible*. This means keeping all Here-Born campaigners and soldiers invisible to them but not unknown—at all times. Including and up to the time of execution, during it and in particular...upon withdrawal from EB.

"But, and here's the key, the UWMD must hit them worldwide and they must not be able to get away from it. I have a fear, though...."

Roses turns my face to her and searches deep into my eyes, hers are filled with questions.

"I cannot get Wernt thoughts. I fear never finding Karrell."

And she takes my hand and kisses it.

"We will solve this," she says.

"We will resolve this before you all leave," Droght concurs.

They nod agreement, but Madsen says, "If Once-Other can't round-n-about get his thoughts, I see no immediate success by him nor anyone else. We can't have him running amok on EB an' all or kidnapping Peter Wernt for his own self-centered reasons and damned be it an' all to we of Here-Born!"

"We will get it done," Droght affirms, a growl in his voice.

And I realize he's speaking to Roses more than anyone else, and she smiles her thanks to him.

We sit silent for several minutes each deep in thought.

After several minutes amble by, Benwarr smiles and says, "You were right Maggie. He comprehends what most cannot. So true your words were...Once-Other knows despite that many times he does not know that he knows."

He chuckles as they all nod in agreement, except for Madsen who glares at Maggie. But for me, my mouth falls slack trying to understand what Benwarr said and why.

Roses slaps me in reprimand of such slowness.

I still don't get it.

Roses shakes her head at me but smiles.

Each of them, once again, scans all of everything over from their own perspectives.

Again they vote.

Again all vote yes.

Next, they take my breath away altogether.

"Desert Drivers are in place and ready," Ozerken says.

"Free Marketeers are in place and ready," Madsen says.

"Nomads are in place and ready," Benwarr says.

"Northerners are in place and ready," Jenk says.

"Let it be done if the vote comes out yes," Benwarr says.

"Damn fine indeed," I add in a shaky voice.

Roses pulls the blankets up and says, "Once-Other is tired. See the haggard upon his handsome face. Note how his magnificent new chest heaves as he breathes."

They stand up, approach and shake my hand.

Ozerken pauses and looks me in the eye and says, "You are welcome in the North. Welcome, as a Desert Driver would be."

"We Northerners second that," Jenk says.

"You are now an honored Nomad," Dew and Benwarr add.

Maggie kisses me, pats my cheek and chuckles.

Droght smiles his pleasure at that kiss.

They leave and Roses and I are alone.

I turn to her and confess.

"I am so ashamed, Roses. None of them realizes how cowardly I was out upon sand. None of them knows how close I came to giving up."

She slaps my shoulder, real hard.

"All of everyone has personal demons Once-Other. I suggest when you are well, you think through what they were expressing. Keep going until you understand what they said and why. Exactly what they said. And don't look at me like that."

She kisses my brow, touches my cheek and says, "Keep in mind…one I love…you kept your promise…to live through it and tell others of what you found."

She pulls the covers up, adjusts the pillows, gazes at me and says, "Now Once-Other my dear. If you are a man of your word. If your commitment is towards marriage. If you desire to consummate this relationship at some time. Oh? I'm so glad we kept your original head. I like it."

I smile.

A quick peck on my cheek and she says, "You best recover your physical well-being before my eyes and desires begin to wander." She chuckles taking the bite out her comment.

The deafening bleat of a camel shakes the tent.

We both glance at the entrance expecting to see its head appear.

But there comes shouting followed by feet scuffing in sand instead.

The camel snorts protests.

Footsteps and camel steps upon sand grow fainter.

We smile at each other over old wives' tales about what camels get up to with tents in bad weather. *

"Sleep now…one I love."

I smile and say, "Roses. So beautiful a flower. So beautiful in you." And I sleep.

*See Glossary: Camels and tents.

# CHAPTER 65

## OF PROPERTY OWNERSHIP AND A PROPERTY'S RIGHTS

The Department for the Assurance of Happiness

Los Angeles Regional District

Motto: Our Monitoring Ensures Your Happiness

Date: Confidential

Document: 798-632

Document Type: Assurance of Happiness Transcript

Requesting Authority: Mister Warrent McPeters

Issuing Authority: Mister Warrent McPeters

Subject Matter: LAX Arrivals

Location: Earth

Methodology: Third-eye camera, audio-visual, Security, and Poip

Transcription Processor: Ms. Agnes Soulone

Environmental: Ratio of one Poip per five people active

Transcript:

Six silver, cigar shaped Star Liners maneuver to docking along an endless shore. The green-gray ocean seethes and churns as landing engines scream, demanding their right of way.

The clang of steel on steel as they edge into docking bays. Metallic thunder echoes and the ocean's waters shrink back as though afraid.

Star Liners hover-in-waiting as their cable lines shoot downwards. Hundreds of electrical motors shriek. Cables tighten, their twangs echoing down the hallways and all the way into the Grand Hall of Arrivals and Departures.

Blasts of hot air follow as landing engines finally wind down. Internal power supply engines hum alive supplying air and all else a Star Liner needs while at rest.

Faces populate portholes. Smiles and stares of awe plastered on each one. Fingers point outwards, tracing the mile upon mile of landing bays shrinking to a tiny dot in the distance.

Frowns cut away smiles as eyes discover the drab gray and green of Government color...everywhere. The eager eyes, though dimmed, remain ever hopeful. This is Earth after all!

The loud growls of exhausting air seem to shake the very core of Earth. The high-pitched whine of atmosphere-engines subsides.

A strange momentary silence ensues.

Steel creaks and groans—airtight hatches open—travelers throng the gangways. The sudden cacophony of human and other voices grows louder, mingles with the patter and stomping of feet along the cold floors and walkways leading to the Grand Hall of Arrivals and Departures.

Peter Wernt enters Arrivals and Immigration amidst the struggling humanity and non-humanity pouring out Security Tunnel 32-LAX like a thick, spiky porridge.

Some appear lost.

Others stare up at the high domed ceiling while many walk too fast on the motorized walkway. Parents call after children. The very confused stare open mouthed at the drab olive green walls, shaking their heads in disbelief.

Young children run ahead, shouting, throwing paper balls.

Poip attempt to intercept them but the children dart away. Poip give chase, lose them, stop up, scan around, and get run into by luggage carts. Poip stumble over their own clumsy feet, right themselves and throw open their arms as they are programmed to do.

Hails and wails sound in almost every Earthbound language and hundreds of off-world ones. Security Scanner 1144-LAX zooms in on Peter Wernt and confirms no dangerous items are on his person nor on that of Property Item D-109.

Peter Wernt has forsaken his air-conditioned suit for a suave, light gray pants and jacket covering a white silk shirt. Slip-on shoes replaced those boots designed for sand and he has apparently matched colors a little like Once-Other does.

Well—*did*.

How terrible my having to view a C-POP execution out upon Here-Born's sand—sometimes duty taxes one more so than Government does.

Oops. That's a no-no—but wait...something else is weird.

Nothing I had seen led me to understand Peter Wernt was wealthy.

But seeing him in his local clothes leaves me in no doubt he is of the one-percent. I mean the cut of his cloth is very expensive—I have seen similar quality on the highest of earners, and no one else. And okay, his fan-n-fit suit was expensive but many tourists headed for Here-Born's blistering heat will break the bank on one.

No way to figure gross income based on those alone.

I wonder what he is...but my mind goes blank.

Suddenly earlier recordings of events on Here-Born come home to haunt me. Haunting visions of what had happened between Peter Wernt and Once-Other upon the sands of Here-Born.

I shouldn't enter anything here about other events, but I can't help myself. I keep thinking about Once-Other never again riding across sand, free under that big blue sky of theirs.

Nor hear him selling pre-owneds to tourists. Never again will he wrestle verbally and bargain fiercely just as Peter Wernt described to Number Six and Eight.

I'm even saddened that Once-Other will never again drive nor smoke, not even those cigarettes Peter Wernt left on his table. I wonder if anyone will find Once-Other out where he was left to die.

Oh dear...back to work.

Must admit here that I have seen very little of the report I am working—it makes me dizzy just imagining what it is all about. I can't understand why my Supe gave me no detailed instructions. Not even a—*what you should be looking for*—nothing.

What is going on? Oh my-my.

Best get back to work—Skellumer is breathing down my neck from across our cubicle. I can smell his breath from here—a mixture of rotting garlic and unwashed socks. I wonder if he's been placed here to keep an eye on me.

They do *sneaky* a lot.

Back to work, I go.

Around D-109's neck is a snug fitting Domestic Neutralizing Collar. It's one of those Autumn Leaf models with tawny brown maple leaves printed on a cream background. A neat and impressive eight-foot chain attaches to it with the other end fastened to Peter Wernt's belt.

Domestic Neutralizing Collars were introduced when Murder in the First Dot One Degree was passed into Law.

When activated they stream electronic pain thus enabling M&M-PBP (the Modification and Modernization of Property Behavioral Patterns).

M&M-PBP was first legalized under the Ownership of Property and Merchandise Obedience Act of 23 August 4294. Merely a couple of years back.

At the time of its passing into law, Criminal Pre-Owned parts were being sold to tourists from all over Inter-Constellation Arena Thirty. The resultant epidemic of heinous crimes brought about the demand for a new law and its enforcement.

Give me a moment to check something.

Okay. I'm back.

"You a jack-in-a-box?" Skellumer asks not looking up from his desk.

I get that personal opinions don't belong in the workplace but Skellumer...urgh! I examine him as he turns and smiles tobacco stains at me.

His bulbous nose most always sports a pimple or four. His small brown eyes ever search for tiny violations, anything that could mar his Right to Assured Happiness and can be reported.

I've been told he was once married. I can't imagine who would do that to herself. How I got him alongside me in my work-a-day cubicle, I cannot imagine either.

Despite all that he is, his eyes are always burning, alive with a something I cannot fathom.

"Skellumer. Don't start on me this early. Got a new project and I need to get up to speed."

"That'd be something to see. Make a hardworking man like me happy to see a young pup sweating some."

"Would make a young pup like me happy getting back to work," I shoot back.

"No one's stopping you," says he-who-must-always-have-the-last-word.

I turn back to work and his eyes bore into the back of my head.

I sigh.

Maybe one day he will retire.

I pause, take a breath, ignore Skellumer's questioning eyes and glance around our office.

I'm looking at eight high, by ten wide, by fifteen long, and twenty long-long years inside these gray walls and drab olive painted window frames. There are two desks of plastic chip-board, the eternal transcriber's keyboard, and Happiness monitoring viewer. Nomadi on my wrist and gooey-sticky used to be red carpets beneath our feet.

I lean forward and there is dust on the outside of the window-pane. Three floors down is the street on which travels public transport and shakedown cabs—tourist artifacts I call them.

Across the road the dilapidated local park waits in vain for the sound of children. Many ADD-Dees sleep on plastic benches, under leaves and in hollows dug into empty flower-beds.

No one is fooled—the shrubs, hedges, trees, and fallen leaves are all plastic. I figure the grass is plastic as well—there has never been a sprinkler in action.

Overhead, black clouds remind of recent volcanic eruptions. I can still smell the soot and magma and burnt earth when outside. I've promised myself one day I'll live out in the country—rumor says there are real trees in places, clean air, and water you can drink right out a stream. Maybe even get married to a strapping farmer's son and raise lots of kids.

Who am I kidding?

Back to work.

I had checked Records to find D-109 registered as twelve years old. He's very tall for twelve, muscular as well. His light desert-suit looks thin and I understand why he shivers with cold despite the stifling heat of LAX.

It's cold here compared to Here-Born. He's lucky, though. With today being an odd-numbered date, the air inside the dimly lit Grand Hall of Arrivals and Departures is turned off.

Per Federal Ordinance Number 560-987 of July 4, 1401, cooling and heating systems must be powered down each odd-numbered calendar day.

Brother Mao, the President of the US of Axis which we rightly call the USA as do most, signed this Ordinance into law after it passed in both the Senatorial Hub and House back on July 4, 1401.

We celebrate it as Independence from Electricity Day.

This Ordinance is Mankind's way of righting the wrongs vested by industry and technology against our evergreen planet. Industry and technology are determined to raise the temperatures inside all households, beyond endurance.

They are too determined to fill the air with nitrous oxide and gangrene spores.

Anyone with an education gets it.

Brother Mao was more than a President, though. He was a deeply religious man—a man of God. He gave to all people a new and beautiful Religion: The Happiness through Eternal Revolutions Church.

Last year they celebrated the Dollar Cultural Revolution in Honor of Brother Mao, who was a dedicated disciple of Saint

Karl. Saint Karl was the author of *Happy Change comes Through Organized Chaos*.

Last year we celebrated the Truth Findings. These revealed that all Banking institutes on Earth were in violation of the Equalness and Assured Happiness laws.

People took to the streets and were encouraged to withdraw all their cash from Banks and all other Financial Institutes and burn them to the ground—adding their own money to the flames for good measure.

How effective those actions were.

Yes. Real change comes only through real chaos.

I sigh with gratitude and glance at a picture of Brother Mao on the wall above me.

Skellumer has one above him as well. We all do.

I bow low but in mind alone.

I know that is wrong, but I can't help myself.

Oops. Did I input that?

It's my mind that so often shocks me with illegal questions like, "Is Change through Chaos the only way to change something?"

I silence my thoughts and glance at Skellumer. He smiles as though he can read them. Folk here like to fake Here-Born skills. I sigh, lift my nose, look down it at him and return to work.

Good thing D-109 didn't arrive yesterday or tomorrow. With the air running on those days his body, accustomed to desert temperatures, would deform right there in the Grand Hall of Arrivals and Departures.

Cold air, like ice, bends and twists their limbs as is outlined in *The Guide to Touring Here-Born*—required reading for all tourist and others headed to Here-Born. It must be tough on

Here-Born's citizens to not be able to touch or eat ice on a planet that hot.

How do they survive over there?

D-109 has not brought a fur coat with him either—that will be a problem. He may catch Attention Deficit Disorder Disease (ADD-D), which can be fatal. Whatever Peter Wernt's perceived value in Property D-109 is, it will all be lost should the disease take hold.

Wait! I have a question.

"Doesn't a disease require bacteria or a virus?"

Oops! Another no-no—questioning one's education.

Back to work.

They make their way over to and stand in line awaiting an Immigration Officer interview. D-109 grows more confused as he watches the hustle and bustle around him. And yes, he is quite cute for so large a boy.

He rubs his nose as several passengers crane their necks to see him. A young boy slips across the lines touches the chain fastened to D-109 and runs back. D-109 stares straight ahead.

Mobile advertising passes close by him.

He blocks his ears and backs away.

Each time one passes him by; he cringes and covers his ears again. The one he backs furthest from has waves crashing like thunder upon a beach as a powerful voice bellows, "Sing a song for ADD-D. Walk along happy and free. Save on energy with ADD-D. No electricity for me nor we. Every other day. Hooray!"

Of course, the dear thing does not understand. You know. The Property having just arrived is not properly educated. I mean. What education could he possibly possess? We realize where he comes from. Don't we just?

Poor unfortunate child.

If he were educated as I am, he would know that the ADD-D disease ravaged Earth back in the mid-twenty-second century. For decades, ADD-D spread across Earth piggybacking on every spore, bacteria, and virus in existence. Everything from the air to moisture, to plants and animals, carried deadly ADD-D.

As usual a terrible grief grips my bosom at thoughts of the devastation caused. In fact, it was so bad that fifty-five percent of Earth's citizens became unable to read and write. Moreover, it has gotten higher ever since.

That is ADD-D for you.

These days I am one of the few able to read and write.

But wait! I've something important to add here.

You must understand that one should not pay any attention to the criminally insane when they insist the Department for Happier Education is directly responsible for the high instance of illiteracy.

How stupid are the criminally crazy?

Do they even entertain a meager understanding of ADD-D or not?

Not!

Praise them. Oh, Praise them on high—the Department for the Assurance of Happiness.

Hallelujah!

Don't we just love Religious Freedom? Of course, we do. We the People have our Right to praise the Department for the Assurance of Happiness by exalting Hallelujah on their behalf anywhere and at any time on any day.

That's a big thank you to Saint Karl Marx, Brother Lenin, and Brother Mao. Hallelujah to them and back to work I go.

But oh my! D-109 is heading for a compulsory History Lesson Unit and so my affection for him takes off and flies wild and free. You see...I have studied history with a passion even my Professor admired.

"Makes me feel lame and tardy, Agnes," he often quipped.

History has been a passion for all my life. I know it is all true—that's what's so appealing. Locked away there are answers that one day when I find them, I'll unlock our world and set...oh dear...I really shouldn't.

Nevertheless, I do so love the accuracy of history. The facts. The dates. The events. Each one precisely recorded, accurate down to the last detail. I've never understood those who look sideways at history. We could learn so much oh dear me...there I go again.

Yes, every time I notice one of them I drift into Historical Fantasyland and this morning I envision what will unfold in 3D fact for D-109. I'm so glad he's interested in this particular period—World War II. It is my favorite.

First off, he will learn how the US of Axis, that be-damned USA, started World War II in 1953 when they dropped atomic bombs on Japan without provocation. Twelve Japanese cities reduced to ashes with no warning, no reason and no justification. Never in the history of Earth, nor since, has such a horrific act of aggression occurred.

In self-defense, Japan attacked Pearl Harbor but the US of Axis was waiting. Seventeen Japanese ships were sunk before a single aircraft took flight. Every Japanese airplane launched was shot down. Any captured sailors or pilots were executed on the spot. *Take no prisoners* being the motto of the US of Axis.

In desperation Brother Adolf, the duly elected leader of the United Republics of German Persons against War called for worldwide peace. He appealed directly to the then President of the US of Axis, a Doctor Hendrik Verwoerd, to end his War of Colonization.

At the same time, Brother Adolf demanded Doctor Verwoerd release all Jews, Arabs, Gypsies, South Africans, Hispanics, Chinese, Australians and Mentally Challenged citizens from any-and-all Confinement Labor Rehabilitation Camps located in the US of Axis.

Unfortunately, Doctor Hendrik Verwoerd was both the designer and author of the Bill of Right Persons and Others. Refusing Brother Adolf, Doctor Verwoerd instead proceeded to use his document to declare independence from the Allied Nations United Against all War in 1948.

And so the US of Axis refused to end its war no matter the keen work of the good Brother Adolf. Instead, the resort town of Dresden located in the United Republics of German Persons against War was bombed to the ground by the US of Axis, which then became a rogue Nation.

This bombing forced the Allied Nations United Against War to declare war. These nations were Italy, Japan, Russia, Germany, France and the United Kingdoms of England prior to 1948.

After 1948, they all changed their names in hopes of escaping History's finger pointing at them in accusation.

Abraham Lincoln, the Prime Minister of the United Kingdoms of England, read the Declaration of War over Radio South Africa, a northern province of Scotland.

At the onslaught of war, the US of Axis was condemned in the New York Letteratti, an English National Newspaper published out of Berlin located in the United Republics of German Persons against War.

Thus began the tragedy now studied as the history of World War II.

We would be illiterate without compulsory History Lessons lending one-n-all illumination.

Hallelujah.

D-109 reaches the end of his chain.

Still not close enough to see a compulsory History Lesson without passengers coming between; D-109 yanks on the chain.

The force jerks Peter Wernt sideways causing him to drop his passport and papers. He glares down at them, pulls his Nomadi out a pocket, enters a four-digit sequence and hits the enter key.

D-109 drops to the floor and lays unconscious.

Thus work Domestic Neutralizing Collars.

Every time I witness a Collar at work I'm reminded of a terrible falsehood.

Someone once mentioned that Collars are based on ankle bracelets used long, long ago to track criminals on probation or when someone was confined to quarters.

How silly an idea.

Right?

# CHAPTER 66

## OF PETER WERNT

Transcript continued: Peter Wernt kneels, slaps D-109's face and says, "Be a good Property and maybe you'll live to be worth something." He deactivates the Collar, steps back and waits.

D-109 gets up and holds what must be his pounding head. Peter turns to the counter just as an overweight Immigration Officer waves him over. He yanks on the chain dragging D-109 towards the counter.

There, he hands over his papers and passport to the Officer, who is sweating profusely upon a Right to Ensured Happiness Walk2Work Corrective Regimen.

On the Officer's shirt is pinned a bright orange badge.

It is a Happiness via Weight Reconciliation smiley.

The Officer accepts Peter Wernt's passport and swipes it through a scanner several times before success. What he reads on the Passport Verification Screen causes him to stop walking.

Not something you want to do on a Walk2Work.

His pain painted face reappears above the counter as he stands up from the tumble he took. Yet he stares at Peter Wernt with distinct signs of well...worship.

Peter waves as to cancel something.

The Officer's mouth works, but no sound is forthcoming.

He jogs faster.

His focus bounces from his Passport Verification Screen to Peter Wernt and back. He twitches as if assaulted by an ADD-D spasm of prophetic proportions.

Peter Wernt waits patiently and by all appearances is accustomed to causing consternation.

D-109 moves backward the full length of his chain. He is a quick learner after all—giving Peter Wernt enough space to complete the formalities of re-entry to Earth's society.

Once again jogging rhythmically on his Walk2Work, the Immigration Officer holds his arms up high and is about to shout Hallelujah or something but Peter Wernt gives him a stern wave down.

Still he blurts out, "You are. You are. You are!"

Peter Wernt leans across the counter. "Let's keep that between us two," he whispers.

The Immigration Officer's face reflects regret. He reluctantly nods yes, stamps the Passport but instead of handing it back to Peter he places it into a drawer safe and locks it. He turns to the document delivery tube, enters a code, types in *Peter Wernt* and waits.

Moments later a passport drops to the counter-top. The Officer checks it, examines Peter's face and hands it over saying, "There you go Mister Warrent McPeters. Your real Passport."

Oh, my Hallelujah!

Peter Wernt and Mister Warrent McPeters are one and the same person! I have to look into this...but wait. I can't stop watching.

Still caught in a rapturous tizzy, the Immigration Officer shuffles folders hidden from view in a drawer safe. Grabs one, opens it and says, "Ah! Your Original Certificate of Ownership for D-109. Sir!"

He hands it over panting faster, hands shaking with excitement.

"Will you require anything else Your Honor?" he asks.

"Please, my name is...."

The Immigration Officer responds in jerks.

"Yes. Yes. Oh. Yes. Sorry. Mister McPeters. Welcome back. I'm so honored to meet you. Is there anything more? Anything at all? Can I get someone to carry your bags? Attend to your Property?"

"I'm good," McPeters says. "Oh? Do you have a Writ of Execution Release?"

The Officer rummages in a drawer finds the unabridged version, hands the document over but fumbles the hand-off.

The sheath of papers slips from his hand and floats away as though a winged glider. It evades McPeters' grasping fingers, floats to the floor and lands between McPeters' feet.

He spreads them, bends over and reaches down.

At that moment, D-109 rushes in and with the quickest, most perfect kick from behind I have ever seen, lands his boot squarely in McPeters' groin. McPeters goes rigid, a statue unto himself.

His mouth snaps open for a moment of silence.

He lets go and bellows a roar of agony that attracts attention far and wide. At the same time, his eyebrows and ears twitch like mad for several moments.

Then all freeze in place and he drops like a felled tree only noisier. For an instant, utter silence reigns as McPeters slowly curls up on the floor.

Next, his howl cuts in and it is the highest pitched male voice I have ever heard. I stare as his hands clutch, with tender care mind you, at his groin.

A crowd, buzzing with curiosity, moves in.

"Hey! That's McPeters!"

"Wow!"

"Get a selfie, sweetheart!"

"I thought he was much taller."

"I like the way he's twitching."

"Me too."

"We'd better get out of here."

The Immigration Officer throws open the bulletproof security screen and with great effort hoists his substantial weight onto the counter. With a plopping sound he rolls across it, drops to his hands and knees on the opposite side and struggles to his feet, snorting.

The crowd backs away.

D-109 works frantically at McPeters belt trying to free the chain. McPeters fights back gasping for breath and howling in pain. D-109 pulls at the chain, and in a jerky fashion, drags McPeters away from the counter-front. McPeters manages to roll over and lie on top of the chain.

Still howling at the top of his voice, he opens his Nomadi, drops it, clutches at it in desperation, gets it and hits a button while still howling.

D-109 collapses and lies twitching on the cold, dirty floor. McPeters' howl subsides, a siren winding down. Silent now, he sucks at air loud enough that I can hear.

An Airport Security Guard rushes in, skids to a stop, fires a High-Tazer and hits D-109 square in the back causing the Property to jerk far worse than I have ever seen before. Guard pulls the High-Tazer electrodes free, pins D-109 to the floor and cuffs him.

McPeters stands up, sways with feet splayed to avoid unnecessary contact between pants and said parts. The Guard offers to assist, but McPeters pushes him aside. The Immigration Officer rushes up and collides with McPeters, trips up the Guard.

All three fall to the floor with the Guard on top.

McPeters says things I am not allowed to enter.

The Guard stands and helps both to their feet.

They look down at D-109.

"Would you prefer Secure Transportation?" the Immigration Officer asks and wipes sweat from his forehead.

Twenty minutes later McPeters exists the Airport with D-109 strapped into a caged electric wheelchair. A Security camera zooms in on dear little D-109.

The Call of the Wild shines in his eyes or perhaps a call for Freedom. Oops. I did not enter that! Or did I? Nevertheless, welcome to Earth D-109. Here a Property is not equal. For that you are to blame—you Here-Born folk—and I know why.

Yes, all has now come back to me. Once-Other and Mister Warrant McPeters have a connection to each other. Dear me…I'd missed the connection because of this *Peter Wernt* identity. But now that he's really McPeters, I understand.

Some time back a C-POP murdered the son of our esteemed Director of the Department for the Assurance of Happiness. The trial in People's Court 90213 was typical, fast and clean. As always the pre-owned Part was judged guilty of Murder in the First Dot One Degree. Our Monitoring Ensures Happiness evidence proved its guilt beyond doubt.

Happiness Monitoring showed McPeters' wife purchasing a pre-owned arm from a vendor named Once-Other, our Once-Other as I now recall. Audio proved she questioned him about the C-POP certificate. He assured her the certificate was authentic. What a load of...oops!

Forensic evidence, however, proved the arm came from a known criminal.

She, the previous owner of the arm, was guilty of child abuse and Murder in the First as judged by their own Here-Born Court. Further documentation placed in evidence outlined how impossible it is to change the status of a Here-Born from a Citizen with Honor (Neatness) to a Criminal Citizen.

Earth's prosecutors presented this evidence just in case someone should question the validity of our own Courts. Next, documentation outlined how legal access to the encrypted Here-Born database was all but impossible to obtain.

Such access is only gained via an application to the highest levels of Here-Born's Government and with good reason—according to them out there in the deserts of Here-Born.

Due to Here-Born's mind-to-mind method of communicating, personal information provides direct access to a mind. Or so they claim. Therefore, they do guard their Right to Personal Privacy in a dedicated manner.

On Earth, we do not use mind-to-mind communication so the Right to Personal Privacy became irrelevant and was abolished centuries ago.

These days' rumors still abound that our Courts and Justice System harken back to the good old days when trials were broadcast over live TV Networks as reality entertainment.

Some desperate perverts even hint that back then News Anchors influenced public opinion and Jury verdicts causing the courts to evolve to how our legal system works today.

The truly depraved even suspect journalist of creating the news. Other wilder theories imagine that journalist would actually, when seeking a scoop, *start a fire* if nothing was happening. And *fire* meant anything, not just fire.

Ridiculous. You'd agree, wouldn't you?

I mean—who would believe such idiocy.

So there, to all those who think we've no Justice on Earth.

We do!

You see, we partake in Trial by Jury on Earth.

We the People are the Jury. We watch. We vote. We take up duty in as many trials as we can, time permitting.

Which proves Freedom of Choice is alive, as well.

All these Rights are part of our Right to Happiness.

That in itself is Truth and Justice for All.

I was so thrilled to find the McPeters' trial scheduled for broadcast on my Service Providers network: *The NonBias Channel.*

I had registered to vote as part of the All Encompassing Jury. This allowed me to watch during working hours. Of the nine hundred and ninety-five thousand votes cast in the McPeters' trial, a meager one percent was for Not Guilty.

I was proud to have a Majority Vote.

See and hear Democracy and Social Justice in action!

Here on Earth, Applied Legal Philosophy using both logic and truth spearheaded the development of our All Citizens are Equal laws to cross-reference the Murder in the First Dot One Degree law.

You see, such an evil act deprives us of our Equality and it is obvious the Guilty Party has denied citizens of Earth their

Inalienable Right to a single child. A three-member family life is a perfectly equal, triangular life...you see.

Thereafter came the Reimbursement for Lessened Equality Law, which restores equality and triangulation by assigning a Here-Born citizen, those awarded as compensation under a Writ of Property, the status of being a Property.

The Ownership of Property and Merchandise Obedience Act then declares that due to Property being owned it, therefore, cannot be Equal.

Hallelujah!

Oh wait, dear me! I should stop right now. I fear all these personal opinions and other things I am entering may get me fired real soon—getting back to work.

I should...no wait...something is nagging at me.

A time out as I check.

I rushed next door to Research.

Urgh! That carpet is so sticky and gooey I fear one day I will lose a shoe because I can't work it free. Oh dear. Well! Moving on.

I grabbed a terminal and punched in Peter Wernt's details. Mister Warrent McPeters' name and picture displayed. I'd never seen him as Mister Warrent McPeters before. I checked the court proceedings record—fascinating.

During the trial, the McPeters family elected to give Evidence without Appearance while Once-Other was tried in Absentia—both these make for cleaner and faster trials.

It was so tragic, the McPeters son's death.

But here now I'll admit to another concern, well almost, there's something about that case that still nags at me.

Some of the items in this current recording bother me, as well.

What are they?

Oops, another no-no.

Back then to the Transcripts.

No, wait—I will look this over!

What bothers me most of all are the things said by Once-Other.

Oh my dear Hallelujah.

So much of what he said to Peter Wernt during their tour made more sense to me than any History Lesson has.

But what was the special something said?

Oh! Wait. Wait. Yes.

While processing the Writ of Execution, McPeters mentioned his wife. Right? What did he say? Think. Come on Agnes. Think.

Oh yes, it was something about how his wife kept going on about this Here-Born Right and that Here-born Right...and still does.

Oh, my? Have to let it be for now.

Dear me, look see, it's time to go home.

Toodle-oo.

# CHAPTER 67

## OF ALL BEING EQUAL

Transcript continued: This morning I am back reviewing McPeters' re-entry. But I can't get my attention off of the Immigration Officer, who jogs on as he does each day.

You see—I bled on those Walk2Work gadgets worse than most.

"You sure lost a lot of weight on one of them," Skellumer whispers so only I can hear.

"How do you know?" I ask.

"Was watching you sweat all day long," he says.

"I don't recall," I reply.

"Of course not," he hisses.

I grunt and get back to work. His eyes continue to bore into me.

"You a spy?" I ask without turning.

"Wouldn't you love to know? Wouldn't you all love to know?" He laughs with not an ounce of mirth.

Just seeing a Weight Reconciliation smiley makes my knees and ankles ache. I've not always been as slim and trim as I am. But a few years back my entire workday was spent on a treadmill—a Walk2Work to you.

Federal Healthcare Laws outline the requirements, qualifications, and rules of why overweight people are excluded from the workplace. In particular, those who drink huge sodas and whom Healthcare can no longer afford to treat.

Gone then the useless drinkers, useless eaters and with thanks to Mayors for Healthfulness!

We also hold dear to our hearts other endeavors done by Mayors for Healthfulness such as the drafting in the Hub of the Healthcare Carelessness Bill. This Bill outlines how and why overweight persons are in violation of our Right to be Equal.

To rectify unbalanced individuals, the Rationalization of Bone Structure to Weight Section of the Bill is used.

This Section states that to be allowed to work one must fall within the required weight ratios of bone structure to fatty tissue present in your body. Those persons who are over the weight ratio and who want to work must walk and later jog while working or be banned from the workplace.

Such logical Laws do not exist on Here-Born!

How do they survive over there?

Here on Earth all Laws reference the All Citizens Are Equal Act—the backbone of our nation. The Rationalization of Bone Structure to Weight Section specifies that the correct ratio of body weight to bone weight ensure happiness and equality for All.

This also ensures equality across all cultures, ethnic diversities, locations, languages, bone structure, body tissue and body weight.

It is never easy, though.

Equality by body weight provides employment and Healthcare to persons within the correct bone to weight ratios. Those who meet these ratios have employment while the useless drinkers of large sodas and the useless eaters of fattening foods lose their jobs.

It is not possible for us to be equal and have equal success nor can we have equal Happiness unless we work to maintain our equality. Weight ratios keep us equal.

This law rectifies this issue.

Hallelujah.

Some have questioned weight ratios and oh so very needlessly so. A simple search reveals the truth to any and all dissenters.

Succinctly put, Psychiatric Surgeons conducted Exploratory Surgery Procedures (ESP) in search of the Source of Life. They discovered a deeply hidden truth; true happiness depends entirely upon the ratio of bone tissue to weight. Period.

Unbalanced ratios cause unhappiness. Unhappiness violates our Equality. Diagrams are available from all Mobile History Lessons.

History Lessons will always assess you and provide your correct weight to bone ratio taking into account height and width.

After all, how important is your health history to you?

When I was overweight, I discovered a Walk2Work was nothing more than an angled rolling floor with a crude braking system. They are uncomfortable, close to impossible to walk on and treacherous to jog on.

The more overweight you are, the more braking is required.

One spends all one's working day on a Walk2Work tread-mill. It is the only way those who violate Equalness by being overweight are permitted to work.

We are serious about being Equal.

# CHAPTER 68

## OF EARTH-BORN'S SIMPLE AND FAIR TAX AND ECONOMIC SYSTEM

Transcript continued: I open Real Time Happiness Monitoring for LAX Arrivals just as lights in the Immigration Dome dim to almost off.

There is no need to panic.

This is standard and in compliance with the Preservation of Green Air and Spore Depletion Act of May 17, 1308...and happens on a regular basis every other day. This gives citizens and corporations the right to reduce energy usage and save on electricity bills.

Paying less for electricity is a happy thing.

We here at the Department for the Assurance of Happiness provide all census information via our activities to ensure happiness. On average, a census originates once every five to ten minutes. As we all know, our monitoring ensures your happiness.

Every minute turned down to half power saves a full one percent off one's annual electricity bill divided by the number of people within a square mile—which number comes courtesy of regular census numbers.

Sing Hallelujah.

"Hallelujah."

Oops.

My Supervisor is here and is both frothing-at-the-mouth-mad and afraid. He barks as never before in his short stint here. "Repair your employee penalties. You have cost me! Do it now."

"Yes Sir," I reply—guilty as charged.

"You input personal opinions," he growls. "Dang. Revenues lost, never to return."

He storms off.

Well. Okay. He is new and being cautious. I understand. I get his angst.

I quickly fix my work status, which repairs our section's one as well, down here at the Department for the Assurance of Happiness. I know. I know. Most people don't get how this works nor how critical to life on Earth it is. So. How does one do this? How does it work?

Okay. Okay. I'll take a little personal time-out and provide a brief outline of the simple actions one takes when doing this correctly.

Learning is a happy thing!

Hallelujah.

First off, I applied for an increase in inflation. Yep. Get it. Understand it. Fill out the application. Which unfortunately has its penalties—but more on penalties in a moment. Secondly, I exercised my right to request a higher Patriotic Status, which fixed the increased inflation penalty.

Okay. Okay! Wait. I'll give a fuller explanation of the above now that colleagues are reading over my shoulder, Johannes Skellumer included.

Apparent to all, I entered personal opinions into a Transcript, which includes my thoughts and observations, which is illegal and therefore penalized. I can't help it...I'm so taxed out it hurts. Oops. Did I say that? Of course, I'm *not* referring to taxation but to workload.

Right? Got it? Workload, not taxation.

Taxation protests are illegal. Yep.

So, getting back to my explanation.

To correct our Section Status and return us to full compliance, I applied for an increase in inflation, which covered our Section's losses. You see personal opinions have no value in a Transcript. So HQ deducts all personal opinion lines as nonproductive which results in a loss of income for our Section.

Yes. We are paid per inputted transcript line.

Not so Hallelujah!

Now the great simplicity here is our Assurance of Happiness Law. It outlines how a loss of income is fixed by increasing inflation. This Law links directly to, and works hand-in-glove with all our Laws of Equality. I know. I know. Hang in a second or so. I'm getting there!

Just realized I'm inputting these explanations into the Transcript. I have no idea of what exactly has come over me. Nonetheless, my co-workers lean in close and read over my shoulder. Let me continue then.

First off a little supporting info for one and all.

Equality Laws provide sufferers of ADD-D and all others suffering from any debilitating illness with equal income, equal pay. As you already know, each section has its allotment of ADD-D suffers—ADD-D refers to all disease. These include all common Work Related Inabilities including the Compulsive Revulsion to Coordinated Work Regimens Syndrome.

So get this first! *Regular* inflation supports ADD-D sufferers. Got it?

I hope so!

Therefore, regular inflation flows into our Section as income and from here flows to our resident ADD-Dees as their pay. So simple no? However, it doesn't end there for me and my current predicament. Oh no!

I now have to compensate our economy because I requested an increase in inflation through my application for a rise in inflation.

Yep. Clear? Crystal.

To repair the damage wrought by my current application, which causes a higher inflation than average regular inflation, I applied for a higher Patriotic Status. It was immediately granted and I have now been promoted into the ninety-seven percent tax bracket. Which balances the higher inflation I just caused by applying for an increase in inflation.

So simple, no?

Hallelujah.

And I thought that is all there was to it—but no.

My Supervisor ambles on over his bemused grin foreshadowing further enlightenment. He stands silent for a moment, hand on my shoulder. I glance at it and he pats my shoulder then takes it away.

I look his gray suit and black shoes over and realize they are not as expensive as Mister Warrent McPeters' are. For the first time, I check him over in detail to find he is tall for a Norwegian and a little stout on the about.

He scrubs his fingers through dark black hair. Points to the far corner where our requisite ADD-Dees are watching TV and says, "Though they don't work they do have the right to equal employment and thereby equal pay. Which means our economy needs *extra* money for them as they do not produce or do anything and their employers, in this case our section, aren't paid for them. Okay?"

"Got it," I say as some earlier confusions evaporate.

He adds. "As we all know; r*egular inflation* is achieved by printing extra money to pay our ADD-Dees. Now since you lowered our income with personal opinions you broke the All Citizens Right to be Equal law. Right?"

And he looks me in the eye.

"Ah? No." And I cross my fingers.

"No?" he says. "Okay. Listen up. Your opinions lowered our income. So how do we pay our ADD-Dees with less income? Never mind! We can't!"

"Got it," I say. "That's not equal anymore."

He nods and says, "Because of what you did, the only way we can *make up the money* and pay our ADD-Dees is with the *increased* inflation you applied for as opposed to *regular* inflation."

I grin, which lets him know I am not tracking with this.

"Now-now," he assures me. "Stay with me here."

I nod and he gets that. Or so his bland smile says.

"Increased inflation prints extra money over and above the extra money already being printed to guaranty a healthy and abundant regular inflation—sort of extra-extra money you could say.

"This extra-extra money is passed to us same as regular inflation money would be and is paid out by us to those over there, our ADD-Dees. Good so far?"

"Got it," we all chorus, Skellumer included.

"So now. Once an application to increase inflation has been approved, which typically happens in ten to fifteen seconds, every applicant such as yourself, must re-balance the National Ledgers via the Inflation Preservation and Nullification Act."

"Oh?" I glance around the other faces and find all their eyes glazed over.

My Supe sighs but doesn't give up on us.

"Okay. Let's back up a little. One. You opinionated on the job in a Transcript. Two. We can't pay ADD-Dees because we receive no income for those opinions. Three. You applied for an increase in inflation. Four. More money was printed—money over and above what's already being printed to ensure a healthy, regulated inflation. Five. The extra-extra printed money is passed on to us. And six. We pay our ADD-Dees with it. But there's still a problem...due to you as well!"

"There is?" I ask my voice a little shaky.

"Yes! You have *increased* inflation by your application to increase inflation brought about by your opining. How are we to fix that? No? Allow me.

"Government can't print the extra money and the extra-extra money at the same time. That's impossible. So how? Through your application to upgrade your Patriotic Status is how. With an upgraded Patriotic Status completed and approved, comes a reward. Yes. Hard to believe you're rewarded for upgrading your Patriotic Status."

"Ah. I am?"

"Okay. Look. Here's how. This reward automatically elevates you into a higher tax bracket. Along with that incredible elevation comes the title of Honored Tax Payer...bestowed upon you by a grateful government. How envious your neighbors will be."

"Without a doubt this all makes sense," I whisper in awe of his sound body of knowledge.

But he's not done.

"With your Honored Tax Payer status you get to pay more money to Government, which deposits into the Government coffers through the inflation Preservation and Nullification Act. This means you have given back to Government money printed by Government because of your application to increase inflation. I see you're not sure—think the extra-extra money I mentioned earlier."

"Ah!" I say. "So with my Honor Status tax bracket I pay back the extra we couldn't print because of extra-extra that had to be printed."

"Now you understand?" He waits, smiling.

The lights turn on and I jump right in. "Yes I do. I increased inflation by applying for a rise in inflation, and so to balance it I'm awarded a higher tax bracket to compensate for the printing of the extra-extra money. And at the tail end Government gets additional revenues from me as I now pay Honor Status taxes."

He jumps back in.

"Brilliantly summarized! I'm sure you are familiar with the advertising done by the Federal Note Printers, Loans and Banking Group—as I am."

"Ah?" I say.

"You tracking here? No? You've seen the promo—*print baby print.*"

"Ah yes," is all I can muster.

He turns to leave, but I grab his sleeve and ask, "If what I'm paying in taxes each month means that to pay my bills I use credit each month. Are we talking inflation as well or something else?"

He stares as though he cannot believe what he had just heard. I hold onto his sleeve and wait him out.

He shakes his arm until I let go, brushes it off and says, "Using credit to pay your bills will never be inflation."

"What we talking then?" I ask.

"Using credit to pay bills is what's called Deflation."

"What?" And I give him my puppy dog look with droopy eyes and a soft smile thrown in for max effect.

He sighs, claps softly and says, "Deflation works hand-in-hand with inflation."

"Okay simple," I say.

"Here's how and for clarity's sake...from the top again so you can understand how this all fits neatly together. First off.

"You applied to increase inflation and so extra-extra money got printed—money over and above the extra money already being printed to ensure regular inflation. Next.

"Increased inflation money, the extra-extra money, flows away from your application and eventually to our Section's ADD-Dees. That action right there is the first cash flow of a balanced economy. You know? Checks and balances. Yeah. You got it. But now you've personally caused higher inflation by applying for increased inflation. Right?"

"Yeah. Okay."

"Next! You applied for a higher Patriotic Status. On approval, you were awarded a higher personal Taxation bracket which offsets the increase in inflation."

"Hmm?" I muse.

"Sigh. Okay. With a higher Patriotic Status, the government collects higher taxes from you to cover the extra money not printed because the extra-extra money had to be printed. So that money can also be passed on to ADD-D recipients without any concerns of unbalancing the books. Okay?"

"Yeah. So I'm paying them...ADD-Dees...either way...right?"

"Yes! How wonderful to hear such happiness in your voice. But! Listen up...it's a little complicated from here on.

"Okay. So while the government is busy printing extra-extra money because of your Increased Inflation Application, they are not able to print the boring extra money for regular inflation as they usually would. And as you can imagine they'll soon face a shortfall of printed money. Well! The Inflation Preservation and Nullification Act is known as the Financial Gate Opener and Flow Neutralizer. Right?"

"Ah?" I say.

He ignores my question and races on.

"Here's how. This law opens the gates allowing money to flow and to keep flowing under certain natural conditions."

I wipe my hands on a facial tissue.

He waits as I toss it into a trashcan and continues. "In the final step you apply for more credit, so money now flows *towards* your Application. That's Deflation. Applying for more credit is financially known as the Balancer. Technically it's referred to as a Balanced Economy—money flows away from you then flows back towards you—and there you have it...balanced you see."

It's hard for me to come to terms with the fact that I did the full educational thing through MBA and didn't understand that an increased inflation Application, followed by a Patriotic Upgrade, is balanced by the Preservation and Nullification Act at the same time a credit Application is approved and results in a Balanced Economy—until now.

When I tell him that my personal debt stands at four-and-a-half million dollars—he congratulates me.

I am shocked by his congrats.

But he assures me that I must hold my head high and be proud that I'm now paying ninety-seven percent taxes.

Apparently, not many people pay so high a percentage.

He confides those others aren't really patriots.

"In fact," he whispers in my ear, "some of them are paying as little as ninety-two percent."

"How come so low?" I groan.

But he leaves, after patting my shoulder.

# CHAPTER 69

## OF DUTIES AND CHANGE

Six weeks have passed since my rescue and events have all but overtaken me. During a briefing provided by Benwarr, he updated me along with all of those who represent our three groups. Ninety-seven dot five percent of Here-Born voted yes to deploy our UWMD, an unprecedented percentage.

Yet it saddens me. EB's citizens have no idea. None.

After the vote, Here-Born personnel heading for EB are mostly senior UWMD staff. As with those placed into position earlier, these come equally from amongst our three groups. From our prison system have risen many volunteers, with Amnesty granted and active upon each one's success.

Most have already departed for EB carrying in their luggage Fraggers of varying power and differing versions and uses. Many got through with others imprisoned. Both results we consider a success.

Such volunteering lifts one's heart.

It was a long meeting during which only Benwarr spoke. I was relieved when it ended. Soon, though, I would undergo the most difficult task of my life.

Reggie, Jiplee's husband, had made application for deployment to EB. It was moved up to the highest ranks. First, it went to Madsen and Maggie and from them to Benwarr and, to my utter astonishment, from Benwarr to me.

I spent some time considering his application and then had Reggie brought in. This despite my being confined to the tent at Roses' orders.

"Good...you're looking well," Reggie greeted me as soon as he straightened from entering the tent, and then his eyes found Roses.

He smiled and added, "The rumors of Roses' beauty do nothing to prepare one for the seeing of her in the real. Congratulations to you, you lucky scoundrel. Forgive me Roses but I am unable to help myself...beauty has always set me mind free and my *mouth* has always spoken what's on my mind."

Roses gently waved his words aside and indicated a cushion.

Reggie sat down, was thoughtful for a moment then said, "But first let's touch upon moments from our past. I thank you for attending Jiplee's farewell, Once-Other. Josh and Alice order me to say *hi* and when are you coming to visit again. Alice also says she's brim full with lots more to tell you about butterflies—*it's going to blow his mind."*

I smiled and said, "They are a treasure, Reggie. And so much so I'm tasked with reviewing your application for active duty on EB."

"Well...to my advantage, Once-Other," he replied. "No one understands what happened and why I must go more than you do."

"We're in a war, Reggie. People will die—patriots all. They will die here. They will die on EB. How many will all told, I cannot imagine."

He waved me silent and said, "I'm already part of the dying. I am willing, my life is yours to send to the depths of danger and if needed, from there never to return."

"I understand. But are you aware of the duty for which you are most suited, Reggie?"

He shuffled closer and leaned in.

"I cannot be readier Once-Other, nor more aware of what is best. I'm informed of your debriefing and of what happened to both Jiplee and Franciscoa. No one stands stronger in readiness than I. My family, my friends, my work companions—have stepped forward. They are prepared to lend a hand, to help with what all and where all—if I'm no longer here—for Alice and Josh. Give me the word and I will serve. In Jiplee's name, I will serve."

Roses helped as I sat up and reached out to him. He took my hand, gazed into my eyes, pleading with me, but his real value lay elsewhere.

"Reggie. This war may be swift or it may be long. Either way, EB will invade us. Either way, many of us must travel to EB. Many who are parents as well. Wait. Please hear me out.

"You have a greater task than for which you've applied. It's much larger than our Campaign and higher even than this war itself. I need you to safeguard our future, Reggie. Okay yes—I am a Colonel. So, I can order you to do what is needed but I'd prefer that you see the future and understand what road best suits your helping hand."

"I will die if I must. Yes. That leaves my children without parents. Be that as it may."

"I'm not looking to send you towards death...but towards life. You are to be tasked with Here-Born's tomorrows. Can you see it? Can you understand why?"

"I see Jiplee's face before my eyes, every waking moment. I see her in my children. Hear her in their voices. The way they move. How sometimes I will look up and find Alice standing there looking at me just as Jiplee did when she and I were young. I die each time Once-Other. Each time."

"Live by Neatness alone, Reggie. Forgive me if you can but these are your orders.

"I am making you entirely and solely responsible for our tomorrow.

"Into your hands alone, I place the life and well-being of every single Here-Born child.

"You will take any and all actions required to search out and find every child who loses one or more parents to this war. You will see to a home, not merely a house nor simply accommodations, but a *home* for them until each finds a loving home with new parents.

"You're free to recruit all the personnel you require—use older people as they know children well. They also understand tomorrow is made for today's child. Care for our children and Here-Born's older people...as you care for your own."

Reggie sat still for a long time staring at the cushions behind me. When at last he looked up, he said nothing in return. Instead, he stood, bowed to Roses and offered me his hand.

I took it and then he said, "Thank you Once-Other. You've eased the weight of Jiplee's death and saved me from a path of revenge and given me a future filled with Neatness enough to serve my name for all eternity. I wish you well. I hope you return from EB and Karrell returns with you."

He stood and walked to the exit, paused and looked back over his shoulder.

"I had forgotten her true self, Once-Other. Pain and loss hid it from me, and even my own words had vanished into the mists of painful grief. I thank you again. I can hear what I'd said, and I see the truth again. *I recall Jiplee harbors no hate for them despite that I do. We believe she lives. We know not where. To my hate, she lends a loving hand which eases my pain and replaces it with that which we all seek—freedom returned!*"

Smiling, he turned and left.

Roses took my hand, kissed my cheek, wiped tears from the corners of her eyes and growled, "Now you sleep."

At this time, I am proud of what Reggie has done.

He has selected a safe location deep in Desert Driver territory. They have constructed standalone and communal homes and all those bound for active duty are contacting them daily. Here-Borns, whose children have flown the nest, are keen to offer their services. I sense Reggie will do well by them all.

On a personal level, my back wounds have healed with proper treatment and the new ribcage bonds well. The impact of Wernt's bullets and my fall down Iron Rock Ridge caused damage enough to require replacement.

On an intimate level, I have recovered well enough to more than commit to Roses. She appears as pleased and satisfied as I am. We spoke for hours afterward, which eventually lead to discussing our going to EB. It was our first battle of wills. There will undoubtedly be many more to come. Strangely, we both won during this one.

I go to EB and Roses goes to EB. However, here today Roses has something special to show me.

I glance up and overhead the Half-Day-Moon rises to welcome midday. Dust-devils dance in circles down streets and between tents. Camels bleat and roar, horses whinny and on occasion a SandMaster roars into action.

I smile that the sound of it now fills me with the certainty of a continuing tomorrow and the fear of before has all but fully vanished. Dissolved by an enlightened acquaintance with all Desert Drivers and how our Founders UWMD works.

With a firm grip on my hand, Roses leads me through the maze of tents which compose Benwarr and family's current campsite. I glance at her pale-blue silk suit and smile. Her eyes ask why I am smiling. My smile says I like how she looks and she smiles.

We reach the center of the campsite.

Pleased to be alone with Roses upon a free sand, I lean against a white corral fence and admire the black-n-white horses within. Roses wipes sand from her silk suit, squeezes my hand, points to the stallion and says, "Dad's given him to us...Prince."

"A damn fine Prince altogether," I admire.

"He's the one who found you, along with his lady friends. They always remain together. They are all trained as rescue horses."

"No," I say.

"Well, they are. Fortunately, we had a Maggie provided shirt of yours—unwashed. Did you leave it in her bedroom?"

"No," I reply in a steady voice.

She chuckles and says, "They go out with rescue saddles and First Aid kits. Because you were unable to mount up, he returned and we followed him back and found you. You were in bad shape. Dad was worried...he didn't know you well enough then."

"He laughed at me," I say.

"I was there, remember. It is just his way of expressing relief. He was apprehensive. He had been monitoring your campaign work for some time. As you can imagine, we get reports from EB. The results from yours were...are...good—actually better than any others."

"I do what I can," I concede.

She slaps my arm, hard.

"And that's for?" I ask sounding more hurt than I am.

"Don't make less of yourself," she says looking me in the eye.

"Oh!" I manage.

"Now you know," she says.

"I do?" I ask.

"You think Dad allows one of his daughters and his favorite at that, to commit to just anyone?"

"Oh."

"Yes. Oh."

"I see. Yes. Fine. Damn fine and all. But? Why put me on a camel if horses...?"

"Anyone who can't mount on their own needs a stretcher. They don't fit on a horse."

"Ah."

"You tired?" she asks.

"No. Why?"

"Oh. Ah. Ah-oh."

"Oh."

We laugh and she hooks her arm through mine and gazes out across the desert. Prince joins us and we stroke his neck in appreciation and thanks. In silence, I consider the future.

From this campground located close to Sand Lake Flats, the D'elti family is leaving for Earth-Born. As mentioned, Roses and I had argued her going. She won. We then discussed the unusual voyage I must undertake getting to EB.

She was also concerned about my extended travel once there in search of Karrell. She had wanted me to let others not closely related, find him. But no—it must be me. I had promised Karrell that I would come for him.

This she understood.

On the other side of the ledger, Wernt departed before Prince found me. Odentien, the Lady, and Mister Conqueror left some weeks later, cutting short their stay as well. Prior to their departure, we worked on getting their thoughts.

Nomad security experts followed them around the hotel, the Mall, the Fairgrounds even during circus acts. These *shadows* were able to monitor some of their thoughts as I had with Peter.

The Twelve...well, these three anyway, were found to be using real-time protocols in a unique fashion. These were not regular protocols like most others, which only lay out the way to present data from one computer to another as all computer-to-computer protocols do. Here we were talking human beings, not computers. We discovered they had added personal life experience to how each accesses the thoughts of one or more of their group.

After much searching and scanning their minds for thoughts, we found four folders common to them all. We named them One2Four.

Folder One and Two contain pieces of protocols but never a complete one. They had even broken protocols apart and spread them throughout the first two folders. To gain access to their thoughts requires joining hundreds of fragmented pieces together and so create a full protocol. However, there was more to learn about how to present the request for access.

We first had to get the protocols themselves, so we kept going at Folders One and Two. These two folders contain actual computer like protocols laying out exactly how to present a query to access thoughts. Once we got that right, we moved onto folders Three and Four, which required adding personal memories to the query.

On reading the report, I was puzzled at how such a crude and basic security system had kept me, or anyone else for that matter, from accessing Wernt's thoughts.

Droght, Head of Nomad Security, joined in as promised. He went out and learned as much as he was able to over several breakfasts and dinners at their hotel.

Thanks to him, we discovered each piece of a memory held in common by the twelve is indexed by year, month, day, hour, minute and seconds down to one-thousandth of a second.

Each was also uniquely named as an *instant in time.*

We suspect they named them as such to echo Here-Born's Moment in Time and so the Twelve have perhaps paid homage to their home world.

Droght tracked their communication in real time and found that each sends out a stream of time parameters for a memory held in common along with the search query. After we had developed a method of application Droght went out and tested, and still nothing.

Time was running out for they were preparing to leave.

I thought through all we had and still found it impossible that such a system could fool anyone with high encryption skills. I got with Madsen, Droght, Roses, Ozerken, Pe'truss, and Benwarr and we worked their system over. And this despite Roses' protests and wishes to drive everyone out the tent and let me rest.

Benwarr, Droght, and Roses put the system together laying out each piece too fast for any one of us to follow. Ozerken and Pe'truss took the Nomad's work and constructed the system itself and presented Madsen and me with the internal workings of the Twelve's security system as complete as was possible.

Madsen and I worked hard with what we had. Yet, no matter which way we approached it we could not gain entry as proven over-n-over each time that someone went out and tested what we had. Two days on, we had made no progress.

On day three, Madsen threw up his arms. "I've about had it an' all!" But I kept going.

Another two days went by during which Roses scolded me for not getting enough sleep, but I found the answer. It too was simple in the end. To gain access we had to send, not just the time parameters of a memory held in common, but the memory itself had to be attached as well.

I trained Droght on it and sent him out. He caught up with Odentien and company at the Departure Gate of Inter-Constellation Port-SLF. On Droght's return, his gloom spoke of failure more so than any words could express.

There was obviously more to it, but we had run out of time.

Therefore, his promise to Roses wasn't kept.

She hugged and thanked him nonetheless.

With the Twelve's thoughts still hidden I must find another way of locating Karrell.

So be it.

# CHAPTER 70

## OF HISTORY, LIES AND BEING ENSLAVED BY IDEAS ALONE

Transcript continued: Interior lighting, typically subdued inside LAX, is dimmer this morning. Visuals are not nearly as bright as when Mister Warrent McPeters returned from Here-Born.

A few tourists hailing from various worlds arrive, straggling along as though they now regret being here. Their faces turn to the drab walls and floors like the hypnotized at a sideshow. In amongst all these arrivals, only a tour group composed of a single family from Here-Born seeks entry.

Up to and until today there had been a higher than usual influx of tourists from Here-Born. News bulletins made mention of this. However, it sounded more like ominous warnings than a tourist season report.

I'm curious about the low-lighting though—this appears to be more than simply lowering their utility payments. One moment as I access LAX's utility bill. Done and yes—just as I had thought.

LAX has exceeded their monthly energy allowance and cannot buy additional consumable kilowatts. They have maxed out on consumed wattage for this month. They cannot purchase any further Unused Consumption Certificates, no matter who is selling.

Compounding this, LAX's Breathable Air monthly usage is way over the top. Too many passengers and others have passed through LAX these last weeks. LAX Admin is in danger of violating several Assurance of Happiness laws, not something to be taken lightly.

Breathable Air in the LAX environment will have to be suspended.

Yes. That's tourists for you...over using and under-taxed.

But let me check into this a little deeper.

A moment as I switch to The Department of Tourism...okay...got it...opening LAX Records, checking pending notifications. Yes. Found the details.

To hand is an unreleased Weather and Catastrophes bulletin. On the cover sheet is a picture of several volcanoes erupting with black clouds billowing overhead and boiling lava pouring down the sides towards a distant city. Dramatic yet false. The bulletin itself is standard issue.

I read it through anyway.

"Due to volcanic activity in the central Northern Hemisphere LAX will be closed to avoid ash and further residues for six weeks. All Travel Tickets and Cargo Assignments remain in full effect and are postponed six weeks, exactly.

"No further notifications will be provided.

"Special offers are available as follows.

"You may verify your new travel or cargo *Departure DATE* for a reasonable fee of $15,000.00 per cargo consignment or travel ticket. Checking *Departure TIME* is a *separate* item and costs the same price of $ 15,000.00 per ticket. Alternatively, pay a mere $45,000.00 and verify both departure date and time simultaneously.

"Also. Please consider the more alluring offer that follows and nab for yourself an incredible Web page access special offer when checking either cargo departure dates or times:

"You can now access the Make a Change web page for a mere $70,000.00 per ticket, which will be added, on your behalf, to the charges outlaid above. With this offer accessing both departure date and time simultaneously, costs a special low, low $159,000.00.

"Return trips are changed and charged separately per the above rates.

"Don't wait—take advantage of this Special Offer right NOW!

"Not included in the above prices, the Department for the Assurance of Happiness collects an additional 75% Assured Happiness Tax on the overall transaction.

"Helping ADD-Dees adds to your Quality of Life and Assures Happiness for One and All.

"Furthermore, Federal Sales Tax of 168% will be charged in compliance with the Verification of Web Site specifications as listed under the Ease-of-Use stipulations for both ADD-D and Non-ADD-D citizens.

"If you so wish, you may cancel a Flight or Cargo delivery and we will send your original purchase costs to the Department for Enhancing the Happiness of ADD-D sufferers. A mere 200% tax on the transaction will be due by you to cover costs.

"No refunds allowed."

Nothing could be clearer, a closure notification which en-sures the happiness of all.

Hallelujah.

Back at my Transcript, I check on the new arrivals.

Security check request, Benwarr, Dewana and Roses D'elti.

Security Check returns No connection to Once-Other/Madsen Somalo.

As a family, they pass through Immigration without inci-dent.

Per the current Assurance of Happiness Directive from Mister Warrent McPeters, which states: Attention. Red Alert. Direct Terrorist Attacks on Happiness. All Here-Born citizens must be assigned Terrorist Status D for Dangerous until proven innocent.

Said status attached to the D'elti family.

On the sidewalk, Benwarr D'elti powers up his Nomadi, turns and looks directly into an Assurance of Happiness cam-era and...

...my screen died and went blank several hours ago. I im-mediately switched to digital audio recording and I am now entering the recorded details. The information I am entering I recorded on my little digital recorder.

Be Ready, Prepared, and Continue is our Section's motto.

Transcript continues with the entering of recorded details:

I turn my monitor off and back on.

Still dead.

I check my Nomadi; its screen is blank as well.

I check Skellumer's terminal—also blank. I step across the squishy carpet and into the hallway and hurry by large offices segmented into cubicles. All the monitors are dead. Faces turn my way and eyes appeal to me. Confusion, fear and here and there, carefully hidden relief, but not carefully enough. I head back to my office.

I sit down just as a picture appears on the screen—it is of the good Brother Adolf. I love this particular photo in which the Cross of Equalness rests easy at his throat and his hand points to heaven while the glow of all Being Equal shines around him.

I glance over my shoulder; the same picture is on Skellumer's screen.

Back to mine.

The clouds glow around Adolf as they always do, the sunshine reflects off his face and his eyes glow with heavenly light. Without warning, something new and terrible happens. The picture becomes animated and the camera pulls back.

I hang onto my desk, arms shaking.

Thousands upon thousands of worshipers stand before him. I never knew his congregation was that large? They are all pointing to the sky and shouting over and over.

What are they shouting?

Oh...at the bottom of the screen.

"Sieg Heil."

Whatever those words mean.

No time to ponder as the commentator is already talking about something called Nazis and a war and a place called Germany and that Adolf Hitler started World War II.

What?!

Tanks, airplanes, trucks, and soldiers all wearing the Cross of Equalness rumble across the screen.

How can the Church of Brother Adolf start a war?

Now, what?

Church members accost persons on the street, storm into homes and confiscating firearms, beating the occupants. People forced into railroad cattle cars, packed like sardines in a can. Young children stare at the camera, eyes dead. On the station platform, a church member draws a firearm and shoots an old man who is unable to stand after being pushed to the ground, kicked and beaten.

Oh no!

I'm looking at thousands of emaciated corpses guarded over by church members wearing the Cross of Equalness. Of course! And reality hits me right between the eyes. This is a new compulsory History Lesson.

At last! All makes sense.

We are learning why Freedom of Religion had to be rewritten then rewritten again to become the original Hallelujah Freedom of Religion and Ensured Happiness Act. I mean...I now know what happened.

A map of the world appears on screen and my headache gets worse. Unfortunately, with this project I have already overused medication, run out of and still face two weeks before the renewal date. I drag my mind back to the screen.

Focus falls on Europe and zooms in on a country or province named Germany. Yes! That's it! Just *Germany*.

To the left of the Western European coastline lie two smaller landmasses named Great Britain. I recognize these as Red Zone GB. Red Zones no longer support human life.

A large piece of real estate further west and down south a little is, of course, the US of Axis. Red Zones are scattered across parts of the continent, particularly along the southern and northern border areas.

Wait. What's that on the US of Axis? I lean closer and read what's printed, and oh my. They're calling the US of Axis...the United States of America. What? The United States of America is further north and over in the Far East. Who are these loons? I mean, that is where I live, I should know where I am. Right?

I stare with eyes so wide they hurt, but what is there keeps getting worse setting off painful flashes that almost blind me. I turn away and bury my face in my hands. After a moment, I rub my eyes but when they scream in protest, I look back at my screen.

A Map of Africa displays. On the southern tip is another Red Zone I know of, but an information box says it is the Union of South Africa (later a Republic) and one of the Allied countries from WW II. Who came up with this junk?

Australia appears, and though it's a Red Zone, it is declared one of the WW II Allies too. No, they were not. Like South Africa, they fought against Brother Adolf alongside the US of Axis in payment for being released from Internment Camps in the US of Axis. That is why they are Red Zoners. Red Zones are Dead Zones are Fellows of the US of Axis and were all nuked to end WW II.

If there is one thing I know, I know my history.

Visuals jump to a picture of the President of the US of Axis during WW II, Doctor Hendrik Verwoerd, but the News Reel calls him the Prime Minister of this Union of this South Africa thing. Please. Try getting your facts right.

Next, it declares the good Doctor to be the architect of something called Apartheid. What's that? Then it makes a big deal of the fact that the Doctor studied in this place called Germany. What does that have to do with anything? Next, it displays the front page of the New York Letteratti.

Love that Newspaper. But wait...under the name banner...something weird...*New York, New York, United States of America*. What kind of terrorist attack is this?

Next, a visual recording of a radio broadcast playing from within a family's home in black and white. I watch and listen as a voice claimed to be the Prime Minister of England declares War on Germany and it's dated September 3, 1939. How can something so old be 1939? The radio is crude, so this News Reel comes from the time when electricity was first used domestically.

Everyone knows we're talking way back during the early 1300's.

And now!

The vast continent of the United States of America is named Communist China. What?

Ahh?!

Now there is a picture of Brother Mao, pimple on chin included. But where's the Stars and Stripes. They always fly behind him. But scrolling now, some horrifying quotes purportedly from Brother Mao:

"War can only be abolished through war, and in order to get rid of the gun, it is necessary to take up the gun."

And.

"Political power grows out of the barrel of a gun...."

And.

"The Communist party must control the guns."

And worse.

"Everything under heaven is in utter chaos, the situation is excellent."

Next a title: Mao Zedong's Great Sparrow Campaign.

In 1958, Mao Zedong demanded all sparrows be killed. The reason given was that sparrows were eating the crops. Millions of peasants spent all day chasing sparrows. The sparrows became so tired they landed and were killed on the ground. When it was found that sparrows ate insects and were actually protecting the crops, it was far too late.

Famine ravaged China.

Soon there was nothing to eat.

People became criminals in pursuit of food. Many killed others just to eat them. It is said even brother ate brother, child ate parent, parent ate child. And those in charge refused the elderly any food at all, allowing these *useless eaters* to starve and die.

It is said that fathers were made to bury a child alive as punishment for a child caught stealing food or complaining about the lack of food, or of hunger.

While the people were dying of starvation, stockpiles of grain sufficient to feed the entire Chinese nation rotted away or was sold to foreign countries.

Some say the deaths happened because of ignorance while others say it was done to decrease the number of peasants whom those in charge viewed as numbers, not as real people.

Does your government see you as merely a number?

My heart races at that question.

I glance about as guilt makes me cringe.

Phew! Not even Skellumer is looking around.

I get back to reading.

The number of deaths during Mao Zedong's reign is estimated to be between thirty and seventy-eight million all told. No one knows how many starved, or were murdered, or worked to death, or were tortured and killed for protesting or speaking out.

This massive number of people died during *peacetime* in that China was not at war.

The total tally of dead for all sides during WW II stands at forty-five million and is lower than Mao's rampage. This makes Mao Zedong or Brother Mao as you refer to him, the greatest mass murderer in all of human history.

I cannot breathe.

I pound my chest and my heart starts again and my lungs inhale air.

I have questions.

What is the horror I am watching?

Is someone trying to brainwash me?

I must be strong because I know my history if nothing else.

Wait.

Is this some kind of a test?

Wait again.

The screen is changing, evolving into desert sand. A shimmering mirage draws closer. In a blinding flash of motion, we are up close. It's a person dressed in an air-conditioned suit with the face-shield down making it difficult so see the face behind.

Eyes shine through the shield, though—intense eyes. They stare into me and into everyone around me and suddenly a powerful voice speaks.

"Have you ever wondered how real the history you've been taught actually is?"

The face waits as silence descends around me. In this utter silence, the people around me crash to become mentally scrambled eggs.

Is everyone thinking *yes* as I am?

The voice speaks. "If yes, understand this if you will. They have lied to you. History was changed. Perverted. Twisted. Good twisted into bad. Bad into good. Heroes are villains. Villains are heroes. Dates were switched and changed around almost randomly."

The head retreats.

Desert evolves into a view of Earth from high above.

The point of view rushes closer and closer to the surface.

The picture of Earth grows bigger.

What is all the surface green stuff? A carpet? Artificial grass? Going down faster, getting closer. It's all trees, a whole continent of trees. What is this? And the voice speaks.

"You have been lied to. What is on screen exists right here, and right now. The green you see is the Rainforest. You've been told it died. Yet centuries ago laws were passed ensuring that for each tree cut down, three new ones must be planted. That was done worldwide.

"You were and are still being told that you must pay for the air you breathe as the Rainforests are gone and carbon dioxide can no longer be naturally converted to release oxygen back into the air.

"You've been taught this can no longer be done by plants and trees nor can it be done by your oceans. For some unknown reason, you've been told these can no longer do this conversion process due to so few forests and stagnant oceans.

Breathable Air of Chicago, Illinois, has lied to you about this. BA has said that it's air they import from planets far, far away. Another lie!"

The image of the beautiful green Rainforests of Earth freezes on the screen.

My hands are shaking.

I glance around.

Most of my fellow staff members are popping pills.

Even my Supervisor is.

I look long and hard at him.

He gets it but shakes his head.

No one is sharing pills today.

Skellumer smirks and does not pop a pill—he never does.

In the far corner, our ADD-D workers are huddled in conversation pointing at their TV.

My screen returns to normal.

But I can't work. No one can.

# CHAPTER 71

## OF DIFFERENCES RESOLVED

Ozerken has arranged a working passage to EB for Madsen and me on board cargo carrier Seattle BA-75. She's docked at port bay Three North. We're headed for Three North in his SandMaster. I sit to the right of Madsen, staring out at the passing desertscape.

In the distance a flock of Arzerns circle, dark silhouettes upon a clear blue sky. Over my shoulder, our trailing sandcloud's tail is crooked as Mourner's Wind has come alive and drives dust northwest.

My thoughts wander and I stare without seeing consumed by Peter Wernt, and afraid of what is in store for Karrell. And worse! How will I find Karrell? Alas! There come no answers. I push my fear mongering aside and glance about the interior.

Ozerken drives as he always does, concentrated, silent, and thoughtful. Madsen stares at his back, eyes blank. Ozerken abruptly turns to us and says, "Something's not right with the BA class of carriers. We hope you two can find out what."

"What round-n-about you an' all mean?" Madsen demands.

"We haven't been able to find out why...but security appears to be almost non-existent on tankers bound for Earth-Born, which is strange, but a secrecy surrounds everything about them. We've made no inroads on this subject."

Madsen nods as though suddenly realizing something new, sits thoughtful for a moment and says, "I understand an' all."

Ozerken says, "Several years ago we became interested in the BA series of Inter-Constellation tankers. Our interest was piqued when we discovered BA translates into Breathable Air.

"We have more questions, though...why are tankers filled with petrochemicals, gasoline or crude oil bound for EB when gasoline and most petrochemical products are banned there? All the way down on that."

He checks ahead, adjusts the suspension and adds, "And another, why are silos and tankers named Breathable Air—BA? Get all you can."

Madsen and I nod, puzzled as well.

The engines roar. The wind howls. Dust billows. Miles pass by beneath our wheels.

I sense Madsen returning to a topic best left alone. But...this is Madsen and he once again says, "It's too dangerous Once-Other. Karrell's predicament will cloud all you do, your decisions in particular. Stay here. I'll go alone."

I shrug it is too late.

He sulks, much as Peter Wernt did.

"I'm going to Earth-Born, Madsen. I'll find Karrell no matter what."

"Even Roses fought against it. An' now we have round-n-about lost track of Wernt since his arrival at LAX. We made contact with Karrell. It was good an' all but not anymore."

"I already know that contact was made and that Wernt has since vanished—Karrell too. Don't forget, I won my side with Roses." I swallow a lump of fear and slump in my seat. "I hear Vicki, your wife, whiplashed you over going as well. Did you argue with her?" His jowls cascade involuntarily. I grin for revenge has a flavor to it.

After several minutes, Madsen says, "At least cover your face when we arrive on EB. If Wernt recognizes you—who knows what an' all he'll do."

I stare off at the spider-web of pipes converging on Oil Depot One from east and west. I nod on seeing the value of Madsen's suggestion and Madsen relaxes just as Ozerken drives up to the South Gate of Oil Depot One.

Like the surrounding fence, it's constructed of armored steel plate, is hung between two concrete pillars and covered with spikes—crude yet effective. Nevertheless, it's worthless when addressed with a Fragger.

I glance around to find no Poip about.

We pull up, showering the real people guards dressed in camo-uniforms with sand. They glare, slap at dust, and three head on over. Two of them keep a distance holding rifles aimed down but ready. The largest guard climbs the ladder, leans in through the open door and says, "Nomadi please."

My heart races as he inspects my face as though something does not add up. He does the same to Ozerken and Madsen. Madsen smiles weakly. The guard grunts and returns our Nomadi and steps down. I silently thank Nomad Security for the professional work done reconfiguring our Nomadi ID's.

Ozerken closes the door.

Hydraulic gate-locks clang loudly.

The gate opens and a guard waves us on.

I glance about as the gates close behind us and as far as I can see not a single person is about. I listen, but the ghostly quiet seems to absorb the throbbing of our engines.

Above us, tall chimneys and latticed steelwork climb the sky. Their entwined shadows creep as ghosts across sand watching the day tramp on by. Higher yet, the latticed steelwork closes ranks to become security screens woven so tightly as to filter the natural sunlight into a subdued hue of gold.

We turn a corner and suddenly enormous upright, cigar-shaped silos surround us. In them is either BA, oil, gasoline or petrochemicals. They stand silent, waiting to inject another payload into cigar-shaped and detachable oil or BA transportation-tanks. The filling of a single tank from a silo takes several days.

We turn a corner and the sudden howl of liquid being pumped through pipes drills holes into my eardrums. Madsen and I cover our ears. Ozerken ignores the noise. To our left, site personnel wearing ear protection rush about their duties.

We turn back northwards and stop hard.

Ahead, a BA carrier hovers over a transportation-tank. Engines grumble like an old lady with aching joints forced to suspend herself in midair. It settles, and we wait as the transportation-tank docks into the cargo bay. We smile fascinated at what appears to be a large white cigar now settled over a smaller one.

All the while white-uniformed workers rush about shouting and pointing. I glance up at the overhead security screen, and it's closed tight.

Prior to takeoff, it opens, allowing for an unimpeded launch. As abruptly as it began work ends and Ozerken heads on northwards. Our engines seem muted in comparison to the screech of liquid rushing through pipes under high pressure and the bellows of the cargo carrier hovering almost overhead.

After an hour, and with not a single worker showing a face, I say, "Are we in a monster's lair, recently deserted?"

Madsen and Ozerken ignore me.

I remain silent as we travel the final ten miles to North Dock. Two-thirds of the way across a Walmer shrills. Instantaneously, workers emerge from a four-story building with lunch boxes in hand and race for seats in shaded areas. And I'm reminded of my last meal with Roses—two weeks ago.

We had lunched through a lingering hand holding farewell in the Mall of Sand Lake Flats. "You should stay here, Roses." I had opened with instead of ordering food.

She glanced my way, patted my hand in a calm-yourself Once-Other fashion and in acknowledgment of silly conversation and returned to her menu. We ate in silence.

Each time I glanced at her hoping she had changed her mind, she smiled and whispered, "I love you too." And she continued eating, still smiling.

I eventually gave up, chuckled and we enjoyed the meal together.

Thereafter, she and her family left in SandMasters for Port-SLF.

I stood atop a dune watching their sand-cloud grow smaller. Madsen, Maggie, Pe'truss, Jenk, Droght, and Ozerken joined me and we stood there until the roar of engines died and the dust dissipated.

Two hours later, I was still gazing at distant dunes. My inner view drifted outwards following them along the fifty miles of desert to Port-SLF. I grinned...the citizens of Earth-Born had no clue what they'd released upon themselves.

Madsen eventually strode stiffly up and said, "I've round-n-about had this an' all."

I nodded and allowed him to drag me away and I helped break camp.

With all ready and loaded we did a lot of hand-shaking as Nomad HQ moved out en masse. Their vehicles snarled up a storm and their roars hurt. Distance soon silenced the roars and the hulking shapes slowly vanished, hidden by dust.

Madsen and I stood humbly upon the empty, silent desert. I felt gutted of life having lost Karrell and now my new friends and family were gone as well. I sighed and climbed into a waiting SandMaster.

We drove north to await passage to EB.

I return from thinking about yesterday and find Seattle BA-75 towering overhead, an enormous python having swallowed a whale. I've been hired on board BA-75 as Coney Jones and Madsen as Jon Green, Facilitation Engineers. What we are to facilitate neither of us knows.

Ozerken again slams the brakes on hard and we slide to a halt. Madsen and I get out.

Ozerken nods to us and I note a troubling smile in his eyes.

We wait, but he doesn't care to explain. I lean in and ask him something I've wanted an answer on for some while, "Why did you cut off your arm like that?"

"Conviction and convincing," he says and smiles.

"Oh!" is all I can manage to say.

Madsen's face remains expressionless.

A single backpack in each of our hands, we bow our heads as the SandMaster roars away blowing sand and dust everywhere. Madsen presses a button mounted on the steel structure alongside the cage door. It ding-dongs.

Minutes later the door slides open, we enter and are whisked up twenty floors to Crew Registration.

"Our heroes have arrived!" the cute Arrivals Executive in a spotless white uniform says and rushes out from behind her counter and gives us each a huge hug, which neither of us understands.

She returns to her desk and pulls up our data on-screen.

Here mouth moves as she reads. Her dark hair is stiff enough to remain unmoving. Done she looks long-n-hard at us with an odd respectfulness and says, "So grand a gesture of you two to stand in like this. So unusual. What heroes you are."

We smile to hide our hidden agenda and confusion at her words.

"Anything for BA," I reply.

She nods her eyes glowing with a strange light. Done with registration she heads off, data screen in hand, two large manila envelopes under her arm. We follow her squeaking boots.

Our collective footsteps the only sound, she leads us along stark white and deserted passageways. We clamber through hatches, up several ladders to higher decks and finally down a long dimly lit passageway where she assigns us to Berth 101.

"Here you go," she says and points.

Our accommodations welcome us to double bunks and trunks bolted to the deck. I run an eye around the bulkheads to find they are either filthy or painted dark brown or both. I decide not to touch.

I check berth numbers and discover my bunk stands directly beneath a dripping from the overhead. The drops are also a dirty brown and the bunk cover is damp and stained.

Upon my already abused ears, musical entertainment comes via snores in various tones and echo modes. I sigh and note we have no exterior views.

"You'll need these," the Arrivals Executive says and hands over the two envelopes. I open mine to find a thin handbook titled: Engineers, Duties of, Facilitation.

"Thanks," Madsen and I say as one and in appreciation.

She checks us over and smiles secretively. Gives us each a peck on the cheek and runs a hand down each of our chests. Walks off backward, steps out into the passage, stands a moment smiling sadly, waves and says, "Good luck," and squeaky footsteps echo a rapid retreat.

A siren screams and eight snoring souls awaken and swing sixteen feet to the deck.

"What you guys do?" asks a lanky one striper pulling on a shirt.

"Facilitation Engineers," we say in unison.

With not a word spoken, they all pack and troop out the door, double time.

"At least we have a place to ourselves," Madsen says.

"Interpreting Ozerken last smile...duly intended," I reply.

And I glance at the contents of the manual.

The first item that gets my attention in a one-two-three altogether fashion is Blockage: Pipes and Joints.

Then another. Solidification: Urine and other Waste Products, Hands on Facilitation Methods 1-22. And another one: Protective Suits, Odor Penetration of, Dry Bathing without Soap—Failures of, Socializing & Movement Restrictions.

# CHAPTER 72

## OF CRIMES AND LIES

My supervisor hands me a new Transcript Authorization without any explanation. "What's this?" I ask. He shrugs an *I don't know*. I connect and initiate playback eager to see what it is all about.

To my shock, it opens to a late night scene inside the McPeters home. We are in the lounge. At first I cannot wrest attention from the abundance of wealth.

Everything is top-of-the-line—the white imitation leather sofa, sprawling armchairs, soft artificial shaggy carpets, and four standing lamps. And beyond all imagination a wall-wide, ceiling high TV.

Am I envious or what?

Mr. and Mrs. McPeters are dressed in twin sets of pale gray nightgowns. But dear D-109 is still wearing the same clothes he was when he arrived. All three are watching one of the most favored TV shows of all time—*The Birth of Truly Equal Happiness*.

Oh no! Appears D-109 has caught terminal ADD-D. Spasms rack him as he sprawls lopsided in the armchair, his attention fixed on the TV. Drool runs out the corner of his mouth and every few seconds he shakes and his heels thump the floor.

A chill tiptoes across my shoulders. I glance around and behind me stands my supervisor staring at my monitor and rubbing his forehead as though it aches. He nods as I do when understanding a terrible tragedy but says nothing, turns and walks out.

Skellumer chuckles as though he knows what's what.

"You're sure to get your comeuppance, Missy," he says.

"Listen Skellumer...urgh...never mind."

I get back to the Transcript.

McPeters points his Nomadi at D-109 and hits a button.

D-109 lurches out the armchair lands on the carpet with a dull thud and jerks something awful. McPeters stands up, stretches, waves at his wife Mary, glances at D-109 and says, "You wanted another kid. Now you've got it."

Mary refuses to look at him. Her jaw muscles flex and her eyes reflect hate. "It's not mine," she says. "Didn't ask for it. Get rid of it. Send it back."

McPeters throws his arms wide. "What's it take? Eh? What? You can program it, make it whatever you want it to be. There's a button for pleasure and a button for pain."

Mary hunches forward concentrated on the TV.

McPeters flaps his arms, his eyebrows twitch as he looks around as one lost. He shudders, washes his face with his hands, looks out between his fingers, kicks D-109 and stomps out.

"Deactivate!" Mary screams.

A moment and D-109 goes slack. Mary stares at the TV, tears stream down her cheeks. D-109 awakens, struggles up and stumbles over to her.

She cringes from him wiping at her cheeks. Moving slowly, he hands her something. After a momentary hesitation, she reaches out a hand. I zoom in—it is a video chip! Where did he get that?

I do a rapid search for a file, find and load the file of D-109's arrival and scan through it. Stop! The LAX Security Guard crouches over D-109, extracts the High-Tazer probes and cuffs him—but nothing more.

Wait. Slow playback down. "Ah ha."

The Guard slipped the chip into D-109's pocket so fast his action was invisible in standard mode. I pull up his details. Quickly attach the record of what he did and forward his picture, transcript, ID and record to the Reports Section here at the Department for the Assurance of Happiness, Attention Mister Warrent McPeters.

Wow. That is incredible.

Hallelujah.

Am I well trained or what?

I am back with the Transcript.

Mary peers into D-109's eyes assessing him and glances with a strange and knowing fear at the chip. She pops a pill then another, inserts the chip into the TV, hits play, and oh my Equalness.

On the screen is their bedroom. Mary McPeters sleeps alone in low ambient lighting cast by a purple bedside lamp. I note the scar on her arm, which indicates she had already purchased her pre-owned arm, the C-POP one.

The shadow of a human form moves along the wall.

I wait tense and afraid.

Phew! McPeters steps into view their sleeping son in his arms.

He places the boy on the bed close to Mary and the little one snuggles up with her and sighs. McPeters takes a spray can of Peace and Sleep out a pocket and sprays a cloud around Mary's face. She breathes in, stirs and settles into Peace and Sleep. He sprays some around his son's face and the child slips into Peace and Sleep, breathing heavily.

A strange thing to do…wait!

He moves Mary's new C-POP hand onto their child's throat pressing her fingers around the delicate white skin. He looks down at them for a minute, nods in satisfaction and exits.

Oh, my Equalness…I hope this is not what I think it is.

In the lounge, he sits down on the couch, crosses his legs, turns the TV on, the sound up high and waits. Fifteen minutes later his Nomadi blinks as the doorbell chimes.

He presses a button and the front door unlocks and swings open. He sprays Peace and Sleep around his own head, tucks the can into a pocket, breathes deeply of the spray and falls asleep.

A shadow enters—a male human form in a black, skintight suit. Gloves hide his hands. A hood with narrow slits for the eyes covers the head—sunglasses hide the eyes. The figure examines McPeters, pats his cheek, waits, pats the other one and heads out the lounge, pauses and glances back and gone.

He enters the bedroom, stands next to the bed, leans over and pats both their cheeks—gets no response and pats again. Still gets no response. He stands motionless for some seconds arms at sides. Moves in and both hands go around Mary's one that is at her son's throat and squeezes—and holds.

I am trying to be professional here.

Oh dear me.

Oh, how their son's little legs twitch and his little feet kick so valiantly but he fights in vain and his struggle is short lived. The dark figure maintains pressure until well after the kicking ceases. He sighs loudly and stands erect staring down at the bed. A blast of trumpets from the TV jolts him alert and he reaches across to the still child.

His gloved hand holds the little boy's nose closed for several minutes. The little boy's mouth does not pop open to breathe. Figure nods approval, lets go, slips out, down the hall and out the front door.

Mary stands up like a cork flying out a champagne bottle. She glares at D-109, sways, and faints. In the same instant, their TV cuts to a blank screen and hisses as though demanding revenge. D-109 catches her and lays her on the couch.

McPeters storms in...no wait. I was not paying attention.

Rewind Happiness Monitoring. Yes. Hidden in shadows and watching all, McPeters! His face a storm of rage, his fingers twitch. Back to when he entered the lounge.

He presses a button on his Nomadi and D-109 flops to the floor and lies there twitching. McPeters rushes over, sits on Mary's chest and sprays Peace and Sleep. She awakens, shocked and horrified at the sight of him.

She fights him while apparently holding her breath. Condemnation grows and fills her eyes. He keeps spraying until she breathes in and condemnation dissolves. He turns to D-109 still twitching on the floor and turns up the power.

D-109 twitches and spasms far worse than before. His feet and arms pound the carpet in a futile struggle to live. I cannot watch poor little boy's torture but must as duty calls.

Several minutes later blood trickles out his nose.

He shudders once, stops twitching and lies still.

McPeters turns the Collar off heads into the kitchen and returns with a cloth. He removes the Collar wipes the blood off and fixes it around Mary's neck. He sets the power to medium and turns power on. I do not want to review what happened—but again I must—and I do.

Mary jerks repeatedly, horribly. He switches power off but leaves the Collar in place around her neck.

In the alley behind the apartments, he drops D-109 into a dumpster. Glancing about he puts a copy of the Writ of Property into D-109's pocket. The lid clangs, bounces twice and closes. He walks away slapping his hands together at a job well done.

Back in the apartment he logs in, finds the Happiness Monitor record of what happened and erases everything. He searches for the original of his son's murder and clears all listings and content.

He destroys the video chip under his heel and kicks the fragments away. Does another search of Happiness Monitoring and finds some details of the death still remain. He erases those. He searches again but nothing further displays.

I rush out the office—Skellumer watches while pretending to type notes into the system. "Comeuppance storming your way, Soulone!" he calls out.

I ignore him as a sudden bout of burgeoning thought along with a new kind of reasoning kicks alive deep within me. Somehow, someone obtained a recording that by all appearances was entirely deleted.

Several hours later, I rush back in—lookup my recent activities and erase them despite that I now know it does me no good. I glance involuntarily over my shoulder. Skellumer makes more notes and slides his prying eyes my way.

I take a deep breath—his stale odor is worse today.

I shrug him off and consider. I have just done something and committed myself to a course of action I dare not think of, never mind mention.

One last check online then. I initiate a new search but my screen freezes, and Skellumer's and all others too.

Today a camera stands mounted on the hood of a truck. I instantly recognize what we are looking at. We're headed directly towards a section of the Razor Wire Zone, but no audio plays.

These razor wire fences cordon off endless miles of decimated land that surrounds all Red Zones. I have traveled this particular road before—I was on vacation and lost. Poip turned me back when I got too close and also provided proper directions.

The camera speeds deeper into the Razor Wire Zone.

At three-hundred some yards from the fence, two Poip step out of hiding with weapons drawn, hands held palm forward demanding a halt. A blinding flash, blades of rainbows, bright white light, a thunderclap and both Poip vanish.

Oh, my. This is not a History Lesson. How did that happen? Was a Fragger used? Oh, dear Equalness. We *are* under attack by Here-Born. After all the years of doubt, proof at last that the citizens of Here-Born are evil. How sick and unprovoked is this terrorist attack?

How much better I feel knowing that my parents won't see this. Most parents of children my age are long gone to that restful place in the sky. That place where peace and fulltime Happiness is abundant. Yes. Few parents live beyond that of a child grown into their teens.

Wait. Personal history is taboo.

And back to my screen.

The hood-mounted camera drives at the razor wire, more flashes and loud thunderclaps open a path ahead. We speed on for many miles of flashes until the ninety-foot high armored wall that seals off the South Central Red Zone comes into view.

A massive burst of light and we are through. More flashes and the lush vegetation and trees around the vehicle explode and vanish leaving a path through the forest...wait a minute!

Forest? Lush vegetation? Can't be. Not in a Red Zone.

Oh, my Equalness and praise be Hallelujah. This I cannot believe.

Red Zones by every description possible are nightmarish—toxic wastelands. Environments so poisonous a fifty-mile-wide no-go-zone surrounds each and every one of them. Our countless Red Zones were defined hundreds and hundreds of years ago.

Nothing flew over them, traveled through nor near them.

Generation after succeeding generation has feared these areas. We have behaved. We have dedicated our lives to conserving the environment. We have loved all living plants and animals as though each was a favorited child.

We sacrificed our luxuries, our automobiles, our vacations, even those children we have never had so that other life forms may live by the grace our sacrifice bequeaths them by means of a decreasing population.

My bladder threatens to gush involuntarily and my headache screams. I rush to the restroom and make first in—first out.

Back in my office I find the screen filled with images of clear blue skies then terracotta roofs and green gardens. Water sprinklers huff and puff spraying rainbows across endless lawns.

Around me staff talk at the same time and loud as all-get-n-go can be. Someone across the corridor growls, "Look at that! That couple has grey hair. They're old. Look at those parents and their kids…those kids are well beyond teenagers.

And our area erupts as hundreds of enraged voices speak as one; which is a first.

It is also the first time I have realized how dead quiet our workplace tends to be.

Voice-Over says, "You have been lied to."

# CHAPTER 73

## OF OCEANS AND A SIMPLE IDEA

The legends are numerous and the investigators split. How did she come to be? Earth-Born, a pearl lost and alone suspended in space too vast to imagine. Light years above her abundant plains blinks a Milky Way—a collection of planets and suns and moons and who knows what more.

Some believe Earth-Born is the central hub of this entire universe. Others look to the stars and imagine great civilizations spread throughout.

Few are certain which is true.

Many ardent and dedicated investigators of worlds and stars insist an explosion brought about all this universe and Earth-Born as well.

Should one inquire after the source of said explosion, one is told something akin to, "*It happened as a spontaneous combustion of unknown quantities and qualities,*" both terse and glib.

That they will rabidly follow up with, "*All comes from nature bringing into being a hodgepodge of accidents and multiple though convenient coincidences.*"

Yet no one asks how this explosion originated nor what detonator was in use. Even scientific illiterates fully understand that for an explosion to let rip matter or material of some kind must first exist. However, any solid, gas, or liquid first requires space in which to exist before it can exist.

Therefore, an explosion can only occur after the creation of space and then of matter within that space because before space and matter...there is no space...there is no physical material, no matter.

Therefore, there is nothing solid.

And explosive material in this universe...those require a detonator for nothing explodes here...without encouragement. If that were possible, we'd be dodging explosions all day long.

So if there is *nothing* to explode and there is *no place* for it to explode inside of there can be *no* explosion. Which raises the question...what exploded thereby creating this the physical universe if prior to said explosion all there was...was an actual *nothing*?

Those scientific investigators reply, "Yap, ha, huh, yap-pity-yap-yapping," on and on.

Be polite and thank them as you walk away.

Yes. Earth-Born's beauty outranks that of planets and other heavenly bodies one can easily see from her. She shines with skies blue, oceans as blue, forests too green but scattered about her countenance are scars, scars that have never healed.

Run an eye along northern Africa, the Middle East, on into southwestern Africa, the deserts of the Americas, Asian and much of Australia.

Tell me...are those old scars?

Scars of conflict like none most of us have seen. Conflicts so deadly in their devastation their scars never healed.

How terrible then, that which rained down upon Here-Born leaving her with scar upon scar, and scars alone.

*** 

Four hours before entering EB's atmosphere we at last got into a wet shower with soap and washed off that odor. We have agreed to never and absolutely not ever mention Facilitation duties...to anyone. Especially the first one when the amidships main pipe was blocked.

We made our way crawling, slipping and sweating through a tangled maze of yellow piping. Closer to the Relief Valve the humidity was thick enough to set our heads spinning while between the pipes was barely room enough for Madsen to squeeze through.

"You should change your physical profile towards the leaner side so—listen to your wife Vicki and—," but he cut me off with a glare.

After slithering between the final barrier of pipes, we found the Relief Valve area. It had almost no room to turn a wrench and none in which to leap clear let alone swing a sand-snail by the tail.

Fortunately, being well hidden what happened remains a secret. On opening the valve, I was amazed at the magnitude of blockage. How can a pipe so long, so large in diameter and with so few crew members become so blocked?

Nevertheless, the post of Facilitation Engineers was crucial in keeping our presence far less than obvious. Any crew seeing us abruptly took another route or retreated, no matter how much further they would have to walk.

Our searches about the interior of BA-75 revealed her cargo of gasoline was not doing duty as fuel nor did it serve to generate Breathable Air. In conclusion, BA-75 heads for EB with a cargo designated as *other wares* but carries forbidden gasoline.

"What do they need gas for?" I asked Madsen.

"We don't need to worry about that," he replied.

I asked why he thought I was worrying over trifles.

He walked off in a huff. Too long in too confined a space I figured.

Now, some weeks later with the crew gathered inside the Briefing Room we wait to enter EB's atmosphere. Cheery voices hum and drone around us. On the other hand, I have had it with all the noisy verbal talking that pounds home every minute. I sigh just as the overhead speakers shout as though we are one-n-all entirely deaf.

"Crew to strap in! Crew to strap in!"

We rush for seats tattered and torn with usage and faded from bright green to a dull dirty green. Slow-Madsen buckles up moments before BA-75 slams into the atmosphere and bounces off screaming, an injured Crier snarling as the scent of Arzerns wafts thick upon its senses.

We hit once more and bounce again as BA-75 screams wilder protestations at the abusive treatment. A heady final dive and the ship groans and wails in anguish.

Every joint, metal plate and beam moans, shudders and visibly bends one way then the other...well...more-or-less. We plunge downwards, suicidal in all but intent. Air pumps howl tortured protest, temperatures continue to soar.

My body shakes as though I am charging across a thousand-mile-wide Crier warren at three-hundred miles per hour.

A pause as engines clear their throats, cough once then roar loudly as reverse thrust takes over. Into this cacophony tinkles the intro bars of Jingle Bells.

Madsen and I stare speechlessly but agree the tinkling got our attention off the scary attempts at reentry—altogether. The vocals start and we are more than a little taken aback at how they and the whole song had been changed leaving only a chorus—with new lyrics.

Taxes high, taxes high.

Taxes are so gay.

Oh how happy we will sigh

when high taxes pave the way.

Hey!

Taxes high, taxes high.

Tax us all the way.

Oh how happy we all cry

'cause taxes are so gay.

Oh!

Taxes high, taxes high.

Tax us when we die.

Oh how happy we will fly

when taxes set us free.

Yipee hee hee heeeeee!

We shake our heads in stupefied awe at the outburst of applause and force ourselves to join in as the ship plunges downwards faster-n-faster.

Just as I fear my brain will dislodge and drop into my mouth additional braking engines fire with a whoosh-n-roar that rips through the entire ship. My brain bobbles instead and my stomach drops like a lead ball as the rest of me vibrates faster than a sand-snail's lure.

Amidst the roar of engines, a screen lights up accompanied by dramatic music to display Earth-Born below us. East and west continental-coast-lines trace paths along an ocean of breathtaking proportions. No photo nor video can prepare one who has lived a lifetime upon sand for the impact of blue ocean from pole to pole and coast to coast.

How terrible circumstances must have been to force our ancestors to bid her farewell and embark upon a journey for a destination known to be pure desert. And there to live upon a planet of no rain, no green and no natural gardens to protect one from a merciless sun.

How strongly must they have protested what had become of life on Earth-Born that leaving had been their only option?

We sit gazing at her beauty and from my Foundation the reason why our Founders were right touches me. Their Letter told why and still does today.

With greater understanding, I realize that it is not possible to flee to freedom. Escape represents but a temporary respite. The slave master soon follows and sets about his task of enslaving one-n-all—once again.

Madsen and I, as the only Here-Borns on board Seattle BA-75, are noticeably in awe of the visuals below. Madsen bumps my elbow. I glance around to find a Poip pair observing us. We yawn close our eyes and pretend to snooze. Through eyelashes I watch them. They lose interest and move on as *Jingle Bells* repeats.

I peer into the future as we Free Marketeers do and scan over the simple yet vital task we are to perform, once landed. We have a precise envelope of time to deliver a message, which will be broadcast later, all across EB.

We'll have our own crew to contend with, Poip on the ground, and possibly swarming personnel as BA-75 signs on and boards an outbound team who'll take off after docking a new cargo.

We land with a loud whoosh and the sad groans of stressed metal as suspensions bounce then settle. Views confirm that we're in, of all places, a desert but one covered in scrub.

Once the thuds, bumps, moans and groans subside, we head for the silo exit as does the rest of the crew. I carry a jerrycan in my backpack. Madsen has a metal pipe in his along with a small acetylene torch and more. We are first out but just before exiting I pull on a mask as I had promised.

We step out upon a wide steel walkway. I close the hatch behind us and Madsen jams it tight with a crowbar we had hidden in a nearby storage locker. He extracts a bolt cutter from his backpack.

Ignoring the calls and whistles and banging at the hatch we hurry to a small green, red and white gasoline pump displaying the BA logo—a red four-leaf clover. My stomach twitches as the walkway clangs and bounces like a trampoline beneath our boots.

I rubberneck far afield, to where the wind carries sand to destinations unknown. Human voices drift upwards from below. I glance around the storage depot. It's filled with gleaming white oil tanks, but there is no one in sight. Around the perimeter, BA's are docked as we are.

The distant horizon carves a rugged line along a blue desert mountain. The sky is clear and eastwards the landscape is dotted with copses, green pimples upon a vast desertscape.

I jolt as Madsen cuts the lock free with a loud twang followed by the sharp ring of metal bouncing across metal. I take a deep breath and the familiar taste of dry air tinged with sand elicits a smile. A wider smile ensues when the sweetness of water permeates the dry.

I search but cannot find a river, pond nor lake.

Seems I'll have to wait to see those.

I turn square on and face the vast and empty facility before us. After opening the can, I hold it upside down to prove nothing is inside. I stick a finger into the short neck to show it's open then pump gasoline ensuring the torrent entering the neck is visible.

Filled and capped, we race to an open cage but not as fast as my heart races in sync with the bouncing walkway. Loose runner-wheels clatter and bang as we rattle downwards toward the desert floor.

Overhead, several crewmembers explode out an alternative hatch, wave, and shout at us but we ignore them. Some head our way in pursuit setting off a racing heartbeat in my chest and drops of sweat on Madsen's forehead.

Ten minutes later, we exit and race across sand our feet pounding the ground, a rock star drummer gone crazy. We stop a good two-hundred sand-paces from BA-75, gasping for breath despite the almost complete absence of gravity.

Once we have recovered, Madsen rams the pipe into sand so it remains upright, lights the acetylene torch and holds the flame to it. Every few seconds he pulls it away for ten to fifteen seconds then back on—over-n-over altogether.

The crew in our pursuit shouts as one over a megaphone, "Kill the torch! Flammable Storage site!"

I splash gasoline over the steel pipe. Madsen sets it on fire and we idle until the flames die while keeping an eye on our pursuer's progress.

"Are you guys insane?" The megaphone bellows.

Madsen once more attempts to make metal burn and fails.

We repeat this several times and mid the last demonstration Poip emerge from behind a massive storage tank. We jolt as though shot, quickly shed encumbrances and race for a nearby scrub.

Behind us, the Jerry-can topples over, gasoline ignites with a wild explosion and sends the can flying in the direction of the

Poip. The Poip dodge around the flames and set off in pursuit of us.

"Halt or we fire!" A-one calls out.

A flash of light, a thunderclap and both are gone. I am well pleased. Madsen sighs with greater relief as he is already huffing-n-puffing. We ease off to a fast walk.

"You need to shed some pounds, Madsen."

"You need to understand I still outrank you."

I smile but not because I am impressed.

# CHAPTER 74

## OF BREATHABLE AIR, HIDDEN AGENDAS AND OLD PLANS

I do not understand why but this lady here, me, I, Agnes Sou-lone, keeps her Nomadi in permanent record mode. Just seems a good idea at this time. I have been doing it since the first Transcript my Supe gave me on this subject.

I sense a purpose and an importance, but I need to learn more.

As I enter my apartment, an alarm sounds and my heart lurches and sets off racing. My BA bill is due at 9:00 PM to-night. Of course, the time is already eight-fifty-nine. If you are late by even a minute, they turn BA off. Immediately, Un-Breathable Air pumps into your home—breathe too much UBA and you soon die.

I grope for my Nomadi and am about to transfer payment when my TV turns on without any input from myself and at the same time my Nomadi freezes. I sit down and oh my Equal-ness!

A typed letter appears on the screen.

Dear Ms. Agnes Soulone,

Like millions of others, your Breathable Air payment falls due tonight.

As with most citizens, you have waited to make your pay-ment until the last possible second.

Please be comfortably seated, watch and listen.

Thank you.

I sit, watch and listen.

The locks on my doors and windows go clunk, locking me in. BA supply groans and turns off. Stale, lifeless UnBreathable Air pours in.

Oh, how gullible I am to have sat here waiting. A new Law must have passed affecting those of us who do not pay our bills on time. How long can I survive breathing this? No need to ask for I already know. Not long at all, mere minutes.

I await my fate as afraid as anyone would be.

But there's hope for tomorrow.

As mentioned, I am recording events for a future in which it may play a role. I check my apartment over for the last time. I won't miss it—there is nothing appealing in its fifteen by ten feet. Neither in its gray walls, gray ceiling, kitchen nook, shower nook, toilet nook and closet nook with its shabby con-certina door.

I check the closet.

He is sleeping—still recovering. Good. He will never real-ize what happened.

Writing on the TV screen fades and hundreds of little squares appear.

I lean closer to find each is a headshot.

I appear in the center of my screen.

Every other one is of a different person.

Some are neighbors, but their faces change too fast to keep track.

Hundreds, maybe thousands, maybe millions of us are sitting in front of a TV. UBA pours into my grim mortuary of a home moaning as though mourning its own insidious duty.

I wait still, cold and silent for soon the genocide will begin.

We are all watching, waiting, afraid. It seems a long time coming.

Time likely slows when Death hovers over one's shoulder.

I focus on the TV and discover that faces never show up twice.

Mine remains centered.

Does everyone pay bills at the last possible moment?

UnBreathable Air now fills the room. I turn this way, that way, but cannot escape the foul stench. Won't be long now. I check the time.

Oh, my Equalness—it can't be. How?

Ten-thirty?

A whole hour-and-a-half has ticked on by.

No one can breathe UBA this long and live.

I rush to the air vent and take a deep gulp of UBA. The stale odor is worse than sickening so close to the source. I gag but do not suffocate. What is happening? I stare at the TV. Thousands of others are checking air vents. They gaze around lost as I am, unable to believe.

I fall asleep on the couch—breathing foul UnBreathable Air.

In the morning when I leave the door is unlocked.

No one says anything in the grim, dark green elevator.

No one needs to.

I note a new kind of silence. One in which we examine each other. A forthrightness never dared before. In every eye shines a little brightness. That tiny spark of hope says we are young, we are eager again and more...a sense of knowing, of learning.

Still, the air thick and stale makes me gag.

We do not give a damn, though—we are alive.

Halfway to the office, traffic grinds to a halt. Cars, buses, trains, moving sidewalks, everything—only stale UBA continues to blow.

Every screen turns on; advertising, Nomadi, History Lessons, even Security. Perhaps every screen on Earth is on.

Across them these words appear:

This happened three days ago. Please pay attention.

Focus shifts, comes back and I lean forward.

Mister Warrent McPeters sits at his place in the Hub.

In awe, I admire the dark wood panels, the wood desks, chairs, and benches. I drool over the silverware. I can almost taste the fresh coffee, orange juice, and pastries.

All are present—the President, the Vice President, their staff and all the Members of Congress. Their suits glow in the way a History Lesson depicts silk garments.

I am envious and sickened.

The hum of voices dies and quiet settles over the Hub. No one shuffles. They all watch McPeters. He waits as the silence deepens. He leans forward and types his eyes fixed on a monitor screen. He looks up and scans the attentive faces for several minutes.

Members shuffle, pat their clothes, glance at him and away.

McPeters speaks softly, urgently. "On this day BA earnings are sufficient to secure our destination—our destiny."

A roar of applause explodes; happiness beams blaze outwards from broad smiles. McPeters inspects their faces and grins, satisfied with what he finds.

"My Fellow Rulers, Welcome. Today we have success. Prince MaChordam Multra and his Court have accepted our current offer for the purchase of Rio-Tero II.

"A quick recap if you don't mind. Unlike Rio-Tero, Two is a world as Earth-like as any that can be found but without desert scarring its surface—not even one square inch worth. Yeah. I don't get why they live on Tero and I don't care. More importantly, we the owners of BA have a stake in this."

Another round of applause erupts.

McPeters hits Enter and the BA bank account displays on a wall screen. The total is too vast to decipher.

He points and says, "Fellow Rulers...time to vote. Yes, and we purchase Rio-Tero II. After that, we migrate all our friends and families from out the Red Zones. From out those our *real* homes...and all which that entails. Yeah. Let me clarify further plans.

"First off! We'll obliterate all evidence of the Red Zones but leave a staffing contingent behind quite capable of following orders and maintaining the status quo. Remote Management via Poip maintains our iron grip upon all those left behind for obedience stands paramount. Or we vote no and remain here...as we are."

A long silence ensues during which McPeters checks each one eye to eye. His nose twitches and so does his eyebrows. It takes twenty-six minutes to look all in the eye and linger a moment.

"Members..." and he pauses dramatically, "our fortunes and futures are on the line. Everything our predecessors and we worked towards over the preceding thirty-five-hundred odd years, perhaps longer, led us here to this—the attainment of the New World!

"But this time an *actual* New World on which we are the sole occupants. Here and now, the ultimate lifestyle lies within our grasp. Yeah! We the Members need no longer brush elbows with those we rule. But! And understand this well...we are risking all for this...our ringing of *that* bell...."

He waits and you could have heard a flea jump.

"The Freedom Bell!" he roars.

A cannonade of applause fires off.

He smiles until it wanes then throws his arms wide embracing the entire universe. "Oil, gasoline and oil derived products along with gold from Here-Born paved the way for this our future. BA having raised the initial finance will continue making annual payments.

"Yeah. BA covers over three-hundred years of mortgage payments and pays as well all salaries for every manager and their staff. Those trained veterans who have chosen to remain behind.

"For them we'll leave a portion of the Red Zones—as mentioned and as agreed."

From the sea of faces, a voice calls out. "What of the future? Our future, our travel, finances—taking into consideration our act of commitment?"

"Excellent question," McPeters replies. "Finances are always critical. Now Rio-Tero holds patents for their much in demand Inter-Constellation travel and they do not care to share. However, they need oil. Does that remind you of anyone?"

Laughter tickles the walls of the Hub.

Into it he says, "Agreements already negotiated and concluded will put in place as many of their Inter-Constellation ports as needed...on Rio-Tero II."

"Who's paying for all this?" calls out a somewhat disgruntled sounding voice.

"Again BA pays," McPeters says.

"What do we live on?" another shouts. "BA can't cover payments for everything, forever."

McPeters nods sagely and says, "True. Hear me now. Attention! Please.

"Here-Born's oil and gold take care of more than everything we'll ever need...what all our future generations will need. Why do you think we negotiated the distribution of their gold across all borders and boundaries real, imagined, current and future?

"We control both products. And that's the *bad* news.

"The good news is that Here-Born will soon become just another State of the United Earth and will soon be subjected to Earth law one-hundred percent. All their assets, wealth, production, and services are soon to be assimilated under the Assurance of Happiness and All Citizens Are Equal Laws as already implemented here on Earth!"

He checks his audience over. They are enraptured.

He continues.

"Here-Born's gold and oil belong to us. We own everything. Everything! Today we vote to make the dream first dreamed in the late eighteen-hundreds become reality."

Twenty minutes of applause ends and McPeters continues appearing to have been humbled. "But please! Let us not forget those soldiers of the past who made this all possible. Without those seasoned fighters, we would not be here today. So let us give thanks as well...to what our enemies refer to as the Tides of Evil and those of 2026 in particular.

"Without whom the International State of Emergency would not be in place. Yeah! We can smile at that. Yeah. It is still in place—that Emergency. Ha-ha. Yeah. We would not have this future sans the dedicated and organized union members...all those our soldiers of yesteryear. And like all soldiers through all of time—they were hired and indoctrinated for nothing other than to fight and die...on our behalf.

"Some died clandestinely while others stood openly before the citizens of their own countries and decried and railed against their own. Many gave their lives on the front lines of civil protests to light the spark of violence. And why so?

"Our opposition refused to engage in violent retaliation back then. They reasoned to out-wait us. Thought they would eventually out vote us and undo the tremendous work done by those who came before. Yeah and Hell no.

"Nothing quite as biased as unregistered voters. But we needed violence in the streets and on campuses. That solely as a tactic whereby we could disarm the public and let loose the hounds of liberty, of progressiveness—so that here today I can speak as I do."

He glances about, dead silence reigns.

"Those early soldiers came from many camps, diverse backgrounds, and so many Unions. Teachers, Federal employees, Firemen, Policemen, Longshoremen, Taxi drivers, Auto Workers, Miners, Truckers, Coffee makers, Hotel Workers, Gardeners, Actors, Writers, Directors, Managers and Executives Unions. And of course, Politicians, and News Media.

"Yeah. I wish I had been alive back in the day. But no...and worse...my forefathers chose to leave Earth. Something I will always regret. Yet now and with you all, I have done my part. All too true what our Fellows said and did back in 2026. Allow me to meander some here.

"True change comes from Chaos my friends—from out of Chaos *alone* comes change. Do nothing if Chaos results. Do something if Chaos results. From out of Chaos comes real change. How many of our past leaders used this technique? Too many to count I'd say. Thank you to them all for their help in bringing to fruition all our dreams here on this historic day...today."

The room goes wild.

Applause and hoots of victory finally settle and McPeters says, "I repeat. The International State of Emergency would not be here today without our unionized soldiers of 2026.

"Here now in victory and for a moment let us be honest. Nothing glows with quite the same radiance and fulfillment as an honest, worthwhile group perverted and twisted in its purpose.

"And in particular, groups populated by those fool enough to believe empty promises. Thank you to all past Unions, TV, radio or elected officials including Government and News personalities who trumpeted our cause. May you Rest in Peace.

"Yeah! And lest *we* should forget!

"These very same people who gave their all to help us arrive here today...were all rounded up and shipped to work camps. There we worked them to death along with those fools stupid enough to have registered for entitlements. Yeah! Thanks for supplying all your info. And so willingly you did. It made finding you and shipping you out a simple task.

"And we enslaved each of you long before we started with those who openly opposed us. Wake up! Come on! You opposed your own government. Now! We are your government. Yeah!

"It follows you will soon fight us. Naw! We had shipped you out before that happened! Yeah, we worked and starved you to death! Yeah! Thanks for registering! Thanks for volunteering! Thanks for repeating the talking points!"

A few snickers circulate the Hub.

McPeters whispers. "Anyone here remember the last time we experienced rioting? Protest marches? Have there been any Union negotiations? Any of such like talks gone wrong? Have you heard of any negotiations on behalf of the worker, ever? Have you attended any negotiations at all? Not in my lifetime."

Their chuckles skitter across the airwaves.

McPeters waves them silent. "Now to the matter of oil and gold. Glance around fellow warriors. Those you see around you are the owners of both—I'm emphasizing that."

They nod eagerly.

"Let us vote," McPeters concludes.

They do so in silence.

Not one No-vote makes an appearance.

The BA account empties as McPeters makes the down payment on Tero II.

All screens gray out and voice-over cuts in.

"You've been cheated, deceived for thousands of years. You've been lied to...but listen well to this, if you so please."

Words appear on screen and voice-over reads them:

"Yet. We the People are the economy.

"Without us where is the consumer?

"Without paychecks, we cannot purchase.

"Without our paychecks and without our purchases there is almost nothing to tax.

"Even at the highest levels of commerce and industry...all filters down to our level...for we are the buyers...the consumers.

"Without us there is nothing worth growing, making, manufacturing...let alone distributing!

"Think about that. Thank you."

# CHAPTER 75

## OF THE CONQUEROR'S MINIONS, THEIR USE, THEIR DEATHS

For the first time in my life, everyone on the bus talks at once, almost drowning the grind of steel wheels on rails and the crackle of electrical sparks from the trolley contacts. Strangers cross age-old barriers to reach out like never before. Each seeing themselves in the faces of others, their lives revealed in another's eyes and we recognize something more, but no one is sure of what.

I struggle, I search and insight touches me lighting a flame within.

My travel companions grapple with comprehension as well—eyes light up one after another. A long silence ensues into which a dear lady whispers, "I'm worth something. I am economically valuable. I contribute!"

The dam walls of personal oppression crack open and splinter apart. We the People of Earth reach out through the cracks hungry for more. First as little drops soon becoming a gentle flow, which rushes onwards as we cascade outwards like a dammed river free to once again seek the ocean...the ocean of ideas.

Some whisper, others speak openly.

"We've been lied to."

"Yes, we have."

"What can we do?"

"Should we be paying for BA?

"What's this stale smell they keep pushing out?"

"I thought it was carbon dioxide."

"Yeah. That stuff kinda kills you dead."

"I've seen someone suffocate from it—over on Here-Born. They got those ditches."

"Me too. Lucky it's got that color and odor."

"Yeah."

"I didn't know people were living in Red Zones. Did you?"

"No."

"They must be maintaining fake homes locally!"

"Yes!"

"Damn liars...all of them today and yesterday!"

"Let's speak as one!"

"Until now...how silent our world...and so too our lives."

"I say leave well enough alone."

"Shut up you!"

"Why am I taking daily drugs? There's nothing wrong with my health. No pain."

"Can you believe what those politicians are doing?"

We come to another unexpected halt.

Every screen buzzes with static and clears.

Again it is the interior of the Hub.

Again the same politicians present.

But this time they are in an uproar, shouting at each other, pointing finger and flapping arms. McPeters stands and holds his hand up for silence and waits until you could detect the sound of a pin dropping.

"Let's be clear here," he says. "Not a single person in the Hub today was unaware of this and hadn't agreed to it. We all paid dearly...commitment came at the highest possible price."

His face red with anger Jimmy Cromwell screams, "Yes. But you had a stepson. A stepson! Others gave their own flesh and blood. I may be one of the Twelve, but I'm not privileged as you are."

Preordained agreement ripples through the Chamber. McPeters watches it hit, a wave crashing upon the beach of mutual discontent. In the coldest voice I have ever heard, he says, "Let me backtrack here for everyone."

He glares a challenge at them and they all fall silent. "Yeah. We agreed to invite certain of Here-Born's politicians to our New World campaign. Right? Don't just stare at me! Right?"

They nod as one.

"Yeah. Did they or did they not deliver all of Here-Born's gold and oil to us as promised along with the real names of actual and suspected campaigners?"

With grim faces and solemn nodding, they all confirm.

"We will make good on our word and release them from prison as soon as our Invasion Force takes full control. Keep in mind that I found out they of Here-Born *are* a divided nation. Yeah. We land within a few days circumstances permitting— sooner if needed. We deliver what we promised. Like every single one here...they paid the entry fee."

"But I say," a Senator with an aged face and wispy gray hair says. "Jimmy, as always, is right. We others made the ultimate *personal* sacrifice."

"Your point?" McPeters snaps at him.

"Ah. I. Ah. Please. Okay. Look. I gave a daughter's life my own flesh and blood."

McPeters snarls, "Are you saying the entrance fee was too high for you, Senator? Are we already forgetting the Rio Teroan's fanatical fixation on the Rules of Evidence? Real Murder in the First dot One…evidence of?!"

"No I. No. Just looking for some justice and truth."

McPeters nods. "Umm? Justice and truth. Yeah. Okay. I'm going to back way up…all the way back to fairness and truth."

He glares without a single twitch and save for a few, every head bows.

McPeters growls in a low hiss, "You idiots kidnaped twelve infants from Here-Born. Me, Jimmy Cromwell there, Odentien, Juana, Sally-Anne, John McIntyre, May-ling and the others no longer with us. Those seven fools tried to go home. Right?"

No one disagrees yet none expresses agreement.

"Now correct me should I be wrong. Yeah. You tried for how many untold centuries to get distribution rights to Here-Born's gold and oil—and failed. Your little contingent plan was our kidnapping."

Heads bow further, glazed eyes point to the floor.

"Yeah! We the kidnaped delivered by training in your techniques and applying our natural skills to your teachings. We took complete control of most of their politicians and got those rights—those untold quadrillions of dollars for longer than we can imagine."

He pauses and glares. Few, other than those of the remaining Twelve present meet his eyes.

"Yeah. We have each paid an entrance fee to our New World. An exact sacrifice—the life of a child. The one permitted us by law, which legislation we have agreed to waive in the New World. I lost my wife. She's gone...yes...still at home but no longer with *me*!"

McPeters steps forward, hands on hips and challenges them—their heads bow even lower. The remaining Twelve smile and sneer.

"Yeah. If I recall correctly, I first alerted us to how and where Here-Born's campaign operated. Mary, my wife, going on and on about Rights sent shivers and alarm bells through me. This Right. That Right. On and on she went, ad nauseam.

"But we were alerted!

"That's when I proposed a course of action. And using their politicians once again we got the real names of these so-called campaigners each time one was discovered and verified. Yeah. Now at the same time, our Laws kicked in on Here-Born.

"Which thus far has worked. Without their politicians' involvement in our campaign, nothing was possible. They were the breakthrough point. Politicians. Oh Yeah. A greedy bunch are we not? So!

"After a period we will no longer just distribute oil and gold as I've already covered. We'll own it. However, we needed and still do need a situation with which to justify our planned invasion of Here-Born. Now.

"Anyone here present forgotten what sticklers the Rio-Teroans are for Inter-Constellation etiquette? What do they say? Oh yeah. Do what you must only—have ample justification. Right?"

All nod yes.

"So we invented C-POP and Murder in the First Dot One Degree.

"We had to use our own children as undeniable proof of Dot One.

"You know this as a deep-seated truth down in your hearts. There could be no trusting some criminal with this task no matter how well paid he or she would have been. When stress hits, lips speak! And so we shared the burden of the act. Each one of us committed the deed for another...all of whom are present and as guilty.

"So keep in mind! It is easy to force any individual to speak. Anyone! But it's far harder to get someone to speak when the deeds are their own and there's no one to point finger at except self! Please!

"Never lose sight of that. Nor of this...our actions were for the greater good of all Mankind. Solely and only for Mankind's future do we tread so difficult a road. It is the correct path upwards to a Greater Race of Human Beings.

"Something only dreamed of since the early days.

"Previous historical giants paved the way...yet failed in the end.

"Fellow Adolf, Fellow Joseph, Fellow Mao, Fellow Lenin, Saint Karl and many less illuminated wannabes. What did we learn from them? Genocide? Not workable. Communism failed. Fascism failed. Democratic elections failed.

"No singular political philosophy brought about what was needed—how precisely that showed up back in 2026. What did work? We combined them all. The use of all those political philosophies swiveling around the central theme...*from out of chaos comes change...change comes only out of chaos.*

"So how would we bring about chaos? Do nothing if more chaos results...do something if more chaos results...drive every confusion or troubling incident directly into chaos and or greater confusion...and so comes about change. The *directed change* that we want.

"Let us not forget those dearly beloved Harbingers of Fear. That old trustworthy News Media. Oh. How they spread bad news and every act of terrorism far and wide. How close that was in the end. Imagine if they'd refused to cover those acts. Imagine if they simply made a two-minute reference to it and never mentioned an act of terror again.

"How would we have spread terror and panic across the world without their coverage? No. That would have been impossible. Imagine hitting New York and only the USA got a two-minute bulletin and nothing else.

"We would have failed miserably.

"And! We took over the poor and struggling by giving them free stuff, those endless handouts, and entitlements and then gave them more free stuff. Promised them a free ride forever and never allowed them time to think it through. Oh! Thanks to a complacent and co-operating News Media once again.

"Imagine if some entitlement junkie had said something like *when we're all on free stuff where's the money to make free stuff going to come from?* Well, slaves are where. And the entitlement poor were the next new era slaves right after those who betrayed their own people by helping us.

"Gone they are.

"So easy to round up registered entitlement receivers. Get on the train, on the bus. You are off to pick up free stuff for yourselves. No! Take the family along that way you can carry more.

"There you go. Step right on up.

"On the other hand imagine if someone had suggested that *if you get free stuff you lose your right to vote—years for each payment you receive.*

"How would we have built a voting bloc of voters living off free stuff if that had happened?

"Thank all Fellows no one thought of that one!"

He drops his arms his face aglow as though a holy light shines upon him. He takes a deep breath, wipes his brow and continues.

"Had those who helped back in 2026 taken some real history lessons we would not be here today. But more importantly, from Fellow Mao onwards we purged anyone who helped us the invader, invade against their own people. May have been earlier, but that is sure.

"And how exactly did we invade and conquer? By using propaganda laced with violence. Propaganda designed to gain popular agreement against *undesirables*. You know who those were. Smokers of cigarettes went first. Lovers of the right to freely own and bear arms went second. Those overweight useless eaters were third. Polluters who refused to drive green cars fourth. Pro-life advocates fifth. Protestors against drug use were sixth—and on and on.

"I...okay here's how. Just find a segment of the population who are easily positioned by propaganda into a group worthy of the hate of others. Get the remaining population to hate that one group. Make people believe that that group has no rights. But!

"Never allow anyone to realize that if they agree that someone else has no rights...their rights will soon evaporate as well. So never leave them to their own devices once you have won. Yeah—once in power we purge those who helped get us there. They are the first to be purged...once the invader rules! Always!

"Perhaps you now fully understand why I so welcome Here-Born's treasonous politicians to our New World."

Heads nod sagely as understanding dawns.

McPeters nods his satisfaction and says, "We must never lose sight of the main thread of a successful invasion...and, in particular, post a successful one. No matter the office they hold, no matter how good the work they have done nor the talking points they repeated until all others believed as they appeared to. They are always purged first...*always*.

"Every invader knows this: if someone betrays their own people, their own Constitution, their own Bill of Rights and thereby their own form of government—they protest authority. Any authority. And so much so they'll commit treason to see their own country surrendered up to an invader—one from beyond their borders or one from within their borders.

"But...now the invader is the government and since we know they protest their own government enough to betray it...they vanished first. And into forced labor camps they went, half-starved and driven till they drop and don't get up. And why so? Because the Invader is now the government and they protest government...don't they?"

Silence reigns, he inspects them and continues.

"And so all the little helpers back when—vanished. Including those of the so-called...News Media."

He claps his hands silently and continues.

"Now. About today. Yeah! Man can now finally rise to heights of socially perfected behavior upon a New World rid at last of those who hang like lead weights around our necks, dragging us forever down.

"No more the drug addict, the whiner, the chronically ill, the naysayers, the indigent, the bum and hobo, the anti-Socialism nuts, the entitlement addicts. And on and on and on!

"So! Any doubters amongst us?"

No one moves, no one blinks.

He takes a sip of water.

"Yeah. Now about what we've done—generally speaking.

"You know we could not afford to bring outsiders in...no matter how loyal they appeared. We used an entrance fee none could back away from without paying the ultimate price...death by extended ADD-D.

"Look around and to see how well this worked. Our Invasion Fleet hovers in waiting—ready to plunge downwards and rain fire upon a desert world. They remain hidden in the dark of space, awaiting orders to deploy a scorched Here-Born policy."

Every face except for those of the Twelve turns gray. The silence grows so deep one can hear electrons orbiting. They had obviously never addressed their plan in so coldblooded a manner.

McPeters is not done and his voice begins to rise growing stronger. "Now you gave over to us the remaining Twelve, full control, and responsibility for the New World campaign. Do you want to take that back?"

He looks them over and nods.

"Anyone here want to turn traitor on the remaining Twelve? Let me remind you of the hundreds of corpses rotting in shallow graves. Do you agree that they gave their lives for our training? Gave them well? Do you now regret the blood on *your* hands?"

A single cough breaks the silence.

McPeters drives on.

"Have we the remaining Twelve given ourselves to you? Have we delivered everything we said we would? Has C-POP Murder in the First Dot One Degree been accepted by Rio-Tero as acts of terror?"

Heads nod eagerly.

"Then trust us to deliver Here-Born and the New World as we've promised and with ample justification for all our acts. In other words...your salvation *is* at hand."

The House Members glance with fear-filled eyes at one another.

"Once again. Anyone here no longer wish to leave their beloved Earth?"

All shake their heads.

"Yeah! Okay then. Remember my—our commitment to you. Yeah.

"You kidnaped us.

"Yeah.

"You took us from the arms of loving parents.

"Yeah.

"You imprisoned us in that horribly cold dormitory...housed like rabbits in a warren. But we each whispered to you the secret of what fuels our hatred...no one from Here-Born came looking.

"No one!

"We gave our commitment to the New World. You still have it! I've long forgotten those of the Twelve executed for attempting to escape. You should forget what you should as well. Yeah! Therein lies your salvation."

And his face twitches violently.

# CHAPTER 76

## OF TWO DIFFERENT CONQUESTS BEGUN

I rush out the elevator to find pandemonium reigns. Hundreds of transcribers mill about, talking up a storm, a mass of swirling gray uniforms just like mine. In the center of all this commotion stands my Supervisor.

He is alone deep in thought with a clear space around him. In one hand, he holds his beloved red, white and blue coffee mug. Steam floats around the rim, slithers upwards and fills the narrow hallway with its fragrant aroma.

In his other hand dangles a lighted cigarette.

I note he is standing directly beneath a smoke detector.

I head for my office. Got stuff I need to check on—right now!

I stride by him and he smiles at me.

"Morning Agnes," he says.

I screech to a halt. Agnes? He knows my name?

"You know...smoke detector...right above you?" I say somewhat lost for words.

He looks up, ponders for a moment and says, "What say you turn this one off?"

"That's illegal. It's also illegal to smoke indoors."

"Yes. I know. Turn it off anyway."

I head to my cubicle, log in and turn the smoke detector off. He wants some real protest—he's got himself a protester.

Now, what is on my mind? Oh yes. I hunt down the third-eye recordings made by Peter Wernt and scan through them and make notes of the information Once-Other passed on with regards their groups, Nomads, Desert Drivers and Free Marketeers.

Oh, my Equalness—everything makes sense.

They are here!

They have taken over everything from our communications systems to electrical grids...absolutely everything. Oops.

My Supervisor is right behind me.

He sure can move quietly and quickly.

He places a hand on my shoulder and squeezes.

Oh no! What is this?

"Agnes. Good work. Excellent. Stay the road."

"Thank you, Sir."

"Call me Pete."

"Okay. Ah? Pete."

"I wonder what's next?" he asks.

"Me too," I reply.

He pats again and heads off.

I'm about to get down to further research, but static waves cut across my screen. They resolve and shadowy shapes evolve, sharpen and become Seattle BA-75 docked on Here-Born. The engines fire spewing flame, smoke, and thunder. The camera follows the tanker until it disappears into the sky.

Screen goes black then activates again.

We are looking downward at another desert.

BA-75 comes in for a landing with clouds of smoke and billowing dust. The engines cut off and heat waves rise. The camera pulls back. BA-75 grows smaller until we are so high we can see the world below, and it is Earth. The focus moves in closer and closer. Two tiny figures exit a hatch onto a steel mesh platform above the transportation tank.

The viewpoint races into close-up.

Oh, my Equalness—it is Madsen Somalo and another.

Why is the other one wearing a mask? Why does anyone wear a mask?

What are they doing? What type of liquid is coming out that silo? We should see vapor spewing if it's liquid oxygen. No, cannot be liquid oxygen—doesn't fit.

Okay. He's done.

They head for the cage their boots clattering across the steel walkway. Going down in the cage. I wait through time-consuming and endless clackity-clack. This is taking forever.

Okay, they are running across the sand now. Okay. We all know that Madsen. Steel pipes do not burn. Give us a break here. Okay. That looks like gasoline. Oh yes. Now the pipe burns. Wait. That silo is filled with gas, not liquid oxygen.

If they are not busy importing oxygen but instead it is gasoline—why am I paying for BA? Why is anyone paying for BA?

Voice-over echoes my thoughts. "Why are you paying for BA when what's being imported is gasoline?"

Madsen Somalo and partner do the pipe and gasoline test a few more times.

Voice-over says, "You have the right to continue paying for BA if you so choose. You have the right to cease paying for BA if you so choose. All Nomadi now provide you the right to continue paying for BA or not to pay for BA anymore. Please check your BA account and select...yes, I want to keep paying. Or No, I don't wish to pay for BA."

Trust me on this. Agnes Soulone selects *No* and smiles.

If there's anyone so stupid as to want to still pay for BA? Go ahead.

Oh dear. There goes Mister McPeters' monthly payment for their New World. Well, from me at the least. Oh, my Equalness wait. The screen changed into a digital counter. Oh my, how it's flying, the number growing too fast to track.

When it stops...it is too vast and below...really huge: 99.999% of BA payments have ended. That's five nines! This is much bigger than I'd imagined. We're watching this worldwide, all times zones, all the time. Oh, my Equalness. Now, what?

The screen changes showing BA's Electricity Bill on one side and their Bank Account on the other. Oops. They are broke after the down payment they made on the Rio-Tero II purchase. Damn fine broke altogether, as they say on Here-Born.

My Nomadi blinks and beeps. I check and the message reads, "BA attempted accessing your bank account. They were blocked. There is no charge for this new service. We appreciate your business."

What an exhilarating feeling but back to my screen.

The camera cuts away then comes back and we're looking down at Here-Born.

Above the desert dark flat ovals with pointed noses and bird-like tails hover-in-waiting. That's our fifteen Troop Carriers and ten Armored Carrier ships poised and ready and just out of range of land-based missiles. I recognize the port buildings...Port-SLF servicing what was Once-Other's hometown but which is located a good fifty miles away from his old business.

Our ships roar alive, orange flames exhaust two-mile long streamers. Their roars rise to screeching howls, flames turn blue and in unison, the ships plunge into the atmosphere. Outer shields soon glow white with heat. They slow their almost vertical dive, pull up and skim along the sand.

As one, they halt and hover and then drop to land sending dust in all directions. Ramps slam open with dull booms, sand-clouds billow and one-hundred and fifty thousand invaders ride out safe and secure inside Armored Troop Carriers, which look much like SandMaster but run on tracks, not wheels.

Troop Carrier engines roar battle cries their guns barking Death's chorus. Port-SLF's control tower rips apart. Flaming shards fly in all directions. The terminal follows. Docking bays cringe as a flaming goo softens them and metal wrinkles then melts.

Wherever the camera is pointed pillars of black smoke climb into a clear blue sky.

Our invaders drive hard marauding through business complexes and suburban communities razing them to the ground. They never stop in their drive onwards toward Sand Lake Flats.

Fighter pilots follow the carnage. They cruise then stop up, hover and open fire leaving a scorched Here-Born in their wake.

Skeletons of buildings smolder, melted tents cringe in sorrow, broken SandRiders spit orange flames and billow black smoke. The corpses of those too slow in retreating lie bent and contorted by the merciless flaming-goo or scattered and ripped apart by swarms of angry bullets.

SandRiders race ahead of the invaders taking continuous gunfire.

One receives a direct hit, explodes, the rider leaps clear, lands, tumbles and in one smooth motion is back on his feet running hard. Another SandRider cuts in next to him and he swings on board looking much like the SandRider act Peter Wernt attended while at the circus.

How odd...I still call him Peter Wernt for those times he was on Here-Born.

The SandRiders accelerate rapidly. My. They must be hitting more than a hundred miles an hour on those things—our tracked armored tanks and carriers cannot keep up.

Nevertheless, our guns fire continuously.

Homes burst into flames. Warehouses erupt like geysers. Parts fly whirring and whining a deadly warning to any who would dare cross their paths. Oh dear, this isn't simply an invasion. This is genocide and a scorched Here-Born policy as McPeters had promised.

Voice-over says, "We wish you no harm. However, do please understand. We will defend ourselves."

Eight hours of destruction later Sand Lake Flats Mall drifts into camera view.

The carousel close to Pre-owneds Galore quivers under the storm of destruction. Around it, tents and buildings erupt into cones of flames topped by columns of dark blue smoke. Tendrils of fiery death flare outwards, adjoining buildings and tents burst into flames.

The shelling ends and I listen to the lick and crackle of flames as tents and buildings die. I yank my attention off the carnage as the roar of many SandRiders cut in seconds before they race into view. The camera view changes to overhead and holds.

Several Armored Troop Carriers release another barrage of fire.

Once-Other's store erupts and vanishes. The carousel wheel spins off across the desert like a weird flying saucer crash-landing. The Mall collapses in on itself and explodes. A few desperate people flee the Mall just ahead of the collapse. At least one does not quite make it.

The towering head of the gold mine remains untouched.

Thus far, no troopers have deployed but every building, tent and home along the way lies in ruins. I verify and yes, not a single oil pipe or goldmine head was touched.

The Invasion Forces leave SLF headed northward to the Highlands and there to take out the Desert Drivers. But on the way they are laying waste to the Free Marketeers without mercy. This leaves the Nomads.

They, using camels and horses, will be easy pickings once all Desert Drivers are eliminated.

No further Here-Born citizens are visible on screen save for those desperadoes rushing ahead on SandRiders racing to get away from the invaders. Only fifteen minutes after reaching Sand Lake Flats, not a single structure remains upright. Every building or tent burns or smolders a charred ruin—save for the goldmine.

The screen visuals dissolve turning flat black.

BA's Electricity Bill reappears and a clock counts down the minutes in seconds. Focus shifts to the Due Date and Time now only five minutes away.

I glance about our silent office. Gone is the click-clack of keyboards, the deep sighs of those working silently under scrutiny. My Supervisor paces the hallway, smoking, salutes me with his mug and says, "Fresh. You want one?"

I shake my head no and get back to work, but cannot...the countdown clock hits 00:01. The screen changes and a document appears. I read it aloud.

"Action to Collect Unpaid Debt.

"Complainant: Eduvision Electrical Corp.

"Defendant: Breathable Air Inc.

"Amount Due: $750,101,749,345,282.95

"Due Date: Overdue

"Interest Per day: 5% compound."

The screen dissolves. Opens to an overhead view of Mister McPeters, Odentien, Number Six and Eight and the other remaining Twelve working at a screen. They are filling out an Application for Bankruptcy on behalf of Breathable Air.

The remaining Twelve's names are listed as the sole owners of BA. I lean closer but find no other names listed.

Fifteen seconds later Bankrupt Status for BA is active.

Quick cutaways show air fans in various locations turning off. Over my shoulder, stale air stops blowing. And it hits me right between the eyes—Once-Other the devious one.

I recall him telling Peter Wernt about the skin cream store, which went out of business after the citizens of Here-Born decided to stop buying their product. Their action was not a boycott, but a Free Market action by individuals exercising their opinions with their Nomadi—or wallets.

Now here we are no longer paying for BA. I never imagined that just keeping my wallet shut or Nomadi turned off gave me so much power in a free market. How clever those rascals from Here-Born are. And! What an incredible weapon for We the everyday People it is! My!

The screen switches to a split view of our President making a call and McPeters answering. "McPeters here!"

The President takes a slow deep breath and says, "President Watters and Harry Bracchion-Brown, Senator from the United Republics of German Persons against War. What the hell is going on? You guys are the sole owners of BA...are you scamming us?"

McPeters hangs up without a word.

More frames appear as other House Members call. Multiple voicemail recordings play. The remaining Twelve sit around their screen smiling at one another. McPeters accesses a second account.

Oh, my Equalness. It's the Treasury of the Federal Government of the United Countries of Earth. Wow—the total climbs faster than did the clock counting down the seconds to BA's failure.

I had no idea our taxes flowed into Treasury so quickly.

I can no longer say Equalness without gagging.

The remaining Twelve put their feet up on the desk, laugh as if it is a joke and watch the dollars increase. And it hits me, Government has access to every Nomadi and business account.

The screen makes a sudden change and switches to Here-Born.

Our Invasion convoy turns off the Eastern Freeway and heads into a vast bowl or basin-like valley surrounded by high dunes. Vehicles park alongside each other, engines die, steel ramps clang open, boots tramp down onto the sand and our soldiers form-up in the center.

The CO climbs atop an Armored Carrier with a microphone in hand.

He's tall, hairless and stands stiffly in a spotless desert camouflage uniform. He strides forward; muscles pop and snap as he moves. He slams to attention, looks his men over with pride and suddenly bellows, "Men! We got us here a mission. A simple task—the final taking of the nut. But! Do you know what they say in the history books men?"

Close-ups of individual soldiers in similar uniforms flit across my screen. Their brown rifles and handguns ready. Not a single face moves nor twitches.

The CO bellows louder. "Soldiers! They say that if you take a People's land you must never leave survivors. We will leave no survivors for if we do on some far and distant day they will demand their land back and they will fight until they get it back. Let us not make the same mistakes those who colonized during the early days back on Earth did. No survivors! No prisoners."

A bloodthirsty human-animal roar explodes. Soldiers leap skywards and hold their fists high in salute to him and one another.

A louder roar cuts in.

The rim of the surrounding dunes erupts into wild sand-clouds. SandMasters thrust up from below the surface charge forward and halt facing down into the valley below.

Fragger units hum, aimed at our Invasion Force.

A cough, clearing a throat barks over a bullhorn and into the sudden silence a quiet yet firm voice speaks.

"Attention! Earth-Born Invasion Force! We offer you this single opportunity in which to surrender with honor."

The Commander of our Invasion Force draws his handgun turns and fires towards the circle of SandMaster.

Blinding rainbows fire in all directions. A sudden flash of white light fills the basin. Sharp thunderclaps resound; echo away and in the ensuing silence puffs of sand settle.

Oh my, oh my.

What an incredible sight. Unbelievable!

# CHAPTER 77

## OF A BATTLE FOUGHT AND WON

Not a single weapon remains—not a knife, a rifle, handgun nor mounted gun. Not a single rocket nor round of ammunition lies in waiting ready to fire, load or launch. Not only are our troops disarmed but dead lies their will to fight.

A single volley of Fraggers has accomplished a complete defeat. I hold my hand to my mouth and chuckle—oh my wowness.

Within the desert basin surrounded by ten SandMasters stand one-hundred and fifty thousand of Earth's finest invaders. Moments earlier they had been snarling, lusting of conquest—they are now like jellyfish stranded hundreds of miles from the nearest water.

I cannot help but smile so broadly my jaws ache.

Our famed invaders stand at stiff attention each and every one of them naked as the day they were born. Not a stitch of clothing, not a bootlace, nor a single band of underwear elastic remains.

A Fragger volley vanished all weapons, all clothing, and all ammunition in one fell swoop.

In a subdued voice our Invader CO commands, "Hup-yur-ho!"

Military training allows hands to move with precise timing. Every hand snaps around front and covers that most private of human body parts from present and future prying eyes.

LWB SandMasters with benches mounted on their beds rumble down dune slopes and stop fifty feet from the Invasion Force. Other SandMasters drive in loaded with boxes from out of which plain white garments peak. They drive by the others and park closer to the Invasion Force.

Around me, fellow staff chuckle while others laugh aloud.

Even Skellumer snickers.

Our naked Invasion troopers file by and are handed full-length gowns, a pair of flip-flops, and are marched to waiting SandMasters and transported away. Even some of our troopers are laughing. In the face of hot enemy fire, there is nothing quite as vulnerable as naked and unarmed soldiers.

The bullhorn comes alive with a squeal of feedback.

"In compensation for your unwarranted invasion all equipment, vehicles and ships are surrendered to Here-Born. And to quote your Department for the Assurance of Happiness...have a nice day."

My screen becomes mine at last.

I sigh in sad relief.

Suddenly the taste of bile is in my mouth and the burn of tears is at the corner of my eyes. Once-Other would have loved the way this has all played out if only he were still with us.

# CHAPTER 78

## OF ALL CITIZEN'S PERSONAL CHOICE

My Supervisor strolls in and pats my shoulder. I admire his uniform—so superior to mine as evidenced by the sheen of quality. "I'm counting on you," he says and walks out his brown leather shoes squeaking as new ones do.

I turn to my monitor where a letter displays.

I lean closer, focus and deep within at the very depths of soul an ache awakens. One I have knowingly suppressed for a very long time.

On my monitor is my life's story, the one of endless misery.

I begin the read not only of a lifetime but also of an awakening.

*** 

Dear Citizens of Earth-Born,

Dead ahead is a fork in Life's road for all of Earth-Born. None of the Rights and Freedoms we of Here-Born take for granted exists on Earth-Born. Nor has your Government mentioned any of these to you.

Please allow us to share parts of ours with you.

Though there are many pages, it will be an adventure.

All we ask of you is a touch of indulgence and a little time in which to step away from the fear of things new. Many who travel this road may come to understand the circumstances under which our Here-Born Founders left Earth-Born, and never returned.

And why it is that we never surrender.

Freedom is our All...you see.

What price would you pay for Freedom?

Or as some prefer...for salvation from the slave masters.

Would some reading be too much?

Strangely, we seek your help in and with our own Freedom.

Please keep in mind, we of Here-Born believe betraying those one politically represent is an act of betrayal, an act of treason. On Here-Born, betraying any sworn oath is legally treason or a High Crime at the very least.

Thank you for your time and any reading you may care to give.

Committee for Self-Defense—Here-Born.

\*\*\*

I gaze about.

Everyone is reading.

Hundreds of pale gray uniforms interspersed with hundreds of beige represent we of Earth. Each sits still with head bent—reading. A quick glance out the window and the streets overflow with people sitting on benches, leaning against poles, standing in the street and on the sidewalks, their attention riveted on Nomadi.

For the first time, I clearly notice the pale gray and beige uniforms. A shudder runs down my back.

I have imagined dresses, suits and other things from out storybooks—until this moment. I rub my eyes and stare until the uniforms are as clear to see as my monitor is. A quick count reveals that four-fifths of us wear them. There is something wrong with that.

Before starting the read, I linger a moment, my eyes focused on a darkened sky. My thoughts swivel away from a dark yesterday towards a brighter future. A future I have never dared think of let alone did I make mention of a wish.

That wish I have all but buried in despair.

Now it is time for Agnes Soulone to read.

After the first glance at my screen, a virtual fist hits me right between the eyes. In the same instant, change comes over me as a warm, comforting hand brushes across my shoulders.

"Agnes," I say to myself, "What you read here you must grasp better than anything before. Do not ask me why Agnes. Just trust me on this. Time is short. Those from Rio-Tero may decide to pay us an unexpected visit and demand a payment we are no longer able to make. Perhaps have no desire to pay either.

"Get to your task Agnes. No rest for the wicked."

\*\*\*

**Excerpt from the Here-Born Declaration of Independence, Constitution and Bill of Rights**

Citizens of Here-Born one-n-all:

Freedom we have won. The War of Independence is over.

We stand free of Earth-Born!

Grasp all you can with hands, hearts and minds.

Drink long and deep from the Well of Freedom.

But keep near to heart a solemn promise to never again surrender for Freedom is hard won and long in returning— once stolen from one's grasp.

We write to elicit your vote.

Your Freedom vote for what we have written here.

Do we stand as one? As a nation united?

Can we face tomorrow as a free people?

Is there a government system designed to protect itself not for hundreds, nor thousands, nor tens of thousands but for millions of years-n-more?

Can we protect it from those amongst us bound and determined to wrest freedom from our grasp so they may tie real or virtual chains around our necks for all of time?

Please read carefully and understand what we are doing for each other, our children and theirs and down through the coming ages.

Since winning our Independence from Earth-Born, we have searched this galaxy and many others. We almost gave up hope of finding any government form that would serve freedom and us.

How very strange it was to find what we had sought for so long on Earth-Born itself. In the finding, the reading and the understanding of this treasured discovery we are moved to write as follows:

### 24th July 4008 EB

We the People of Here-Born, adopt the full and *original* Constitution and Bill of Rights of those United States of America, a Republic. We thank them for the document they left behind—we consider it a treasure.

With the benefit of history, other technology, and our own requirements, we have added new ideas and clarified all we can as best we can. This we have done in defense against those amongst Mankind who insist upon enslaving their fellows.

We the People of Here-Born condemn all forms of slavery whether physical, mental, financial or spiritual. We hope all of Mankind understands these are inalienable Rights, are God-given and may only be removed by God—and by God alone.

Live by Neatness alone fellow citizens.

However, from human history comes a clear message to one-n-all.

On the day that a worthwhile Constitution and Bill of Rights are enacted, some amongst us are already plotting its downfall. These schemers are wily, patient and willing to wait hundreds of years to gain victory.

Their victory is our freedom lost.

Never lose sight of this.

We wish to prevent what happened to the United States of America from happening to us.

Those United States of America vanished.

An Empire of Freedom vanished without a trace.

Live by Neatness alone fellow citizens.

\*\*\*

I glance up as Skellumer giggles.

"Those Here-Born dopes. I can't figure what they're talking about. What is this Bill of something and Constitute something and this the United States of America something? Where does this come from?" He scratches under his beige collar.

I always imagine fleas or something worse.

"Let's read...see if you find anything worthwhile," I say.

"Not likely," he says.

I wave him off and scroll down to the next section.

I catch my breath, screw up my eyes, note our ADD-Dees clustered around our Supe and listening as he reads it to them, and I start reading.

\*\*\*

**Excerpt from the Here-Born Tax Code**

Schedule 1-4 is the only Tax Code legal on Here-Born.

All taxes are collected at the State level as a State's Right.

Each State independently possesses the Right to withdraw financial support from the Federal Government. This State's Right is inalienable and is a defense against Federal Governments going rogue.

Within the consideration and agreements of We the Citizens of Here-Born, the costs of life, of business and of living may never to be taxed.

Living life can often be tax enough.

The Annual Taxable Income (ATI) will always be income *over and above the basic costs of life*, of living or of running a business and of all education which also includes all the listed items on which Government may spend Tax Revenues.

Schedule 1-4 outlines the percentages of ATI paid per year for individuals, any business, and all corporations. These are based upon the income remaining (the profit) after subtracting all deductions from Gross Income. Therefore, net income alone is taxable and is the ATI.

Schedule 1

Below fifty thousand dollars, one pays 10%.

Schedule 2

Fifty thousand but less than one-hundred and fifty thousand dollars, one pays 7.5%.

Schedule 3

One-hundred and fifty thousand but less than three-hundred thousand dollars, one pays 5%.

Schedule 4

Three hundred thousand dollars and up, one pays 2.5%.

ATI percentages may never be increased.

They can and by the same amount for each Schedule, be lowered.

Once lowered they may not again be raised.

How Government obtains, revenues for programs not part of Schedule 1-4 is covered later.

The first time an individual (eighteen years or older) or a new for-profit business enters the Here-Born economy their ATI is fixed at the lowest percentage for a period of five years.

This is currently 2.5%.

This allows a five-year period of opportunity, of building, of learning, of training on the job and allows for an organization to become profitable or for an individual to become a professional.

Persons under eighteen pay no taxes neither may their parents nor any others be made to pay taxes on a minor's earnings.

Minors are free to work upon their own self-determinism.

With this system, we encourage success.

***

And I, Agnes Soulone, feels happy with 97% in taxes every year?

I suspect I may live to regret reading this. Maybe not. Maybe if I save and scrimp, I could go live on Here-Born. I glance about. Silence paces the halls of the Department for the Assurance of Happiness, like never before.

Yes, no work getting done. Agnes goes back to reading with her face quite pale but mutters to herself, "I note that Here-Born's citizens have prohibited certain forms of taxes. Won't such ideas get them into trouble? We can't even mention lower taxes or complain about them without getting into trouble."

"They must face prison time for their crimes," Skellumer growls.

I wave him silent.

"You watch your high-minded ideas I see them plain as writing," he says. I go back to reading. So does he.

***

Prohibited forms of taxation follow.

These are listed solely and only in defense against any who may wish to invent other Tax Codes in the future and call or name them something other than a Tax.

This is not a full list at all.

Sales Tax

Property Tax

Taxes on Service provided

License or Permit Fees of any kind

Parking Fees for parking on Public Land, streets or roads

Citations and Fines of any kind or type

Any form of general or specific Usage Fees

Excise or Trade Tariffs

Utility Tariffs or Taxes

Energy Usage Fees or Taxes

Communications fees covering usage of, installation of, maintenance of or any other form of fees or taxation

Oil Taxes

Gasoline Taxes

Energy Taxes

#

How to determine taxes due each year:

The highest dollar amount due over two succeeding years—the current one and the previous year will be the amount paid.

All Government spending is restricted to Section 12 of the Tax Code.

No new nor other forms of government expenses may be created in the future.

A person or group attempting to add items to Section 12, or even proposing such is committing Treason against the People of Here-Born and will be prosecuted.

\#

Section 12

Government employee's salaries

Elected Officials Salaries

Office Supplies

Office furniture

Travel and accommodations while conducting proven Government business

Communications systems hardware, software, support, and services

Data and IT systems hardware, software, support and services

Maintenance of Buildings and Grounds, interior/exterior

Transportation for Government purposes

Maintenance of Public Land, Roads, and Streets

Percentages required and set aside to the Self-Defense Fund

Government's purchase of Utilities

This concludes Section 12.

All levels of government from City to County, to State, to Federal voted yes to be restricted to Section 12.

Section 12 may not be added to for any reason whatsoever.

Not by the People's vote.

Not by Legislation.

Not by any means whatsoever.

Items can be removed.

Once removed they may never be added back in.

Any person or group attempting to add items to Section 12 is to be charged with Waging Economic War for the purpose of the Economic Enslavement of We the People of Here-Born.

The charge is, therefore, one of Treason.

Military Self-Defense was voted a State's Right by all.

Federal Military involvements are restricted to a Federal Liaison Office. All States elect their own Representatives to Federal Departments as well as to the Federal Liaison Office. The Federal Liaison Office provides coordination between States for Self-defense purposes alone.

\*\*\*

Okay—been staring at my screen all day and thinking, thinking, trying to figure why I must know this not just need to know.

What drives me? I'm not sure. I check behind me and again he is there. I have noticed my Supervisor keeping a watchful eye on me from a distance. Don't know if it's something I've done or not done, but it's time to head on home.

Behind me, Skellumer closes out his first and likely only relatively silent day.

"Tomorrow Skellumer."

"What trash. I can't even make myself read more. This'll never work. Those people are idiots."

"Toodle-oo Skellumer."

"Here-Born morons!" he mutters.

# CHAPTER 79

## OF ENTITLEMENTS AND MORE

It's morning, I'm back at the office...and I've had a change of heart. Last night I read into the wee hours and at first I figured to leave out of this Transcript much of what I'd read last night.

But on the way in I realized I can't...I mustn't...so I won't.

Yes, I've continued thinking about what I've learned these past days enough so that my head aches—all the time. I need to understand...how this information could work here on Earth. Here is what I read last night:

*∗∗

**Excerpt from the Here-Born Declaration of Independence, Constitution and Bill of Rights**

Public land, buildings, grounds, parking facilities, offices, warehouses any and all real property is on loan to the Here-Born Government at all levels. These are given into Government's temporary care by We the People who remain the Rightful and Registered Owners thereof.

Privately owned property cannot and may never be confiscated nor become Government owned through legal action, regulation, law, propositions nor confiscated in any manner whatsoever by any part of Government at any level.

Hereby, Eminent Domain is removed from the Here-Born Constitution and so too any form of confiscation for back or unpaid taxes.

No Government entity may obtain credit in any manner nor for any reason whatsoever.

No new Government Sections, Departments, Group, Division, Commission or Body may be created in the future for any reason at any Government level for any purpose whatsoever.

Government bodies may not raise funds through any means other than the above Schedule 1-4 and as outlined below.

On Here-Born the purpose of all Government, all Public Officials, all state hired employees and those elected to Office *is NOT* the continued and ongoing drafting of new Laws, Propositions, Bills nor any other form of legislation nor regulations.

Their duties instead are the administration and management of our World, our States, our Counties, our Cities, our Towns, our Villages and our Hamlets and done so within the budgets made possible by Schedule 1-4 and nothing else.

\#

**Entitlements and all other Here-Born voting requirements**

We the People of Here-Born believe that all Citizens who desire a Government Program have the Right to have such a Program brought into existence for their use.

We the People of Here-Born believe that no citizen who does not wish to participate in a particular Government Program shall have such a Program forced upon him or her. Nor shall the Taxation required to fund such a Program be forced upon him or her.

We the People of Here-Born believe that anyone wishing to assist with the financial support of any Program yet not use the Program themselves may do so at their own self-determinism alone. Such participation would be tax deductible.

We the People of Here-Born declare that any person who requests and then receives payments from an Entitlement Program into which they have *not* contributed in the past or signed up for, loses the right to vote for a period of six years— for each payment received.

Example: If one receives ten such payments, whether these payments are extended over time, in a single month, or on a single day; one loses one's vote for sixty years.

See the Letter to All Citizens Current and Future for why this penalty exists.

In that, any form of Political campaigning is illegal and that those running for office may not advertise either; We the People of Here-Born operate *without* an Electoral College or Districts.

We've adopted a democratic system of voting. Therefore, each State irrespective of the population will have the same number of Senators and House Members representing them. Each State has 2 (two) Senators and 2 (two) Representatives.

This ensures each State as a whole, equal representation in the Federal Government.

All voting, whether in an election or for Laws or Propositions will always be done by a popular vote alone. This may never be changed.

Our reasons for this are obvious.

Every Earth-Born country in existence perverted the use of the Electoral College or Districts. Districts were redrawn and redrawn and filled with the loyal voters of one Party or another. And Electoral College members often came together to vote into Office someone who failed to garner enough votes.

Our system ensures every vote is of the same value as every other one.

Nevertheless, our system prevents oppression by a majority.

May it never be said upon this world of Here-Born, "*Your vote has no value!*"

Any Program, Law, Legislation, Entitlement, Proposal or Proposition must follow steps 1-12 as below and this includes those requiring additional tax revenues over and above the solely legal ATI of Schedule 1-4. This requirement may not be changed by a future Citizens vote nor in any other manner. The attempt to do so is Treason.

The 12 steps are as follows:

1. All proposed Entitlement Programs must be written up in detail, outlined and budgeted for yearly running costs in less than twenty-six pages, 8.5 x 11, in either ten or twelve font size and posted on the Election Website by the individual who is running for Office.
   The full document must be posted a minimum of three months prior to the Date of the Election. Once posted, no changes may be made to it. All other forms of Legislation follow this same route but exclude additional taxation requirements.

2. Entitlement write-ups must provide an actual first Annual Budget. It must also show the exact monthly tax payment for participation due by each Citizen who votes Yes on it.

3. The Entitlement document must list exactly the number of Yes-votes needed to cover the Program's budget for the first year. A Yes-vote for an Entitlement is an automatic sign up for that Entitlement.

4. For an Entitlement Legislation to pass, Yes-votes must at a minimum count equal to the required number of participants to cover the annual budget. If the turnout is a little low and the predicted yearly per person tax payment can be slightly increased to cover the budget, the increase may not be more than 10%. When the increase is greater than 10%, the vote will be counted as a No-vote, will fail to become Law and cannot be passed on to the President for signature.

   All other Programs, Laws, Legislations, or Propositions require a 69% Yes-vote of and by all citizens qualified to vote. Each fails on anything less than a 69% Yes-vote. For all elections and all voting, citizens may 'stay home' without fear a *majority vote* may take away their Rights because each Non-vote is automatically counted as a No-vote.

5. Every Program, Bill, Proposition, Entitlement, proposed Legislation, Law or Proposal must incorporate one subject only and cannot co-join, nor reference, similar or dissimilar Entitlements, Projects, Programs, Law or Legislation, whether new or old, authored by the same person, another, or other persons. It must be in plain language.

6.  After the election, if changes are made in the House or Senate to the Program or to any other proposed Law or Legislation it must again be displayed on the Election Website for an additional ninety days for each change made.

    Each change that is made must be advertised to the Public daily, on and in all media, on each day of each ninety-day period leading up to the final vote. No changes may be made to the document in the last fifteen days prior to the voting date.

    Any failure, which restricts or prevents access to the website and documents of any Program or Proposal, must have its duration added to the ninety-day period required for each change made. Whether access denied is global or local.

7.  When changes are made in the Senate or House, no references to other Legislation, Laws, Propositions, Proposals or any other document or Law may be part of any Legislation, proposed or otherwise.

8.  Person who first authored and listed the new Legislation when running for Public Office must have been elected to Office for the legislation to proceed. Proposed legislation fails when the author fails to be elected. Legislation may only be proposed by those running for Office and so prohibits those already in Offices from presenting any new proposals. A proposed legislation cannot be offered by multiple individuals running for office. It is restricted to the author alone. On inspection should it become obvious that

many have worked to bring multiple, though slightly different versions of legislation forward to be voted on all participants will be charged with a High Crime.

9. All Legislation must pass by a 69% Yes-vote in the House or Senate, being the one into which the Official WAS elected.

10. All Legislation must pass by a 69% Yes-vote in the House or Senate being the one that the Official WAS NOT elected to.

11. After #9 and # 10 above, all proposed Legislation must appear on the Confirmed in Congress Website for ninety-nine (99) days without change. On the one-hundredth (100th) day of being visible and viewable on the website the final vote by We the People takes place. Access failure conditions apply here as well.

This final vote is when the no less than a 69% Yes-vote is required of all of Here-Born's voters so that Legislation of any kind may become Law but which excludes Entitlements voting which has its budget to meet via the number of required Yes-votes. Any and all voting must be a separate vote to any election or any other Proposal, Proposition, Legislation, Law or Bill. This second vote gives Citizens a defense against bringing into Law Legislation, which has been secretly changed or altered or knowingly or unknowingly voting on multiple items with one vote. The First Vote for new Legislation is cast by We the People when the author is voted into Office.

Citizens:

The Original Copy and all other copies must be downloaded to your Nomadi when first placed on the Election Website, which is when the author is running for Office.

If you support a Proposition or other legislation and intend voting Yes, you are urged to compare each version up to and including the final draft. Ensure each edition represents what you first voted on when voting someone into office.

Please be vigilant. Download newer versions and compare them before you vote the Final Vote.

Backup all copies in which are new or additional changes. Do so in defense against those who in the future may attempt to redefine its meaning or change the wording or cause the originals to vanish. If you don't like what's happened to it or don't support it at all...*simply stay home.*

12. Only at this point, and upon acceptance by We the People as per steps 1 through 11 of this Section, can a new Program, Law, Legislation, Entitlement, Proposal or Proposition be signed into law by the President. Any legislation failing as above may not be passed on for Presidential signature.

Suggesting, by spoken words or written that the required voting percentages on Here-Born be changed is a High Crime. Attempting to alter them or actually altering the required voting percentages is Treason.

Therefore:

Each Here-Born citizen qualified to vote, being those 18 or older, shall be provided with an Electronic Voting Card referred to as an EVC. EVC's are used solely and only to vote Yes for Legislation that requires financing over and above Schedule 1-4. These are Entitlements only. EVC's are not and may never be used for General Elections nor any other type of voting. No similar cards for General or other Elections may be introduced now nor in the future.

When voting Yes for a Program entry fields will pop up on a Nomadi. A voting citizen must enter their EVC Voting ID and Password. The Monthly Dollar amount due in taxes will display.

All voting on Here-Born is done via Nomadi and requires log-in names, secret questions, and passwords. Voting and counting servers are local to voters; in their neighborhoods.

Local servers carry no more than the number of names that allow neighbors to check those who voted Yes, No or a Non-Vote (also a No-Vote) by simply knowing each voter's name when viewed.

For security reasons, false neighborhood Voter ID's can be entered and kept secret at the local level. At least one false ID for each voter and created by the voter—the actual number is decided on by each neighborhood voter. This makes voter fraud more difficult as hackers will have to find which Voter ID is real and which isn't.

All voting servers from neighborhoods to Final Tally servers go live five minutes prior to the vote. They are dark at all other times. This makes hacking more difficult as well.

These servers will provide totals of Yes, Non or No-votes. This allows citizens to monitor their own voting neighborhood after voting closes by temporarily isolating their voting server, have all neighborhood voters login and verify their vote on a separate neighborhood server. And compare them.

They can then verify that these tallies match the official recorded local vote—many neighborhoods now meet and do this with all neighbors present who are normally only the yes voters. This same verification is available at each step up the server ladder all the way to the Final Tally Servers.

For the Tally Servers to be correct, neighborhoods must share and update voter registration real time to all local Nomadi and servers. Local servers and citizens must verify all new entries of newly registered voters.

Many neighborhoods have set up their own servers to which all other neighborhoods, Here-Born wide, share voting tallies. These servers are on secure private pipes. This allows full verification of the vote count as every neighborhood server total should match the Tally Server's total.

All citizens who voted Yes for an Entitlement Program shall share the first annual budget of a Program as an additional tax payment over and above, and in addition to, the taxation in Schedule 1-4 but only when and if, the Legislation Passes into Law as above.

Citizens may withdraw financial support for and thereby use of any Program by giving a minimum of three months' notice prior to the end of the Financial Year, by or on December 31st.

They will continue to be responsible for the current Financial Year. Citizens, when providing an End of Financial Support and Participation notification must use Verification of Receipt return mailing.

Upon receipt of the End of Financial Support and Participation Notification, Government will immediately cease to receive, demand or acquire payments for that Program from a citizen at the start of the next Financial Year.

Government carries the onus, duty, and responsibility—solely and only—to cease any acceptance of payments, attempt to demand payments or any other actions or efforts to collect revenues once a Citizen's financial support ends at the beginning of a new Financial year. Attempts to continue receipt of payments is a crime, all participating in such will be charged.

Citizens have the Constitutional Right to inform their Banking Institution of an End of Financial Support and Participation notification. Citizens must provide their Financial institutions with a Verification of Receipt along with Certified copies of their signed End of Financial Support and Participation Notification. If Government fails to sign and so return a Verification of Receipt, your record of purchase and official stamp on it will suffice.

Banking or other Financial Institutions must then immediately block all requests by any Government Section and in particular the Treasury Department at any and all Government Levels from access to these citizens accounts. And must forbid any payments from these accounts for programs from which a taxpayer has withdrawn financial support and has provided the proof as outlined above—once a new Financial year starts.

Financial institutions must, by law, inform customers of any and all attempts by any section of Government to withdraw funds illegally as above.

Citizens who voted No for any such Program may not now nor in the future be made to, nor forced to pay such additional taxation.

Citizens wishing to receive the services or advantages of Entitlements but who voted No may commit to a twelve-month taxation commitment, upon their own free will alone, at the same annual amount as those who voted Yes are paying.

Their withdrawal from such a Program is done as above.

Any Program, which due to Citizens withdrawing financial support from the second year of the Program onwards must cease to operate if the budget can no longer be met by those remaining in the Program.

Citizens may not be forced or encouraged or sold on paying more than the original amount.

On the Second vote for an entitlement program, should an up to 10% increase be incurred, all Citizens must be informed of the increase immediately. The up to 10% increase is valid once only and may not be exercised again. Attempting to do so is fraud and perpetrators will be prosecuted.

Once new signups for an Entitlement program that failed to meet its budget reaches the number of participants needed in the original proposal to carry the budget, the added 10% is then no longer required and must be deducted from all payments and all Participants must be so informed.

Government must stop collecting revenues for any Program no longer active or about to be shut down. Once a Program has been closed or fails to meet its first annual budget or the person running for Office is NOT elected to Office the proposed Legislation may not again appear to be voted on at all, nor under any other name. Nor may parts be integrated into new Proposals or in any other form of Legislation.

Here-Born does not operate under or with inflation. Therefore, inflation cannot be used as a reason or part of a formula to increase payment amounts.

Each running Program must be listed by name on the current Government Programs website. The Program document must be one page, letter-sized and provide a full description of its services and additional monthly Taxation costs.

Programs may not be advertised beyond this.

# CHAPTER 80

## OF THE DEFENSE OF RIGHTS AND A WEAPON TO HAND

As they say on Here-Born, "Damn altogether!"

I'm on the bus and still reading—my pale green uniform feels thick with sweat. My black shoes squeeze tighter than before.

On leaving, even Skellumer was looking less Skellumer—despite his beige uniform being in desperate need of a wash. But! If he changes, watch out, for everyone on Earth will have changed long before he does.

The key goes in smoothly and turns, but the dark brown and tattered door hesitates to open. My shoulder applied does an open sesame.

I kick the front door closed and in the same instant catch a glimpse of him ducking back into the closet. Looks to me like he took a shower today—good for him. Well...he's coming around.

I make some stir-fry, which would be excellent with meat but who can afford meat these days.

I leave a little where he can get at it.

I eat and read the last few paragraphs of the excerpt.

\*\*\*

**Excerpt from the Here-Born Declaration of Independence, Constitution and Bill of Rights**

For changes to be made in whole or to any portion of the Here-Born Declaration of Independence, Constitution or Bill of Rights a 97% (ninety-seven percent) Yes-vote is required. This vote is of and by all of Here-Born's citizens who are eligible to vote. This means ninety-seven percent of all citizens of a voting age whether registered to vote or not and whether or not they have ever voted before.

This DOES NOT MEAN 97% of the turnout of voters.

This DOES MEAN 97% of ALL ELIGIBLE VOTERS.

More so than any other time the Non-vote is equal to a No-vote!

And again!

This ensures Here-Born voters and all citizens of the Right to opt-in to any and all Programs, or Laws, or Legislation, or Propositions, or any change or addition by voting Yes as opposed to having to opt-out by voting No.

The opt-in Yes-vote, including the automatic Non-vote equals a No-vote applies to all the voting done on Here-Born.

This allows voters the Right to *stay home*, without fear a *majority vote* may take away their Rights.

All Citizens are eligible to vote at the age of eighteen.

\*\*\*

A new morning, and dressed in a pale green uniform with black shoes I have added a touch of lipstick. Cannot figure why but I did. I bought the green ones on impulse as well.

I can hear him in the closet—talking to himself. I'm sure he's muttering one or two curses under his breath. He ate the stir-fry last night—good. I was worried. He eats so sparingly.

I take my time over breakfast—thinking the weirdest imaginings possible. They are so far and beyond me I cannot as yet put words to them. I'm reaching for a future with all this pondering.

I see myself somehow embracing thousands of others. I now have a little hope, but I'm having trouble envisioning how everything slots together. I at least have a sense of why I'm reading what's being displayed, so avidly.

I'm not relaxed, though, not at ease. Something new or perhaps a higher intensity of an old ache turned on when I awoke.

It's the knife of fear that cuts me and for no apparent reason, no obvious cause. I take precautions nonetheless and leave a bowl of cold soup on the closet floor before heading out for work—in case I fail to return.

During the trip to work this morning nothing untoward occurred. I felt a new anticipation in the air. One I noted shone in the eyes of my fellow commuters as well. The bus was full yet quiet, but not that quiet of old, a new contemplative one.

Not even standing room was available.

Everyone ignores the overdone, overrun History Lessons, which never stop running. I had not realized how irritating they are. So much of the history provided conflicts with the data and information of these last days.

Which is true? How to find out?

I adjust my pale green uniform and stare out the window. The clangs and rumblings of our trolley's progress grow faint— my thinking wanders over new landscapes. History versus history. Here-Born versus Earth. Real versus Propaganda. Solutions slither away ever elusive.

I make it to work as we used to every morning.

Is it all over? Is that it? Is there nothing more to it?

I enter my office.

"You believe this junk?" Skellumer asks.

I note he washed his pale beige uniform and shirt, a touch of shine on the worn shoes.

"Don't know that belief comes in," I reply. "It's starting to make sense to me."

"You've gone mad, Soulone," he says but without the venom of old.

Nevertheless, I wave to zip him up and get to work but he refuses to stow it.

"Who is going to pay ADD-Dees under a Here-Born system?" he asks.

I glance at them sitting in front of the TV.

I had not thought of them lately—I do now.

"Well, Skellumer. We'll figure a way to get them productive and valuable economically. Do that and they won't need handouts."

"Who's the fool now? Wishful Miss Agnes Thinking."

"To work I go Skellumer."

I turn to the tired old desk I've sat behind for too many years to count.

Seated, I reach for the keyboard but the screen flashes to black. I am again unable to access Monitoring Assures Happiness Records.

Hallelujah...I decide to stop saying Hallelujah as well.

You could taste it throughout the building, anticipation met as utter silence falls over us. My Section, Happiness Records and Verifications, has never been this quiet despite the quiet bouts of late. I frown at all the strange scenes playing across the monitor screen.

I check around the office. So is everyone else—back to my screen.

Okay. I get what I'm looking at, World Capital Buildings, Washington DC but a long time ago.

Subtitle:

Washington DC, United States of America 19th to 21st centuries.

Weirdly dressed people march by. Long hair. Odd circular sunglasses. Pictures of flowers. Flowers pinned into hair. Many carry posters.

Does Peace get a Chance? End the War. War is hell. Get Government out my Life. Stop Spending. Lower Taxes. I'm happy with my Healthcare.

No Socialism for me.

Lots more. Way more. Wow.

Fascism sucks. Communism kills success. Every mad assassin or mass killer is or was on psychiatric/mental health drugs—all of them—check it out. Down with the USA. Democracy urinates. Long dead the Queen. Stop the bombing, and so many more.

Hundreds of cops in black uniforms with white helmets sporting transparent shields and carrying truncheons surround the protesters.

Screen changes to scenes of police removing protesters with not a single Officer smiling. Most protesters or demonstrators refuse to move.

None of them fights back. Instead, they sit as though glued to the road. Police struggle to move them. It takes two to three officers to drag one protester away.

An older black and white recording that shows people marching in protest. Announcer mentions a Gandhi leading Peace movements against British rule in India.

The view switches to another location. Here, they refuse to carry Identification Cards in India. Cops charge beating at the protesters. Some cower, others run, yet others stand their ground and are beaten to it.

Through all the attacks they keep moving forward, marching on.

Back to DC

More protesters dragged away. Officers struggle in tandem to get them into wagons, not easy work.

Officers getting mad. Protesters are silent, passive, unmoving.

Message on my screen:

Dear Citizens,

If you prefer, a Government that governs for All the People.

If you would like taxes that allow personal success to be rewarded.

If the Right to keep most of what you earn makes sense to you.

If you wish for a Government wherein charity is not enforced but done by personal choice.

If you desire a smaller Federal Government as well as at all other levels of government.

If you demand your elected officials represent you and your fellow citizens.

Please use your Nomadi and vote Yes.

If you don't want to change anything. Please vote No.

Thank you.

Oh, my wowness!

I glance around and everyone I can see is voting.

I turn back and on my screen, the Treasury Account displays. The dollar amount of our taxes keeps climbing. To be honest, spending the entire day watching the voting percentage climb and the tax dollars collected climb should be boring.

Trust me—not so. I miss lunch because I do not want to move. My Supervisor brings me coffee and a cookie. Bless him.

"You're welcome," he says as though he had read my thoughts. I do not turn around not wanting to take my eyes off the screen.

Inside my head, something changes and new ideas nip at me. Still, I haven't come to terms with all I've seen and read yet...but I've petted it some.

Come clock out time and the Yes let us change this hits the eighty percent mark.

I think we are going to change our lives.

Anyway, I hope so.

Toodle-oo.

At home I find he finished the cold soup.

I give him hot soup and fresh bread.

Showered. Yep. The water still works. Dinner and TV and as usual one is tasteless, the other entertainment-less. Nothing to view until programming dies and the Hub appears.

All of our Representatives sit in attendance. I again note the fancy suits, ties and the abundance of delicious food and drink on display.

The President rises, sips a little red wine and with his usual dignity addresses the nation.

"My Fellow Citizens,

"I am here, though with a heavy heart, to address you to-night. Generally, I would not bother you at such a late hour but on this day, I feel I must.

"Here in my hand is an Ultimatum purported to come from *We the People*. I doubt the validity of such a statement. Too broad and encompassing I'd say. Oh, wait! Am I not of We the People? But let me read this to you. I'm sure you will be as amused as I was."

He glances at his fellow Officials who smirk as he continues.

"You will come to understand the nonsense written here and you'll not wish to become anarchists. Those of Here-Born want us to swallow this all without so much as a protest. Yes, just swallow it hook, line and sinker and so become anarchists! I'm so pent-up at this monstrosity.

"But...I will now read it.

"We the People by a Legal expression of our wish for a Government vested in us, for the right to peaceful and fulfilling lives, to remove excessive taxes from the Statutes and get Government out of our lives, do hereby declare that all persons employed as Government workers and all Elected Officials must immediately resign."

He stares into the camera with his favored expression of incredulity, raises an eyebrow and continues.

"A bare minimum of the hands-on Department Representatives and staff will remain at work until a new Constitution and Bill of Rights is drawn up, voted into Law, signed and enacted. One which We the People agreed to and voted into existence."

He throws his arms wide. Gazes around the Assembly at all the smirking faces and in his most solemn voice says, "Please fellow citizens stop this nonsense—you already have *that* Government."

The Speaker of the Combined Houses stands and says, "We will vote on this *Measure*."

Tears whelm in tune with my sinking heart.

I knew it would happen this way.

Still, I had hoped for something else.

They all vote No.

"The Measure fails."

Like I needed to be told.

The screen goes blank.

Minutes later, another a letter on my display addressed to us:

Dear Citizens,

Washington DC houses the Senatorial Hub and House.

If you'd like to bring to their attention, non-violently, what your wishes are, please gather and march by in DC with signs expressing your wishes—be polite and well mannered. That's a winner always and especially with the signs used.

Taking into account that a passive protest will be violently attacked with many innocents arrested and charged we suggest between three and five million citizens arrive and maintain a continuous march-by.

Best not to camp but instead rotate people daily and only a march by. Don't occupy the buildings. Camping and occupying government property are illegal. It follows a law will be passed making a march-by illegal.

We'll deal with such a law when and if it happens.

We suggest any who are arrested be replaced.

Let's not forget Food Vendors, Rest Room Vendors, Sanitation and Refuse Removers and Providers of Security. You are all invited and bring your services along.

Again, please do not camp—but do keep marching.

Washington DC awaits you.

Thank you for your attention.

Oh my! And the screen goes blank, and I head for bed with a glance towards the closet, he's peeking out tonight. That's a good sign. I point to the couch, but he closes the closet door.

Oh well—to bed I go.

This morning my commute goes by as always.

But the screens are active when I arrive.

Even my Supervisor watches, Skellumer too. It's the Assembly again and it seems none of them had gone home. They are tired and grumpy.

Coffee, muffins, and bagels await their pleasure.

Many have their feet up and snooze.

Those still awake watch the Treasury Bank account collecting taxes.

They smile and nod victory nods.

The screen dissolves and a new document appears.

# CHAPTER 81

## OF THE SLAVE MASTER'S SALES PITCH AND NEW RIGHTS

I download it to my Nomadi right off. I'm one-two-three damn sure altogether that I want this as part of my record.

As an aside, I have stopped taking my required daily medication since I ran out. Must admit I am thinking a little clearer since and feel more energetic as well.

As I read, I can't help imagine the Founding Fathers of Here-Born arguing and shouting in their Halls of Government as they developed their Constitution, Bill of Rights and wrote The Letter.

Here is what is on my screen right this moment.

***

**A Letter to all Here-Born citizens, current and future**

Dear Citizens,

Amongst Mankind, there are those who are continuously dishonest and unethical in life. Sadly, they have always been amongst us.

Through all our history they have given us war, destroyed economies, brought us slavery under the whip or sword or gun, under drugged and/or electronic control and under financial duress. And in more ways than can be quickly listed.

No economy, religion, organization, group nor political system has to date been free of him nor her.

Now!

It's generally known and fully understood by all that excessive taxation will slow an economy and eventually destroy it.

It is on our part *dreaming* that those imposing excessive taxation will realize the error of their ways and change when they note how excessive taxation hurts an economy, and thus the people.

Because, if we know what excessive taxation does to an economy—so do they! Yet they impose it.

Therefore, if politicians pass Laws that usher in excessive taxation in all its myriad of forms, their only purpose is to bring slavery to one-n-all under the whip of economic and financial duress.

Therefore, anyone selling the idea that taxation beyond Schedule 1-4 is required; is selling slavery for you, for your friends, for your family.

But please...do be careful.

They will tell you just how deeply concerned they are about your and others welfare and to help you they will need to tax *someone else—excessively*. Beware! That is the Slave Master's most cherished sales pitch!

Think of it as the Slave Master selling slavery to a slave. The other sales pitch the Slave Master uses is directed straight at the worker.

Workers are told that owners and management are crooks and criminals who live by greed alone. That management must not be tolerated because they grow rich at the expense of the workers. Therefore, the worker must refuse to accept management offers and proposals...always.

Yet success requires both the worker and management.

And truly...all success lies in the hands of the worker, but not alone.

Success requires close co-operation and good communication between the worker and management. Yet the evolving Slave Master encourages the Worker to refuse to speak with management and insists workers not tolerate Management one iota. And we all know that one-hundred percent intolerance is by definition—hate.

And the evolving Slave Master encourages hatred between people with different views. Which people are required to work together for there to be a viable success, in any sphere, any activity—work or play.

But when hate wins—management moves on to other places, other endeavors. And for the worker the job has gone—never to return.

This is when the evolving Slave Master offers more entitlements to entice the unemployed worker deeper into slavery.

You'll see and hear the Slave Master telling you to hate another or others more than before. Telling you that you can only be free by destroying the company who provides your work opportunities and that you not listen to anyone else and refuse to talk to or with those *others*.

Yet. You will also find the Slave Master refusing to tell you and management what exactly they are doing and what their agenda is. And while they condemn Management they pass laws and regulations that make it impossible to have a business in your hometown, your County, your State and finally in your Country.

Using laws and regulations, they send management fleeing to places where they *can* do business. So. While the evolving Slave Master promises you the worker freedom that freedom comes with a price.

Those companies where you work move away and there goes your job never to return. And you end up with no job, no honor, no dignity as the price you paid for *freedom*. And this they hide from one and in a blinded lied to fashion one travels the road to becoming a slave—willingly.

Our ancestors left Earth because of the International State of Emergency declared in 2026 though they left many hundreds of years later.

As of 24th of July 4008, it is still being enforced. Which includes all Rights suspended, the Constitution overthrown and elections ended.

Those in Office back in 2026 served for Life for there were no further elections and that is why they were so uncaring in passing laws against the Will of We the People. Their intention before the State of Emergency was the establishment of a dictatorship, but they referred to it an organized community.

Increased taxes they promoted as a means to spread the wealth so that the poor and underprivileged may attain their deserved restitution. No such massive handouts to the poor were ever given.

The poor simply got poorer.

Instead, the money went to make themselves and their sponsors wealthier and to pay Government workers to run Government Programs. That is where and how wealth is distributed with only a pittance going to the poor.

We of Here-Born have found satisfaction in a different way of life.

For us, the only way to receive what is justly ours is by increasing our own economic value, each individual doing so personally. That is done with education, training and experience towards greater skills that lead to bigger paychecks.

Therefore, it is written here in the Here-Born Declaration of Independence, Constitution and Bill of Rights that We the People do fully understand that Government will *always* attack Freedom.

This is done through the undoing of a Constitution and Bill of Rights. And further! Via instigated mass rioting and by cutting communications media not favorable to Government. Via the Declaration of an Emergency and the suspension of Elections due to public disobedience and especially due to rioting.

Which disobedience and rioting was, is and always will be provoked, sponsored, condoned, and support by those wishing to enslave We the People. And the war you will fight will not always be a violent one.

Instead, and in particular with Socialists, they will attack from within with *ideas alone.* Weapons are *no defense* against ideas. Ideas breach armor, bullets, and bombs and enter minds moving from one to another.

With ideas alone, Communists take control by organizing the community. The National or Nazi Socialist organize at the national level. Each uses violence as a means to an end. And continue the violence once empowered.

They sell the same ideas...as above. They repeat them over and over until a nation accepts them and then they take over control. That is when the horrors begin. Wealth is confiscated (stolen). Even their supporters are tossed out of house and home to wander the streets penniless.

And so comes forced labor. Worked until you die. Always. Always!

But why forced labor? Because they destroyed your economy first.

Therefore, it is declared an Inalienable Individual Right that at any time Laws are enacted which violate our Declaration of Independence, our Constitution, our Bill of Rights and this Letter; from the date of their enactment such Laws are here today and for all Eternity Declared to be Illegal Laws and Unenforceable.

Citizens!

Any Freedom gained must be fought for on every day of every person's life. Once gained it must be defended.

This does not *always* require violent conflict.

The First Defense is education. Education freed of Government control of its teachers, its Institutes, and its curriculum. But primarily by an education in and of our Declaration of Independence, Constitution, Bill of Rights and this Letter. Then as well in factual and honest History where the student is allowed to discover his or her own *lessons learned*.

And all these can only be understood if the basics of reading, writing, and mathematics are taught in a way which requires a student's skills be measured in his or her application of them out in life—while still a student. Teach too the skills of honest research and data analysis for these two skills are one's armor against falsehoods and insidious lying.

The Second Defense is our Ultimate Weapon of Mass Destruction.

The Third Defense is the right to fight back which includes armed self-defense. This does not suggest nor condone initiating violent attacks upon another or a group. This condones self-defense only.

Keep in mind that ill-intentioned persons, those who wish to be our Slave Masters and/or their minions can sound civilized, even heartwarming and beneficial to oneself. They can even be well-mannered, reasonable, logical or raving mad.

They will creep up on you over decades by dumbing down education, filling entertainment and news broadcasts with false information, decrying and condemning any and all who dare insist on good moral conduct. Let alone the Constitution or the Law of the Land.

These black-hearted and ill-intentioned persons will erode justice in defense of those who support them. They will abuse Justice and the Law to destroy any who challenge them. Their explanations will sound reasonable and so it sneaks up on you in a manner that appears to give one more freedom.

But there are none, neither supporters nor protesters let alone the minions, who will escape the evolving Slave Master once he's empowered to rule over us. None will escape him— no matter how much you may have assisted the evolving Slave Master to attain power or what you were promised.

Therefore, the right to personal self-determined decision and choice is the Right of all citizens. The Right to be individually responsible for self or others by choice is an Inalienable Right for All.

Added to the above is the Right to create jobs. This includes freedom from Government regulations and interference. Never again will government intrude upon the creativity of the entrepreneur nor the enterprising person, nor those who wish to carve their own business paths.

Furthermore, all citizens owning businesses, small, medium, large companies and corporations have the Right to Create Programs for the Employment of Government employees who refuse to obey illegal orders.

This removes the threat of being fired and then being unable to support one's family—for all government employees. This allows as well for citizens in times of oppression to know that those left in government are abusing the laws of the land and are thus criminals.

Websites should go up so that government employees may apply in secret and all parties know that new training may be required and so most starting salaries will merely cover an applicant's monthly bills and costs of living.

Citizens! It is not possible to Flee to Freedom.

Eternal vigilance is a must in every life and every day of your life.

Teach it to your children. Teach it well. Never assume they know of what is written here or of what Freedom is or what Slavery is—in all its insidious forms.

And may you never need violent conflict to resolve these.

And may you never find lost your Right to defend your Life and that of Family and Friends.

And from this day on you have in your hands the Right to Defend your own Sanity—forever.

Signatures:

| | |
|---|---|
| John Ashley McGregor | Jensen R. D'elti |
| William Tshabalala | Jessica Ozerken |
| Charlene Joanne Chu | Diana van den Jaarsveldt |
| Arnold Washington | Maureen Wagenaara |
| Hendrihetta Schwartzlauda | Johnstone Mokoena |
| Ozwolde Okada | Mathieu du Fleurs |
| Herbert K. Somalo | Javier Oritz |

# CHAPTER 82

## OF STEPPING UP AND TAKEN DOWN

This morning my Supervisor is noticeable by his absence. The one at home seems to be doing much better, but I have no time to ponder as, throughout our offices, screens display that same black screen and static snow. A terse message appears, and my heart thumps painfully.

Dear Citizens,

Go to your Nomadi and vote Yes or No.

Yes, means you still wish to continue providing your current Government with tax revenues.

No means you no longer want to support your current Government, which is dedicated to governing for the few by penalizing the majority.

Thank you.

Voting begins.

No one works. We stare at screens on which are two counters. One counts the votes climbing the other displays the Tax Revenues increasing on the Treasury Account.

Like, everyone, I sit watching both numbers going up and up.

My Supervisor arrives and prowls the hallway coffee in hand.

BA remains off and our offices smell fresher. Even thinking of BA makes me mad. Imagine. Paying for air when there's more than enough to go round. How important that Letter from Here-Born's Founders has been for them.

Come noon, tax revenues start to slow. If BA went down fast what's going to happen to our Government when or if the money stops? Wait.

Another scene from Washington DC.

A large crowd marches by the Senatorial Hub. Police face them and cordon off a no man's land between the marchers and the Hub entrance. A counter turns on: one-hundred and eighty thousand people in but a few hours.

My Supervisor paces. His footsteps elicit squishing sounds from the carpet. He is still busy chain smoking and chain coffee-ing. His Nomadi held tight to his ear, his eyes on me. I scratch the itch that his stare elicits.

After looking at the screen for some time but not actually seeing it anymore, something yanks at my attention. I focus as Poip emerge from the Hub and take up formation behind the police.

I note the counter again—one and a half million marching by—must be worrying for them inside the Hub.

My Supervisor is suddenly behind me.

I sensed him at first and then got a whiff of coffee and tobacco.

He leaves after patting my shoulder.

It's 2:00 pm and two-and-a-half million people march.

The police remain at attention, ramrods awaiting orders.

New motion grabs at me. A figure emerges from the Hub via a side door obscured by shadows. I lean in closer.

It's Mister McPeters! He climbs into a black limo.

Where's he going? Will he come home to LA? To his wife? How's she doing? A non-stop flight can deliver him home in four hours. You'd think he'd want to be at the Hub.

What's so important to make him leave? On the other hand, is he headed for his Red Zone home and safety?

My Supervisor places a hamburger, fries and soda at my elbow. Stomach growls a response to the enticing aroma. Wait. What's gotten into him?

Okay. Never mind.

I eat, check around and find everyone still riveted to his or her displays. Day marches on, silent as never before.

Eventually, when I notice the crick in my neck, there are three-and-a-half million people marching by the Hub...and my mouth drops open.

Hundreds of policemen drop their shields, their truncheons and with hands held high, join the parade of marching citizens. Folks offer them signs, which the police eagerly grasp.

Many walk by and slap each officer on the back.

It seems not all public servants just obey orders.

I glance up.

My, it is 11:32 PM and the place is deserted except for my Supervisor, still smoking, still coffee-ing. The counter keeps going as I turn Transcribing off, grab my coat and head for the elevator.

My Supervisor leaves at the same time. He lingers on the sidewalk when I get on the bus. I wave to him through the window as we drive away. He waves back. Weird.

I sit down and look around. A strange calm is present—a new quiet. Even the empty streets feel different. Yet I'm afraid

Government will use their Here-Born attack strategy against us—there's a lot at stake for them—especially since so much of what's happening on Earth was revealed to us.

Despite this, people I see out and about are more relaxed and talking to each other without that regular furtiveness. Is this the calm before the massacre? I hope not.

Yes. Life is going to be bad, real bad—for a while.

The bus turns the corner and I glance back, but he's gone. I should get his full name someday. He hasn't been with us long. He is kind of aloft but not in a bad way. Attractive as well, in a sort of devil may care fashion.

I'm having weird thoughts tonight.

I sit back and about to relax when a chill breeze wafts by.

I freeze up tight as the hairs at the nape of my neck snap to attention. I snug my collar down and scrutinize the passengers, but no one else does so. I go over each commuter one at a time then the street and sidewalks for danger but find none.

I run a hand over the tight knot of hair calming it and whisper, "Something needs doing here, Agnes. Yes! Something needs doing."

All the reading I've done and monitor screen images I've watched since Here-Born's invasion, rest heavy within me. But I can't put a finger on what's with myself. Hope I do so soon.

It's time for me to get off the bus. I hasten down the aisle. The doors whoosh and slide open. I step off. Urgh. Gum stuck to the sole of my left shoe. Urgh.

I fiddle the key in the slot and those nape hairs jump to attention once again, but it is too late. Something hits me square between the shoulders with the driving force of a bus traveling at fifty miles an hour.

I'm thrown forward. The front door snaps open in two halves, left and right—so much for security I think and sprawl to the floor taking the skin off both knees.

The sound of soup being slurped. I glance up.

The TV displays millions marching at the Hub.

He's come out the closet good and proper at last and is sitting on the couch drinking straight from a frying pan. He peers over the rim at me. Glances at something behind me, fear flashes in his eyes, but it is instantly vanquished by the fires of anger.

A blur of motion to my left far too fast to perceive what. A flash of movement at the couch and then all motion stops. Oh, my deepest wowness.

Mister Warrent McPeters crouches at the far side of the lounge his arm crooked around the neck of...oh...he's still holding my pan in his hand.

Two more blurs rush by, one to either side of me.

McPeters moves and becomes a blur. The pan falls and slithers across the carpet. Soup splashes on the carpet and on the walls. Loud thuds and bangs echo. The coffee table breaks. The couch tilts backward then rights itself. Another loud noise stuns me. A groan of pain and all motion ends.

I stare more amazed than I have been these last few days.

My Supervisor kneels at McPeters left fixing handcuffs to him. Once-Other kneels at McPeters right attaching the other end of the handcuffs.

Done Once-Other looks up and the happiest smile I have ever seen lights his eyes. "You alright Karrell?" he asks being polite and all by speaking out aloud.

"Knew you'd come, Dad," Karrell whispers hoarsely. Well, he has recovered enough to speak a little—well done on his part. They hug a long time.

My Supervisor helps me to my feet and brushes my coat off while frowning down at my knees. I don't dare look down. Nice of him though and anyway who is this guy?

"Well Agnes," he says. "You're one for the records."

What's that mean? I stare him in the eye and they smile at me. Okay. Not an insult. Okay. Good. Now, what? I gaze about a little overwhelmed.

McPeters groans but no one pays him any mind except for Karrell who picks up the frying pan and looks a long silent moment at McPeters. Suddenly he swings the pan and smacks McPeters on the back of his head. Dead silence as McPeters tips forwards and falls flat on his fact.

Karrell grins and says, "Take that! Property D-101!"

Laughter explodes from all of us.

Wiping at his tear filled eyes, Once-Other comes over, shakes my hand, keeps a hold of it and says, "Thank you for what you did. It was very brave."

"Anyone would have done it," I reply.

"No," he says. "And please...don't make less of yourself. That man is, *was* the most influential person on Earth-Born. He writes legislation in real time and approves it for the whole Hub and could have sent a thousand Poip to your door upon a whim."

I swallow against a tight throat but manage to say, "I know. But Karrell...when...what McPeters did. I had to help. And. What all they had paid for their New World. No!"

"You are brave," my Supervisor says matter-of-factually.

In all that just happened I had missed something or maybe it missed me. Now it hits home and I blurt out, "Once-Other? How do you come to be here? You were left for dead out in the desert...by him. How?"

"Well dear me Ms. Soulone. That is a long story. One for the books I'd say, altogether. What all we have done here these last weeks may never be revealed. Perhaps history my eventually demand answers."

"No answer eh?" I say and look about, mind racing as questions spring to life.

Once-Other smiles and says, "I do have one answer for you. Seek out a Jonathon Andrew...work with him to evolve to a new political civilization here on Earth-Born."

I look for more but he just smiles broader. "Okay. I'll find him. Oh? So where's Madsen? You were the masked one with him doing the *burn a pipe* thing."

"I ordered him home," Once-Other says.

"Ordered? Wasn't he your senior?" I gasp.

"He was. Circumstances changed. No, well I made them change. He needed to go home...for a while," Once-Other murmurs.

I nod and reply, "I understand."

"I figure things are going to be a little chaotic for a while General," my Supervisor says.

Once-Other nods yes.

"You a General?" I ask rather ill mannered.

"Certainly," he replies.

"Right," is all I can say. "There's a new certainty about...."

"She sounds ready," Once-Other says.

A little afraid to ask for what exactly I am prepped, I glance from him to Karrell and back and wonder how they came to be here and it hits me clear as daylight. I turn to my Supervisor.

"You saw Karrell on that Happiness Monitoring at the McPeters place and followed what I'd done. Right?"

"She's perfect," Once-Other says in answer to my Supervisor and me.

"For what?" I ask.

Behind me, boots scuff on the carpet fuzz. I turn and recognize the D'elti family standing just inside the front door with two police officers behind them.

"We'll take him off your hands, Madam," the larger Officer says as they move past me.

What's he call me Madam for I ponder and why has no one answered my question?

My Supervisor hands me an eChip and says, "Here's the evolution that occurred after our people won and declared Independence from Earth-Born, the first time.

"You've read everything we displayed over screens these last few days and as always you've kept records. On this chip are links to all the documentation you will need. It includes direct contact info for everyone in this room, except him."

He nods at McPeters and turns back to me. "Agnes, keep in mind that the techniques used at this time to free you are the last resort save for a violent overthrow."

He stares hard at me. I nod I get it. He nods in return. "It is far better to build what we of Here-Born have alongside what currently exists no matter how bad it has become.

"So! Allow what *is* to continue while quietly building a new Political Civilization parallel to it. Never bother asking permission to do so. Never fight the old for you will, like every revolutionary in our history, naturally become exactly like that which you've set out to fight.

"Oppressive regimes are born in revolution.

"You must *evolve* to a higher Political Civilization to avoid destroying the lives of every citizen via revolution. It's tough. It feels wrong. It takes a little longer but it's the right way."

He raises an eyebrow.

I nod agreement as some of my recent thinking falls into place. I sigh happily for tomorrow shines a new light upon all those of Earth. Yet the unpleasant.

"What will I do with him?" I ask as McPeters is walked out the door.

Once-Other turns to me and says, "Our prison system and penalties are included on the chip—you will find those who commit Treason don't get a firing-squad. They do get to spend the rest of their lives making up for that Treason, though. Find some Dung Duty for him."

He smiles and says, "You will also find links to your own history. What may interest both you and most all citizens could be your own history. It is listed chronologically—and visual as can be got. It should untangle the mixing up and hiding of dates and who's who for you."

While he was talking, I'd held onto a burning question but can't anymore and ask, "The UWMD? Which one? Fraggers? No longer supporting something via your wallet or your vote? Wait! Building the new alongside the old? Wait! The unelect and repeal websites? Wait! All? No! Never mind Fraggers. Humm? Oh! Takes three to create! One, your Constitution. Two, your Bill of Rights. Three, the Letter to all Citizens. Right?"

"You're ready," Once-Other says and they all smile, turn and head for the door.

"Keep in touch," I manage to say.

Karrell comes back and hugs me long and hard almost as long as Roses hugs Once-Other.

Benwarr and Dew smile a lifetime's worth of joy at Roses then at me.

"Don't suppose anyone cares to clean up the mess you made?" I ask.

They check the place over and look to me.

"You'll be able to hire someone to do that by tomorrow," Once-Other says.

"You sure will," they all chime and one of the Police Officers steps forward and volunteers with a smart salute.

I feel strangely elated and terrified all at the same time.

Dear me, what is to become of Agnes Soulone?

Once-Other comes back, leans close and whispers in my ear. Nothing anyone has ever done has placed that much trust in me before nor since.

I gasp, peer into his eyes and he adds, "Never make less of yourself, Agnes. Ordinary people are more often extraordinary people and most will rise to the occasion."

# CHAPTER 83

## OF RIGHTS FOREVER

Editor's Note: What does not come across well in this edition is that during this speech and the following excerpts screens both at the event and across Earth displayed many different aspects of Earth's real history during the ceremony. This included actual dates of the events. So! Imagine! We'd been taught that Independence from Electricity Day was first celebrated in 1401!

There was no electricity back in 1401!

History we have since discovered has been but an ocean of lies.

***

From the Archives, Library of Congress, Washington DC.

Inaugural Speech, First President of the United Countries of Earth.

"Ladies and Gentlemen. Citizens one-n-all. Your First President, Agnes Soulone."

Footsteps, muttered greetings, microphone noise as it is bumped.

Cough.

"Thank you. Thank you All. I am so glad at the almost complete absence of those awful uniforms. You look incredible today. Agnes Soulone is pleased."

Applause.

"Welcome one-n-all and thank you again. I do admit to having some trouble finding the words especially the ones I would most like to say. A sense of being overwhelmed I suppose. But not as much as I first was. I'm sure many of us feel the same.

"Thank you for all you have done.

"However, a thank-you will never do it justice.

"Well! Here we are! I dare say many of us were surprised to discover we live here...in the US of Axis. Ah-ha! And that where I previously worked in Los Angeles...the coast there is *not* the Pacific coastline of China. On the other hand, we were told what is now again actually China was the United States of America. We've removed that old *Axis* title. Dear me! Education...gone awry."

Roars of laughter, hoots, cheers.

The President waits for silence.

"About our previous elected officials...I will never mention their deeds nor discuss them in any way whatsoever. To do so gives life to what they did and who they are. The cold facts will be in all history lessons.

"Now let's get to the matters of today.

"First off I confess that when Once-Other and the others left my old apartment I felt very lonely, terrified really. I went to work the next morning with no idea of what needed doing.

"Pete, my Supervisor, ex-Supervisor, was still there smoking and coffee-ing as usual. He handed me what I thought was a new Happiness recording to work with—but it wasn't one. What it was, was a copy of their entire Constitution and Bill of Rights and Letter to all Citizens.

"And now it's ours. And we all know what it really is.

"I read it all. I asked him what I should do. Being from Here-Born he smiled and walked out.

"Well...I spent a lot of time working with them and others—long distance. During that time, I picked up a great deal of information. Much had to do with our invasion. There was interesting data as well as news both saddening and disheartening.

"As many of you have already read the details. I would like to touch on something that speaks of why war and violent conflict should be avoided. And of why communication between groups must not be torn asunder when our apathy allows people of ill intent to make us slaves once again.

"And so I make my point though I would have much preferred having no example by which to make it."

There's a long silence and then the President continues.

"Possibly the worst news I received was that Maggie Schwartzlauda was killed during our invasion of Here-Born. Droght D'elti I'm told is inconsolable. They were working together in the Mall of Sand Lake Flats at the time.

"When the Walmer sounded they headed out the Mall but on the way heard some children calling for help. They went back in and found several tourists from Earth trapped in the elevator that takes you underground. Working together, they got the door open and those people all made it out.

"Droght and Maggie did a double check to ensure they had found them all. That is when the rain of fire from our forces leveled the Mall and left only the gold mine museum intact. To my horror, I witnessed it on screens as it happened.

"She had been close to Once-Other. I know how much he liked her as I had worked with the Happiness Monitoring records on which she appeared with him.

"I regret that invasion and am still angry it was done in my name...in our name. But you know? They of Here-Born will not tell us how many of their own were killed. They merely ask how I'm doing and now I can tell them *damn fine and altogether.*"

A few people laugh.

"Staying sober for another moment I'd like to inform you of something I still have trouble believing. No matter how many times I've asked, the Here-Born government will not reveal how many of their soldiers were found by Poip here on Earth and imprisoned or worse. No records of that exist or are *missing.* Let us have a moment of silence, please."

Silence.

"Thank you. And now. A moment of humor is called for.

"It has come to my attention that the sight of our invasion troops standing proudly upon Here-Born and in the next instant completely naked is making the cyberspace rounds in a viral fashion. It's garnered many comments and some of them very amusing indeed. I too was stunned at the manner in which our invaders were conquered by Here-Born."

For the first time in hundreds of years, thousands laugh as one.

Laughter fades.

"For myself...I hope to live up to your trust. I thank you for your Yes-vote on my program and proposed legislation which encompasses getting rid of the old and, in particular, the endless reams of regulations that accompanied previous legislation—and which is now illegal.

"I thank you for also voting yes on our adoption of the Here-Born Constitution and Bill of Rights as our own. Though it is a little like making our own...our own once again and then some.

"I know many of you must have been terrified of voting for this. I mean. There I was the sole person in charge of this great world of ours making promises to you.

"Trust me on this—so too was I."

Applause explodes.

As it fades, President Agnes Soulone says, "Thank you to all the multitudes of helpers who stepped up and grabbed hold of the various political reigns and interim Government duties and who took responsibility.

"A special thank you goes out to all those military, police, and government personnel who stepped away from the previous regime at great peril to themselves and stood shoulder to shoulder with us.

"Thank you from the bottom of my and our Nation's heart.

"I've too much to say yet I pause again...to pay special tribute to one of us who, beyond measure, helped to bring *us* to where we are today. Thank you to Jonathon Andrew for all his help and his understanding of what a free people value most.

"His input during the drafting of our acceptance of the new Constitution cannot be adequately rewarded. What is strange is no one really knows him as he is a private person and seeks no fame. I had promised not to mention him...but I have.

"Thank you, Jonathon. But where are you? How do you disappear without a trace?

"Well, as usual, no answer. So! With his and your help we have set up State's Rights and you have here today sent your

Representatives to the Hub. We have worked together as a nation and here we are and who knows but that tomorrow is ours!

"We are all to one degree or another familiar with our Rights. But I'd like to take the time to bring Religious Freedom to our attention.

"It is significant because it guides us now as it did in the past and will again in the future. It has always painted a path that leads to Personal Freedom—and that is why those wanting to enslave us target religion.

"Should it ever die again it will be because the Slave Masters amongst us have once again taken hold of our lives. And he again reigns over our economy, our hearts, our minds, our freedoms and has already murdered Religion.

"Let us never again remain silent when those who wish to control us destroy Religious Freedom.

"It's true that they compound that death with even more oppressive taxes, endless regulations and deliberate violations of our Rights. Never forget that they are actively destroying our Constitution in attacking us and bringing to bear upon any person who dares to speak out against them, the full force and power of a government gone mad.

"We must never remain silent again.

"We must never fear them again.

"If we once again remain silent, we condemn our children to worse than what we will suffer by speaking out.

"No paycheck is more important, no mortgage is more important, no job is more important, no self-perceived status is more important than your Rights, your Freedom. If you love your children never remain silent ever again. Never silent again!"

And the crowd roars in return, "NEVER SILENT AGAIN."

A few moments of silence, the President says, "Thank you all. That is a lesson we must all teach our children starting today.

"And speaking of children...just as Here-Born's Constitution and Bill of Rights embraces the concept of the individual being not wholly a physical being but a spiritual being that lives onwards into the future.

"And taking into account the possibility that at the time one passes away you may in the next moment be associated with an unborn child's developing body...abortion is now a crime.

"It's been centuries since last a mother-to-be died from birth complications. We have those issues pretty much covered, medically. Most who have suffered that misfortune were usually too distant from Emergency services to be helped...at the time of crisis. At this time, even Emergency service personnel are trained to rescue an unborn child should the mother-to-be pass away due to a tragic event.

"And the majority of mothers are saved as well.

"Well. There's another aspect to Religious Freedom. As I've heard a Here-Born or two say, *even the fouled mouthed religion haters got the right to say what they do about religion—from Religion—they have just not realized it.*

"Sounds accurate to me. Religious Freedom initially gave us Freedom of Speech though that is not the same as the Freedom to Lie in a publically damaging fashion.

"Allow me to quote from Freedom of Speech.

"*Crimes include lying in News or other Media reports and claiming or pretending it's all fact or factual while it's actually falsehoods, lies or simply isn't what it's stated to be.*

"*This includes biased reports or failures to report when favoring a particular person, group or politician.*

*"This includes as well any form of false statements verbal, visual or written that are designed to destroy the reputation or honor or integrity or good standing of another or others.*

*"Whether such destruction or damage occurs or not.*

*"In short...Freedom of Speech does not include the freedom to lie."*

President Soulone pauses.

"And so...Freedom of Religion...and its importance.

"Everyone here was handed a copy of why there's Freedom of Religion and why it's important. Please take it home and read it. Let your families, neighbors, work companions and strangers know they should download, read it and understand that it ensures our tomorrows and that of our children and their children.

"Even those who have no Religion get *that* Right from Freedom of Religion and nowhere else! You should study our new Constitution too, as it is a weapon.

"In fact it's Here-Born's UWMD. Oh yes! Now I know it for sure.

"It's been an enormous task and I am proud to say that those of Here-Born, Once-Other and others, were not quite able to leave as obviously-invisible as they had hoped. And ever so very grateful I am.

"And We now move on for a new future awaits us all.

"I have heard your call for a return to cultural identities and sovereignty. These are important and as critical to our future as open communication and freedom of travel. Barriers and walls destroy communication. Endless, ongoing regulations that create difficulties with moving products or hinder travel from one state, planet or country to another is what needs to change.

"For if we are all truly of Earth then we should act as friends do and work with each other. Yet in a united nation, a united world of multi-cultures and races, there is ample room for individuality and differences in culture, beliefs and expectations. Diverse cultures will thrive if each is willing to be communicated to and to communicate with cultures different from one's own.

"We have spoken on this at length. There is a proposal in the making wherein we hope to bring all elected officials from all *States,* as the old countries are called, together. Yet, we will all remain united under the banner of our new Constitution and Bill of Rights. There's support for this idea.

"We are also working to keep the Hub as the center of all Federal government so that National governing bodies from all states are in one place. While back home, in the countryside so to say, States run their own affairs.

"It seems to me the best road back to cultural identities.

"An enormous amount of work still needs to be done and we will get it done. To that end, I'll be keeping a careful eye on our un-elect website. I ask of you to use your voting power on the Legislation website to remove any legislation you no longer desire.

"Please use the same power to vote someone out of office as well. Yes! We can now undo any and all legislation and any regulation. How those politicians of old must be turning in their graves, shuddering."

Laughter.

"I'm greatly encouraged by the promise Once-Other and others made to us—to our Grand Masters of Enterprise that is. I had my doubts. But is appears to be true, to have worked and still does.

"You know they told me that those good old boy monopolies and dedicated government contractors from way back during the Free Market system which used to earn millions or billions will *not*...once a balanced economy kicks alive...disappear and die.

"Instead, they will find, if they look at it the right way, that those billions will translate into trillions or even quadrillions of dollars. A few have already mentioned this is true. But...they imply that they had to look at the free market system in a new way...and the floodgates opened for them.

"We all love that...they make so many of us wealthy.

"Another change we've made is regarding patents and copyright of technology. This is done to protect we consumers. As of now, any time an owner of technology of any kind whether transportation, space flight, computer or software or garden hoses retires a version of theirs, that version immediately becomes public domain.

"Thereafter anyone or any enterprise can and may pick up full support and further development for the product due to having access to the patents and copyrighted materials for a specific version.

"Finally Fellow Citizens, I bring to your attention a poem titled *Chains and Dreams*. A citizen of Here-Born who was once my Supervisor wrote it. I have asked him several times if his real name is Tull-Tor Hawkur, but he never answers, only smiles.

"It is my hope he will step forward and take credit for it. I hope you will take it and the Freedom of Religion brochure home with you, read them and consider on each.

"Thank you, one-n-all!"

Applause.

***

**Religious Freedom**

As taken from the original Here-Born Constitution:

All citizens of Earth have an Inalienable right to Religious Freedom.

And to the practice of their Religion anywhere including in public. To the practice of their Religion in private and upon all property occupied by any and all Government entities.

To the beliefs of their Religion.

To the right to speak freely of their Religion and or beliefs, anytime and anywhere.

Under the possible circumstance wherein future generations may seek to circumvent Criminal Laws enacted on Earth it is separately declared that: Any criminal act incorporated into a Religion and then practiced under the guise of the Freedom of Religion is not held free of Criminal Law but is subject to it.

Examples of current criminal acts are: Murder, Rape, Theft, Fraud, Terrorism, Blackmail, Treason, Assault, Torture be it spiritually, physically, mentally or emotionally.

No Law may be enacted that declares any Religion or Religious practice to be criminal.

No Government entity has now, nor in the future, the right to Legislate nor in any manner whatsoever define what Religion is. Nor which Religion is acceptable, or which are not acceptable, or what Religious Belief is acceptable or what constitutes Religion or Religious Beliefs.

**Separation of Church and State**

CHURCH is here defined as those individuals or groups who form the legislating, ruling, management, administrating or governing body of a Religion whether that religion is formal or informal.

STATE is defined as those individuals or groups that form the legislating, management, administrating or governing groups, or individuals, or entities of Government or any Public Office.

This includes all Government at all levels of government.

It is here declared that a governing body of the CHURCH may not be the same governing body of STATE and thus bring into being one governing body that rules, administers, legislates, manages or directs both Church and State. Which includes any Church and any Government from Federal Government to State, to County, to City or town.

This includes covert or overt co-operation between such groups thus rendering them factually as one.

This does not now nor in the future exclude from Public Office any person with a Religion or Religious beliefs. Nor does it exclude any Public Official or Citizen from the practice of their Religion as above and below.

The purpose of the Separation of Church and State is to ensure that no Church can decree by official Law what form of Government is acceptable. Nor what Laws must or must not be passed nor what person may serve in Government.

Secondly, this is to ensure that no Government body, group or individual can by Law decree what a Religion is. What Religion is acceptable, define Religion or ban any Religion or its practice.

### Religious Practice and Worship

Any individual or group may practice their Religion upon the exterior grounds of all Public Property including Government buildings at any time. This is a Right.

Blocking of entrances or exit paths is not included here.

No Law may be passed banning the practice of any Religion at any specific time or in any location save as written here. Therefore:

All Government buildings must provide rooms for the practice of Religion. The practice of any Religion is confined to these rooms inside all buildings used as Government offices or other Government use.

It's predicted that at times many different Religions may be in practice at any one time and mixed in a single room. This is how it shall be. If space allows, more than one room per building should be provided. Anyone is free to practice in any room if more than one is available.

Participants are free to make agreed upon schedules if so desired.

Private enterprise has the Right to formulate their own rules regards the practice of religion on company premises during and after work hours.

This must be documented and be part of all employment contracts. A copy must be provided to all new employees as well as a hardcopy placed permanently on Bulletin Boards and an eCopy on a public website.

The private sector by Law must include within the body of all Contracts of Employment the rules that allow or disallow the practice of religion at or in the workplace in everyday language. This provides all applicants the option to accept or reject any offer of employment based upon their personal religious requirements.

Some employers may wish to provide quiet environments at the workplace for the practice of religion during working hours. Some employers may prohibit the practice of religion in the workplace altogether.

These are their Rights.

In this here, we understand that citizens who seek Public Office will inevitably bring into any Office and any Legislation they propose some measure of their religious beliefs.

Per our Constitution such Legislation appears on the Election Website at the time a person is running for Office. This gives Earth's citizens the opportunity to accept or reject the individual running for office and any proposed Legislation at the same time.

The above from the Here-Born Constitution and Bill of Rights is included in the United Countries of Earth's Constitution and Bill of Rights in honor of the fact that Religion brings change for the better in any society.

It is Religion, which keeps the Flame of Freedom burning.

Extinguish Religion and the Flame of Freedom dies.

Using Religion to maim, or murder, or slaughter is a greater crime than the murder of Religious Freedom itself.

# CHAINS
# AND
# DREAMS

Upon the Tomb of the Slave Master it is written:

All people are honest. All people are honorable.

In some, though—these are deeply buried.

Despite this, they do reside in all people.

That is a truth.

It serves all people of goodwill well to note that the Slave Masters that are amongst us and those who wish to become such rely heavily upon that truth.

And so it came to pass that our honesty and our honor opened the door to making us slaves.

Listen carefully those who may wish to be free.

The Slave Master knows that once we give our word once we've agreed to that we will forever keep our word.

And so they lie and cheat and thus elicit from us our Word of Honor.

But in their telling they leave out vital information.

And when we discover how truly well we've been lied to what do we do?

Alas! We still keep our word.

For we are honest and honorable.

And they know that.

And they know too that for us our word is as sacred as our honor.

But for them it's something to be spat upon and is merely the bait they use to draw us forever into slavery.

And so we find we would be slaves rather than break our word once given.

For we have given our word when declaring, we will keep our word.

And so we keep our word forever.

Do we not?

But is it not now time to assign ourselves a new Right?

The Right to change our minds about keeping our Word once given.

Let us then ably take back our Word exactly as previously given *and* retain our Honor.

Especially when we've been lied to.

And greater Freedom shall belong to all.

But here now at this reading's end let us too consider another response.

We all know just how dedicated those who wish to enslave us are.

How ardently they repeat those well-learned talking points.

Propaganda learned until the minions have become naught but a collection of repeating audio files.

And each audio file waits to be played yet again each time we are careless enough to express our hope

for but a little freedom for ourselves for our children.

Should we not admire such automated dedication on their part and simply smile their endeavors aside?

Tull-Tor Hawkur

***

**24th October 4318**

Dear Students,

Travelers stopping off at Inter-Constellation Port-SLF and who venture into Sand Lake Flats itself will find as they leave the Terminal a monument honoring those who lost their lives.

This includes Franciscoa, Maggie, and Jiplee.

The statue itself is that of a single Arzern, wings spread, carving an arc across their blue sky. The poem first read by our First President, Agnes Soulone, is set in stone at its foot.

There are many such monuments across all of Here-Born.

A particular note of interest for the many students who have asked after Once-Other.

It is rumored that Martin du Fleurs was Once-Other's actual name. His last name, Maggie's, and some others are signatories on their Declaration of Independence and Bill of Rights.

Look it up.

Tull-Tor Hawkur signed his poem three days after Agnes Soulone's inauguration.

Other than Once-Other's name—real ones appear in this edition.

It is also rumored, that on the day Karrell was rescued and Agnes Soulone was given the eChip, Once-Other had whispered his real name to her.

In my humble opinion keeping Karrell's presence secret during those times and not allowing herself to enter it on record was a tough task. As are all tasks requiring one not do something.

As historical records show, Here-Born's invasion of Earth was unique in all of history. Unlike any before they did not attack us nor did they attack our institutes nor our government nor anything else—with violence.

There has been endless discussion of the fact that they used our own systems and technology and bypassed everything including our previous political system and its embedded government apparatus—The Department for the Assurance of Happiness.

Here-Born's mission commanders made no effort to destroy what was in place, but it vanished as a new political system was built parallel to it in a truly rapid evolution.

In so doing they have given us our own UWMD, which is now part of our Constitution.

Should it happen that our government goes rogue in the future, there will be no need to try changing it from within itself should it be beyond repair as it was before.

Instead, we will do as Here-Born did to us and set up a parallel political system. One that returns us to what we adopted back in the day with active defenses in place. Thereby we leave the corrupted one to evolve into the new. In its end, only the corrupt and criminal will continue to cling to it.

And should we, perchance, fall back to the times when vast sums are donated to election campaigns we'd simply set up the election website again. And using said donations we'd advertise the utilization of the election website and promote candidates who enroll to run for office via the website *alone*. And use its reach to explain and to get more candidates to run there too.

This starts a new evolution, not a revolt nor revolution.

That's why the website and the voting system.

It's so easy to change something by setting up the new without attempting to undo, let alone destroy what is. The chief difference will be time involved for we will be evolving to a new system not starting and running a revolution to get a new system. Neither is it an endless evolution but instead a short and fast one of but a few years.

A welcome change from history past.

And so those of us who care to ponder on it realize that we have not as yet qualified to receive Fragger technology from Here-Born.

But as President Agnes Soulone said in her acceptance speech...the Here-Born UWMD is now a part of our Constitution and Bill of Rights.

And it is a weapon.

Yes. It is the ideas of our Constitution and Bill of Rights that defends us for all time, not weapons, let alone Fraggers.

Not that we shun active defense as and when needed.

And may the practice of *divide and rule* never again be exercised upon us.

And as they say on Here-Born, "Live by Neatness alone fellow citizens!"

Well. Time for me to go—they're here.

Yes!

I am looking to get up into the 5% tax bracket.


Willard Williamson.

Chief Assistant to the Librarian.


### THE END


**Dear Reader,**
**Building the Road to a New Political Civilization calls**
**for an Army of Patriots beginning here in the USA and**
**then spreading to every country in the World.**

Individuals are the cornerstones of every worthwhile endeavor to ever rise to success here where we live—Earth.

It is possible to achieve what we have here in this book, and in those books to follow, peacefully as outlined. All that's needed is enough folk understanding there is a way to be had.

To make this plausible and Once-Other known all I ask of you is the four items listed below:

- Leave an honest review on Amazon and any other online bookstore you are able to or so wish.
- Word-of-mouth is the most powerful tool We the People have and which cannot be stolen from us no matter what.
  Please tell others about Once-Other.
- Request a copy every time you visit your local Library. Search them on line as well and electronically request a copy.
- Request a copy from your local bookstores including Barnes and Noble.

In doing so I will be there thanking you each time you do so. Our children will thank you for the all of time.

*Obviously parts of Once-Other remain fiction, such as the One World Government, but the Road to a New Political Civilization we can build within each Country on Earth as laid out, though 'many hands' will be needed.*

Many thanks to you—Lawrence.

686

**Currently under construction:**

THE

123<sup>RD</sup> ROOHLI H.

**another novel by**

LAWRENCE M. NYSSCHENS

**And headed towards**

**a New Political Civilization**

AS WELL!

**No details at this time.**

**But check lawrencemn.com regularly**

# GLOSSARY

**24th July, 4008 EB**...date Here-Born adopted the original Constitution and Bill of Rights of the United States of America...date of their Declaration of Independence from Earth at the conclusion of their First War of Independence.

**Adieu**...goodbye.

**Abeyance**...a state of temporary disuse or suspension.

**Akin**...of similar character or type.

**Allied Forces**...WW II countries that fought against the **Axis** Forces. Principal countries were United States of America (the real USA) and Great Britain along with Canada, and other British Commonwealth nations such as Australia, South Africa, India and many more.

**Altogether**...expression encompassing all that *can be inferred.*

**Ad nauseam**...to a tiresomely excessive degree.

**Antarctic**...a wind on Here-Born blowing out the southeast.

**A-one and B-one**...a two-part system of **Poip** robots.

**Apartheid**...a system of segregation and discrimination on grounds of race in force in South Africa 1948–1991. From Afrikaans, literally 'separateness', from Dutch apart 'separate' + -heid (the equivalent of -hood). **See Verwoerd, Doctor Hendrik**

**Apoplectic**...overcome with anger.

**Arzerns**...predatory birds, most have about a three some **sand-paces** wingspan and stand around two sand-paces high the largest stand about three sand-paces high.

**Assuage**...make an unpleasant feeling less intense.

**Asunder**...archaic or literary meaning...apart.

**ATI**...Annual Taxable Income.

**ATV**...All-Terrain Vehicle.

**Audrey**...waiter at the Top of the Mine restaurant.

**Auspicious**...indicating a good chance of success, favorable.

**AWOL...Absent Without Leave.** Military, meaning don't have a pass to be off Base.

**Axis...Axis Powers...**these were the actual Axis countries during WW II...Germany, Japan, and Italy. They fought against **the Allied Forces.**

**Bade...**past tense of bid.

**Balanced economy...**no inflation, no deflation.

**Benguela current...**a cold ocean current in the Atlantic Ocean on the West coast of Africa.

**Bequeath...**hand down or pass on.

**Betwixt...**between; used mostly in the South Midland and Southern U.S.

**Biased...**to be heavily in favor of, or for, or against, a thing, idea, view, or person.

**Brother Adolf...**see Hitler, Adolf.

**Brother Lenin...**see Lenin, Vladimir.

**Brother Moa...**see Zedong, Moa.

**Brother Sun...**Here-Born's sun.

**Cactus (plural cacti)...**tall upright cactus with blades arms growing out them.

**Camels and tents (briefly, from Arabian Nights)...**One cold night, as an Arab sat in his tent a camel thrust his nose under the flap and looked in.

"Master," he said, "may I put my nose into your tent? It's cold out here."

"Certainly," said the Arab and turned over and went to sleep. A little later, the Arab awoke to find the camel had not only his nose in the tent but his head and neck as well. The camel then said, "I will take but little more room if I place my forelegs inside and out of the cold."

"Yes, place your forelegs inside," said the Arab making more room in his small tent. Woken once again the camel said to him, "May I not stand inside? I'm holding the tent open by being half in and half out."

"Yes," said the Arab. "Come inside. It will be good for both of us."

The camel crowded the Arab into a tight corner near the entrance where he went to sleep. When he awoke the next morning, he found himself sleeping outside while camel had the tent all to himself.

**Campaign**...Here-Born's first method of self-defence

**Capital Square, Washington, Here-Born**...international Capital City.

**CO2 captures**...massive and deep ditches dug in the sand into which CO2 flows and from there into Converters where carbon and oxygen are separated and oxygen is released into the atmosphere (Plants, trees, and oceans do this naturally). CO2 is heavier than air and so sinks to lower elevations.

**CO2/CO**...carbon dioxide...the gas that comes off most anything that burns, too much will suffocate one, it is heavier than air and so collects in low-lying places. CO (carbon monoxide) is what automobiles exhaust. It can be burned with oxygen and then becomes CO2.

**Collect-n-grind**...a flexible pipe-like rock grinder which moves on wheels and can be guided, which ingests rock, crushes it into a fine powder in stages, and like a vacuum cleaner sends the resulting powder to the surface.

**Colloquialism**...not formal or literary.

**Comm-link**...a communications link.

**Comeuppance**...noun, informal; a punishment or fate that one deserves.

**Constellation**...a way to break up the sky. Stars (Suns) in a constellation can be many light-years apart. Some constellation names are Ursa Major (Great Bear), Centaurus (Centaur) and in Once-Other the fictional Rio Tero (River Tero).

**Countenance**...a person's face or facial expression.

**C-POP**...Criminal Pre-Owned Parts.

**Crier fan**...a handheld fan used when taking water from a Water Crier.

**Cromwell, Jimmy**...a senator from Earth.

**Dallied**...act or move slowly.

**Deflation**...goods get cheaper, there are more goods/services available than money, buy more for less cash.

**Deidre**...Once-Other's ex-wife.

**Della Comfort**...Once-Other's favorite armchair.

**D'elti, Benwarr**...Roses' father, a leader amongst the Nomads.

**D'elti, Dewana called Dew by all**...Roses' mother.

**D'elti, Droght**...son of Benwarr and Dewana D'elti.

**D'elti, Roses**...daughter of Dewana and Benwarr D'elti.

**Department for the Assurance of Happiness**...the ultimate entitlement program and surveillance system.

**Desert Drivers**...inhabitants of the northern regions of Here-Born, descendants of Here-Born's original soldiers.

**Director of the Department for the Assurance of Happiness, Earth**...Mister Warrent McPeters.

**Dirge**...a lament (lament—song or poem) for the dead.

**Drinks-n-All**...bar, restaurant, and dancing.

**Earth slash Here-Born Accord**...economic, trade, policing, education and political agreement between Earth and Here-Born.

**Earth-Born**...how those of Here-Born refer to Earth.

**EB, EB's**...short for Earth-Born.

**Edification**...instruct or improve morally or intellectually.

**Eduvision Electrical Corp**...planet wide Electricity provider, Earth.

**Erg**...an area of shifting sand dunes in the Sahara.

**Evac**...Emergency Evacuation.

**Fairing**...a structure added to increase streamlining on a vehicle, boat, motorcycle, or aircraft.

**Fan-n-fit**...skintight suits that are air-conditioned using Quaaseon gas.

**Finger**...a measurement about one inch in length (finger's width)

**Foundation**...Here-Born's term for one's Education.

**Fragger**...from fragmenting...technology that turns solid matter into fragments or close to vanishing it.

**Franciscoa (Franci)**...Once-Other's store assistant.

**Free Marketeers**...one of the three population groups on Here-Born, who are business orientated.

**Galore**...in abundance, lots of.

**Ghutra**...Arab headdress to protect mouth...worn in desert conditions.

**Hangdog-garb**...and so it is, I got that, whatever, depending on usage and attitude when spoken.

**Harken**...to give attention to what is said; listen to.

**Hellbent**...Once-Other's SandRider.

**Here-Born**...desert planet to which citizens of earth emigrated in 3776 EB.

**Here-Born Residentia**...hotel in Sand Lake Flats, Here-Born.

**Hew**...conform to.

**Hitler, Adolf**...Nazi (National Socialism) dictator of Germany.

**House and Senatorial Hub of the United Countries of Earth-Born**...the central government city of Earth.

**Hunduranda**...a SandMaster dealership that also provides work to prisoners.

**Ilk**...of the same class or kind.

**Inflation**...goods and services get more expensive, the value of money decrease, buy less for more cash.

**Insinuate**...suggest (something bad) in an indirect and unpleasant way.

**Inter-Constellation Arena Thirty**...a politically affiliated group of thirty constellations with Rio Tero the leading constellation and to which both Earth and Here-Born are parties.

**Inter-Constellation flight**...Rio Tero space flight service between the thirty affiliated constellations.

**Introspection**...the examination of one's own thoughts or feelings.

**IP**...Internet Protocol, the standard computer language used by applications and computers to find and speak to each other across a network in the workplace or over the Internet.

**Iron Ridge Mountain**...far northern mountain ranges of Here-Born.

**Iron Rock Falls**...vast, wide and high sand-falls down which sand thunders like waterfalls do.

**IV-line**...an intravenous line, a tube inserted into a vein via a needle.

**Karrell**...Once-Other's son (Deidre is his mother).

**Lady**...the Earth-Born Asian female in the Museum, dressed in white silk and hiking boots.

**LAX-EB**...Los Angeles Inter-constellation port on Earth.

**Leeward**...on or towards the side sheltered from the wind.

**Lenin, Vladimir**... was a Russian **communist** revolutionary, politician, and political theorist. He served as head of government of the **Russian Soviet Federative Socialist Republic** from 1917 and of the **Soviet Union** from 1922 until his death. Under his administration the **Russian Empire** was replaced by the Soviet Union; all wealth including land, industry and business was nationalized (confiscated/stolen from those who owned it). Based on **Marxism** (see Karl Marx) his political theories are known as **Leninism**.

**Lowlands**...all sand below the northern plateau and the Iron Ridge Mountains.

**LWB**...Long Wheel Base, a truck manufactured with a longer payload area by extending the rear wheels further back.

**Madsen Somalo**...Once-Other's Campaign senior and childhood friend.

**Magnetos**...a small electric generator containing a permanent magnet and used to provide high-voltage pulses, especially (formerly) in the ignition systems of internal-combustion engines.

**Malstrado the Rat**...Once-Other's favorite rock star.

**Marx, Karl**...a German **philosopher, economist, sociologist, historian, journalist,** and **revolutionary socialist**. Marx's economics laid the basis for much of the twisted understanding of labor and its relation to capital (free economy—though more so Capitalism, which is not the same as a free economy). He published numerous books during his lifetime, the most notable being *The Communist Manifesto* (1848) and *Das Kapital* (1867–1894). Marx's theories about society, economics, and politics – known as **Marxism** – holds that human societies progress through **class struggle**. The basic idea is that there is a conflict between an ownership class that controls production and a labor class that provides the labor for production. Marx believed capitalism produced internal tensions which would lead to its self-destruction and would be replacement by a new system: **socialism**. He argued that class hatred under capitalism would result in the working class' conquest of political power and eventually establish a classless society, **communism**. Marx actively fought to bring about communist socialism, arguing that the working class should carry out organized **revolutionary action** to topple capitalism and so bring about social and economic change. So much for the 'natural conflict' idea.

**Maureen**...a tall black haired fortuneteller located at the fairgrounds in SLF

**McPeters, Warrent (Mister)**...Director of the Department for the Assurance of Happiness.

**Midst**...being surrounded by other things or parts or occurring in the middle of a sequence of actions

**Mister Conqueror**...male with **the Lady** in the gold mine, dressed in a red-n-black checkered fan-n-fit suit.

**Mister Warrent McPeters**...Director of the Department for the Assurance of Happiness.

**MM-PBP**...Modification and Modernization of Property Behavioral Patterns.

**Moment in Time**...an action done one-on-one by parents with a child that brings about a conceptual understanding of the child's education by the child.

**Mother Wind**...all the winds of Here-Born collectively.

**Multra, Prince MaChordam**...ruler of Tero and Tero II.

**Naught**...zero, nothing.

**Neatness**...an unwritten code of conduct lived by on the planet Here-Born in which personal honor is all-important. Neatness embraces personal honor, personal integrity, personal ethics, all existing moral codes, even tidiness and especially *wholeness of self.*

**Nettler, Bordt**...was a good friend of Once-Other.

**Nomadi**...all-purpose personal communications device.

**Nomads**...one of the three population groups of Here-Born.

**Nordt, Jenk**...a Northerner, provides pre-owned parts to Once-Other. Travels by walking.

**North Guard**...mountainous dune just north of Sand Lake Flats.

**Nother, Meredith**, Senator voted into the Federal Senate for the Upper Highlands of Here-born by the Northerners.

**Number Eight**...also Mr. Conqueror, disgruntled male from Earth, an associate of Peter Wernt.

**Number Six**...Asian female from Earth, an associate of Peter Wernt (also, The Lady).

**Odentien, Gordon**...Earth-Born tourist with horizontal mustache begging a trim, who meets Once-Other at the Drinks-n-All.

**Olfactory**...relating to the sense of smell.

**Once-Other**...name of the main character, hero, protagonist (in Here-Born grammar, both words are capped).

**One Grain o' Sand**...a nightclub in Sand Lake Flats.

**One-on-one**...a tour on Here-Born with the tour guide going one-on-one with a tourist.

**One-two-three**...an expression encompassing the order of certain occurrences.

**Ozerken, Mawlendor**...a Desert Driver from out of Plaeth City, Far North Highlands.

**Pernicious**...having a harmful effect.

**Peri-peri**...a chili sauce sometimes referred to as African bird's eye chili.

**Wernt, Peter**...Once-Other's new tourists and campaign target.

**Poip**...Police over Internet protocol, a two-part system, A-one and B-one models, considered a plural in grammar.

**Port-SLF**...Inter-constellation port at Sand Lake Flats, Here-Born.

**POV**...Point of View.

**PoW**...Power over Wireless.

**Pre-owneds Galore**...the name of Once-Other's store.

**Pre-owneds**...human body parts in good enough condition to be reused.

**Quaaseon gas**...fictional gas used to cool a fan-n-fit suit similar to how air conditioners work.

**Quashes**...to suppress something.

**Rehabilitation Road**...how prisoners gain an education, economic skills, and a paying job while imprisoned.

**Rio-Tero II**...a second planet owned and ruled by Rio Tero, which is much like Earth but absent any desert.

**Rio-Tero**...planet from which the dominant technology comes and political decisions are made...a desert planet similar to Here-Born.

**Roanark Braer**... a beige-n-black deer-like animal with a donkey face and Kudu like horns which roams the Highlands, and which brays like a donkey and eats cactus.

**Rocklands**...vast stretches of dark brown rock covering parts of the surface of Here-Born.

**Ruing**...to bitterly regret and wish it undone.

**Saint Karl**...see Marx, Karl.

**Sally forth**...to set out briskly or energetically...Forth...onward or outward in place or space; forward.

**Sand Lake Flats Review (The)**...city's eNewspaper.

**Sand Lake Flats (SLF)**...Once-Other's hometown and location of his store Pre-owneds Galore of SLF.

**Sand**...the equivalent of earth on Earth. Here-Borns never say: '...the sand.'

**Sandfalls**...like waterfalls but over which sand and rock fall like water over a waterfall.

**SandMaster**...eight wheeled, two engines, two gearboxes armored vehicle on Here-Born.

**Sand-pace**...one sand-pace is approximately five feet.

**SandRider**...wheeled sand rider with motorcycle style saddle and fairing.

**Sans**...literary or humorous, without.

**Schwartzlauda, Maggie**...an intriguing wisp of a brunette with deep blue eyes who is in charge of refreshments at the SLF gold mine museum.

**Sieg Heil**...a victory salute used originally by Nazis at political rallies...literally, 'Hail victory!'

**Skellumer, Johannes**...old male transcriber works alongside Agnes Soulone.

**Slack**...a depression between hills, dunes, in a hillside, or in the land surface.

**SLF Mall**...Mall of Sand Lake Flats.

**SLF**...Sand Lake Flats.

**Sloppy**...careless and unsystematic, very casual.

**Sloth**...reluctance to work or make an effort, laziness.

**Soonsaan**...childhood and current friend of Once-Other, owner of Soonsaan's SandRider Sales, Repairs and Maintenance of Sand Lake Flats.

**Soulone, Ms. Agnes**...pronounced Soul-one, transcriber of Assured Happiness monitoring records at the Department for the Assurance of Happiness, Earth.

**Specter**...something unpleasant or dangerous imagined or expected.

**Stay**...stop, delay, or prevent, suspend or postpone.

**Supe or Supervisor**...male supervising Agnes Soulone at the Department for the Assurance of Happiness.

**Tack**...a boat's course relative to the direction of the wind.

**Thermocouple**...a device (massive ones on Here-Born) made up of two dissimilar materials that are conductors, as copper and iron are, by which an electric current is generated when the two materials are subjected to extreme temperatures.

**Thobe**...an ankle-length robe with long sleeves worn by some Arab men.

**Toip**...Taxation over Internet Protocol (see IP).

**Top of the Mine**...restaurant in the Mall of Sand Lake Flats.

**Tower Dune City**...a large city in the Here-Born northern region.

**Trepidation**...a feeling of fear or agitation.

**Tull-Tor Hawkur**...poet, political columnist and commentator on Here-Born.

**UBA**...Unbreathable Air.

**Unequivocally**...leaving no doubt.

**US of Axis (USA)**...United States of Axis.

**UWMD**...Here-Born's Constitutional Ultimate Weapon of Mass Destruction.

**Verwoerd, Doctor Hendrik**...7th Prime Minister of South Africa. He is the person behind the conception and implementation of *apartheid*, a system of **racial segregation** dividing ethnic groups in South Africa. Historical: Justice Millen, in a judgment delivered in the Transvaal (a Province of South Africa) Supreme Court on July 13, 1943, pronounced that He (Verwoerd) did support Nazi propaganda, he did make his newspaper a tool of the Nazis in South Africa, and he knew it." This case arose out of an action, brought by Dr. Verwoerd (as editor of the Transvaaler—an Afrikaans newspaper) against the Johannesburg Star (an English newspaper), for publishing an article, entitled "Speaking Up for Hitler", in which the Transvaaler was accused of falsifying news in support of Nazi propaganda and generally acting like a tool of the enemy. Dr. Verwoerd lost the case. In a lengthy judgment, extending to more than 25,000 words, the judge found that Dr. Verwoerd had in fact furthered Nazi propaganda. The defendants had proved, said the judge, that Dr. Verwoerd "caused to be published a large body of matter which was calculated to make the Germans look upon the Transvaaler as a most useful adjunct to this propaganda service." On another point, the judge said: "This is a falsification of current news which was approved by the plaintiff. It was calculated to cause alarm and despondency, and it is not open to doubt that it was of great service to the enemy in the way of supporting his propaganda for the damaging of the war effort of the Union of South Africa." Like so many racialists, Dr. Verwoerd had early training in anti-Semitism. In the mid-1930's, when he was Professor of Applied Psychology at Stellenbosch University (Afrikaner-dom's oldest seat of learning), he accompanied five fellow professors on a deputation to the South African Government to protest against the admission into South Africa of Jewish refugees from Hitler's Germany. Verwoerd studied Applied Psychology in Germany. His use of the news media as a propaganda tool is done by all Socialist groups including those in the USA, Europe, Austral-Asia, Africa, Central and South America & Canada, etc.

**Vested**... a personal stake in something, project, action, deal, etc.

**Wagenaara, Pe'truss**...Desert Driver and companion to Ozerken.

**Walmer**...a siren like those used to warn of dangers such as in WWII bombing raids.

**Water Criers**...a wolf-like animal with a pouch on its back in which their young reside until old enough to venture out on their own.

**Williams, Jiplee**...the first Here-Born casualty of the undeclared war.

**Wise**...a way of doing or proceeding or considering, a manner, fashion.

**Wrought**...made or fashioned in a specified way

**Zedong, Mao**...Communist Socialist dictator of China (deceased).

\*\*\*